A CHOICE OF EVILS

By the same author

The Gossamer Fly
Last Quadrant
The Bonsai Tree
The Painted Cage
House of the Sun

A CHOICE OF
EVILS

Meira Chand

Weidenfeld & Nicolson
LONDON

First published in Great Britain in 1996 by
Weidenfeld & Nicolson

The Orion Publishing Group Ltd
Orion House,
5 Upper Saint Martin's Lane,
London, WC2H 9EA.

A catalogue reference is available
from the British Library

Typeset by Deltatype Ltd, Ellesmere Port, Cheshire

Printed in Great Britain by Clays Ltd, St Ives plc

For
Zubin, Aditya and Natasha

I have taken some liberties as a novelist that might seem inappropriate to academics. All Chinese spellings are in accordance with the now out-moded Wade-Giles system. Since this was the method of romanized spelling used in the era this book is set in, it seemed fitting to adhere to it rather than use the modern *pinyin*. I have also continued to call the old capital by the familiar name of Peking, rather than Peiping as it became known after Chiang Kai-shek established his centre of government in Nanking. Since Chiang Kai-shek is recognized in the West only by the placement of his surname first, as is the custom both in China and Japan, I have set out other Chinese names in this way. However, I have set out Japanese names in the Western manner of surname last, to fit in with other characters.

CONTENTS

One does not become enlightened by imagining figures of light, but by making the darkness conscious.

C.G. Jung

If only there were evil people somewhere insidiously committing evil deeds, and it were necessary only to separate them from the rest of us and destroy them. But the line dividing good and evil cuts through the heart of every human being. And who is willing to destroy a piece of his own heart?

Alexander Solzhenitsyn

SOVIET

R. Amur

Manchouli •

THE
**JAPANESE
EMPIRE**
AT THE TIME OF
PEARL HARBOR

Peking
Vladivostok
Tokyo
Shanghai
Hong Kong
Bangkok
Saigon
Singapore

INNER **MONGOLIA**

Jehol •

Paotao •

Peking •
Tientsin •

R. Hwang Ho

Yenan •

R. Hwang Ho

Taierchuang •
Hsuchow •

• Sian

CHINA

Wus
Nanking
Wuhu •

R. Yangtze Kiang

Hankow •

Chungking •

PROLOGUE

1

1937

Nanking, China

'I have seen her, Mama,' Lily announced. 'She has bright red hair, like a halo of fire. Is she really from Russia? How long is she going to stay with us?' She pulled critically at her fringe. She was stuck for ever with her dark Chinese hair and eyes black as the pip of a lychee.

'As long as Bradley thinks best,' Martha Clayton replied from behind the *China Weekly Review*. She lowered the newspaper, looking over half-moon glasses at Lily. The child was easily bored, always seeking new diversions. Perhaps their guest, sent to them by Bradley Reed, would stem her restlessness through the school holidays. Martha leaned back in her chair, glad to relax before dinner; it had been one of her operating days at the hospital. She sipped the plum wine she made each year. It had been a particularly difficult day, each operation on her list demanding. It was so different from her own childhood. Her father had struggled not only with hygiene but with the distrust of his Chinese patients in the isolated area where the mission had functioned. He wore Chinese dress, Martha remembered, and his blond hair hung in a pigtail. He also operated in this attire; they all wore Chinese dress in those days to allay suspicion. Her father had been a good doctor and a good preacher; she feared she had failed his high standard.

She stared over the newspaper at her daughters. Lily stretched out on the floor beside her. Flora was lost in a book, curled up on a rattan chaise. Both girls were back for the school holidays from Shanghai.

'I told Miss Komosky dinner was at seven.' Flora looked up from her book. 'Lily, her hair just has to be dyed. Nobody has hair *that* colour.' She admonished her sister then turned to her mother. 'Is she here for the Encyclopaedia?'

Martha nodded, taking her glasses from her nose and folding up the newspaper. 'She is Bradley's chief assistant.'

She had met Nadya Komosky on her arrival and been surprised. She would have expected Bradley Reed to employ a different type of woman, someone of a quieter nature, more scholarly in appearance. And older. The girl upstairs must be no more than twenty-eight.

'The Encyclopaedia is nearly finished. It is already partly in proof. She needs to stay a while in Nanking, to supervise any last changes,' Martha explained.

'That book will never be finished. It's been going on for as long as I remember,' Lily yawned.

Soon this impetuousness of Lily's would need proper direction; she was already fourteen. She seemed always to slip from Martha's grasp by mercurial means. There would be no such anxiety surrounding Flora's future. Martha moved her gaze to her natural daughter and saw safety in her grave face. Flora, with her measured thought, seemed older than eighteen.

Many doubts beset Martha at the time of Lily's adoption. Her husband, Bill, was no longer alive. He had viewed the adoption of a Chinese child as acceptable only if a couple had no other children. If there were natural children, Bill believed the Oriental child would feel inferior and the Occidental usurped; instead of love, hate would grow between them. Chinese orphans should be cared for in a Christian orphanage. Martha had accepted these views without question, until they found Lily. It was Flora, only four years old at the time, who insisted they adopt her. Martha's father, Dr Keswick, had still been alive, and running the old mission hospital. She remembered the dispensary of that hospital, always crowded with patients, each conscious only of their own need, each wanting to see the doctor first. Crying babies with mothers who never followed prescriptions. Patients who refused to divulge symptoms but expected her to take the three pulses of the wrist as did Chinese doctors. Tubercular coughs. Women in protracted labour, smallpox and typhoid cases, one fan to cool a temperature of a hundred degrees. As a child she remembered the sight of bandit victims stumbling, minus ears or fingers and sometimes noses, into the dispensary. She had lost her own husband to a bandit uprising. She reached hurriedly for her wine to banish the painful pictures.

Martha's worry now was not just for the development of her children but for their very future. On her knee the paper was full of the ominous. War hovered upon the horizon, threatening to engulf them. Even Bradley had the wind up him. He had seen no need in the past to hurry the completion of the Encyclopaedia. Like everyone else Martha had hoped the Japanese, after their occupation of Manchuria and the failure five years before to take Shanghai, would be content with their gains in north China. Bradley's letter had disturbed her more than she wished to admit.

The Japanese are only waiting for an opportunity to push further South, Bradley Reed had written to Martha.

> *And who will stop them when they're ready? We don't know what's ahead, except trouble. I want the Encyclopaedia finished. I am sending Miss Komosky to sit in Nanking, to breathe down their necks and make them see urgency at the university. I have to be here in Shanghai. Miss Komosky is a pleasant young woman, and an efficient worker. If she could stay with you it would be a great help to us all. You will find her no trouble, you have my assurance.*

Martha had known Bradley Reed since childhood. Their families had met aboard a ship while returning to China after home leave in America. After disembarking at Shanghai, they had shared a further ride on a crowded barge up the Grand Canal to their respective missions. It was the middle of winter and Martha wore a padded Chinese coat for warmth. The families huddled together in a small, cold cabin, on deck Chinese passengers chattered. Through the window she and Bradley peered out between a row of feet at market towns, earthen farmhouses, temples and everywhere graves, like large molehills littering the ground. Only the icy draught through a broken pane occasionally drove Martha back from the window. After the break in America she did not wish to miss an inch of China. She knew she was home when the stone walls of the city loomed before her. Over its gates, like rotting gargoyles, were the decapitated heads of criminals. She did not give them a second glance. The Chinese towns she had lived in went by many names, but the sights were always the same. She was excited to be back. She had not felt at home in America; some vital ingredient was missing. The ease was almost uncomfortable. Other children found her conversation outlandish and adults were shocked by her tales of discarded babies in dry riverbeds.

Bradley Reed was now a famous man. Although from a dynasty of missionaries, he was a Renaissance figure who had branched out as an academic, businessman and publisher. He had also lived many years in Japan. His influence was considerable. A department had been established at the University of Nanking, of which he was head, to deal exclusively with the business of the *Encyclopaedia of Chinese Sources and Traditions,* or TECSAT as it was called.

The Encyclopaedia was Bradley's brainchild, a monumental undertaking, written in both English and Chinese. Work had been proceeding on it for years. Hundreds of students and experts at Nanking University were involved in contributing and compiling the statistics needed to fill its many volumes. The cost was enormous but had been backed by the Rockefeller Foundation and other wealthy institutions. In America the name Bradley Reed carried clout. The Encyclopaedia had also the personal backing of General and Madame Chiang Kai-shek. The book was to be a source volume for all areas of Chinese life, from religion and agriculture to sexual mores. This information was now stacked in bundles about the compilers who worked on the Encyclopaedia in a barn-like building east of the Drum Tower.

'Mama, why is Agnes Smedley not yet here?' Lily enquired, watching the clock edge towards seven. She admired the notorious Agnes Smedley who, once before, had appeared at their home like a sudden storm, obscuring normal vision, flouting all convention with her outlandish tales. Lily could hardly suppress her excitement at the thought of soon observing at the dinner table, not only the extraordinary Agnes, but also the red-headed Russian.

'Agnes Smedley will arrive when she chooses to arrive, as she always does.' Martha answered with a sigh. 'She is coming down from the north. It is a long way. We will not wait for dinner. No doubt our Miss Komosky is hungry.'

She did not look forward to the difficult Agnes, who was forever in trouble with the authorities. She had agreed to accommodate her for a night at the request of the Bishop, who was returning the following day from a visit to Hankow. Agnes was collecting medical supplies for the Eighth Route Army and Martha, again at the Bishop's request, was to arrange a part of these supplies. Not long ago the Christian community would have wanted little to do with activists like Agnes Smedley, or the Eighth Route Army. Now, together with other political and religious factions, the community stood behind Chiang Kai-shek and the newly formed coalition of the United Front, working as was necessary to fight off the Japanese.

Martha turned to watch the last of the setting sun through the open window. Beyond Nanking the land stretched away, flat and green; the rice bowl of China. This year, as always, rain and wind had repeatedly smashed up crops and homes, killing men and animals. She thought of the mud-walled farmhouses beyond the town, and the people to whom she ministered, who endured only hardship. Suffering bent them all. Men or mules with packs strapped to their backs, women with children strapped to their backs, children with smaller siblings tied to them; no one walked without a burden. In China nothing had changed since her childhood; she had known no other home. Now, as she grew older, she wondered if the country would ever digest her. Within herself it seemed she had no landscape to call her own. The desolation she had felt as a child often settled upon her now. She clung to her work. When she was younger there had been religion, upon the order of her father, adhesively binding her to life. But later, after her husband Bill's death, there was always the feeling that the old demon, God, had disowned her. Many said it was she who had turned her back.

Upstairs, Nadya Komosky saw by the clock in her room that it was already five minutes to seven. She brushed her hair vigorously, then looked in the mirror, giving the scarf at her neck a last tug. About her the room was plain, but adequate. Although she had been many times to Nanking for Bradley Reed, she had never met Dr Clayton. Bradley had failed to tell her, when he arranged this accommodation, that Martha's home was in the compound of her hospital. He had not mentioned that the view from her windows was of uniformed nurses in the wards opposite, rows of beds and supine figures. Nadya would have preferred a glimpse of Nanking's ancient city walls, or the gleaming Yangtze River. The house was separated from the hospital by a patch of lawn bordered by shrubs and a clump of trees. Beyond the hospital she could see the curling roof of the vermilion Drum Tower. She would keep her eyes upon this elegant structure, Nadya decided, when the alternative view proved tedious. She was not usually put off by circumstances. She had already learned the strangest opportunities were sometimes found in the most barren of places.

She made her way downstairs. Dr Clayton sat in a chair with her teenage daughters curled up like young puppies about her. She rose as Nadya entered the room, and offered a glass of wine. Her smile was spontaneous, but her eyes remained cool and left Nadya with a desire to recheck her appearance. She wished now she had not worn earrings. Bradley Reed insisted few people worked as tirelessly for the betterment of the Chinese as Dr Clayton; Nadya regarded her curiously. Martha's skin was scrubbed smooth and her hair, prematurely grey, was pulled tightly into a knot. If her eyes were less sharp, Nadya would have described her as remote. If the motivation of doctoring did not impel her so strongly, Nadya could visualize Martha as a depressed and troubled woman. She had been told by Bradley that Dr Clayton's hair had turned grey overnight at the news of her husband's death.

'I make it myself,' Dr Clayton announced, pouring the wine from a crystal decanter.

Nadya sipped the cool, sweet liquid. The girls sat up straight to observe her. Above the rim of the glass Nadya met their discerning eyes. She had

7

heard from Bradley the story of the adopted Chinese daughter, Lily, discarded at birth and found by Flora.

'Your hair is too red. Do you dye it?' the Chinese child asked. She gave a broad grin of welcome.

'Lily!' the older girl, Flora, exclaimed. A measured expression shadowed her eyes, echoing her mother's circumspection.

'She has every right to ask questions,' Nadya laughed.

'I like the colour of her hair. I want mine to be the same. That's why I'm asking,' Lily explained. She turned with a frown upon her sister and then stared again at their new lodger. She was nothing like the masculine Agnes Smedley who, until now, had been pinioned in Lily's mind, exotic as a fly in amber, as something of another world. Nadya Komosky was much more.

No one before had been so pretty. Scarves hung extravagantly about her. Her hair swung and flamed about long earrings. Everything appeared in constant motion; earrings, skirts, scarves and hair. Grey eyes, pale as water, threw out a bold but quizzical stare. A strange energy seemed released from her. Lily glanced at Flora's sobriety and the resolution of her mother, then returned her gaze to Nadya. She sighed, taking in once more the flaming hair and pulled at her own dark fringe.

'My hair is not dyed. But I learned to rinse it in beer when I came to Shanghai. Better than beer of course, is champagne. But it's too expensive, even in Shanghai.' Nadya's voice filled with regret. She saw no reason to mention the regular use of henna.

A slight frown creased Martha's brow at these whispers of Shanghai decadence, but Lily breathed quickly. These were the things she wanted to hear, reports from another world. She was forced by her mother to shampoo her hair with spirit of soap from the hospital dispensary. She hated the green, unlatherable stuff with its medicinal odour.

The dinner was simple but good, and Dr Clayton talked of her friendship with Bradley Reed. It was warm even under the fan. Moths were thick at the window screen. A whiff of night soil upon the air reminded Nadya again that Nanking was a pedestrian Chinese town, not a cosmopolitan metropolis like Shanghai. There was none of Shanghai's wanton clamour, swelling to fill the night. Here, all was order and decorum. Nanking lacked Peking's majesty, and was devoid of Shanghai's hedonism, crowded masonry and rapacious pleasure. Nanking had no foreign concessions. Unlike Shanghai its expatriates were not rich businessmen but professors, missionaries and the diplomatic corps. Yet, in spite of its staid reputation, Nanking was by day a bustling, populous city. Above it rose Purple Mountain, changing colour by the hour through a spectrum of blues and mauves. It was home to the golf club and Sun Yat-sen Mausoleum. At its base a spirit road of massive stone animals, standing or kneeling in pairs, led to ancient tombs. As the new capital of China, Nanking was seeded but ungrown. It was a town of avenues waiting for buildings. A main road bisected the city upon which stood the Metropolitan Hotel and the main ministries. There was only one fashionable shopping street. Nightclubs were few and the smoking of opium was frowned upon. The Government aimed at grandeur and modernity. Glamour was supplied by the presence of the Generalissimo and more visibly by Madame Chiang Kai-shek. For Nanking a new flowering seemed imminent. But some ambassadors as yet refused to move from Peking fearing dullness, and came and went between the two cities. Unlike Shanghai, Nanking disdained an élitist mentality. Its foreigners mixed easily with Chinese society.

Friends in Shanghai had groaned at the news of Nadya's banishment. Nanking is a missionary convention, or a YMCA meeting, they said. She bought a new evening dress with gold trimmings and was warned frivolity was frowned upon; better to dress for a funeral. The only thing that appeared the same in each town was the rarity of young, unmarried, foreign women. Every night in Shanghai someone different had taken her dancing.

She did not wish to move to Nanking, but there was no refusing Bradley Reed. When she had arrived, almost penniless in Shanghai, he had given her a job without even a reference. She had only her experience on the *People's Paper* of Blagoveshchensk, where she had worked as a proof-reader. Even there her opinions were too outspoken and, for her own good, she had been moved to a section of the Town Planning Association, compiling reports about roads and drainage. Once more her unguarded views had raised eyebrows.

'I don't go by curriculum vitae. I rely upon instinct when employing people. I've never been wrong as yet,' Bradley said at the interview. She was grateful for this sweeping gesture.

When Bradley had first employed her, Nadya travelled regularly between Nanking and Shanghai. Usually she chose the night train, steaming into Nanking in the morning as they served a glass of tea. From the station she went straight to a hotel and then to the university. Rushing back to Shanghai she took charge of the proof-reading as the pages came off the presses of the *China Weekly Review*, which was printing the book. She was working directly under Bradley, supervising the documentation of TECSAT. It would be a while now before she saw Shanghai.

Across the table Lily continued to stare relentlessly. 'Your English is funny. Where are you from?' she asked, breaking into the conversation.

9

'Lily,' Flora hissed. 'I told you, from Russia.'

'Before Shanghai I was in Harbin, which is in Manchuria, and before that I lived in Blagoveshchensk, which is in Russia. Originally, I was born in St Petersburg, but I hardly remember it,' Nadya answered. The shadow of ornate stone buildings passed like half-obscured pictures through her mind. Then, she saw again the rough wooden houses of Blagoveshchensk, muddy roads and factory chimneys. Bleakest of all had been the gold mine with its convict labour that her father managed. Now, as an adult, things were revealed with exactness to her. As a child she had accepted her environment in the way a child accepts.

'Do you have a husband?' Lily enquired, putting down her knife and fork to concentrate the better. She ignored Flora's kick beneath the table.

'Not at the moment. But there was one. He came and went so quickly I hardly felt married at all,' Nadya replied. It was unnecessary to reveal to this child that she had not in fact been married to Sergei. Lily expelled her breath slowly.

'Why did you leave Russia?' Flora asked, unable to stop the question, then blushing in embarrassment. Lily turned in triumph and returned the kick beneath the table.

'To be free of the Communists. I fled with my husband. His name was Sergei Lekhovich. We hid on a boat and escaped to Harbin. Blagoveshchensk is a border town on the Amur River. If we had lived anywhere else we might not have thought to escape. The Amur River is joined by the Sungari, flowing away from Siberia to Manchuria and Harbin. Many people have escaped on those rivers.'

'Oh,' Lily breathed, leaning forward to cup her chin in her hands. 'It's like a fairy tale.'

'Siberia is a place of snow and exiles.' Flora recalled a geography lesson.

'There is snow and there are exiles. But there is also much more,' Nadya answered shortly, suppressing the complex mix of emotions stirring within her. She remembered wild duck against a winter sky and ripe wheat beneath the sun, rushing away to the distant horizon.

'If you are from Russia, why do you speak English?' Lily demanded.

Nadya laughed. 'Because my father spent much time in England and France as a young man. He loved those countries. He saw that I learned their languages. I had an English governess, and a French one too for a while. But things changed in Russia, that way of life died. And my father moved from St Petersburg to Blagoveshchensk. Even there he saw that I continued to learn languages, teaching me himself.'

At the end of the table Martha listened to the interrogation, content

10

for her daughters to ask the questions she herself would have put more discreetly. Lily's excitement was plain to see; no emotion stayed hidden for long in Lily. Flora was different. She had been so small when her father died and yet, it seemed to Martha, Bill's death left a residue within the child. In her early years she had absorbed too intent a knowledge of sorrow.

Bill had been killed in a year of great flooding and rain. Vast swathes of land disappeared under water, crops were ruined and famine began. Impoverished peasants swelled the bandit ranks and marched as an army upon a nearby market town, killing and looting, carrying off the rich for ransom. Parcels of ears and fingers returned to waiting relatives. The horde moved on from town to town, each day edging nearer the mission. The hospital courtyard was already full of the wounded. Terrified refugees camped beside them.

Flora's second birthday arrived in the midst of the panic. Bill carried her on his shoulders, her sandy curls mixed with his own. He galloped around the verandah, into the house and out again. She screamed with laughter as he stopped abruptly in front of Martha.

'I don't think we should leave the mission,' he said. 'We should show these bandits we're not afraid, that God protects us.' Some of the other missionaries in the area had already left their stations for safer places.

'What about Flora?' Martha replied. It was a Sunday and she sat reading on the verandah. She tried to show no fear, but Bill did not know China well. She knew what hunger could do to men. The Chinese doctors at the mission had assessed their countrymen and also urged evacuation.

'I think we should stay,' Bill repeated. 'The brigands will stop before reaching here. There's no need for panic.'

'That's what father said at the time of the Boxer Uprising. In the end we ran for our lives. We were hidden in a loft by Chinese Christians for a week. Murderers climbed on the roof and peered through the windows. We lay flat on our stomachs all day so as not to be seen. It was summer and the heat was well over a hundred degrees. Food and water were only brought to us at night. The smell of our own stench was sickening.'

She could never forget that time, like a deep well in her childhood, bottomless and black in its terror. 'Eventually, we were smuggled in coffins to the Yangtze, and hidden again in a boat. It took ten days to get to safety. We hid in that boat like we had in the loft. My brothers were small and their health so broken when we reached our destination that they caught typhoid and died. I don't think we should stay here.' She had never opposed Bill before.

11

'We live by faith, otherwise we would be continuously running from this or that in this benighted country,' he answered.

She remembered then her mother's faith throughout the Boxer ordeal and her strength in the midst of grief, and felt ashamed. She rose and put her arms around him. Still upon Bill's shoulders, Flora laughed and pulled at Martha's hair.

In the evening Bill got out his old motor bike. At the beginning of their marriage she had watched him drive out on it to the dispensaries. It had been Dr Keswick's idea to open small clinics in the countryside and to use them as feeders for the main hospitals. He had looked out across the plains of China with a proprietorial light in his eye. He saw the dispensaries as evangelistic agencies. Martha decided maternity clinics must be incorporated in them. Then she had discovered herself pregnant with Flora, and Bill had gone off alone.

'I'll show you there's no need to panic,' Bill said pushing the motor bike out of the mission compound. Before them the countryside was serene.

Martha rode pillion as Bill roared up grave mounds still soggy with rain, raced along the pulsing river, and then up the steep ramp to the top of the city walls. The evening blew in Martha's face, the sun set in the trees, illuminating the yellow roofs of a pagoda, sinking towards the grey mud walls. Bill was damp with sweat. The smell of him mixed with petrol fumes and night soil from the fields. She clung to his body. The memory of those odours remained with her still.

'There is nothing to be afraid of,' he said. 'We're together and God is with us.'

His faith had been no protection against fate. Eventually, after he went missing, his body was found in a faraway place, spliced and hacked to pieces. Martha's father, Dr Keswick, would not let her see the remains. The coffin was nailed down, even as she struggled against it. Martha pushed away the images filling her mind, and returned her gaze to her daughters who appeared already in thrall to the Russian woman.

'Why did your father move to Siberia?' Lily demanded of Nadya Komosky, visualizing inhospitable wastes of snow.

'I don't really know,' Nadya replied. It was the truth. Something had gone wrong in St Petersburg of which she knew little. Gold mining under the Tsars had been a government monopoly. All mines belonged to the Imperial Court. No private individuals were allowed to search for the metal. Whatever the mistake her father had committed, his punishment had been mitigated. His exile to Siberia had been in the superior capacity of a government job. He was to mine gold for the Treasury.

12

'Weren't your parents worried about your escape?' Flora asked, concerned about filial matters.

'My mother died when I was small, soon after we arrived in Blagoveshchensk. And my father a few years ago. I had only a horrid stepmother.' Nadya laughed. Although she had tried to obliterate his memory she had suddenly, because of this conversation, to think of Sergei again. Even the thought of him made her angry. He had touched a wildness in her of which now she was ashamed. And she had also to think of her father. The anger in her doubled.

There was a rapid knocking at the front door, followed by the hurried footsteps of a servant towards it. 'Here is Agnes,' Martha said, putting down her coffee cup.

'Agnes is a kind of Communist,' Lily leaned forward, her tone conspiratorial. 'What happened to your husband? Where is he now?' She was anxious to know the end of the story before Agnes Smedley appeared.

'He ran off to America with a man called Ivan Shepenov who was on the boat which brought us to Harbin,' Nadya replied briskly.

'A man?' Lily's eyes widened at this strange adventure. 'Were you heart-broken?' she asked. Listening to Nadya was like opening windows on to exotic landscapes.

'On the contrary. I knew by then I did not love him. The shock was only to discover a man might love another man,' Nadya answered.

'A *man* can love another *man*?' Lily did not dare look at her mother, fearing the condemnation in her eyes at these wanton tales, more decadent by far than Agnes Smedley's stories of political adventure. She heard an intake of breath from Flora at this sudden education.

'I also discovered they were both spies. Shepenov was an important spy and had recruited Sergei, who was no more than a tadpole, in Blagoveshchensk. The only money Sergei and I had were the few jewels my mother left me. They stole those from me and vanished.' Nadya appeared unfazed by such duplicity. Lily sat back as if in a trance.

Martha cleared her throat. The sound was not one of approbation. Bradley Reed or not, Lily knew her mother capable of finding alternative accommodation for a woman she considered unsuitable for contact with her daughters. Beside her Flora's silence was ominous, merging with Martha's disapproval. And yet, neither had stirred at the sound of Agnes Smedley's arrival, held to the table by Nadya. Lily crossed the fingers of both her hands. She would rather die now than lose Nadya Komosky.

There were footsteps in the corridor and the door was thrown open. Nadya looked in amazement at the woman before her in a dusty khaki

13

uniform, threadbare puttees and muddy shoes. If she had not already heard about Agnes Smedley, Nadya might have been unsure of the gender of the figure in the doorway. Agnes pulled off her peaked cap, revealing hair cropped close to her scalp. Nadya was introduced.

'She washes her hair in champagne. She was married once very quickly, but her husband was a spy and fell in love with another man. She hates Communists and left Russia to escape them,' Lily burst out in a rush. Agnes Smedley turned to give Nadya a critical look.

'Straight from the front, I presume?' Martha interposed hurriedly, seeing the expression on Agnes's face. She wanted no trouble from the unpredictable Agnes.

'We were covered with lice,' Agnes announced, running a hand over a head of stubble. 'I had to have lice like everyone else, otherwise they said I couldn't claim to belong to the army. Cleanliness is unproletarian. Share and share alike.' Her blue eyes scanned Nadya who had lit a cigarette and drew upon it through an ivory holder. Agnes Smedley's face was tanned as a peasant's. The skin peeled off her nose.

'Whar army?' Nadya enquired. She thought Agnes Smedley looked ill beneath the weathering, as if she had a history of sanatoriums behind her.

'The Eighth Route Army.' Agnes regarded her with pity.

'Agnes needs a bath and some clothes. Flora, what can we lend her that might fit? She has grown so thin in those mountains.' Martha hurried to change the subject.

'There is nothing but millet and salt turnips twice a day and sometimes not even that,' Agnes informed them, going out of the door with Lily and Flora.

'Is she really a Communist?' Nadya enquired, as Agnes left for her bath.

Martha caught the edge in Nadya's voice. She shook her head in perplexity. 'Let us just call her an activist, a pro-China person like Edgar Snow or Anna Louise Strong. Agnes is also a writer and one of the few foreigners to have lived in the communist stronghold, Yenan. But I should tell you, she has never liked Mao Tse-tung and I believe he ordered her out of Yenan, branding her a troublemaker. She believes in the people of China, as do we all. Of course her views differ from mine about Chiang Kai-shek and many other things, yet you cannot but admire her courage. In these days of the United Front, the Christian community does what it can to help her. Everyone must work together to rid the country of the Japanese. She has come here now to get funds and medical supplies for the partisans and the Eighth Route Army. Argue with her at your peril,' Martha advised.

'Then she is an exhibitionist. But one who might also do some good work occasionally,' Nadya ended hurriedly seeing the look on Martha's face. She inhaled deeply on her cigarette. She had the feeling lodging here might be no easy task.

At last Agnes Smedley reappeared and sat at the table in a skirt and blouse. She appeared out of character in these accoutrements. 'We need Thomas splints for broken arms and legs,' she announced to Martha. She began to eat at a rapid pace. Joan of Arc, thought Nadya, must have looked like this, with her rejected femininity, cropped hair and fighting clothes. The same spirit might have burned in her.

'Thomas splints are imported items but I can lend you one that could be copied by the local factory,' Martha suggested.

'You cannot imagine what it's like up there,' Agnes said, shorn head turned away from Nadya. 'The poverty is ghastly. The partisans fight the Japanese night after night in temperatures below freezing with neither shoes nor socks. And yet they fight on. In the winter their hands swell and turn black from frost-bite. Then, there is no choice but to amputate. There are no medicines or surgical instruments. Yet still they come, to join the army and fight. The Eighth Route Army and the partisans have nothing and yet they share everything with the civilians.'

Nadya shifted in discomfort at these descriptions. She saw Siberia again in her mind, a line of figures with bowed heads, bent backs and dragging feet, straggling across its limitless space. Women and children had trailed behind their men into a cold waste-land. Siberia was the symbol of the Tsars' despotic rule. Her father knew too well by what whisker of fate he had escaped sharing the destiny of these exiles. He was a good manager who, as best he could, saw to the welfare of those who worked for him in the gold mine. Yet, as a child, that line of figures stumbling against the frozen landscape, had been stamped for ever upon Nadya's mind.

The exile ranks of Siberia were swollen by intellectuals, with whom her father spoke late into the night. He always boasted he had met the banished Lenin. And Stalin, on one of his many penal adventures, had escaped from servitude in a neighbouring mine. When the Revolution came in 1917, her father had embraced it. And some years later he had disappeared from Nadya's life, not only pulled forward upon a wave of political idealism, but fuelled by love for a new woman. Nadya was left with her stepmother Anna. They had lived then with the chaos of an unknown Russia, tossed brutally between anarchy and famine. She remembered only fear through those bleak years, her wretchedness compounded by the coldness of Anna, and the absence of her father.

The line of figures still moved across the limitless land, sent now not by the Tsars but the Central Government.

Nadya turned to Agnes Smedley with new energy. 'I'm sure Bradley Reed will donate towards anything you may need.' She took a risk on Bradley's generosity. Agnes looked at her with new interest.

'We need *everything*,' she replied. Her commitment was infectious. It was impossible for Nadya to sustain her own memories of Russian Reds before the energy of this woman. It all seemed something apart.

'China *is* different,' Agnes insisted when Nadya voiced this thought. 'The Russian Reds don't even recognize the Chinese Communists. Their backing is with Chiang Kai-shek, if he wants it. Here in China only the Communist guerrillas can fight the Japanese and give this country back to its people. Chiang Kai-shek's Kuomintang are corrupt capitalists. All they think of is power for themselves. Especially that feudal bastard, Chiang,' Agnes growled after Martha left the room to see about the splints. Then her eyes settled again upon Nadya who continued speaking of Russia.

'You should go to Yenan. You might make a good activist, fighting for China.' Agnes appraised Nadya anew after hearing of life in Siberia. There were things she had not noticed before, deterrred by the swing of scarves and earrings. She saw metal now beneath the fine bones with their slightly Slavish tilt. Nadya Komosky's face pandered to no one. It was self-sufficient and self-contained.

'*Activist*.' Nadya tried out the word. 'I do not object to that term. It has not the same connotation as Communist, and it is better than being a White Russian. We are seen as dressmakers or prostitutes, objects of charity queuing at soup kitchens, or eccentric nobility in fraying clothes. Foreign firms sack men who marry White Russian women,' Nadya's voice was bitter. Experiences in Harbin and Shaghai flooded her mind.

'You should not put up with it. I've made it a principle to refuse compromise,' Agnes responded. 'I was always in trouble in Yenan for arguing with the women. In spite of equality, those women up there are all incredibly prim.' Agnes had not been popular with the women of Yenan.

Nadya laughed. Through Agnes Smedley she glimpsed another China that had nothing to do with the decadent world of Shanghai that had briefly trapped her. The world of Agnes Smedley was not for her, but she saw now, as if through a break in the clouds, the living flesh of a different China.

'Now tell me, when my hair grows, should I really use beer or champagne?' Agnes asked.

The next day Agnes was gone, to stay with the Bishop who had returned from Hankow. Within a few days Martha's verandah filled up with splints. Agnes Smedley returned from the Bishop's to examine each one before packing them off to the partisans. Soon she left, but already Nanking impressed Nadya with its commitment to a new China. She saw too that Martha Clayton, although of missionary stock, was no proselytizing Christian, in spite of the distance in her eyes. She had Nadya's begrudging respect.

At the university Nadya's room was little more than a large alcove off the huge vaulted hall where the compilers worked on the Encyclopaedia. She was at her desk the morning after Agnes Smedley's departure when the man was shown in. At first she thought him Chinese, until he introduced himself.

'I am Kenjiro Nozaki. I have come to complain,' he announced with a bow. 'I am from the Japanese Embassy,' he added, seeing her incomprehension.

'I had wished to see Professor Bradley Reed, but I am told he is not at present in Nanking. Instead, I was sent to you.' He spoke fluent English.

'I am his chief assistant,' Nadya confirmed. The man was exceptionally tall for a Japanese, with a smooth, fine-featured, intelligent face. She remembered Harbin again.

She had arrived in Harbin with Sergei to find the town awash with Japanese soldiers. In the hurry to escape Communist Russia, she had minimized the knowledge that Manchuria was now under Japanese control. It did not take long to realize, one tyranny was much like another. She stared at the man before her now and remembered those Japanese soldiers in Harbin, standing guard on every corner. She remembered ill-coloured skin and lips blue with cold. It had been difficult to read expressions, their features were so alien; they had instilled only fear. This man was nothing like them. He took a seat as she indicated, and placed his hat upon the desk before he began to speak.

'In this week's *China Weekly Review*, Professor Reed has advocated an even stronger drive by the various parties of the United Front against the Japanese. He has also written that should our nation advance further into China, we will destroy all the universities. This is not true and his blatant anti-Japanese stance does nothing to make the task of our Embassy here in Nanking easier, nor the lives of our many peaceful Japanese citizens in China. Professor Reed should refrain from writing such ill-advised comments. Please be kind enough to convey this message to the Professor on behalf of the Japanese Embassy.' From a skylight above sun streamed down upon the woman's red hair. He stared at the fiery blaze. It was said only devils had hair that colour.

'I have not read the article yet,' Nadya replied, taken by surprise. An obvious distress punctured the man's suave demeanor. She offered a cup of coffee.

'It has been a hard year for us here, since the United Front was formed. We wish only for peaceful co-existence in China,' Kenjiro Nozaki informed her. He appeared in no way aggressive and she wondered whether he voiced his own opinions above those of his government in Tokyo. She had never spoken to a Japanese before. The man did not fit the pastiche she had put together from Bradley Reed's talk of ambition and war, or her own memory of the soldiers in Harbin.

'Is Professor Teng Li-sheng in this department?' he asked. His eyes remained unrelentingly upon her, although there was nothing licentious in his appraisal.

'Professor Teng is head of the Department of Eastern Religions, but is involved with us of course. A good part of TECSAT concerns his subject. We all work together,' Nadya replied. The man's concentration upon her was now discomforting.

Kenjiro Nozaki nodded and at last looked away. 'Professor Teng and I were students together in Paris. Professor Reed may talk as he wishes but I can tell you from my own viewpoint, I feel the deepest friendship for China. It has been a difficult year,' he repeated, lifting the coffee-cup to his lips.

Kenjiro Nozaki had arrived in Nanking in December of the previous year, two days before General Chiang Kai-shek was kidnapped in Sian by his protégé, Chang Hsueh-liang, son of the murdered Manchurian warlord, Chang Tso-lin. The country had been in an uproar. For three days nobody knew where Chiang Kai-shek was, if he was dead or alive. He had been forcibly detained in Sian to persuade him to drop his war with the Communists and instead form a coalition with them against the real enemy, Japan. Eventually agreement was reached. Madame Chiang Kai-shek and W. H. Donald, the Chiangs' Australian advisor, flew into Sian. Chiang Kai-shek bowed to the demand for a United Front, and the need to stop civil war. Negotiations were opened with the Communists. Overnight it appeared to the world that Japan, not the Communists, had become Chiang Kai-shek's chief enemy.

It had been a difficult time at the Japanese Embassy, with the country solidifying around them, leaving them like an island in the middle of Nanking. They had kept a low profile and listened to the news, while preparing for an emergency. Little had happened beyond an expression of hostility on the faces of shopkeepers. Life, even after Chiang Kai-shek's return to Nanking, went on as usual. To most people the Japanese were in the north, and unlikely to desire control of the rest of China. It had been a tense start to Kenjiro Nozaki's posting.

He stood up, retrieved his hat and placed the official letter of complaint from the Embassy before Nadya. He glanced again in consternation at her flaming hair. He wished there was reason to sit longer, but could find no further excuse.

'My wife was French,' he gave a slight smile before turning away. 'Her eyes were the same colour as yours. Forgive me for pointing this out.'

She watched him walk towards the door at the far end of the room. For a moment she felt perplexed. She would have liked him to stay. Then she shrugged and returned to her work.

PART ONE

Beginnings

1901–1937

1

1901–1937

Sword of Power

The Crown Princess of Japan, Sadako, was sixteen years old when the child, Hirohito, was born on 29th April 1901. At seventy days Prince Hirohito was taken from his mother to be reared away from her. Later the Princess bore three more sons, and these too were taken from her.

Once Sadako had produced an adequate number of sons her husband, Crown Prince Yoshihito, lost interest in her, returning to debauchery. Unlike his father, the Emperor, Yoshihito was sickly. The residual effects of childhood meningitis left him mentally and physically unfit for most of his life. In winter he left the capital for the balmy climate of Kyushu and, even when he returned, seldom emerged from the veil of wine and women.

Hirohito saw little of his father and throughout his childhood met his mother only once a week. The ritual separation of royal heirs from their parents was thought to build character, cauterizing softness from a future monarch. The custom sprang also from earlier intrigues, when unscrupulous uncles and concubines sought to establish their own offspring with the demise of the Emperor's son.

Almost from birth Hirohito was surrounded by military men. The first three and a half years of his life were spent in the home of a vice-admiral of the Imperial Navy. He was charged to instil into the heir a spirit able to withstand all hardship. Hirohito was a child apart, withdrawn and painfully aware of the attention surrounding him. He understood that he was different. Already in his tiny life there was deference but no love.

Before Hirohito was four the vice-admiral died and the child returned to his father's palace. He saw no more of his parents than before. He was established with his brothers, Chichibu, Takamatsu, and Mikasa, in the grounds of the Akasaka Palace in a separate establishment from his parents, with maids and retainers to care for the children. The court official in charge of Hirohito's new home, Takamasa Kido, was a favourite of Emperor Meiji and had been partly educated in America. His son, Koichi, was fifteen and became a big brother for small Hirohito.

Marquis Koichi Kido, who would later become one of Emperor Hirohito's closest civilian advisors and his Lord Privy Seal, introduced the child to his teenage friends, the sons of other court aristocrats. Prince Asaka and his half-brother Prince Higashikuni. Prince Kitashirakawa and his half-brother Marquis Komatsu, and the young Prince Konoye, later to be twice Prime Minister. They had all attended the Peers School, founded for the children of the nobility. Hirohito would also later go to this special school. They made a fuss of their young royal friend, enjoying his awe of them, telling him stories of war, playing the soldier to him. They spoke with teenage idealism of Japan's mission to lead Asia from Western bondage. Talk of war, intrigue, conquest and a new Asia surrounded Hirohito in the company of these older boys. Bonds were formed with these young men that would last Hirohito all his life.

Soon Hirohito's real education was begun. A kindergarten was arranged, with Chichibu, the eldest of Hirohito's younger brothers, and five small boys of court officials. Chichibu was free of the restraints imposed upon his older brother. He was an extrovert, leading all games. When the kindergarten children climbed a wall, Hirohito was lectured by courtiers on the unseemliness of such antics in a future monarch. He was forced to stand alone, watching the others scramble up and down, listening to their enjoyment. By nature obedient and sensitive, physically smaller and less aggressive than average, Hirohito did not chaff at the restraints imposed upon him. Led by Chichibu, the children grew scornful of Hirohito's timidity.

'The trouble with Hiro is that when he falls down he doesn't know how to get up,' Chichibu jeered and the others screamed approval.

There was a monthly outing from the Palace for the royal kindergarten. Invariably Hirohito chose to visit the Zoo and in this wish was indulged. The children ran from cage to cage, giggling at monkeys, awed by tigers, pulling faces at the bears. Only Hirohito, in his usual role, was forced to follow some distance behind, lectured on animal life by the superintendent of the Zoo. On one visit they reached a small cage containing a newly captured badger. The creature trembled with fear, pressing itself against the far bars, its moist bright eyes upon Hirohito. The child stood in silence, biting back tears, identifying as the other children could not with the animal's terror and isolation.

'I don't want to look at it any more. I want to go home,' he sobbed. The other children tittered.

Hirohito's guardians accomplished their work as instructed. The training of imperial children bred the habit of docility and a rigid pattern of behaviour. By five, Hirohito was a grave and lonely child. The tipsy, debauched promiscuous life at court had already been revealed to him in the most frightening manner. On a rare visit to his father Prince Yoshihito, he was plied with large quantities of sake and drank in filial obedience until he keeled over. His father and the courtiers roared with laughter. Hirohito was ill for days, and although only five, never forgot the experience. He became for life a teetotaller. In contrast to his father and grandfather he lived until his death a prim, monogamous, austere life.

Hirohito quickly learned to mask emotion, giving no sign of mortification, comforting himself like a true prince of the Imperial line. He submitted to grim routines to improve his posture and poor, myopic eyesight. There were attempts to eradicate his extreme clumsiness and the inherited shuffle he walked with, a defect passed on from his grandfather.

Emperor Meiji received the progress reports Hirohito's father refused to see. Meiji had already dismissed his son as being without substance, and placed his faith in his eldest grandson. The affection his father denied Hirohito the child tried in vain to find in his grandfather. But Meiji, libertine and architect of modern Japan, preferred Hirohito at a distance. His virility was legend and projected itself in his commanding figure, short beard and piercing eyes. He enjoyed claret, poetry and beautiful women. He was a marathon drinker, his court permanently shrouded in an alcoholic haze, but, unlike his son, he could surface from debauchery to steer his monarchy as needed.

The years of Hirohito's boyhood coincided with Japan's growth in world stature. Fifty years before, Commodore Perry's black ships had demanded commerce at gunpoint, ending several centuries of isolation. Meiji was the first Emperor in modern times to be more than a puppet living in Kyoto. He was reinstated to power by his supporters, who wrested back the monarchy after centuries from the Shogun, the military ruler of Japan. In 1868 Emperor Meiji, then a boy of fifteen, was moved by his supporters from Kyoto to Tokyo. It was hoped under the young Emperor to rid the land of foreigners, holding modernization in check. Then the country would be returned to its hey-day when no barbarian could enter and no Japanese leave, without the sentence of death.

But there were also progressive men about the young Emperor Meiji who knew the barbarians would not leave so easily. The isolation of centuries had left Japan impoverished in a larger world. Already, with their massive ships and guns, the Westerners had demonstrated superior power. Until Japan had adequate knowledge of all things modern, she must learn to live with the barbarians and more important, learn from them. This modernization of Japan took up the next three decades.

Imitation of things Western spread like a fever through the land. Young men were sent abroad in droves to seek the desired knowledge. Battalions of Westerners were imported into Japan. Engineers, school-teachers, lawyers, architects, scientists, military and naval instructers were persuaded to divulge the secrets of modern development ignored by Japan through her centuries of isolation. The Emperor himself, avid and youthful, urged his court to think progressively. He installed electric light in his palace, but rarely used it for fear of fire. Court ladies were encouraged to wear crinolines, and to speak aloud instead of whispering behind their hands. In the street children bounced a ball to the 'Civilization Ball Song', listing things coveted by the nation; steam engines, gas lamps, cameras, telegrams, lightning conductors, newspapers, steamships and hansom cabs. The world was surveyed and institutions picked, suitable for use in Japan. From France came a conscript army, from Britain a navy, from Belgium banking and fiscal reform and from Germany a constitution.

With its isolation lifted at last, Japan now looked for the first time about the modern world and saw that the great land it had regarded through history as the centre of the world, was at the point of disintegration. China, weak and disunited, had become a colony of foreign powers. Japan saw those great powers, Germany, Britain, France, Russia and the United States, grouped before her and feared for herself. Small, vulnerable, newly born into modernization, Japan was a mouse before an elephant. Only the resource of ingenuity seemed available to Japan. It was decided offence was the only defence.

Japan's new Western trained army went to war with China in 1894. It overran Korea, then Taiwan and demanded China allow Japan to move into the Kwantung peninsula of south-east Manchuria. So alarmed were the powers of the Western world by this upstart behaviour that Japan was forced to relinquish her slice of Manchuria. She watched Russia take over instead. But in spite of this loss, a new confidence was born within Japan. The sacred dream of past Emperors, laid down at the birth of the nation, was for Japan to eventually fulfil its predestined place as ruler of the world. A first step had been taken towards this vision.

It was decided to go to war again, this time with Russia, on 6th February 1904. Once more Japan relied upon ingenuity. She moved forward with silence and stealth. Although war was not formally declared until February 10th, a surprise attack was launched on February 8th crippling Russia's Far Eastern fleet at Tsushima. What was left of the

Russian fleet fled to the stronghold of Port Arthur, on the Kwantung peninsula.

This act of stealth by a tiny nation, inferior in strength and size to Russia, caught the imagination of the world. *The Japanese navy has opened the war by an act of daring which is destined to take a place of honour in naval annals*, enthused *The Times* in London in 1905. An identical act of stealth, played to the same rules, began the Pacific War many years later at Pearl Harbor, and brought then a different reaction from world opinion.

Before Russian reinforcements arrived it was imperative for Japan to capture the garrison at Port Arthur. Emperor Meiji turned for this task to his favourite General, Maresuke Nogi, calling him out of retirement. Nogi knew Port Arthur well; his brigade had captured the town from the Chinese in the earlier war. He had taken the place in a day with the loss of only sixteen men. He remembered it as an easy target and saw no need to bother with a new assessment. He took his two sons into battle with him. In 1904 Port Arthur was no longer the place Nogi had earlier defeated; time had moved on. Weapons were improved, thoughts upon strategy had altered, and Port Arthur was now Russian territory.

As he had previously, Nogi hurled wave after wave of infantry at the forts of Port Arthur, but without success. *The Times* reported the battle as a succession of Charges of the Light Brigade, made on foot by the same men, over and over again. Death was certain and the methods innumerable. There were bullets, shells and shrapnel. There were mines, torpedoes and hand grenades, pits of fire or stakes, and poisonous gases. Besides these was the dread of disease; typhoid, dysentery, beriberi and always the ever present danger of gangrene for the wounded. A new era in warfare had dawned. Now, at Port Arthur, General Nogi could simultaneously look back to the Middle Ages, and forward to an even more brutal age of warfare. His men, in heat and rain, advanced towards both boiling oil and electrified wire. They struggled against planks speared with nails to tear their feet, and the new devices of searchlights and magnesium flares. Against this illumination men wandered blindly, while machine-guns targeted them in the beam.

Both Nogi's sons died. He watched them through binoculars, waving their swords at the head of their troops. By the time General Nogi had taken Port Arthur observers noted that *corpses do not appear to be escaping from the ground as to be the ground itself. Everywhere there are bodies, flattened out, stamped into the earth as if they were part of it. What seems like dust is suddenly recognizable as a human form, stretched and twisted and rent to gigantic size by the force of some frightful explosion.* It seemed to the

27

world that the Japanese Army won its battles by accepting a price in human life no other nation was prepared to give.

Devoted to his Emperor, this price in human life and the death of his own two sons, was even too much for Nogi. He prepared to commit ritual suicide. Emperor Meiji forbade it.

'As long as I am alive, you must remain alive also,' he ordered. General Nogi retired again.

In 1908 Emperor Meiji called Nogi to him once more and entrusted him with a new order. He was to be mentor to seven-year-old Prince Hirohito. In retirement General Nogi now spent his time imparting to the sons of the aristocracy the Way of the Samurai; the ethics upon which he had been raised. He was headmaster of the Peers School.

Nogi, white-bearded, elderly and one-eyed, vintage warrior, scarred in face and body by sword, arrow, bayonet, bullet and shrapnel wound, should have been intimidating to a seven-year-old. But General Nogi was a Japanese gentleman of the old school. Besides the *will that knows no defeat* he also cultivated the art of calligraphy, tea ceremony and flower arrangement. His hobby was growing bonsai trees. He constantly mourned his lost sons, just as the child put into his care looked always for a father. The affection that grew between the old man and the child, was said to have made life almost happy for Hirohito.

Nogi saw Emperor Meiji regularly to report about the child in whom he now took such an interest. Meiji's trust was a source of pride to the General. He saw his last task in life as forming the young Prince in the image of his master, Emperor Meiji. He spent many hours with Hirohito imparting his knowledge of the great battles of Japanese history, reliving the pain and glory of Port Arthur, reiterating a vision of Japan as the premier force in the world. This vision of Japan's place in the world and the ethics of the Samurai code threaded through Nogi's stories of battles and strategies in the mind of the growing boy.

It was Nogi's task to bring the introspective child out of his shell. There was nothing, Nogi insisted, that could not be overcome by practice and will power. Hirohito came to idolize Nogi, with his military mind and military bearing. To gain Nogi's approval he became a competent sportsman and put himself through hours of study and physical training, standing under glacial waterfalls until he could control his shivering. He aped Nogi's Puritanism, his contempt for sexual pleasure and his thrift. Nogi took an unassuming lifestyle to extraordinary degrees.

'Be ashamed of torn clothes, but never of patched ones,' he told Hirohito.

He insisted the child wear coarse cotton underwear and kimono; he

28

should not be softened by the touch of silk on his skin. Under Nogi's influence Hirohito began to hoard things. He used his pencils until the stub was too small to grasp, and rubbers were worn down to a crumb.

Each day in the school the children bowed towards the Imperial Palace and repeated the Rescript on Education. After this they sang the national anthem.

'What is your dearest ambition?' General Nogi then asked them.

'To die for the Emperor,' the children replied.

Hirohito bowed with the other children, but was already aware this national sublimation would one day be directed towards himself.

In 1912 the Emperor Meiji died. Nogi was away at the time, sent by the Emperor as his representative at the Coronation in London of King George V. By the time he returned Meiji was dead. The State Funeral was held on 13th September.

The evening before the funeral General Nogi called Hirohito to him. They sat either side of a low table and discussed the calligraphy Hirohito had done that day. Then followed a lecture by Nogi lasting almost three hours. Hirohito sat motionless trying not to betray his physical discomfort or fatigue.

'I am satisfied with your progress while I have been away,' General Nogi said at last. 'Please remember that my physical presence is not necessary for me to be with you in your work. I shall always be watching you and your welfare will always be my concern. Work hard, for your sake and for the sake of Japan.'

Hirohito bowed and left the room. Within an hour Emperor Meiji's funeral cortège began its journey to his resting place in Kyoto, the ancient capital. A cannon thundered in the distance and prostrate subjects lined the route to Tokyo Station.

General Nogi observed the start of the cortège and then returned to his house in Azabu. His wife waited for him. They bathed and dressed in white kimono and bowed before an autographed portrait of Emperor Meiji. His wife passed General Nogi a cup of sake from which he took a sip. He turned then to bow to her. At this sign Countess Nogi drove a dagger into her throat cutting the artery. General Nogi then thrust a short sword into his bowels, pulling it crosswise and up, falling forward upon the knife in the required manner. He had kept his promise to his beloved Emperor Meiji, made after the death of his sons at Port Arthur. He had lived until his master died.

When told the news the twelve-year-old Hirohito heard it impassively, in the manner General Nogi would have wished. If he stiffened, if desolation consumed him, he showed nothing to the courtiers before him.

'Japan has suffered a regrettable loss,' he said with the composure that befitted a new Crown Prince.

At Emperor Meiji's death, Prince Yoshihito, Hirohito's father, ascended to the Chrysanthemum Throne, taking for his era the name of Taisho. His reign was short and undistinguished. His behaviour became increasingly erratic; court officials feared any public appearance. At a military parade he slashed soldiers with a riding crop, ordered a man to unpack his gear and then repackaged it himself. Such behaviour soon forced the Regency upon seventeen-year-old Hirohito. What small freedoms he enjoyed now vanished. His every move was monitored, his words and gestures coached. Courtiers hemmed him in.

An early marriage for Hirohito was now considered a necessity. Empress Sadako was progessively minded and wished her son to have some say in the choice of his wife. She had married her husband without so much as a glimpse of him. Marriage promised Hirohito a relationship closer than any as yet experienced in his life. Beauty was not what he looked for in this rare opportunity. He passed over the prettier applicants for the role and settled for the homely Princess Nagako. She was the niece of Prince Higashikuni and Prince Asaka, his heroes during his childhood in the Akasaka Palace. Her family, dashing in comparison to the one he lacked, made his choice immediate. After a considerable wait the marriage took place on 26th January 1924. Immediately, speculation began as to when Nagako would produce an heir.

At the end of the following year, as Nagako recovered from the birth of a girl, Emperor Taisho died and Hirohito became the new Emperor. Tradition demanded that ancient Kyoto, not modern Tokyo, was the venue of Hirohito's enthronement. The Coronation ceremony was on 6th November 1928. From the previous evening people crowded the route in Kyoto along which the Emperor would ride in a horse-drawn carriage. They were ordered not to defile the roadside. Bowels must be held. As the weather was cold and kidneys less obedient all onlookers were urged to carry a bottle. These must be corked and at the end of the festivities deposited at collection centres for disposal.

Such clarity of detail did not stretch to all issues surrounding the Coronation. There was confusion about the title of the new Emperor's reign. A name must be chosen by which his era would be posthumously remembered. The Mainichi *Daily News* announced that the Hirohito era would be known as Kobun, light and literary achievements. This news was leaked from the palace as Emperor Taisho lay dying. Hirohito was furious and to punish the paper altered the name of his reign to Showa, enlightenment and peace. Many said it was a bad omen to change the name of a reign in this manner.

Religious rites initiated the new monarch into the Shinto priesthood. His position was that of supreme intermediary between the world of the living and the world of the spirits. He planted shoots of superior rice, whose lush maturing would symbolize the harvest of his reign. In ritual celebration he descended for a night into the womb of the Sun Goddess, to be reborn divine. No Emperor could rule without possession of the Mirror of Knowledge, the Sword of Power and the Jewels of Antiquity, bestowed upon him by the Goddess. This Imperial regalia was officially transferred to each new monarch. From now on Hirohito must speak regularly to his Imperial ancestors before the Mirror of Knowledge, reporting the events of the reign of Showa. He was twenty-five, and his sincerity and optimism were undeniable. He wrote the first Imperial Rescript of Showa himself, determined his own words should shape the expectations of his life. From where the new Emperor stood the future looked golden.

Hirohito saw the reign of Showa as fulfilling the prophecy of his ancestors. The first Emperor of Japan, the legendary Jimmu Tenno, had laid down for the nation a vision of its true destiny. *Hakko Ichiu* meant the bringing together of the eight corners of the universe under the roof of Japan. There was nothing Hirohito wanted more for his reign than the fulfilment of this prophecy.

Hirohito was a quiet, thrifty man. The lessons of austerity learned from General Nogi were never forgotten. He cut down immediately on extravagances, including the number of clothes given to courtiers and the presenting of dried fish on occasions of note. The corridors of the Imperial Palace had reeked with the smell of these gifts at his enthronement and disgusted him. He updated his office with Western furnishing and installed a telephone for direct access to whoever he chose. He built a miniature golf course in the Palace grounds. He wished his reign to embrace the modern world. And he desired his lifestyle to follow that of the British monarchs.

Since a visit to England when still Crown Prince, Hirohito had retained a warm admiration for the British royal family. He looked back upon the visit as one of the happiest times of his life. 'I knew freedom as a man for the first time in England,' he later told his brother Chichibu. While staying at Buckingham Palace, Hirohito had been surprised by King George V who had walked into his room unannounced, half dressed, in slippers and braces. Such unprecedented informality had upset Hirohito's retainers. The Crown Prince himself had never forgotten the King's paternal warmth as he put an arm around Hirohito's shoulders and sat down on the bed to chat. The Prince of Wales had been a constant companion on the visit, and Hirohito was much in awe of his carefree manner and elegant clothes and his ability at golf. He was also impressed by the immense affection in which the British public appeared to regard their royal family. It was his first view of a constitutional monarchy of this kind and the memory never left him.

Although, as monarch, Hirohito was above politics and day-to-day decision making, he had no desire to be a shadowy figure hidden away behind moats and walls, or a puppet in the hands of ambitious men. He wished to be rid of the image of the father who had filled him with shame. He wished to propel Japan to her rightful place as a powerful, modern nation and, to this end, his daily life was that of any hardworking statesman. His meticulous, methodical nature, obsessively concerned with detail, missed little. He put his seal to nothing he had not evaluated, and knew at all times every move within the Government. But the formality of court life that encouraged Hirohito's obsession with detail, also weakened his initiative. He had been trained since birth to fit the patterns of protocol. Above all the correct discharge of his duties was ever uppermost in his mind.

In childhood Hirohito had wished to be more like his suave younger brother Chichibu, Oxford-educated, avidly sociable, who played tennis and listened to jazz. Chichibu with his outspoken ideas, who refused to conform, occasionally referred to his brother as 'slow coach'. Hirohito once sadly confided to a court official, 'He has so many attributes of royalty which I lack. He is a natural leader. He has no reticence about showing what he feels, and knows what he wants from his ministers or his people. The business of kingship comes easily to him.'

Unlike the extroverted Chichibu, Hirohito was withdrawn. His greatest interest had always been the study of marine biology, a subject upon which he was already an expert. He had the circumspect nature of the scientist and was never happier than at his microscope with his old tutor, Professor Hattori, or collecting specimens on the beach at his Summer Palace at Hayama.

Lacking Chichibu's forceful characteristics, Hirohito relied on other traits of survival, honed through his unhappy childhood. Secrecy and guile, he discovered, achieved as much as Chichibu's forthrightness. The lessons of military strategy learned at General Nogi's knee, and at which he excelled with brilliance, he applied to games other than war. He was an adept player in the intrigues of his court, playing the Military against the Government, the army against the navy, one person against another with consummate ease to get his way. No criticism could be levelled against him, and responsibility for any misjudgements was assumed by those beneath him. As Emperor, Hirohito was infallible. As a man things did not always go according to his will.

The country had been polite in its welcome of the new Emperor's daughter and hoped a son would follow. Instead, before his marriage was five years old, the Emperor had fathered three daughters. Whispers began at court of the need for the Emperor to take a concubine, to give the nation an heir. He would have nothing to do with the plan. He felt affection for his homely wife. Her support and the birth of children gave him for the first time the feeling of a home.

Empress Nagako was acutely aware of her failure to produce a son, and no stranger to the habits of the nobility. Her own father had produced nineteen children from a swarm of concubines. Court intrigue abated only when Nagako's fourth pregnancy was announced. Once more a daughter was born. Eventually the Empress became pregnant again and at last gave birth to a boy, Prince Akihito.

The first five years of Hirohito's rule had not been easy. Pressure was all about him, not only in his personal life but in his public duties. Plots abounded in which his name was always invoked. Fanatical devotion to the monarch was the excuse for secret societies to act against supposedly political or moral deviation. Rightist plots, hatched by the Black Dragon Society and Shumei Okawa, or army plots by ambitious officers like Kingoro Hashimoto or plots in which these two factions worked together, blew like an ill wind through the first years of Showa. The number of dubious secret societies proliferated, as did the plots they hatched. March Plots, October Plots, December Plots, February Plots. There was a tight, idealistic circle of comradeship amongst the brightest of young right-wing minds in Japan. The ambitions of these men abounded about the Emperor who remained secluded in his palace, far from the grassroots of his nation.

The world was seen by the Emperor through the four courtiers closest to him; the Imperial Household Minister, the Lord Keeper of the Privy Seal, the Emperor's Aide-de-Camp and the Grand Chamberlain. There were also *genro*, state-appointed counsellors. Hirohito's *genro* was Prince Saionji, the last survivor of a small group. The Prince had spent his working life in the service of both the previous Emperors. The breadth of his mind and vision were almost unparalleled in Japan. He was seventy-two when appointed as *genro* to Hirohito. It was his job to temper the royal judgement for the good of the nation. He saw Japan's future in co-operation with the West and rejected her military past. His advice was unfailingly for the moderate course. His views were not always in tune with an idealistic young man in his twenties. Sometimes, Hirohito, irritatingly restrained by Saionji, found ways to disregard or manoeuvre around him. But for many who were also of liberal mind, the old man's place beside the Emperor was seen to bode well for the era of Showa.

Even before Hirohito's ascension to the throne, the name Manchuria spelt magic. Across the water it beckoned with limitless land and resources. Its acquisition was the natural beginning of *Hakko Ichiu*, that mythological vision of a united Asia under Japanese leadership which Hirohito cherished. Within his court, distanced from the world of men, Hirohito dreamed his dreams. But in a modern and aggressive age, the vision of *Hakko Ichiu* had become for many fanatical right-wingers a megalomaniacal symbol of world domination through military force. The young militarists about Hirohito looked not to the south but to the north to begin this march towards an Empire. They aimed to secure Manchuria in readiness for a strike at Russia.

Hirohito distanced but did not deter the young militarists about him. Silence was the constitutional course and for Hirohito silence was convenient, both as a weapon and as a screen. Ambiguity had its uses. Officially, he could not be seen to agree to a plan that might commit Japan to a future of unknown ramifications. Unofficially, the young officers involved in preparations for the taking of Manchuria assumed they had his backing.

There were differences of opinion upon this subject in the army, and political unrest in the country. Keeper of the Privy Seal, Count Makino, begged Hirohito to be prudent. Prince Saionji, finding army attitudes increasingly unreasonable, argued the sense of going to war. He was also not always happy with the opinions of his Emperor who appeared in turn to blow hot then cold upon a variety of matters. As the band of aged Western-leaning moderates like himself grew smaller, it appeared to Saionji that the influence of fanatical young officers and upstart radicals about the monarch grew ever more dangerous, even though Hirohito continued to act with propriety. He was particularly alarmed by a rumour that Hirohito planned to encourage the moving of troops to Manchuria without official sanction. Eventually a compromise was reached in the Diet, the Japanese parliament, and the war was sanctioned. The nation knew nothing of these plans. As anticipated, the conquest of Mukden, capital of Manchuria was bloodlessly over in a few hours on 19th September 1931. It took only a further few months before the whole of Manchuria was under Japanese control, and the new state of Manchukuo proclaimed on 1st March 1932.

Some years later on New Year's Day 1936 Hirohito wrote a short but apprehensive poem about the future.

> *As I*
> *was visiting*
> *the Shinto Point in Kii*
> *clouds were drifting far*
> *over the sea.*

His private life was on an even keel, Nagako had given birth to a second son, but his reign had textured since its early days, and events piled up in complexity. The army's expansion from Manchuria into China continued unabated. The strength of the Military could no longer be denied, nor the difficulty in ruling it. Its ranks were subversive and divided, filled by officers from poor rural areas whose minds were crammed by schemes of grandeur. Whatever early support Hirohito had given the army seemed to have gone to their heads. There were those in the army who now wanted an Emperor who could be presented to the people as a monarch but manipulated by those in power behind the throne. They condemned all liberal elements in Japan which encouraged the Emperor to think of his role as more temporal than divine.

An ugly mood grew in the army and soon after the election of the new Diet, on 26th February 1936, a revolt began. Murder squads went out to eliminate any government leader or elder statesman who was seen to advise the Emperor too liberally. Old men who had served Hirohito were cut down. The former Keeper of the Privy Seal, Count Makino, escaped as did Prince Saionji. Those in the army who favoured caution were shown no mercy by the revolutionaries.

Within the Palace, Hirohito was beside himself with anger, appalled at the murders, and the terror suffered by his closest advisors at the hands of radical restorationists. 'The army are using silken thread to suffocate me. I want this rebellion ended, and its instigators punished. Do this,' he ordered his War Minister.

The revolt seethed a while and was put down. Hirohito wanted no martyrdom for those involved and would agree to no compromise. He was particularly upset that Prince Chichibu, whose right-wing radicalism had grown apace, had supported the rebels. Prince Saionji did not discount the fact that, had the coup been successful, the rebels might have put Chichibu on the throne if Hirohito were not compliant enough. 'Japanese history has . . . considerable examples where, urged on by hangers-on, a younger brother has killed an older brother to ascend the throne,' Saionji said.

Hirohito's wrath shook those about him. Executions of the culprits were without formality and no ashes returned to their families. Many others were sent in disgrace to cool their heels in Manchuria. Such tactics of strength from the usually passive Emperor shocked the army command. He had asserted himself as never before. Even those who disagreed had obeyed him.

By the following year the thought of war with China could no longer be avoided. Chiang Kai-shek had joined hands with the Communists against Japan. This alone was a terrifying thing, and pushed Hirohito towards compromise with his rebellious army. The army feared a Communist bloc of Russia and China, if it ever came about, would eventually annihilate Japan. Already a pact with Hitler pledged Japan to act with Germany in resisting the spread of Communism. The war the militarists sought at last coincided with Hirohito's own dreams of mythological conquest. There was also the Emperor's added desire to safeguard his homeland from any threat of Communism, however remote, coming over the water from China.

In spite of Hirohito's brief assertion of strength after the 1936 February revolt, the power of the rightists and the army was now established to such a degree that prime ministers rose and fell in quick succession when they did not meet army requirements. Finally, in 1937, Prince Konoye became Prime Minister. As a child Hirohito had admired Konoye. He was one of the 'big brothers' introduced by Marquis Kido when Hirohito moved into the Akasaka Palace. He was elegant and debonair and had the audacity to sit with his legs crossed before the monarch. Beneath this show of sophistication, Konoye was a man who lacked judgement and dithered. He did what he could to seek a negotiated resolution with China, but was powerless to control the flow of events. One month after his investiture, Japanese troops clashed with Chinese outside Peking at the Marco Polo Bridge. An era was begun from which there was no turning back.

War, as it now evolved, might not have been of Hirohito's making but, conscious always of his duty, he turned his precise mind to its detail. Those heroes of childhood, his uncles by marriage, Princes Asaka, Higashikuni and Kitashirakawa, were tough professional soldiers who held important posts in the army. Even though they were many years older than himself, Hirohito was now their Supreme Commander. He ordered a Supreme War Headquarters to be built in the Palace, to personally oversee on maps and table-tops, each battle as it grew. All moves were to be reported to him. The ultra rightists and the militarists who now had his ear were delighted with his enthusiasm. The ideals of pan-Asianism, absorbed as a child from his teenage friends at the Akasaka Palace, the stories of battle told by General Nogi, those dreams of colonization passed down from Emperor Meiji and before, and his own dull, circumscribed life, came together now for Hirohito. On a table-top in his War Headquarters, Hirohito plotted strategy. He watched the tiny flags of advance push down on the map deep into China. Tientsin was taken and then Peking. The sudden offensive of the Chinese military in Shanghai further forced the Imperial Army to look south to protect its interests in that city. Then, Chiang Kai-shek's new capital of Nanking appeared the ultimate glittering prize.

From the sidelines Prince Saionji, now eighty-eight, watched sadly. His life work appeared destroyed. He had envisaged a modern, internationally minded Japan, and had encouraged the Emperor towards this. Instead, he had seen Japan become a pariah nation after the conquest of Manchuria, withdrawing from the League of Nations. He had condemned an arms race and watched money poured into war preparations. He had advised friendship with Chiang Kai-shek and instead saw the Emperor agree to war against the Generalissimo. He advocated close relations with Britain and the United States, and instead the anti-Comintern Pact had been signed with Nazi Germany. People of dubious worth were being promoted about the Emperor, cutting him off in a ring of security as never before.

When he heard of the elevation in court of people whose views he considered extreme, Saionji sighed. 'It comes as no surprise . . . that is the trend of the times and there is nothing to be done. It is a great pity for the Emperor's sake.' Saionji's grumbles were distant. Hirohito did not hear.

Emperor Hirohito spent each summer at Hayama. In this fishing village thirty miles from Tokyo, he forgot the weight of monarchy. He became a man, walking the beach, trousers rolled above his ankles, fishing, swimming, his mind wandering from affairs of state to wider reveries. The greatest irritant in this idyll was an excess of mosquitoes.

The Summer Palace was of weathered wood, modest compared to the house of an American neighbour a distance along the beach. There were no telephones, refrigerators, electric stoves or air-conditioners. At dawn in the garden Hirohito relaxed chopping wood. In rock pools he gathered the marine specimens on which he was an expert. Years before upon the beach he had discovered a spotted red prawn. This creature had been overlooked by the cataloguers of marine biology until Hirohito's identification. The discovery of *sympathiphae imperialis* had been a proud moment in Hirohito's life. So introspective and bizarre a hobby as marine biology, was earlier deplored by Chamberlains when Hirohito was Crown Prince. Only when Hirohito's interest in military history reached a level of equal obsession, did murmurs of displeasure cease.

In the summer of 1937 the Emperor left Tokyo and drove once again to Hayama. The weight of war in China depressed him. It was more, he had discovered, than a game upon a map, more than dreaming the dreams of his Imperial ancestors or the glories of General Nogi's tales. At moments the reality came through to him. His subjects suffered. Young men in droves must be shipped off to die far from home. Taxes burdened his people to pay for the war in Asia and to float the Japanese Fleet. In his name the common people must suffer all manner of hardship. These were things not thought about in the rush to enter China. Even this annual visit to Hayama had been forbidden at first by court officials. It appeared ostentatious for Hirohito to relax when men were dying on the battlefield. But the vision of *Hakko Ichiu* superseded all other considerations. For such a dream some sacrifice was inevitable. Hirohito was still impatient for the fall of China, still impatient to move on, to Hong Kong, Singapore, Malaya. His mind was filled with strategy and an ultimate glory.

Now, briefly, at Hayama he could forget the events of the day. He stood once more on the deck of his motor launch in a white linen jacket and straw hat and dropped starfish and sponges into his pockets. He read Aesop's *Fables* on the beach, picnicked, swam, built sand-castles and raced with his children. He spent many hours at the microscope studying the specimens caught at Hayama; there he entered the only world in which he was truly happy. By mid-August he relinquished these pleasures and returned to Tokyo, to the khaki uniform he now wore. It had been decided by the army chiefs that he should make Iwane Matsui, an ageing, retired General in the reserve, Commander in Chief of Japanese forces in Central China.

It was an honour, but also a mystery to General Matsui, why he of all people should be reactivated from the reserve to take command in China. He was sixty, frail and tubercular. His weight on a five foot frame was down to no more than seven stone. He was given to recurrent fevers and coughs. He had been retired at his own request four years before in disapproval of the army's outrageous plotting to conquer China. He espoused the Strike South, but also recommended friendship with China. In retirement he had set up the East Asia League in Japan, a society to work for a united Asia and prevent a war with China. He had gone to Peking to establish a branch of this society but the Chinese were suspicious; Manchuria had given the Japanese a bad name. Asia for Asiatics sounds like Asia for the Japanese, they told him as they turned away.

Now that war was upon them, General Matsui could no longer talk of prevention. His speeches to the East Asia League advocated a quick drive up the Yangtze to take Nanking. Once in occupation Japanese actions must be exemplary. They must persuade the Chinese a Japanese administration was preferable to the deviousness of Chiang Kai-shek.

Everyone knew Matsui's convictions. He took his new command to be a sign of temperance on the part of the army and the Emperor. If a man of his mind was being reactivated when others, both active and able were bypassed, it must mean a change in attitude by the high command. Perhaps now they saw the wisdom of a negotiated settlement with China. That wheels within wheels still turned in the Military, or that to all he appeared a dispensable man, did not occur to the General. In the Phoenix Hall of the Imperial Palace, Matsui's medal-encrusted uniform weighed heavily in the August heat, his sword knocked against his knees. His face twitched uncontrollably. He bowed then knelt before his Emperor to receive command of the Imperial Army in Central China.

On his departure from the Palace, General Matsui shared a car with Prime Minister Konoye. Matsui was still dazed by the honour thrust upon him, still warm with thoughts of all he must do.

'There is no solution except to break the power of Chiang Kai-shek by capturing Nanking. That is what I must do,' General Matsui promised.

There was to be no delay. Two days later the East Asia League gave him a hurried farewell dinner. General Matsui made his last speech.

'I am going to the front not to fight an enemy but in the state of mind of one who sets out to pacify a brother.'

In the magnificent Phoenix Hall with its motif carved in silver or wood, painted on lacquer or woven into brocade, Hirohito became the nation's high priest, unapproachable, speaking in archaic words and voice. After the departure of General Matsui, Hirohito walked back to his workroom in the Imperial Library. In that room he was a man and fallible, he could discuss events with other men. The sincerity of Matsui was unmistakable. If his health held up, it would be good to have such a man in the field. Hirohito wanted the war over quickly. What had to be done, had to be done, but he wished the nastiness finished and China under his thumb. Only then could the rule of Showa begin to spread Enlightenment over greater Asia.

2

1928

Tokyo

Kenjiro Nozaki put down his pen and listened to the sound of his father's return from Kyoto. The powerful voice carried through the house before it died away. Beyond the room a spider's web spread under the eaves of the verandah. Beads of rain from a recent shower hung within it, like jewels against old lace. Such an intricacy of construction, he thought, for the harbouring of death. In the morning a maid would sweep it away, and the insect begin its work again.

As he watched, old Chieko appeared, hobbling painfully upon arthritic feet about the verandah of the house, her white hair pulled back into a thin knot. He saw her glance up at the spider's web, noting the need for demolition. She had looked after Kenjiro from birth, and grown old in the Nozakis' service. There had been, he remembered, the perfume of soap about her. It had stung sweetly in his nostrils as she nursed him to sleep. She still fussed about him as if he were a child. At his window she stopped with a toothless smile, and knelt to chat of Naomi's doings. The odour of rotted teeth hung about her now.

'Naomi is nothing like you. You were a terror. You must marry again and give her a mother.'

'Go away, old woman. I'm not ready to remarry. Leave the shutters open. And don't disturb that spider's web,' he ordered.

Old Chieko sighed and stood up. She pulled the heavy wooden doors half across the window in compromise to his request.

'Once you would never have spoken like that. You wanted my breast, not your mother's. And what is this about leaving the windows unshuttered? Is this what they do in foreign lands?' She hobbled away, pleased to have scored a point with him.

At each window about the wings of the house Chieko stopped to drag the shutters from their boxes. One by one the windows were closed for the night. The bright pictures of life Kenjiro watched were cancelled, like the slamming of a cover on a picture book.

He switched on the reading light and tidied the papers on his desk. A maid had already laid out a cotton kimono to wear after his bath. His father would take some time, he had first privilege in the bath, Kenjiro would follow and then his mother. He looked down at the page of writing before him, and wondered at its value. Why was he saying these inflammatory things? He was neither journalist nor revolutionary. His first article had been published some days before in a leftist magazine. There had been telephone calls immediately from unexpected people, mostly Communists, asking for interviews, further articles or his allegiance. By attacking the numerous extreme right-wing organizations in Japan, and especially the dubious personality of Shumei Okawa, Kenjiro had put himself in danger. With Mitsuru Toyama of the Russophobic Black Dragon Society, Okawa controlled the dark, reactionary infrastructure of the country. Instead of fear, Kenjiro felt only exhilaration. He waited as a swimmer waits for an incoming wave before a rocky shore. He chewed the top of his bamboo brush, the tang of the wood pricked his tongue. From the inner garden beyond the verandah came the scent of wet stone and leaves. He turned his attention to the writing again. The long list of right-wing associations lay before him. The Cherry Blossom Society, the Dark Ocean Society, the Stars and Ocean Society, the South Seas Association, were only the most influential. Besides these were more sinister organizations that he had yet to touch. The name of Shumei Okawa hung like a shadow over much of this list.

A maid slid open the door. 'The master asks that you join him after your bath,' the woman announced, kneeling.

Kenjiro frowned. His father rarely spent an evening at home, preferring to relax at a few select tea-houses or the premises of his mistress, Oyasu. He must wish to discuss the Emperor's Coronation from which he had just returned. He would use his invitation to the event as an object lesson, dropping names with which to impress his son of the importance of secular power. Kenjiro put down his pen in annoyance. A summons from his father could not be refused. The maid rose and began to lay out quilts for the night. He heard Naomi crying.

'What's wrong?' he asked.

'She found some newborn kittens under the verandah, and wanted to keep them. It is her bedtime, she is tired,' the woman laughed.

Through the half-open shutter he saw Naomi, clinging to the hand of a maid, practising her first steps along the verandah. Her hair was wet from her evening bath and she wore a brightly-patterned cotton kimono. Sometimes he took his daughter to the Zoo, a beach or a shrine. The occasions were rare and, much as he wished, he could not enjoy them. When he looked at Naomi he saw Jacqueline. In the delicate bones and hazel eyes, in skin like the lining of a shell, his wife appeared

41

seamlessly within the child. It was over a year since Jacqueline's death. Memory still gripped him unbearably.

The garden of the house was fading into darkness. Usually he enjoyed this hour, on the cusp of day and night, but this evening a restlessness filled him. He looked again at the paper before him and cut a word here or there. He knew he was writing to empty himself, pressured not only by grief but by the months of stress in Japan. After Jacqueline's death the anger in him mounted; everything exacerbated his loss. His life seemed manipulated to confine him.

Kenjiro watched as Naomi was restrained by the maid from climbing off the balcony into the garden. She struggled, flailing against the woman. Although she was installed with a maid in the furthest wing, her cries crossed the garden to Kenjiro. The baby cried, said his mother, no more than all babies, no more than Kenjiro himself as an infant. But at night in his dreams her sorrow mixed with his own.

Jacqueline had decided before the birth that, if the child was a girl, they would call her Naomi. Although a common Japanese name, its biblical connotation beyond Japan made it appear bi-cultural. Jacqueline felt this an appropriate way to set about the naming of their child. After the birth she lived only long enough to hold Naomi and whisper her name.

If he had not insisted they return from France, perhaps Jacqueline would still be alive. French doctors might have handled the birth differently, in a hospital instead of at home, with the right equipment at hand. Kenjiro blamed himself. His father had not agreed to the match. They married in Paris without his consent. Within a few months Jacqueline became pregnant and Kenjiro decided to return to Japan. He had grown weary of exile in France. In Japan a diplomatic career awaited him, he had already passed the Foreign Service exams. Kenjiro had secretly hoped for a son, and wanted him born in Japan, to deepen the hybrid rooting. And anxious by now for the restoration of his only son, Yuzuru Nozaki encouraged the idea. His letters were brushed with compromise. If Jacqueline was alive Naomi would not have cried. Probably, Jacqueline would have kept a kitten. The old weight in his body returned at the thought of his wife.

In a remaining illuminated window Kenjiro glimpsed his father on his way to the bath. The light in the corridor shone on his bald head. Virility powered his stance, his walk, the directness of his stare. A maid scuttled behind him, to scrub his back. He was a handsome man, barrel-chested and of unusual height; perennially attractive to women. His face was heavy with thrusting features and deeply-hooded eyes. Kenjiro had inherited his height but was slim, with his mother's sensitive boning. At last Kenjiro undressed, tying the thin blue kimono about himself, and followed his father to the bath. Eventually, he walked to the room where his father waited, a porcelain flask of sake already before him.

Kenjiro bowed, then sat at the low table opposite his father. A maid hurried in with more hot sake for Kenjiro. Yuzuru began to talk about the Coronation in Kyoto. There had been many Shinto rites of purification. These esoteric ceremonies were hidden from the mass of guests, in the innermost chambers of court buildings. Many banquets supplemented the formality of ritual, and these Yuzuru had enjoyed. Kenjiro listened patiently. His father's face was inflamed by drink and pride at his own eminence. Not many bureaucrats had received invitations from the Imperial Household.

Kenjiro knew his father had taken Oyasu with him to Kyoto. For many years she had been Yuzuru's chief mistress, set up in a house of her own. He had watched his mother pack a suitcase for the visit to Kyoto. In it she included a medicinal soap his father used after an amorous hour, and an aphrodisiac to be drunk twenty minutes before intercourse. She did these things unemotionally; her duties lay elsewhere. Had a son resulted from the liaison he might have come to live in the main house, to be reared by Kenjiro's mother. They were spared this trauma as Oyasu had never carried a child full term. If there were offspring from other liaisons, Kenjiro knew nothing of them.

'There was much talk in Kyoto of Chang Tso-lin. They say his death was the work of Manchurian bandits,' Yuzuru announced, refilling his glass.

'It is the official explanation, what else could they say?' Kenjiro replied, watching his father throw back a small cup of sake. The controversy raging throughout Japan about the death in China of the Manchurian warlord, Chang Tso-lin, had quieted during the Coronation when the newspapers had other matters to report.

'It was a plot by our Imperial Army. He was not assassinated by his own people.' Kenjiro met his father's eye. In spite of the difficulties of their relationship, in the area of political argument they found a meeting place, like two boxers in a ring.

Yuzuru sipped his sake. 'Chang Tso-lin fought with us against Russia in the 1905 war. He was our best insurance against Russian encroachment in Manchuria. He should not have been killed.'

'Chang Tso-lin was the main obstacle to our *own* encroachment in Manchuria,' Kenjiro replied. 'The problem of Manchuria will grow and colour the whole of the Showa era. It may be the new Emperor's greatest test. Already there are people in Japan who dream of one day conquering China. Why must we want what is not ours?'

43

'Because Japan needs land and raw products to survive. Because the Chinese are weak and the Manchurians so disunited they allow themselves to be governed by whoever wants the job. If Russia gets into China they'll soon flood over the water and attempt to conquer Japan. That's what Russia has in mind. We have no choice but to see that day never comes. We must advance instead before Russia takes a step.' Yuzuru finished his sake and then continued. 'Of course for this to happen our army will have to come down off their high horse and make some compromises with the civil sector. The money of the big business conglomerates is needed if we are to take over Manchuria.' Yuzuru refilled the sake cups. He flexed the muscles of his jaw, anger flushed through him.

'In Kyoto I was confronted by that weasel, Tajima. He was sent to warn me you are in great trouble. You know the power of a man like Okawa, and his connections with Toyama. You have gone too far with these stupid writings. Who gave you these ideas? There is a limit to how much my name will protect you, or how much the right-wing organizations and men like Okawa will tolerate. I have been told that if you leave the country immediately, these articles will be overlooked. If not, the risk of arrest is great. Have you ever considered my feelings or those of your mother? She has not slept for nights.'

Kenjiro started in shock. 'Have you seen the article?' It had not occurred to him that his father would know about his writing.

'I do not need to. I can imagine only too well.'

Yuzuru Nozaki looked at Kenjiro over his cup of sake. He was not pleased by his drawn expression, nor by the outrageous articles. More than this he was worried. Kenjiro faced danger from the growing reactionary elements in the country. There were escalating arrests of young men with dangerous ideas. *Ideas*. It was easy to do no more than talk. The boy took after his mother. He suspected his wife might even now encourage the growth of her son's *ideas*. She herself had once had leanings in that direction, but the cement of marriage and its duties soon eradicated this.

He gazed in irritation at his son, and saw only weakness. He knew the naked rise of sympathy that could spread like a blush through his face. The smooth boning and unobtrusive jaw did not appear manly enough. The deep-set eyes, elongated lids drawn taut, were better made for a woman. He wore his hair too long and did not drink enough. There was too much restraint where there should have been none, and too little where discretion was needed. Only in the sensuous mouth could Yuzuru see himself in his son. He gulped back his sake in anger.

In his youth Yuzuru Nozaki had made a Grand Tour of Europe. He

44

found Japanese compatriots in Paris of all ranks. The taste of their rumbustious life and the seductiveness of the women, made him loath to return to Japan. Those Paris friends were now men of power in the military and Civil Service, and Yuzuru himself a bureaucrat of some standing. He had entered the Ministry of Commerce and Industry, realizing the importance of the stock exchange in the financial world. In this ministry he also saw quick promotion and had risen speedily.

When a foreign tour was arranged for his son, he warned him from experience of the dangers that might allure. Of the sermon one morning Kenjiro remembered little but excitement at the very things his father suggested avoiding. The women, Kenjiro was advised, were for use and not attachment. From France he might bring curios, silks, fine porcelain, sophistication and sexual experience. He was not to return with a wife. Such liaisons were lower-class and exposed men who could not control their emotions. All advice was forgotten before Jacqueline.

'What will be the state of this country if all free thought is suppressed? What future will there be under a military regime . . .' Kenjiro began to protest.

'I also met Watanabe,' Yuzuru interrupted, his face red with fury. 'I spoke with him about you. As you know he is in the Gaimusho. He holds a high post in the European and American Affairs Bureau. He will do what he can; he owes me a favour. Before you went to France you were ready to enter the Foreign Service. I suggest you waste no further time but take up your career immediately. You are already twenty-five. Leave off this radical nonsense. It is the stuff of students, not grown men. Watanabe will see you get a good posting. Perhaps you will find yourself back in Europe. I expect that would please you.' Kenjiro let his father's rage explode before replying.

'We must fight the ideas of Fascism . . .'

'I have had enough of your ideas.' Yuzuru struck his fist upon the table. 'The Western-style democracy you preach has no place in Japan. Our traditional patterns of obligation will never change.'

'Which means the influence of the men like Okawa and corrupt political and financial cliques will continue to supersede the will of the people. This frame of mind will bring us disaster,' Kenjiro insisted.

'Bah!' Yuzuru raged. 'At the moment it is you who is facing disaster.'

Kenjiro could not sleep. Only through his father's contacts would he now be taken into the Foreign Service and given a posting abroad. Even then he would be watched by the Military Police wherever he went in the world. He would have to be circumspect. He was to leave Japan because he could not agree with the trend in the country. Yet, to escape, he must enter the very bastion of those mores he disagreed with; the representation abroad of the Government and country. How would he cope, he suddenly wondered, with the crucial choices of this conflict?

In the dark Kenjiro listened to the creaks of contracting wood in the old house. He thought he heard Naomi cry but when he listened it was only a cat. Whatever the future he felt impatient to get on with it. The stress of the past two years had calcified about him. He could not wait now to get away.

The cat wailed again. Kenjiro raised himself on an elbow. He had opened the shutters after Chieko closed them, as he did each night. It confused her to have her routine disturbed, but he liked to see the first light break. After Jacqueline's death he moved from the Western-style room they had shared. Now, he slept Japanese style again. His room opened on to the verandah and the garden. He often woke early and from his quilts watched the old lantern come into focus and the camellia gather light. The garden was part of his childhood. The lantern was old and weathered green with lichen. It stood like a sentinel amongst the rocks and small pruned shrubs, impervious to time. The Great Kanto Earthquake had toppled but not broken it. Each morning, from his bed, he watched it re-form with the light.

The sound came again; the creak of wood on the verandah. He wondered if a maid was moving around, but the footstep was heavy. There was a full moon and it showed a man, trying the shutters of each window. The shape of another intruder appeared, the moonlight gleamed on a gun in his hand. Kenjiro drew back inside the room. The men were not common thieves. No pilferer carried a gun. To arrest him, even at midnight, police would come straight to the door. These men must have been sent by some vindictive right-wing organization.

There was the creak again of wood. The men slipped through a door to the servants' quarters. Kenjiro made his way silently to the phone in the main room and dialled the police. His father kept several swords wrapped in silk in a chest in his study, family possessions of another era when men of standing all wore swords. There was also a revolver, he remembered. He walked quickly towards the study.

Before he could reach the room, screaming began. The servants had woken. There was the vibration of running feet, falling screens and voices. Gun shot spat out. For a moment in the darkness all movement stopped. Kenjiro slipped into his father's study, opening the chest where the swords were kept. He found the revolver and drew it from its case. It was old and there were no bullets. He heard another shot.

The corridor was dark. At the top of the stairs light shone from his parents' room. His mother screamed and Kenjiro ran forward. Above him two men backed onto the landing. He flattened himself against the wall as they came down the stairs. If he was quick he could take them by surprise. He stepped out of the shadow, gripping the gun, hoping the bluff would work. The men turned, wild eyed. Scarves were wrapped around their faces.

There was a sudden movement above them on the stairs. Old Chieko stood upon the top step, staring fixedly at Kenjiro. The men looked up. The crack of a gun burst in Kenjiro's ears. Old Chieko swayed, clinging to the banisters, her eyes still fixed upon Kenjiro. The dark stain of blood spread slowly through her kimono. Her knees buckled beneath her and she slid down the steps like a limp sack of grain.

From outside the house came voices and a banging upon the door. The police announced their arrival. The men with guns turned and ran into Kenjiro's room, dropping down into the garden from the verandah. They swung themselves up through the branches of a pine, jumped over the wall, and ran off into the night.

Kenjiro bent over Chieko. Her limbs were splayed out at odd angles, like the rag doll Naomi played with. He knew she was dead. The parted kimono revealed her legs, thin as a bird's above split-toed white socks. She had taken the bullet meant for him. He thought suddenly of Naomi and turned towards her room.

'She's all right,' his mother shouted from the top of the stairs. He looked up and saw his father, a towel pressed to his arm, the sleeve of his kimono wet with blood.

'It's only a graze, nothing more,' Yuzuru said.

'Call the doctor,' Shizuko Nozaki ordered a servant.

The police were all around now, running after the intruders, examining Chieko. The chief officer was already questioning the servants.

Yuzuru led the way to the room where earlier he and Kenjiro had eaten dinner. A servant brought tea for the police and brandy for Yuzuru and Kenjiro. The doctor arrived and Yuzuru retired with him to another room for the wound on his arm to be dressed. The police officer was a local man, known to the Nozakis. He was apologetic, affronted by the audacity of the event.

'They are not ordinary thieves,' he announced. 'Thieves do not carry guns.' Kenjiro said nothing but Yuzuru, returning to the room, was direct.

'There is the possibility of some misunderstanding. The men may be acquaintances under the wrong impression concerning the politics of my son. I do not wish you to pursue the men, nor for you to record the incident. Do me this favour please. It is a matter that we will settle amicably.'

The police officer understood. 'If that is your wish, if no harm has been done, then of course I respect your feelings.' He looked through the open door at Chieko's body, covered by a sheet.

'She was an old woman,' Yuzuru said, following his gaze. 'She has no living relative. Even the shock of such an upset could have given a heart attack to someone of her years. She has been in weak health for some time.' The officer nodded and with his men soon left the house.

Kenjiro watched him bow low before his father. The next day a gift of delicacies and money would be sent from the house to the police station. The doctor who dressed Yuzuru's wound had not been informed of Chieko's death. Soon they were alone. Shizuko sat in a corner, dabbing her eyes with a folded square of muslin. The bullet had not entered Yuzuru's flesh, the wound was light. Kenjiro sat silent before his parents. At last Yuzuru spoke.

'Tomorrow you must go to your Uncle Juichi. You will be safe there. Your mother and Naomi will go with you. I will arrange things at once with Watanabe. As soon as he has secured a posting you can leave the country, and after that your mother and Naomi will return. Some country air will do them good.' Yuzuru's voice was calm.

Uncle Juichi lived in the remote mountains of Nagano, a cousin of Yuzuru's whom the family considered a country bumpkin, in spite of his wealth from considerable holdings. Kenjiro bowed before his father, his brow touched the matted floor. He was grateful to be spared any outburst. His father made him feel as he had in childhood, inadequate before his superior talents.

3

1930

Toyko

The train journey from Kobe to Tokyo took many hours. The train steamed through land textured by paddies, tea bushes, fields of radish and the constant shadow of mountains. Although he had been ten days in the country, it was Tilik Dayal's first proper glimpse of Japan. So much had happened in the last few weeks. His life had been stood on end.

It was the season to flood the paddies. The land was a jigsaw of watery mirrors. Thatched farmhouses rose like islands above the deluge. The movement of clouds and the ridges of hills reflected at his feet. It seemed a strange reversal of order for Heaven to fall to earth in this way. Refracted in the window his own face skimmed over the aqueous kingdom, insubstantial as a ghost.

This land was different from India. Everything was crushed together into the frame of the window; houses, bamboo, pines, worked fields. All was neat, terraced, lined, an obedient and precise formation. Nature seemed manipulated to the will of men. Hills, thick with trees blocked the eye everywhere. Here there were no far horizons.

On the train journey from Delhi to Bombay to embark on the ship to Japan, there had been nothing but horizon. Tilik remembered a thousand miles of dry brown land, dust in his mouth and the baking sky. Occasionally the figure of a woman walked into view, a brass pot of water on her head, its dampness the only gleam of moisture remembered on that journey. Man appeared powerless before such terrain. Where had he come to? What had he done? He could never return to India. In the panic of the past weeks, he had forgotten he was fleeing into exile. The finality came to him now.

He drew back from the window and stared at the flooded world about him. He had the feeling the neat demarcations of this land must fit the nature of its society. The hard wood of the seat pressed against his back. Before him a man unlaced his shoes and placed them neatly upon a newspaper, tucking his feet up beneath him. The woman beside him did the same. They opened lunch boxes of cold rice covered with strips of seaweed.

Towards the end of the journey Mount Fuji appeared, sweeping into the sky like a tall grey funnel. Since summer approached, the cap of snow depicted on picture postcards was missing. Tilik stared at the toy shape. In the train people rushed to the windows to gaze at the icon. Tilik did not stir. In India the Himalayas soared beyond the grasp of men. His awe was reserved for Rash Bihari Bose, the object of his own pilgrimage.

From his pocket Tilik pulled out the letter of introduction carried with him from India, and read it for the umpteenth time. To his mind it did not say enough. After stating his name it spoke only of the coming death of White Rule in India and the glory of Independence. All it said otherwise was, *Please Honoured Sir, Great Patriot, be kind enough to help this young man in his hour of need. He will tell you his story himself.* Would this be enough to interest Rash Bihari? The letter was signed by Patel, the commander of the revolutionary group Tilik belonged to. He had not thought to ask Patel if he knew Rash Bihari personally. Now, as the train clanked heavily over the tracks, taking him nearer the Great Patriot, these questions and more filled his mind. What if Rash Bihari turned his back upon him? A great amount of his remaining money was invested in this railway ticket. On the telephone, requesting an interview, Tilik had been tongue-tied, and had not missed the weariness in Rash Bihari's voice when he at last agreed to meet him.

Tilik had once seen a picture of Rash Bihari Bose. It showed a strong face, a thick head of hair and a moustache above full lips. The freedom fighter, wrapped in a shawl over a high-necked jacket, projected dignity. His patriotism was an example to generations. He became known in India and abroad after a bomb attack on Lord Hardinge. As the hunt for him intensified, he was persuaded to leave India and continue the struggle for freedom elsewhere. He had fled long ago to Japan. Tilik already felt close to the man. He too had fled India on account of a bomb.

He took a taxi from the station to Rash Bihari's home. A maid showed him in. Tilik sat down and waited in trepidation. Out of respect he had worn a tie, but he loosened it now in the heat. He studied the walls of thin varnished wood and the threadbare patch in a rug. The stale odour of Indian spices hung on the air. He picked out the sharpness of mustard seed that had filled his own home at cooking times. And behind it the perfume of incense. Emotions, tightly suppressed for weeks, rocked abruptly through him. He remembered the smell of frying savouries, the odour of burning cow dung, and the perfume of ripe mangoes. There was the taste on his tongue of the bitter almonds he had picked from trees as a child, and the oily delights of the sweetmeat shops. His senses were tormented. He would never return to India. Soon he heard footsteps outside the door.

Rash Bihari was now neither young nor thick-haired but a portly, balding, elderly man in a crumpled Western suit. The ordinariness was disconcerting after the legendary tales. His smile was warm, he seemed pleased to see a countryman. Tilik's throat grew suddenly tight. This was the first Indian he had met since arriving in Japan. Emotions overcame him. His first words to the patriot emerged as a stutter. He pushed forward the letter of introduction.

The old man read it then refolded the paper, handing it back to Tilik. 'I do not know these people. Many know me whom I do not know. But it is of no matter. You are here for reasons I understand and appear in need of help.' Rash Bihari sat down and called for some tea. The words rehearsed for this moment shrank upon Tilik's tongue. He sat looking at his hands.

'You have family in India? A wife?' Rash Bihari asked, trying to help. His expression was benign and yet there was detachment. He had a quiet, forceful manner.

Tilik shook his head. 'My father died in Amritsar, at Jallianwala Bagh, and my mother some years ago. Had she been alive I expect she would have been looking for a suitable girl for me to marry. I'm already thirty-three. I was an only child. My father would follow only Gandhiji. To him revolutionary organizations were unusable as a tool for civilized men. His death opened my eyes to other more forceful ways,' Tilik explained. 'I chose then to follow Subash Chandra Bose.'

He wondered how one acquired the kind of aura Rash Bihari carried. Was it zealous patriotism to a cause? Did exile establish it? Would people one day feel about him as he now felt about Rash Bihari? Even as he asked these questions he knew the quiet certainty that emanated from Rash Bihari was something more than all these things.

'Ah! Amritsar,' Rash Bihari sighed.

'I hate all Englishmen,' Tilik burst out.

'We must hate them collectively in order to be free, but there are decent and reasonable men amongst them. This you should not forget.' Rash Bihari spoke mildly. He listened attentively as Tilik told the story of his father's death at the hands of General Dyer. He watched emotion tremble through the young man's body.

'My respect for Gandhiji is without words,' Rash Bihari said when Tilik finished. 'But only force, not passive resistance, will drive the British from India. Only young leaders like Subash Chandra Bose, whom you follow, can take us to our goal. For Independence to be achieved Subash must stay in India. He must not, like you and I, be driven into exile.' Although they shared the common Bengali name of Bose, there was no relationship between the two freedom fighters, Rash Bihari and Subash Chandra.

The maid entered and set down the tray of tea. Rash Bihari poured it out himself, setting a strainer over each cup. 'I do not believe we are men of true violence for all this talk,' he sighed. 'We hold ourselves above the common criminal because of our sense of mission. But then again, why should intellectual ruminating in any way set us apart? Death is death and its perpetration cannot be ameliorated whatever the cause. Now, as I grow older, I think about these things. Of course, when I was your age and hotheaded, such thoughts were far from me.'

Tilik stared at the stream of tea Rash Bihari poured carefully into the cups. He saw the liquid was dark and thick; leaves, sugar, milk and cardamoms all boiled up together. His mouth began to water. He had not drunk such tea since leaving India. He realized once more how far he had drifted from all that was familiar.

'This tea is sent to me from home. You cannot get Nilgiri tea here, you cannot get any good tea at all. The first thing we all have to do in exile is to arrange our supplies of tea and spices.' Rash Bihari chuckled.

Tilik found no humour in these facts. Who was to send him this tea? How was he to pay the sender? What was he doing in a country that could not even provide him with tea? His life as it now unfolded had not been mentioned in his horoscope, charted at his birth.

Rash Bihari Bose stared at the young man opposite him, nervously turning the cup in his hand. A high-ridged nose dominated his face, his brows met in a bar. His wide mouth had a looseness that seemed to Rash Bihari to weaken his expression. His eyes burned with the earnestness of most young zealots and protruded slightly, as if pressured from inside. He would be prey to men of stronger character who sided not with right, but with the trite truths of a personal agenda. There was something lost about him. Rash Bihari remembered his own early days in Japan, and felt sympathy. Probably he would find his way.

'And what of this recent incident that caused you to flee to Japan?' Rash Bihari asked, settling back once more, balancing his teacup on the wooden arm of the chair.

'I was working in a firm of British accountants in Delhi, McGregor, McGregor and Anderson. My qualifications were Indian ones, so I had no hope of rising above the level of a clerk. I could only watch the rise of the White Sahibs. But at college I had met many who felt as I did. I was already working actively in revolutionary groups. Of course at McGregor, McGregor and Anderson they knew nothing of this . . .' Tilik's voice trailed off.

'The incident?' Rash Bihari reminded him, stifling a yawn in the hot afternoon. Tilik cleared his throat, and groped for words with which to describe the bungled bomb attack in Delhi on Police Commissioner Tegart.

Once more, as he finished his story, Tilik found he was shaking. Rash Bihari reached forward, took the cup from his hand and set it on a table for safety. 'You must remember that violence, even if we believe its use achieves something for our people, is still violence. It belongs to the active, insidious, creeping power of something so dark it can swallow all reason and destroy the personality. This, to me, is the greatest personal battle we face when we choose revolutionary ways. Regard yourself as a swimmer in a vicious sea. Your job is to keep your head above water, while the body is submerged. All about you are men of dubious nature, who would use you for their cause.' Rash Bihari spoke quietly while looking hard at the young man before him.

'Now tell me the rest of your story,' Rash Bihari continued.

Tilik forced his mind back again to the failed bomb attack. 'The police saw me clearly as I ran. They put out a description of me. They wanted to hang me for the attempted murder of Tegart. I had an uncle in business here in Japan, in Kobe. He said he would give me a job. The commander of our group had contacts at the Japanese Embassy in Delhi. A Japanese there by the name of Kenjiro Nozaki, who was sympathetic to our cause, arranged special papers for me. I was smuggled aboard a boat at Bombay. I arrived in Kobe to find my uncle had died the week before. My Japanese aunt closed the business. In Delhi, before I left, they told me to make contact with you, they gave me that letter. It has all happened so quickly.'

'There is a role for those of us outside India,' Rash Bihari told him. 'Only Japan is in the position to stand by the oppressed Asiatic and to liberate Asia. Japan encourages us to continue our own struggle under their protection. They know as long as British imperialism rules India they cannot expect a final victory in Asia in this battle. I have worked many years here to establish contacts with the military and civil high commands, and to impress upon them the necessity of helping India in her struggle. Subash Chandra Bose looks to Germany and Hitler for help. In my view he should look East, to Japan.'

The stress he had lived with since he arrived rose up again in Tilik. He was without contacts or friends. He could die in this land and no one would know. He had neither money nor a language in which to communicate and no country to return to. He recalled once visiting a relative in a dilapidated building due for demolition. During his visit the floor had vanished beneath him, leaving him clinging to a beam, treading air. This was how he felt now.

'There is much here for an energetic young man to do,' Rash Bihari announced. 'You must travel and talk of our Indian cause throughout Japan and the Far East. Japan is on the brink of extending its power into Manchuria and this will widen our own theatre of agitation. There are very few of us in Japan with experience in anti-British activities. Most Indians here are merchants.' Rash Bihari's tone was fatherly.

'But I know nobody, what can I do?' Tilik could not keep the desperation from his voice. Rash Bihari laughed.

'You must meet Mitsuru Toyama. He is an old man now with a white beard, but his vigour is undimmed. And Shumei Okawa. If you know these men all doors will open. Without their help we can do little.'

'Are they so powerful?' Tilik asked.

'Toyama heads an extreme right-wing nationalist group in Japan. He is the main force in the Black Dragon Society. His power stretches from the palace to the peasants. Like you, I knew nobody when I fled here. Then I met Sun Yat-sen, who had also been given asylum. He introduced me to Toyama, who has been my protector ever since.' He stood up and crossed the room to some bookshelves.

The afternoon sun filled the room. Rash Bihari bent forward, peering at titles. Tilik thought again of the photograph of the man in his prime and observed the portly form at the bookshelves. Now he wondered if exile would produce in himself the same aura of sad irrelevance. He shook these thoughts from his mind. The small standing fan turned on a table, its breeze sweeping over Tilik at intervals.

'Take these English translations and read them, they are the writings of Shumei Okawa, Toyama's protégé.' Rash Bihari pushed several books into his hands. Tilik turned the pages politely. They were well thumbed and spotted in places by mould.

'Patriotism like ours, aimed not only at a free India but also at an Asia free of Western domination, has values close to Toyama's own heart. He arranged my safe hiding in the beginning, in the home of a baker called Soma. For Toyama the family took the risk of protecting me. Those were difficult years. I married their daughter Toshiko. She was a brave woman.' Rash Bihari's face filled with emotion. 'The marriage was arranged by Toyama. He thought it a good way to bind me to Japan and our common cause. We were happy while she lived. She died when our children were still small.'

54

They sat in silence for some moments before Rash Bihari spoke again. 'We live in a troubled era, the reign of the white man is ending. All over East Asia there are Indian freedom fighters. We need an Independence League, to give shape to our struggle in a co-ordinated way. We need to utilize the changing situation in East Asia to further our cause. Toyama talks in far-reaching ways. We have also an ally in Okawa, who has studied our culture and language. These men are leaders in Japan. If Japan rises to free Asia, they will march with us into India.'

New strength rose up in Tilik. For the first time, listening to Rash Bihari speak, the confused weeks behind him had meaning. He saw a pattern in his destiny. His eviction from India was not to enter limbo.

The weeks that followed had a breathlessness. Tilik was employed in a trading house in Tokyo, and as language was a problem, was settled in the accounts department. He was to board in the home of Ichiro Ohara, a partner in the firm. All this he gathered was arranged by Mitsuru Toyama at Rash Bihari's request.

Mr Ohara spoke passable English and was proud of his cosmopolitan attitudes. The family made an effort to welcome Tilik and brought out forks and spoons even though he insisted on eating with chopsticks. The younger children stared curiously. Only twenty-year-old Michiko, the eldest daughter, ignored Tilik and his efforts with chopsticks and the language that reduced her siblings to giggles. However badly she snubbed him, the adrenaline raced through his body in a pleasant but disturbing way.

Each morning Tilik set out for the office with Mr Ohara, and in the evenings immersed himself in Japanese lessons. Soon the linguistic mysteries about him lessened. Outside office hours he wrote anti-British literature. Through Mitsuru Toyama's influence much of this appeared in the Japanese vernacular press after it had been translated. Invitations began to come to give public lectures. Among the friends he acquired at the Black Dragon Society and elsewhere was Jun Hasegawa who, as a close associate of Mitsuru Toyama, acted as his intermediary. Hasegawa worked with Army Intelligence. His English was perfect. When Tilik tried his Japanese, Hasegawa became annoyed.

'Please let us speak in English. Every time I hear a foreigner speaking Japanese I have a strong desire to strangle him.'

One September evening Hasegawa summoned Tilik to a restaurant they frequented. He entered, beaming. He had a new mistress and the grey hairs apparent in the year Tilik had known him were now covered by ebony dye.

'Women keep me young,' he said when Tilik commented on his

appearance. 'If you don't start soon your balls will dry up.' He ordered iced beer and food. The heat had not yet abated. The door of the restaurant stood open to the sound of traffic from the main road.

'We've gone into Manchuria,' Hasegawa announced after a long drink of beer, his colour was high. Tilik did not understand. He was hungry and his attention was on the man behind the counter, fanning their dinner over charcoal.

'We've taken Mukden,' Hasegawa explained. He spoke in a low voice so that nobody else should hear, trying to suppress his excitement. 'The whole country is waiting for news. The morning newspapers will be full of it.'

'I've heard nothing of it,' Tilik replied. Hasegawa re-filled their glasses with iced beer.

'How would you, you're a foreigner. There has been hardly anything in the press, although for months now many people have known this was in the air. As a nation we are able to keep a secret.' Hasegawa's voice was full of pride. His eyes were hooded and his chin receded abruptly. He had the look of a lizard; sleepy, wary, arrogant.

'I've heard Manchuria talked about. I thought it was economic chat, about the need for their raw materials and markets for your products,' Tilik replied. Hasegawa smiled and shook his head.

In the restaurant was a tank of live fish. Hasegawa leaned forward and discussed the merits of each creature intently with the cook. A crayfish was at last chosen and brought up in a short-handled net. It was laid flapping on a block of wood. In a single movement the cook half flayed it as it writhed. It was placed on a plate before Hasegawa, garnished by a yellow flower. In spite of Hasegawa's insistence, Tilik had declined the dish. Hasegawa began to eat, the creature flapped weakly before him. Tilik watched, sickened yet excited.

'We need Manchuria, we cannot continue to grow without it,' Hasegawa told him, wiping his mouth on a napkin, as he finished. 'We also need it as a buffer state before Russia. Many people think Russia is our number one enemy, and we should Strike North and take Siberia. Others think we should Strike South at Western colonies in South-east Asia rather than first at Russia. There is a mystical prophecy that 1936 will be a turning point in Japanese history. To some it is the year to take China, and to others the year to take Siberia. Many people think if we Strike South it will end in a war with the United States. But they also must realize we can only successfully strike at Russia when we have at our disposal the manpower of Asia. Then it will be a proper war. The Asian races against the White race. In the future all war will be Racial War.' Hasegawa's eyes gleamed in animation. He turned to a plate of grilled chicken liver.

'I remember the night Emperor Taisho died and the Crown Prince became the new Emperor,' Hasegawa continued. 'I was with Shumei Okawa and a crowd of young officers from the Emperor's retinue. We were all drunk with celebration. Even then Okawa jumped up to drink a toast to the conquest of Manchuria. As we walked home we passed the Palace. In the moonlight we saw country folk praying for the new Emperor. We felt ecstatic, as if the conquest of Manchuria was already assured.' Hasegawa had a faraway look in his eyes. Tilik shifted nervously. For the first time he grew fearful of the power around him. He sipped his beer, made a start with the chicken liver and let Hasegawa ramble.

'Our people will spread and multiply across Asia. Those races we have conquered or shall conquer, will disappear eventually. The Koreans will be assimilated by us; the Chinese and Manchurians will be the victims of opium; the Russians ruined by vodka. The destiny of Japan has been outlined by the Gods. Asia could soon belong to us, if we take it carefully.' Hasegawa stopped suddenly.

Tilik looked into his beer. These were the schemes of men to whom megalomania was plausible. He thought suddenly of Rash Bihari. The caution he exuded was a dull thing before Hasegawa's charisma. Perhaps Rash Bihari was no more than an old man with scruples. Tilik could already see the reproof upon his face, and for a moment grew confused. Was Hasegawa a man to follow? He observed the empty shell of the crayfish, and felt a new twist of exhilaration. Hasegawa's contemptuous eyelids flickered.

'If you look at Japan on the map of the world, you will see our position is not without significance. We stand alone before the rest of Asia, advancing bravely into the Pacific towards America. At the same time we appear ready to defend Asia from attack. Geography has positioned us for a special destiny.' Hasegawa finished the last of his beer and then turned abruptly to Tilik.

'We will immediately be setting up our own administration in Mukden. Soon all Manchuria will be under our rule. Your cause serves our cause. A foreigner on the side of Japan, interested in Asian nationalism, has great use for us. In the new state we will need an ever more diligent Intelligence. There is much you could do to help us that is impossible for a Japanese. For your own cause you would have extended territory, as I have explained to you.'

Tilik was taken aback. Hasegawa would not let him interrupt. 'I am to go there myself, to assist in setting up the new administration. It is based on the principle of the unity of the five races living in Manchuria. Japanese, Koreans, Chinese, Mongols, and Manchus. I have been closely involved with the planning of this party structure. We have to guard against differences of ethnic opinion and anti-Japanese views. I have planned an anti-Western campaign which I feel will help unify people against a common enemy. If this could be spearheaded by a non-Japanese who is also an Asian, it would be a help. Will you do it?'

'Yes,' Tilik answered, all hesitation suddenly gone, his path clear at last before him.

It had happened as Hasegawa said; a bomb on a railway line, an attack on a garrison, the taking of the walled city of Mukden, and towns falling like dominoes along the track to Port Arthur. Mukden had been taken in a single night. By noon on 19th September the war was finished and Mukden under the Japanese flag.

'We knew something was in the air,' said Mr Ohara, translating a newspaper article for Tilik. They sat in rattan chairs on a narrow verandah. 'If this had only happened earlier it might have saved me.'

'How would it have saved you?' Tilik enquired.

'It might have brought new growth to my business, as it will now for many people. Without Toyama's help we would have been bankrupt. He bailed me out, and persuaded our present company to take us over. Our name and face have both been saved.' Ohara sighed. It was the first Tilik had heard of his story.

In turn, Ohara knew little of Tilik's activities at the Black Dragon Society. The hours Tilik spent working in his room he assumed were in learning Japanese. He was not interested in India or its battle for freedom. He feared and respected Toyama, and repaid his obligation by installing Tilik in his home.

Everywhere parties of celebration for the conquest of Manchuria were in progress. Hasegawa called Tilik with an invitation to an élite geisha house in Tsukiji. There were a large number of guests, all important men. Mitsuru Toyama himself nodded to Tilik from afar. Hasegawa came to settle him in and introduced him also to the famous Colonel Hashimoto who, with Shumei Okawa, had masterminded so many plots.

A geisha plied Tilik with sake and attention. Small, low lacquer tables were arranged along three walls of the room. Tilik was seated alone in a humble position, at an end table near sliding doors. The noise was robust and the drinking heavy as the party became progressively bawdy. Men who were household names in the country did conjuring tricks or stood on their heads. There was a wheelbarrow race with the geisha as barrows, their bare legs protruding from kimono about the hips of drunken men. Tilik watched Mitsuru Toyama join in these antics, unabashed. This unloosed Toyama was as unnerving as the austere old man at Black Dragon Headquarters.

There, when Tilik had first met the great man, Toyama's eyes had sent a coldness through him. Behind round spectacles they were sunken and flinty. A white beard straggled over his dark kimono. He had the look of a mystic, yet he was a famous fixer of death. His smile, it was said, could make a Prime Minister tremble. A strange force streamed from the grim old man.

Tilik remembered that meeting when, later, Toyama squatted down beside him, flushed by drink and abandon. But behind the high colour his eyes were the same, unmoving as a reptile.

'You need a Japanese wife,' Toyama announced in a jocular tone. 'It will smooth your way in your work here and cement the ties between our countries. I shall arrange your marriage, just as I arranged the marriage of Rash Bihari. If I know anything, I know how to choose a woman,' Toyama chuckled and spluttered.

It was Michiko Ohara whom Toyama had in mind as a wife for Tilik. With the identity revealed of his prospective bride, Tilik spent the day in a daze. Everything seemed suddenly heightened; the sun on the leaves in the garden, the sleek gleam of the crows on the telephone wire, whose grumbles now sounded harmonious.

'This will finally free me of my obligation to Toyama. You mix in important circles, even if you are a foreigner. But you must give Michiko time, this marriage is not to her liking. She will come round to sensible thinking,' Ohara explained, surprisingly anxious for the match.

Such resignation did not encourage joyousness. Mrs Ohara hurried past on the stairs with a worried smile. There were sounds of hysteria from Michiko's room. Trays of food were carried in and out to her, as to an invalid. In spite of the atmosphere, Tilik could not rid himself of buoyancy.

'Time, give her time,' Ohara counselled.

The year drew to a close. 'I cannot wait for Michiko for ever,' Tilik pleaded.

He had orders from Hasegawa, who had already left for Manchuria, to follow as soon as possible. Not only Mukden, but all Manchuria was now under Japanese control. The world was not pleased with this aggression. The League of Nations appointed a Commission under Lord Lytton of Great Britain to enquire into the affair.

It was Toyama himself who brought about yet a further delay to the nuptials. No one at the Black Dragon Society was happy with the Lytton

Commission, snooping about Manchuria. There was the smell of trouble ahead.

At the Society Headquarters Tilik listened to Shumei Okawa outline a campaign of anti-Lytton Commission agitation. Okawa's intensity filled the room, and quickened the blood in Tilik. Okawa's close-cropped hair and neat moustache emphasized the pent-up energy radiating from him. This energy brought converts as much as his ideals.

'The Western powers in the League of Nations *will* hear us. What right have they to interfere in our affairs in Asia? They themselves are colonists, with no right to investigate anything.' People began to cheer.

'You can help us,' Okawa said afterwards to Tilik. 'This is an excellent chance for you. We will arrange for you to speak at our gatherings. The thrust of your speeches I suggest should be the futility of countries represented on the Commission trying to solve a problem best settled by Asians amongst themselves. Tell them Lord Lytton is from a country that is holding India in bondage. Who could be more unsuitable to deal with the Manchurian problem?'

The next weeks were busy. Anti-Western, anti-Lytton Commission demonstrations were organized all over the country. Tilik was sent from town to town. His speech was the same and so often rehearsed that he spoke it with easy passion. His theme, Asia for Asians, went down well not only with right-wing organizations, but also with the unpolitical. As a non-Japanese he appeared to bring into stark relief an issue closer to heart than previously realized by many people.

The wedding finally took place at the end of February 1932. It was a quiet family affair on a cold morning at a Shinto shrine. Afterwards, Toyama himself made an appearance. Almost at once Tilik and his bride prepared to leave for Manchuria.

On 1st March, Manchuria became the Republic of Manchukuo, and Kang'te or, Henry Pu-Yi as he was known to the West, last Emperor of the deposed Ch'ing dynasty, was declared Regent to a fledgling puppet monarchy. On that day Tilik and Michiko began the long journey to their new future.

Michiko had come to terms with Toyama's order. She was sullen but no longer distraught. At times she made a dutiful effort at conversation. For Tilik it was enough. He had patience and Manchukuo already appeared before him as a land of milk and honey.

PART TWO

East of the Drum Tower

China 1937

4

April 1937

Meetings in Manchuria

Donald Addison ordered an egg and after an hour was served a whole roast chicken. Such things happened on the Trans-Siberian Railway. It was not easy to convey in pantomime the need for a soft boiled egg. He had, thank goodness, brought his own marmalade and some biscuits. The windows of the train were never opened, nor the bottles of wine on the tables in the dining car. Butter was finished as the journey began and tea spilt in his lap. He did not complain; he liked train journeys. Outside, the sun shone weakly on an empty land. Siberia was flecked with the dark, tapering shadows of trees. The evening was setting in. Soon the window offered nothing but his own face. Tomorrow he would reach Manchouli, a village on the border of Russia and what had once been Manchuria before the Japanese invasion. Now Manchuria was renamed Manchukuo. From the border he would cross into a land where his father had never been.

Manchouli was an insignificant village, but the new flag of Manchukuo flew above the station building. Donald Addison disembarked from the Trans-Siberian Railway and was issued a visa for a country recognized only by Salvador and Japan. Now he had crossed the border he need no longer lie about his profession. In contrast to the Russians the Japanese liked reporters, especially those with superior credentials. Correspondent for *The Times*, carried its own introduction. The Japanese were anxious to be liked.

'Please write good things about Manchukuo and Japanese people in your London newspaper,' said the official who took him to collect his visa. The Lytton Commission's report to the League of Nations on Japan's occupation of Manchuria had not recommended acceptance of Manchukuo. The League had voted accordingly and Japan had withdrawn in protest. Since then its international image had suffered.

Donald boarded a train of the Chinese Eastern Railway and rattled on. The train was patrolled by armed guards. In the middle of nowhere they stopped for a wagon of dead Japanese soldiers, killed in a skirmish, to be

63

coupled to the train. Suddenly, Japanese with guns were everywhere in the already crowded carriages, many of them wounded. They were grim-faced young men, far from home, without the smiles of the Manchouli officials.

Beyond the window barren plains stretched to a horizon of hills. Camels and herdsmen stared at the passing train. Flocks of wild duck wheeled up over the wastes of northern Manchuria. Donald gazed at the nothingness and was filled with euphoria. The journey through Russia had been impeded by thoughts of his father. It did not matter that twenty years lay between their visits. His father's shadow still crossed the Russian steppes and darkened each Russian town; people remembered his name. John Addison's book on the 1917 uprising was a classic for students of the era. For the first time since he left London, Donald felt free. His father's eye had not rested on this land, his opinion had not weighed its future, or his tongue pronounced its slippery names. China could be his.

Few Westerners had as yet crossed the lines into Yenan, the blockaded Red area in north-west China, or met the rebel leader, the guerilla Mao Tse-tung. Little was known of the Communist movement, all news was forbidden by order of Chiang Kai-shek. What variety of Communists were these Chinese Reds? What kind of men were their leaders? What ideology gave them strength to endure battles, disease and death? Only Chiang Kai-shek's hatred of the Reds was documented. His suppression was brutal. Students opposed to Japanese aggression, peasants, workers and intellectuals, risked all to join the Communist party and the Eighth Route Army in its struggle against Chiang Kai-shek's dictatorship. Under Chiang thousands had been arrested, tortured and executed. To be a Communist sympathizer was a crime punishable by death. And yet, people still flocked to join the movement.

This was the secret agenda of Donald Addison's journey. His book on Red China would equal his father's on Red Russia. The only way to learn about the Reds was to get to their hideout, whatever the risk. Many had tried and failed. He stared out of the window at the barren land. For the first time in months excitement filled him. But immediately, as promised for *The Times*, he was to investigate the Japanese occupation of Manchuria.

It seemed he had entered another world when at last he reached Harbin. It was a Russian town on a Chinese plain, its schizophrenia compounded by the shadow of the Japanese. Fear in the town was endemic; men with guns were everywhere. Soldiers and police patrolled, civilians armed themselves against attack and no foreigner walked alone.

'You need a bodyguard, sir,' the manager advised as Donald left the hotel. 'Harbin was always a violent place but now, since the Japanese, words beggar all description.'

Donald nodded and walked out into the night. At the corner, as he had been told, a vagrant pleaded for alms. He met the man's eyes and knew he had found his guide.

'Go tomorrow to Hengtao. Book into the Railway Hotel. Amleto Vespa will see you there,' the man informed him and turned away.

It took some hours to reach Hengtao. The Railway Hotel was a collection of disused coaches in a siding. He ate a late lunch in the dining car and walked back over the tracks to his coach to wait. He began to think the trail might be nothing but a wild goose chase. Why should the notorious Amleto Vespa risk meeting him?

Lennox Simpson had put him in touch with the right people in Harbin. Donald had written to Simpson before leaving London. He wanted a meeting with the Irregulars, the bands of White Russian ex soldiers and officers who were clandestinely fighting the Japanese. Simpson had once edited the English language *Harbin Herald*. He had criticized the high-handed actions of the Japanese and his paper was ordered to cease publication. All the presses and type were confiscated and Simpson expelled from Manchukuo. He fled to Dairen and began proceedings for redress. Donald waited for Vespa without expectation. Probably he would not come.

He had almost given up hope of Vespa appearing when at last the door opened. There was a rush of cold night air and the smell of men and damp wool coats. Vespa entered with several Russians, others with guns stood guard outside. The carriage was suddenly full. Vespa drew the blind down at the window as he introduced himself.

'How d'you know Lennox?' he asked.

'Through my father. When Lennox was expelled from Manchukuo my father was instrumental in getting his case presented in Parliament,' Donald answered. Vespa nodded and sat down, pulling off a pair of torn woollen gloves.

'It's dangerous for me to see anyone like this,' Vespa stared at Donald assessingly. 'I work for Japanese Intelligence only because I have to. I have three children and a wife in bad health. If I do not do as they wish we would all be killed. They've told me this cold-bloodedly. They hold me to ransom by threatening my family. For their sake I swallow my feelings and obey. But their methods of subjugating Manchuria repulse me. I can take no more. I'll answer any questions you want.' Vespa then nodded in the direction of a bear-like man.

'Colonel Zayazeff of the Irregulars,' he introduced and Donald extended his hand.

'Everyone here is with the Irregulars,' Zayazeff said, gesturing to the men with him. 'Hengtao is about to be attacked. The town was surrounded by us this afternoon. It is the avowed purpose of every Irregular to do what he can to destroy the Japanese, who call us common bandits. *Bandits!* They have stolen our country, our property, and massacred our families. They wish to discredit us in the eyes of the world and justify their activities in Manchuria.' Zayazeff's beaming face turned suddenly dark.

Vespa sat down. Fatigue gutted his thin cheeks and hawk-like eyes, his beard was two days old. 'I've been in the Secret Service since 1916. I worked for Chang Tso-lin for eight years. He was a man of honour, fearsome but fair in my opinion. Manchuria has always been a seedbed of violence. After they murdered Chang, the Japanese wanted my expertise. For Chang Tso-lin I had to hunt down bandits, smugglers of arms and narcotics, and white slave traders, to maintain some semblance of order in his territory. Where we could not eradicate this scum, Chang used them. Like the Japanese, he offset his military expenditure against his gains from these people. But, unlike the Japanese, Chang Tso-lin killed no one who did not deserve to die. But now on everything the Japanese Army in Manchuria hold monopolies. From these dark trades they make much money.'

'Some people say the Occupation has grounds, that it has saved the country from Russia, and from the chaos of other parts of China,' Donald interrupted and saw he had hit a nerve. It was difficult to know how much to trust the opinions of the Italian. His colourful life had started early when he ran off to Mexico from Aquila, to join the Revolutionary Army there. From Mexico he had travelled the world and, surviving escalating adventure, come to rest in Manchuria with Chang Tso-lin, and taken Chinese nationality.

Vespa glared at him. 'Manchuria is a disillusionment for the Japanese. Manchukuo was to be their Utopia. It was always a mirage and is now a burden of increasing weight.'

'Some men must have had a vision for the place?' Donald insisted. He pulled his notebook from his bag and began to write.

'My Chief put me in charge of recruiting bandits to round up villagers, and set the Chinese farmers building Japanese-style houses for Japanese settlers. We promised the Chinese new land, new seed and implements for themselves when the building work was done. But instead I saw those farmers turned over to the Japanese Army to be used for bayonet practice by new recruits.' Vespa's eyes grew fierce. His voice became hoarse.

'I saw these atrocities, and many more. The Japanese use the Chinese like slaves to work land that once belonged to them. Japanese immigrants, who were impoverished farmers themselves, find they are now members of a ruling class by virtue of their race alone. Overnight they who were serfs are now feudal lords. I protested to my Chief after those Chinese farmers became bayonet fodder. "Do you fish?" he asked me. "No one is sorry for fish. You must assume the same attitude." '

Vespa accepted the vodka Donald poured from the bottles he had brought for this purpose. He took a gulp and continued. 'Military expenses are their heaviest burden. Today after six years of occupation there are still Irregulars and bandits left in Manchuria, harassing as they can everything Japanese. And of course, the Soviet Government maintain several hundred thousand crack troops near their border, which obliges Japan to keep at least as many men ready to face them. Things are not easy for Japan in Manchuria.' Satisfaction edged Vespa's words.

'Away from the railway lines, we are the real masters of this land. We may present only a small threat to security, but we irritate the Japanese as would a mosquito bite.' Zayazeff's deep voice filled the carriage. 'The sheer vastness of the land will defeat the Japanese eventually. They make a point of concealing their losses. But I can assure you, hardly a day goes by without an attack by us, and we seldom fail to destroy what we go after. Very soon we shall attack this town and you will see.'

Donald scribbled down notes but was stopped by the sound of machine guns. The crack of bullets ricocheted through him. He gritted his teeth, so that his reaction would not be seen. Vespa and Zayazeff looked at the door.

'The attack has started,' Zayazeff announced. 'Our part was done in the prior arrangements. Let us drink, we've a few hours now to spend together.' He tossed back his vodka.

Outside the carriage the firing continued. Soon Zayazeff squeezed his great bulk into a corner, yawned loudly and closed his eyes. Sleep settled suddenly upon the men in the carriage. Only Vespa seemed in no need of repose.

'You have family?' he asked.

'I'm divorced,' Donald replied.

'No children?' Vespa questioned. Donald shook his head.

'Then you don't know what it's like to sell your soul to save your children. In the beginning they gave me some money, now it's like getting water from stone.'

'What does your Chief have to say about that?' Donald enquired, stifling a yawn, his hand ached from taking notes.

' "Japan is poor," he says. "Our first task is to lighten the burden of our military expenses. We did not take Manchuria to spend millions on it." Then he gets excited and jumps up and down. "Make money," he screams. "Increase the rackets, multiply the monopolies, arrest more people, more kidnappings, bigger ransoms. Money. Money. The Japanese Army must have money." The cold-blooded exploitation of narcotics is their best revenue, you know. They manufacture the stuff themselves. The whole of Manchuria is hooked on it, from schoolchildren to old men. Only the Japanese don't touch it. Their Army Handbook proclaims, *The use of narcotics is unworthy of a superior race like the Japanese.*' Vespa shook his head sadly, and continued with detailed revelations.

Eventually Zayaeff grunted and sat up. 'There has been no shooting for an hour,' he said, shaking people awake.

'How do you know? You were asleep,' Donald inquired with a smile. Zayazeff gave a loud laugh.

'You are mistaken. I never sleep. Let's go.'

Outside, in the dark early morning, their breath froze on the air. Donald buttoned up his coat. Vespa looked at his watch. Zayazeff walked off to speak to a group of Irregulars who had been involved in the attack.

'My work is done here,' Vespa said, clasping Donald's hand. 'I have a train to catch, when trains begin running again. I must report to my Chief that the town has been taken by Irregulars.' He gave a bark of a laugh and then walked away, his lean frame quickly obscured by ground mist and the smoke of a belching train.

Zayazeff returned to Donald. 'It's been a success. Many Japanese soldiers were killed in their barracks and the rest taken prisoner. The officers were all in the brothels and unarmed. They too have been taken prisoner and have already started the march to our mountain camp. You too must come to our camp. You would think it a Japanese encampment. Everything we have is taken from them; uniforms, caps, bedcovers, radios, canned food and knives and forks, not to mention rifles and grenades. We have also two mountain cannon. Of course we badly need an airplane, but we have not succeeded in capturing one yet. With our two Japanese anti-aircraft guns we have brought down five of their planes, but they were too damaged to be of use,' Zayazeff finished sadly.

'Will you kill your Japanese prisoners?' Donald asked.

'Oh no,' Zayazeff laughed. 'We'll hold them hostage and then Vespa, no doubt, will be sent by his Chief to negotiate their release in exchange for captured Irregulars held in Harbin. How we laugh when this happens. Whatever the Japanese may suspect, they have no proof of Vespa's real work. I pray they never will.'

They walked into town. People were beginning to emerge from their homes. A few soldiers strode about. Walls were poxed by bullet-holes, bodies were strewn around. The first light was breaking and already Japanese planes circled above, looking for the raiders. Zayazeff shaded his eyes, squinting up at the sky.

'Brave, hard fighting enemies have always paid each other the tribute of admiration. But not the Japanese. The better the enemy fights the more resentful they become. They have only contempt for those who oppose them, no matter how heroic the defence. There can be no heroes but Japanese heroes, no bravery but Japanese bravery.' Zayazeff sighed and turned to face Donald. 'Well, I too must now leave you now.'

Donald watched him march away.

The sun broke through the clouds. Donald unpacked his camera. He adjusted the focus, squinting through the lens at bullet-scarred walls, the circling Japanese planes and prostitutes shivering outside their burnt brothel. This was what he liked; to frame emotion, pinning it down to consumable size, allowing nothing to escape. He looked into the camera and things filtered through in a manageable way, distanced from his emotion. Even as a child he had felt like this, from the day he owned his first camera. His father had laughed.

'Following in my footsteps?' There was pride in his voice. He had been presented the week before with an award for photo journalism.

'Not *all* your footsteps, I hope,' Donald's mother replied. Even now he remembered the tightening of her voice. She wore a green dress, close about the midriff. The colour reflected her sea eyes. He remembered the brittleness of her laughter. That night, like most others, she cried.

Now, in Hengtao, he walked forward to frame the prostitutes in his camera, their clothes bright against the charred remains. He stumbled against something and found the corpse of a half-dressed soldier at his feet. The man must have rushed from the brothel, pulling on his breeches. Donald pointed the lens to the ground. The man's head appeared before his eyes, a bullet through his brain, another in his jaw. He stepped back quickly.

The shock lasted with him as he walked back to the Railway Hotel. It was the first dead man he had seen since his father's suicide. Now, in the cold early morning, he could no longer escape his memories. He cursed aloud. Crows replied from the bare branches of a tree. He saw Cordelia again, slim, immaculate, sitting at her office desk, the noise of Fleet

Street drifting up through an open window. *Cordelia.*

The next day Donald returned to Harbin. He began to look for copy again. The Japanese Military Command were helpful, anxious to show their best to the world. An expedition was suggested.

Donald flew in a military plane to Pao-tao, a dusty Muslim town on the edge of the Gobi Desert. From there, by camel caravan, he would journey to a Japanese military outpost some distance beyond Ujino. The town was one of the last Mongolian settlements on the border of Inner Mongolia. A month before fifteen Japanese soldiers had been sent to this outpost with a wireless set. Their presence was intended as proof of Japanese expansion into Inner Mongolia. There had been no news for some time from them. A Japanese military group was on its way to investigate.

Pao-tao was a rough trading town with a predominance of mosques. Dust dried the throat and settled in a powder over skin and bread. The town was a centre for wool. Great camel caravans coming down from Tibet and Mongolia and Sinkiang converged on the town before travelling south to Tientsin to trade. Donald did not know what he hoped to gain by this journey. The opportunity had presented itself, and the thought of the desert drew him. Its vastness would empty his mind. He knew nothing of the region.

There were ten camels and four mules. Captain Nakamura was going to Ujino with four other army personnel. Travelling with them was a monk in robes that seemed Tibetan, although he appeared of Indian origin. He sat aloof upon his camel, speaking only in Japanese with Captain Nakamura. He looked at Donald and then away.

Tilik Dayal was not happy to see an Englishman as a travelling companion. His face took on a sullen look.

'Who is he?' he asked Nakamura. 'Is he a merchant, a dealer in wool? Why can you not get rid of him?'

'He is a reporter,' Nakamura replied. 'We're supposed to take him to Ujino. He has papers with him from some military high-up, and has been put under our command. I don't know what he thinks he'll find; a lot of sand and camels?'

'You know why I'm here. What will we do if he finds out the purpose of my journey? He could spoil my plans if he wanted. It is better for him to think I do not speak his language. Remember, please. I don't like Englishmen. I have no wish to talk to him. An Englishman killed my father. I will pretend to go into deep meditation the moment he troubles me,' Tilik warned. Nakamura laughed.

'Why are you wearing these ridiculous robes?' he enquired.

'I always wear them while travelling in this area. It fits me into the religious lifestyle of the people, inspires their confidence and gives me instant information. There is nothing these people respect more than a religious man.' Tilik grinned.

In Hsinking, the new Japanese capital of Manchukuo, Hasegawa had thought the disguise a splendid joke. So much humour had been generated at his cost in the Japanese Military High Command that Tilik's feelings were ruffled. He himself could see little humour in the disguise, only a brilliant convenience.

Surveying the sea of sand beyond the dusty town, he wondered what this journey would yield. He stared surreptitiously at the Englishman, so obviously awkward upon his camel, resisting the animal's lurching gait. Soon he would have sore buttocks. Tilik smiled at the thought of the man's discomfort. His face was red as a pomegranate from exposure to the sun. Bitterness curdled in him. How far had he been forced to travel in life by this arrogant, red-faced race?

Children ran about the camel's legs, begging from the man. Tilik watched Donald Addison empty his pockets of small coins. No white man knew how to deal with poverty. Either they arrogantly ignored it or, like this man, made fools of themselves. They had no idea who to give to or when, nor even how much. They had no knowledge that in some places organized begging was a trade like any other. The animals stamped their feet and sand blew up in a fine cloud of dust. A hot wind stung his cheeks. Tilik wound his draperies about his face.

He had woken one night with the plan fully formed in his mind. He shook Michiko awake and told her. He had continued talking long after she went back to sleep. The next day he discussed it with Hasegawa who became uncharacteristically excited. He had immediately spoken on Tilik's behalf with the Military High Command who appeared taken by the novelty of Tilik's idea.

'Anything that minimizes British influence in China is to our mutual advantage,' Hasegawa declared. 'If all the wool in this area can be shipped to Japan instead of Britain, that is also to our advantage. Go and see what you can do, then we will work on Tokyo,' Hasegawa had ordered.

It was a good plan. All the wool of Tibet, Mongolia and Sinkiang entered Pao-tao on the backs of endless camel trains. From there it travelled on to Tientsin where it was bought by British merchants for transhipment to Britain and the mills of Lancashire. Just as Gandhi had brought about the boycott in India of British goods and textiles, so Tilik wished to prevent Mongolian wool from ever reaching England. One more round of meetings with the headmen in this area and the plan would be ready to implement. Before the wool caravans reached the British merchants in Tientsin, a Japanese purchasing commission would buy up the wool in Pao-tao at the same price it was sold in Tientsin. After this trip, with his facts complete, Tilik would return to Hsinking and maybe to Tokyo for discussions at government levels. In collaboration with the great textile combines of Japan a purchasing depot would be organized in Pao-tao. In one stroke he would cripple Britain and enrich his adopted country. On his camel Tilik surveyed the desert, stretching void to the horizon. The useless, barren landscape now appeared a place of power.

The land was shifting, the wind moved dunes overnight. Day ran into day upon the camel's meandering gait. The desert did not have the effect upon him that Donald desired. Instead of erasing sensation, the emptiness appeared a crucible for his blackest feelings. Emotions burned through him, more painful than the desert heat searing his skin through his shirt. He was powerless to stop the vivid intrusion of unwanted thoughts, like a reel of film gone mad, flapping about in his mind. His father. Cordelia. His father again. The sobbing of his mother. The sound of the gun, and the dripping, bloodied wall down which had slid his father's brains. Against this bitter, inner world, the wastes he traversed faded to nothing.

Hour after hour the sun beat down, eroding will. At night the moon and stars appeared magnified. Donald lay on the cool sand in the dark and stared up at their strange beauty, finding relief. He thought of the remoteness of this tableland between China and Russia, once the domain of Genghis Khan and his grandsons. The Land of the Blue Sky, it was called. He had the feeling he stood at the top of the world. Distance meant nothing to those of this soil, endurance was in their genes. Even now, in terrain that flattened him, others spent lives of transit. Caravans of a hundred thousand animals and men, traversed without thought thousands of miles. From these wastes Kublai Khan had swept down to conquer Japan. In sight of the country, but before he could land, a typhoon destroyed his ships. Now, seven hundred years later, the Japanese returned the gesture, sweeping over Manchuria, struggling like ants over an unsubduable wilderness. He wondered at the need in man to conquer and to kill.

'What are you Japanese going to do here, in this dust bowl?' Donald asked Nakamura the next day as their camels lurched forward together. Nakamura sighed. He spoke good English, and had taken a degree in the language at university.

'In Japan the eye is never stretched but pulled up short everywhere by mountains, hills, forest, cultivation. Everything is scaled down, knitted together, compressing the individual,' explained Nakamura, as he rode beside Donald. 'Here the eye is pulled to its limit, there are no boundaries. And I do not mind telling you, I am frightened by this space. We Japanese are not used to such freedom. We are comfortable only where there are limits. We have a need for tight controls about us in all areas of life. In a larger figurative expanse we are lost and do not know what response is demanded of us.'

It was clear something of this anxiety filled the Japanese soldiers with Nakamura. They constantly enquired of their guides if they were lost. Only the Indian Lama sat immobile on his camel; Nakamura told Donald he had come this way before. The day's purpose was always to locate the next source of water. The guides gave prayers of thanks before removing the planks that covered each well and pitching camp. Gradually, Donald learned to trust the guides, knew water would be there at certain points, as would, eventually, a destination. He made several attempts to communicate with the Lama, but each time the man turned away.

Finally, the desert did its work. Donald's mind slowly emptied of the nightmares. His thoughts stretched to nothingness over vistas of sand. He wondered then at the shape of his own life, locked in by boundaries of fear and frustration, and glimpsed a desert more parched than any before him. Immediately, he pushed this uncomfortable vision back within himself.

They came at last to the desert town of Ujino. It was no more than a cluster of tents, but they were received hospitably by the headman of the community. For the first time in days they washed, and slept under substantial cover. They ate a feast with their host who slaughtered a goat for the occasion and forced upon them a noxious drink that went to their heads. The Indian Lama was in conversation with their host. He spoke in Japanese to the interpreter.

'How does he speak your language?' Donald asked Nakamura as they sat together in the great tent. They were replete with food, and Nakamura's face was reddened by drink. A close smell of roasted meat and unwashed clothes thickened under the canvas. Lamps of animal fat left a rancid smoke upon the air.

'He has lived in Japan, and has a Japanese wife,' Nakamura answered. He appeared very drunk, and began to sing a Japanese song.

'But he is a Lama,' Donald protested.

Nakamura shook his head. 'That is his disguise; I'm not supposed to tell you. But what does it matter? He is on some kind of reconnaissance work for the Japanese Government. We've been told by High Command to help him.'

Nakamura shut his eyes and continued with his song. His voice trembled in sadness. Then, unexpectedly, he rose to his feet and began to dance. His hands moved to left and right, graceful as a woman, his body was taut with emotion. In the tent there was silence and his song, if not comprehensible, released its melancholy into the night. At last he sat down and refilled his glass.

'What was the song about?' Donald asked.

'About the role of a man in life. About duty and virtue. About how we must leave all those we love, and the beauties of this world for the greater beauty of valour. It is a song about war, to strengthen the mettle of the soldier's soul.'

'It did not sound like a war song,' Donald replied.

'Not a war song, a soldier's song,' Nakamura corrected. 'We are not a warring people. We fight when we have to but it does not come easy, and we must prepare our soul for the task, for our country and our Emperor. To overcome our own desires before duty, that is virtue in our eyes.' Nakamura began to sing again, translating into English.

> I see those faces, hear those voices.
> My wife and son are waving,
> Waving their flags until they break.
> Their message to me is to fight well.
> I look at the sky, and in the spaces
> Between the clouds I see them waving still.
> From the deck of the great fleet of battleships
> I say good-bye to the land of my birth,
> Goodbye to my wife and son.
> I look at the place where the sky arches
> Above the Imperial Palace
> And I swear I will fight well.

The Lama was given a tent of his own. Donald shared one with Nakamura. He could not sleep and went out into the night to sit upon stones amongst the shrubs about the well. He could hear the Lama coughing, then suddenly there was a scream.

In the moonlight Donald saw a snake slither from the Lama's tent. He walked over quickly and lifted the flap. The Lama was making incomprehensible sounds. Donald struck a match and lit the oil lamp in a corner.

'Do you understand English? Did it bite you,' he asked. He was amazed to hear the man reply in perfect English.

74

'Yes to both questions. It is poisonous, they all are here. Oh God, I will now die.'

'Show me the bite,' Donald demanded. Tilik stretched out his arm, already swelling.

'Wait,' Donald instructed.

In his own tent he took from his rucksack his razor and a flask of brandy and then returned to the injured man. He struck a match and ran it along the razor's edge. After pouring brandy on to Tilik's arm he made a quick incision. Putting his lips to the cut he sucked hard. The metallic taste of blood filled his mouth. He spat out and sucked again and again, then rinsed his mouth with brandy. By now Nakamura had also arrived.

'It should be all right, if you're lucky.' Donald tied a bandage Nakamura had unearthed about the wound. The Indian's thanks were mumbled in a begrudging tone when at last Donald stood up to leave.

'If you speak such good English, why did you not talk to me earlier?' Donald asked. The man glared up from his pallet.

'Because I have no wish to communicate with an Englishman.' Tilik spoke rudely, confused in the extraordinary circumstances. 'But I wish you to know I am grateful.'

Donald frowned in exasperation as he lifted the flap of the tent. 'Well, I suppose that is something. Goodnight.'

In the morning Tilik was feverish but sitting up when Donald again returned to his tent.

'I am going to live,' Tilik announced. He had decided he could not be churlish, even if the man was a white-skinned colonial who held his country hostage. His life had been saved. 'Where did you learn this snake bite technique? Are you also a doctor?'

Donald shook his head. 'Once in Rajasthan, in the same way, someone saved my life,' he replied.

'You have been in India? It is very strange that my life should be saved by an Englishman,' Tilik said. It was impossible to even explain to the man just how strange it was.

'You would, I hope, do the same for me,' Donald smiled.

'I doubt it,' Tilik replied. 'I have no love of you English people. I would have wished you dead. An Englishman killed my father. This I can never forget.' There was both resentment and bewilderment in his voice. 'Now, instead, I must thank you.'

Donald laughed and sat down on the floor beside Tilik's pallet. 'Tell me why you are here, in these robes, with the Japanese? I know you are not a Lama,' Donald insisted.

Tilik sighed. He wished to speak to the Englishman. There was a likeable quality that he had not expected to find in a man of his race. Words poured suddenly from him. The Englishman listened attentively.

'The Japanese are supportive of India's cause. I carry on the struggle for Independence from here,' Tilik confided at the end of his story.

'They would like to exchange white colonialism for yellow, you mean?' Donald replied.

'I do not think so,' Tilik stiffened, aware suddenly of the need for caution. He knew nothing of this man.

Donald scratched his head. 'We English are not all so bad, you know. Mr Gandhi has some sensible things to say. I respect him greatly. I met him in India on my first visit and again in London.'

'*You* have met Gandhiji?' Tilik sat upright in amazement.

'I have just published a book on India. I know also of Subash Chandra Bose, although I have not met him.'

Tilik shook his head in perplexity. 'You are the first Englishman I have ever heard talk like this,' he replied. 'What do you think, some say even Jawaralal Nehru will follow Subash in the end?'

'Nehru will follow Gandhi. He's his political protégé. Through Nehru the old man has access to the young and Nehru's political future is assured through his alliance with Gandhi,' Donald answered without hesitation. Tilik looked at him in renewed amazement.

Donald laughed. 'Even Gandhi has English disciples, who are dedicated to him and the Indian cause.'

'That is true,' Tilik nodded. Until now he had only half believed such things. 'But they are exceptions. I suppose you are too.'

'We will meet again, God willing,' Tilik said the next day, as the main caravan departed. He was not going on to the military outpost. There were headmen to meet in other villages near Ujino.

'I'm a believer in destiny,' Donald grinned. He rode on and saw Tilik in his phoney Lama robes grow small against the desert.

It was still a long ride to the outpost but time was now meaningless. Donald had learned to swim with the unhurried rhythm of the camel, his thoughts spun out, unworried. The terrain had now changed. They traversed rocky plateau land, with spectacular views.

At last they reached their destination. The outpost, on a crag of rock, had been wiped out by guerrillas. The bodies of the fifteen soldiers were already half-buried in the loose sandy soil. What remained of the corpses had a leathery look. Most had already been carrion to the vultures wheeling above.

'This is the work of Communists,' Nakamura said.

Later he demanded they drink the remains of some beer they carried, not only to fortify themselves but in farewell to the murdered men. That evening Nakamura did not dance, he spoke bitterly in a low voice, almost to himself, as he sat alone beside Donald.

'We are being drawn into a trap. We have a large, modern, well-trained army and it is pitted against a poorly-equipped but mobile and invisible peasant force. For our country we gladly die. Young men in mountain villages leave the beauty of Japan, and the rice fields in season reflecting Heaven. They leave this peace to enter the military, to fight for Japan. Gladly, I tell you, we do this. But when I see fifteen men sent across a desert, to live on a piece of windy rock, facing a wilderness hiding enemy hordes, all in the name of expanding our territory, I wonder at the sanity of those we obey. This is not death in valour for our Emperor. This is death for stupidity, for arrogance, for the vanity of an ignorant command of which our Emperor knows nothing.'

'Look at this land,' Nakamura swept his arm before him. 'How can we ever hope to control this continent? It is immeasurable. We can take towns, but that is all. The vastness of the countryside has already slipped from our grasp. This peasant force, these Communists, with their thousand-mile lines of communication, already control this land as we never can. It will never be truly ours, even though we may eventually command it. How many young men must we lose in this madness?' Nakamura drank down his beer and walked off into the scrub. For a long time he could be seen, sitting on a nub of rock before the barren hills.

The men were buried and the caravan turned back to face the desert once more. Again the rhythm of the camel and the sight of the endless horizon engulfed them. Nakamura's face was now without expression. Donald thought again of Kublai Khan. Ambitious and brutal, he had risen out of this soil, was of its essence and timelessness. He had been defeated in his conquest of Japan by elements that were alien to him. So too now the Japanese, however stoic and hardy, were scaled down by existence on their tiny island. They compressed further all those things about them, trees, homes, lives, poems, nature itself, in order never to touch the unbounded. How could a people used to so tight a circumference of things, ever grasp the immensity of China?

5

May 1937

Unreliable Men

The weekend after Agnes Smedley's departure with a further load of medical supplies, Nadya took a walk on top of Nanking's old walls. Near one of the gates was a steep cobbled ramp leading up to the summit. The walls were higher and wider than they appeared from below. In places between the crenellations grass grew like a field. Through its history the town had been razed many times and preserved few distinguishing features. Nanking had known greatness but was haunted by sacking and retained an exhausted air. Patches of wasteland still stood in memory of distant scars, like an index to its past. The town spread flatly until arrested by moats and the massive old walls. These encompassed an area twenty miles by fifteen, punctuated by sixteen gates. They were closed each night and opened each morning on orders beaten out from the Bell and Drum Towers. Whatever the traumas of the past Nanking still stood, its walls refusing to crumble.

Up on these walls a peacefulness filled her, as if all her disparate parts had locked into place. Nadya remembered such a feeling on walks long before, across the steppes in the spring with her father. She remembered that land, wet and green after the thaw, the sun setting slowly in the sky. It was always the land she remembered now, when she thought of Russia. It filled her like an ache. The towns of the steppes were all frontier towns with squat wooden houses and rough-hewn telephone poles. Their ugly monotony and impermanence had settled into her bones as a child. But the indomitable land, harsh and sweeping in winter, glowing and expansive under the summer sun, had entered into her soul. The Siberian summer was as profuse as a wild-flower garden. She remembered swinging a purple music case on her way to piano lessons, wet grass soaking her stockings about the ankles. She remembered the dappled Siberian orchids she sought on walks with her father. There had been one with neither roots nor true leaves. Her father had uncovered the coral-like base and explained how the plant derived its nourishment in symbiotic association with a fungus. He admired this hardy perennial whose survival he said was a miracle. We must all be like this in these terrible times, he had told her, able to grow anywhere. The memory of her father filled her as always with desolation. The old feeling of abandonment crept through her. He had taught her early about endurance, she thought in sudden bitterness. He had given her no choice but to learn to live like the strange rootless plant, devising her own survival.

'We're not supposed to be here, you know.' The voice came from behind her.

She turned to face a tall blond man. He stood silhouetted against the sky on the very edge of the ramparts. Wind billowed up his trouser legs and his jacket flapped like wings. His hair stood on end in the breeze. She had the impression he might take flight, disappearing over the wall like an eagle. He laughed and jumped down to shelter.

'I love the wind. I wish I were a bird, gliding on the currents. They don't let you walk on this wall. There's a sentry already, to escort us down.' He pointed to a soldier coming towards them.

'Why can we not walk here, what is the harm?' Nadya frowned, the old anger at her father still nagging.

'I didn't make the rules, it's not my town,' the man grinned at her expression.

'Why are you here then? How do you know this?' Nadya asked.

'They told me at the YMCA, where I'm currently staying. However, I thought I'd see how far I got. I like seeing how far I can get with things. Bad habit. Doesn't lead to a peaceful life.' He looked out across the city to where the Yangtze glittered, stretching far into the body of China, and drew a breath. For a moment they stood in silence together, observing the distant river.

The breeze blew in Nadya's face and whipped her skirts away behind her. The massive ramparts and watch-towers of the wall snaked into the distance. Evening was approaching. The sun stained the sky vermilion, gold edged a few dark clouds. Beyond the town was the watery world of the Lotus Lakes where thick cascades of willow trees dissolved into a blue mist. East of the Drum Tower, where much of the foreign community lived, she picked out the hospital with the green square of lawn in the compound. Beyond it the areas of the old town were a concentrated jigsaw of tiled roofs. Houses, hovels, temples and tea-houses were threaded by narrow lanes. There was no air to breathe in these packed quarters, pungent with garlic and night soil, charcoal and opium, frying food and drying fish.

The blond man turned towards her as the sentry approached. 'It's worth it, isn't it, even if only for a few minutes? I'll try again another

79

day. My name is Donald Addison,' he said. The sentry gestured an order to descend the stone ramp.

'Where are you from? England? Why are you in China?' Nadya asked. She stared at him enquiringly.

'So many questions.' Donald raised his eyebrows but gave a potted account of himself. The woman before him had a fierce, defensive manner. Something flamed through her, lighting her up. He could not imagine her in repose but only in constant, mercurial motion.

'I came to China to investigate the Japanese in Manchuria. And then to visit the Communists in their blockaded area,' he told her, his eyes travelling over her face.

'What do you want to mix with them for?' She remembered Agnes Smedley's defence of the Chinese Communists even as she said the words, but the man was the kind who could not be agreed with. Everything about him demanded, if not a battle, then some manner of sparring. His eyes never dropped their quizzical amusement, nor left her face for a moment. Once or twice, in embarrassment, she was forced to avert her gaze. He left her with an uneven feeling.

'Research purposes,' he smiled. 'I believe they're the *only* hope for this country.'

'I came out of Russia to escape the Reds.' She remembered the sound of gunfire and bodies on the roads in Blagoveshchensk. Against her will she was sucked in by some disturbance, dark and strange, within the man. She could not establish distance.

'I suppose you support Chiang Kai-shek whose Blueshirts exterminate students and intellectuals?' He shook his head sadly as he spoke. She remembered Agnes had called Chiang a feudal bastard.

'I see *no other* hope for this country but Chiang Kai-shek,' Nadya pushed up her chin. 'He has brought more unity to China than there's ever been.' She did not know enough about Chinese Communists to argue for them one way or another. The talk of people like Bradley or Martha was all of Chiang Kai-shek.

'Chiang seems more interested in suppressing the Reds than fighting the Japanese. In spite of the United Front he'll make a pact with Japan and lose the whole of China,' Donald replied. The setting sun dazzled him for a moment and glowed within the woman's hair. He had a desire to reach out and touch her.

'Are you a Communist? There are people who think there might be more stability in China if the Japanese were here,' Nadya retorted. She did not know why she was arguing so heatedly with this stranger, saying things she did not believe.

'These *people* are foreigners no doubt. I don't think you'll find many

80

Chinese of the same persuasion. I'm not a Communist, only a hack reporter. I'll soon know more of the Generalissimo as I hope to interview him.' Donald spoke to Nadya's back as he followed her down the stone ramp. He felt forced to keep his gaze upon her, as if to photograph her in his mind. He observed her legs and the way she placed her feet to break her descent upon the steep cobbles. Beneath the thick fall of hair her neck was lightly freckled.

They reached the bottom of the ramp. Nadya turned to nod good-bye and walked towards Martha's hospital with the wrought-iron letters of its name arched above the gate, the William Clayton Nanking Hospital for Women and Children. She was glad Agnes Smedley had not been near to hear her exchange with this man. He was the type of person to whom words were ammunition. To defend oneself it was necessary to grab whatever thoughts flew by and fling them at him like a pile of stones. Agnes would have put him in his place with a few terse phrases and her knowledge of Yenan.

The Yangtze was busy with war ships coming up to Nanking from Shanghai. The HMS *Danae* and the gunboats, USS *Panay* and the HMS *Ladybird* and the HMS *Bee* were often in port, along with many other vessels of different classes. So frequent was the arrival of these ships that the social life of the town improved. There were dances at the International Club and dinners on board the ships. Bands played and couples whirled on the roof of the International Club.

At these times the town seemed alight to Nadya. After a day of documentation and the smell of paper, crammed yellowing onto miles of shelves, it was a relief to throw herself at the night. The gold-trimmed evening dress and the fashionable clothes she had brought from Shanghai at last had a place in her life. And there were the naval men, smart in their uniforms, thirsty for pleasure without involvement.

Nanking was not without interesting men, some were even famous in scholarly ways, but there was no one she felt drawn towards. They passed her in the TECSAT Department, and talked of statistics for the husbandry of pigs, or an addition to the pantheon of Chinese gods. Some took her out to dinner or danced with her at the Club. As always they were eager, but she could summon no interest.

At last Bradley Reed journeyed up to Nanking to assess the progress of his project. The few days of his visit were chaotic. Bradley stirred energy wherever he went, demanding the impossible, pushing people to extremes. He left the Department breathless, but on track for his autumn deadline.

Before leaving he came to dinner with Martha. She was relaxed in

Bradley's company as she cut an almond cake for dessert. He entertained Flora and Lily with tales of their mother's childhood.

'We travelled on a boat up the Grand Canal. From the window of our cabin we had a great view of the feet of the peasants who sat up on the deck above us. Remember Martha how we complained of the smell of those feet?' Bradley laughed. The girls giggled and looked at their mother, unable to imagine the child in her.

Over coffee Bradley turned his attention to Nadya. 'I have been talking today with Madame Chiang Kai-shek and W.H. Donald, their Australian advisor. They want regular reports on our project. I have suggested you keep them up-to-date. I want you to take in a progress report once a fortnight.' The light above the table polished Bradley's white hair. His face had the tough, soft look of old chamois leather.

'Madame Chiang Kai-shek? What is she like?' Nadya asked. She knew Bradley had easy access to the Chiangs, whom he had known many years.

'Very persuasive,' Bradley said. 'But I was even more so; she is to write a foreword to our great work. I told them you would take our proofs in as soon as possible.'

'To Madame Chiang Kai-shek?' Nadya repeated.

'Well, to W.H. Donald at least, I am not sure you will see Madame. I have already discussed all that is necessary with her. She is a busy woman.' Bradley devoured his almond cake.

'Who is this W.H. Donald?' Nadya asked, taking the cup of coffee Martha passed her.

'He is an advisor to the Chiangs,' Martha explained. 'He has been thirty-five years in China and never returned to Australia.'

'He arrived first in Hong Kong and worked as a journalist for the *China Mail*,' Bradley remembered. 'He was one of the first ninety overseas war correspondents to reach Japan after the outbreak of the Russo-Japanese war. The scoops he scored were so numerous he was signed up as correspondent for the *New York Herald* in China.' Martha nodded, as Bradley concentrated on another slice of cake and continued with more information.

'So great is his intimacy with the Generalissimo and his wife that he calls them to their faces, Gissimo and Missimo. They call him in turn, Uncle Donald. There seems no historical event he had not been party to in his years in China. Before advising Chiang Kai-shek he worked for the Manchurian warlord, Chang Tso-lin and then his son, Chang Hsueh-liang. He helped Sun Yat-sen organize the Chinese Revolution, and worked also for the Viceroy of Canton, an imperious old Mandarin.'

Martha smiled at the apprehension on Nadya's face. 'He's not as frightening as he sounds,' she laughed.

Both she and Nadya had come to reassess their first opinions of each other. Martha knew more now of Nadya's story. Behind the defensive exterior she saw a depth she could respect. She saw also in Nadya's commitment to her work, a discipline that surprised her.

'The Generalissimo, Madame and W.H.D. That, according to a standing joke, is China's Foreign Office in a nutshell. No one can see the Chiangs without W.H.D.'s permission, even the Generalissimo's body-guard, who is a heel-clicking German who quarrelled with Hitler,' Bradley informed them.

'No one, except for you, I suspect,' Martha smiled. She felt implicit support from Bradley. Their memories ran in parallel threads back to the mesh of childhood. No one understood her like Bradley. Once he had asked her to marry him. Her reaction had been shock; she thought of Bradley as a surrogate brother. Soon after his proposal she had met Bill, and Bradley had married his wife, Claire.

Bill Clayton had come out to China to be her father's assistant the year before Martha returned from America. When Martha had left to study medicine in America, the mission hospital had been small and her mother still alive. When she returned to work with her father, it was a sprawling complex, but her mother was dead. Bill Clayton was full of religious zeal and a brilliant doctor. Within a year they married, much to Dr Keswick's delight.

The thought of Bill filled her suddenly. He had always got on well with Bradley, although she had never told him of his proposal. At the end of their first year together she and Bill had moved to Soochow, to take over the hospital there. Their bedroom, she remembered, was painted cream and apple green. She could still see Bill in the doorway, tall and loose-framed, his hair copper in a shaft of morning sun, freckled and sandy all over. She remembered watching him from the bed, pulling on his clothes to go off to an emergency. An old man had been caught in a factory press. They had been in the midst of making love, and Bill had left her quickly. He was brisk and tender in his embrace. If she had not welcomed it, she felt no great aversion. She found her pleasure in Bill's own. Desire and passion, so idolized in literature, so tempting to the upright man, was still a mystery to her. It was as if a contagion had passed her by. She thanked God for freeing her from those struggles of the flesh. And yet in that room, on that morning of hurried love-making, she had conceived Flora. Remembering, she felt as rarely while Bill lived, a sudden wave of lust for him. She turned quickly back to the conversation at the dinner table, shocked at this rogue response to memory. Bradley still spoke about W.H.D.

'Even I have to approach the Chiangs through W.H.D.' Bradley sighed. 'I go back to Shanghai tomorrow.' Turning to Nadya, his tone changed. 'Phone W.H.D. for an appointment,' he ordered.

'What does W.H.D. stand for?' Nadya asked.

'I have never met anyone, even his group of intimates, who know what the initials stand for. D is for Donald, that's all anyone knows,' Bradley said.

'I have heard that name,' Nadya replied. Almost at once she realized it was not W.H.D. she had heard of. Donald was the name of the man she had met on the walls of Nanking. She realized now she had thought of him often since that day.

Nadya did not sleep well that night. The face of the man she had met on her walk atop Nanking's walls came constantly before her, and would not be willed away. The fan whirled above in an uncertain manner. She feared it might crash down upon her. A faint edge of carbolic hung in the air. The impending meetings with W.H.D. and Madame Chiang Kai-shek filled her with apprehension. The past seemed to crowd up behind her. And thoughts of Sergei pushed again into her mind as fast as she thrust them out.

She had known him only three months before they escaped to Harbin. A fire destroyed his accommodation and the Blagoveshchensk Committee assigned his family a room in Nadya's home. The house had long ago been repossessed by the government, and divided up. Sergei was consumed by the convenience of the Amur, and their proximity to China. His father, a former court architect famous for his role in a political conspiracy, had been imprisoned then released to Siberia. Prison affected his lungs and he died, but Sergei could not forget Imperial Russia. He longed for an end to penury, for holidays at German spas again, and for the dacha on a lake in Finland where he had hunted with his father. This residue lined his mind while he worked in a machine tool factory.

It began as a game. They sat in the orchard on summer evenings. Laundry was strung between the trees and flapped and dripped upon them. They spoke in whispers, elaborating on Sergei's plans. He was inspired by the escape to Harbin some years before of Konstantin Rodzaevsky. At twenty-five Rodzaevsky was now General Secretary of the Russian Fascist Party in Harbin and working to free the Motherland. Sergei spoke of this man in a reverent tone. They lay in the grass under the trees and the sun flamed above.

'Take me with you,' she demanded.

'Escape is not for women,' he argued.

'You need money for a good escape. I still have my mother's jewellery,' Nadya reminded him.

A breeze stirred the laundry and filled out shirts. A damp vest blew down upon them. Sergei had not yet kissed her. She leaned forward and shut her eyes, but as he made no move towards her she placed her lips upon his mouth. Although she trembled his body was passive, waiting for her to draw away. She had never been kissed before, and found nothing extreme in his response.

'If we delay the river will freeze,' he told her as she opened her eyes.

There had been no moon the night of the escape. The wind smelled of winter. Thin ice formed already about the edge of the river. A man was waiting.

'There are soldiers returning to duty on the borders of Manchuria. I didn't know we were to carry them. I cannot take you on the main boat, it's packed with those soldiers.' He lifted the tarpaulin on one of a train of barges filled by sacks of potatoes. The craft sat low in the water. 'You'll have to make do with this.'

Beneath the tarpaulin the odour of the river pressed upon them, as did the manure from the soil about the potatoes. They awoke at first light. With a sudden jerk the boats began to move. Lifting a corner of the canvas they watched the town drift away. Then, for the first time, Nadya realized not only the town but the country itself was slipping away from her. Panic overwhelmed her. She knew then she would never return. A skin was being ripped from her. Images of the past and of her father thrust up within her, filling her with desolation.

Once her father had taken her with him on some business, to the boundary of Mongolia. It was not a land to press upon a child, and yet he had taken her there. She remembered still the smell of his heavy woollen coat as he held her against him. And she remembered the strange barren hills of that vacant land stretching into the distance. She was sure that, when she reached the horizon, she would be able to sit and dangle her legs into empty space. The land appeared on the edge of nothingness. The unknown place she travelled towards now with Sergei seemed suddenly an equal void.

On the journey to Harbin Sergei made no move towards her. It was she who initiated their first coupling, its awkwardness compounded by the sacks of potatoes upon which they were forced to lie. It was as if he lent himself to her, allowed her to sit astride him. He offered no help and she, unskilled, had only a fire in her body to guide her. She was unprepared for the pain that skewered her upon him, or for his abrupt recoiling. He seemed suddenly to shrink within her. He pushed her off and turned away.

'Next time it will be better,' she whispered, afraid she had upset him, unable to tell from experience what her sensations should be. The heat had seared on in her belly for hours, as the barge rocked rhythmically over the water.

At last, where the Amur River met the Sungari, they were smuggled aboard another boat. As they stepped from the gangplank on to the deck, a blond man with green eyes, much older than Sergei, appeared and clasped him tight. For the first time then she saw the emotion she had sought in Sergei's face. He stood with his arm about the strange man, a light took hold of his eyes.

'This is Ivan Shepenov,' Sergei introduced her. 'I know him from Blagoveshchensk. He sails these boats between Russia and Manchuria. But for him we could not have got here.' She knew then, instinctively, that they were lovers. He told her later, easily. He told her also that Shepenov was a spy.

In Harbin they went to a friend of Nadya's stepmother. The Primakovs were émigrés who had fled Russia ten years before, when exit visas were still easy to obtain. The house was warm and filled by the sweet smell of baking. Mrs Primakov poured tea from a samovar and served warm bread fresh from the oven. It was early morning but her husband had already left for his job on the Chinese Eastern Railway. She asked questions about Blagoveshchensk and Nadya's stepmother. Sergei was silent, concentrating on his breakfast.

'I need a job,' he said when Mrs Primakov tried to draw him out.

'Work on the Chinese Eastern Railway is difficult to get, but my husband will help,' Mrs Primakov offered.

'I do not want to work on the railway,' Sergei argued.

'This town overflows with refugees. Half the Russian men are unemployed. Women take any degrading task to keep their families together. Children have learned to beg in half a dozen languages, or sell themselves on the street.' Mrs Primakov's mouth grew tight. 'From nowhere the Japanese suddenly came, when all the time we expected the Soviets to invade us. Blagoveshchensk was rough but Harbin is now worse. We have become a town of robbery, kidnappings and bandits. Russian deaths exceed births by two to one thanks to assaults, abortions and alcohol.'

In Blagoveshchensk they had not thought of Harbin as other than free. Compared to all they lived with in Russia, the Japanese had seemed no menace. Nadya was filled with sudden trepidation.

'I will find a job for myself,' Sergei told Mrs Primakov. He wiped his mouth on his sleeve and pulled on his coat. He had an address he wanted to trace, and showed Mrs Primakov a scrap of paper.

'This is the Headquarters of the Russian Fascist Party,' Mrs Primakov frowned. 'You must not mix with them.'

'They're working to free Russia from the Soviets,' Sergei replied.

'These people are dangerous. They've been bought by the Japanese Army. Since the Japanese we're flooded with drugs, prostitution and extortion. With the Russian Fascist Party as a front, the Japanese are behind all the kidnappings, for which they take a cut from the gangs. This is their way of exploiting Manchuria, of making money from our destruction. Harbin is awash with heroin and morphine. It can be bought anywhere, delivered at home or at the school gates.' Mrs Primakov spoke in an impassioned way. Sergei turned his back upon her.

At the front door she drew Nadya aside. 'It is my duty as a friend of your stepmother to tell you I do not like this young man. I ask you to take care,' Mrs Primakov urged. She presumed Sergei was Nadya's husband and, in the interests of propriety, Nadya did not disillusion her.

Soon Sergei found the Russian Fascist Party Headquarters, where Shepenov waited for him. From then on he went out alone, leaving Nadya with Mrs Primakov. He returned late each night smelling of vodka. Soon he did not return at all. Nadya knew he had finally gone when the diamond brooch and rings, and a thick gold chain with an emerald pendant that had belonged to her mother were missing from their velvet pouch. The last tangible link with her dead mother vanished. The loss cut her adrift, more than the humiliation of Sergei's disappearance. He was seen leaving Harbin with Shepenov. Later she heard he took not only her diamonds but money from the Russian Fascist Party Headquarters. She stood on a precipice with nothing beyond.

'I must find work quickly,' she said. She could not take the Primakovs' hospitality indefinitely.

'You have the right spirit,' Mrs Primakov nodded in approval.

Nadya discovered then another Harbin, apart from the town of solid stone edifices patrolled by Japanese soldiers, that resembled provincial cities upon the Volga. Harbin had first appeared to her as a fragment of pre-revolutionary Russia in the middle of the Manchurian plain. The cupolas of Orthodox churches rose against the sky. Tramcars and droshkies and horse-drawn sleds clattered along cobbled streets. Hotels, theatres, shops and banks proclaimed a bourgeois vitality. Now, she noticed hovels constructed of wooden scraps and discarded boxes, where the poorest Russians lived. Girls of eight or nine in cotton print dresses offered themselves to men. She learned that for an exiled Russian woman there was little work beyond what her body could earn. She went through advertisements in papers that listed typing as a requirement. On the way to interviews she observed Russian women walking the street, staring men boldly in the face, whispering a word. She passed the doors of cabarets and bars and sensed diseased life within. It was as if this world drew her slowly to it. She had heard of the district of Putevaya, where Russian prostitutes laboured day and night. She thought of it as she journeyed back to the Primakovs after each unsuccessful interview.

'It's not your fault you cannot get work, unemployment is our affliction here. Everyone is leaving for Shanghai. All kinds of work are available there. We have a little spare money, it will buy you your passage. And you can live with Mr Primakov's sister until you find your way.' Mrs Primakov rolled dough, her hands white to the wrist with flour.

From the first moment Shanghai filled Nadya with optimism. Within a few days she saw Bradley Reed's advertisement for an assistant in a newspaper and applied for the job. She was lucky. In general, the work available for White Russian women in Shanghai differed little from in Harbin. Now, in Nanking, she turned restlessly, the past fragmenting behind her. She closed her eyes and slept at last, as the first light speared the room.

Nadya was nervous, and put off phoning W.H.D. for some days. Asking around, she heard tales of his power. There was talk of genius, but also of sycophancy. Whatever he was, W.H.D. appeared larger than life. At last she picked up the phone.

'Why didn't you contact me before this? Come today at three o'clock.' The order was barked down the wire.

He was as big as his voice but at once assumed a paternal air, ushering her into his office, calling for tea. Her fear of him ebbed away. 'And cakes. Do not forget the cakes,' he demanded of a secretary.

At six o'clock she still sat listening over cups of tea to his talk of China, past and future. He seemed in no hurry to let her go, enjoying his captive audience. She did not mind, he was far from dull, and spoke with authority. However colourful his tales, she doubted he embellished much; his life had been extraordinary.

'I'm like a little boy who dare not go to sleep for fear I will miss something,' he told Nadya.

'As soon as I arrived in China I began to win the reputation of being a foreign-devil who speaks the truth, who can't be bought, who does what he wants and who is generally good joss. I think I can say my name is tagged on to every convulsion that has hit China since I arrived. And it won't be long now before the Japanese know exactly who I am.' W.H.D.'s voice boomed out, even though there was no one to hear but Nadya. He leaned forward over his desk towards her.

'The Japanese beat Russia but one day that victory is going to cause their downfall. Beating Russia began their almighty thoughts about world hegemony. The world press lauded Japan to the skies as the Oriental David slaying the Russian Goliath. We inflated their heads and one day we are going to suffer for our later failures to see beneath their smooth skins. The Japanese have fooled everyone but the Chinese.'

It was not until six o'clock that he finally asked, 'Well, what about Bradley's great book?'

She had not expected to see Donald Addison again but he stood unexpectedly before her in the same linen suit, his tie off-centre, his hair still without direction. She had come to the International Club with a group of people from the university. There was dancing that night on the flat, terraced roof of the club. The band played loudly behind Donald Addison. He grinned and held out his hand, giving no more than a cursory nod to the people at her table. She stood up to dance and was immediately angry at her obedience. He swept her away without a greeting, humming above the music.

'And how was the Generalissimo?' she asked.

'I have not yet succeeded in seeing him. There is some all-powerful Australian guarding him, who seems even fiercer than his Hitler-trained bodyguard. I had an appointment which he cancelled.'

'W.H.D.? He is not so bad,' Nadya replied. She had already now met him twice, but of course she had Bradley Reed's introduction. 'Maybe you have upset him.' Donald Addison was pressed firmly against her. In spite of untidiness there was a clean, scrubbed smell about him. She had been waiting to see him.

'Why should you think that?' He slowed his step and drew back to regard her. It was difficult to know if he joked or was genuinely upset. Once more, as on the walls of Nanking, she had the feeling of playing a game of words.

'Because you look like someone who upsets people,' she replied. His grip tightened as he pulled her towards him again. In spite of the prickly banter of words, her body was at ease against him.

'Now, how do you know all these things?' he asked. He had been told he might find her here at the Club. It had not been difficult to make enquiries.

'You have not yet said good evening to me,' she complained.

'Haven't I?' Still humming above the music, he pressed her closer. He had seen her a score of times each day, etched indelibly on his mind. She was always silhouetted against the fiery sky, the sun burning in her hair. He could not rid himself of her.

'Why should W.H.D. cancel your appointment?' she asked.

'Because he said I was dangerous stuff. In my opinion, I simply tell the truth. That is my job. There was a recent article on him in *Time*. It was not by me but something I had written ages ago about China, mentioning him, was quoted out of context. He said I had insinuated he was an opium dealer.'

'And is he?' she smiled, leaning back to look at him anew. She enjoyed his sense of mischief.

'I shouldn't think so. But I have been damned. I suppose I would feel the same in his shoes.' He began to laugh.

'I could speak to him. My job brings me into contact with him. He either likes or dislikes people, nothing in between.' The offer was out of her mouth before she could suppress it.

'Are you going to be my guardian angel? If so we should get to know each other better. I have heard it is pleasant to boat at night on the Lotus Lakes,' Donald replied. He drew her close again.

'I have an appointment to see W.H.D. tomorrow.' She was suddenly angry with herself. Why should she bother to seek involvement? What did it matter to her if he got his interview or not? It was as if in some way he controlled her.

'I do not like being beholden to women. But I also do not like being snubbed. As it is I left a file in his office that I must pick up. I might see you there tomorrow. And the Lotus Lakes?' he persisted.

'The day after tomorrow is full moon. It's a good night for a picnic on the water.' Something quickened in her, already she felt enmeshed. The music stopped and he returned her to her table.

'You're going?' She thought he would join her friends.

'I came for a drink. This kind of evening is not my type of thing. Besides, I've written so many rude articles about expatriate communities around the world, few will have me at their table.' Donald bowed in apology to the people before him.

He looked over his shoulder before he left the terrace and, seeing she stared after him, smiled with the look of a naughty child. She could not deny his strange charm. Nadya turned back to the people at the table who were immersed in a discussion about agricultural fertilizers. Her feelings were confused.

The next day she entered W.H.D.'s office in trepidation. Donald was there, the forgotten file already in hand, talking to a secretary.

'He won't see me,' Donald announced as she walked up to him. The secretary pursed her lips and shook her head. 'I even told her to say you recommended me.'

'Why did you say that?' Nadya asked with a frown.

'Was that wrong?' Donald asked.

'I told you to leave it to me. I know how W.H.D. can be.' A wave of annoyance filled her.

When she entered W.H.D.'s room she found him at his most volcanic. His eyes blazed behind his glasses. 'What have you brought this man here for?' W.H.D. demanded. 'Do you know anything about him?' She shook her head.

'Well, let me tell you, he's notorious. Not at all the type for a nice girl to see. All kinds of rumours abound about him in Fleet Street. His father was a famous man, a journalist of integrity, which the son is not. I am a journalist myself, and I do not like sensationalism, or unproved sources. Because of his loose comments, some people now say I'm an opium dealer. Few people realize it but, the fact that China is no longer thought of as a backward country of dragons, curios and laundry men is in no small part due to myself. I am proud to say upon my advice to our Generalissimo, China's voice now rings out on international platforms.'

'You like the game but not the spotlight,' Nadya smiled, trying to keep things light. Whatever W.H.D's opinion of his influence might be, Nadya found it difficult to imagine the suave and crafty Chiang Kai-shek hanging slavishly upon the Australian's every word.

'Dear lady, you are right,' W.H.D. stormed. 'Do you know, there are regular attacks upon this innocent child, to get him kicked out of China? I am sick of being picked upon. It is bad enough here in China, but when people who know nothing of me, like your friend, add their two pennies' worth, you can be sure I will retaliate. And why does he need you to plead for him. Can he not face me himself?'

'It seems to have been a misunderstanding. He says he was quoted out of context. He is here only to pick up a forgotten file, and I'm not pleading for him, only telling you the facts. He seems an interesting man and in his position with *The Times* could surely be more useful as a friend than an enemy,' she suggested.

W.H.D. sat down at his desk again. 'Are you trying to tell me what to do? I don't want to hear that man mentioned again.'

Nadya pushed the latest report from the TECSAT department across to him. 'Things are going well. We should be able to finish by the autumn as Bradley wants.'

'If the Japanese don't attack,' W.H.D. growled.

'You think they will?'

'Matter of time. If we have a Japanese occupation you can be sure that book will never be finished. Everything will be destroyed. China must remain united and fight them. I maintain the Japanese can never really conquer this country. If we are unlucky they may hold power for a while, but no more.'

'Perhaps Mr Addison should interview *you*,' Nadya suggested.

'*Mr Addison*. Well, since you have taken such a shine to him, and I am not untouched by your feminine charms, let us have a compromise. Why don't we let him interview Madame? *She* will put him right,' W.H.D. relented suddenly.

'But *I* have not met her yet,' Nadya protested.

'Well you are going to, right now. Come on, I am on my way to her office. She does nothing without my advice and I handle most of her correspondence. She said she wanted to meet you.' W.H.D. gathered his papers together and steered Nadya from his office. Outside Donald sat on the corner of a desk, still talking to the secretary.

'Shall I bring Mr Addison?' Nadya whispered. She looked over her shoulder at Donald. He raised his eyebrows in enquiry.

'Certainly not. God damn it, *he* will need an appointment.' W.H.D. spoke loudly, marching Nadya forward. Donald began to laugh.

Madame Chiang Kai-shek sat at a desk in a crowded office. She was dressed in a suit of black crepe with yellow piping. Her beauty was legendary, she had no need of the heavy make-up she wore. She greeted Nadya in fluent English. She appeared more American than Chinese, with a vivacious manner and jerky movements. Her mind ran at breakneck speed. The telephone rang and she gave brisk orders, then turned to Nadya.

'This book is important, you understand. Never before will there have been such a complete, such a thorough compilation of all the facets of our great, unwieldy nation. Much divides us but much more unifies us. This is what Bradley wishes to put across; all the things in our nation that make us one thinking, breathing mass of people. These strengths we need to know, to be proud of, and draw upon in the future.' Behind the charm was efficiency, not warmth. It was said her sister, the widow of Sun Yat-sen, was the mother of China, and Madame Chiang Kai-shek its governess.

'I want you to be personally responsible to me for this book. I am very interested. It must come out as quickly as possible, as Bradley advises, for we do not know what the future holds. There could be much destruction of our infrastructure, artefacts and culture. Things that emphasize our greatness and oneness are doubly important at such times. If some symbol of our culture is concretely before us, we cannot forget easily who we are. This great book is very symbolic to me.' She nodded and turned to the telephone again. The interview was over. Nadya left Madame with W.H.D. and went to wait in an outer office.

There was a clear moon that evening, silver light flooded the water. The Lotus Lakes spread out before them like a secret, enchanted world. They chose a punt and the boatman poled off from the shore, gliding smoothly forward.

'Well, what was the Madame like?' Donald asked, leaning back, trailing his hand in the water.

'Energetic, intelligent, ambitious, charming, beautiful, but I think without a heart.' Nadya tried to sum up all the dazzling qualities of Madame Chiang Kai-shek.

'Who needs a heart with such qualities? A heart makes a mess of life,' Donald said. He sounded bitter. Shadow hid his expression.

'What a terrible thing to say,' Nadya sat up in the boat. 'Life is only about having a heart.'

'Evaluate,' Donald demanded, sprawled on a rug. Behind him the boatman poled the craft with small, soft slaps of water. 'Is there anything in your life you would honestly say has come about through obeying your heart?'

'If I had not obeyed my heart I would still be in Russia, maybe shot dead or put to hard labour, starving and fearful at the best,' Nadya concluded.

'I only respect my head,' Donald decided firmly.

Nadya thought again of Sergei. The moon cut across the water and hung low above the crenellations of Nanking's old wall. There was the croak of frogs and sawing crickets as the boatman steered along the shore. At places the walls of the city almost met the lake and dense shadows fell upon them. She told him then about Russia, about Blagoveshchensk and the escape. The memories came alive to her again, under the moon on the swaying boat, the smell of the lake about her. She felt a grief whenever she thought of Russia. The harsh, rolling landscape, within which was seeded so much of her life, filled her unbearably.

'And what did you feel when Sergei left?' Donald asked. There was none of the usual edge in his voice. Instead she sensed companionship, as if he too had experienced some form of betrayal. There was a keenness in his gaze, as if he assessed her anew.

'I was relieved.' She trailed her hand in the water, memories overpowering her.

The relief had surprised her, she remembered. Beneath the fiction of romance and adventure, there had been hard facts of feeling hidden away. She saw now the relationship had been illusory. Sergei had used it to escape from Russia, and she to lose her virginity. Deep within herself she had discovered a woman whose sensual needs had driven her out of Russia.

'Will you be here for long, in China?' She had not questioned him before.

'I have nothing to hurry back for,' Donald answered and fell abruptly silent. She could tell immediately her question had jolted to the surface some unwanted thought. It was as if they played a game of hide and seek, revealing surreptitiously small clues to their buried lives.

Donald had been happy these few moments on the moonlit lake, listening to her story. He wished she had not reminded him of the blow he had recently taken. From Manchuria he had flown down to Peking in an army transport plane. In Manchuria news had been sporadic and censored by the Japanese. On arrival in Peking the name Edgar Snow hit him with cruel force.

There was no one who had not heard of the famous American journalist, Edgar Snow, who had arrived in Shanghai in 1928. Snow spoke Chinese and was an activist who had contact with the country at a level other journalists found difficult. Now the world was talking about the articles he was publishing after spending four months with Mao Tse-tung in his Communist capital. Mao had dictated to Snow his life story, and the history of the Eighth Route Army. The rebel leader had entrusted Edgar Snow to alert the world to the Chinese Communist movement. Snow was writing a book about the experience, holed up in his Peking home. Already, as Snow released parts of the incomplete work to the press, *Red Star Over China* was being called a classic.

In his hotel room in Peking, Donald had sat with Snow's reportage before him. Words seemed to rise from the page, embedding themselves deep within him. For some days he wandered about in a daze, spending long spells in bed, too lethargic to rouse himself. It had not occurred to Donald that someone other than himself might be destined to unravel the Red enigma. His life appeared suddenly to have been arrested, his future stretched aimlessly before him. Once more God had cheated him of what seemed his. All he wanted to do was to leave Peking where Edgar Snow was at work on his book. He travelled to Shanghai and then Nanking, unsure of what direction now his time in China should take. In one stroke he had been diminished to the status of a hack reporter. He had no golden egg to lay.

'Perhaps someday I shall go to Hong Kong or Europe,' Nadya conjectured. If she let herself think about the shape of her life, panic sometimes seized her. Since childhood it seemed there was only flight, abandonment and confusion behind her. Work held her in China, but she still felt ungrounded in dark moments. And, in spite of her words, how would she easily travel anywhere? She possessed neither passport nor country.

'Europe's no Utopia at the moment. Hitler there, the Japanese here. Better to stay where you are. Could be bad times ahead everywhere,' Donald remarked.

'Do you think there will be war?'

'Here? Probably. Perhaps I should also go,' he mused.

'You have no family, no wife, waiting for you at home?' She tried to sound casual. He was silent.

'I never found the right woman,' he replied after a moment.

She saw the distress in his face. The jocular façade was gone and he appeared another man. In this unguarded stance there was a new vulnerability in his expression. She knew then he was afraid to show this part of himself, but that it was there, like a fearful animal, trapped within him. She sensed things had happened in his life that made him need to hide.

She unwrapped the picnic of cold meats and wine, pies, bread and fruit. Martha had donated some almond cake. The white light of the moon gleamed upon the oily surface of the water and the smell of the lake was strong about her. The rocking boat stirred memories again of the unrequited longings of her body, pulsing through her unattended, on that journey out of Russia. Her body was full of useless needs. She dare not look at Donald Addison, dismayed at the emotion engulfing her. These feelings led nowhere, and no man had adequately stemmed them. She looked up to find him staring at her.

'Did you love this Sergei of yours?' he asked. He had seen the expression on her face.

'I thought I did. But the relationship was really to get out of Russia.'

'See, you followed your head, not your heart, even if you don't believe it. That is why you're here,' he smiled, triumphant, sipped his wine and looked out across the lake.

He was all façade, Nadya detected. Behind the cleverness and the restlessness she saw a troubled man. She met his eyes and did not look away. He was afraid of life in a way she had never been. She was no longer apprehensive of him.

'I followed neither my head nor my heart, I followed my body. It was no good, he preferred men, but I was already out of Russia.' There was a need to be honest with him.

He raised his eyebrows. 'I hope you're not so frank with every gentleman you meet. You might give the wrong impression.'

'I thought I should tell you the truth,' she said. The moonlight drained the colour from her blue dress, put new shadows in her face.

He leaned forward to refill her wine, then raised his glass in a toast, as if something was settled between them. He held out his hand and she took it.

6

July 1937

A State of Alert

To reach Teng Li-sheng's house Kenjiro Nozaki had to pass through the old districts of Nanking. The narrow streets were crowded with stalls selling roasted singing birds skewered on long sticks. Oil lamps flared. He visited Teng when possible at night. As always, he felt he was followed. If he turned quickly he imagined a figure slipped into a doorway. Or, perhaps, his mind only played strange tricks. He reached Teng's lane, an alley no wider than a rickshaw, and knocked on the gate. Behind him the road was empty. The old servant came, coughing.

'Is Professor Teng in?' he asked.

'He will be back soon.' The man opened the gate.

Kenjiro followed him across the small courtyard, into the house. The living room was furnished with a table and desk, cane chairs and an armchair poxed with burns from cigarette ash. As Kenjiro sat down, the loose springs of the chair moved beneath him.

The old man reappeared with jasmine tea. Kenjiro took the blue patterned cup in his hands and leaned back. There was a peace in the room he found nowhere else in Nanking. He liked its battered sparseness and the view of bamboo outside the window. Something here returned him to himself. He had known Teng since their student days together in France. When Kenjiro was posted to Nanking he had been delighted to find Teng still in his job at the university, head of the department of Eastern Religions. Kenjiro sipped the jasmine tea and looked about the room. Books clothed the walls floor to ceiling, mostly on religion, magazines and gramophone records filled the table. As long as Teng had his books and music he needed little else, thought Kenjiro. Already, the anxiety that had stressed him all day began to drop away.

There were sounds outside and Teng hurried in. 'I've been at the university, everyone is working flat out. Bradley Reed has set a new deadline for the Encyclopaedia. He fears there may be war ahead and wants the work finished quickly. He's sent his red-headed Russian assistant from Shanghai to breathe down our necks. She's very pretty, so nobody minds.'

Kenjiro was about to tell him he had already met Bradley Reed's Russian assistant but Teng was regarding him with enquiry. 'Has something happened?' Teng asked, perceptive as always. Then, immediately, he waved aside Kenjiro's first words of reply. 'Wait, let us eat first. Bad news is always better on a full stomach.' Teng ordered the servant to bring food.

He strode across the room and began searching for a book on the packed shelves. The long blue Chinese gown with its high collar was dusty about the hem. Behind steel-rimmed spectacles his eyes were deep-set in a fleshy face, and framed by unruly grey hair. He sat down at the table, pushing the gramophone records to one side, and poured some Chinese wine into two small glasses. Drinking it down in a single gulp, he refilled their cups immediately. The servant returned to place steaming bowls of food before them. Kenjiro could no longer withhold his news.

'The Embassy is in a state of alert. News started coming through yesterday. There's been a skirmish outside Peking.'

'What happened?' Teng asked, spooning vegetables into his bowl. 'The ginger pickle is good. Please help yourself.'

'A detachment of soldiers was on night manoeuvres at the Marco Polo Bridge. One of our men left his unit and supposedly went missing. Not much provocation is ever needed as you know. There is a Chinese fort at the bridge. It didn't take long before shelling started.'

'There are continual skirmishes,' Teng replied. 'Every week brings news of yet another. Now, take some of this pork, the old man cooks well but has outdone himself today.'

'This time I think it's serious,' Kenjiro replied. His anxiety spilt into impatience with Teng. On the wall hung a calendar, its date already two days old, 7th July 1937. Kenjiro tore off the couple of pages.

'Remember this date. You might soon wish you could forget it.' He slapped the pieces of paper down on the table, pushing the red number seven before Teng.

'As bad as that?' Teng asked, looking up briefly over his bowl and chopsticks. 'Sit down, my friend. You're overwrought and lonely. You should have married again after Jacqueline. You're not a man to live alone, like me. I should introduce you to our Russian beauty at the university. She might persuade you there is a lighter side to life,' Teng chuckled.

'I have met her,' Kenjiro announced and explained the circumstances. He detected no evidence that Teng had comprehended yet the seriousness of his news. The breeze from the fan lifted the calendar sheets from the table. The red numbers fluttered across the floor.

Kenjiro leaned forward. 'Peking will fall quickly,' he warned. Japan saw the Chinese Army as ludicrously untrained, and the country as an amorphous mass with a government powerless to maintain order. Although he said nothing to Teng, Kenjiro knew hundreds and thousands of troops would be despatched into the area and ordered to attack Peking.

Teng put down his chopsticks and wiped his mouth on a handkerchief. 'I hope you're not right. No doubt General Chiang Kai-shek will now move in his best troops, those trained by his German commander. The "critical hour" he's always talking about may soon be upon us. Or perhaps, as my sources tell me, if there is war he'll leave the north to its fate and concentrate on defending the south. He will prefer to fight on home ground, Shanghai and Nanking are more easily defended.' Teng's voice hardened suddenly. He surveyed the dishes before him and helped himself to some rice.

'Leave Nanking, go inland where it will be safe.' Kenjiro picked without appetite at the food. His apprehension was not just for the possible approach of war, but the stress of his friendship with Teng. Where would it lead him? The first time they met it had led him to Jacqueline. It had been Teng who convinced him to follow his feelings and ignore his father's wrath. Meetings with Teng were rarely innocuous in Kenjiro's experience. And yet, already the difference was clear. They were no longer two radically minded students in France, but adult men involved in critical times.

'I cannot leave here.' Teng threw up his hands. 'First the Encyclopaedia must be finished. Do you know how many years and how many people have been working on it? At last now the end is in sight. Let us see what happens with this particular skirmish.'

'I came here to warn you,' Kenjiro sat back, defeated.

'I thank you old friend, but I must make my own decisions.' Teng smiled sadly. It was no longer possible to talk as they had in their student past. Words were no longer innocuous things. Now, if war began he would be needed. The United Front had been forced upon Chiang Kai-shek. Even though differences between all the political parties had been put aside to fight Japan, Teng could not see it holding. Chiang feared the Reds too much. Instead of fighting the Japanese Imperial Army, he still turned to fight Communists whenever he could. His Gestapo, the Blueshirts, still arrested Communists and exterminated Red troops or villages that supported them. Yenan was as blockaded as before. The Eighth Route Army would need arms, money, whatever could be raised, the peasants whatever help could be given. With or without the Japanese it would be war with Chiang. If the Japanese occupied China, the Communist task was only doubled. If there was war, Teng would be in the thick of it; his support for the Communists was wholehearted. He could never admit the real depth and direction of his political commitment. Such admissions would endanger both himself and his friend. Kenjiro knew him to be a liberal minded man; that was enough weight to place on the trust between them.

Across the table Kenjiro observed Teng's impassive face. He hoped his liberal views were not propelling him towards danger. Was it possible that Teng was a Communist? He pushed the uncomfortable thought away. In those Paris days it did not matter that they were infatuated with liberal ideals. Communism had the glamour of a new age, all their friends discussed it. Now, it was dangerous to sit on the borderline of such thought. In Nanking, the centre of Chiang Kai-shek's Nationalist regime, those who supported the Communist underground movement put their lives at risk. But, as always, Teng appeared an extraordinary character releasing Kenjiro from a stifling world of bureaucrats. He could think no further than the need to break out of that rigid world. It was as if some dark substance were cleansed from him when he was with Teng. Afterwards, he was left with a loathing for himself. Contact with Teng only made him aware of how, each day of his life, he betrayed even further his own ideals.

They seemed to pick up where they left off in Paris, debating with a frankness Kenjiro had forgotten could exist. They still spoke in French and sometimes Japanese, which Teng had studied. It was Jacqueline who had introduced them; Teng was with her at the Sorbonne. To Jacqueline then all Orientals had appeared as one. They had spent much time in those far off days, enlightening her about their ethnic differences. In speaking of such things, the long-held barriers of national distrust were broken down between them. Teng's wife had remained in China while he studied in France. The marriage was not happy and ended soon after he returned to Nanking. He had never remarried, and had once told Kenjiro he had taken a vow of celibacy. Even in their student days he had the look of a monk about him. Through Teng, like the scent of old perfume released from a long closed cupboard, Kenjiro again touched Jacqueline and that other life he had once lived.

'Why must there be war?' Teng sighed now across the table. 'Why can Japan not leave us alone?' It was inconceivable they could soon face each other as enemies.

Kenjiro pursed his lips. 'What are we as a nation before China, before your great history. What does Japan have that is not taken from China, from chopsticks and Buddhism, to rice and city planning? Sometimes I think there is a need in our national subconscious to avenge this debt, to show China we have come of age.' As he spoke Teng's expression changed to sudden fury.

'To hell with your national subconscious.' Teng shouted, thumping his fist upon the table, making Kenjiro start. Then, with an effort, he collected himself. There was much he wished he could say to Kenjiro and dare not. He had a secret life, unknown to the people he met each day at the university. Just that morning he had visited Grandma Chao, a famous old rebel, unlike any other bandit. She was an apparently respectable grandmother, fifty or sixty, totally illiterate. At present she was hiding in Nanking, gathering arms and ammunition to send to her group of guerrillas. She was from Manchuria, and had tasted Japanese rule. She knew of murder and rape and looting. Her family were wiped out by the Japanese army in 1932. Teng had promised to raise two thousand dollars for her, but he could tell none of this to his friend.

Kenjiro was shocked at the anger in Teng's voice. Annoyance pulsed through him. He was not without pride in the expansion of Japanese power, the might of a small nation against the giant. He was still a patriot. It was only too clear where he and Teng now parted in the matter of ideals.

'Are we to take sides against one another?' he asked. Teng ignored the remark. Kenjiro tried again.

'For forty years we have been wresting territory from China; Taiwan, Korea, Manchuria, Jehol, Inner Mongolia. Now it seems we want what is south of the Great Wall. Even though I suspect the United Front is not so united, to Tokyo it makes our policy of leisurely annexation obsolete. There is no place in Japan for sceptics like me. I have this terrible feeling inside me. When I think of the future I see a black cloud. I saw such a cloud once from a burning village our army had sacked in Manchuria. I keep seeing that cloud now again when I think of the future. Marco Polo Bridge is not a passing incident, it is the spark to light a fire.'

'Wait, see what happens, we have had months of these skirmishes,' Teng repeated. His tone was now one of weariness.

It was a hot morning. A ceiling fan swept round above Kenjiro's chair. There was a note from Fukutake already upon his desk. Kenjiro wiped the sweat from his neck with a handkerchief and sipped the clear tea in a glass before him. The desks of four colleagues pressed about him in the office, making the room seem even smaller and hotter. From the window he had a view of Ginling Women's University, and beyond it the red walls of the Drum Tower upon its raised island of greenery. It was impossible this morning to ignore the buzz in the Embassy. As he had indicated to Teng, the Marco Polo Bridge skirmish was no ordinary clash. No doubt Fukutake wished to see him in relation to the event.

Fukutake's office was large as befitted his superior status, with the desks of only two assistants in a corner. Kenjiro was at ease with Fukutake. Although he was older than Kenjiro, they had been at the same school and then at the same university together. Fukutake's father had worked in the Ministry of Commerce and Industry under Kenjiro's father. They had been posted together once before in Delhi.

Across the desk Fukutake shuffled a pile of papers. He gave a cursory greeting and told Kenjiro to sit down. His usual affability was absent. He pulled a document from the pile before him and ordered his assistant to take it to another department. He waited until the man left the room before turning to Kenjiro.

'There is a complaint against you. It has travelled at this point no further than my desk.' Fukutake stared at him fixedly.

'Complaint?' Kenjiro frowned, his mind ran over a list of possibilities.

'You have a Chinese friend, I believe. Although nothing has yet been proved, there are some worrying rumours surrounding his politics. I would advise you not to see him again.' Fukutake kept his voice low in the empty room.

Shock flushed through Kenjiro. He remembered the shadows that seemed always behind him. In the Embassy at Nanking, as in all his other postings, Kenjiro was conscious of how he conducted himself, how others saw him. At the beginning of his career it had been difficult to swallow down opinions, to agree with views that were not his own. But in time he became adept at lies.

'He is an old friend from my student days in Paris,' Kenjiro protested. 'It is not my fault he lives here. Would you have me ignore a friend?'

'I understand,' Fukutake said. 'Believe me I sympathize, but these are difficult times. You are no longer a student but a diplomat. We may soon be at war with China. We cannot fraternize too freely with these people. It has been rumoured your friend may have Communist ties. I tell you this for your own good.' Fukutake spoke with the frankness of old acquaintance.

'How do you know I have met this man?' Kenjiro controlled a sudden surge of anger.

'Do not ask me that.' Fukutake held up his hand. 'I can only say it is none of us here in the Embassy who have imparted this information,' he added quickly, lowering his voice even further. The *Kempeitai*, the secret police, must be even more active than he had thought, Kenjiro decided. There was no other way Fukutake could know of his visits to Teng.

'Nozaki, listen. I know you have a past, and these are dangerous times. We must all toe the line. Only the most foolhardy would step out of order,' Fukutake advised, dropping all formality. He spoke in a quiet, pointed manner, looking directly at Kenjiro.

'Who has been talking to you?' Kenjiro asked, anger flaring anew in him. How could Fukutake know why he had left Japan? 'My *past* is a few student thoughts and a rash article or two.' Would he never throw off doubt in establishment eyes? Was his name to be listed forever in the thick files of the *Kempeitai*?

'That may be, but you know as well as I, many are in prison for less.' Fukutake leaned forward, his voice filled with urgency. 'This is a good posting, do not spoil it for yourself. It means something to be here in China, especially in these times.'

Kenjiro bowed in reluctant submission. Fukutake was right. He had been surprised at his posting as Cultural Attaché to such a diplomatic hot-bed, in the immediate firing line of Japanese ambition. To be sent to Nanking seemed a sign from the powers above that he might soon be rehabilitated; silence and diligence had proved his remorse for earlier misguided ways. It was nearly nine years since he had left Japan. As always his father was at work behind the scenes, doing what he could.

Returning from Fukutake's room, he busied himself at his desk, refusing to join his colleagues talk about the incident at Marco Polo Bridge. He had a sudden feeling of isolation. Were any of these men, he wondered, in the pay of the *Kempeitai*?

'What has happened to you Nozaki? You appear to me as if shut up in a box,' Teng had said at their first meeting in Nanking.

'That is *exactly* how I feel,' Kenjiro had answered with a laugh. He could think of no one in all the years since Jacqueline's death with whom he could share not only memories, but such freedom of expression. He felt boxed in more firmly now than ever before.

At last, in the early evening, he was able to leave the Embassy. He made his way to the hall where the Asia Conference was to be held. A banner, draped across the front of the building, proclaimed in red letters, 'Asia for Asians'. Kenjiro stood back. Evening darkened the sky but a light had been trained on the words. The Asia Conference had been arranged jointly by the Japanese Embassy and the Free Asia Movement. He had been involved in securing the venue and accommodation for delegates. The conference had created considerable interest. Participants came not only from all over China, but from other Asian countries. The last conference in Dairen several years before had been a success.

The hall was already filling up. Kenjiro took a seat next to Fukutake.

The Ambassador was to give an opening address. At first there had been hesitancy; nobody knew how far Japan should be seen to support the conference in these difficult times. But from Hsinking came orders from one of the Generals to do whatever was needed to give the conference a boost. It appeared one of the main organizers was an Indian, with connections in Manchukuo. Kenjiro had not yet met the man. He had arrived from Hsinking the night before and others had taken care of him.

At last people settled and the Ambassador stood up to give his address, speaking obliquely of Asian brotherhood in a world of new perspectives. He trod a fine line of diplomacy, although he was a supporter of the military. After the Ambassador came the Indian. His eyes protruded slightly behind a sharp nose, filling his face with an earnest, fanatical expression. He was at home on the platform, surveying his audience, waiting until he had their attention. He spoke with a practised fluency, as if reciting well-worn words.

'Why has China united against Japan, a nation that wishes only to see her advancement, and to protect her from the threat of Russia, which is even now massed on the borders of Manchukuo? In the event of a fight with Japan, where will Nanking turn for help but to Britain and America. And will these nations not later demand their pound of flesh in return for the help they give China? Do you think a China, armed and aided by Britain and America, if it defeats Japan, will then become the dominant power in Asia? Do not deceive yourself. If Japan were ever defeated, then China would pass under American or British control. That would be a tragedy for China and for the whole of Asia. White domination is what we must co-operate to rid ourselves of. It is Russia with her encroaching ambitions we must prepare to fight, not each other.'

It was the same old propaganda, but people listened. The man had the power to project himself. Kenjiro wondered at the zeal that could emanate from unassuming individuals once a missionary chord was struck. The Indian's face was transfigured by an uncontrollable energy. A voice that had begun persuasively now harangued the crowd. There was also something familiar about him. Kenjiro realized, with a start of recognition, that he had once arranged special papers for Tilik Dayal during his posting to New Delhi. He remembered a bombing and the need for the man to seek asylum in Japan. He looked at Tilik in amazement, and walked forward to introduce himself after the meeting was over. Tilik recognized Kenjiro immediately. As they stood talking, a tall Englishman pushed his way through the crowd. He slapped a hand upon Tilik's shoulder.

'So, you too have come to hear me speak,' Tilik smiled broadly at

Donald Addison. 'Will you report my speech in your English paper? I know I can trust you to be fair,' Tilik turned to introduce Kenjiro to Donald.

'I might even do an article on the further growth of anti-British sentiment in south-east Asia,' Donald agreed with a laugh.

'You could interview Mr Nozaki also for his views upon this subject,' Tilik enthused. Kenjiro protested in alarm; he wanted no further prominence after his talk with Fukutake. He tried to take his leave. Tilik Dayal placed a restraining hand on his arm.

'I have had two surprise meetings, and both with people who have saved my life. We must celebrate.' Tilik insisted they go to a restaurant known for its Peking cuisine. Eventually, they left in an Embassy car for the restaurant.

'Now what will you say about the conference?' Tilik turned to Donald as soon as they settled at a table.

'You will see,' Donald teased. 'How is the wool trade?'

'Captain Nakamura is dead,' Tilik replied. His voice took on a new edge. A sullen look filled his face for a moment. Things had not gone as he wanted.

A new Japanese Army High Command, in spite of Hasegawa's intervention, had not liked Tilik's idea of paying the wool traders the same price they would get from the British in Tientsin. It ordered prices dropped to levels that exploited the traders. As a result there was a new explosion of discontent against the Japanese amongst the Chinese traders.

'All the units in that area, including the one to which Captain Nakamura was attached, were massacred by Chinese guerrillas,' Tilik announced.

'I liked Captain Nakamura,' said Donald. It unsettled him to think the rational, friendly Nakamura was dead.

Kenjiro sipped a beer and listened to the conversation with a slight frown. He did not know what to make of Tilik Dayal. 'You have come a long way since we last met,' he remarked. Tilik nodded, anxious to give proof of the distance travelled.

'I have been given great support in Japan for the Indian cause. Both Shumei Okawa and Mitsuru Toyama are my benefactors. Toyama arranged my marriage for me,' Tilik boasted, happy to drop these powerful names. Something in Nozaki's restrained manner made him feel he must defend himself.

Kenjiro put down the beer to suppress the sudden wave of alarm flooding him at the mention of Okawa. He did not miss the look of satisfaction on the Indian's face at the impression these names had made on him. Kenjiro picked up his chopsticks and assessed Tilik Dayal anew. What a useful tool he must be to the militarists. Obviously, they paid him well to further their propaganda. There were things he was tempted to say, but swallowed them down with a mouthful of pork and cashew nuts. He should not put himself in further danger. Nowadays trust was a scarce commodity. He picked up a fresh mouthful of meat.

Donald sat back, his eyes alert. 'What are you doing in Hsinking?' he asked Tilik. He sensed an undercurrent between the two men before him. If he could get him alone, he had a feeling the Japanese could tell him a thing or two.

'In working for India I am working for Japan, and vice versa. I have been given the opportunity to publicize the Indian Freedom Movement over a wide area.'

'Hence of course the Lama disguise when we last met,' Donald interrupted and turned to explain the desert journey to Kenjiro. A look of annoyance passed across Tilik's face. It was not necessary for the Japanese to know these details.

'The defence of Manchukuo is increasingly important,' Tilik announced, seeing the intensity with which Kenjiro was now listening. He remembered the terror that had filled him the last time he had met this man in Delhi. He must have appeared then an abject sight. The desolation of those days welled up before him. A sudden panic overcame him.

'I had not realized the time. Forgive me,' he rose hurriedly as they neared the end of the meal, 'I am supposed to see a group of the conference delegates.' After promises to meet again soon, he left Donald and Kenjiro to finish their meal together.

'Who are Toyama and Okawa?' Donald asked as they watched Tilik depart. He observed Kenjiro in a leisurely way. The man seemed more approachable than many of the Japanese he had met. He remembered Nakamura again and felt a wave of regret.

'Toyama and Okawa are men who are not to be taken lightly,' Kenjiro replied. To speak these names aloud unnerved him. Donald looked at him enquiringly, but Kenjiro did not elaborate.

'How did you find Manchukuo?' Kenjiro changed the subject. He realized Tilik had left him to pay the bill from the Embassy's conference expenses. Although this was in order, he felt another spurt of impatience.

'Manchukuo was interesting,' Donald was careful not to give vent to his criticisms. He gave Kenjiro a penetrating look and then decided to chance a little more. 'I thought when I came here I might investigate the

106

Reds, but now I find someone else has got there first.' He was surprised he had suddenly, inadvertently, decided to risk such a slippery admission. But as he suspected, Kenjiro reacted without censure when told about Edgar Snow.

'China and Communism are bigger than the scope of one man,' Kenjiro replied after Donald had explained the situation. He saw Donald's eyes were bloodshot. It seemed the Englishman was carrying great disappointment with him over this Edgar Snow. In different circumstances he might have thought to introduce the man to Teng. But in these uncertain times, such fantasy could not be sustained. There seemed suddenly so much to hide since he arrived in Nanking. The posting he had been delighted to take as a step to better things seemed now like a minefield before him.

'Do you know what is happening up in the north?' Donald had lowered his voice. 'It is rumoured there has been some trouble that could ignite further. Can you confirm there has been an incident near Peking?'

For a moment Kenjiro hesitated. He looked about guardedly before he spoke. 'There has been an incident near Peking at the Marco Polo Bridge. We are doing what we can to contain it. We have, I assure you, no wish to provoke the Chinese into expanding the conflict for reasons of their own.' Kenjiro was murmuring the information. Donald leaned near him to catch the words.

Kenjiro looked furtively about him again. He had said nothing that would not soon be known. Guilt was driving him paranoid. He took a deep breath to control himself. 'If you are finished, perhaps we should go,' he said, taking his wallet from his pocket and putting down several notes on a plate with the bill.

Outside, he left the Englishman and walked quickly away in the direction of the Embassy. The car had gone with Tilik Dayal and he was glad of the chance to walk. The evening was warm and above him the sky was star-filled. He observed Orion the Hunter arched above Nanking. Up north, over the Marco Polo Bridge and in the sky above Peking, Orion must be as visible. Or were the clouds of battle already blotting out with smoke and death the three stars of Orion's sword? He returned his gaze to the road and looked quickly back over his shoulder. Behind him the street was dark and quiet.

Donald Addison hurried towards the Nanking office of the *North China Daily News* who, by arrangement with *The Times*, allowed him use of their facilities. The article was already formed in his mind. He had a scoop, he was sure, with the incident at the Marco Polo Bridge. No one had as yet reported the news and the Japanese had now confirmed it.

7

August 1937

War

It was the suddenness of the event that shocked. The summer was stifling, the heat packed densely about them. The war had rolled on, unseen, a thousand miles or more beyond the horizon. Then, like a dark cloud blown invisibly southwards, it burst upon them. Peking and Tientsin had already fallen. Now it was heard that a Japanese force had landed in Shanghai.

Nadya walked quickly through the ward behind Martha. The August heat was in hiatus, cooled abruptly by an approaching typhoon. Rain beat down and wind whistled in the hospital windows. Adrenaline quickened her heartbeat, making her movements jumpy. She tried to ignore the fear somersaulting through her. Martha's back was calm and straight before her.

'Ostramalicia,' Martha announced, watching a woman totter forward upon tiny feet. 'In its advanced stages it makes normal childbirth impossible. There are countless still births and tortured deaths during agonizing labour.' She walked on up the ward between the rows of beds.

'Ostramalicia comes from calcium deficiency and is aggravated by bound feet. It produces a mincing walk throwing the pelvis out of pivot until it is grotesquely malformed. A Caesarean section is the only way these women survive childbirth. That is why we do so many,' Martha continued.

Nadya nodded, concentrating on the even voice. Martha appeared unflappable. It was the first time Nadya had been on a ward round with her. For some weeks she had been doing auxiliary work in the hospital in her spare time. She had also been given a course in First Aid by the matron of the hospital. It had been Martha's idea that Nadya should prepare for the uncertain future.

'We did a Caesarean on this one last week,' Martha smiled at a young woman breast-feeding her baby. 'The child had prenatal rickets. Look at its legs. This is her third child. With each confinement the ostramalicia gets worse. All food goes first to the men here, the women get only leftovers. A pregnant woman is further deprived by the new life within her. A calcium deficient girl baby begins life on the calcium deficient milk of her mother. It's a vicious woman wasting cycle that seems destined to sustain itself forever. What will they do now, these living we try to help live better, if there is war? There will be time only to tend the dying.'

'The buses have already been camouflaged green. But houses are painted black,' Nadya said. Fear rushed through her again. War seemed to follow her, like a shadow.

'Black is to prevent glare during attacks.' Martha's tone remained practical. 'It is said they will bomb us from the air, my dear, even though international agreement demands civilians should not be targeted. War tactics are increasingly unscrupulous these days. I am *not* painting this place black. Who would dare bomb a hospital? We'll paint American Hospital in Chinese and English on the roof. I put my faith in Chiang Kai-shek. He'll drive them back,' Martha decided. 'Now let me see you change that dressing. If there is war we shall need a good nurse more than a good proof-reader.'

'At the moment the proof-reader is still needed,' Nadya protested, bending to change the bandages on the infected foot of an old woman. 'Bradley is going mad. With all this sudden talk of war, there is chaos at the university. We're in the middle of printing the last chapters of TECSAT. I'll have to go to Shanghai to supervise things. The department at Nanking University is being packed up and carted inland for safety, as are all the other departments. In Shanghai they say even factories are being dismantled and taken inland.'

'We must save what we can by whatever means possible. The Japanese will be out to smash everything. There is no doubt of the panic. Everyone is leaving. Even the Chinese have begun an exodus inland,' Martha frowned. 'I'm afraid that's always a bad sign.'

She continued to the next bed. 'This young girl swallowed a needle and is lucky to be alive.' Martha examined the stitches on the woman's abdomen and remembered another case of needles.

He had been her father's patient and she then only eight years old. He was a tailor who inadvertently swallowed a needle. It went down headfirst with the knotted silk still attached to it. Many attempts were made to recover it by pulling on the thread. The man was half-dead when at last brought to the mission. Martha knew her father was perplexed because he turned to prayer. Eventually, he found his answer in a rubber tube. More thread was tied to the remains in the man's mouth, the tube was slid over it and down the tailor's throat. The rubber dislodged the needle passing it into the stomach from where it was drawn out through the tube. She had never forgotten the tailor's amazement. Such creative medicine, conjured up by her father when his back was to the wall, further spread his reputation. If he were still alive, what advice would he give her now as they faced a war like none he had known.

'Come,' Martha said as they reached the end of the ward. 'Let us go back to the house. The girls must be waiting for lunch.'

Rain whipped their skirts as they left the hospital and ran across the compound to Martha's house. 'The girls are supposed to leave tomorrow, but now I don't know what to do,' Martha confided as they reached the front door. Lily was returning to school in Shanghai, but Flora was departing for college in America. 'I was going to Shanghai with them, to put Flora on the boat.'

'Well, you can't do that now. No one knows what will happen, especially if there is fighting in Shanghai,' replied Nadya. The comforting smell of roast chicken greeted them as they opened the door of the house and folded their umbrellas. Flora and Lily already sat at the table, listening to the English language radio station from Shanghai.

'It's Friday the thirteenth. Imagine, a war starting on this of all days!' said Flora.

'I doubt the date means anything to the Japanese,' Martha answered as she sat down. She made an effort to sound unconcerned. The cook brought in the chicken and Martha folded her hands in grace. The radio droned on behind them. A fan swept the ceiling, stirring the tablecloth and their hair. Rain beat against the window. The voice of the radio announcer intruded, detached yet intimate.

The first shooting has occurred between Japanese and Chinese troops today. Shanghai has been preparing for war without let-up. Ten thousand Chinese soldiers have piled up sandbags around North Station. It is clear Chiang Kai-shek is determined to hold Shanghai even as twenty-one Japanese warships move up the Whangpoo and anchor off the Bund. Tension continues to mount in Shanghai. Rainy weather preceding the approaching typhoon adds further gloom to the spirit. Today, after the shooting, the city is on alert and mobilization orders for the Shanghai Volunteer Corps were flashed on cinema screens across the city. People in the audience applauded as young men stood up and left the cinema. War now seems certain. Banks are expected to temporarily close. Mail and communication with the city are likely to be cut. All passenger ships bound for Shanghai are expected to be diverted to Hong Kong, Yokohama or Manila in the interests of safety.

'There is no ship to sail to America on, Mama,' Flora was unable to keep the relief from her voice.

'So it would seem,' Martha replied. She got up to adjust the volume on the radio. 'This is not the time for you to leave.' The decision was immediate now she knew there would be war. Should she not send the girls inland? She pushed the thought away. The Japanese might never reach Nanking if defeated in Shanghai.

'Will school open if there's war?' Lily asked.

'Of course not, Silly,' Flora replied.

'Let us wait and see,' said Martha. 'Situations change overnight in China.'

We may not win, but we can ultimately exhaust the enemy, Chiang Kai-shek had said. Like most Chinese, he saw in years not in days and cast his mind forward to essentials. As far as Martha knew, the Chinese had absorbed all their past conquerors. Perhaps it would be the same again. If the Japanese were victorious in Shanghai, Chiang Kai-shek would be forced to surrender and Nanking would be occupied peacefully. There was time yet to decide about the girls.

By the next day the typhoon had veered away. The clouds cleared, and the sticky heat returned.

'I hate August,' said Lily. 'So hot all the time you could die.' She threw herself on the bed. 'I'm so bored. We can't do anything because of this war.'

'When we were small we went to the sea at Tsingtao, remember? Now Mother has no time, she's working too hard. Next year, when things are normal again, we'll tell her to take us there,' Flora replied, sitting before a trunk, preparing to unpack all they had packed up the previous day. The heat pressed about them in the room.

'Will there really be war?' Lily asked, catching Flora's tone of bravado.

'Probably,' Flora attempted to keep her voice light. She left the trunk and came to sit on the bed beside Lily, picking up a mirror and a pair of tweezers.

'I'll tell Mother you're at it again,' Lily remarked, watching Flora pull stray hairs from her eyebrows; Martha was not for improving nature in the interest of vanity.

'No you won't,' said Flora.

'If there is war will we die?' Lily asked, staring up from where she lay on the bed at Flora.

'We are not Chinese. It's not our war,' Flora replied, immersed in clearing the unsightly merger of her eyebrows. She realized immediately what she had said.

'What about me?' queried Lily, sitting up promptly.

'What about you? Aren't you an American? Look at your passport,' Flora tried to defuse her mistake.

111

'Yes, but . . .' Lily fell silent before the confusion corroding her. She frowned, putting her thoughts in order.

'At school they don't think I'm American. They say I'm Chinese.' She spoke the words in a rush.

'I've told you before to take no notice of *that.*' Flora looked up from her mirror.

'How would you know what it's like?' Lily replied. It was the first time she had talked in this way to Flora. She was fourteen and suddenly everything raised a query.

'They also think I'm strange at school,' Flora reassured. 'At home we don't go to parties or picnics or have new clothes each week, like Shanghai girls. We speak Chinese and know about things up country.' The life of smart schoolgirls in Shanghai was another world. Flora was pointed out at school as the daughter of William Clayton. Her father's death at the hands of bandits was a well-known tale. She had no memory of her father, yet she carried his death like a badge of the bizarre upon her.

'Well, you are not as strange as I,' Lily interrupted.

'I'll be even stranger in America,' Flora said, lowering the mirror at the thought. She dreaded that hidden landscape. She had never been to America and her patchy vision of it was intimidating. In spite of letters from great aunts and second cousins, it remained a distant place.

'I don't want to go back to that school without you. What'll I do?' Lily asked.

'You'll do very well,' Flora replied, raising the mirror again. She wished this uncomfortable talk would stop. She did not want to think of the battles Lily must fight now on her own.

'Mother doesn't love me like she loves you,' Lily announced suddenly. The thought had appeared abruptly, like a piece of debris in a well, released to rise to the surface. Once it had the shape of words she saw the thought had always been with her.

'How can you say such things?' Flora replied, discarding the mirror and tweezers in shock.

'Because it's true. Sometimes, I wish Mother had never adopted me but left me to be eaten by dogs as my real parents intended when they abandoned me. She says it's a miracle she discovered me. Because of me all her orphanages were founded. I was a stepping-stone to many things. She didn't adopt me because I was *me.*'

'I can't believe you're saying this,' Flora was lost for a reply. The guilt she felt at not being adopted gave her relationship with Lily a special dimension, and overwhelmed her now.

'Perhaps if she hadn't found me, my real mother might have come back for me,' Lily mused.

'By then it would have been too late,' Flora snapped. A memory returned to her suddenly, of sitting as a small child on Martha's lap watching Lily playing with a doll on the floor beside them. Even then she had understood the exclusiveness of the love between her mother and herself.

'Why should she have adopted you unless she loved you?' Flora argued, suddenly desperate. 'I love you. They say I cried and cried until you were allowed to stay with us for ever. Don't forget it was me who found you.'

'You see, that's it,' Lily replied in a pert voice. 'If you hadn't cried, Mother would have put me in an orphanage.'

'You're mad,' Flora screamed.

'It's true,' Lily said.

'How can you say such terrible things?' The tears were all in Flora's eyes. Lily remained unmoved.

'I hope this war lasts forever. Then I need never go back to school,' Lily decided.

Flora stared at her sister. The war faded suddenly. Nothing now seemed more terrible than Lily's impassive face.

The day was punctuated by radio bulletins from Shanghai. In Martha's sitting room hospital staff gathered to listen to the unfolding events. An extra fan was brought in and refreshments served. There was an atmosphere of subdued partying.

In Shanghai the bombing had begun, but not in the way expected. The Chinese Air Force took the offensive, with American-built North-rops and inexperienced pilots. Their aim was to annihilate the Japanese warships on the Whangpoo. Instead, inept and ill-trained Chinese fighter pilots bombed but failed to damage some Japanese owned cotton mills, and fell short of the flagship *Izumo*, anchored off the Bund. By Saturday lunchtime the roof-tops of Shanghai were packed with spectators, avid to view the show. On the streets below, the weekend crowds were in a holiday mood. The familiarity of the radio announcer's voice was now that of a trusted friend.

'*I could hear the crowds cheer as the bombers soared up and then the booing as they missed their targets. Their bombs dropped harmlessly into the river. Shanghai is in a state of great excitement.*' The radio announcer was hoarse across the crackle of interference. When the carnage began in the afternoon, incredulity preceded all other emotions.

'*Three bombs have been carelessly and accidentally dropped on the centre of*

Shanghai by China's own Air Force. Even the Japanese could not have done worse. How is this possible?' the announcer pleaded. At last people had begun to realize the extent of the Chinese Air Force's ineptitude.

'The first bomb landed on the roof of the Palace Hotel and the next across Nanking Road on the Cathay Hotel. Fifteen minutes later the third bomb fell on the crossing of Avenue Edward VII and Thibet Road.

'The air is foul with smoke and burned flesh. Shanghai is in shock. Terrified crowds of fleeing refugees are blocking bridges and roads. Everywhere are streams of blood and the mutilated bodies of men, women and children. At a traffic light a line of vehicles has been caught by the bomb, their drivers burned to a crisp. I have seen a disembowelled child and a European, his head cut cleanly from his white linen suit. Craters and falling masonry and glass are all around. The blood of victims drenches the sofas and chairs of the Palace Hotel. Furniture vans are carrying away the dead. Foreigners and Chinese lie dead together. In this hundred-degree heat the smell is excruciating. The pavements are sticky with blood. This is going to be worse than 1932. Already they are calling today, Bloody Saturday. And the Japanese have yet to attack. This is unbelievable slaughter by the country's own Chinese troops.'

Martha sat silent before the radio. Fatigue spread through her. The war had started with such stupidity it could only mirror the way ahead. All the years of turmoil littering her life in China seemed to culminate in the description on the radio. In her mind she could already see the hospitals in Shanghai, the amounts of morphine needed, the bodies left to die in corridors, the endless amputations. Outside, on the street the stench of blood would not be put down by sand and disinfectant. How would they bury so many, so quickly? She made a note to order coffins and extra morphine for her own hospital. Until now she had refused to notice the sandbags and dugouts appearing about Nanking. Before they had even struck, she saw now the Japanese might make short work of the Chinese Army. As the main broadcast ended people began to leave the room, returning to work in the hospital.

She must get the girls inland. The thought was like a stone. It did not occur to Martha to leave; she had never left any situation. As always in emergencies, her mind moved about a structure, and fear retreated. She turned to Nadya who sat with clenched hands.

'You must leave the country,' Martha told her.

'Where will I go? I have not even a passport,' Nadya protested, her agitation clear. Picking up her bag, she prepared to leave for the university. 'I must see the Encyclopaedia finished.'

Nadya too clung to the structure of work, as to a raft in an uncertain sea. But she had not, like Martha, an optional world, a country to return to. Her past was like a cupboard to which she had thrown away the key.

A sudden fear pulsed through her. Dark memories of childhood filled her mind. She saw again the file of convicts struggling against the frozen land, and later the crack of guns in the streets of Blagoveshchensk. Mayhem had driven her from Russia, and now stood before her again. She knew the fear of a cornered animal, unable to run in any direction.

'Then go with the girls when I send them inland. They should not stay here. I cannot go, I shall be needed in case of attack,' Martha replied, ignoring her daughters' terrified protestations. Nanking was the capital of China, Chiang Kai-shek himself lived in the city. There was now no doubt in her mind that Nanking, not Shanghai, would be the real theatre of Japanese interest.

'In Shanghai they say Father Jacquinot has set up a safety zone for the Chinese who cannot go inland,' Martha continued. 'There is talk amongst a group of us here, doctors and missionaries mostly, to do the same in case the Japanese take Nanking.'

'How long will the war last?' Lily demanded, shaking Nadya's arm.

'Who can say,' Nadya replied, trying to keep her voice steady. She brushed a stray hair off Lily's brow, wishing there was some way to alleviate the stress in the child's face.

'I want it to last for ever, and never go back to school.' Lily turned fiercely upon her mother. 'Why must you send me away? Is it because I am Chinese? They won't bomb you, but they might bomb me? Am I a danger to you all?'

'Lily,' Martha frowned. 'You are an American. I want to hear no more of this.' She had no energy, in the midst of panic, to deal with Lily's confusion.

Smoke was thick upon the air and drifted through the university windows, settling in drifts below the skylights of the great hall of the TECSAT department. The sun pushed down in smoky shafts upon Bradley Reed and Nadya as they stood sorting through piles of paper.

'All those, I think, can safely be burned. I have already sent copies to America.' Bradley waved his hand at a box of papers. He drew on a cigar, gritting his teeth about it as he spoke, his hands filled by sheafs of documents.

The university was in chaos. Bradley Reed had rushed up to Nanking on a night train, leaving the hostilities in Shanghai, bringing news of events first-hand. He explained the situation as he and Nadya worked together.

'The International Settlement and French Concession will not be touched. We will be all right, I think. Shanghai is a Treaty Port. There are too many foreign nationals in the Concessions, too many foreign powers who might be angered and encouraged to join the fray on China's behalf. The Japanese do not want that. They will be careful to ensure the safety of all foreigners. But Nanking is another matter. This is a Chinese town, no Foreign Concessions here, nor even many foreigners. A few hundred at the most I should think. They will not discriminate here where they bomb. We must get everything out of Nanking quickly. I want you back in Shanghai. You will be safe there in the Settlement. And besides, there is work to be done. We must be through with the printing of TECSAT before the city falls.'

Huge boxes now filled the rooms of the TECSAT department. The miles of shelves were emptied of their yellowing paper. Each time she entered the great room with its vaulted ceiling Nadya was filled by desolation. The rows of desks where the compilers had worked now lay empty before her. Footsteps echoed. What was not packed to be sent inland or stored in cellars, was burned outside the building. This dismantling of the long-established department unsettled her greatly. It laid bare as nothing else the brutal probability of the future.

Bradley interrupted her thoughts. 'Chiang Kai-shek has sent the cream of his troops to Shanghai. Those German-trained boys know how to fight, not like the rest of the Chinese Army. The Japanese will not get to Nanking too quickly if they come at all. There is time to clear up before you return to Shanghai. Of course, the railway may be bombed, then you will have to travel by road.'

'The railway bombed?' Nadya echoed.

'This is war, my dear, although there has been no declaration. The surprise of it has people reeling. Nobody thought the Japanese would decide to attack Shanghai. The city is unprepared for war, but Nanking has time to ready itself.' Bradley began to cough with the smoke. Outside the windows the flames of bonfires sprouted high above the yard.

The packing and burning went on for days. Eventually the fires grew less and smoke diminished in the courtyard. Bradley Reed returned to Shanghai with the bulk of the TECSAT manuscript. Nadya was to follow with the remaining proofs.

It did not take long for Japanese bombings to target Nanking. The first strikes were aimed at the aerodrome and military installations, but soon Nanking's Medical Centre was hit. It was chosen as the target of the first two thousand-pound bombs. The attack was a failure, leaving two craters in a field of red mud. No one was hurt.

'It's a miracle,' said Martha, shaking her head as she walked round the grounds, inspecting the damage with a group of medical people. It was her first experience of bombs. Their use against civilians was almost

116

unknown. The buildings were the pride of Nanking. It shocked Martha to see the smashed wall of the auditorium pocked by sharpnel, but the greatest shock was to her illusions. In all her years in China she had never known a hospital singled out for attack.

'Do not bomb us,' Martha cried out, waking in terror later that night.

She poured a drink of water. It had been only a nightmare. Yet the fear it released forced her to face the immediate dangers of the situation. She really must arrange for the girls to go inland. Yet, each time she began preparations the same enormities appeared. What if she were killed in an air raid? What would the girls do then? Even her dream she realized, had resounded with images of Bill. She saw again his last wave of good-bye. How could she have known then that she would never see him again? How would she now part with her girls? She sank her head in her hands, and heard Lily's absurd, accusatory words about being Chinese and a danger to them. She thought again of how Lily had come to her.

It had been October and over a year since Bill's death. Winter already filled the early mornings, frosting the hoof marks of water buffalo. Each afternoon she walked with Flora along the wide path atop the walls of Tsingkiangpu, the town they lived in then. Here Dr Keswick, Martha's father, had built his hospital. Buildings huddled below them as they walked, clouds swooped near their heads. They found some wild flowers and Flora had knelt to pick them. Many feet below was the moat, green and sluggish with lichen. It was Flora who saw the baby, lying naked in the mud.

'It's alive, Mama. I saw it move,' she said. Martha looked down at the still body and did not believe it lived.

Usually she did not take Flora to that part of the wall. Much of her own childhood had been spent in this town, and she knew it well. She had walked this way each day to the schoolroom and passed the place for throwing out babies. Female children were regularly discarded. None were ever buried. The Chinese believed that if a child was buried before cutting its teeth, evil spirits would return for another. There were always small corpses in the mud of the moat and scavenger dogs abounded.

As a child, her father had used Martha's horror of those small bodies to compare the callousness of heathendom to the kindliness of Christianity. It did not comfort her. Once, she had seen a man carrying a small bundle across the moat to the field of grave mounds. He had stood a while beside the body before he turned away. When Martha returned from her lessons dogs were already devouring the corpse. She threw stones at the animals and they ran off, one carrying the head, the others dragging the body. She knew then that, Christian or heathen, it made

117

no difference. It was not easy for anybody to leave a baby to be eaten by dogs. She remembered the stance of the man as he stood in the field, and knew callousness was not in him. She had been eight years old, and angry her father did not understand her feelings.

'See, it's alive,' said Flora.

Below them the child moved. In the distance a dog approached. Martha left the wall and ran through the nearby gate to where the baby lay. Above her, Flora peered over the ramparts. The child breathed and gave a cry. Its eyes were yellow with pus, green flies covered its body, already blue with cold. Martha wrapped it in her cardigan. In the hospital the child was cleaned; it was white and thin, and wheezed when it breathed. 'She may not live,' Martha warned Flora, as if they had found a stray puppy.

'We must hope and pray God will let it live,' Dr Keswick told his granddaughter. 'But it may be better if He takes it home, out of this vale of sin and tears, where its parents cared no more than to throw it away before it even died.'

Flora hung her head and prayed. In the morning the baby was still alive. By the end of the week she had gained new strength and the pus had cleared from her eyes. Flora visited the child each day. Soon, she was well enough to be moved to an orphanage.

'No,' Flora cried. 'She's mine. I found her.'

'We cannot keep her,' Martha explained.

'She will grow to lead a useful life. He has let her live so that her soul may be saved and won to Him. Rejoice in this, Flora my child,' Dr Keswick remonstrated.

'No,' Flora screamed. 'I want her.' She built up a great hysteria.

The thought of adoption came suddenly into Martha's mind. Dr Keswick was amazed. 'It is easy to misread our feelings, to think we hear His wishes when in fact we hear our own desires. Foster the child if you will, there is no need for adoption. You are now without a husband and must bring up your own child alone. Martha, this is madness.'

For once her father could not dissuade her. She called the child Lily, like the flowers that bloomed in the moat, rising above the fetid water. After the year of grief, a healing was begun.

'Lily.' She whispered the child's name again now, and knew she could send her nowhere. Safety was only by Martha's side. In this country Lily *was* a Chinese, whatever her passport might say. In these violent times she could be prey once more to scavenger dogs of an entirely different kind.

The war came at an opportune moment for Donald Addison. His

depression due to Edgar Snow had left him deeply lethargic. Now the war, bowling in upon Shanghai, filled him with new purpose. He would go up to the Red areas after the war, when new angles on Communism might be needed. His adrenaline flowed again. He was impatient for events to warm up, to sink his teeth into real action.

The clouds of war brought also for Donald the long-awaited interview with Chiang Kai-shek. Suddenly, Chiang was not averse to publicity before the new menace of the Japanese. But the interview had been a bare five minutes. He had sent a copy to *The Times*, and also a local foreign-run paper, that had risked printing excerpts. It had enraged W.H.D. who summoned Donald immediately.

'What the hell is this?' yelled W.H.D. throwing the newspaper down before Donald. He sat behind a desk in his makeshift war headquarters beyond Chungshan Men Gate. Both he and the Chiangs had moved hurriedly out of the centre of Nanking to relative safety beyond the city walls. 'You are not allowed an interview with the Generalissimo to put about rubbish like this. He hardly ever gives interviews to foreign journalists.'

'We live in a democracy,' Donald shrugged.

'Madame is hopping mad. She and the Generalissimo are to publish a book in the West of their account of the Generalissimo's kidnapping last year in Sian. Publicity like this doesn't help them. I see no sense in such aggressive reporting. In my day the ethics of journalism were different.' W.H.D. gestured angrily.

'It's not unfair. Chiang Kai-shek has great presence. I have quoted nothing that was not said to me,' Donald protested, controlling his impatience.

'What do you mean by calling it, "The Man Who May Lose China"? Or by saying that even now the Generalissimo is not wholehearted in his fight with the Japanese? Or by saying that in fulfilling his own ambitions of power he believes he is serving China? He serves *only* China. Don't you know that but for the Generalissimo, there are many who would have sold out to the Japanese long ago? The Generalissimo is above the corrupt shenanigans that I admit do at times permeate other factions of his party. You are not fair to a very great man.' W.H.D. glowered behind his spectacles.

'Chiang has said that for China the Japanese are a disease of the skin, the Communists a disease of the heart. I asked him about his comment, nothing more. My time with him was too short to determine very much that is not already known.' Donald remained cool.

'Well, let me tell you, young man, a secret directive to the Eighth Route Army from Mao Tse-tung has recently come into Nationalist hands. It states the Sino-Japanese War will afford an excellent opportunity for Communist expansion. First, there will be a show of compromise with the Nationalists behind which the Communist Party will quietly develop. Next, laying the foundation for power, they will break with the Nationalists. Thirdly, there is their offensive, when leadership of China would be wrested from the hands of the Kuomintang.'

'May the best man win. And may I quote what you've just told me?' Donald was pleasantly aware of how much his manner annoyed the sycophantic W.H.D.

'If it brings your brain into line with reality,' W.H.D. stormed. 'Madame is particularly upset that you have mentioned the Generalissimo's early days with such emphasis, saying he struck a bargain with rich gangster protectors to finance his revolution, if he kept leftists out of his government. This kind of embroidery helps no one. Why do you write in this way?' W.H.D. sounded like an angry schoolmaster.

'Perhaps contact with the great brings out the worst in me,' Donald grimaced. 'A man's vulnerability increases in direct proportion to his eminence. I call it Addison's Law. The higher a man's temporal place, the greater the incongruity between the real and the ideal. I make it my business to approach all eminence with this scepticism.'

'Indeed!' W.H.D. glowered. 'Madame and the Generalissimo rise above rubbish like this. But I can have you put out of Nanking, or even out of China if I wish. This interview was given because of your friendship with Nadya. I doubt Madame will wish to make so much use of her now,' W.H.D. threatened. 'Get out of my sight. You are just a troublemaker.'

As he left W.H.D.'s makeshift headquarters in a black-camouflaged house, Donald looked across the road to the bungalow where the Generalissimo and Madame Chiang Kai-shek now lived. The small house was so packed with items from the Chiangs' official residence that it resembled a furniture store.

Ten days before in that house, Chiang Kai-shek had stood before Donald Addison in a dark blue gown. Taller than average, his cheekbones were high above forceful lips. He was a handsome man, bald, imperious, straight backed with dark, aggressive eyes. He had all the eminence Donald required. His thin frame emanated power, his silences were disconcerting. In spite of himself Donald was impresed. He was willing now to believe the Generalissimo's battles with his own split Kuomintang Party might, in some part, be responsible for the more questionable aspects of Chiang's power. As the interview began there was an air raid. The Generalissimo led the way to the courtyard to observe the bombs dropping about them. He seemed to have no physical fear. The interview was too short for proper discussion. Within five minutes an aide appeared to shepherd the Generalissimo to an unscheduled meeting. In spite of Chiang Kai-shek's apologies, Donald was left with a list of unanswered questions, forced to provide a portrait rather than an interview. Donald would have liked more time with Chiang Kai-shek. The man's powerful charisma remained with him.

Donald had rented a battered car from a local garage and as he drove out of the gates he turned in the direction of Purple Mountain where he and Nadya had arranged to meet. He parked the car and climbed to a clearing amongst the trees that they had recently discovered.

'I may have lost you your job, or at the least your popularity.' He sat down on the ground beside Nadya and explained his meeting with W.H.D.

'I do not understand why you have to make everything you write so like *needles*,' Nadya replied, searching for the right word. When angry her English sometimes deserted her. She could not hide her annoyance at the damage Donald might have done her. So much of their relationship was fraught with her exasperation. She continually wondered what drew her to Donald. Yet, when he was absent the need for him became intense. She remembered the evening on the lake, and the man he had revealed to her.

'Barbed, you mean,' Donald corrected her English. 'There are some who appreciate my style, although of course not W.H.D.,'

'I told you before the interview, if you said the right things, many doors would open for you here. Now they are slammed in your face. Pow! Pow!' Nadya slammed doors in the air. Her tone was still angry. Thank God TECSAT was finished, and she had no further need to face Madame Chiang Kai-shek.

'I say what I think is the truth, not what people want to hear. The only doors that have been shut to me are ones I don't care to have opened,' Donald retorted.

'All you want opened are Communist doors. Never did I think I should be so foolish as to get involved with a man who was a Communist admirer,' Nadya answered. The energy the relationship demanded exhausted her.

'I'm only interested in the *unfolding* of Communism in this country. This is an historic era.' He tried to explain.

'All you want is to write your great book, which has already been written by this Snowman.' She knew the cruelty of the remark.

'I'll hit you one day,' he yelled. Nothing touched him deeper than the reference to Edgar Snow.

121

'Every time I try to help you, this is what you do; get me a bad name.' Nadya turned away.

'I'm sorry,' Donald put an arm about her.

'This is not the way out, just kiss-kiss and make love.' She shook him off.

'What have we come here for then?' he growled.

'To watch the bombs,' said Nadya. In the distance a siren wailed over Nanking. She did not really know why she came to observe the war in this careless manner. It was Donald's idea. Their disassociation with the emotion of the town seemed not to worry him. His inventory was always the same; the number of planes, the number of bombs, the precise location of a disaster. How many were killed or maimed was not part of his game. He cut off abruptly at this juncture, while she was left in acute discomfort.

Donald picked up his binoculars. Some distance before them was the airfield and to the right the southern wall of the city. Climbing high into the mountainside were the white steps and blue roofs of Sun Yat-sen's Mausoleum. Below the hill was the spirit avenue to the ancient tombs. The white stone animals like the rest of Nanking now wore a coat of green camouflage paint. Autumn already rusted the slopes of Purple Mountain. Donald looked into the binoculars. Within the lens the sky was a blank pale disc. They might wait hours before the second siren warned of approaching planes.

'Come here,' said Nadya suddenly, pulling him down beside her. 'The second siren will tell us when they're coming. Once you get behind a lens you're lost. I know you can sit like that, looking at nothing for the next two hours. Maybe you find it easier than looking at me.' She felt desperate to break the confusion of feeling that attacked her on this mountain slope. There was the strange grip of attraction to Donald, and behind her dark memories of Russia and its violence. And now all about them was a growing fear of what they might yet face.

Donald swung the binoculars upon her, his eyes still pressed to the glass. 'Is this better, now I can see more of you?'

Part of her face came before him, her mouth moist and magnified. Suddenly he saw his mother's face in the lens of that first camera long ago. And then Cordelia, her lips stretched back against her teeth, smiling like Nadya. The image in the lens appeared suddenly like the grimace of an animal. He stared as if transfixed.

'What's the matter?' said Nadya, pushing the binoculars from his face. 'The reality is here, not there.' Before he could reply the second siren wailed. They both sat up.

'I can see them, three, four, six . . . nine,' said Nadya, squinting up at the specks in the sky. 'They're so high.'

'They must be flying at fifteen thousand feet. All bombers. They're releasing bombs now. Watch the airfield,' Donald commanded, holding the binoculars on the aircraft.

'They've hit the airfield, and a building I think. I can't see much there's so much smoke. It's all white so they couldn't have got any oil tanks,' Nadya reported. Up here war became a game. Donald still followed the planes. At this distance there was little sound, death was a silent business. There was only the song of birds and a breeze soughing in the trees.

'More bombs, over the town. Indiscriminate bombing. Bastards,' Donald swore.

'Two, three, six, eight explosions. I can't even count them any more. It's just dust and flames and smoke.' Nadya shaded her eyes with a hand. There were dull thuds in the distance as the bombs hit the ground.

Donald lowered the glasses and together they watched the smoke billowing up from different points in Nanking, expanding then thinning, merging with the sky. The silence was thick about them. It was better than lying in an odorous dugout or the cellars under the university and hospital.

'They've gone,' Donald said and turned to Nadya, pushing her down beneath him. He could feel the beating of her heart, still digesting the murder only moments before in the distant town. He began to loosen her clothing.

She arranged her body in the ways she knew would please him and extract the greatest pleasure for herself. He had never known anyone with so little reservation. This thought was always with him in the midst of love. In these moments, with the sulphurous smell of the bombing drifting towards them, their love-making had an edge not found at mundane times. Each grasped at pleasure as if to reconfirm the life that about them was ending.

Her nails pressed into his flesh, like the claws of a cat once aroused to gratification. Beneath him she was lost to his presence, although he filled her. He envied her this abandon that, in spite of the urgency of his body, his emotions could not follow. Since Cordelia it was as if something severed him from himself. He heard her cry out and her body slackened. He climaxed immediately, his relief more than the assuaging of physical desire. The act of sex now appeared emotionally distasteful to him.

He turned on his back, lit a cigarette for Nadya and another for himself. He would have been happier now if she were not there. He was always left with the reflection of her desire, unslaked until he himself was exhausted. In the aftermath of love making the very essence that drew him to her, now began to repulse him. Lust in his mind became greed, impetuosity turned to wantonness. He feared the energy she radiated. Love, he had decided, was not as yet part of the pact between them. Confusion flowed through him. She was no better than a prostitute, no better than Cordelia. The same lust had driven Cordelia to destroy his life. Sometimes, these thoughts came to him in the very act of love and immediately his body refused to function. Then Nadya took his failure as a personal affront and demanded to know her affliction. It was impossible to reveal to her the complexity of his emotions. He had not told her about Cordelia, or that China was his escape, nor the reasons why. *Cordelia.* He had only to silently say her name for bitterness to drown him again. He remembered the morning he met her.

It was her first day on the paper and the men were already placing their bets. She was the daughter of a well-known peer, but had a reputation of her own as a journalist. She had come to the paper from a women's magazine.

'I've heard of your father,' Cordelia said when Donald introduced himself. She stared up at him. 'I read that book of his on Russia. I've read some of your stuff too.' Her nose ended pertly, her eyes were grey and always surprised.

'I'll be going down to Sussex at the weekend to see my father. If you come with me, you could meet him too,' he teased. By the end of the day she had agreed to a trip to Sussex.

'Never know who I'll find him with,' Donald joked as they drove down. 'He led my poor mother a dance.'

Since his wife's death John Addison had abandoned all discretion and no longer hid his love affairs. Donald could never see what it was that drew women to his father. As a child he had observed him only through his mother's pain. Twice she had left the marriage, taking Donald with her, but each time returned. On those occasions when they lived separately, Donald was happy without his father, alone with his mother. Some nights he slept in her bed, climbing in for comfort in the dark, seeking the warmth of her body. The bed was high and he was small. He remembered her still, lifting him up. When she cried she held him close and the anger within him turned savage.

'I'll kill him, Mama,' he vowed. On the pillow her hair was damp. Strands stuck to her cheeks and frightened him, as did her swollen eyes.

'I'll take your picture,' he said, sitting up in bed beside her, putting on the light and picking up the toy camera he always kept beside him. 'Smile Mama. Please smile.'

He pressed the camera close to his body. He still remembered his feelings of desperation at her grief. Yet far away, framed in the distant lens, her tears had not seemed so apparent. The terror in him lessened and, eventually, she smiled.

'Funny boy,' she said and put her arms about him, rubbing his head in the way he liked. He tasted the salt of tears on her cheek. He licked them off as always, until she began to laugh. He breathed in the smell of her body, her perfume, and was glad his father was not there. Even now the odour of wet hair or the taste of salt from the sea reminded him of her. She had entered his body with her tears. When she died in his teens he raged at his father.

'You killed her. All my life, every day, I watched her die.'

'Cancer killed her.'

'*You* killed her.'

'Stop it, I tell you.' He could not believe his father would cry. He turned away in disgust.

'If she had not been so unhappy, she might not have got cancer,' Donald replied. He heard his father's intake of breath and felt some satisfaction.

It surprised him as an adult to realize his father was at heart an inflexible, reactionary man who, in his famous book on Russia, had refused to come to terms with a new world order. He remembered the day at Oxford when this realization had tumbled upon him as he sat in a vaulted university library. He had thrown a book in the air and laughed, knowing at last he was his own man. He never considered any profession but journalism.

'So you want to compete?' John Addison had asked, a certain grimness in his tone.

Donald made it a point to defy in print every ideal his father stood for. He began to be read for his radical views; old men in clubs shook their heads. His father backed Empire and Donald the downfall of colonialism. John Addison deplored Communism and his son sighted a brave new world. The ball was thrown between them. Soon Donald's reputation was secure, as a reckless but brilliant character; a risk for any editor.

'Let's go,' Donald said suddenly, rousing himself, realizing where he was. On Purple Mountain the birds still sang. His mind was suddenly full of discomforts.

'Can you never sit still five minutes?' Nadya complained, smoothing her clothes into place.

She picked crumbled leaves from her hair. Her limbs were scratched from the rub of stones and twigs. In those moments when he filled her nothing mattered but the race of her body to its destination. There was a truth she knew then about herself that caused her trepidation. There was nothing, she realized, she would not do for the slaking of this need in herself. It was as if an unknown woman controlled her. Where this woman led she would always follow, against judgement, to the basest of places. She bit her lips in self-censure. Donald seemed never to join her at those wanton limits, but stood back, as if watching her abandon. He left her always with an edge of shame. She had learned not to ask him for explanations. In the beginning she had remonstrated, and glimpsed within him at these times such a churning beneath the surface that she backed away.

'I have to go to Shanghai where the action is, I should have been there on the first day,' he told her at last. 'I thought here, in the capital, I could watch developments, learn the political lay of the land. Mine was the first report to reach *The Times* about the incident at the Marco Polo Bridge. I met a chap from the Japanese Embassy who gave me that scoop. But that was all. Now I've got to get to Shanghai. For once I want to be in the right place at the right time. Come with me.' He did not want to let her go, whatever the complexity of his feelings.

'You know I'm going anyway in a few days, with those last pages of TECSAT,' Nadya said, thankful the war pinned Donald to China.

The afternoon was fading. She had not realized how long they had spent on Purple Mountain. They drove through the old town, Donald pressing the horn of the car continually. Everywhere was chaos. Families with bundles tied to their backs packed the streets, beginning the trek inland. In the dusk the first oil lamps were being lit. Before them the road opened suddenly into a square before a temple.

'Professor Teng is on the other side of that temple,' Nadya said in sudden recognition. 'I'm supposed to pick up some papers from him.' They left the car and entered the temple to walk across to Teng's home.

The graceful buildings and sweeping roofs were set about a series of courtyards. People walked slowly or sat upon the stone balustrades. There was a sense of vacancy. In spite of the crowds there was silence. 'I never like this place. There are always so many people, all staring at nothing, nobody speaking.' Nadya grimaced.

'They've eaten "dream medicine". Opium,' Donald explained laughing at Nadya's ignorance. He took her arm, guiding her through the somnolence.

Amongst the passive crowd a man walked briskly at a distance, his pace and smart Western-style clothes picking him out. He looked over his shoulder in a furtive way. As they neared him, the man stumbled against an old woman who lurched before him. He fell down a flight of steps while trying to avoid her, and winced in sudden pain. Donald bent to help him and saw it was the Japanese, Kenjiro Nozaki, who had confirmed the rumour about the Marco Polo Bridge incident.

Kenjiro looked up, the fear in his expression changing to amazement at the sight of Donald. He gripped his arm, speaking quickly.

'Mr Addison, please, if anyone approaches, I shall say you are writing an article on the advantage of the Japanese presence in China.' There was something desperate in his face. His trouser leg was wet with blood.

'We are going to a friend's house, why don't you walk with us. It will look more natural,' Donald replied, as he helped him up. 'You can't walk far with that leg, it's bleeding. We'll get it cleaned up and then drive you back to the Embassy. What are you doing in a place like this?'

'I have been to visit a friend. I may have been followed by our Japanese secret police; this town is full of spies. These are difficult days for us Japanese civilians.' He spoke nervously.

'You will be safe with Professor Teng,' Nadya stepped forward, seeing the Japanese who had visited her at the university. 'You told me he was a friend.' Recognition suddenly filled Kenjiro's face.

'Of course, you are Bradley Reed's assistant. Perhaps it is better if I just get myself home.' Kenjiro was unwilling to risk another visit to Teng in the company of these foreigners. The real direction of Teng's political affiliations had been unknown to him when he had asked Nadya about him at the university. Even today, after all Fukutake had said, he should not have risked a further visit to Teng. Why had he not resisted the impulse? He felt Donald grip his arm and steer him forward, ignoring his protests.

Teng greeted them with amazement. He ordered the old servant to find some first aid and bring tea. After bandaging Kenjiro's leg, he went to the desk for the papers Nadya needed.

She looked curiously at Teng, wondering about his friendship with the Japanese as she pushed the documents into her bag. 'The packing is finished and I will go now to Shanghai for final proof-reading. Will you stay here?' she asked.

'Soon I'll go inland,' Teng replied, turning away from her. 'There is a war to be fought. I must do my part. This is just the beginning.' He sat down and lit a pipe. The scent of tobacco filled the room.

'Do you expect it to last some time?' Donald enquired. He settled himself in a rickety cane chair. Something in Teng's face drew his interest. Instinct told him this was a man to talk to.

'The Japanese are going to take Shanghai and then Nanking and blockade the sea coast,' Teng forecast. 'There will be no stopping them. Then it all depends upon the morale of our people. If it breaks, China is finished. If not, the burden of war will fall upon the common people and they will have to endure great suffering.' He spoke between puffs on his pipe.

Nadya said nothing, unsettled by the discovery of this unfamiliar Teng, talking not of religion but war. She had looked upon the Professor as an unworldly scholar, poring over books. 'How will you fight?' she whispered. Agnes Smedley's tales of frozen hands came back with force.

'There will be many ways to fight this war. Some will fight with guns and others must help those who have no guns. Each man, woman and child will have their own way to fight. Already there are tales of barbaric brutality wherever the Japanese Army go.' He looked straight at Kenjiro in a sudden, fierce condemnation.

News of atrocities had come over the wires at the Embassy. Nobody believed they were anything but isolated and grossly exaggerated happenings. Kenjiro tried to explain. 'Disorganized incidents, nothing more,' he turned, appealing to them all.

'There are only refugees and guerrillas inland,' Nadya declared to Teng. 'Is it not better for you to stay here?'

'What is the difference?' Teng replied, his voice sharpening suddenly. 'Refugees and guerrillas are just people driven from their homes. If they can fight they are guerrillas, if not they are refugees. The whole country is already full of self-defence groups, Grandma Chao and the Eighth Route Army are amongst the best armed. Others are just peasants in their villages.'

'And you think peasants can win a war against the Japanese Imperial Army, who are highly disciplined and committed?' Donald asked. He found Teng more intriguing than anyone he had yet met. He wondered if the man might not be an underground Communist sympathizer.

'You must understand the nature of this war. It is not a war in the usual sense, between two armies equally matched on a battlefield. It is going to be a war against an entire people,' Teng replied.

'What about Chiang Kai-shek . . . ?' Nadya began. Teng turned upon her, his face contorted. Nadya drew back in her chair, alarmed by this side of the professor that she had never seen.

'Nothing has unified this country as much as hatred of the Japanese,' he thundered, pulling the pipe from his mouth. 'And I don't mind repeating it in front of my friend, even if he is a Japanese.'

'What are you saying?' Kenjiro felt his pulse quicken. He could not believe he was listening to Teng. Nor that Teng would humiliate him in this way before other people.

'Believe me, Japanese soldiers will continue to be as brutal as they are now. Cities will be burned, peasants will leave their homes and cattle, people will become slaves, women will be raped, babies bayoneted, prisoners burned alive and all this on a scale rarely seen before. Mr Addison speaks of discipline, and I beg to differ. The Japanese Army has another side that only their defeated victims see. It is like an army of bandits, beside which military operations lose significance. Atrocities are happening wherever they go.' Teng was beside himself. 'Why do the Japanese people let their soldiers disgrace themselves if they want to conquer China?'

'These things are only disorganized incidents,' Kenjiro repeated helplessly. The blood surged round his body, as if his anger would burst a vein.

Teng's passion would not be expunged. 'Atrocities are indeed happening, and will continue.' Teng raised his voice, his face red with emotion, turning directly to Kenjiro. 'My information is more exact than yours, it comes from the common people to whom all this is happening. Believe me, all you hear is true.'

Kenjiro turned, feeling as he had not since Jacqueline's death, ripped through by loss. He looked at Teng, now pouring tea from a vermilion pot, and saw only that they stood either side of a boundary. What he dreaded had happened at last.

'Hatred can be forgotten, but not contempt,' Teng's voice was hoarse with emotion. 'Once you lose respect for your enemy on the grand scale that is happening now, you lose it forever. Even in fifty or sixty years' time, this war will not have been forgotten. It is not good for the Japanese.'

The words followed Kenjiro out of Teng's house. He knew the old world they had shared was gone and would never be re-entered. The loss filled Kenjiro anew.

The railway line between Nanking and Shanghai was officially closed, but trains ran sporadically as far as they could. By the time they were ready to depart the line was bombed again.

'Then we must go by road,' said Nadya. 'Many people are still journeying up and down. It is not yet too dangerous. Bombing is only about the towns. Madame Chiang Kai-shek is even planning to visit her dentist in Shanghai before the city falls. Besides, I have luggage, a car might be easier.' Nadya looked at the box of proofs.

In view of the circumstances the garage would not allow Donald to drive their car to Shanghai. As they searched for alternative transport it was rumoured another train might run; the line had been temporarily repaired. They left at once for the station.

The train ran at night in blackout for safety, and was crowded with anxious people. Bundles of possessions, food and water, weighed everybody down filling all corners of the train. It was uncertain how far they might be able to get. The terror of bombing permeated the packed, swaying carriages. Nadya sat squashed between Donald and an elderly woman who coughed excessively. No lights were allowed and no siren could warn of attack from the air. Nadya's limbs were stiff with tension, the heat was oppressive. Babies cried, women moaned. The ripe smell of bodies was intense.

The dim memory of another train, long ago, drifted before her each time she closed her eyes. She could have been no more than three or four years old on that long tense train journey from St Petersburg to Blagoveshchensk. Although they had travelled with dignity at the front of the train, a long line of rough trucks was coupled to the back within which were packed the convicts, bound for hard labour in Siberia. Somewhere, the train had stopped and a man escaped. There had been the crack of a gun. In her mind she saw a man falling, as if in slow motion, until he hit the ground. She remembered soldiers about him, pounding his body with their rifle butts in the way that workmen, on a building site near her home in St Petersburg, had pounded stones to break them. Then her mother pulled her close, so that she should see no more. She had pressed her face into the velvet of her mother's skirt, breathing in the faint scent of mothballs.

There was so little she remembered of her mother. The emerald pendant on a gold chain that Sergei had stolen, she saw again against a bed of lace upon her mother's breast. She had also the obscure memory of a white mouse that had been kept in a Lalique glass bowl. She remembered the sea-green tint of the thick glass, foamy as a wave. She remembered the mouse, with black liquorice eyes, crouching in her mother's hand. Of her death she remembered nothing. She recalled only the sound of weeping that had come each night from her father's room. All her life she had wished for the balm of some further memory, but little arose to fill the emptiness. Later her father had married again, to Anna, a local woman in Blagoveshchensk.

At times the train stopped for unfathomable reasons, then Donald climbed down, and sat beside the tracks. Nadya seemed able to snatch at sleep in a manner that evaded him. He stared out at the impenetrable blackness, smelling the odour of the land, ripe with fresh manure. At times the moon emerged and showed him a distant roof, or the outline of some trees. In the darkness the dislocations of his life seemed to grip him anew. *Cordelia.* Hate rose up within him. He stared into the night about him, but the memories would not retreat.

'Mmm,' Cordelia had murmured on that first Sunday together, as he drove her down to Sussex to meet his father. Her eyes were closed, her head thrown back. The window was open and the smell of the fields had filled the car. It was a hot and perfect day. Her hair blew about in the breeze. He could not wait for his father to see her. Even then he recognized the need to flaunt her before him. The adrenaline had raced through his body.

John Addison sat on the lawn drinking gin and lemonade. His eyes were hooded, his paunch spilled over his shorts. Janice stopped mixing ice in the jug and stood up to kiss Donald. He was glad it was Janice who was there, and not somebody younger. Cordelia looked delectable against the foil of maturity.

They ate cold ham and potato salad, washed down with spiced lemonade. Cordelia stretched out on the grass, leaning back upon her elbows. Her shoulders were bronzed by the sun, her neck arched, the long hair swung down her back. Beside her sat John, an expression on his face Donald recognized. At Donald's side Janice chatted on about the horrors of vivisection. Against the sun he watched Cordelia in conversation with his father. Under half-closed lids his observation was intense. He knew then he would marry Cordelia. Nothing else would do. How could he then have known it would end with the bloodied mess of his father's brains, over the desk and the wall.

'I'll kill him, Mama. I'll kill him.' His own voice echoed up from childhood. He had not been back long from India before John Addison committed suicide. Cordelia had encouraged him to go to India, although they had only been married a year.

'Won't you miss me?' he had asked, uncertain even then of the ease with which she was letting him go. 'I may be away some months.'

'You must do this book,' she insisted. 'The Independence of India is an important matter. It is rarely tackled from the Indian perspective, especially by the British. It will cause a stir.'

He wished now he had never gone. He had known at the time the decision was wrong. Why then had he deliberately set off, and stayed away so long? His constant, needless courting of fate was still a mystery to him.

The book on India was published a year after his father's death. The reviews were mixed, but Donald had by then lost interest in its reception. On the day of its publication his divorce from Cordelia came through. The newspapers no longer asked questions about the nature of his father's suicide, but its residue afflicted Donald disastrously. He found himself prone to bouts of fury, followed by heroic drinking after which he was maudlin with guilt. He saw nothing of Cordelia, although on the Fleet Street grapevine he sometimes heard her name.

He had gone to China to forget about his father, to forget Cordelia. He cursed them both loudly, as if the invocation would banish them from his mind. How far must he travel this painful inner road before they would release him? He climbed back into the railway carriage and pushed his way back through the crowd to Nadya.

Eventually the train stopped in the middle of fields, a distance from Shanghai. The track had been destroyed by a bomb, and repair was impossible. People left the train and melted into the night. A truck passed and stopped. For a fee the driver agreed to take Nadya and Donald to the outskirts of town. They heaved their belongings on to the truck atop a pile of vegetables. The last pages of the TECSAT manuscript balanced on a mound of radish.

Above them the sky was lightening. As dawn broke over the fields about Shanghai the extent of the destruction was clear. In the distance was the sound of guns.

8

October 1939

Shanghai

Even as Donald reached Shanghai he had no sense of real direction. He had come to China to investigate the country, not to face a war. The unexpected scoop of Edgar Snow with Mao Tse-tung had forced him to face an unsavoury conflict to ensure professional survival. Now the battle took him unawares. It was one thing to follow distant bombers from Purple Mountain, another to enter the theatre of war itself. He was not a hard-bitten battle-scarred correspondent. Nadya, however, knew nothing of this. She found Donald fractious and drinking more than usual, in the bar of the Metropole Hotel.

In the haste to get to Shanghai the mundane details of war had been far from Donald's mind. Now, he discovered the sound of gunfire reverberated unendingly in his head. Other guests at the Metropole seemed no longer to hear it. By evening all Donald wanted was to lose the sound in drink. In his dreams the guns condensed each night into the same one shot, over and over again. Each night he awoke in a sweat, to see his father's body slumped over a desk. He was not made for war, he decided. Other reporters appeared honed from more seasoned wood, and were all about him now.

The world's press had descended upon Shanghai. Men who followed the trail of war from one country to another, political analysts, old China hands well known to Donald Addison, were staying at the Metropole. Nadya joined him there at the bar each evening, after work with Bradley Reed. The smell of beer and cigarette smoke hung thickly in the room. Donald pointed out faces, but the names meant little to Nadya.

'That's Hallett Abend of the *New York Times*, Harold J. Timperley of the *Manchester Guardian*, Ed Walden of the *Daily Telegraph*, Victor Keenan, *Herald Tribune*. That group is Reuters. There's Associated Press drinking with United Press. *Daily Mail, Chicago Daily News, Chicago Tribune, Daily Express*. God, who isn't here.'

It was a strange war, undeclared, relegated to the terminology of

133

incident rather than aggression. Strange also was its geography within Shanghai. It did not touch the International Settlement or the French Concession, full of foreign nationals under treaties of extra-territoriality. It raged in the China beyond this minute island. Sandbagged, but alert for accident and falling shrapnel, life went on almost as normal within the Settlement, intact in the midst of the smoking town.

Nadya drank Martinis and smoked Sobranis as she watched Donald circle the bar of the Metropole each evening. He returned to their table one evening with his arm about the shoulders of a balding man. Donald's voice was slurred by drink.

'This is Hugh Smollett. I haven't seen him for years. We were at university together. He's with Reuters now.' Donald swayed slightly on his feet. In Nanking he had not been driven to this excess of drinking.

Hugh Smollett sat down and began to complain about Japanese reporting. 'Tokyo's blaming Britain now, harking back to the Shanghai disturbances of '27 and '32 in which we were involved. That's going to make for a lot of anti-Japanese feeling in the Settlement,' Smollett leaned forward over the table to Nadya, there was whisky on his breath. 'General Matsui, the Japanese Commander, thinks because he's careful not to lob shells over the Settlement everyone will ignore what he's doing around it.'

'I've heard he is quite a favourite with Western newsmen and has been invited to dinner at some of the best foreign homes,' Nadya replied. 'They say he has even donated money to the Safety Zone.'

Donald pulled out a paper from his pocket. 'Matsui or not, those Domei chaps, who are the official Japanese news agency, do nothing but write garbage. Perhaps Matsui should have a word with them. Here we sit, bombs falling about us, carrying on as best we can amidst the sandbags, tending the wounded, burying the dead, toning down our parties and all they do is write stuff like this: *Japan has no territorial aspirations in China. All China has to do is to go on quietly with her occupations and leave her policing to us. We will afford her innocent peasantry, now shamefully oppressed by warlords, our disinterested protection. Unfortunately foreigners do not sufficiently understand our purity of motive. It is up to the British residents here to make it clear abroad that we are only working for the salvation of China.* Are we supposed to laugh or cry?'

'The Domei lot are over there. I've a good mind to have a word with them,' Smollett announced. He attempted to rise from his chair but losing his balance fell back, spilling his whisky. Donald laughed, not yet as drunk as Smollett.

'If you want a fight go out to the front lines and watch one,' Nadya

134

raised her voice in exasperation. War was a stress Donald could not take. And yet he pitted himself against it.

'I'm going out with Smollett tomorrow,' Donald turned upon her. They seemed constantly to argue now. The incessant sound of shelling set her own nerves on edge.

She watched Donald walk across the room with Smollett to the table of Japanese, and bow with mock deference. An exchange took place and then Donald guffawed and hit Smollett on the shoulder. Smollett returned the blow and, hardly able to stand, raised his fists to Donald in horseplay.

Nadya was busy supervising the proof-reading of the last two volumes of TECSAT coming off the press. It was stuffy in the office and fans were still needed. They had two rooms in the building of the *China Weekly Review*. Bradley's office led to a larger one where Nadya worked with a group of editors and proof-readers. Once the room, like the TECSAT department at the university in Nanking, was padded with documents. Now this too was bare, great boxes of papers already departed for safer destinations. Extra typesetters, employed in desperation by Bradley, had been squeezed into an additional space across the corridor. Each day further pages of TECSAT appeared from the great presses of the *China Weekly Review*. The race against time pressed upon them all, little chat was to be heard.

The summer heat lingered, no longer humid, edged now by the odour of the burning land. Ash blew in through open windows, spreading a layer of grime on the freshly printed papers, on desks, typewriters and potted plants. A boy was employed just to dust away this residue of ash. Staff were diminishing daily as more and more people fled Shanghai. Nadya was forced to proof-read for long hours herself, with little relief. Even Bradley now put aside other work to tackle this menial job. She looked down at the proofs before her. She was tired of the prolific number of Chinese ghosts.

The dry atmosphere of Peking in winter is conducive to electric sparks when friction is applied to fur or hair. Spirits are scared by such illuminations, and can therefore be prevailed upon to depart by a strenuous rubbing of the scalp.

Another ghostly manifestation is the Kuei Tang Ch'iang or Wall Building Ghost. This erects a wall around a traveller at night and follows his movements, never letting him escape . . .

She sighed and leaned back in the chair. It was lunchtime but she was not hungry. Bradley was at a meeting. The room was empty, the others having gone for their meal. From the drawer of her desk she pulled out the binoculars Donald had used on Purple Mountain. As she often did now, she climbed the narrow staircase to the flat roof of the building. There was a view from there over the war lines. Even within the relative immunity of the Settlement, there were growing reminders of the true state of affairs. From her office window Nadya looked out to the Whangpoo River, clogged by a line of Japanese warships. The freighters of Jardine Matheson, Butterfield and Swire and the Mollar Line, sides painted with giant Union Jacks, edged past the Japanese ships to bring the Settlement its supplies. For the Chinese beyond the Settlement boundary, only starvation and terror were in ample supply. Refugees crowded the foreign concessions, sleeping in doorways, begging at corners, dying on pavements of wounds or disease.

She held the binoculars to her eyes. The plains about Shanghai stretched out, blackened and smoking to the horizon. Each day dark sulphurous clouds billowed from new areas. Through the glasses she surveyed the charred land. The battle had intensified to take the last stubbornly-held perimeters of greater Shanghai. The crumbled ruins of the Chinese areas of the city now proliferated with Japanese flags; poached eggs, as the foreign residents of Shanghai disrespectfully named them. They flapped starkly in the wind.

In the distance was the sound of gunfire and the drone of planes once more. It was always Japanese planes by day, Chinese planes by night, as if a rule had been applied. Nadya swung the glasses up upon them. She watched as three Japanese aircraft circled in search of a target, then dived. Bombs dropped from the low flying planes and ploughed into an old building. A great cloud of dust mushroomed up. Across the creek she could see street fighting and naval shells crashing into the Chinese positions. She turned the glasses down again and saw ragged children still at play on the banks of corpse-ridden Soochow Creek.

Suddenly, far away, still small even through binoculars, she made out a line of Chinese prisoners roped together, digging a trench. She could see the dark soil mounded beside the hole, and the rough gesturing of soldiers. As she watched the men were lined up beside the trench, as if for some drill. The soldiers stepped back and levelled their guns. The men fell neatly, one by one, into the open seam of ground. She tore the binoculars from her eyes. Then slowly, against her will, raised them again. There was nothing now to see but a brisk shovelling of earth by the soldiers into the hole. She stood with the wind in her face, viewing death as she would a film. The shame of such omnipotence filled her.

'I cannot forget it,' she whispered to Donald, lying in bed late that afternoon in his room at the Metropole.

'It was too far away for you to be sure of what you saw. Perhaps you were mistaken.' He pulled away from her and turned on his side.

136

'I saw it clearly. They fell like ninepins. It was too far to hear the guns. It was like those bombs we watched drop on Nanking, while birds sang on Purple Mountain.' She felt uncomfortable now when she recalled their cavalier attitude to those first bombs upon Nanking. The sky outside the window reddened with the setting sun. A few miles away the sky for others was ruddy with flame. Something seemed terribly wrong. She lay here, languid, safe, her body replete with pleasuring, while only miles away others died, tormented. She remembered Professor Teng's outburst in Nanking, and his tales of horror. She turned again to Donald, but he was not interested.

'What does it matter, a few Chinese more or less who would anyway die of starvation or disease?' Donald insisted. He did not want to hear about it, did not want the weight of her revulsion added to his own. Each day it was as much as he could do to suppress his own confused emotions. She leaned over him and stroked his bare chest in an absent manner.

'I felt paralysed. They were dying and I could not even hear the gun.' She tried to analyse her reactions. 'Perhaps if I could have heard the gun, I would not be able to turn my back so easily upon their death. I would have had to carry some echo of their fury within me. But there was only the sound of the breeze in my ears as they died. Nothing more. It was too distant for involvement.' She searched for words to explain.

'Sometimes you talk nonsense,' Donald answered. The sound of constant gunfire affected him badly. Nightmares continued to wake him. He pulled himself above her, thrusting her limbs apart.

'Again?' She abandoned herself to the moment. He pushed himself deeper within her.

Later they slept but when she awoke the thought was still lodged in her mind, like a stubborn seed between her teeth. 'Why can I not forget it? Why do I wish I had heard that gun?' She gripped his arm, looking up into his face.

'I should be glad not to have heard it. Now forget it,' Donald told her, struggling to sit up and pull on his clothes. He could take no more of her odyssey of guilt.

'You don't understand.' She groped for words, exploring the dilemma. 'A cycle of conscience is somehow unfinished, because I heard no gun. It was the same on Purple Mountain. We stood outside experience. We trivialized death on Purple Mountain.'

'What melodrama.' He buttoned up his shirt. If he kept his mind on the work of factual reporting, he could function. If he attempted to expose his emotions, a nightmare at once began.

'Let's go down for a drink,' he suggested.

She sat cross-legged on the bed before him, her hair holding the sun beyond the window. The gold light settled on her bare shoulders, spreading a translucence over her breasts. The sheets creased about her. She had the look of a Renaissance painting. He knelt before her, cupping her breasts in his hands. He could never catch the mercurial light in her hair any more than he could, however many times he possessed her, be sure he held her secure. She seemed ready always to slip from him. It disturbed him to think their relationship insubstantial, and yet in himself he knew he erected barriers to its growth.

'I cannot sit like this, an immortal on a mountain looking down untouched upon the world. I keep thinking of those things Professor Teng said.' She swung herself slowly off the bed.

'What are you doing, what is your war effort?' Nadya demanded gathering her clothes from the floor where, in their haste for love, they had strewn them.

'I'm reporting the horror to the world. War is war and a nasty business,' Donald snapped. 'I'm not required at this moment to do more than write it up as I see fit.'

In the lift, on the way down to the bar, she continued to worry. 'On a street along one side of the *China Weekly Review*, I counted sixty-three refugees. They were sleeping in alleyways, doorsteps and windowsills, anywhere they could find a ledge. The autumn is coming, last night it rained heavily and they have no blankets. Most of the babies were almost naked. All I could hear was the crying and coughing of sick children. These refugees are not beggar class, they're peasants, driven from their homes by Japanese bombs or the fires set by Chinese troops to cover their retreat.' Nadya sat up and looked out of the window at the distant haze of smoke.

'At least they're safe in the Settlement,' Donald replied. He had reported these facts in his last cable to *The Times*. He did not want further involvement. *Report the fact and move on to the next. Dwell upon nothing.* These were the rules he had devised for himself. *Keep moving as fast as possible.* He steered her towards the open door of the bar, avid to begin the daily round of amnesia.

'But the Settlement is already full, they've put up barbed wire to keep out more refugees. Father Jacquinot's Safety Zone is now the best sanctuary,' Nadya replied. She thought suddenly of Martha in Nanking and wondered if the preparations for a similar safety zone were also underway. Nadya walked before Donald into the bar and was dismayed to see Smollett waiting.

In the countryside the battle escalated. Japanese planes carpet-bombed the Western districts of Shanghai. Ambulances and fire-engines screamed out to the suburbs. From the opposite direction, laden with bundles, new refugees trailed into town.

Near Nadya's flat a school had been turned into a hospital, as were cabarets, cinemas and brothels. Space was at a premium, funds to care for the refugees continually solicited. The expatriate community battled alongside the bombs with the usual round of parties, but the Settlement acquired a beleaguered air. It had become a city of bachelors and grass-widowers. The majority of expatriate wives had been evacuated to Hong Kong or elsewhere by official order. Lonely and curfewed, the remaining male residents lived ever more furiously. Nightclubs, cabarets and dance palaces now persuaded customers to stay for breakfast. Shanghai lived feverishly, lost to the erotic and the exotic beneath searchlights and tracer shells. All the while the Settlement bulged with the destitute Chinese population of the outlying areas. No road was now without its pavement population, filthy, hungry, ill.

As the summer heat cooled the incidence of cholera lessened. Consumption now became the main fear for the refugees. The Whang-poo was awash with bodies. Officials reassured the Settlement that drinking water drawn from this source was adequately filtered and disinfected. Amongst the cattle herded into the Settlement, Foot and Mouth disease broke out. The food situation was deteriorating; fewer ships were allowed up the Whangpoo. The intersecting creeks flowing out of Shanghai into the Yangtze valley still managed to supply most produce. Junks and sampans glided in on the wind carrying eggs, chickens, vegetables, coal, fish, pigs and bamboo. Under the bombs peasants risked their lives in the fields, and risked them again on the way to market.

Slowly the Japanese advanced. Their flag flew over North Station. The areas beyond Soochow Creek were methodically bombed. The retreat-ing Chinese Army blew up the main bridge behind them. Everywhere there was burning. Yet the buildings of the Foreign Concession rose almost untouched in the smoking, flattened plain. Through the railings surrounding the Concession, Chinese destitutes observed the expatri-ates drinking coffee in cafés.

Most days Nadya went out to Father Jacquinot's Safety Zone or to one of the dozens of refugee camps that now littered Shanghai, and were supported mainly by European money. She had joined the National Child Welfare Association in a voluntary capacity. Above all, it was the children who affected her. She had learned to look at many things, but the small stiff corpses gathered on carts for cremation, the stacks of tiny coffins in Dr Fu's children's hospital where she worked, the bloodied, shattered infant limbs and the staring orphans, touched her at a different level.

Dr Fu's hospital helped to provide the refugee children with nutrition. The hospital made its own soya bean milk with primitive equipment. Beneath the usual hospital smells the odour of cooking soya beans pervaded, rising up from the basement kitchens. Each day from Bradley Reed's office or from the *China Weekly Review*, Nadya went straight to the hospital, grateful for Martha's training. Sometimes she drove the van with its vat of milk out to Father Jacquinot's Safety Zone.

Father Jacquinot had persuaded the Japanese army authorities of the need for a safety zone for Chinese refugees. Part of the old walled city of Nantao, adjacent to the French Concession, was ringed with white flags for this purpose. Two hundred and twenty-five thousand Chinese refugees were now living in the area. The winter was ahead and apart from food the need for thick clothing was urgent.

White-bearded Father Jacquinot, in black cassock and beret, dared bring down his artificial wooden arm upon the heads of Japanese soldiers who refused to respect his Safety Zone. The headquarters of the committee was in the premises of an old fire station. When Nadya arrived with the soya milk, Jacquinot was on the phone berating the Red Cross for delivering less than four hundred thousand buns.

She delivered the milk and drove back down the boundary road separating Japanese-occupied territory from the Safety Zone. Soon, she approached the barbed wire barricades of the Settlement, guarded by police. These gates were now closed as the Settlement could take no more refugees. Yet the destitute still picked their way over the remains of the mined bridge towards them. Women with children slung on their backs or filling their arms crowded before the barricades. The International Police pushed back the crowds and Nadya showed her Red Cross pass.

'Drive through, lady.' The police officer, a Scotsman, ordered the barrier rolled back for the jeep. A detachment of Volunteers from the Settlement controlled the crowd as she drove through. She looked straight ahead so as not to see the women holding their children up, imploring her to help. Against the pressure of bodies, the barricade was closed again.

'Why can't you let them through?' She turned to the officer on the Settlement side. The agony of it all tore at her.

'Full up, Miss. We've nowhere left to sleep 'em. They bring disease as well.' The man had a ginger moustache.

'But you're sending them back to sure death. Only the Settlement is safe.' She could hear her own voice, like a thing apart, flailing about the man.

'No need to shout, Miss. We're only obeying orders.'

As they spoke, Japanese planes winged out of the sky, diving low over the lines of women and children, splattering machine-gun fire. The crowd turned in a single movement, like a shoal of fish, and swarmed back towards the ruined bridge. The planes returned, spitting more bullets. Bodies now choked the bridge, dead mothers fell into the water, live babies in their arms. Nadya jumped out of the jeep, running back to the barricades.

'Let them in,' she screamed, trying to tear at the gates.

'Get down, Miss!' The man with the moustache pushed her behind an armoured car.

Already, she saw that someone at the barricades, against orders, had rolled back the gates. The hysterical crowd flowed through, babies in baskets suspended on poles, swinging from their mothers' shoulders, toddlers carrying younger children, others lugging bundles bigger than themselves. Abruptly the barricades were closed again upon the order of an officer who appeared in a car. The crowd still pressed against the thorny wire, regardless of injury. The planes streaked off, there was silence again.

'It's over, Miss. You can get up now. Nasty bit of work.' The officer helped her up. 'No need to upset yourself. They're Chinese. Death stalks them closer than it does us. And they've a different attitude to dying. They expect to. We do not.'

Her face was wet with tears.

The tower stood near the Waterworks in the French Concession. They were not supposed to be here. Donald had bribed some Chinese soldiers with packets of cigarettes to let them through the front line. He raced towards the water-tower, but was forced to stop and crouch for safety against a wall at a fresh barrage of firing.

'It's all right,' he yelled to Smollett who followed behind. 'It's between the lines of fire.' The tower was high and above the fighting. These were the last days of the battle for Shanghai. Only a few stubborn Chinese battalions now held out on the far edge of the city.

'It'll give a bird's-eye view and terrific pictures,' Donald slung his camera round his body.

'We'll have to climb up eighty feet or more,' Smollett looked apprehensively at the tower. 'I'm not much good at heights, Addison.'

'There's a ladder,' Donald replied, taking no notice of Smollett's protest.

'There are some American Marines over there on that balcony and French soldiers near the Waterworks. Nobody's on the tower. We could join the Marines,' Smollett suggested.

'They're not journalists looking for pictures. Wait for a lull in the firing.' Donald ran to the base of the tower. Smollett followed reluctantly.

Donald began to climb. Near the top of the tower was an observation platform. The stairway was narrow and, as he gained height, a strong breeze whipped about him. The sound of gunfire was fierce. Looking down he saw Smollett's face staring up fearfully. He would have given anything, Donald was sure, to retreat back down the ladder. He had never liked Smollett and now knew why. Smollett appeared the personification of all those fears he suppressed in himself.

'Addison, I can't go on.' There was terror in Smollett's voice.

'Don't look down, we're nearly there now.' Donald pulled himself onto the platform. He reached out a hand to Smollett who snatched at it desperately.

Far below the creek was lit by sun. The water cut in a ribbon of light through the cratered, smoking land. From the tower the view of the battle was spectacular. The crackle of machine-guns and the smoke of mortar fire floated up to them. The sky arched above, immeasurable. Clouds drifted by, untouched by the chaos below. Donald looked into the camera lens and began to snap the scene below.

'Addison, I shouldn't have come up here. I can't stand heights. It makes me feel sick.' Smollett edged round the platform to where Donald stood. 'I won't be able to get down again.'

'Well, you're up here now, and I'll help you down. You won't get any pictures if you stand back there,' Donald spoke briskly, preoccupied with the camera. He hoped Smollett was not going to be a nuisance.

'I don't think I can stand at that rail like you, Addison.' Smollett's voice was hoarse, Donald turned to look at his white face. The wind flapped about them, cutting their words adrift.

'I'll stand behind and hold on to you,' Donald suggested, moving over to him.

'It's cold up here.' Smollett began to shiver.

'Take hold of yourself. Don't waste the climb. Get your shots and we'll go down immediately.' Donald took Smollett's arm and steered him to the rail. Smollett raised his camera while Donald hung onto his jacket. Suddenly Smollett twisted in panic.

'Addis . . .'

There was the clank of bullets hitting the metal struts of the tower. Donald's arms were suddenly covered in blood, and yet he felt no pain.

It was Smollett's blood he realized, as he ducked down. Smollett's body shook as bullets sank into him. Then he slumped heavily forward over the rail. Donald edged backwards, pulling Smollett's inert body with him.

'Smollett.' Donald reached out and shook him. He put a hand to his pulse and felt nothing. Smollett lay face downwards, blood dripping through the slatted floor. Donald flattened himself beside Smollett's body. The firing went on. Bullets struck the tower, thudding against the metal structure. They ricocheted down upon Donald, spent but powerful enough to scratch and bruise, like a shower of stones.

'Oh God, God,' he muttered, shielding his head with his hands. He had not prayed since he was a child. His hands were sticky with Smollett's blood, his face cut by deflected bullets.

The firing stopped suddenly and continued at ground level again. Donald did not move. At last he heard the tower being climbed. A new terror took hold of him. The Japanese were coming. They would appear on the platform with their bayonets and finish him off. He began to pray again. Instead, an American Marine arrived and others followed.

'Are the Japanese coming?' he asked in confusion. The Marine knelt beside him and shook his head.

'The battle is over here. The Chinese all retreated into the French Concession at the time you were fired upon. Your friend is dead.' French soldiers were also now on the platform.

Donald was helped up. Below the tower, on the Chinese side, bodies were strewn about like a heap of dolls, tossed on the floor after play. The Japanese appeared to have had few casualties. They had already packed up their guns and left.

'One of the Japanese gunners elevated his fire. Maybe they thought you were Chinese snipers. This French soldier here ran out at great danger to himself while they were gunning you, to hang up a French flag on the tower. That's when the firing stopped.' The Marine nodded towards a French soldier who was examining the bullet-scarred metal.

Smollett was lowered on a harness of ropes. Donald followed, climbing down awkwardly. As he reached the ground his knees buckled beneath him. Someone gave him brandy and dressed his cuts. Smollett's body was laid in the back of a jeep, under a canvas sheet.

'The battle for Shanghai is over. Chinese troops have orders now to withdraw and the Japanese are advancing into the Yangtze valley,' the jeep driver told Donald as they drove towards the Settlement.

'Has the Chinese flank been turned?' Donald asked. His teeth chattered, obstructing his words, shock still convulsing him.

That evening Donald drank heavily. He could not believe Smollett was dead. If the firing had started a moment earlier, it would have been he, not Smollett who died. Instead, Smollett's body had protected him.

'Addis . . .' Smollett's voice came to him again. The memory of holding him against the rail, impatient with his fear, would not go away. He gulped back neat whisky. As the bullets pumped into him, Smollett's body had shuddered in a sickening way.

'But this is ridiculous,' Nadya argued. 'It was an accident. You did not kill him.'

'He tried to get free even as I gripped him. He saw them raise their guns. But I forced him to that rail,' Donald's voice cracked. Nadya held him in her arms until he quieted. Later, she undressed him and put him to bed.

That night, as Shanghai had dreaded, the suburb of Chapei was put to the torch. Eight miles of fire roared up across the land behind Shanghai, to cut off the retreat of the Chinese Army. Nadya sat up until late, watching Donald. Beyond the window the holocaust lifted the roof off the night. It was as if in his dreams Donald could see this surreal sunset. His sleep was fitful. In repose his expression was vulnerable. Awake, he now wore isolation like an armour. Nadya wanted to know more about his family and his past life, but he cut off questions with a flinty tongue. Once, he had told her his mother died of cancer. He had taken a creased picture from his wallet. She had stared at a young face, humour hidden by a careworn smile. I took that, he said, with my first box-camera, when I was ten years old. Of his father he would not speak.

She wondered why he had never married, but he would not be drawn on this subject, evasive as always. This deliberate withholding of information disturbed her. Sometimes, like water imprisoned in an underground place, she felt the silence pulsing within him, as if it would break out. On the walls now, the reflected glow of Chapei grew stronger. Perhaps, like that burning city, his memories too must await their immolation. She settled back in the chair and closed her eyes, but her sleep was no less fitful than Donald's.

In the morning smoke from Chapei still drifted over the Settlement. A charred space spread where once the bustling suburb had stood. She knew then that Shanghai had finally fallen.

General Matsui's press conference took place in what had once been a schoolroom. It was bare of all but two vases of yellow chrysanthemums on a table covered by a white cloth. The journalists filed in and took their seats. The day before they had gathered at the cemetery on

144

Bubbling Well Road, to bury Hugh Smollett. A translation of a report sent to Tokyo by the Shanghai correspondent of a Japanese newspaper had been circulated that morning. The report alleged that Smollett had not been killed by a Japanese machine-gunner, but had died as the result of wounds received several days before in a scuffle with another British correspondent at the Metropole Hotel. Smollett and Donald's horseplay before the Domei reporters had been seen by everyone in the bar of the Metropole, and the absurdity of this report raised much ire. Donald found himself elevated to hero status. The mood in the room was not sympathetic to General Matsui.

'We're going to be told to suppress anti-Japanese feeling,' said Art Fabian of United Press, sitting next to Donald.

'They're planning a victory parade through Shanghai and the Settlement. They're not the best nation for public relations. More like putting your foot in it,' Donald replied.

At last General Matsui appeared. He strode into the room, smaller by a head than the military men who surrounded him. This aroused some amusement amongst the journalists. He settled at the table, a tiny figure between the yellow flowers. There were no medals on his uniform and his voice, when he spoke, came as a surprise, echoing strongly about the room.

'When I left Japan I thought to do my best to co-operate with the officials of other nations in Shanghai. During the two and a half months I have been here the situation has changed in London, Washington, Paris and Brussels, and I am disappointed in what officials of other countries now say and do here in Shanghai. I cannot accomplish co-operation with these officials as I had hoped. This is unfortunate for the peace of the world.' General Matsui gazed about the room and then leaned forward towards the correspondents. A lost tooth gaped under his moustache.

'Do you think the International Settlement is carrying out its duty of neutrality?' he demanded. There was a stir of annoyance in the room. The translator pointed to the raised arms of correspondents in quick succession. Questions were thrown at General Matsui. He gave his attention to each, his expression alternatively amused or serious.

'I wish to assure you I have no intention of taking advantage of the present state of things, of either violating neutrality or favouring the Chinese, in order to take the International Settlement into my hands. But as things have gone, I repeat, co-operation cannot be obtained,' said the General.

'What should the authorities of the International Settlement do to prevent you feeling a need to take any steps against it?' Donald asked, standing up to face General Matsui.

'The fundamental thing for all people to understand is that Japan is not an aggressor, but came here to rescue the civilian population of China,' Matsui answered. An aide stepped forward and spoke in a low voice to the General. Matsui stared at Donald.

'How far will your army continue the Shanghai drive? Do you intend to take Nanking?' Donald stood up again and asked the question on everyone's mind.

'For future developments you had better ask Generalissimo Chiang Kai-shek.' General Matsui gave a chuckle. 'It is up to the Chinese to cease hostilities. We do not know whether we will go to Nanking or not. It all depends upon Generalissimo Chiang.'

The conference was ending. 'We are an honest country,' General Matsui promised by way of conclusion. 'Whatever Japan may do, nothing brutal or foolish will happen here.'

Correspondents filed out of the room, but as Donald moved towards the door a military man hurried after him. 'General Matsui wishes to speak to you. Please return to your seat,' said the aide.

Donald turned and bowed his head slightly in respect to the General. He sat down on the chair the aide pulled forward close to General Matsui. There was a flush to the old man's face, as if he had a fever. A nervous tic twitched at his chiselled features. The General leaned forward.

'The occurrence the other day in Nantao was most unfortunate. I wish to convey my condolences on the death of your friend. It was thought you were Chinese snipers.' General Matsui spoke without emotion. He lit a cigarette, his eyes upon Donald.

'I wish you to give a personal message from me to the world in your London newspaper,' Matsui continued. 'I have been made very angry by reports from America and England revealing foreign expectations that the Japanese Army under my direction would grab everything in Shanghai and would imperil all foreign rights and interests here. Nothing is further from my thoughts.' The General looked sternly at Donald.

'I am more than happy to convey with every sympathy your message to the world,' Donald replied. What private agendas and political infighting must this tiny General face, he wondered. General Matsui smiled.

'New York, Washington and London seem to think I am a Japanese version of a looting Chinese warlord. Please disabuse the public in the

Western world,' General Matsui drew on his cigarette and began to cough.

'I wish you to make it plain to your readers that, despite some destruction of foreign properties in and around Shanghai, my whole campaign was directed with the determination to protect foreign interests. All military experts will agree that I could have captured Shanghai in less than half the time, with less than half the Japanese losses, and half the expenditure, had Shanghai been a Chinese city without foreign areas which demanded consideration. In fact I do not mind telling you, for this consideration to your Foreign Settlements, I have been much criticized in Tokyo,' General Matsui explained. Donald nodded and scribbled in his notebook.

'The many American and British facilities and warehouses are all intact,' Matsui continued. 'But we are now masters of Shanghai.'

'And Nanking?' Donald asked again. The General glared.

'I am no longer needed in Shanghai. The battle here is over. I move on to the battleground north of Lake Tai, to direct the advance on Nanking, if indeed we are forced to advance. Everything depends upon Generalissimo Chiang Kai-shek.'

General Matsui stood up. 'I shall wait to read your report. You will be my publicity man.'

Donald appeared the man of the moment. The misadventure with Smollett and the scoop it provided made a hero of him. General Matsui's favour only added to this aura. Donald felt a swell of support about him in the bar of the Metropole. But this did not help in the matter of self-knowledge. He knew himself for a sham. Only to Nadya could he admit his guilt about Smollett.

Now, he sat before a typewriter in the editorial room of the *North China Daily News*, the foremost British paper on the China coast. The clack of the machines filled the room like an army of desperate cicada. There was an air of urgency beyond the usual newsroom pressure. Since Shanghai had fallen everyone knew newspapers were in danger. A Japanese-held Shanghai would tolerate no pro-Western propaganda.

'We'll be muzzled, and forced to parrot official lines as Domei does,' said Joe Russek, one of the paper's key reporters. 'I'm leaving.' He leaned on the back of Donald's chair, trying to read what he had written.

'Is everyone going?' Donald asked, looking up from the typescript in the machine before him, and then rolling it hurriedly to the beginning of the page before Russek's inquisitive eyes.

'Most correspondents I know are moving on. I've bought my ticket back to Australia. I'm going via Japan, thought I'd see what was happening there. No point now in remaining here. The best is over with the fall of Shanghai. The Japanese will go on to Nanking, but that will be no more than a technical occupation. There's no doubt Chiang will surrender now. Shouldn't think he has any other choice,' Russek answered.

Donald shrugged. He wondered what he himself should do. He could not think clearly since Smollett. A Chinese assistant came up to him and Russek turned away.

'This cable has just come through for you.' The boy held out a piece of paper. It was from London.

Regret Smollett death, but story excellent. Trail Matsui, your position invaluable. Suggest return immediately Nanking. Rumoured Chiang will not give in.

He stared down at the cable. Already, *The Times* considered him as good as any of their better-known war correspondents. He saw again that China could indeed be his, in an unexpected way. His father had done nothing like this. Donald turned to the paper in the typewriter:

Foreign holders of bonds secured by the Chinese maritime customs should have no fear that their claims might be endangered by Japan's control of Shanghai customs, said General Matsui, Japanese commander, at Shanghai today.

General Matsui, who discussed the Chinese situation with this writer for nearly two hours today, intimated that the Japanese control of customs would not be carried out in a manner that would ruin China's huge domestic bond issue.

General Matsui wishes the readers of this paper to be, in his words, disabused of the image of him as a looting Chinese warlord. He wishes readers to know the great pains he has taken to protect foreign interests in Shanghai . . .

He listened to the frantic clatter of machines about him, and observed the bent heads of the men before them. What could they say that was not now a repetition of each other's reportage? Only he had the first-hand story of Smollett. Others had written from his copy. Only he had the trust of Matsui. For the first time in days, a new determination welled up in him. He returned his eyes to the keyboard and began to type with vigour. The road ahead was clearer now.

The Japanese Victory Parade took a route through the Foreign Settlement and the French Concession, much to the distress of its residents.

'Whatever Matsui might say about not entering the Settlement, this is the thin end of the wedge,' said Donald. He stood with Nadya on a corner of Nanking Road. 'This is foreign territory. It is not part of the Japanese victory. They've no right to parade through here.' Donald clicked his camera.

Thousands of marching feet vibrated through the town, blending with the hooves of horses, and the wheels of artillery and mounted guns. Planes flew overhead. The fears of childhood returned to Nadya on the Shanghai pavement. She had heard these sounds before as the Red Army marched through Blagoveshchensk. Her fear was not of Russians or Japanese but of men, brutalized and trained to kill.

The Japanese residents of Shanghai were closely stage-managed, brought by bus to Nanking Road, their cheers recorded by microphone and transmitted by radio to Japan. Newsreels of the parade were made, police precautions were intense. The Settlement was out in force, its mood surly and unbowed.

'We'll have a better view up there,' said Donald.

He pushed through the crowd to climb onto a plinth below a bank, pulling Nadya after him. The ledge was precarious but the view cleared the heads of the crowd. Before them the twisting body of a khaki serpent stretched away through the Settlement. Beyond, a blackened plain reached to the horizon. Rising Sun flags flew everywhere, sun caught the rifles of the marching men.

'Will nobody stop them?' Nadya asked.

As she spoke an explosion sounded. The troops fell to the ground, fixing bayonets. Smoke rose above the mass of people. An order was shouted and the soldiers leaped up, barring all escape routes.

'Someone's thrown a grenade,' Donald clicked his camera fast. A man ran from the crowd followed by a Chinese policeman. A shot sounded and the man fell, writhing a moment before his body stilled.

'Thank God the Chinese got him before the Japanese.' Donald's face was contorted with emotion. Soon the parade moved forward again.

'Chiang put up a fight for Shanghai, but taking Nanking will be only a technicality.' Donald was changing the film in his camera beneath his jacket. 'I predict he'll withdraw into the interior and leave Nanking undefended. The Japanese will enter without a fight, set up a puppet government and order will be restored. I must get to the front lines and then to Nanking. The centre of action has already moved.'

'I thought you weren't interested in being in the midst of things,' Nadya replied.

'Well, I've changed my mind,' Donald answered. 'I feel I owe it to Smollett. And *The Times* has ordered me back there.'

149

9

December 1937

Return to Nanking

Already a cold and bitter wind cut through the Settlement. W.H.D. had come to Shanghai. He had only an hour and they spent it in the Chocolate Shop, which had recently been the meeting place of Shanghai's élite bohemians. Now it was deserted. The menu was reduced. Nadya drank a diluted hot chocolate, W.H.D. a diluted coffee. He turned down his mouth in disaste.

'The Generalissimo and Madame are leaving for Hankow, and I go with them. If the Japanese advance towards us, we'll move on to Chungking. A temporary government will be set up there and resistance reorganized. Surrender is the last thing on the Generalissimo's mind.'

It was the second time in a few weeks that W.H.D. had been in Shanghai. Previously, he had accompanied Madame Chiang Kai-shek who wished to visit her dentist and inspect the front, before the fall of the city. The trip had been disastrous.

'Our car blew a tyre. Madame flew over my head and landed in a mud hole. I thought it was the end. She's a brave little woman; continued the trip in spite of a broken rib. You take your life in your hands now, travelling that Shanghai–Nanking road.' W.H.D. shook his head. Just days before the British Ambassador's car was fired upon by a Japanese plane, in spite of a Union Jack painted upon its roof. The Ambassador, Sir Hugh Knatchbull-Hugessan was seriously wounded. In London tempers were incensed by this wanton act.

Upon Bradley's orders, Nadya handed W.H.D. a copy of the penultimate volume of the Encyclopaedia. TECSAT was finally printed and being packed for removal to Hankow with Chiang Kai-shek's effects. 'The last volume will be ready in just a couple of days. Maybe I'll bring it myself to Nanking.'

'Stay here, foolish woman,' W.H.D. advised. 'Nanking is no place now, everyone is leaving the city.'

In spite of Bradley's sense of urgency, the printing of TECSAT had taken time, due to the departure inland of so much of Shanghai's labour force. The Japanese had not interfered with TECSAT, although they were now in control of the Settlement. Donald too had stayed on. A further cable from *The Times*, suggested he report upon Shanghai under the Japanese occupation before leaving for Nanking. The Japanese Army's advance towards the capital was a drive of terror. Until some days before Donald had seen no urgency to depart Shanghai. Now, as Chiang Kai-shek showed no sign of surrender, it seemed the fall of Nanking was imminent.

'Donald is going back, to be in the thick of it,' Nadya replied.

'Fool. How is the boyfriend?' W.H.D. frowned in disapproval.

Nadya shrugged away the enquiry. She had no wish to explain to W.H.D. the episode of Smollett or its effect upon Donald.

'Cooling off? I'm glad to hear it.' W.H.D. pursed his lips.

Nadya had refused to see Donald for some days. Smollett's death had affected him badly. His behaviour had become unstable, swinging between moods of blackness and drunken bravado. He spat vitriol without provocation. Nadya backed away and each time he followed, meek with apology, only for the cycle to begin again. After tolerating his perversity, she was exhausted.

W.H.D. finished his coffee and ordered another. 'You're well rid of that young man. Arrogant, unstable, his reputation precedes him everywhere. He likes to shock. I suppose it's not easy to have a famous father, nor to have him shoot himself in front of you. I cannot see what you find in him. Besides, he's married. What future can you have? A nice girl like you needs security, a husband and children.' W.H.D. patted Nadya's hand.

'He's not married.' She sat unmoving. And she had heard nothing about his father shooting himself.

'Not told you, has he? The bastard.' W.H.D. swore. 'You should have asked me. After that article in *Time*, I learned a few facts. The mystery about his father's death was never cleared up. I should think there's a lot he hasn't told you.'

The blood throbbed in her head. She did not want to admit she knew little of Donald but what passed silently between them. The unspoken rule of their relationship was that she should ask him nothing. Now, in the Chocolate Shop, with the hum of war planes overhead and the aroma of cocoa and coffee about her, anger flooded through her. W.H.D. was delighted.

'I met his wife once, in London at a party. Beautiful woman, journalist, daughter of a famous Peer. There was a rumour about for a while that father and son both shared her. John Addison was a real womanizer. Just rumour,' he added, seeing the look on Nadya's face.

He glanced at his watch and picked up the edition of TECSAT. As they left the Chocolate Shop the cold wind whipped about them again.

Donald was nowhere. At last she got through to a friend of his at Reuters. 'He left yesterday on a Japanese troop train. He's trying to get back to Nanking.'

She replaced the telephone. Thoughts sat like pebbles now in her mind. There was nothing in the time she had known Donald to prepare her for W.H.D.'s revelations. And why should he disappear in this manner, without a word, even if she had refused to see him? A note at the least was owed her. For the first time she saw Donald three-dimensionally. The image hit her with unexpected power. The shadow of another life swung away behind him. She had accepted a cardboard figure, reading into his life and their relationship whatever she wished. All the while his responses came from experiences hidden far from her. He had not lied, but he returned nothing in exchange for her openness. She remembered the night on the Lotus Lake, she remembered her wish to be honest. And yet, his own secretiveness had forced some measure of the same upon her. Where was trust if no confidence could be exchanged? What was the essence of such a relationship? Perhaps she meant nothing to him.

It was impossible then not to re-live every moment of their relationship, and see herself in an unflattering light. She blushed at the things she had demanded of him in their most intimate moments. Bewilderment dissolved into fury in the light of W.H.D.'s remarks. Donald was no different from Sergei. He walked out of her life, as if nothing had passed between them. He took her trust and tossed it aside, hiding truths about himself.

Anger raced through her. Donald's things still littered her apartment. She gathered them up in a sudden fury, stuffing them into carrier bags, and put them outside the front door. A briefcase was left and she opened it, rifling through the papers inside. There was nothing to connect him to the things W.H.D. suggested; no letters from a wife, no diary of confession. She straightened up in a rage. Everything between them until now had been a lie. There were other methods of rebuttal less cruel than he had chosen. She could not understand him.

For a long time she sat, knees drawn up under her chin, on the bed where so much of their relationship had evolved. She stared from the window across the Settlement roof-tops, to the smoking ruins of greater Shanghai. Weeks ago the view had been green, with the straw hats of peasants dotting the fields. The rice bowl of China was gone. How would they eat? What seed was there left to regenerate life for those that might survive? She remembered the line of roped prisoners, falling one upon another into their grave. She saw again the carts of bodies in the Settlement, the orphaned children, the refugees beaten by wind and rain, pressed against the walls of buildings. On every corner now children were for sale. Before her everything converged in hopelessness. The cruelty of Donald seemed only an echo of the greater savagery around her. Donald could go his way, but the need to confront him consumed her. All her relationships seemed without resolution. Men slipped into her life and slipped away, without an explanation. Even her father. One moment they were there and the next they were gone, and she of no importance.

She remembered her father and then, almost immediately, the governess, Mussya. She had been as plump and affectionate as Anna, Nadya's stepmother, was bony and tense. Nadya had grown up in terror of Anna. A terror she suspected her father shared, always silent before the woman. Even in a childish way Nadya understood her presence was a threat to Anna. She exploited the discovery boldly, a weapon in the battle between herself and Anna for her father's affection. When he returned from work each day Nadya had run to him, fussing about him, demanding attention. But her father was too much in awe of Anna to play the game to Nadya's satisfaction. He took the child upon his knee, but under the sour eyes of his wife, his caress became half-hearted.

Once, Anna went away, back to her family home to nurse a sick sister. Nadya stayed with her father and Mussya. It was summer. Even now she could not forget those three months. Her father was as if reborn. And Mussya seemed no less so. They had celebrated Nadya's twelfth birthday with abandon. There were picnics and outings and expeditions to find wild flowers. Every hour her father could spare from work was planned with jubilation. In the evenings he played upon his balalaika and sang Siberian folk songs while Mussya accompanied him.

And then there was the dancing. Mussya danced like the village woman she was, unable to resist the rhythm of the music, caught by swirling emotion. It infected her father who stamped and laughed aloud while he danced. Nadya watched until the delirious throb drew her into their abandonment. In the end she and Mussya collapsed in a breathless heap of laughter. Her father flung himself into a chair. Taking Mussya on one knee and Nadya upon the other, he squeezed them both enormously.

At night, in the quiet house, she heard movement and whispering in

153

the next room and knew Mussya was there with her father. At first this seemed strange and disturbed her so that she lay awake, straining her ears to make sense of the sounds, or catch a conversation. But, quickly, she took comfort from Mussya's new status. She hoped Anna would not come back and that Mussya would be her new mother.

Instead, Anna returned. And with her homecoming Mussya was promptly dismissed. No entreaty from Nadya brought an explanation. The house became silent, only Anna's angry voice echoing each night through closed doors. Then, one day, her father was gone, vanished into the snowy steppes after Mussya. Even now that moment of abandonment lived with Nadya. She had waited for him to return, then waited for his summons. No message ever came. Or perhaps, it later occurred to her, Anna intercepted messages, holding Nadya hostage. When finally, after many weeks, he did return Nadya had clung to him, desperate. There had been much shouting and a policeman was called. In the end her father departed alone into the night. He walked away, in spite of her cries, without a backward glance. She knew by the set of his shoulders the effort it was not to turn to her, to carry her off with him. She could understand nothing of the matter, defined by adult rules. There was only the knowledge that he had left her to Anna's harsh resolve. All her life she bore the brunt of Anna's festering bitterness.

Later, she heard there were children by Mussya; he had no more need of Nadya. He regularly sent a small financial provision for Anna and herself, but Nadya saw nothing of him. He did not return, nor invite her to stay with his new family. Many years afterwards, as an adult, Nadya understood that perhaps her father had been refused the right to see her by the connivance of Anna and the police. Perhaps the price he paid for Mussya was the loss of his own daughter. Perhaps this loss was Anna's revenge. But as a child, the pain of abandonment inflicted upon her, was all Nadya understood. She was in her mid-teens before she saw her father again. For some reason then, unexpectedly, an invitation came to visit him and Mussya. She had travelled to their home full of trepidation. And discovered the worst; nothing could be rebuilt between her father and herself. There was only distance now between them, and a dark, sharp hate in her heart. There was no place for her in the circle of contentment her father had built with Mussya. Small children played and shouted. The love he could not give to Nadya, she saw he now squandered upon them. At the end of the visit she had returned to Anna, her anger so great tears would not moisten her eyes. She knew then he was finally lost to her.

The years with Anna were filled with grim emotion. She could not say Anna treated her badly. In time she even appeared to take strength from

Nadya's youthful determination. He never loved me, she repeated bitterly, over and over again. She seemed to shrink, the wiry tenacity turning to frailty. Those years alone with Anna were also a time of great turmoil in Russia. Her father's abandonment of Nadya coincided with this political chaos. It was as if she and Anna were forced to cling to each other in a treacherous sea. Anarchy, typhus, famine. Reds, Whites, bodies in the streets, the rule of the gun. And then the brutalities of the first Five Year Plan with its relentless industrialization. All these things swirled about her after her father left.

Eventually Anna took a lover, a minor Party official in Blagovesh-chensk, who came and went as he pleased, turning a roving eye upon Nadya. When he appeared she hid herself away, terrified he might approach her. As soon as she could Nadya had gone to work at the Blagoveshchensk *People's Paper*, unaware of its future usefulness in employment with Bradley Reed.

Now, in Shanghai, the desolation she had faced at her father's desertion, filled her again when she thought of Donald. She knew suddenly then she must return to Nanking. She could not let Donald go, turning his back upon her, as she had let her father go. She had the power now to take her life in her hands, directing its destiny. The explanation she had never received from her father, she needed now from Donald.

And on another level, there was a necessity in this war to do something crazy, to push away the shadow of death that hovered always before her. Nadya got off the bed with new energy. As the war spread to surround Nanking, she could perhaps play a part in the Safety Zone; she could be of use to somebody.

There was a press pass in Donald's briefcase, stamped with Chinese characters. Donald had several passes allowing him access to areas of military sensitivity. She put it in her pocket. Journeying to Nanking was no easy matter. Troop trains such as Donald had used were infrequent. She had no transport but a bicycle, in the garage beneath her apartment. Why should she not cycle to Nanking? A German, she heard, had recently cycled as far as Hankow. If she kept close to the railway line her direction was clear, and a train might pass. She began to pack a rucksack. The journey should take no more than a few days. Every time fear overcame her she remembered Agnes Smedley. A bicycle trip from Shanghai to Nanking would be nothing to Agnes Smedley.

December frost hardened the ground, and wet leaves were slippery underfoot. She picked from a cupboard a padded Chinese suit and pulled on thick underwear and sweaters beneath it. She would appear no different from afar than the fleeing refugees. Her red hair she hid

155

under a woollen cap. She packed some food in a rucksack and pushed in the last volume of TECSAT, ready just that afternoon. It would be needed in Nanking; Chiang Kai-shek and W.H.D. had not yet departed the city. She left a note for Bradley who was soon to return to America. The office was disbanding. With the completion of TECSAT, her work with Bradley was finished.

She left in the early morning, mist still hung upon the road. At first it did not seem too hard. A stream ran alongside the railway. Few people were about. The land was charred as far as she could see, an unrecognizable landscape. She kept close to the railway line, hoping at each station to find a transport train. The Chinese refugees kept their distance from the line and any chance of contact with the Japanese. The first stations she passed were deserted. She sat on the bank of the stream to eat breakfast and later some lunch. Shanghai was already a distance behind her.

At places the track had been bombed and repaired. She cycled on the clay border paths beside the rails. The day was cold but sunny. Some distance ahead was a shallow ravine. Bombing had destroyed the bridge and it was crossed now by makeshift struts. She started across, cycling carefully over the narrow planks. Immediately she became aware of a stench rising up from the ravine. Looking down she saw the bodies of Chinese soldiers. They had been machine gunned and appeared to have lain for days in the narrow furrow. Their shabby blue padded jackets, not unlike her own, had been ripped open by bayonets or animals, the white quilting strewn about like candy floss, burnished by days of rain. The stench made her retch. She was terrified of losing her balance on the bridge and plummeting down upon the bodies. She pushed forward, not stopping until distance was achieved. The day had turned rancid upon her.

At the next station were six Japanese soldiers. They had no English but were jovial, offering food. They examined her press pass and its red seal. Already the dusk faded into darkness. They showed her a station bench with a pillow and blanket and she accepted the offer. She felt no fear, surprised at the affability of the soldiers. She slept fitfully and in the morning they gave her a breakfast of dried apricots and small loaves of Chinese bread. She set off again with replenishments of food in her rucksack.

Late in the day she stopped a group of peasants, asking in her broken Chinese the distance to the next station. They stood beside the railway line, scratching their heads. She saw a sudden flash of light ahead. A trolley-car, used for running up and down the track, was coming towards them, filled with soldiers. There was immediately panic amongst the peasants. They jumped over the steep bank beside the rail, pulling Nadya with them. She rolled down the slope, scratched by shrubs and undergrowth. There was a sudden, sharp pain in her head.

When she awoke it was night and cold. Above, the stars were like chips of ice in the black sky. She sat up, but felt sick and lay down again. She must have hit her head as she fell. The peasants and her bicycle were gone. When she awoke next it was daylight, there was a pain in one eye. She pulled herself up to the top of the bank and lay beside the railway line. If a trolley-car passed, they would see her. Eventually she heard a rumble, and saw a train had stopped. Soldiers peered down at her and she was lifted aboard.

'I want to go to Nanking,' she said and remembered nothing more. At times she awoke to the rhythm of the train and the voices of the soldiers. Occasionally it seemed day, occasionally night. She had no sense of time until shaken awake. The train had stopped. She was helped out and sat upon a wooden box. One of the young soldiers spoke some English. 'Wait, please,' he said.

It was a large station, and beyond it there appeared to be a sizeable town. The boy returned and escorted her to another area. 'The Major want see you. You are feeling better now?' he enquired. She stumbled and the boy put a hand beneath her elbow to help her along.

'You like this war?' she asked.

'I must fight for our Emperor. Maybe I must die for him.' He sounded cheerful.

The press pass was already upon the Major's desk, as were the contents of her rucksack. A small, swarthy man with bandy legs introduced himself as an interpreter. She did not like the look of him. The edition of TECSAT was open before the Major.

'You are Russian,' declared the interpreter as the Major held up some papers of identification from her rucksack. He spoke fluent English. 'Where are you going to, walking alone in the middle of nowhere? The Major says we must decide if we will shoot you.'

The Major had a square, protruding jaw. The whites of his eyes were yellowed, like old eggs. He stared at her red hair, and instinctively she took a step back. Her head ached badly still.

'The Major says, all Russians are spies. If you were a Chinese we would shoot you, right now. Or, if you were carrying a gun or a knife. What is this book?' The interpreter looked from Nadya to the Major. The Major glared at Nadya and prodded the pages of TECSAT. He struck the desk with his fist and shouted.

'Major wants quick reply. Speak at once,' the interpreter urged. She explained about TECSAT and her involvement in it. The Major rapped the desk again.

'Is it not a code book? Are you not a spy? What organization do you work for?' the interpreter enquired. The absurdity of the charge made her want to laugh, instead she felt she might cry.

'You can see what the book is,' she shouted.

'Do not raise your voice to the Major,' the interpreter said. He lifted an arm, as if he might hit her. 'The Major says you are to get off this railway. You cannot walk here, it is highly strategic. You are near the front lines. You will stay here until the morning. We will then decide what to do with you. It is better to tell us now who you are working for.'

'I have told you all there is to tell,' she began to shout again. The interpreter hit her across the face.

She was given a straw mat in a small room. A filthy toilet led off it. Some rice, tinned fish and pickles were brought to her. She lay down on the mat, the odour of excrement filled the air. At moments she felt she might vomit. It grew dark and finally she fell asleep. The next morning the young soldier who spoke English returned with green tea and Chinese buns. He brought also a mirror and hot water, which she took gratefully. Looking into the mirror she saw that her hair stood on end and bits of leaves adorned it. Her face was streaked with mud, her eye was ringed by a bruise. In her pocket she found a comb and a handkerchief and did what repair work she could. It was midday before she was summoned again by the Major. Beside him in the room sat an Indian man. Nadya looked at the foreigner in surprise, wondering if he too was a captive.

'The Major tells me you want to get to Nanking,' the Indian said. His eyes protruded slightly behind a sharp nose, his hair was thickly oiled. From his manner it was clear he was no captive. He spoke in Japanese and the Major appeared respectful.

'Who are you?' she scowled. It was as if she had entered a maze.

'My name is Tilik Dayal. I am on my way to Nanking. I can take you there.' He smiled.

'Will he allow it?' Nadya glared at the Major. Tilik laughed.

'I have come down the line from the town ahead to pick you up. They do not know what to do with you here. I am also on my way to Nanking. I have a car, we are to go by road. The railway line ahead is bombed. We can leave at once if you wish. I will be your chauffeur.'

A battered car was provided, food and flasks of water. Tilik drove out of the station, a Homburg hat on the back of his head, as if in a holiday mood. Nadya was bewildered at this sudden release, everything seemed unreal. Now, on either side of the road, she saw devastation. Corpses were everywhere, limbs stiffened grotesquely, half-eaten by dogs. Surviving villages flew Rising Sun Flags. Planes droned overhead and Nadya held her breath. There was nothing to stop them being machine gunned in the car, no indication of who they were. Tilik conversed in Japanese whenever soldiers stopped them and showed his documentation.

'How is it you can drive to Nanking in an army car?' she demanded, unsure of what to make of the man.

'I have safe passage. I am on my way back to Manchukuo from Shanghai. The hostilities there detained me,' he explained, his eyes upon the road.

'You are in league with the Japanese military. Maybe you are the spy, not me.' No ordinary foreigner commanded such co-operation from the Japanese Army.

'But for me you would be interrogated today by the Military Police. No doubt you have heard of their methods,' Tilik replied, turning his head to look at her.

'You haven't answered my question,' she insisted. She felt no fear of this man. 'Are you in the pay of the Japanese?'

'I work from here to free my country of alien rule. Japan supports the freedom of India. I can turn you out of this car, right here. I can report you as a spy to the nearest command,' he answered. There was something disturbing in her presence beside him. He kept wanting to turn and observe her. In spite of dishevelment her hair glowed in the sun like burnished copper. He had never seen hair that colour.

'You do not frighten me,' she replied and settled back in the seat.

'There are many thousands of Indians all over Asia like myself. One day we will march with the support of the Japanese military into India. We will set the country free.' He was anxious to impress her.

'And then India will be part of the Japanese Empire instead of the British, and you will have brought it about,' Nadya retorted. 'I fled Russia with my husband, to Harbin. There too there were people working to free the Motherland with the help of the Japanese. I know the kind of things they did.' She spoke bitterly, remembering Harbin and Sergei's admiration of Konstantin Rodzaevsky, whose vile crimes were reported in the newspapers.

'So your husband escaped to Harbin? Why is he not with you now?' Tilik had orders to find out more about Nadya. The Major was certain she was a spy.

'I do not know where he is. He ran off with a man called Shepenov, to America. That Shepenov was a real spy. Tell them to go after him.'

'Shepenov?' Tilik frowned. The name was familiar. He was sure the man was listed as a double agent, part of a Russian organization recruited to work for the Japanese. He had been used for responsible work but had vanished with his male lover and a suitcase of Japanese money. If he was in America that was news. The woman must know more.

'So you were alone, a young woman with no work. How did you keep yourself?' Tilik asked, swerving to avoid a bomb crater.

'It is none of your business,' Nadya replied. 'I am going to sleep.' She closed her eyes, soon exhaustion overwhelmed her. Occasionally then he turned his head and looked his fill at her. She awoke as the car stopped abruptly.

'We cannot go on. It's too dark and the headlights are damaged,' Tilik announced, turning the car off the road. 'There's a building over there.'

He left the car, carrying a torch, and returned a few moments later. 'There's a barn. We'll rest for the night and go on in the morning.'

Nadya followed him to the ramshackle structure. Inside she sat down on the piles of dry hay that still filled the barn. Tilik lit a hurricane lamp and set out a meal of cold rice, tinned fish and pickles.

'Is this all they ever eat?' Nadya asked. Tilik nodded.

'Japanese army fare requires little cooking. They are the most mobile of armies. They need no kitchen. The Major gave me some Chinese wine.' He poured some into a chipped cup and handed it to Nadya. She drank it back and asked for more. Tilik sipped sparingly at his cup.

'Drink it up,' Nadya ordered. 'In Russia we throw back our vodka like that.' She snapped her fingers in the air. Tilik refilled their cups. Nadya reached for a ball of cold rice and began to eat. There was nothing to say. They ate in silence until the sparse meal was almost finished, keeping aside something for the morning.

The lamp threw long shadows about the barn, the rafters were black above them. Her eyes were like a cat's, Tilik thought. In India cats were evil creatures. Tilik had been taught from childhood to avoid them. He looked at her apprehensively. With those cat-like eyes and flaming hair she appeared a creature from another world. She unbuttoned her padded jacket upon a close-fitting sweater. He was unused to women who displayed their bodies so unconsciously. She began to arrange the bales of straw into a bed for herself. Soon she turned her back upon him and settled for the night.

Tilik lay down a distance away. The moon thrust in through the rotted roof, washing the barn in colourless light. Nadya breathed evenly, her shoulders rising and falling. Tilik could not sleep; the barn seemed full of the woman. He moved nearer, wanting to look again at her cat-like face; he had seen Western women only from a distance. In the half-light he could smell the scent of her skin and see the shadow of her eyelashes. The drink had made him bold. In the moonlight her face took on a translucence. The red hair was drained to a yellow fire. He had seen such faces in American movies, and Christian pictures of angels. He breathed quickly.

Suddenly she stirred, and he drew back hastily. She turned and saw him, inexplicably near, pushing awkwardly away. Her eyes blazed up in fury. She rolled clear of him in a single movement and picked up a hay fork from a corner. He fell back in fear.

'I would not touch you,' he protested. 'I was just looking at you.'

She stood over him with the fork, as he retreated on all fours. He was out of his depth. Michiko's modesty and predictability had not prepared him for this harpy. The fork was poised in her hand, as if she would castrate him. He pulled back against the wall.

'You can sleep in the car for punishment.' The absurdity of the moment struck her and she began to laugh. Tilik crawled from the corner, pleading his cause, but Nadya prodded him firmly towards the door, pushing him out into the night, like some unsavoury insect. She wedged the door shut behind him.

It was icy in the car, and humiliation filled him. Even the wine was inside the barn, and also the remains of the food. The sound of her laughter still filled his ears. He struck the dashboard with his fist, he would report her as suggested by the Major with all the additional details of Shepenov. There was no doubt she was a spy. What right had she to dismiss him in this manner? She was one more example of the arrogance of the white-skinned race, even if she was not English. He was here in China, in this freezing car, with not even a ball of cold rice at hand, because of the attitude of such people. Even now he remembered the moment this hatred for Westerners had begun, setting his life upon its particular axis.

He had been eight years old the day he saw his first Englishman, a sweaty, sunburned soldier. In innocence he had swaggered up to the man and demanded, 'Why is your face so red?'

'Because I eat only tomatoes,' the soldier replied, lowering his gun.

From nowhere then Tilik's father appeared, sweeping him up like a sack of grain, backing away in apology. The soldier's laughter arched over the carts and people crowding the narrow road.

Tilik had not asked the question in disrespect but rather in admiration. However much his father might rant about the injustice of British Rule, it was clear to a child who was superior. For a week Tilik had refused all food and ate only raw tomatoes. His mother screamed and locked him in the storeroom, the doctor was called and laughed. His father shrugged and declared, 'Let him find out for himself.'

He had emerged from the experiment chastened. The mirror showed the same dark eyes and skin like the bark of the mango tree. He knew then he was bolted forever to his limitations. Anger overwhelmed him. When he listened then to his father speak of the persecution of Indians upon their own soil, his rage was no longer directed at his father for deprecating a people who should be admired. For the first time he identified with the powerlessness his father must always have felt. It was as if in those weeks he left childhood behind. Something awoke, like a seed that has stirred, and begins the first movement of growth.

He did not sleep well in the car, the cold biting into his bones. He dreamed of Michiko and longed for her familiarity. Nowadays fatigue was always with him. The journeys he was sent on from Hsinking by Jun Hasegawa seemed endless. He repeatedly traversed barren rocky land, to people who welcomed him apathetically. He worked more to consolidate Japanese power than for Indian Independence. He was a paid puppet on a string who jumped to the command of the military. Nobody cared about India; the talk was all of Japan. Hasegawa laughed if he dared to grumble.

'Have we limited your activities on behalf of India? Our Empire is at your disposal to spread your propaganda.' Then Hadegawa would outline the next journey to some far-flung perimeter.

'Send me to places where people have at least heard of India. What do camel herders care?' he insisted.

'Asia is one. An Asia for Asians will work to your end. Only keep your mind on that. All things will come in time.' Hasegawa dismissed him.

Tilik knew Hasegawa well enough to sense a distancing. Since the collapse of his wool trade project in Pao-tao Tilik felt a diminishing interest in him. In Tokyo the blame for this loss of trade had been placed squarely upon him. So also had the deaths of Japanese soldiers killed by the Chinese in revenge for the lowering of the wool tariffs. The tariffs has been lowered against Tilik's advice by a new Military High Command. Yet it was suggested Tilik had put the cause of India before the safety of the Japanese. One hundred Japanese soldiers had died because of his plan, including Captain Nakamura. His protests had not been heard.

Rash Bihari had not been happy at this news, when Tilik visisted him on a trip back to Japan. 'This is not the way to help our country. You have allowed yourself to be trapped. Even if you were not directly to blame, do you think they will recognize that? In all these years I have made sure I kept my independence. But you have become their creature.'

Now, in the freezing car Tilik drew his coat about himself, remembering Rash Bihari's words. Soon he fell into a fitful sleep. He saw Rash Bihari shaking a finger in anger at a coat Tilik had designed. It had broad lapels and brass buttons, and was to be worn over a uniform. It was a coat for marching into India, a splendid coat in which to turn out the British. 'This is a winter coat, for the snows of Manchukuo. It is not a coat for our Indian climate. Have you forgotten who you are? I am the Indian, Rash Bihari Bose. Who are you?' his mentor asked. Tilik awoke with a start. Shame still pulsed through him. Shame at betraying himself and India, shame before the Russian woman, shame at colluding with the Japanese military. He whimpered in his fear.

In the morning the woman acted as if nothing had occurred the night before. They finished the rice and a bottle of cold tea before travelling on. The terrain had changed.

'We've crossed the front lines,' Tilik announced, trying to mend the bridge between them.

Now, instead of a scorched landscape, the earth flourished with vegetation again. On the road they overtook a stream of refugees pushing carts, carrying bundles, babies or old people on their backs. Small children, sewn into their padded winter clothes, trudged towards Nanking and the hinterlands beyond. Bands of Chinese soldiers in retreat, bedraggled and bloodstained, carried their wounded. As the miles to Nanking grew shorter, the river of people increased.

Tilik no longer assumed his cocky manner and spoke no more Japanese. He played the role of a confused and frightened foreigner, desperate to reach Nanking. Nadya observed him in disgust. Before night they finally reached Nanking. The Yangtze stretched wider, the terrain grew more hilly and then Purple Mountain appeared. Nadya sat up in excitement. The sun set behind the grey walls of Nanking, rising up now on the horizon.

Tilik stopped as directed by Nadya before Martha's hospital. After Nadya walked off he drove on to the Japanese Embassy, and sought out Kenjiro Nozaki. He filed a report as the Major had suggested and added the details he had learned of Shepenov. With the disapproval of Hsinking's Military High Command now stacked against him, he could not afford to miss an opportunity to deepen his credibility.

Nadya found Martha in the hospital, dressing the wounds of a Chinese soldier. 'What have you come back for? This is not the place to be. We're preparing for attack,' Martha scolded.

'I thought I could be of some use,' Nadya insisted, handing Martha a pair of scissors with which to cut a bandage.

'We're taking in soldiers, as well as our usual women patients,' Martha replied.

'Do you know if Donald is in Nanking?' Nadya enquired as casually as she could. She sat down on the floor, too tired to think any more.

'I heard he was here. But I think he left with most of the other correspondents, to wait out the attack up river, on the USS *Panay*. The Japanese have asked all foreigners, for their own safety, to leave before they take the city. On the *Panay* I suppose Donald will be near the action and be able to enter with the Japanese. As far as the city is concerned, there'll be little action I think. There has been a retreat. Chiang Kai-shek and his entourage have left for Hankow. A division of Chiang's soldiers are still here, but what can they do? It is better the town surrenders and we get the whole thing over with quickly. We'll have some peace again, once the Japanese enter.' She bent down to where Nadya sat. 'You're not in a good way. Let me examine that cut on your eye. Afterwards, you must have some hot soup and get to bed.' Martha pulled Nadya to her feet.

'We have a Safety Zone set up like Father Jacquinot's in Shanghai,' Martha explained. 'The Government, before they fled, turned over administrative responsibilities for the city to the Safety Zone Committee. There are twenty-three of us who have decided to remain here to run the Safety Zone. The Zone measures three kilometers by two about the Drum Tower. It encircles several embassies, including the Japanese. Their staff have been helpful. These Japanese civilians are different from their military, and most of them are not happy with what is going on. The Zone will protect Chinese civilians for the few days it might take until the Japanese have completed their occupation, and established law and order in town.'

Nadya winced as Martha examined the cut. 'Where have you sent Lily and Flora?' she asked.

Martha stopped swabbing. 'I have sent them nowhere,' she replied. 'I am sure this occupation will be quick and bloodless. The Japanese will not be opposed by Chinese forces, as in Shanghai. It seemed as safe to keep the girls with me as to send them off somewhere. As a child I sat through much worse.'

Martha had found herself unable to make the decision to send the girls away. All advice to evacuate had run off her. Each morning she decided to go ahead and began arrangements. Each night the possibilities inherent in that parting returned, destroying her resolve. Nadya looked at her in surprise. Martha turned away, as if not wanting to meet her eyes.

'Maybe you are right,' Nadya replied, too caught by the pain of the swab to argue with Martha. 'Nanking is not Shanghai. The worst might be over in a day.'

As General and Madame Chiang Kai-shek had already left for Hankow, Nadya found a group of officials who were departing the following day. She gave them the final edition of TECSAT to deliver to W.H.D.

PART THREE

The Rape of Nanking

Nanking, China, December 1937

10

December 1937

Last Chance

General Matsui was confined to bed in Soochow with tubercular fever when news of his promotion came through. He dismissed congratulations with a disapproving silence. All it meant was that he was no longer Commander in Chief of the army about Nanking. There had been criticism in Tokyo of things in Shanghai. The Emperor had wanted only a brief undertaking, instead the battle had stretched into months. Now the Emperor had relieved him of personal supervision of the field. General Matsui was elevated to overall command of the Central Chinese Theatre. Hirohito had appointed his relative Prince Asaka, to replace Matsui in the taking of Nanking. General Kesago Nakajima and General Heisuke Yanagawa and their men, who with Matsui and his divisions had made up the greater part of the Japanese force, were now accountable to Prince Asaka. Promotion rendered Matsui obsolete in all but responsibility. He had no control of hour by hour movements and plans. His command had been distanced from him.

He put a hand on the table and with an effort pulled himself off the hard bed. He called an aide and gave orders to summon all staff officers. The coughing began again. It had not been easy to find a billet in good condition. Soochow was in smithereens from ferocious bombing. Little was left of the famous pagodas, gardens and ornate bridges. In the past he had visited the city and been captured by its legendary beauty. It saddened him to see its destruction. Beyond the window of his room, General Matsui looked out on a mess of smashed trees and stones. A light frost covered the frozen ground. The house had already been looted by Japanese troops before his occupation. Women had been molested and civilians needlessly killed. Nerves were at breaking point but his staff officers were taking few counter measures. Soldiers were soldiers and war was war. Incidents inevitably happened, but unnecessary excess was not to Matsui's liking. Ill health sapped his energy. The dark hours on his sick bed were filled with terrifying premonitions.

He ordered hot water and shaved, clipping at a grizzled moustache. In spite of the heavy uniform he shivered, there being no heating in the room. The army was ready to enter Nanking. The city's walls had already been breached by bombing and artillery fire, but Chinese resistance still kept Matsui from the city. Fifty Japanese tanks were massed upon a highway one mile from the southern gateway. Air bombardment had destroyed the railway north of Nanking and an important arsenal. Wuhu, a distance south-west of Nanking on the Yangtze, had been occupied the day before with little resistance. Chinese troops dissolved before the Japanese, escaping across the river or discarding weapons and uniforms to masquerade as civilians. This ploy was frequently used by Chinese soldiers to escape detention. No Japanese would act so cowardly, proud only to die in uniform.

It was rumoured that with the fall of Wuhu, there would be an immediate withdrawal of the remaining Chinese troops from Nanking. How Chiang Kai-shek expected hundreds of thousands of men safely to cross the fast-flowing Yangtze, in full view of the Japanese Army and with inadequate transport, was difficult to imagine. It would be no less than a duck shoot.

A group of foreigners had repeatedly asked for assurances, impossible to give, that the Safety Zone they had set up, copying Shanghai, would be respected. Nanking was not Shanghai. It was an entirely Chinese city, and the seat of Chiang Kai-shek's government. The town had no foreign concessions whose destruction would bring the wrath of world powers. General Matsui was clear in his mind upon this issue as he pinned on the full weight of his medals. No time need be wasted as in Shanghai, pussy-footing about foreign property. He gazed unduly long at himself in a splinter of mirror. With Prince Asaka's arrival Matsui would be placed beyond the reach of his men. This was his last chance to address them directly. At the time appointed he strode from his room into the icy courtyard. He suppressed a cough as the frozen air gripped his infected lungs.

He surveyed the officers before him. New faces had appeared. In the past weeks a number of staff officers from the Emperor's cabal had been injected into his command. He frowned, uneasy, and controlled a shiver. No one must think he lacked stamina. In Tokyo a Grand Imperial War Headquarters had been established in the palace. It was as if the Emperor himself now watched each movement of the war. He must not let the Emperor down, and yet Matsui felt frustrated. Orders from Tokyo appeared to come direct now from the new Imperial Headquarters. And sometimes, he suspected, orders came in sets of two, one for Matsui and another of varying instructions for the hand-picked officers who now stood before him. Already he felt undermined. In Tokyo the General

Staff made a show for the Western press, drawing lines on maps to indicate where the advance would stop. When troops reached these lines they simply regrouped and moved on according to secret orders. In this manner the impression was created of the men at the front being out of control and moving forward on their own. Nothing was what it seemed.

Matsui drew himself up, and made an effort to control the twitch in his face. His voice was strong and filled the room. He was determined, to the extent of his capacity, to make sure the occupation of Nanking was orderly. He wished no harm to the population. The order he issued was for his armies to pull up three or four kilometers outside Nanking's walls. Then he cleared his throat and fixed his eyes sternly upon the men.

'Go into the city with only a few well disciplined battalions. This occupation must be carried out in such a way as to sparkle before the eyes of the Chinese and make them place confidence in Japan. The entry of the Imperial Army into a foreign capital is a great event in our history, and will attract the attention of the world. Therefore, let no unit enter the city in disorderly fashion. Let the units chosen to enter know beforehand the matters to be remembered and the position of foreign rights and interests in the walled city. Let them be absolutely free from plunder. Appoint sentries as needed. Plundering and causing fires, even carelessly, shall be punished severely. Together with the troops let many military police enter the city and thereby prevent unlawful conduct.'

Once the officers departed he sank down again upon his bed. There was nothing more he could do. No one was more aware than he of how easily his orders could be usurped.

On Sunday 5th December Prince Yasuhiko Asaka left Tokyo and three days later arrived at the front to take up his post as Commander of the Shanghai Expeditionary Force. His old friend General Kesago Nakajima, once head of secret police in Tokyo, was confined to an abandoned country villa some miles south-east of Nanking. On the day Prince Asaka left Tokyo, Nakajima, in a flurry of enemy activity, took a flesh wound in his left buttock. From his bed he reported to his former patron the success in breaking through the outer Nanking perimeter. There had been unexpected resistance along the battle lines. Chinese artillery still hammered at the Japanese, preventing the establishment of positions from which heavy guns could be brought to bear upon the city. Chinese lines still held and they had even recaptured a village. Nakajima estimated Japanese forces had sustained many casualties in the present fighting. Prince Asaka absorbed this news. He was also informed of the instructions General Matsui had issued on troop deportment in the city and his hope that Nanking might surrend*r. Prince Asaka returned to his own headquarters. From there he issued instructions to his staff officers, marked *secret, to be destroyed.* The orders were to kill all captives.

The stillness was unnerving. After weeks of gunfire, Matsui's men now faced Nanking in silence. The wind whipped across the frozen ground, soughing through the grass. A light snow settled on their khaki coats and melted. The battalion spread across a wide area, a line of armoured cars in front. General Matsui shrank into his greatcoat, a tiny, skeletal figure. The sides of the car were open and gave him no protection from the biting wind. In spite of the distance Matsui had no doubt the Chinese commander General Tang, still in the abandoned city, observed them through binoculars. If Tang held the city at all it could be for no longer than a few days. Japanese bombers stood ready to fly from Shanghai, loaded not with ammunition but champagne, for a victory celebration. Yet, Matsui was determined, in spite of Prince Asaka, to give this last chance of surrender to the capital. He knew the general impatience in the Military High Command with his scruples towards Nanking. He hoped the city would have the sense to surrender. Leaflets urging this decision were now to be scattered over the town. So great was his anxiety that General Matsui had supervised the wording of these pamphlets himself.

> *My outposts east of Nanking must receive your reply by noon Friday. My representative is prepared to negotiate on the spot concerning the procedure of surrender. If no answer is received by the appointed time, we will attack.*
>
> *Abandonment of resistance will spare the city its historic relics and spots of beauty. The anticipated hostilities bode no good for anyone, only harm. If you continue resistance Nanking will witness the nullification of all its constructive efforts of the last generation. I advise you to surrender.*

In the distance the walls of the town rose like old grey gums on the plain. A charcoal-coloured ice lay underfoot. The ground, burned by the retreating army, had quickly frozen. Mud-walled villages were empty, their population bundled inside Nanking. Akira Murata was one of the battalion chosen to accompany General Matsui to this strategic spot. The empty land before them and the silence, broken by a shout of command or a shuffle of boots, seemed more ominous than the rattle of gunfire. Akira Murata looked up at the sky. The wind unravelled clouds to stream across space and pile up behind the town. A kestrel wheeled above. He drew a breath, icy air filled his nose making him sneeze. The commander turned in disapproval. Akira stifled another sneeze. Once more they silently surveyed the prize that would give them control of China.

Purple Mountain was already under Japanese command. The great gates of Nanking had shut, and the ragged Chinese Army was in disarray. The town was naked of any real defence. The best troops had already departed Nanking with Chiang Kai-shek, leaving the town to its fate. Only a small force still remained inside the walls.

The wind cut about Akira's cheeks. An old wound in his leg ached in the cold. He had been shot in a skirmish outside Peking, near a bridge named after an ancient explorer, and was returned to Japan, to a military hospital. On recovery he had rejoined his regiment in Shanghai. The kestrel still glided above. He wished he were a bird.

The bleak winter paddies, textured now by burnt stubble, reminded him of home. On the advance from Shanghai they had passed through villages like his own. He came from an area famous for its pottery. In the Chinese villages he had seen kilns, some of intriguing ingenuity, that he examined surreptitiously. He had watched as stacked pottery was kicked to smithereens when the lust of the troops was unslaked. He thought of the men who had shaped those pots, whose life was spent bending to plant or harvest rice. What was the difference between them and himself? There was nothing he liked about the war.

Above him now the sky was full of sound. The noise resembled the echo of cannon fire within the clouds. At last several planes broke free and were caught by a ray of sun. They flew low over the city. Paper leaflets spewed suddenly from each plane, like flurries of whipped snow. Then, flake by flake, they sank slowly to blanket Nanking. There was a stir amongst the men. The planes sped back into the clouds. The sky was clear again.

For some time they continued facing Nanking. Would the gates of the town swing open, would a party appear to meet General Matsui? Akira strained his eyes hoping to see a white flag upon the walls of Nanking. Nothing appeared. At last the armoured cars spluttered and revved, turning one by one away from the town.

From his car General Matsui observed the battalions standing to attention in the icy wind. The men were weary and over-strung by months of fighting. Their lips were blue with cold. An assault on Nanking would be to nobody's advantage. Chiang Kai-shek had already retreated to Hankow, Nanking was not to be defended. In all but name it was already taken. Chiang Kai-shek would do best by everyone if he deferred to Japanese demands. The Generalissimo was not like Sun Yat-sen who, more than twenty years before, had talked wistfully with

Matsui of Oriental unity and brotherhood. Now General Matsui had twenty-four hours. If the gates of Nanking did not open he was powerless to avoid more carnage. Already an insupportable number of Japanese had been lost since the Shanghai battle. Chinese losses were unknown, but must be far greater. If Chiang Kai-shek did not surrender, how many more would die? The campaign could last for years. General Matsui began to cough. Sickness always caught him when health was needed most.

Matsui could not rid himself now of unease. Rumours blew about and his intuition was alerted. General Nakajima and General Yanagawa, in command of the divisions who with Matsui's own 9th had advanced from Shanghai to Nanking, were younger men who in their youth were posted to Paris with Prince Asaka.

Lean and silent Asaka was a professional soldier who, in spite of privilege, had enjoyed few favours in his career. In the army mutiny the year before he had sided with the military revolutionists, and been censured by Hirohito. His appointment to the front, by order of the Emperor, must carry some special directive. If performed according to Imperial wishes it might be a way for Asaka to return to favour.

Yanagawa's command did not trouble Matsui. Yanagawa, disgraced like Asaka after the mutiny of 1936, would do anything to return to Imperial favour. 'It is as if I were recrossing the Styx out of Hades; I can see the light ahead,' he declared at his sudden resurrection.

But everyone knew Nakajima's reputation. He had been chief of the *Kempeitai*, the secret police, a specialist in thought control, intimidation and torture. He was known to everybody as a man of sadistic personality. Many tales were told of his grim exploits. It was whispered he had come to Nanking with special oil from Peking for burning bodies. Such rumours did not set Matsui's mind at rest.

In the forward regiments, under these commanders, battle-fever raged, soldiers taut with nervous exhaustion. The traditional inter-unit rivalries ran easily out of control. In the heat of the race up the Yangtze delta men were frantically burning villages, slaughtering cattle, carrying off women, to deprive other units of billets, food and entertainment. Such things happened, General Matsui knew, when men reached a razor's edge.

Akira Murata unrolled his blanket and settled down in a corner of a ramshackle hut. The billet was better than those of the last few nights. There was little sleep to be had in a shallow, muddy, frozen trench with no protection from cold or snow. At times it seemed the Army expected them to sleep while on the march. Once they were clear of Shanghai, it had become a race to reach Nanking. The chronic stress of battle, with little sleep, poor food, forced marching, and an unpredictable enemy had reduced them all to exhaustion. Every night they slept with freezing gales whipping around them, hunger unappeased. The smell of filthy uniforms was overpowering.

Akira never talked much with the other men. A few already slept, a group chatted in a corner. Others scribbled in notebooks; most of them kept a diary. Through the crumbling wall Akira could see the distant glare of fire. The routine was always the same. Whenever they entered a village the first priority was to steal the food. Next was to rape the women. Then there was the killing. Men, women and children, not one must be left. To leave a single witness meant risking the Chinese troops learning of their locations. To sleep easily at night they must exterminate each village. These were their orders. All the way to Nanking they were to employ a scorched earth policy, burning as they went. On the other side of the Yangtze, the other divisions would be doing the same.

Such things were all done in the name of the Emperor. They were fighting his sacred war. Soldiers were instructed to die with his name upon their lips, but in their last minutes most men seemed only to call for their mothers. When Akira began to think like this nothing made sense any more. He stared out through the broken wall at the blazing horizon. The majority of men in his unit were decent types, concerned for their families at home, not the kind of men he would readily think of as doing the work they were put to do here.

When he rejoined his regiment in Shanghai after his leg was healed, he had hoped the war would soon be over. They had waited in boats to land on Chinese soil. It was dawn and Shanghai was still some distance away. On the open deck their guns were greased and bayonets polished. As the light grew a thick mist was observed. They had come in quietly over the water, protected by night. There had been little rest in the dark hold of the swaying ships. On deck in the cold, they waited, sleepy. Through the fog came the grumble of anchor chains, winches creaked as assault boats were lowered. There was a ripple of query through the rows of men, unable to tell how far from shore they were. All they knew was they faced the Yangtze delta. A man coughed, another sneezed.

At last the mist began to rise and the green line of the shore was visible. There was the outline of a walled town, and its first dawn stirrings; the call of a cock, and the work chants of coolies coming over the water. The shoreline was laced by canals crowded with sampans and junks. Had they attacked in the mist, without a view of the terrain, confusion and casualties would have resulted. On the shore figures moved who would

175

not live to see the day. Row after row, the men stood silently on order, and filed to the waiting assault boats.

They were crammed in so closely Akira's arms were pinned to his sides. The recruit next to him was a white-faced youngster on his first sortie. All types were coming out now from Japan, most with little experience. He gave the boy a word of encouragement.

'I had only a few weeks' training. I've never killed before,' whispered the boy. His face was long and pale. Dark rings smudged his eyes and, in spite of the cold, a line of sweat edged his upper lip.

'You only kill the first time, after that it's all the same,' a man across from him shouted. 'And afterwards you get to fuck any women left over.' The boy cringed.

'If you don't want to do it, just tell them to drop their trousers so you can have a look. They never wear any underwear. They're just the same as other women. You'll soon be doing it like everyone else. While you fuck 'em they're human, when you kill 'em they're pigs.' The man laughed, not unkindly, at the boy's shocked face. 'Listen, it's against official military regulations to have 'em, so you've got to destroy the evidence. Even the commanding officers will tell you to do that much.'

'You've shot birds, killed a rat, cut off the head of a wriggling fish? These Chinese are no better than animals.' An older man with a tough peasant face leaned towards the boy. 'Don't look at their eyes when you stab. Remember that and you'll be fine.'

'It is for the Emperor. It is his will,' the first man reminded. Others in the boat nodded assent.

It went smoothly. The Chinese soldiers in the area were not the quality of the men fighting nearer Shanghai. They were country boys with little training and straw hats. They ran in all directions and fell like pigeons on the wing. In the village the Japanese soldiers wasted, as ordered, few bullets, stabbing instead with their bayonets. By midday Akira's uniform was wet with blood. He hardened himself against those he struck. Their screams seemed of no more importance than the crash of waves on the beach behind him. Someone threw a baby in the air and he caught it on his bayonet. The bodies cowering before him, pleading, screaming, were only objects to be stopped in their tracks, contained in the town, killed in one stroke for economy. They were not people.

In the evening they had made camp. Men went off to look for women who might be hiding about the ruined town. Then they pushed on the next day, moving from village to village. Through the weeks, with each mile they took, with each new district under their belt, the sense of excitement mounted.

Now, the sight of bodies, bloody, mangled, charred beyond recognition or chewed by hungry dogs appeared no longer abnormal. Killing and the sight of killing, day after day, had also entered the sphere of normality. All sense of horror was gone. Akira could look at these sights now, as could they all, without emotion. The nature of their circumstances no longer struck them as extreme. It was kill or be killed. From some deep place, a hidden splinter of themselves stepped out, anaesthetized to horror, to do what they were asked. Things that in ordinary circumstances they would shrink from, were now done without emotional involvement. Akira too observed this mechanical creature step from himself, to perform his obligations. Death appeared more common than life. For the first time he understood its place in the order of things. And yet, in spite of all he had done, he could not boast of his exploits as the others did. Instead, against his will repugnance threatened to overwhelm him. The others seemed not to share the emotion. Shame of this aberration consumed him and would not go away.

So much of his time seemed spent hiding this disability. Already the others thought him weak. The shadowy double he summoned forth to wield his gun and bayonet, he could not stow back within him. He felt disorientated, unbalanced. Others appeared comfortable to live beside their double. They allowed it to strut permanently about, absorbing guilt and query, as if a bargain had been struck with this other man. What price must later be paid though, Akira was not sure.

He opened his diary. His corner was dark, a hurricane lamp swung from the end of a rope, but gave little light. He watched a man shut his notebook and settle to sleep, and wondered what he had written; the number of miles marched, the score of Chinese killed? Men boasted of the numbers they had dispatched. No one voiced distaste. There was even the rumour that two officers in another detachment were in competition to determine who could cut off the more Chinese heads. The minimum number was to be one hundred. It was said the race was being reported daily back to newspapers in Japan, and followed at home as if it were sport. Akira was confused. He could not sort out the strange conflicts within him. Those like himself, suspected of strange scruples, were made to feel their distance from the core of things. He looked over at Ida who snored open-mouthed. He was a Christian and had funny ideas, yet he did his work efficiently. I am first a Japanese, he said when goaded by the men. And they left him alone, satisfied by proof of his deeds in the field. It was only by intuition that Akira knew those who felt as he did.

It was difficult to understand whether the feeling that gripped him was cowardice, or some integrity of his former life, clinging to him still.

Those others whose thoughts matched his own also kept to themselves, ashamed of their innermost feelings. In an indirect way each knew who the other was, like a secret group within the group. They aimed their guns clear of a target or disappeared from the scene of a rape, and kept silent with regard to these miscarriages of duty when they noticed them in others. There were one or two who had gone mad with it all, and they disappeared mysteriously. There was also the case of Takahashi, who sobbed and refused to bayonet, and was shot by an officer before them all. Akira looked at the blank page of the diary before him and began to write.

Today I killed a child, a boy of about thirteen, no older than my brother Jiro. I had no choice. I might have pretended not to see him or to misaim, but he was there in the hamlet we entered and saw what was done to the women. He was hiding under some bales of straw. We pulled him out. It appeared his family had already fled but he had been left behind in the hurry. The men treated him like a toy. They shot bullets about his feet so that he jumped and squealed. I too used my gun, it was harmless fun. Then there was talk of how to kill him. In spite of the blindfold he began to cry. I remembered Jiro and suggested they let him go, for he was but a small shrimp. He will report on what we have done. We have been told to do away with those that can report, even the women, they said. Besides, he will grow to hold a gun at us. I felt the old suspicion turn upon me. You kill him, they said, and we will watch. Those that felt like I did looked down at the ground and did not meet my eyes. I remembered Takahashi and could not help but feel some sympathy for him. I knew I must steel myself. It was my duty and he was after all only a Chinese, but the image of Jiro would not leave me. It was made worse for me by the crying and sniffling of the boy. It suddenly struck me that perhaps I could help him in his last minutes. I said a few words to the others to set their minds at rest and then removed the boy's blindfold. I told him as best I could in sign language and the one or two Chinese words we had all picked up, that he was free to return to his mother. I told him to run off as fast as he could. He wiped his eyes and stared at me disbelievingly. Then he turned and ran. My aim is good when I want. I shot him in the head before he was but a few yards away. The others were pleased with me and laughed thinking it all a great joke. But I felt differently. I wanted only to help him die without fear and with the hope of seeing his mother again. He did not have to face the point of a gun, waiting for death, snivelling and trembling. However deluded, he died free and instantly. It was all I could do. Such are the ways I now devise to avoid the feeling blunt killing gives me. I admit I am a coward. I despair of myself and am filled with shame at my failure to do my duty. I know these Chinese are our enemy and it is our duty to kill them, but sometimes I feel these common people know as little as we do as to why we are here. If the others had known how far my thoughts and motives were at that moment from their own, I would be gunned down no doubt, like Takahashi.

He closed the diary and lay down. It was true, nobody really knew why they were here, living like animals, doing things that in normal life they would refuse to do. To the best of their knowledge they understood only that this was a war initiated by the Chinese against the Japanese; that was what the newspapers said, what their commanders said. It was called a sacred war. They were to liberate the Chinese from the oppression of their own kind. Why then was the killing of innocent peasants actively encouraged? It appeared they had been sent to terrorize rather than to liberate. If liberation was the quest why did they not enter undefended villages peaceably, why was their presence not greeted by cheers?

Now, he recalled again the anti-war graffiti he had seen scratched on the walls of station toilets or factories when he had been released from military hospital in Tokyo. He remembered one statement.

Even if we fight China, it is certain we shall lose because Russia is behind China. In Russia if a worker dies his funeral is paid for by the State, but our Japanese government will not do such a thing. In times of war we poor people become depressed and cannot make a living. The government should stop this war. I am against the war because it kills people.

They seemed to him now like the true feelings of the nation, scratched out with a nail in the dark when no one was looking. Even the military hospitals now gave only cursory treatment and returned men to the front before complete recovery. More and more men were shipped to hospitals in Korea or Taiwan so that in Japan the real number of casualties would not be known. There were even reports that some hospitals were free of badly wounded men, fanning rumours that such patients were done away with. Kill or be killed. There seemed no choice now. All Akira could remember was the eyes of the boy who looked like Jiro.

179

11

December 1937

The Panay Incident

The weather had brightened. Donald Addison stood on the deck of the gunboat, his face to the December wind. The Yangtze was broad about the *Panay*, anchored near the Nanking Bund. In places the sun reflected opulently, then grew sombre under clouds. He imagined the river stretching across great swathes of China, goring through rock, spilling over plains, unifying the immeasurable. Day and night, life and death, good and evil were as nothing to the pulse of the river, constantly forming itself anew. A kestrel wheeled overhead. He followed its flight, high above the sudden burst of flame from inside the walls of Nanking. Soon, another orange flowering exploded in the town. Already, the first Japanese detachment had entered Nanking, breaking through the Kunghwa Gate. He returned his eyes to the kestrel high above the placid water. River or bird, they were without boundaries. His vision drew back from the arch of the sky to his feet on the deck of the boat. In the distance was the crack of guns. He seemed forever trapped within himself.

The *Panay's* engine purred, then cut out. The silence was sudden about him. He listened to the lapping of the river against the bow. The American gunboat stood by on the Yangtze maintaining communications with the outside world, ready to take on any expatriates still in Nanking. The boat was to anchor in midstream until the battle was over. The remaining staff at the American Embassy slept on board and returned to the town by day. Foreign correspondents crowded the ship, converting the sick-bay into a newsroom. In Nanking the only foreigners who remained were four reporters and the twenty-three men and women who had opted to organize the Safety Zone. At the urging of the Japanese almost all other foreign nationals had fled. That day the last city gate had been closed, and the foreigners left in Nanking had forfeited their right to board the gunboat. Soon the Japanese would launch the last onslaught.

'Come for a beer, Addison,' Marco Mariani, a cameraman with

Movietone News, shouted as he came along the deck. Donald shook his head.

'No good, all this thinking,' Mariani scolded. His short plump shape rolled with the rhythm of the ship. A cigar hung from the corner of his mouth. He stood at the rail beside Donald.

Some days before Mariani had borrowed a car on Movietone's account, and with Donald drove out of Nanking into the battling countryside. Mariani had a name for catching on film the rawest moments in the rawest manner. There was no war he had not covered. He approached death with blatant objectivity. Donald admired the coolness of the Italian who drove as if on a Sunday outing through the embattled countryside. He stopped once to film a cart of charred corpses, pushing away sobbing relatives to better record the grimace of death, his camera cranking noisily on a tripod.

Every mile along the roads they had seen barricades ready. Trees and bamboo were felled to a knife-sharp stubble, to hinder the approaching Japanese. There was the permanent odour of smoke on the wind. From a hillock they had looked down upon roads thick with people trudging inland. Across the burned winter countryside the lines of refugees appeared in the distance like long, grey caterpillars creeping slowly forward. The whole country seemed on the move.

Nearer Nanking fires raged everywhere, set by the Chinese to clear all cover for the invading army. There was something medieval about these open field engagements in sight of walled towns. Sixteen miles from Nanking they drove into a village where the remnants of a Chinese division were billeted. The Captain offered to show them the front.

Skirting a hill, they came into full view of the battle lines. Chinese and Japanese emptied their guns at each other across a narrow valley. The horizon was rimmed with smoke. In the distance dark clouds billowed from the blazing ruins of a town taken by the Japanese.

'We're fighting a losing battle,' said the Captain. 'All we can do is make the Japanese advance costly and slow. Already, they have taken Purple Mountain which commands all land and river approaches.'

'Without planes for aerial reconnaissance you'll always be outflanked,' said Mariani, using his usual provocative approach, puffing on his eternal cigar. 'Why you don't give up? Maybe a Japanese government is good for China.'

'We will never give up,' replied the Captain.

As the Chinese spoke, a Japanese plane droned above. They ducked for cover as machine-gun fire splattered about them. Only Mariani stood erect by a bush and set his camera whirring. Several of the Captain's men were wounded. Mariani took more photographs.

Back in Nanking Donald sent a long cable to *The Times* and left again. Within the city it was impossible to gauge the daily rhythm of battle. There was just the mounting tension, the rain of bombs and preparations for weathering the assault. The ragged remnants of the Chinese Army, retreating across the countryside before the Japanese, were left to fight as best they could. The city was swollen with refugees, renewing provisions or seeking rest before continuing inland. Like other journalists, Donald made the *Panay* his base, its neutrality an island in the war.

The smell of the river filled Donald's head. A sudden memory of the Lotus Lake and that first evening with Nadya filled his mind. An image of her, naked, cross-legged on the bed, pushed itself before him. To thrust the picture away, he held his camera close, concentrating on the lens. The oily surface of the water, a clump of rushes and some water fowl were suddenly framed before him. Half-hidden by the reeds a body lay face down in the mud. Beside him Mariani squinted at the shoreline. The odour of cigars lifted comfortingly off him.

'Do not waste film, Addison,' Mariani advised. 'In a war bodies must come in excessive quantity or bear some horrible scar to qualify for our cameras. This one, sodden, submerged corpse, what can it mean for the newspaper? Nothing. Death itself no longer shocks us now. Everything becomes normal when we see enough. This is a terrible fact, but it is true. Our compassion becomes fatigued. Now, I look only for the best corpses. Of course, before this war is finished, I may become one also. Now how about that beer?'

The Italian was insistent. Donald explained the need to type up a cable to London and Mariani ambled off at last, trailing the scent of cigars. The smoke of bombing still ringed the horizon like a smudged pencil line. What Mariani said was true. Now Donald must remind himself that, behind each plume of smoke, lay death.

The engine purred suddenly, vibrating beneath Donald's feet. There were shouts as the anchor was hauled up with a cranking of chains. Soon, the boat began to move. Donald swore out loud. That morning shrapnel had showered the *Panay*. A decision had been made to sail up river and wait out the fall of the city in safe water near Wuhu. He had intended to report the taking of Nanking from the Japanese perspective, entering with the main troops. To be so far from action at a vital moment was not part of his plan, but he was already aboard the *Panay* when the decision to move was made. Perhaps, later, he could get ashore and make his way back to Nanking. In this last effort to breach the walls, the shell fire was intense. By the afternoon Nanking was expected to be in Japanese hands.

The boat slowed again and stopped in midstream. He stared down into the water. The dark forms of fish swarmed beneath the surface. Below them was the blackness of a hidden world. That world bore no relation to the reflective surface of the river stretching into the distance, golden with the morning sun.

The *Panay* made noises of movement again. The dark brood of fish, disturbed by the sudden kick of the engine, dispersed. He saw then that they fed upon the dismembered torso of a woman. Without the weight of the fish upon it, the lump of flesh rose slowly towards him. Before it could break the surface the fish returned, dragging it back into the gloom, covering it with their bodies. He shivered. Instead of a shining reflective path he saw an image of the river dried, its muddy bed cracked into patches, its hidden booty exposed. Amongst old pots, kerosene tins and broken chinaware, were the bloated remains of death. All the killing of the past months had been emptied into the Yangtze. He wondered how the river still flowed, clogged as it was with such debris. At night he imagined it released the anguish of those murdered spirits. He was not a religious man, and vowed his disbelief repeatedly. Now, he grew afraid of his thoughts.

As the *Panay* began to move again, the fish were left behind. He drew back from the rail and made no further attempt mentally to plumb the river's depths. The shelling from the shore was reckless. In spite of immunity under the American flag, painted on its bows and deck, the *Panay* could be caught in cross fire.

Donald made his way to the upper deck to type up his report in the temporary newsroom. A tier of iron bunks and shelves of medicine bottles still confirmed the room's original use. A couple of desks and typewriters had been squeezed into the cramped space. There was already a queue for the typewriters. Donald sat down on a bunk and took out a pencil and small pad and scribbled the beginning of a cable for *The Times*.

The first Japanese detachment to enter Nanking broke through the Kunghwa Gate shortly before 5 o'clock yesterday afternoon. Stubborn resistance was met inside Nanking. Field radio reports from Japanese headquarters outside Nanking at 9 a.m. this morning reported that during the night the Chinese launched two violent counter-attacks against the Japanese at Kunghwa Gate. Both attacks were repulsed but the Japanese suffered serious losses. They charge the Chinese made profuse use of gas shells.

Eventually, a machine was free, and Donald sat down to type. At last the *Panay* had reached a quieter stretch of the Yangtze and dropped anchor.

Nearby were two vessels of the Standard Oil and Asiatic Petroleum, which had been fitted out as temporary floating hotels to accommodate four hundred Chinese and a number of foreigners, including several diplomats. All wished, like those aboard the *Panay*, to return to Nanking as soon as was safe. Nobody visualized more than a few days of inconvenience, until the city was in Japanese hands and order restored. The Standard Oil vessels hooted a welcome to the *Panay*.

The drone of approaching planes streamed over the clank of typewriters and passed. Donald looked up, but could see nothing from the porthole. Harvey Quest of the *Herald Tribune* met his eye. Donald watched him turn back to the typewriter and pause for thought before a last word. The noise of planes returned, flying low above the *Panay*. As Harvey pulled his sheet from the typewriter, an explosion burst through the boat. The *Panay* rocked violently. Water slapped the portholes of the sick-bay, men were thrown from their chairs. A sharp pain stabbed Donald's ears. He hung onto the frame of the bunk beds. Then, steadying himself, he rushed upstairs.

Johnson of the American Embassy was already on deck with his binoculars. He thrust them into Donald's face. The boat still rocked sickeningly. 'Tell me I'm not dreaming. Tell me those are not Japanese planes,' Johnson yelled.

Donald raised the glasses to the red circles on the departing aircraft. 'How can they hit us? The American flag is plastered all over us.'

'You tell me,' said Johnson. 'They're coming back for more. Get down.'

The boat shuddered from a new blast. Water showered the deck, drenching them. Donald stumbled awkwardly along the wet and listing deck back towards the sick-bay. As he reached the room another explosion rocked the boat, igniting the pain in his ears. The vessel heaved about alarmingly. He had a vision of it keeling over, trapping them beneath it. There was the sound of breaking glass and the bunks came down on top of him, pinning him to the ground. Everything went black.

When he opened his eyes the sound of planes was still overhead. Broken woodwork and smashed glass littered the floor. Harvey Quest lay in a pool of blood. Donald listened to the spit of machine gun bullets still hitting the hull of the ship. The iron wall of the room was ripped open by shrapnel. A pale finger of sky appeared in the rent. Someone bent over Harvey. Donald struggled clear of the bunks. He had seen enough bodies, he knew Harvey was dead. There was nothing he could do.

He ran back towards the companionway. The metallic rain of bullets continued to pound the ship. He looked up at the narrow stairway to the upper deck, and saw the machine guns of the *Panay*, manned by sailors stripped to the waist, stuttering with fire. The boatswain's mate, caught in the bath, naked but for a towel, operated one of the guns himself. Another explosion threw Donald half-way down the stairs. He burst into the petty officers' mess and found it full of crouching people. A man groaned in the rear. He saw it was Marco Mariani.

'I'm hit. I'm dying.' He clutched at Donald's shirt. 'Help me Addison. Find doctor, find priest.' Mariani bent double in agony, blood spilt from his waist over his knees.

'Where's the doctor?' yelled Donald.

'Try the engine room,' somebody shouted.

He groped his way down corridors and stairs. The boat listed badly, making speed impossible. He wondered how long they had before it began to sink. At last he found the room, deep in the belly of the boat, reeking of oil and blood. There was only the light from a small generator. The wounded were laid out on the metal gratings, the rattle of guns was far away. The groaning of men, limbs mangled by bullets and shrapnel, sounded like a pack of muzzled animals in the airless iron room. The doctor came with him to Mariani.

'This is crazy. We're American. We're not supposed to be hit. What are the devils playing at now? I'm not equipped for this kind of emergency,' Dr Grazier exploded.

'His stomach is full of bullets,' he said after a glance at Mariani.

'I'll get him down to the engine room. Do something,' Donald insisted. The doctor pursed his lips and shook his head.

'Leave him here, I'll give him some morphine. I've still a drop left. Lieutenant Anders has been hit in the throat, but he is still in charge of his vessel. Soon we'll have to abandon ship.' He administered the morphine to Mariani and hurried to the upper deck and Anders.

Donald crouched beside Mariani and saw the pain ease in his face as the morphine took effect. Mariani reached out and gripped Donald's shirt, pulling him close. His voice was hoarse.

'Addison, in these moments I have been thinking. I understand God is not pleased with me, in spite of my going so regularly to mass. Very rarely I miss it, you know. This has happened to me because I no longer take notice of death. I am so fed up with corpses I no longer see them even as human, with life once, and love and family. Only they are corpses for me to photograph, to make me famous Italian war correspondent. They must be burnt black, like chicken you roast for too long, or perhaps without head to qualify for my camera. I feel nothing any more. This is God's punishment to me. Now, I am dying and I tell you, that corpse you looked at with your camera, that one I told you to ignore, he *is* important. He is like me, one small man with life and feelings. I do not want to die.'

'Shut up Marco. You're not going to die.' Donald did not like the dried up smell of Mariani's breath or the way he hung on to his shirt. A putrid odour filled his nostrils. His own throat had constricted with terror. Perhaps he too would be in Mariani's state before the day was finished. Already, his shirt was red with Mariani's blood.

'We're sinking, Addison. We'll all go down with this boat, you know,' Mariani screamed suddenly.

'Listen, I'm going to get a pillow, to make you more comfortable.' Donald stood up.

'Get me priest, not pillows,' Mariani sobbed. The boat gave a sudden lurch and listed further starboard.

'We've no chaplain or priest aboard,' said the doctor when Donald found him, kneeling beside Lieutenant Anders.

A bloody bandage was wound about Anders' throat. He was writing messages on a pad of paper, which were then chalked up upon the white paint of the Bridge. The sky was clear above the *Panay*, the planes had disappeared. 'They'll be back,' said the doctor, following Anders' gaze. 'They've not finished with us yet. Nobody knows what the buggers are playing at.'

Leave the ship. Send the boats back. Stay near the shore. Word by word the new message was chalked up. Lieutenant Anders grimaced above his bandage. In the distance the drone of planes returned.

'You're unhurt. Help get the wounded to shore,' the doctor ordered Donald.

The grey surface of the river stretched out, the sun picking up each ripple. It was roughly a quarter of a mile to shore, Donald gauged. How would they make it to safety before the planes returned or the *Panay* was sucked below? Panic gripped him.

He went down to the engine room. Every few moments the ship groaned and shifted beneath his feet, tilting further. Manoeuvring up and down the narrow stairs beneath the weight of wounded men, was not easy. Donald was thrown against walls. The men howled in pain and cursed. Most of the lights had gone and he groped his way in semi-darkness. In spite of the cold he was sweating. His clothes were now sodden with the blood of the wounded. A sour metallic smell rose off him and made him want to vomit.

At last all the wounded were brought up from the engine room. The worst cases were carried on makeshift blanket stretchers and lowered into the lifeboats like rolled-up carpets. Donald knelt by Mariani, who

186

had also now been brought up on the deck. In the distance Donald could make out a desolate stretch of muddy shore up which the wounded were being hauled to safety. Mariani had not gone ashore in the earlier boats. His entrails spilled over his trousers, gleaming like offal in a butcher's shop. He waited for the doctor to bind up his wound, securing his insides under a corset of lint.

'Don't leave me Addison,' Mariani whispered as he was lowered into the last boat. Donald embarked beside him.

At water level their vulnerability was overwhelming. The small boat was overloaded with men, the water inches from the top of the craft. The river was icy. The shadow of the boat hung beneath them, dark and still. A water bird screeched. There was no sign of habitation along the frozen river bank. Mariani groaned again as more men jumped down into the boat, rocking it precariously.

'We'll sink,' Donald called out in panic. He tried to stand up. The wind blew his words away behind him. Someone pulled him down. Then, suddenly, they were moving.

The oars cut through the water with quick swishing sounds. Waves slapped the sides of the boat, splashing upon him. It seemed they must sink, so low were they in the river. Donald squinted up at the sky. He felt like a duck stalked by the gun of a hunter. If he survived he would never again shoot a water bird.

'I promise. Dear God, I promise. Only let us get to safety.' Donald mumbled the words aloud.

'What you are promising, Addison? You think God is listening to you in these circumstances? If you die there is no time to keep your promise, and if you live you will anyway not keep it. Even though I have been a good Catholic all my life, I am now seriously wondering about God for the first time in my life. There are terrible thoughts in my mind. Perhaps there is nothing there.' Mariani leaned heavily against him. Far away the black dots of planes became visible again against the clouds.

The roar of aircraft burst above them in a sudden crescendo. The planes dipped, speeding towards them. Donald could see the rivets on their undersides. They swooped down above the tiny lifeboats. In a cockpit Donald glimpsed the small goggled head of a pilot. Bewilderment and anger surged through him. He had seen a human face. Suddenly, everything took on a new meaning.

'Why are you doing this.' He yelled at the departing plane, shaking a fist in the air. The surprise of that one small face overwhelmed him.

Bullets hit the water, spitting like stones across the surface. Men shielded their heads with their arms. The boat rocked violently. A bullet thudded against the far side of the boat, passed an inch from Donald's knees and lodged itself in the wood beside him. Water now spurted into the boat through numerous holes.

The planes returned yet again, diving low. Their shadows winged over the water, like savage, prehistoric birds. Mariani moaned. Donald hid his head beneath his arms as the next hail of bullets began. He muttered the prayer his mother had made him say each night as a child, kneeling at his bed. His lips formed rustily about the words. Once more the planes lifted and were gone. The lap of water about the bows filled the sudden silence. He raised his head and felt the adrenaline burst in his chest. Looking up he saw the sky was clear. *He was not dead.*

Somebody handed him a tin hat and he began to bale water that was seeping quickly into the boat through bullet holes. After a moment he stopped to prise out a bullet from where it was lodged in the side of the boat. He tested its weight, observing the gleam of metal as it lay in the palm of his hand. Then he closed his fist about it, and slipped it in his pocket. The oarsmen began to row again. Slowly, the grey line of the shore came closer. At last there was a shudder as the boat hit ground. Before them was a forest of impenetrable-looking reeds.

Several men had been hit in the attack, including the *Panay's* storekeeper, who lay dead in the bow of the lifeboat. Donald took hold of Mariani, half-carrying him over his shoulder, and staggered towards the bank. Thick, icy mud sucked at his feet, pulling him down. If he stayed more than a moment in each spot he knew he would sink to his knees in the stuff. The weight of Mariani and the gluey mud made negotiations difficult. He pulled each foot free with difficulty, then stumbled suddenly. Mariani pitched out of his arms with a scream of agony.

Far away was the hum of planes once more. Panic gripped him and he began to mutter old prayers again. He reached Mariani and took hold of the Italian, dragging him forward by the armpits. At last the tall rushes surrounded them. Donald could see between the high, dense mass of stalks the crouching shapes of those who had landed before them. The noise of the planes grew louder. He wriggled further into the reeds, pulling Mariani with him. Mud now covered him in an icy poultice. A late afternoon sun spiked between the reeds. Mariani appeared unconscious.

Donald stared up, as if through a thick green grille, hardly breathing. Once more the planes would dive down, and bullets strike him at last. Suddenly he felt calmer. Either he would die, or he would not. He prayed only to die outright, not to be ripped apart like Mariani. That seemed all that mattered now, quick death. He was to go with a bullet, like his father, like Smollett, he realized. Was this retribution? He looked up at the sky and swore, whether at God or at the planes, he was no longer sure.

The aircraft still circled overhead, wings agleam in a shaft of sun, like the fins of sharks. Their shadow passed over the reed beds. He ducked down beside Mariani, waiting. The drone of the engines grew louder, then retreated into the distance. Donald sat up in surprise.

Instead of swooping low, the planes sped on across the river towards the oil vessels, anchored near the opposite shore. A shower of black pellets detached themselves from the aircraft and hurtled downwards. The boats burst suddenly into flame with a massive explosion. The vibration of the blast shook the reed beds. High above, the planes jumped away from the wall of flame spurting up uncontrollably. A thick black bellow of smoke curled into the sky.

In midstream the *Panay* now lay at an odd angle, the American flag still flying from the after mast. A chugging sound carried over the water. Donald saw a Japanese military craft heading for the *Panay*. It threw out a volley of warning shots as it approached the gunboat. Japanese soldiers boarded the *Panay* and in a few moments, finding it deserted and near its end, returned to their own craft and quickly steamed away. Almost immediately, the *Panay* turned on her side and vanished beneath the water. She went under with a great sucking sound, like water down a drain. Suddenly, there was silence.

When it was clear the attack was over, Donald stood up. The reeds closed above his head. His knees hurt and he realized now the blood on his leg was not Mariani's but a scratch from a bullet that had entered the lifeboat. In the mud, at his feet, Mariani groaned. Donald could hear shouts ahead, but the tall mass of rushes hampered his view. He took hold of Mariani again and staggered forward in the direction of these sounds. The reeds were rough and cut his arms and face. Eventually, Donald stumbled onto a dry patch of land in the midst of the reed bed jungle. The first man he saw was Dr Grazier, who came forward to help with Mariani.

Most of the survivors were already assembled in the clearing. Flames from the Standard Oil vessels lit the growing darkness. A derelict motor launch, abandoned by its Chinese crew, had been found. It was decided the worst of the wounded should be placed aboard and floated down river. The *Panay's* crew knew of a hamlet some distance along the shore. Five more miles inland lay the walled town of Hohsien.

'The Magistrate there should know we are coming,' Dr Grazier informed Donald, bending over Mariani. 'Johnson of the American Embassy has already gone on ahead to warn them. If the town has not already been attacked by the Japanese, we can get news to the world of what has happened. Hohsien has a hospital.'

The sky was aflame with the light of the blazing ships on the further shore. Occasionally, a new explosion roared out of the bowels of the oil vessels, sending up fresh sheets of flame. Fragments of hot metal dropped out of the sky, hissing and smoking in the icy water. Evening was setting in and the December cold, lifting off the river, froze the thick skin of mud that caked them all. The motor launch now holding the worst casualties from the *Panay*, was silently tracked down river until the hamlet was reached. The village was no more than a few mud-walled houses and a well. The ragged population ran out to meet them, their broad anxious faces lit by the flares they carried. Stretchers were improvised for the worst of the wounded from the doors of pig pens, and coolies engaged for the long walk to Hohsien.

Mariani was by now delirious. The morphine had worn off and no more was to be had. Donald walked beside the makeshift stretcher carried by two emaciated Chinese. A blanket had been found to wrap about the Italian, who shivered violently. The trek to Hohsien was along the banks of a creek. Frost covered the short grass and crunched underfoot. The pain in his leg from the bullet scratch now caused Donald to limp. The sky hung above, secret, black and cavernous. Stars sparked like flints in its frozen depth. The Standard Oil's inferno still lit the night for miles behind them in a ruddy artificial sunset. Once, an alarm was raised as two junks were sighted and everyone climbed down into the safety of the reeds again. Crouched in a tight ball, knees beneath his chin, it seemed suddenly to Donald that this position, taken so instinctively, was not only that of pre-birth but also of primitive burials. He stared up again into the impenetrable night. Mariani continued to jabber incoherently, tossing beneath his blanket on the strip of wood.

'Addison,' he whispered, trying unexpectedly to sit up. Donald put a hand on his arm.

'Lie down. I'm here,' he said.

'I feel my skin has scales all over, like an alligator or a snake.' His voice was suddenly strangely clear, as if more morphine had been administered.

'It is the mud. We're all covered in it,' Donald replied.

'I feel also a grime on my inside,' Mariani whispered.

'You're wounded, you've a fever. Tomorrow you'll feel better, after we get to Hohsien. There is a hospital there,' Donald reassured. Mariani shook his head.

'It is this war, all this horror and killing, these bands of men trained to

190

exterminate each other. It is this talk about *the enemy*, as if they were a species different from ourselves. Men are persuaded so easily to act against their better selves. It is like training rats in a laboratory.'

'It is the mud,' Donald repeated, unwilling to hear more.

Mariani shook his head. 'I see it as the Devil. Yesterday I did not believe in such nonsense, but now I see the Devil everywhere. I close my eyes and I see monsters. They rise up before me and fill the sky. I assure you, I would prefer instead to see God at this time, but he refuses to come near me. I cannot blame him.'

'You are hallucinating,' Donald replied. Mariani's delirium seemed to rise again. He began to pant, pushing words through his lips with difficulty.

'Evil contaminates, creeps into us unawares, cell by cell, getting us used to its inhumanities, until we are caught and can look the monstrous in the face. Until, like myself, I can turn my camera upon anything without discomfort. Until I can be selective about my corpses, demanding evidence of unusual gore or torture before I waste my film upon it. All this is not to shock the world, to warn it of man's capacity for barbarity. If this was so then I might be forgiven. It is the seeking merely of perfection in my work. All my life with my camera I have trailed death. If there is no war, then death by violence or the bizarre; New York murders, Mafioso killings. Mariani, he is always the first to be there. Now, sometimes, the Mafioso, they call me. They tell me where to find some new, important body. They want me to be the one to photograph it. They know I am the best. And I am proud of this morbid reputation. I see all this too late.'

'You are talking nonsense. Don't exhaust yourself like this.' Donald patted Mariani's arm.

'But I may not have much time. Maybe this next minute, I close my eyes and *pwuff*, I am dead. And I understand as yet nothing of my life. It now looks like a piece of knitting unravelling before me. All this pride in my work I now know is only a way for the evil trapped in me to find its way out. The worst thing about the Devil is that he seems so ordinary, so plausible a fellow. His schemes and reasoning are so persuasive. He makes upright men seem like liars.'

'We all have a stage manager hidden within us, policing our actions, pulling our strings until we dance like marionettes,' Donald gave a short laugh.

'We live with illusion, deluding ourselves about who we are or what we are. I am no better than those Japanese out there who kill and bayonet. And as they kill what do you think they feel? Why, only that they are doing a good day's work for their Emperor. Are they not deluded creatures? I thought I was a passive observer, recording for the world. I too am deluded. Why do I choose to observe only atrocity and death?' Mariani grabbed Donald's sleeve and held it fast, an expression of terror on his face.

Donald searched for words to reassure the Italian. 'When I was a child I used to wait for those moments I could see my shadow following me in the sun. When I couldn't see it, I imagined it tucked away inside me, a twin self into which was stuffed all the dark emotions I could never show the world; my hate for my father and every other despicable thought. That way I could show a clean face to the world, free of my real feelings. Sometimes, I would think of killing my father, and it was always my shadow that did the deed. I used to feel sorry for my shadow, weighed down with all these heavy feelings. I wished I could let it out more often into the sun. I felt the more it could show itself the lighter its burden might become; the less it would have to hide. I remember running outside whenever I saw the sun, to let the poor thing out of myself.' Donald laughed. Until now he had forgotten that childhood relationship with his shadow. He saw it suddenly in a new perspective.

Mariani gritted his teeth and groaned. 'Just hang on,' Donald urged. 'I can see Hohsien ahead.' Lights flickered in the distance.

The Italian shook his head. 'If I had the time, all my photographs now would be for a new purpose. I am famous only as a sensationalist, a corpse eater. Maybe I could change this, but now it is too late.'

'Stop talking,' Donald ordered. Mariani lay back with a sob.

'See, the gates of the town are opening for us. They'll patch you up as good as new.' Donald looked down at Mariani's ashen face.

Hohsien had been attacked three times by Japanese bombers. The remains of the hospital were perched on a hill, the debris of bombing raids littering its interior. Its doctors had fled to cramped but safer premises. The wounded were now carried to the hospital's ruined rooms. Dr Grazier inspected the battered operating theatre and found it usable. Soon medicines and instruments were brought up from the town.

'I can't promise a thing,' Dr Grazier said, looking down at Mariani. His voice was grim with exhaustion. He had operated without a break for several hours. Already the dawn was breaking. Mariani had lain semi-conscious from the time they entered Hohsien, his breath faint.

'Go back into town. Get some rest, I'll do what I can for him here,' the doctor advised. Donald shook his head and sat down on the floor outside the operating theatre.

The door had been blasted out in an air-raid, a sheet hung across the entrance. Below it Donald could see Dr Grazier's legs and those of the nurses he had found in the town, clustered about the operating table. He heard the clink of instruments, and wondered at Dr Grazier's methods of sterilization in these primitive conditions. A ripe smell of putrefaction overcame him. The world seemed steeped in this smell. The need to shut his eyes seemed to obliterate every other sensation. He lay down against the wall, pillowing his head on an arm. Dried mud from his shoes crumbled about his feet and had left a filthy trail behind him down the corridor. Perhaps the trail of his own life, like that of a slug, might appear like this to whatever God looked down upon them.

He awoke to the blood-splattered front of the doctor. He wondered first if the blood was Mariani's or the wounded man's before him, or a mixture of everyone's pain. The doctor shook his head. 'He went before I finished. There was nothing we could do.'

Donald nodded and with an effort stood up. He walked back down the corridor, kicking aside the fragments of mud that had earlier fallen from his caked feet. Outside, he sat on the steps and watched the winter morning creep over the battered, sleeping town and thought about Mariani. It was strange to feel tied to a man he barely knew. This time the day before, Mariani was still snapping corpses. *Come for a beer. Why do you spend so much time at the rail?* He heard the Italian's voice again, urging him out of reverie. *Before this war is finished, I may also die.* Mariani had chuckled, not expecting the event so immediately. Who could say what was ahead or how soon? The unfinished quality of Mariani's going was what disturbed Donald most. Old men had had their chances, and seemed less deserving of sympathy at death than Mariani in the prime of life.

The sun rose slowly, staining the sky with pink light. In the distance the Yangtze was caught by the day. He saw then that the pink glow in the sky came not from the dawn but from the remains of the Standard Oil vessels, smouldering still at their moorings. The horror of the night came upon him again. Why was he whole and Mariani dead? Had fate kept him for a worse ordeal? He thought again of the strange conversation with the dying man. Below, in the town, he watched a child lead a water buffalo to a pond. A man collected barrels of night soil placed outside each house. Each did what they had always done to tranquillize the terror.

Donald stood up. The steps fell away before him. A bush of winter jasmine cascaded over a wall, the wind blowing petals onto the huddled roofs below. The yellow tiles of a temple gleamed in the morning. He thought again of the conversation with Mariani and of that childhood relationship with his shadow. He knew nothing of that sad, angry man he kept hidden in himself. Yet, the words spoken the night before, coming from he knew not where, had given it life once more. It swelled within him again. He could not die like Mariani, before his time, knowing nothing of this other man.

Hohsien was not safe. The *Panay* survivors voted to push on inland, carrying their wounded with them once more. They would journey in open junks twenty miles along canals to Hanshan, outside the area of hostilities. From there they might get to Shanghai.

The decision came to Donald suddenly. He must return to Nanking, into the face of aggression, into the evil itself. A certainty filled him. Beyond the darkness, if only he could stay the path, might lie wholeness of some unknown kind.

He made his way down the steps, pitted by blasts and gunfire. Slowly the town rose up about him, its pathetic reality forcing away the brave abstract thought that came upon mountain tops. Fear grew in him again.

12

December 1937

The Rape Begins

International Committee for the Nanking Safety Zone
5 Ninghai Road
Nanking

14th December 1937

Mr Kenjiro Nozaki
Cultural Attaché to the Japanese Embassy
Nanking

Dear Sir

We petition you in the name of humanity that the following steps be taken for the welfare of 200,000 civilians in Nanking.

1. That the burning of large sections of the city be stopped and what remains of the city be spared from either reckless or systematic burning.

2. That the disorderly conduct of Japanese troops in the city, that has caused so much suffering to the civilian population, be stopped immediately.

3. In view of the fact that the looting and burning have brought the business life of the city to a standstill and consequently reduced the whole civilian population to one vast refugee camp, and in view of the fact that the International Committee of the Safety Zone do not have unlimited supplies of food to feed these 200,000 people, we most earnestly beg you to take immediate steps to restore normal conditions to civilian life in order that the fuel and food supply of the city may be replenished.

We plead for the bare essentials of normal life: housing, security, food.

Most respectfully submitted

The International Committee for Nanking Safety Zone.

International Committee for the Nanking Safety Zone
5 Ninghai Road
Nanking

17th December 1937

Mr Kenjiro Nozaki
Cultural Attaché to the Japanese Embassy
Nanking

Dear Sir

We are sorry to trouble you again but the sufferings and needs of the 200,000 civilians, for whom we are trying to care, make it urgent that we try to secure action from your military authorities to stop the present disorder of Japanese soldiers wandering through the Safety Zone.

There is no space here to go into the cases that are pouring in faster than we can type them out. But last night Mr Norris of our Committee went to the University of Nanking dormitories to sleep, in order to protect the one thousand women who fled there yesterday because of attacks in their homes. He found none of your gendarmerie on guard there as requested, for the protection of the women in our Zone from your soldiers.

At 8 p.m. Mr Strang and Mr Reeves took Rev. Moeran to Ginling Women's College, next to your Embassy, to sleep in a house near the gate, as one of us men has been doing each night, in order to protect the three thousand women and children who are there in one of the buildings. They were roughly seized by a searching squad of soldiers and detained for over an hour. Miss Nadya Komosky and Dr Janet Allen who were in charge of Ginling College, were lined up at the gate and kept there in the cold and roughly pushed about. The officer insisted there were Chinese soldiers in the compound and he wanted to find them and shoot them. Finally we were allowed to go home, but Rev. Moeran was not allowed to stay, so we do not know what exactly happened after we left. We heard only that there were many vicious rapes by gangs of your soldiers, and many more women were taken away.

With the panic that has been created amongst the women, from terrorization and rape by your soldiers, growing numbers are flocking to our camps, leaving more and more men alone. The public institutional buildings that originally were listed to accommodate 35,000 must now accommodate 50,000. Already two more public buildings, the Ministry of Justice and the Supreme Court, have been emptied of men to

196

accommodate the growing number of terrified women. Each night brings more and more to us.

If the panic continues not only will our housing problem become more serious but also the food problem, and the question of finding workers will also increase. This morning one of your Embassy Staff, Mr Fukutake was at our office asking for Chinese workers for the electric light plant. We had to reply that we could not even get our own workers out to do anything. We are only able to keep rice and coal supplied to the large concentrations of people by Western members of our Committee and staff driving trucks of rice and coal. Our Chinese food Commissioner has not dared leave his house for two days. The second Chinese man in our Housing Commission had to see two women of his family raped last night at supper time by Japanese soldiers. Our Associate Food Commissioner, Mr Havers (a Theological Professor) has had to convey trucks with rice, and leave the 2,500 families in his Nanking Theological Seminary to look out for themselves. Yesterday in broad daylight, several women at the Seminary were raped shamelessly and publicly by your soldiers in the middle of a large room filled by men, women and children.

We twenty-three Westerners cannot feed 200,000 Chinese civilians and protect them day and night. That is the duty of the Japanese authorities. If you can give them protection, we can help feed them.

In the name of humanity we once more request you to please take steps to return Nanking to an orderly way of life. We assure you of our willingness to co-operate in every way for the welfare of the innocent civilians of the city.

Most respectfully submitted

The International Committee for Nanking Safety Zone.

Kenjiro put down the letters, then reached across and placed them on top of a tray containing a further pile of such missives. Every day they came in from the Committee for the Safety Zone, hand-delivered by one or sometimes a delegation of the Westerners. He stared out of the window of his office. Ginling Women's College was next door to the Embassy. Kenjiro had heard the screams of women the night before and gone himself, unable to bear it. Soldiers had surrounded the gate. They refused to let him through. He had returned to his office and Fukutake, who was also still in the building. They walked back together to the college. The hysteria inside was clearly audible. Once more the soldiers had refused to let them through, in spite of Fukutake's threats. They had laughed in his face, liquor upon their breath.

'We have no influence upon them at all,' Kenjiro said. 'We can do nothing.' Distress filled his voice.

'It is not our business,' Fukutake replied grimly. 'It does not do to forget we are civilians. We too are under command of the Military. The whole thing is sickening and shameful. If we make too much fuss, you know what our fate will be. The *Kempeitiai* are already thick on the ground here. General Nakajima himself is in command in Nanking.'

Kenjiro was sure Fukutake, like himself, could not have slept that night. He tossed and turned and in the end got up as the first light broke, and drank some brandy that he kept in reserve at the back of his cupboard.

The Embassy had already protested to the military high command at the behaviour of these soldiers. In the wake of the troops had come Japanese officials, including the diplomat, Counsellor Shunrokuro Hidaka, who had been aghast at what he saw. Kenjiro had gone in a delegation with Hidaka, to protest to General Matsui. Hidaka asked if the troops had not heard the orders of their superiors. Matsui had only muttered that it seemed the superiors themselves were to blame. Hidaka had also visited Prince Asaka to express his horror at the state of things. Little had come of the visit. Back at the Embassy Hidaka had fumed.

'Nothing of what is happening in Nanking may ever come to light in the Japanese press, but you can be sure the world press will spread it over every newspaper page. With all these foreigners here, how can it be otherwise? The situation is intolerable. It is a disgrace to the name of Japan. How has any of this been allowed to happen?' His disgust was palpable.

Hidaka had written a detailed report, and cabled it back to the Foreign Ministry in Tokyo. A copy was also sent to the War Minister. Tension pervaded the Embassy. If someone of the stature of Counsellor Hidaka had failed to halt the war of punishment, their helplessness was assured.

'My report will cause some uproar in Tokyo, of that you can be assured,' Hidaka predicted as he left.

The sky was blue behind the vermilion Bell Tower, but about its sweeping roof the city lay in rubble. Through the months of air raids life had been a continual race from desk to dugout and back again. At the end, exhausted and fatalistic, most people had no longer heeded the planes, but sat stoically at their desks. All that was now stopped. Japanese troops had poured into the city with tanks, artillery, infantry and trucks. The population of Nanking had hesitantly welcomed the troops, sure peace would at last prevail with the occupation. Instead, it seemed they had entered hell. Kenjiro stared at the curling eaves of the Bell Tower. His head ached. Chaos instead of order, terror instead of calm was all the army had brought so far. A clerk entered to announce Mr Strang of the Safety Zone Committee. Kenjiro waited for Mr Strang and more letters of complaint.

'Let us hope it does not snow.' Kenjiro shook Mr Strang's hand.

'Too many already endure deprivation without deteriorating weather,' Mr Strang agreed. 'How long will this go on?'

As long as thought necessary, Kenjiro answered silently. He was under no delusion about the Military; 20,000 more troops were due to stream into Nanking.

'Things will be better soon, I hope,' he replied aloud.

'A few days of chaos were expected while Chinese forces withdrew and you Japanese began the occupation. After this we hoped normality would be restored and the refugees could return to their homes. The disorder has got to stop. We have as yet received no answer to our previous letters.' Mr Strang spoke firmly. 'It is not much to ask, just an answer to a letter.'

Kenjiro sighed. It was not pleasant to be the repository of antagonism between the Safety Committe and the Japanese Embassy. Because of his fluency in English and French he had been appointed to deal with the foreigners.

'There are bound to be a few disorderly incidents in circumstances such as these.' The words reverberated uncomfortably through Kenjiro. He had said the same thing to Teng at their last meeting.

'There is a general terror of your army. There has already been more looting by your troops than by the retreating Chinese soldiers. Our trucks and cars are being stolen. These are essential to us for delivering rice and coal to camps in the Safety Zone.' Mr Strang drew himself up to full height.

'The army has also commandeered our Embassy cars. You must understand, we are not allowed to recognize your Committee or the Safety Zone,' Kenjiro replied.

Some time before General Nakajima and Colonel Muto had entered the town, rolling in on a stream of armoured vehicles. With their divisions there would now be eight thousand Japanese soldiers in Nanking. Prince Asaka had put General Nakajima in charge of maintaining public peace but, as far as Kenjiro knew, no more than fourteen policemen had arrived with Nakajima to assist him in this order. He did not tell Mr Strang this.

Colonel Muto, responsible for the billeting of troops in the Nanking area, had already informed the Embassy that the camps outside the city walls were inadequate and the army would billet as they wished in town. Nakajima had been late in arriving. The news at the Embassy was that he had taken ten thousand captives outside the walls of Nanking. Through the night his men had exhausted themselves herding prisoners to the edge of the Yangtze. Their fingers grew sore from machine gunning, and the river ran red with blood. By morning bodies clogged the shore like wet sandbags. Kenjiro pushed this disturbing picture from his mind and listened again to Mr Strang.

'The Safety Zone has received full recognition from the Chinese authorities. In Shanghai there was never a problem. General Matsui himself donated money to their Safety Zone. We have been hit many times in the southern part of the Zone, killing nine innocent people. Your soldiers stream through it and terrorize everyone.'

'Nanking is not Shanghai. The Embassy will do what it can to help you, these conditions are not to our liking. Although we cannot officially recognize you, we will treat you as if we did recognize you. At the beginning of December the Ambassador made it clear to your Committee that this is all we can promise,' Kenjiro replied.

'These are our complaints and requests to you for today.' Mr Strang placed several envelopes upon the desk.

The military had advised all foreign nationals to leave Nanking. It was not pleased that twenty-three Westerners remained in the city. Get them out, the military commander who visited the Embassy ordered. A ship is being sent from Shanghai; put them on it, he demanded. It was pointless to explain to him the uselessness of such imperatives with committed Westerners.

'Posters have been put up all over town by your military, advising soldiers to give themselves up and trust to the mercy of the Imperial Army,' Mr Strang continued. 'At the Safety Zone Headquarters we are in the process of disarming those Chinese soldiers who have come to us in obedience to this announcement. We are doing what we can to persuade them they will be fairly treated, in accordance with the Geneva Convention.'

'For every one that voluntarily surrenders himself there must be two who have already discarded their uniforms and merged with the civilians in your Zone,' Kenjiro pointed out.

Mr Strang ignored this observation. 'We would appreciate you coming to Headquarters, to report on the surrender. We wish it to be official.'

'If you are not recognized, nothing can be official,' Kenjiro argued. His headache was worsening. 'I will come if it pleases you, but I can do nothing.' Mr Strang nodded and soon left.

Within an hour Kenjiro left the Embassy for the Safety Zone Headquarters. A gust of wind hit him as he stepped outside. He tightened the scarf about his neck. There was dust in his mouth again. It blew on the breeze, swept up from the heaps of rubble littering the town, remnants of the recent blitz. Beyond the Embassy the city was in ruins. Outside the gate he climbed over a pile of bricks, once part of the Embassy wall. By the time he reached the road his trouser legs were ringed with chalky grime. People no longer hurried about between sirens, glancing anxiously at the sky. They walked with the vacant look of sleepwalkers, unable to take more stress.

In the distance Kenjiro saw the flicker of flames and watched a group of soldiers before a burning house. Carts, wheelbarrows and rickshaws trundled past bearing the contents of Nanking's prosperity. Soldiers carried away sewing machines, blackwood chairs, or embroidered quilts upon their backs, bent double under the weight of loot like a trail of loaded ants. An army truck passed bearing two grand pianos and a grandfather clock. All shop fronts were smashed. Smouldering debris was at every corner. Bodies lay by the roadside, some horribly bayoneted. Bands of soldiers appeared to roam about at will, without command, free to pillage. There was a wild look about these men, their faces reddened by the drink they found in the shops and homes they smashed. Fukutake had mumbled that he had some suspicion the army also issued them liquor, along with orders to terrorize. In the distance the sun flashed on the blades of bayonets. Kenjiro shivered and drew his coat closer. There was menace, sharp as acid in the air. Its essence pervaded everything. He was one of the victors, with no need to fear the conquering horde, and yet panic flickered through him. Stray dogs appeared suddenly fat, fed upon a deluge of corpses. He hurried on.

Soon he came upon the building where the Chinese soldiers were being disarmed. It had once been a grand place of courtyards and gardens. One wing was in ruins but the others remained, springing up from the dust like a phoenix, yellow tiled roofs alive in the sun. For a moment, seeing the reflection of the sun and the past, Kenjiro's heart lightened. Teng would also probably be here. He liaised between the International Committee and the Red Swastika Society, the Buddhist Red Cross with whom he now worked. Instead of leaving for the interior, Teng had stayed on in Nanking.

He trembled at the thought of Teng and laughed at himself. Teng was not a woman that his emotions must be tied in knots. They had not met since the day Teng worked himself into a rage, turning upon Kenjiro in front of the Russian woman and the English journalist. Perhaps it was an illusion to think their friendship could survive this war.

He reached the first courtyard through a side gate. It was packed with the remains of the ragged Chinese Army. They appeared an exhausted, undernourished, tubercular lot. There was the constant sound of hawking and spitting. Kenjiro wore the armband of a Japanese official and men parted before him, the scent of terror thick amongst them at the sight of him. He walked up the steps into the entrance hall.

The kerosene stoves barely eased the chill in the cavernous, stone-flagged chamber. The queue of men had filed through the room for hours, surrendering rifles and bayonets. Many were still in army attire but others, in panic, had already discarded their uniforms and joined the force of labourers in the Safety Zone. Now they surrendered themselves as the International Committee advised. They wore straw sandals that made no sound. It was the Westerners, with their thick, hard shoes whose footsteps echoed. Everywhere he looked he saw, standing out from the compact Asiatic bodies, the tall awkward foreigners with their bony faces.

'I have no doubt your army will treat these men mercifully for their surrender. We have assured them of it,' said Mr Strang, coming forward to greet him. They stood in a cold corridor, their breath clouding between them.

He followed Mr Strang to view the procedure of disarming and saw Teng in the compound where the soldiers were collecting. He was supervising the distribution of rice. As soon as possible Kenjiro made his way towards him. Teng looked up at Kenjiro's voice, but continued with his work.

'These men are terrified,' Teng announced. It was as if they had met only yesterday. The bucket from which he ladled out cold rice had a broken handle. There were dark food stains down the skirt of his gown. He had not shaved for days, growth sprouted unevenly from his chin. His hair was uncombed, giving him the appearance of a wild hermit.

'The Japanese Army needs these men for labour,' Kenjiro replied, trying to sound in authority.

'Can you tell me, as POWs will they be treated according to the rights laid down by the Geneva Convention?' Teng asked. He gripped the handle of the pail until his knuckles grew white. 'All this trust of the Japanese military by the Safety Zone Committee is the naïve thought of Christian missionaries. Good people, but not realists,' Teng growled. 'They are prepared to risk their lives to save Nanking, but instead I fear their naïvety will be the death of thousands. These foreigners have failed to assess the Japanese Army correctly, especially in its new role of conqueror.'

'Why did you not leave Nanking?' Kenjiro asked. He ignored Teng's heated remarks.

'There were things to finish up here. The gate closed almost literally in my face.'

'I am glad you are here,' Kenjiro admitted. He wanted to know their friendship remained, beyond wars or the plans of unscrupulous men. Nothing seemed more important.

'I have been busy, burying the innocent victims of your army. That seems our main work in the Red Swastika Society. There are many monks in the organization.' Teng ladled out the last portion of rice and made his way to a tap in the corner of the courtyard to wash out the bucket. Kenjiro followed, feeling a flicker of anger. He did not like Teng's tone and this talk of *your army*, as if Kenjiro was part of a conspiracy.

'I am nothing to do with the army,' Kenjiro burst out. Teng looked up with a mild expression.

Near the tap a plum tree clung to a moss-covered rock, its bare roots gripping one side of the stone. A few early blossoms had opened. Large, craggy boulders and others worn to strange shapes by the erosion of river currents, were arranged about a pond.

'This was once a beautiful place,' Teng sighed looking about the garden that had formerly belonged to the Minister of the Interior. 'Each of these boulders has been carefully chosen, and hauled from the beds of deep rivers. Nanking will never look like this again.' He sat down on his upturned bucket. *'What shall we be rid of if we want peace and happiness? What shall we do to be rid of sorrow? What is the poison that devours good thoughts?'*

'What are you chanting?' Kenjiro asked, unable to keep the edge from his voice.

'The Song of Enlightenment; you have forgotten. I remember a time, many years ago of course, when you were interested in Buddhist sutras.'

In Paris Kenjiro recalled they had studied the life of the Sixth Patriarch and the Buddhist sutras of the Ch'an school of Buddhism that in Japan had become institutionalized as Zen. They had both been drawn to this school of sudden conversion, free of ritual and idolatry. Much time had been spent in educating Jacqueline in this esoteric learning. That life seemed now another world away. He could not remember a single sutra whereas Teng still chanted them fluently. Teng kept the company of monks, as well as Communists, Kenjiro suspected. In the middle of the crowded, busy, depressing place, Kenjiro felt alone. Beside him Teng sighed and rubbed a hand across his brow.

'We have come a long way,' Kenjiro said in a low voice.

'Too far,' Teng replied. 'Look at these poor men. We are both, you know, in the midst of national tragedy. The fall of Nanking will do Japan no good. It is the beginning of the end for you. And as for China . . .' His voice trailed off before he continued.

'Three hundred thousand soldiers were left to defend Nanking, you know. They were trapped in a triangle, with the city at its apex. Against all advice General Tang volunteered to defend the city. With the breaking of the Chinese Line at Soochow, the Chinese retreat became a rout. The defence forces were three separate armies. When they withdrew into the city to take up positions for street fighting, they found General Tang had fled without leaving orders for defence. The army collapsed then, like a body without a head. Panic ensued. Some soldiers discarded their uniforms and arms and merged with the civilians in the Safety Zone. Some, half-mad with terror, tried to cross the river letting themselves down over the city walls with ropes, puttees and torn clothing. Many fell and were killed. Thousands more drowned as overcrowded junks capsized and sank in the Yangtze. There was no organized transport across the river. Any system would have collapsed under the hundreds of thousands fleeing for their lives, waiting on the banks for a few junks. The river gates were jammed with stalled trucks and cars that overturned and burned, killing hundreds more. Trampled, stinking corpses piled higher and higher, blocking all traffic. I was there, I can tell you.' Teng spoke without intonation. He sighed and then continued.

'Has there ever been a war like this? Do you know since August millions have been forced to flee their homes in this Shanghai–Nanking area? It must be one of the greatest migrations of people in history. They flee mass slaughter brought about by an incomprehensible invasion by an incomprehensible army. The countryside is depopulated and barren. The Japanese march on hoping to catch up with wealth and the disintegrating Chinese Army. But they will find neither. The army has already withdrawn and will reorganize. And China's wealth is in the industrious character of her people.' Teng stopped and the strength seemed to fade from him. Kenjiro said nothing.

Teng raised his head and pulled back his shoulders. 'The terror of this war is not that of battle, of shells and tanks and guns. It is not even the terror of bombs from the air, terrifying as that may be. Shanghai or Soochow, wherever the bombing has been intense, no one had fled their homes. No, the terror is of what men of one race can do to fellow men of another race. The stories we hear are not fiction but authenticated crimes.'

Kenjiro sat down on a stone beside Teng. He felt suddenly responsible for his blinkered nation. 'I've heard enough about the exploits of our

Army on the way to Nanking. We're talking about war, and war does strange things to people.' Kenjiro felt ill listening to Teng.

Across the courtyard he suddenly saw the Russian woman. She was helping with disarming soldiers. She stood behind a trestle table handling guns with a practised hand, first checking barrels for ammunition, before registering each man.

'She is still here?' he asked. Somehow, he had convinced himself that she must have left.

Teng nodded. 'Nadya is working with the International Committee. She could have left, but didn't. She has the right spirit; even returned here from Shanghai.'

'Maybe she is a spy,' Kenjiro mused. Teng began to laugh.

Kenjiro had not meant it as a joke. The Indian, Tilik Dayal, had filed just such an accusation with him, backed up by reports from a military man at a railway station near Shanghai. Fukutake had ordered Kenjiro to investigate but each time he picked up the woman's file a deep reluctance filled him. In the end Kenjiro did nothing with Tilik's report, but tucked the papers away. He hoped it might be forgotten.

'She attracts you, my friend?' Teng murmured, looking into Kenjiro's face.

'All attractive women attract me, I am no different from other men,' Kenjiro laughed to rid himself of embarrassment, shocked Teng had seen so acutely. He had not realized himself, until this moment, that he was drawn to Nadya. Had he filed away Tilik Dayal's report for this reason?

Several hundred Chinese soldiers now packed the courtyard. They were to be transferred to another building and kept apart from the other refugees, until they could be officially handed over as POWs to the Japanese. They stood silent, unsure of the wisdom of their decision to surrender.

There was a stir in the courtyard. A Japanese military official arrived. Kenjiro pushed his way through the crowd and introduced himself to the officer. The man reached no higher than Kenjiro's shoulder. His eyes were small as currants, deep-set beneath his brow. To Kenjiro he appeared of peasant stock, a country man who had come up through the ranks to his position. He spoke with a flattened dialect that might be, thought Kenjiro, from Kyushu. He gave Kenjiro a cursory nod. Mr Strang hurried forward. The other foreigners came into the courtyard, obscuring his view of the Russian woman. The officer turned to Kenjiro, pushing his chin in the direction of Mr Strang.

'Tell them six thousand uniforms of the Chinese Army have been found so far in town. They have here no more than a few hundred men.

Many soldiers have deserted, discarding their uniforms and mixed in with the civilian population. We will not tolerate this. All former soldiers must surrender, or sacrifice their rights as prisoners of war and be subject to the death penalty as spies.' The officer spat out the words. 'We will take the men here now. We will expect more tomorrow.'

Mr Strang stepped forward, his voice boomed out commandingly. Kenjiro interpreted for him. 'The International Committee wish to be assured of their good treatment.'

'They will be treated as promised,' the officer replied. His nostrils flared and his lips tightened. The unit of accompanying soldiers behind him stood unmoving. Kenjiro glanced at their stony faces. The blades of their bayonets gleamed in the thin winter sun. The power of authority was a heady thing. Men found themselves in the position of God, and dispensed the judgement of Devils. The officer turned and barked an order to his men. They began to rope together the prisoners in groups of four or five.

'Where will you take them? What will you do with them?' Kenjiro asked without Mr Strang's prompting.

'That is the business of the military, not you diplomats,' the officer replied.

Suddenly a woman's voice was heard over the heads of the bound men. 'What assurance do we have that they will not be killed?' It was Nadya. Kenjiro moved forward to stand beside her and repeated her question in Japanese. The officer glared. Kenjiro looked down at Nadya's impassioned face. He had seen a similar flaming in Jacqueline's eyes many times.

'Do not provoke him,' he murmured.

'To my mind it is not provocation but my right to ask their fate,' she hissed. The man grunted in rage and turned away.

'He is doing his duty,' Kenjiro replied.

'Duty?' She looked at him, aghast.

Mr Metzger of the YMCA, Chairman of the International Committee, suddenly appeared, thrusting his way through the crowd. He came straight up to Kenjiro. 'These men are not going off like this unless we have written assurances of their safety, in compliance with the Geneva Convention. We cannot hand them over without any formality. We have persuaded them to surrender and we are responsible.'

'I will tell him what you say, but I doubt he will give such an assurance. Your Zone is not a recognized entity,' Kenjiro explained.

'We have received no answer from your Embassy to that request.' Mr Metzger's thin face was firmly set.

Kenjiro spoke again to the officer who, in answer, silently pursed his lips. His men continued to bind the prisoners together. The first group were being marched away. The officer barked rapid orders, supervising their departure.

Mr Metzger began to shout at Kenjiro. 'I demand that you stop this. It is unlawful.'

'There is nothing I can do,' replied Kenjiro. He knew the hopelessness of his position and that of the captive men.

'How can we be sure they will not all be killed?' Nadya turned upon him.

'I can do nothing,' he repeated. He saw his impotence as the foreigners must see it.

'Nothing?' Nadya shouted. The blood rose in her face. She pushed herself in front of the officer, pulling at his sleeve. Anger spluttered through her.

Surprise turned to fury in the man's eyes. He looked down at Nadya as if he had suddenly seen an insect upon his uniform. He shook her off roughly. Mr Metzger's voice rose in support of Nadya. The officer raised his arm and brought it down, flinging Nadya back upon the floor. Kenjiro turned in distress to help her up.

'This is not the way to behave,' Kenjiro could no longer control his voice. The officer took no notice of him.

How could he explain to these people the web of order and obligation that held him in a vice, even in this situation. Not only was the Embassy impotent in the face of military rule, but it would be unheard of to interfere between an officer and his duty. The man was doing as ordered. To cause him loss of face was unthinkable. There were other ways to handle the matter, indirectly and through the right channels. He must be allowed as ordered to take away his prisoners. Suddenly he was aware that Teng had planted himself before the officer.

'Do you think Nanking is some unseen backwater? The eyes of the world are upon Japan here, as everywhere. Have you no respect for the name of your country that your soldiers behave in China worse than animals?' Teng spoke in broken Japanese, but what he said was understandable. His voice was hoarse with suppressed emotion, his eyes blazed. He swayed from one foot to another, like a boxer anticipating a blow, his body taut with anger. The officer looked at him in amazement.

'Who is this man?' he roared at Kenjiro.

'He is a professor at the university. A respected man,' Kenjiro pleaded, horrified at the sight of Teng.

'University man? Look at his hands. He is no more than a common soldier.' The officer grabbed Teng's hands, pointing to the dried blisters on his fingers. 'Such calluses are found only on soldiers from the handling of guns. Take him,' he ordered a subordinate.

'These are the marks of handling a spade, digging graves for the men and women you murder.' Teng raised his voice. His wild eyes and dishevelled appearance did him no good.

'Take him.' The officer roared again. His soldiers came forward to grasp Teng's arms.

'He is a well-known man,' Kenjiro lost his calm.

The soldier turned. 'You would raise your voice to an officer? You would try to save a miserable Chinese, a soldier who has discarded his uniform and now masquerades as a civilian, who shouts abuse at his conquerors? I shall speak of this to those who matter. Tell me also the name of that foreign woman who dared to put her hand upon me? I have seen enough insolence.' The officer's face was now ruddy in colour, his eyes bulged.

'You have made a mistake, he is not a soldier. He is an educated man.' Kenjiro tried again. He made an effort to keep his voice even. Already Teng had been roped to other men, and his tousled grey head was pulled further into the crowd of prisoners.

It was as if he were trapped in a nightmare from which he could not wake. Kenjiro wanted to shout Teng's name, to tell him it was a mistake, release would come soon. And yet he stood, hands at his sides, and watched Teng led away. He must go at once to the Embassy. Fukutake would help him. Nadya dashed forward once more, pulling again at the officer. He turned and slapped her face.

Kenjiro stepped forward. 'It is useless. This is not the way to free the professor. The army is all powerful. Here, in front of us, this officer will not admit he is wrong. I am going now to the Embassy. Something will be done.'

'I will come with you. I will tell them who the professor is,' Nadya insisted.

He shook his head. It was the last thing he wanted. The *Kempeitai* would be immediately alerted. Eventually, he would have to file Tilik Dayal's report on Nadya or the Indian himself might file it directly to the military. What explanation could Kenjiro find if asked, for pleading with a suspected Russian spy for the freedom of a suspected Communist? Who nowadays believed in innocence?

The courtyard was emptying. The last men were led away. Teng turned his untidy grey head, shoulders bent. There was blood at the side of his mouth from a blow. For a moment his eyes held Kenjiro's before he was gone, led out of the gate on a rope.

Nadya took another step forward but stopped, seeing the uselessness.

'I will take a petition to the Embassy, and to the Military Commander himself if need be.'

'You will do no such thing. You must leave it to me.' Kenjiro spoke quietly. He could smell the fresh scent of shampoo from her hair. She shrugged and turned to disappear into the interior of the building.

Soon, after reassuring Mr Strang and Mr Metzger that something would be done, Kenjiro left the Safety Zone Headquarters. The things he would say to Fukutake buzzed in his head, he could still not believe Teng had been taken. As he made his way back to the Embassy, he saw Nadya walking ahead of him, red hair swinging, a shawl pulled tightly about her. He hurried to catch up. She glanced at him quickly and then stared ahead as she spoke in a low fierce voice.

'Once, in Shanghai, I watched from a roof-top while men were shot by your army. They dropped into a grave they had dug for themselves. It was at a distance, but I have not forgotten the feeling of helplessness, unable to even hear the gun that killed them. I could of course have done nothing, but that feeling of impotence has stayed with me. Now, Professor Teng has been taken from under my eyes. He might have been shot on the spot, and I would still have been unable to do a thing.' She walked with short quick steps, head down. Kenjiro said nothing. Nadya began to speak again.

'These soldiers have the power of the Devil. Even if for different reasons we are both exempt from being hounded like animals by your army, we are not exempt from the contamination about us. We have already absorbed it by being encircled. It will stain us for life, one way or another. Every time we shut our eyes we will re-live this. How will we ever be whole again?'

The image of Teng being led away came forcibly again before Kenjiro. Yet, he realized in self-disgust, in spite of anxiety for Teng, he could still watch the swing of the woman's red hair, and the spring of her breasts as she walked. He turned his eyes away. Once more the bleak landscape was before him. A terrified child sat in a doorway. A dog ran by with three fat pups. He could find no explanations. He needed his energy to survive.

'Get Professor Teng freed,' she ordered sharply, stopping to search his face. Her pale eyes met his and he could not look away. She turned towards a brick building that he saw was one of the foreign hospitals.

'I live here, with Dr Clayton,' she said, opening a gate in a side wall, leading to a garden.

'Something must be done,' Kenjiro leaned forward in his chair and thrust the words at Fukutake.

'I have warned you once before over the matter of this man,' Fukutake answered. He played with a pencil and stared at Kenjiro across the desk, noting the stress in his face. 'He is a Chinese. Do you not understand the position?'

'He is my friend,' Kenjiro replied.

'I can only repeat what I have told you before; these are dangerous times.' Fukutake sipped a cup of green tea. 'As you know, an investigation was made. Although nothing was proved it was thought the man might be a Communist. Events overtook us, otherwise a further investigation would have proceeded. With such suspicions as these, it is best to leave him alone.'

'I have know him for years. He is a respected man,' Kenjiro pleaded.

'Respectability can be a front for many things. Think of your own skin. Why is this man so important to you? Do you not understand the *Kempeitai* will have their eye upon you? Do not forget, you carry your past about with you still, it will never leave you. You must always be circumspect. That is my advice as a senior and a friend. Forget this Professor Teng.' Fukutake shuffled papers upon his desk to indicate the discussion was over.

'Think of some way I can get him released,' Kenjiro demanded.

He could speak to no one else but Fukutake like this. Apart from being at school and university together, there was an extra tie that silently bound them. During the time Fukutake's father had worked in the Ministry of Commerce, Yuzuru Nozaki had once helped to prove him innocent of leaking secret information to the press. The knowledge of this obligation still remained between Kenjiro and Fukutake.

'All you can do, and I doubt it will work, is to put in a plea on behalf of the Safety Zone Committee that this man be released. It will have to be worded carefully, so that you appear uninvolved. Nothing more than this can be done, as you well know.' Fukutake remained firm.

Kenjiro returned to his desk to write out the plea for Teng's release and hurried back to Fukutake.

'Why should I put my seal to this, why should I stick my neck out?' Fukutake wondered, pressing his ivory seal in place beside Kenjiro's. 'If there are any repercussions, I will have to admit you know this man. I cannot protect you for ever. You have put me in a difficult position.'

Kenjiro bowed low in thanks. As he opened the door to leave the room Fukutake spoke again. 'I have been asked about that Russian woman. If you have not yet investigated, hurry up. Mr Dayal has spoken of the matter to the *Kempeitai* and they are awaiting our report,' Fukutake reminded him.

'I have already made a preliminary investigation,' Kenjiro lied.

210

Returning to his office, he sat down at his desk. He could no longer now avoid the matter of Nadya's report. Nor could he allow his feelings to sway him; he had no proof she was not a spy. Reluctantly, he picked up his pen. He was under no obligation to the woman.

Immediately, as he began to write, his head was filled by the thought of her. He saw again the brisk walk, the angry eyes, the pull of the shawl about her shoulders, smelled again her shampoo. He put down the pen. How could she be a spy? How could Teng be a dangerous man? Why was he now interlocked with them both in such an impossible way?

Such interlockings seemed the pattern of his life. Events that at the time of their happening appeared solitary things, seemed now to reverberate through his memory, in ever widening circles of association, like ripples on a pond. He thought briefly of the terrifying intrusion of those armed men into his home long ago, forcing him to leave Japan. But more than that, he remembered the time of the Great Kanto Earthquake. He saw it now as a catalyst in his life. He willed the memory not to rise, but it returned, like a curl of smoke across time.

Tradition stated that a monstrous catfish lay beneath Japan. This creature stirred whenever the Sun Goddess frowned upon her Emperor son. At such times the worst earthquakes occurred and had caused past monarchs to abdicate. The catfish stirred on 1st September 1923 and all Tokyo had fallen.

It had been midday. Chacoal braziers were alight beneath meals. Workmen put down their tools to stretch out in the shade with a rice ball and cold tea. Kenjiro returned after lunch to the university, where he was a student. There, on the seismographs in the science department, early tremors rocked the needles at first no more than was usual in volcanic Japan. Soon they mounted by the second, merging to a single swell, billowing like a wave. Kenjiro was thrown on his back, the earth retched and opened. When he regained consciousness, much of Tokyo and Yokohama had disappeared. He stood up and shaded his eyes with a hand. A flattened plain stretched out before him, a woodpile broken by the remains of a few concrete buildings. Charcoal fires still burned under the debris and soon engulfed the ruined city in a holocaust of flame. He stumbled forward. All landmarks were gone.

He did not remember how he found his way home. The house stood miraculously, only one wing had collapsed. The garden had risen like a cake, regurgitating trees. The pond had cracked, leaving the carp to thrash and gasp. In the Nozaki kitchen the soup had tumbled, but the rice in its heavy iron pot still sat upon the hearth.

At one point on the journey home Kenjiro found himself near the moat of the Imperial Palace, ringed by the flames of the city. A hysterical mob fought to jump to safety in the water. The crowd surged against police lines, a man clambered onto a fallen tree and shouted. 'Remember Russia!' Kenjiro hurried on.

Later he heard about the man, an anarchist named Osugi. He was tracked down by the secret police and arrested. Taken with him was his wife and seven-year-old nephew, all later murdered in their cells. After this the secret police, anxious for a scapegoat, put about a rumour that the catfish had turned for exceptional reasons. Koreans and Socialists had offended the Sun Goddess. It was announced they took advantage of the disaster by setting fires and looting shops. The secret police, aided by vigilantes of the Military Sports Club and thugs of the Black Dragon Society, hunted down individuals with Socialist leanings and Orientals who spoke Japanese with an accent. Four thousand Koreans from the slums were given mock trials or linguistic tests and beheaded in the street. One such man had died before Kenjiro. Even now he could not forget.

He heard again the fellow's blubbering and saw the sudden spurt of blood. The man had looked like a rickshaw puller. His boney rib cage was painfully visible on his half-naked torso, but his calves were developed, veins knotted like blue rope. A soldier berated him in the street as a crowd of silent people watched. The armed man roared and strutted, power swilling through him. His sword moved like a tail at his side. Then it streaked with a flash through the air, taking Kenjiro unawares. One moment the rickshaw man jigged about yelling, the next blood fountained from a stump. In the dust his head rolled and grimaced, words stopped upon its tongue. It fell from his body with a thud, like a turnip from a table. The soldier wiped his sword on a paper and sheathed it smartly again. At Kenjiro's feet blood spilt as if from an uncorked bottle out of the headless body. The crowd cringed and backed away.

Kenjiro had stared in disbelief at the two parts before him that had once made a man. All he absurdly registered was that they could not be rejoined. Sensation, he found, only followed an event. It took many hours for emotion to surface. His thoughts awoke later as the shock leaked out. For days, if he shut his eyes, he saw again that spurt of blood and the collapsing body. If he turned his head, the hiss of the sword, breaking space, stopping time, travelled again by his ear. And if all these memories were obliterated one image he knew would stay forever. More than death or its violence, the executioner's eyes remained with him. Even now he remembered the soldier cleaning his sword, expression absent from his face. Each time the same sick feeling filled Kenjiro. Killing was as nothing.

212

He willed the long ago memory away and turned to the window of his office. Almost immediately, the image of the Russian woman was before him again.

13

December 1937

Caught in the Storm

Flora thought of her father each night. In the past he had not materialized with regularity. Now he seemed constantly beside her. She told Lily tales of his bravery, heard from Martha, and also the exploits of Dr Keswick, their grandfather. China was a country where it was necessary to nurture the mettle in one's character. The things their mother had endured sounded like pure fiction.

'We're being tested,' Flora decided, prodding Lily's spine as they lay side by side on Flora's bed. 'When this war is finished we too will have tales to tell.'

Lily lowered her book and looked over her shoulder. 'I already have tales to tell. I was put out to die, don't forget. I just missed being eaten by dogs.'

'Why don't you stop dwelling on that?' Flora frowned. Whenever she could now Lily brought up the subject.

Lily pouted and returned to her book, filled with anger at Flora. There were things about herself, Lily saw now, that she had completely misjudged. For the first time she perceived the originality of her jigsaw self. Sandwiched between Flora and Martha she had suffered from a smallness of bones, a narrowness of eyes, the way people looked at her, especially at school. She realized now, she was a mirror to no one. This time last year she detested herself. Now everything seemed changed.

'I know this war means nothing to you. But it's not like that for me. I am Chinese. This is my country.' Lily slammed shut her book and turned on her back.

'For goodness sakes, I was born here, so was Mama. This is our country too. Why are you making yourself out to be different? Your name is also Clayton.' Flora sighed in exasperation.

Lily no longer slept in her own bed, but without a word had moved into Flora's. To voice fear was to invite it into the room and allow it to order all movement. Nothing was said between them. No reason was

214

given for the sudden nightly telling of Flora's brave tales. Lily listened in silence; even when the culprits were Chinese she did not interrupt. Afterwards, in the dark, they listened to sounds of the city's terror before they fell asleep. Lily's hand moved into Flora's. She clung to her when dreams became strident. Flora, waking in solitary panic, lay rigid until her heart stopped pumping, making no sound or movement.

They had not been allowed beyond the hospital compound since the fall of the city. It was enough to see the bandaged, bleeding bodies in the hospital and the hysterical women, to imagine what went on. Within this enclosure Flora was pushed into another world. Within herself also some line had been crossed. A strange inner landscape stretched bleakly before her. This was adult land, upon which men and women carved pieces for themselves, bounded by deceit. She had not known what it was men did to women to produce a child. Now, day after day, there were whispers amongst the nurses of things that made her sick. She had learned the word *rape*, and it chilled her. Terror fizzled in the air.

From the windows of the hospital each day she watched the demolition of the city. The banks of green that once clouded Nanking had vanished. Trees stood charred by bombs or felled by soldiers for firewood. Why could they not have gone away before it all began? People were shocked to hear they were staying and begged to be allowed to take them to Shanghai, Hankow, Chungking or wherever it was they fled. Martha stood firm and shook her head.

'Should we not go?' Flora whispered once, secretly crossing her fingers for her mother to agree.

'Are you afraid?' Martha asked. 'The worst is almost over. Once the occupation begins everything will quieten down. I faced dangers as a child that far exceeded this. We are foreigners, not part of this war. We have little to fear from the Japanese.'

She did not speak coldly but with concern. Flora was ashamed to fear a war through which it appeared they walked inviolable. There was also an intensity in her mother's eyes that she knew too well. No words were needed to explain the fear Martha had of separation. It had followed Flora through her childhood. She knew how her father had died, and understood she must give no more pain to her mother. The rules were firm between them.

Only Lily was free of this responsibility, being a daughter of circumstance, not of blood. Lily, Flora realized now, must always have felt outside the core of Martha's love. Flora remembered the sense of triumph she had often felt over Lily as a child, and of which she was now ashamed. Like their mother, Lily had suffered enough. She too must have no more pain. A sudden weariness overwhelmed Flora. It was exhausting to stand forever between these two, absorbing sorrow for them.

Since the occupation began Lily and Flora saw less than ever of Martha. The old Amah slept in their room each night, as she had when they were small. Martha hurried in distractedly for meals, between endless operations. Whatever the sights in the hospital, she remained calm and brisk. So used was Martha to the results of strife, to mangled, pain-filled bodies, that she minimized the effect such images might have upon her daughters. She demanded a war effort that shirked no task. They were ordered to work under Nadya, and each night reported to Martha on the hours of rolling bandages, stacking or changing babies' nappies, taking temperatures, comforting the sick. Flora remembered a child who had died that day, its belly ripped open by a bayonet. Who could do such a thing, she wondered? Each day threw her further into that dark terrain of terror she had so abruptly entered.

Martha glanced out of the window of the operating theatre. Across the compound the lights were out in Flora's room. She had not expected the occupation to be like this. An orderly transition of power was what everyone had expected. She should not have let the girls stay in Nanking. Why had she not sent them away? She returned her attention to the man stretched out on the operating table. It was another of the interminable cases of bayonet wounds. She inserted thread into the needle and nodded to the anaesthetist, Dr Chen. There was the faint hum of the generator, pushing light into the room. That morning Japanese soldiers had tried to steal the ambulance. The rubber bladder of oxygen inflated and deflated at the end of the table.

The noise of breaking glass and distant shouting came suddenly. She looked up and knew she had been waiting for this moment. Other hospitals in Nanking had already been entered and terrorized. Even as she stitched up the flesh of the man before her, she listened to the wild sounds. They seemed sickeningly familiar, echoing back over the years. She remembered again the Boxer Uprising, and the death of her two brothers. Each part of her life seemed hinged together by the same chilling chorus of brutality.

About her the nurses shifted nervously and murmured amongst themselves. The noise continued, growing nearer. Martha did not move but continued to suture the unconscious man on the table. The wound was cruel about his neck, severing vital muscle. She had been told he was taken by the Japanese from the Safety Zone to carry ammunition to Hsiakwan with a band of other men. When they deposited their loads,

216

they were bayoneted. He survived and dragged himself to a hospital. Many cases with such tales to tell were arriving now, as were great numbers of maimed women.

She motioned for a swab. The heavy scuffle of boots, and the screams of nurses were almost upon them. Martha knotted the thread upon the wound, pulling the flesh together. Some junior staff had already fled the theatre. Martha continued to sew. There were further sounds of smashing windows. She knotted the last thread and turned to Dr Chen to indicate she was finished. Then she scrubbed her hands unhurriedly before marching into the corridor. No one must know how she trembled. Until this moment she had held everything in place. Even now, to her medical staff, she appeared to stride forward, unafraid. She stood outside the operating theatre, feet planted apart to steady herself.

A mass of men swelled the corridor. A river of khaki bilge seemed to roll towards her. She saw faces now, and reddened cheeks, heard the guffaw of lewd laughter. She saw their eyes were glazed, skating on power, touched only by dark instinct.

'This is a hospital. Remove yourselves,' Martha shouted.

Their faces pushed closer. The rough cloth of their uniforms touched her skin. Her heart pumped in her chest. A soldier took hold of her arm and ripped her watch from her wrist. The Chinese staff were cut off against the wall. Someone pulled at the chain around her neck, drawing it up, warm from her breasts. She saw fingers close about her locket with Bill's photograph. *Bill.*

Fury spat from her in such a wave they stopped their drunken caterwauling. Their eyes focused for a moment. For the first time it seemed they saw she was not Chinese. For the first time she saw they were not a sea, but only six or eight young men. They began to back away.

'Your mothers would be ashamed of you,' Martha yelled. Suddenly now there was Nadya behind her. Confronted by a second foreign woman, the men appeared confused. They looked down the corridor for a way out.

'They're everywhere,' Nadya announced. 'All the staff have been robbed. And they've taken some nurses.'

'Go to Lily. For God's sake, go to Lily,' Martha cried. Nadya ran down the back stairs.

Martha turned again to the soldiers, eyes blazing. 'I have seen the desperation of starving peasants, settling on towns like locusts to devour and loot, to kill and ransom, to keep alive their own families. I have seen the frenzy of the Boxers who came to murder me, like the children you kill and rape. I saw the hate in their eyes for us foreigners. And I could understand that, insinuating ourselves into their country, why should they not wish to kill us? But what I see in your eyes is only drunken arrogance, the mindlessness of power. Get out of my hospital. Get out.' They backed away before her down the corridor, her anger communicating itself above incomprehensible words. She followed them down the stairs, anger palpitating in her chest, and slammed the door behind them.

There must be other soldiers still about in the hospital, and those nurses already dragged from the building might never return. Her thoughts returned to Lily and then to those nurses who must still be upstairs in the dormitory. The Chinese staff had vanished. Only Dr Chen followed her as she climbed the stairs. At last she reached the top floor of the hospital, expecting every shadow to release a khaki figure. The door of the dormitory was open. No lights were on in the corridor, but the moon reflected in the glass of pictures upon the wall. There were sounds, like geese when a wolf prowls near, escaping the room ahead. She knew what she would find.

One man held the gun, swinging it back and forth before his body in impatience. In the half-light the other two men appeared like crooked-legged satyrs, half-dressed above and naked below. Their testicles hung like dried fruit. It was clear they had already begun their devilry. The women huddled together before the swinging gun. Martha stepped into the room, her anger destroying all fear. The man with the gun looked at her aghast, too surprised to react. She wrenched the weapon from him. He stepped forward in fury, but she levelled it at his head and, muttering curses, he backed away. Dr Chen snapped on the light, breaking the spell of the gun.

'Get out,' Martha directed the women. The half-naked men turned, angry as lions denied their meat, as the women scattered before them. They pulled on their breeches. For the first time Martha realized the power she held, quite literally, in her foreign-made bones. She saw the men out of the hospital, pushing them forward with their own gun.

Glass splintered beneath her feet, and the moon glowed icily through smashed windows. She leaned against a wall to catch her breath; she must get Lily. She began to run again. At last she reached the door of the house and found it already open. Her heart lurched in new terror.

'The girls are all right,' said Nadya, appearing suddenly, taking her by the arm. 'Nobody came.'

Martha pushed her aside and ran up the stairs to Flora and Lily's room. They were asleep, unaware of what had happened in the hospital. In the corner, on her mattress, the old Amah stirred.

'Nobody came?' Martha shook Flora awake.

Even as she stared into the sleepy faces of her daughters, Martha remembered that time in the loft during the Boxer Uprising. She remembered her father's prayers and her life welled up in her throat.

'Who would come, Mama?' Flora asked, sitting up, terrified at the distraught appearance of her mother.

'What has happened to you?' Lily pouted. 'We can look after ourselves.' It frightened her to see her mother like this, eyes ablaze, hair disturbed, coolness cracked open like a walnut, to show its strange inside.

'Look after yourselves? What are you saying? Do you know what is happening in this town? No woman is safe.' New frenzy glowed in Martha's face.

'Calm down. They're all right. You are frightening them.' Nadya attempted to pull Martha away from the bed.

'Why should we not be safe?' Lily was insistent, in spite of the pinch Flora landed on her wrist.

'I'll tell you why,' Martha hissed, her face thin and white, the hair falling from her bun, pins scattering the floor. She took Lily's arm and pushed her face close, fear and rage locked into her bones. 'Because you are Chinese.'

'My name is Clayton,' Lily said, drawing back in the bed. 'I am American, not Chinese.' There was no movement in her face.

'Mother!' Flora looked in horror at them both.

Suddenly Martha let go of Lily and sank down on the floor beside the bed. She began to sob uncontrollably. Her hair spilt down her back.

'Soldiers came into the hospital. They have done much damage. She was afraid they might have come here too, and harmed you.' Nadya stepped forward. 'It is all over now. It has upset her. Nothing more.' She spoke to calm the children, bending to pick up the scattered hairpins, handing them to Martha as she helped her up. Standing again beside the bed, Martha now turned upon Flora.

'Keep near Lily. Don't let her out of your sight. Do you hear?' Her voice was unrecognizable. Flora nodded, pushing back against the pillows to distance herself. Nothing yet had been as bad as this fractured vision of her mother.

Suddenly it seemed finished. Martha smoothed down her skirt. She rewound her hair and secured it anew with the hairpins. 'Stay here. I am going back to the hospital to look over the damage. Try and get to sleep.' Martha turned abruptly. Her back straightened, her face closed, her voice returned to its familiar expression. She walked unsteadily from the room. Lily and Flora observed her in silence.

Lily spoke first, her fear spilling into anger. 'What does she mean, calling me Chinese when she has always told me I'm an American, a Clayton?'

'A few hours ago you were disowning all Claytons. She means no Chinese-looking person is safe,' Flora replied.

The fear was now a dense mass in Flora's body. It was not just the sight of her mother's panic. It was all to do with that one word she could not even speak, *rape*. Nothing had the power to chill her more than that silent word. Was this word at the bottom of her mother's panic? Was that the damage in the hospital? A few soldiers and some broken glass would not drive her mother insane.

'Are the nurses all right?' she enquired of Nadya while Lily's attention was diverted.

Nadya shook her head. Truth was best, Flora was no child. The communication passed between them unseen by Lily. 'I'll get you both some hot milk,' Nadya said.

As she reached the door the old Amah returned after hurrying downstairs to investigate. Clucking in fright, wheezing for breath, she lumbered towards the girls. 'Is there no end to this terror?' she asked and collapsed in a heap by the bed.

Lily began immediately to question her about the damage in the hospital. An inventory began. How many windows were broken? How many watches were stolen? Did Dr Chen lose his fountain pen from England? War could still be a game to Lily.

Flora stared at the ceiling. Her mother's face was before her again. That word, *rape*, was wedged permanently in the cold lining of her stomach. That word had now damaged the nurses across the compound. What had been done to them? The iciness gripped her anew. And as always, beyond this new terror, she must deal with the old weight. She must stand guard, ever more vigilant, absorbing pain, deflecting danger, between her mother and her sister. She had been ordered now not to take her eyes off Lily. If anything happened, it would be her fault. Tiredness overwhelmed her. When the war was over she would sleep for a hundred years.

Soon Nadya returned with mugs of hot milk. After some time, when she was sure they were calmer, Nadya made her way back downstairs. Lily's voice followed her. It was ignorant of any real danger, lost still in a child's world. It was Flora she worried for, whose face was now stilled of all expression.

She saw a man in shadow at the bottom of the stairs and drew back, prepared for anything now. Her hand gripped the banister rail. Donald Addison stepped into the light and looked up. His face was ashen, leaves stuck in his hair. Stubble darkened his cheeks and his clothes were torn.

It was as if she had been hit. She gripped the rail tighter as he walked forward unsteadily. There was a vacant look in his eyes. 'I thought you had left Nanking.' She collected herself and spoke coldly, determined to show no more chinks in her armour.

'I was on the *Panay*. It was sunk. Where's Martha?' He sat down on the bottom of the stairs.

Suddenly Martha appeared, coming back through the front door from the hospital. She stopped in surprise at the sight of Donald, and looked up in query at Nadya who now descended the stairs reluctantly. She wanted nothing more to do with Donald, Nadya decided. Once she had confronted him she would cut him away from her mind and body. Donald sat slumped below her on the last step, leaning back against the wall. She could see now he looked very ill.

'Help me get him into the lounge,' Martha ordered. Donald appeared almost half-conscious, and groaned.

'He has a high temperature, whatever else may be wrong,' Martha said. 'Where has he been?'

'He said something about the *Panay* being sunk,' Nadya answered, supporting Donald until he lay back upon the sofa.

'The *Panay*? So many people were on that boat. There is no way to get news here now.' Martha frowned. She appeared herself again. Her hair was coiled tightly at the back of her head, obedient to her will.

Donald stirred. 'Got a room here Martha? I've nowhere to go. Everything's boarded up or burned down.' He closed his eyes again.

Nadya looked down at his thin body. His clothes were torn and his face was streaked with dirt. All the feelings she had vowed to eradicate regarding Donald stirred again within her. Love for him was the expectation of sorrow. He had no belief in happiness. At its first shoots he sought to destroy it.

That night she could not sleep, knowing he was in the house. His presence seemed to override the earlier terrifying intrusion of the soldiers. And her anxiety for Professor Teng welled up anew. Had the Japanese man from the Embassy been able to free him? Where was Professor Teng now? Had he been shot like thousands of others, tossed into a mass grave? Something must be done.

In her room Martha too could not sleep. She sat for a while at the window, looking out into the blackness at the fires that still bloomed in Nanking any time of day or night. How much, she wondered, could there be left to burn? She swung the curtains together blotting out the scene. All she had kept in place for so long boiled dangerously within her now. She dreaded going to bed, switching off the light. Not since the time of Bill's death had she been so little in charge of her emotions.

'There is nothing to be afraid of,' Bill had said on that last day she had seen him, so long ago now. 'We're together and God is with us.' And she had believed him in that year of terrible famine. The desperate peasants swelling the bandit ranks marched nearer, capturing town after town, killing and looting, carrying off the rich for ransom. Soon it was feared that they would reach the mission.

Martha's father and Bill were persuaded at last to flee before the approaching bandits. They were taken in by friends up river. At last the bandits were stopped by government troops. Bill and her father insisted on returning at once to the mission.

'There will be wounded,' Dr Keswick had said. 'You must wait on here with Flora. It is not safe enough yet for a child.'

Eventually, after some time, word came from the mission for Martha to return. When she arrived Bill was away on a round of the outlying clinics. She had returned to her routine of outpatients and surgery, to a queue of stab and bullet wounds and the many maimed victims of kidnapping. Two days passed; it was not unusual for Bill to delay if work demanded. On the third morning her father interrupted the surgery.

'Martha, I must talk with you child,' Dr Keswick said. She took a stethoscope from an old man's chest and looked at him in surprise. It was exceptional for her father to interrupt the morning clinic. He led her back to the house.

'It is best to be direct. No news is made better by beating about. They have taken Bill.' He stood before her, his agitation clear.

'Who have taken Bill?' At first she did not understand.

'Bandits, my child. Bandits.'

'What proof is there?' she demanded.

'A note of ransom, nothing more,' her father replied.

'Nothing more?' she queried.

He shook his head and reached for her hand. That no parcel of bloodied parts had arrived seemed somehow to give hope.

'What are we to do?' she cried.

'Wait. Pray,' her father replied. Everyone knew missionaries paid no ransom.

Her hands were permanently locked in prayer, her knuckles white with the pressure. She pulled Flora close for comfort, but the child struggled from her and returned to play, unaware. A storm blew up and she thought of him, hidden in a shack or an underground hole, clothes sodden, mud sliding down upon him; cold, starving, beaten. It became unbearable.

'Pay Father. Give them what they want. Write to the Head Mission. If *you* ask they will pay.'

'What are you saying?' Dr Keswick demanded. 'We are in God's hands. Cast thy burden on the Lord, child. *Call unto Me and I will answer thee.* We have no resource to His Will but prayer.'

'Stop it. Stop it,' she screamed.

Eventually, Bill's dismembered body was found. A last sight of him was denied her on Dr Keswick's orders. The coffin was hammered down. She began to scream. They held her down and splashed cold water on her face, slapped her face, and still she screamed.

'Let her be,' Dr Keswick decided. 'Let her exhaust herself. Let it come out.'

She knew then there was no God. Her scream became a scream of relief. Dr Keswick approached with a hypodermic. The dark limbo it brought lasted over a year, until the day Flora found Lily.

Martha sunk her head in her hands now. Outside, in the distance, came the sound of marauding soldiers. She began to shiver. If now a scream escaped her she knew it might never be stopped. She pressed her lips together in an effort of control. She would not give in to the frail creature she saw so clearly within herself.

The next morning Donald's fever had dropped and his general condition had improved. He told Nadya and Martha the story of the *Panay*, and the way he had returned to Nanking over enemy territory. He had climbed a breach in the wall to enter the city.

'Keep him as quiet as possible, he is still very weak and his fever will go up again,' Martha warned, as Nadya followed her to the dispensary to collect Donald's medicine.

Quietude was impossible while the sack of the town continued only yards outside the window. All they did was talk. Donald asked questions that forced Nadya to re-live the horror of the last few days. She told him also about her own journey back to Nanking.

'Why did you leave without a word?' She could not hold back the question.

'I had to get away,' he answered, and turned his face sullenly to the wall.

'From me?' she questioned.

'I don't know from what,' he replied. His expression was lined with fatigue.

'It's all because of Smollett,' she told him angrily.

'How do you know it's Smollett? It's nothing to do with him,' he yelled suddenly, trying to sit up in bed.

'Well, perhaps it's because of your father then, or your wife,' she spat out the information W.H.D. had imparted.

'I am already divorced, so what need was there to mention it. And yes, my father shot himself. He left no note, so I don't know why.' He looked suddenly so haggard she regretted the inquisition.

'I suggest you not believe any more rubbish that bastard W.H.D. has to impart. All he wants is to get back at me.' Donald's voice was suddenly calmer.

'You should not be here, in this terrible town,' Nadya worried. 'You should have gone back to Shanghai with the others.' The state of Nanking could do nothing but damage his fragile emotional balance further.

'I cannot tell you why I need to be here,' he answered, unable to explain even to himself the strange inner journey he was embarked upon.

Nadya observed him, distressed at his agitation. Something appeared to erode the very fabric of his soul. The anger in her diminished. The emotions forged between them were without any tangible explanation. The resolve to be free of him had already disintegrated. She told him then about Teng.

'If he's still alive we'll get him freed,' she said. 'I have a plan.'

14

December 1937

Second Thoughts

There was no heating in the room at Military Headquarters. Tilik Dayal sat on a chair near the door. He watched a trail of ants scurry along a seam in the marble wall. His position was that of an outsider. They did not want him in Nanking, but would not let him go. Sometimes his opinion was asked for upon trivial matters as a form of politeness. It was known he knew Generals of the top rank in Manchukuo.

The building had been one of Chiang Kai-shek's Ministries. Its rooms were cavernous and echoing, staircases spiralled before stone walls. Tilik, alone in this freezing mausoleum, was without a role. A faint smell of blocked drains pervaded the place. Why were they keeping him here?

At the end of a long table Prince Asaka talked strategy. Asaka was small, compact, hard. His skin was drawn tightly across the bone. There was a thin gleam in his eyes, like metal caught by the sun. Commanders pressed around him. Nearby was Colonel Kato, who was assigned to Tilik's welfare. Tilik returned his attention to the ants. For the first time he felt fear.

On a previous visit to Nanking for the Asia Conference, he had walked about the town early each morning, as was his habit wherever he was. Now, he stayed in his room, in a house used by Embassy personnel. If he looked out of his window he could see the road to one of the city's seventeen gates. From that window he had watched the army entering Nanking. Because of a poverty of transport they had come in on donkeys and carts, besides tanks and trucks, covered in mud like farmers. There had been a crushing roll of wheels, the vibration of boots, and the neighing of animals. The army had appeared a dark, exhausted mass of men. Few streets were lined in welcome; people hid behind locked doors. Soon afterwards it had rained. Depression had overwhelmed him. It had not been Tilik's intention to stay in Nanking. He felt like a guest at a party who cannot depart without permission.

Prince Asaka stood up and prepared to leave. There was a clicking of boots and saluting as Asaka walked past. He limped from an old wound

225

received in a car crash in Europe. Colonel Kato strode beside him. Prince Asaka inclined his head slightly to a chosen few, and walked on. Tilik noticed the clipped moustache, the colours of command upon his breast, the straightness of his back. The flinty eyes remained with him. A door was opened, Asaka disappeared with a phalanx of officers. With his departure the room relaxed. Green tea was offered around. Colonel Kato reappeared beside Tilik.

'Now you have met our great commander,' he said, gesturing to Tilik to follow him across the room to a knot of officers. The men turned at their approach, making room for Tilik.

He bowed politely. All the men in the room looked the same to him whatever the shaping of their bones. They had faces of stone, and were lean on skimped rations. They were weathered by winter winds rolling against them day and night across the plains from Shanghai. Their talk was exclusively of the lesson to be taught to China. Tilik was filled by unease. Clearly, this was a war of punishment.

All these years, thought Tilik, he had scurried like a mole through the underground tunnels of command, his gaze secured between narrow walls, never glimpsing the upper world. Now, suddenly, it was as if he had surfaced into gaunt reality. These strutting men, and rolling drunks, this desecration of a city, the rape of women, the killing of children; had he unwittingly, been part of this? These thoughts now kept him awake at night. He missed Japan. There, near Rash Bihari, he felt part of the bigger scheme of things. Here, in China and Manchukuo, there was not even news of India. Where now was Subash Chandra Bose? He knew nothing.

'You are our eyes and our ears in places we cannot reach,' Kato said. 'War is a brutal event. There are unfortunately foreigners still here who might misinterpret our actions. They refuse to leave the city although we have offered them every assistance. It is easy for you to mix with them, to know their thoughts. This way we can contain the wrong information getting about in the world. A Russian is amongst these people, a woman, whom you yourself have reported to be a spy. She may be part of a ring. We have asked the Japanese Embassy to watch her; their relations are tolerable with this Safety Zone Committee. Go amongst these people, let them think you are one of them, find out what you can.' Kato smiled blandly.

Eventually the meeting ended and Kato gave Tilik a lift in an armoured car to his room in the Embassy accommodation. The car drove at speed through deserted streets, scattering dogs. At the sight of the car people fled, diving into doorways. Soon they arrived at the house and Kato nodded his dismissal.

226

Tilik climbed the stairs slowly to his room. On the same floor lived Kenjiro Nozaki. It was a comfort to know a friend was near. He felt he could talk to Nozaki, who listened when others did not. There was no need to watch so closely what one said, or afterwards scour a conversation for what could be misconstrued, as was the case with Jun Hasegawa. Tilik shut the door and lay down on the bed, pulling the blankets over him for warmth. He was always cold these days.

Outside, the noise of firing continued sporadically. The sounds spat viciously into the silence. He shut his eyes and began to shiver. The shots echoed through his head, throwing him back to Amritsar and the day his father died. He had heard no gun since that terrible day, seen no bodies since that moment. For seventeen years he had worked to forget. Why must he now be pinioned to Nanking, forced to watch its destruction? He was no more than a puppet on a string; Japan ordered, he obeyed. Day by day, inadvertently, he had helped to realize this nightmare, thinking he worked for India.

He remembered that soon after he and Michiko arrived in Manchukuo, he had persuaded Rash Bihari to travel to their new country on a lecture tour. Rash Bihari insisted on only addressing Japanese audiences, speaking fluently in the language. His astringency was shocking. He dared to criticize Japanese policy in Manchukuo and the treatment of the Chinese. Tilik had been forced to apologize behind his back for such unorthodox behaviour. The tour had ended in Dairen. Rash Bihari expressed distress at all he had seen. Before embarking on his ship he dispatched a telegram to War Minister General Araki in Tokyo, voicing his disgust. He signed it, *The Indian, Bose.* Many people were upset, for he was a naturalized Japanese.

'It will put you in a bad light with the Japanese Government. Is this really helping our Indian cause?' Tilik worried. Rash Bihari gave him a long-suffering look.

'My Japanese citizenship is for my survival. In all my thought and actions, I am an Indian. I will take responsibility for the consequences of my action.' His voice was firm. Tilik remembered his face, lined and strong. He knew now he would never be like Rash Bihari, could never hold such single-minded principles.

From outside the window the sound of shooting came again, and a sudden crescendo of screaming. Once more women were being dragged from their homes. His stomach tightened, he put his hands over his ears. In desperation he got off the bed and from a drawer took out Rash Bihari's last letter. It was written some months before. It gave news that Subash was once more in jail, arrested at the Bombay docks on his return

227

to India after a time in Europe. Hitler had refused to see him, but Mussolini had been eager.

'Hitler,' wrote Rash Bihari, is not interested in India. He sees us freedom fighters as Asiatic jugglers. India as a country has no strategic or commercial interest for him. Even his Nazi philosopher, Rosenberg who is credited with such insights into our Indian culture, calls us poor bastards, and says from the German point of view British rule in India must be supported. And Hitler has advised the Englishman, Halifax, that the problem of Gandhi is simple: 'Shoot him.' Yet Subash continues to be convinced that something can be salvaged if only he and Hitler can meet. Rubbish, I say. The way lies in the East through the united strength of our people outside India, and through Japan. Yet so immersed is Subash in his anti-imperialist campaign that he now talks of preventing the growth of Japanese imperialism in Asia. 'If tomorrow China could be strong and unified; if tomorrow India could be free, I am sure it would influence the balance of power in Asia, and serve to check the spread of Japanese imperialism.' This is what he says. These are nice thoughts, but look at the reality. Only Japan can help us now.

Just to see the old man's writing spread across the page, was to touch a friend. But the contents appeared as remote as news of another planet. The sense of distance from those very issues that had sustained and directed his life, filled Tilik now with a new consternation. He was no more than a piece of driftwood pitching about on an ocean, without a shore in sight. India was far away. He got up and paced the room.

Michiko had returned to Japan, and was living in Tokyo with her family. She was about to give birth to their child. Her letters were also with him. He pulled her last one from a pile, glad to know that someone missed him. But her news seemed trivial after Rash Bihari's and distant from the reality of things as he knew them.

We wait every day for the fall of Nanking. Each district has everything ready. There are to be special noodles to eat called Nanking Noodles. At night each district will hold lantern processions in celebration. All the children will carry lanterns. In the dark they will form a great swelling river of light. It will be beautiful. Imagine, all over Japan and its colonies, the same processions will take place to celebrate the fall of Nanking. How happy the people of China will be, to be free and under benevolent Japanese rule at last. It is all so exciting, and to think that you are there!

Tilik put away the letter. Michiko knew nothing but what the newspapers told her. Even if the true facts were known, who would dare speak out against authority? He felt even more depressed. Here in Nanking everything appeared surreal. He was safe in his tiny room while outside his window people died, shot at like clay pigeons. He remembered Colonel Kato's face only hours ago at Military Headquarters. He remembered Prince Asaka's flinty eyes and felt a new deepening of fear. He focused on the window again.

A distance away stood an open truck. He saw now what all the commotion had been about. Twenty women or more were crushed in the back of the vehicle. Soldiers stood about, bayonets at the ready, flashing them at the terrified women. Suddenly, Tilik stiffened. Before the truck in the road, women were already being raped. Soldiers had set upon the hysterical women like a band of rutting hobgoblins. Tilik stared at the gross tangle of limbs and the crazed screaming women. He turned, his heart beating in shock.

He ran from the room and down the stairs, but before the door he halted. If he went out would they stop? Perhaps the soldiers would shoot him. Then he heard the grate of gears. The truck was already driving off, its captive cargo huddled in the back. Already the incident was over. He went back upstairs and returned to the window. In the street two women lay bleeding from bayonet wounds, another ran off in escape round the corner. Slowly, people crept out of their houses to help. Tilik found he was shaking and sat down on the bed. He had done nothing to stop the terror. He had been as helpless as that day in Amritsar.

Then he had been nineteen and living with his parents in Delhi. His father had been called to Amritsar to advise an old friend on a law suit. Tilik had accompanied him, for he had never been to Amritsar. They arrived to find a smouldering city. Two famous Nationalists had been arrested; the town was mad with anger.

'The British opened fire and killed many people. Now General Dyer has arrived to take charge of things. He has a bad reputation,' their host explained.

Tilik remembered the question of college had been the bone of contention between his father and himself the following day as they made their way to Jallianwala Bagh, to a meeting the elder Dayal wished to attend. Tilik wanted to study in England like his father, either accountancy or law but, in thrall of Mahatma Gandhi's ideas, his father refused to consider study abroad, or even a Western-style university in Delhi. A Hindu university was all he would allow.

'These British institutions are citadels of slavery. There the white men begin our training for slavery. Do you want to push a pen in an office, to be the victim of business and industry, to be an unwitting tool to further build their imperial, degenerate civilization?'

'Many men who have received Western education still serve India well. Are the Nehrus slaves to the British, are you, is Gandhiji?' Tilik raged.

'We have survived it. I am saving you the struggle,' his father announced. 'The British Empire today represents Satanism, and they who love God can afford to have no love of Satan.' People clogged the narrow road behind them. They were pushed forward until they reached Jallianwala Bagh, as if entering the great body of an octopus through a narrow tentacle.

Jallianwala Bagh was an irregular shaped wasteland. The crowd was immense in the hot afternoon. Under a peeple tree was a well and near the centre a shrine. Peasant families, in Amritsar for the festival of Baisakhi, with no interest in politics, had camped in Jallianwala Bagh during their stay. Tilik and his father settled near some old men throwing dice. They were a distance from the speakers' platform, but had a good view of the rising ground at the end of the enclosure.

The meeting started with a condemnation of the firings on innocent people. As poems to the dead were read, men played cards or gossiped. A monkey in a pink satin skirt turned somersaults at the end of a chain before a group of children. The short swords the Sikhs wore flashed in the sun. A hermaphrodite quarrelled with a beggar. The arch of the sun approached the horizon, shadows stretched longer under the trees. The peasants waited, hoping for some entertainment after the politics.

'Now someone else has arrived,' Tilik's father announced, observing the stir about the entrance.

It began without warning. Soldiers appeared. They marched into Jallianwala Bagh and were deployed by their commander along the length of the rising ground. They were Gurkhas and Baluchis with long rifles. Before them strutted an Englishman, stiff in his uniform, barking orders. His hue was deep as a pomegranate, the sun sparked on his many brass buttons.

The Gurkhas and Baluchis raised their rifles and at a command began to fire into the crowd. Bullets sprayed out like a shower after a crack of thunder. The crows in the trees rose up at the shock, squawking and flapping. The children about the dancing monkey lay dead, the hermaphrodite fell by the beggar. Buffalo stumbled, bleeding. Men ran towards the entrances blocked already with trampled bodies. They scaled the walls of the garden, clambering one upon another, and were picked off like clay ducks on a fairground stall by the marksmen. Children ran screaming across the ground, women rushed to the well and jumped into the darkness. Bodies were heaped one upon another, suffocating those still living. The Englishman marched behind his soldiers, directing them to fire where the crowds were thickest. From the windows of houses overlooking the gardens, people watched helplessly.

'Why is the Englishman not stopping them?' his father gasped. He gripped Tilik's arm.

'Because it is *he* who is giving the orders,' Tilik screamed above the chaos.

His father had suddenly thrown himself down, pulling Tilik with him. Stretched out beside him Tilik prayed to survive. The echo of guns rattled through the earth, ricocheting in his head. Above Jallianwala Bagh the crows circled, their cawing drowned by the fire. He opened his eyes and saw blood in a pool about his father. A man fell upon Tilik, then another. The weight of the bodies crushed his chest, the stench of their blood filled his nostrils. The firing went on and on.

At last it stopped abruptly, as if ammunition had been exhausted. The soldiers turned and marched back into the alley behind them. There was silence in Jallianwala Bagh. Tilik struggled from under a pile of bodies and pulled his father free. The crows returned to the trees, settling back with loud grumbles. The wailing of children and the cries of the wounded filled the silence. He did not know his father was dead. All about him lay bodies, like the pictures he had seen in history lessons of the battlegrounds of wars.

'Why is there no doctor? Why can nobody help?' Tilik yelled.

A man stepped forward from the shadows, his turban askew, his teeth chattered in shock. 'He has given orders that nothing be done for the wounded.'

'*Who* has given orders?'

'The Englishman. General Dyer.'

'But the wounded will die.'

'That must be the intention.'

'Why has he done this?' Tilik sobbed.

'That we do not know.'

Tilik raised his head. For a moment he was unsure of where he was, until he looked out of the window at a group of people carrying the wounded girls off the street. The memory of Amritsar still absorbed him powerfully. He knew suddenly what he must do.

The next morning he went searching for the Russian woman. He walked quickly to keep warm. A cold wind cut about his neck. Ash on the roads covered his shoes, and settled like black sawdust between his lips. If it snowed he thought, even the snowflakes would be black. He remembered the recent vibrancy of the town as if on an old photograph. Now bodies lay at every corner. There was an order to let them lie, as an example to others. An example of what? Stiff, bloated heaps of discoloured rag, poxed by bullets, slashed by bayonets. Tilik could not relate them to life. He kept his head down. The smell of death impregnated the town. It grew steadily riper each day, making him retch. It blew in through windows, pervading his dreams. He burned sandalwood incense in his room, but nothing held back the abominable odour. If they did not clear the bodies, disease would soon begin.

He looked up and found he stood before the hospital. He pushed open the door and breathed in with relief the smart of disinfectant. Immediately, he felt safe. Before him the corridors were lined with people. They stared about vacantly, faces wiped clear of all expression. Nurses hurried about, white uniformed, like small pertinent birds on a seashore of driftwood.

'Where is the Russian woman?' Tilik asked. He was directed up flights of stairs, along more corridors, until he stood before Nadya. After a brief glance, she made no further effort to acknowledge him. Tilik shifted his weight apprehensively from one foot to another, observing the curve of her back as she bent over a patient.

'They think you are a spy.' He blurted it out at last, like a stone that was stuck in his gullet.

She shrugged, not raising her eyes from the young woman whose wound she dressed. 'To all people, all Russians these days are spies.'

The ward was crowded with people and beds. And yet there was a calm and cleanliness unknown beyond these walls. He had been returned to the order of a recognizable world. Nadya made no conversation but proceeded with her work. Tilik hung about awkwardly unwilling to leave. The sun shone into the ward and set aflame Nadya's hair. Tilik stared anew at the incredible sight.

'What happened to your windows?' he asked, looking at all the broken panes patched with old newspaper, trying to find a way to make her talk.

'Soldiers came in,' Nadya answered. 'Why do you not go? You are with *them.*'

'What is wrong with her?' he asked, staring at the woman she tended, taking no notice of Nadya's remark.

'She was pregnant. She was raped. She went into premature labour. The baby is well, but she is hysterical. She has bayonet wounds. Is there anything else you wish to know?' Nadya turned upon him angrily.

'I came only to warn you.' He sought some way to appeal to her.

'I don't need your warnings.' She walked off down the ward. Tilik gazed after her, wringing his hands in agitation. Eventually he turned back into the corridor. It was lined with pallets upon which lay the wounded, groups of relatives squatting beside them. He made his way towards the stairs, pushing his way through the crush of people and then stopped. He did not want to leave this place, nor return to Military Headquarters and Colonel Kato's face. In this orderly world, in spite of the distress it ministered to, his thoughts linked together in a way that had defied him for weeks.

Until the closing of Nanking's gates his purpose had not flagged. What happened about him seemed of scant importance so long as it led to the freeing of India from British Rule. Why suddenly now did so much crowd up before him? For the first time he saw that Indian Independence was the decision of time and destiny. The immediate judgement of history was here and now in Nanking. He remembered the women in the truck again, driven off to torture and death. He turned and walked back up the corridor. The Russian woman was still in the ward.

'Give me something to do to help,' he demanded, his voice rising. 'I cannot work for *them* any longer.' He remembered her laughter as she threw him out of the barn, prodding him with the pitchfork.

'There is nothing for you here.' She turned determinedly to another bed. 'Have they sent you to spy upon us?'

'You don't understand.'

She looked up at him then, hearing the crack in his voice. He shifted about still wringing his hands. His face had a worn, compressed look. He was not the man she had travelled with to Nanking. She remembered his arrogance in the car, his audacity in the barn.

'All this,' he waved his arm in the direction of the town. 'It has changed everything for me.' Nadya steeled herself not to feel sorry. It was possible the Japanese had put him up to this play-acting.

'You are in their pay,' she reminded him, crossing her arms.

'Japan supports the Indian cause. And yes, they have asked me to report on you all, I don't mind telling you. But I cannot sit here while they wipe out this town. I have lost faith in their ideals. The reality of their regime is here about us now. I just want you to know these are my feelings.' His face was a knot of emotion.

Perhaps he spoke the truth. These were special times. She tried to detect duplicity. Instead, she saw nothing but the same weight of horror that filled them all. 'I can see it might not have been easy for you.' She sighed and he appeared to brighten at her acceptance. At last he turned away.

She watched him hurry down the corridor like a frightened animal.

He was not a bad man, however much he might irritate her. Some fragmentation in his life had driven him into exile. Further desperation to survive had perhaps thrust him into places never contemplated. Was it not the same for her, for Martha, and for Donald? Were they not all in exile from themselves? Something similar must afflict the Indian. Why else was he here, fighting for his cause in a foreign land, and not safely in his country?

15

December 1937

Escape

'You went there? Alone?' Kenjiro asked. A weak sun escaped the clouds and filtered through the office window.

'I told Commander Kato he was an old friend of yours,' Nadya replied. Kenjiro looked at her in dismay. She had gone by herself to Military Headquarters to plead for Teng. He was thankful he was alone in the room, that the others were not at their desks to hear her.

'And *I* told *you* I would see to the matter. Why did you interfere? I received information Teng was not shot with the other prisoners. I know where he is.' Kenjiro fidgeted with a pencil, his voice grim. Nadya looked at him in surprise. She had expected him to be pleased. Instead Kenjiro continued to frown.

She had come here, to the Embassy with her information, asking to see him. Fukutake had shown her in and raised his eyebrows in question to Kenjiro. At her news an abyss had opened before him. He saw himself tumbling into blackness.

'I could have gone there like that myself, but it was not the right way,' Kenjiro replied at last. He could not yet take in the damage she had done.

'It worked,' she shrugged, unaware of the reality of the situation for him. 'They did not shoot him. I know he is still being held but, we have time now to find a way to get him out. You got your information about Teng only after I spoke to that commander, didn't you?'

He did not bother to reply, staring at her, still fiddling with the pencil. His mind refused to work. 'Tell me exactly what happened there,' he demanded, leaning forward over his desk towards her.

At first they would not let her in. The sentries at the entrance to Military Headquarters had barked incomprehensibly at her. She reiterated the name of the Safety Committee. When that did little she showed them Donald's press pass stamped by an influential commander, that she had carried with her from Shanghai. It had served her well on that journey. It appeared to help her again. They had let her through the door.

The huge building had echoed, its stone corridors freezing. It reminded her of the burial chambers of old tombs. Uniformed men filled its corridors, striding like automatons up or down stairs. She had entered the very machine of death she realized in a moment of terror; the orders for killing went out from here. Perhaps, she would never leave the place alive. She was escorted up great flights of stairs to a large, well-furnished room.

An officer entered who spoke fluent English. He introduced himself as Colonel Kato. He seemed a different type from the soldiers in the street. He called for some coffee and listened to her story, nodding in a reassuring way. Lighting up a cigarette, he offered her one, almost as an afterthought. She took it, inclining her head in thanks. Leaning forward to light it, he scanned her face in a familiar way, then dropped his eyes to her breast. Instinctively, she pulled her jacket about herself, but returned his insistent gaze. If some harmless flirtation helped she was prepared to humour him.

'There should be more men in your army like yourself,' she told him, daring to be coquettish. 'Your soldiers are not making a good impression in the town.' She felt sick to speak with such flippancy of all that was occurring.

He shrugged. 'The ranks of any army in times of stress are mostly conscripted men; farmers, fishermen, people of the soil. Command is with career soldiers. You are sure you are not French? I spent some years in France. French women are popular with Japanese men.'

'Why should I lie, you can easily check.' She felt she had established a rapport with him. Leaning back in the chair she crossed her legs and noticed the red velvet curtains at the windows were covered with dust.

'Now tell me more about this man. Why should we not hold him? What proof is there he is not a common soldier?' Kato's tone was conciliatory. He refilled her cup with coffee. It was then that she told him.

'He is known also to your Embassy personnel. He is an old friend of Mr Nozaki. They were in France together as students. Mr Nozaki had a French wife.' If Colonel Kato felt the Embassy was involved, they might then release Professor Teng.

'He will vouch for the Professor,' she promised in a rush.

'He has said nothing to me as yet. And you too know this Mr Nozaki?' Colonel Kato raised his eyebrows.

'I met him at Professor Teng's,' she confirmed.

'At his house?' Kato enquired. Nadya nodded.

236

'Then certainly we must release Professor Teng. I had no idea he was known to so many important people,' Kato agreed. She did not like his tone of sarcasm, but he called in a subordinate and wrote out a message on a piece of paper.

'I cannot of course guarantee he is still alive. Our soldiers are sometimes impetuous in meting out executions to those prisoners who unfortunately must be seen to in this way. If we can find him we will bring him here. Some formalities and questioning will be needed before his release. I will send a message to your Headquarters about your friend's position.' He gave a curt bow.

She was suddenly anxious then to distance him, and walked quickly back down the echoing corridors, her heels clicking on the smooth stone. The men hurrying past turned to stare. Her heart beat erratically. Beyond the gates she leaned against a wall, weak with relief.

'You don't know what you have done.' Kenjiro observed her in disbelief. 'Kato is part of the *Kempeitai*.'

The skin around her eyes was white, almost translucent. A great desire for her overwhelmed him. In this terrible place she seemed suddenly the only thing of beauty. He searched for a way to understand her effect upon him at this dangerous moment.

'Now they will torture Teng.' He stood up in distress and stood looking out of the window, his back to her. His agitation was divided between his anxiety for Teng, and shock at his feelings towards the woman seated at his desk. How could he feel lust in the midst of disaster?

'Why should they do that?' she asked, the confidence draining suddenly from her voice.

'To find out who are his collaborators.' He still spoke with his back to her, trying to calm his emotions.

'Collaborators?'

'Professor Teng is a man of liberal politics, as you know. There are even some who say he is a Communist sympathizer.' He turned and immediately was gripped again by his physical feelings for the woman.

'What proof do you have? Just because he is a liberal?' Nadya asked. Teng's angry patriotic outburst of months before came back again to her now.

The way Kenjiro looked at her was disturbing. Her emotional discomfort had now nothing to do with anxiety for Professor Teng. It was as if a thread twisted tautly between herself and this man. She recognized too well the nature of the sinuous feeling winding through her body.

'The Communists are peasants,' she protested trying to discipline her confusion.

'Led by intellectuals,' Kenjiro replied. He turned back to the window again. 'Liberal means Communist in this country, the line is negligible.'

'Why should they guess Professor Teng is a Communist, even if he is?' Nadya answered. He does not want to look at me, she thought, staring at Kenjiro's back.

'Because of you. It has been put about that you may be a Communist spy.' Kenjiro spoke without inflection.

'What do you mean? That is nonsense.' Nadya leaned forward, her face tight. Perhaps the intensity between them was only his disapproval of her action, of the danger she had unwittingly placed them in.

'You and I are both implicated now.' Kenjiro turned and watched her eyes widen.

Already he knew the wheels that would have been set in motion beyond this room. The silence about them was deceptive. Even Fukutake could not help him now. With no more than a few words she had linked him to Teng and to herself. His past would be exhumed and bear a strange new fruit. He was finished. And yet, all he could think of was how this woman would feel, naked beneath him. He shut his eyes in protest at his own thoughts.

'You are being watched. Friends of Teng will all be branded suspect Communists, and I will now be included. I once courted arrest in Japan years ago, because of youthful leftist thought. In our country such things are not forgotten. The Military will want to see my records now. Suddenly, in their eyes, we will all appear to be suspiciously tied up together. Comrades in arms. A spy ring complete. What more could they want?' He pursed his lips, his voice bitter.

'But it is not true,' she exploded.

'What does that matter? Moscow has well-established spy rings everywhere, to warn them of any Japanese plans to invade Siberia. And an attack by Russia is always Japan's worst scenario. Japan is paranoid about Communists and Russia. They see spies where none exist,' he told her.

'What shall we do?' Nadya twisted her hands in her lap.

Kenjiro stared at her over the desk. Before her everything seemed to fade. He could think of nothing but his need to touch her. 'There is one man who might help.' He spoke suddenly as the thought came to him. 'Let me see what I can do.'

He watched her leave, listening to her footsteps fade away down the corridor and sat for some moments unmoving at his desk. Then he opened the drawer and took out a photo of his wife. He remembered the day it was taken. Jacqueline had sat upon the verandah, facing the old lantern, her feet on the stepping-stone to the garden. The summer heat had already begun, pushing deep into the house. In certain rooms, he remembered, tatami mats had been changed, filling the house with a fresh ripe smell of dried grass. The wooden boards of the verandah seared hotly beneath his feet as he knelt with the camera before her. Her belly swelled gently with the child. She had enjoyed that time of year, stretching her bare arms to the sun, meeting its fiercenes head on. His mother, beneath the shade of a linen parasol, frowned at such a foolish husbandry of summer. Jacqueline did not care. She smiled at him still from the photograph. A gingham dress revealed to him even now, her slim tanned arms, her neck thrown back, the crease of her smile. Her eyes. She had torn through his life, displacing those balances distilled since childhood. She had turned an axis, so that even now he seemed forever angled asymmetrically to the world.

As a child he had watched sand crabs on the beach struggle out of their burrows into the sun. A wave washed over them and afterwards the sand about them was smooth and hard and their place of refuge was gone. So it seemed with him. He returned the photo to its drawer. In the room the light perfume of the Russian woman still hung about him.

Kenjiro let himself into the house. He went first to his own room for a bottle of brandy before knocking on Tilik's door. When he entered the room, he found Tilik sunk deep in an armchair. Depression creased his face. Kenjiro poured out two glasses of brandy and sat down in an opposite chair. He took a breath and began to explain.

'Why should I help?' Tilik replied, looking immovably sullen as Kenjiro finished.

'Remember, I prepared your papers in Delhi. You could say I got you out of India. You should know what it's like to face death, to be in need of help.' Kenjiro replied as persuasively as he could. He let the brandy burn down him. He had little trust of Dayal, and knew he was taking a risk with the man.

'My position is difficult,' Tilik answered, his tone evasive. 'If the woman is a spy and the professor a Communist, where does that leave me? Sooner or later the truth will out. I might face death on their account.' He had seen three men gunned down that morning like rabbits, for no reason other than that they were walking along a road.

'Many terrible things are happening about us.' Kenjiro frowned, speaking slowly, searching for words. He took another mouthful of brandy. 'In these circumstances we all fear for our lives. We are submerged in something none of us understand. It is a horror beyond anything we could ever have imagined. We have become part of it just by being here, by absorbing its sickening knowledge. We are imprisoned in this *evil*.' He hesitated before speaking the word. It was full of Christian connotation to him and yet, in these circumstances, it had taken on for him a new resonance. It was as if he understood the word for the first time in its true blackness. Before him Tilik sat silent. Kenjiro began to speak again.

'I am not religious. I attend to the rites I was raised to perform, and have never thought about these things too much. In Japan we accept that a man has many facets. The part of him that is aggressive is given its place in the balance of things. But what we see here in Nanking is beyond all concept of man's small irregularities. This blackness blocks out our very humanness. It casts us beneath even the level of animals.' Kenjiro's voice was thick with emotion. He paused to swallow more brandy and then continued.

'I find myself forced to seek some way to live through what has caught us here. I fear the future will be little different from the present we have created. And the past will fill our minds forever. If we are cowardly enough to leave within us the residue of this horror, to allow it silently to enter us, it will destroy us eventually, like a cancer. It must be fought. We must know in the future we opposed it in however small a way. Only then will it not destroy us completely. In silence we will die one inner death or another, that only we will recognize.'

Until the words were out of him he had not even known these were his thoughts. He was filled with relief to hear himself. At last he saw his direction. It was as if he had faced a fork in a road and knew irrevocably now which path he must take. Whatever danger or disgrace might later overtake him, he knew suddenly he had no choice but this one way.

Tilik Dayal seemed not so sure. He stood up and began to pace the small room. His expression was tense. 'You are a Japanese. How can you of all people speak like this?' His tone was angry, his equilibrium further dislodged by Kenjiro's reasoning. 'You are asking me to stick my neck out for people I do not know and whose innocence is questionable. You are asking me to put my years of work here for India, and my reputation with your military and government on the line. For what?' Emotions churned through him.

'If you do not know what to say to me that means you are not sure of what you feel,' Kenjiro said quietly. He sat looking down at his hands, afraid any physical movement might frighten Tilik away from a decision. He appeared like a thirsty animal that has seen water but is afraid to drink for fear of an attack.

Tilik turned in fury raising his voice to Kenjiro. 'You do not know what you are asking of me.'

'You are angry with yourself, not me,' Kenjiro replied. He could understand the man's dilemma. He himself felt calm now he had made his own decision. 'Do you not understand, even to come and ask this of you is to lay myself open to your trust. I could be shot tomorrow if you wished. You have only to speak to Colonel Kato,' Kenjiro explained.

'How are we to go about it then?' Tilik shouted, anger suffused him. He could not believe he was agreeing to help an unknown Chinese professor, at the probable risk of his own life. He had been pushed into a corner. And he could see how Kenjiro had tricked him. He had thrown himself upon Tilik's trust. Why should he feel trapped by this thing called *trust*? A gate had suddenly shut behind him that could no longer be unlatched. Wild images flowed suddenly into his mind. He saw himself beside Kenjiro, lined up before a firing squad.

'I can't believe I'm agreeing to help you.' His voice broke on the admission.

'You are agreeing because, like me, there is still something left within you that knows we must not be part of this,' Kenjiro answered.

Tilik sat down heavily in a chair, his shoulders slumped. Kenjiro leaned forward and pushed the glass of untouched brandy into the Indian's hand. Tilik raised it slowly and wetted his lips with the spirit. He was not used to strong drink and it fired through his head. He stood up and began to pace about again.

Once more he saw in his mind the women on the truck, some still little more than children. He remembered his cowardice before the soldiers' guns. Every day now, each intolerable sight seemed to penetrate his body and fester there. He felt ill with the weight of it all. Unlike Nozaki, he had no time or inclination for painful self-examination. All Tilik knew was that the regime he had joined so glibly had deceived him. It would also destroy him if it saw a need. Hasegawa came into his mind, devouring the live crayfish so long ago, on the evening he had told Tilik about the conquest of Manchuria. Fear gripped him anew.

'Tell me what to do.' He stopped pacing about and turned to face Kenjiro. Even as he said the words, something seemed righted within himself.

He sat on for a long time in a chair after Nozaki had gone, sipping at the brandy. It swirled in his head. He looked back on his life in distress. Whenever courage was demanded he had fled or taken the road to easy gain. He thought again of the failed bomb attack so long ago now in Delhi. He had set out to kill an Englishman, and instead killed a

241

countryman through his own cowardice. If it had not been for this cowardice he would never have left India. The memory swept powerfully over him, the brandy releasing his shame. Because of him Jai Singh had died. The memory he suppressed with such effort returned again to him now.

Tilik and Jai Singh had been sent by Patel, the commander of their revolutionary cell, to get rid of Police Commissioner Tegart. The man had come to Delhi from Calcutta with letters seized at the time of Subash Chandra Bose's arrest. In these letters Subash argued for more violent action to achieve Independence. The letters were to be delivered by Tegart to the Viceroy.

They had made a wide berth of the station and came out on the road Police Commissioner Tegart would take. Tilik shone his torch on the rutted road. There was open land beside the road and the ruins of a mosque. After the explosion they were to pedal their bikes through the crumbling building and onto the adjacent road which was alive with festivities for the opening of a new temple. Jai Singh unstrapped a wooden box from the back of his bicycle and began to unpack the contents. Tilik's torch illuminated a group of monkeys, thronged about the pothole in which they had decided to place the bomb. Tilik drove the creatures off with a stick, while Jai Singh placed the bomb in its hiding place.

'There are two detonators, just to be sure. We will each have one. We must not miss,' Jai Singh instructed.

In the distance the headlights of Tegart's car, like a pale, swaying flower, moved steadily towards them. Tilik's hiding place was beneath a bush. In the darkness he held his breath listening to the rumble of Tegart's car. In the warm night he began to shiver. He thought of Jai Singh further up the road waiting, plunger in hand, to arrest destiny. If Tegart died or was injured and they were caught, prison would end in a hanging.

The trundling cars bore down upon them like a herd of cattle, vibrating through the hard-packed earth. Tilik rested his head on the ground and the noise filled his ears. Something drew tight in his stomach, his lungs refused to expand. There was just the sound filling him up, ringing through him as it had before in Amritsar. He scrambled out in panic from under the bush.

'Get down, fool,' Jai Singh had screamed. For a moment the headlights blinded Tilik as he stood at the edge of the road. He picked up his bicycle and pedalled as fast as he could towards the ruins. Behind him he heard an explosion.

That night he slept in the grounds of a temple, a disturbed sleep,

242

punctuated by the tubercular coughs of beggars and his own wild dreams. In the mist of early morning, he retrieved his bicycle and rode back to the road. There was little to see but the mangled bodies of monkeys and a trail of blood about the spot where Jai Singh would have been. The pothole was empty of its incendiary device. Tilik made his way to Headquarters.

Jai Singh had been shot through the head by Tegart's men, alerted to the ambush by Tilik's panic. In the headlights of Tegart's car, Tilik had been clearly seen. Overnight he was a wanted man. At Headquarters they thought Tilik had been seen *after* the explosion. They commended him for his bravery.

Now in Nanking, the brandy ran hotly inside him. He took another mouthful of the fiery liquid. Across the room a small mirror showed him his face, filled with resentment and indecision. For a moment he saw himself as others must see him and discomfort overwhelmed him. He threw back the last of the brandy. His mind was made up, whatever the risk, to do as Nozaki suggested. At last he had an opportunity to balance past cowardice and the long-ago death of Jai Singh in Delhi.

Colonal Kato offered him a cigarette. Tilik took it gratefully.

'We have the man detained here now,' Kato confirmed in reply to Tilik's query upon the matter.

'I would like to see him. There was a high-ranking Communist in Manchukuo whom we had captive. He escaped and it was rumoured that he came south, to Nanking, to organize a new cell. I can tell immediately if he is the man.' Tilik did not lie. If Colonel Kato checked he would find such a man had existed and escaped.

'That can be arranged,' Kato replied. 'What about the Russian woman? Have you more information?'

Tilik shook his head. 'It is possible she is innocent. The report I filed was a hurried one. I have not as yet come upon anything that confirms my initial suspicions.'

Kato laughed. 'She is an attractive woman. Has she charmed you maybe? These people can lay low for a long time. They are adept at diverting attention. Continue to observe her. Now this man downstairs, if he is your Manchukuoan Communist I need to know. Go and look at him. We have tried to get him to talk, to find out who his collaborators are, but he is a hard nut to crack. Your Russian woman came to plead for him here. Is this not suspicious? It seems he also has contact with one our Embassy personnel, but that is another matter.' Kato picked up a phone and arranged for Tilik to see Teng. 'Maybe he will talk to you.'

Teng was locked into a small dark room in the basement of the building. The only furniture was a chair, to which he was tied. The glass at the window had long ago been smashed and an iron grille inserted. A biting chill swept into the room, the walls gleamed with patches of dampness. Teng's head was sunk upon his chest. Tilik nodded to the guard to leave them. The door closed and Tilik listened to the lock bolted into place. He took a step closer to Teng, but he did not move. Tilik cleared his throat. What if the man was unconscious? After a while Teng stirred, lifting his head.

'I have only a few moments,' Tilik told him. 'This room backs onto a field. There are no guards outside, they are only at the front of the building. The bars at the window are thin. You can get through them easily with this.' Tilik took a file from his pocket and placed it between the folds of Teng's gown and the chair.

'Who are you?' Teng asked, his voice a hoarse whisper. He had been beaten badly.

'It doesn't matter,' Tilik answered, loosening the rope about Teng's wrist. 'Keep your hands behind you, I've not untied you completely.'

The man's eyes were swollen, his face bruised. Tilik looked down upon a head of unkempt grey hair. He wondered why he was risking his life for this unknown man. One mistake and it would be he who was tied to this chair instead. 'Once you get out make for the road behind the field. A friend will be waiting there. Start as soon as it is dark,' Tilik instructed.

He turned and hammered on the door for the guard to let him out. Teng hung his head again. The soldier opened the door and peered inside until satisfied.

Tilik returned to Colonel Kato and shook his head. 'He is not the man. But it was best to be sure. The man we had in Hsinking was half his age, a different fellow completely.' Kato nodded and offered another cigarette. Tilik sat down and chatted of other things.

Darkness encompassed everything. Kenjiro had taken the risk of bringing a car, careful nobody saw him. He was unsure if any of the plan would work. How would Teng find him in the dark? He dare not put on the headlights. Every once in a while he flicked on the pilot lights as a signal to Teng. The moon slipped in and out of cloud. It was impossible to tell how long he must wait. Or if Teng could even escape at all. Maybe he would be too weak to saw through the bars, or to haul himself out.

Kenjiro shivered in the dark. He was filled with reckless energy. Every part of him seemed exposed to hazard. His life could end at any moment, the balance of everything seemed suddenly changed. With the decision to help Teng he need now only obey those inner forces propelling him, without the fettering of obligation. Such freedom left him feeling unbalanced. He had stepped beyond every rule. He thought of the Russian woman but instead Jacqueline's face came into his mind.

Against the car windows the night pressed blackly. Far away across the field beyond the car the lights of Military Headquarters blazed out, showing Kenjiro the faint outline of an irrigation trench and the rubble of bombed huts. The cold numbed his feet and fingers. He leaned back in the icy leather seat, and fought for a moment against fatigue, closing his eyes. It was not the Russian woman or Jacqueline he saw now, but his father who came vividly before him. He had seen his father once with a woman. It had been in the tea-house at the end of the garden. Yuzuru Nozaki sometimes relaxed with the ritual of tea-making. Kenjiro had been ten years old and had followed a butterfly to the thatched tea-house. Through the open window he could see his father with the woman. At first he did not realize she was naked. The shadows of trellis and leaves seemed to clothe her. He moved closer to the window. A pile of bright silk was heaped about the woman. His father's face seemed buried deep within her body. He remembered still the cleft of her buttocks and his father's hand, like a swarthy insect, around the swell of her hip. He fell back from the window in shock, running over the stepping-stones that traversed the beds of moss.

Now, as he sank into a dream, it seemed his father chased him in fury. The bright kimono of the woman in the tea-house flapped in the air about him, like so many butterflies. His father was shouting. The words came to Kenjiro clearly. 'You have married a foreign wife and contaminated the bloodline. There will be children who are not Japanese and so cannot be in the hierarchy of ancestors. There is no place for you on the family register, you cannot continue the line. You must establish a register of your own. That is the law of the country.' Humiliation overwhelmed him. When there was business at the ward office and his file was produced, he was always noted by even a common clerk as a man with no direct line to his ancestors. He fitted nowhere now in the order of things.

He awoke with a start and realized some time had passed. Teng might have failed to find him in the dark. He flashed on the pilot lights again. Within a few minutes there was a scrabbling at the window. He opened the door and Teng climbed in.

'I knew it would be you who was here,' Teng sank back on the seat, exhausted. Kenjiro started the car and drove forward.

'You must get across the river,' he urged. 'I have packed a bag of clothes and food. I will get you to the wall. There is a place where it has been badly destroyed, some distance from the River Gate. It is away from the centre of things. I don't think many soldiers will be about.'

'The bars were thin. The place was not built as a cell. It won't take them long to know I'm gone. They wanted me to talk about you. But I told them nothing. Nothing,' Teng explained.

Soon they approached the wall. Kenjiro slowed down and drove without headlights. The moon broke free of the clouds and showed them the great shadow of the fortifications, breached deeply in places.

'You can get through there and then down to the river. After that it's up to you. I can't do any more. If there are soldiers, I'll distract them long enough for you to slip through. Be careful.'

'Be careful yourself, my friend. And thank you. When this war is over, I'll look for you.' Teng slipped silently from the car.

Kenjiro turned on the headlights and drove forward. A handful of soldiers slept near the wall. Others patrolled, pacing up and down. Kenjiro pulled over to the side of the road. They had only to turn to see Teng.

'Have you seen anyone here trying to escape?' he called out. They lowered their guns immediately hearing their own language.

He got out of the car, and the soldiers came towards him. For some moments he held them in conversation, until he saw Teng's shadowy form climb stealthily over the rubble and disappear. Then Kenjiro returned to his car and drove briskly away. He was filled with elation.

It was not yet so late. If he stopped by the hospital it would arouse no suspicion. He went there often enough to meet members of the International Committee. He wanted to tell her. The recklessness in him overpowered all other feelings.

Nadya opened the door herself. He had not expected to see her so suddenly before him. 'He is safe,' Kenjiro whispered.

'How? Where is he?' she insisted.

'I cannot say anything, but he is safe.' He turned back towards the door.

'And you?' she asked.

'I don't know. You and I, we must wait and see.'

You and I. He had said the words unintentionally but they hung in the air between them. She stared up at him, not showing anything in her expression. At last he let himself out of the door.

16

December 1937

The River Gate

Besides Donald, there were still two other journalists left in Nanking. When the remaining newsmen boarded the *Panay*, Art Morton and Rod Smythe had stayed in the town. Donald was as anxious to get rid of them as they were now to leave.

'It was foolish to even think we could get to Shanghai by road. We're going now on a Japanese ship.' Smythe tilted his hat to the back of his head and lit another cigarette.

'You were damn lucky to get off the *Panay*,' Morton told Donald from where he sat in a rattan chair, his shoulders hunched stiffly. Martha's sitting room seemed removed from reality. Morton gazed at the leafy plants banked in glazed pots before a window. Beside him Smythe stubbed out a cigarette.

Donald suggested a beer. He knew Morton wanted him to talk about the *Panay*. The thought of it made him tired. And he had no intention either of giving Smythe or Morton flesh for the bones of their next reports.

'After all the efforts of the Japanese to get us aboard the *Panay*, it's ironical that the ship was bombed while we were safe in Nanking. God, how I want to leave this town. I've seen enough. A Japanese ship has been sent from Shanghai with messages of apology for the *Panay*'s loss, and to evacuate the last foreigners,' Morton informed them. 'We're going back to Shanghai aboard it.'

'The ship sails this afternoon.' Smythe raised an eyebrow in query to Donald. 'Coming with us? Your report will cause a sensation. *Eye-Witness Account of Panay Bombing*. You'll be a bloody hero again.'

Donald shook his head, and gazed at the bottom of his empty beer glass.

'Don't know why you won't go. Nothing more can happen here,' Morton said.

'Don't know myself,' smiled Donald.

He always lived by instinct, obeying those currents twisting him like a compass in each new direction. It was enough that he *felt* he should stay.

247

Since losing the story of the Communists to Edgar Snow, he intended to lose nothing more. This war was for his convenience. It had come to him, unasked. He got out of the chair and went to find another beer. He returned to the room and held a bottle up to Smythe, who declined.

'Find it difficult to eat or drink with all these things happening about me. The old ulcer is playing up.' Smythe looked at Donald with some disapproval.

'There's great disappointment on the part of the Japanese that the International Committee of the Safety Zone are not rushing to get on the ship,' Donald announced as he threw back the beer, wiping the foam from his lips on his hand. The Japanese wanted no observers. Whatever it was they did not want observed, thought Donald, he was here to report in detail. He said nothing to Smythe or Morton that might whet their appetite to stay.

'I'll drive you down to the ship,' he offered.

'This is not a Sunday afternoon outing, you know,' Smythe retorted, annoyed by the flippancy of Donald's tone.

'I came off the *Panay*, don't forget,' Donald replied, without looking up from his beer.

It was not as Smythe thought. Donald contemplated the drive to the River Gate with dread. He had heard it was still impassable. He had offered because there was nobody else, and he realized now, to test himself. He wished he could stop his self-flagellation. What did it matter how much he could face? What did it matter if Morton or Smythe walked down to the river?

'We'll get our bags then.' Smythe threw him a strange look.

Within an hour they set off in Martha's old Austin. It was the first time Donald had been beyond the hospital compound since his return to Nanking; his first look at the town since the occupation. In places the devastation was great. Donald remembered driving this road before, between soaring masonry, or near Western residences open to view, and enigmatic walled Chinese enclaves. He remembered a patch of long grass blown sideways in the wind. Washing lines. A window-box of petunia. The long pink tongue of a water buffalo lowering its head to drink. The bowling wheels of rickshaws. Now, there was nothing but this crumbled town locked into winter and grief. Within the circle of its indestructible walls, it seemed Nanking's fate was to be razed and re-built for eternity. Streets were bare. People huddled in their homes, heads down before the wind of terror. Beyond the centre of town direction became uncertain; many of the old landmarks had vanished. Life was uncharted and unchartable.

And he too, since the *Panay*, was changed. He could look at corpses

248

now. He did not jump at gun shot. He congratulated himself for overcoming old bogeys. Nothing seemed to touch him. He had found a way to survive. Except for the dreams. These still came at him aggressively. Either he died, blasted apart by grenades or was eaten by vicious creatures. Or he fell into madness, swirling down chutes like sewage pipes into cells of bedlam. Each night he tried to put off sleeping, dreading his entry into this world the moment he shut his eyes.

There had been a brief burst of sun in the morning but now the clouds returned. A breeze had got up and cut about his neck. He took the usual route to the River Gate, along wide boulevards, which had once been shaded by a canopy of foliage. Now the road was denuded, the trees felled by the army for fuel. They looked at the streaked and shrapnel-pitted surfaces of Chiang Kai-shek's great buildings. Most of these municipal structures still stood.

'Can't blame the Japanese for that one,' Morton said as they passed the gutted Ministry of Communications, Nanking's most ornate building. 'Retreating Chinese troops set it on fire. It was filled with munitions. Those explosions set up such a racket it added to the panic at the River Gate. The Chinese thought the Japanese had already entered the city and were firing at them. Bloody well hope that Red Swastika Society have cleared the bodies at the gate. Did you come back into Nanking by the River Gate, Addison? How *did* they let you in?'

'Climbed the wall.' Donald's tone shut off their further questions. He saw Smythe and Morton exchange a glance.

A sudden cold sweat broke out on his brow. He did not want more probing. It was over and done with. He had survived. Mariani and those who had not must by now be in Shanghai, their coffins carried down the Yangtze on ships with flags at half-mast. Already there were holes in his memory. He recalled as if in a dream the nights spent on wet grass, exposed and cold, the pocketful of cooked rice, eked out for two days, mouthful by mouthful, sour and mixed with weevils. He had survived on trapped rainwater wherever he found it. Fear had flattened him to the earth each time a plane flew overhead. He remembered only running. Running. Always beside the river. Twice he drank from that foul water but as he swallowed the memory of half-submerged bodies rose. Fever had gripped him, thumping in his head. The dark mounds of moving crows or the heaving backs of dogs showed him where bodies lay unburied. Once he stumbled on a rotted head. Above him was always the arch of the sky. Endless and unconcerned. There were also things he could not remember. Without memory he was safe.

Donald drove on. As they drew near the Ministry of War they were flagged down. Trucks blocked the middle of the road. A soldier pointed a bayonet at them. The strap of his helmet cut into his chin, the metal dented on one side. He stared at them with puffy, bloodshot eyes, shouting incomprehensibly. It was clear they were not to continue.

'Back. Back.' He yelled suddenly in English, as if remembering a schoolroom phrase. 'Here no.'

'Why?' Donald asked smoothly.

'Don't annoy him, Addison.' There was fear in Morton's voice. He jumped visibly at the sudden crack of guns a short distance away.

For some reason, when the first shot sounded, Donald mistook the noise. From bombed houses sometimes there were strange metallic hammering sounds from scraps of metal that had been left suspended. The sounds drummed through his dreams. Morton and Smythe stiffened. The soldier grunted angrily and waved his bayonet.

'Get out of here, Addison,' Smythe hissed.

The shots grew into a deafening crescendo. They burst like a long tail of firecrackers at Chinese New Year. On and on. Beyond the trees they could see an army of Chinese prisoners, crushed body to body in the Ministry compound. They were trussed, hands behind backs, in batches of ten or twenty. They were shot in groups, each line falling like skittles upon the line before.

'They're shooting the poor bastards like a herd of swine,' Morton's voice cracked. He twisted to look from the window. Donald backed the car, turning with a screech of brakes.

'Slowly Addison, no need for panic. We don't want to overturn.' Smythe sounded breathless. Behind them was a sudden silence. Then the firecracker noise began again. In the car nobody spoke.

'I know some back roads to the River Gate,' Donald said at last. Morton and Smythe sat in silence as Donald drove on. As they approached the river the stench that hung in a permanent miasma over the city grew even stronger.

'Tie a handkerchief over your nose,' Donald said, pulling one from his pocket. He tried not to breathe.

They were stopped again, a considerable distance before the River Gate. They craned their necks but could see little except the walls ahead. Again the soldier spoke no English and waved his bayonet. He wore a muslin surgical mask.

'H.I.J.M.S. *Seta. Seta*,' yelled Smythe, pointing wildly towards the river. The man went away to talk to others who also wore white masks. The great wall towered grimly in the distance, its shadow darkening the road. A pale winter sun glinted through the arches of the River Gate. Eventually the soldier returned to the car and they were allowed to pass. They jolted forward and turned a bend. Behind him Donald heard

Morton gasp as he swerved to avoid the wreck of a tank. For a moment the car came to halt and they stared at the scene before them.

It was as if they had stumbled suddenly into an immense metal scrap yard through which an alley had been cleared towards the River Gate. The carcasses of trucks, cars and tanks, burned to their iron bones, stood about overturned or piled one upon another. They resembled, thought Donald, the skeletons of mammoths who had died upon their feet.

It took some seconds to realize that amongst the twisted mounds of metal was debris of another kind. The dead were everywhere. An army had died at this gate. Some bodies were roasted to blackened sticks. Some had been layered up by the sides of the road like stiff brushwood, limbs protruding awkwardly. Other corpses crouched upright, or seemed to kneel in supplication, while yet others writhed in agony. Now, it appeared they had stumbled into a diabolical stonecutters' yard, with figures tossed in careless mounds before the gates. It was a compost heap of rotting human waste, forked up in piles and covered by straw matting. They drew shallow breaths, afraid the thick and rotted air would contaminate the living fibre of their body.

Donald saw then that they drove on a road of straw, uneven, and ascending like a springy ramp between the arches of the gate. Beneath the straw was a turf of bodies, layers deep beneath the car. He drove on, keeping his gaze on the shining opal sky through the arches of the gate. Beneath him the road had the feel of sponge. His fear was that the car would stall upon this avenue of stacked corpses, and he would be forced to walk upon it to crank the engine up again. At last the great stone arches of the gate closed over them, echoing and damp. Donald fixed his gaze once more on the distant sky at the end of the tunnel of stone.

Beyond the gate the road broadened suddenly and was clear of bodies. Now they saw thousands of ropes hung over the top of the wall, on the riverside, flung down by those Chinese soldiers who had tried to escape in the hysteria of retreat. The great wall resembled a giant unstrung loom, thick with mismatched threads. Puttees and jackets were knotted together, twisted lengths of sheets were tied to shirts and vests, or rope to leather straps. They draped the wall and blew like streamers in the wind at some drab village fair. Few soldiers had managed to escape this way. The dead were piled up in a thick plinth at the base of the wall, as they had fallen.

At last they reached the jetty. The *Seta* was moored in midstream. The Rising Sun flag flew from her mast. Morton and Smythe stumbled from the car and stood staring numbly at the water. There were several Japanese from the Embassy waiting at the jetty to board the ferry going out to the *Seta*. Kenjiro Nozaki was with them. Donald greeted him with

251

a nod. After the experience of the *Panay* he felt he had nothing to say to the man. But Nozaki was courteous as ever. It was difficult to pin a nation's blame upon him. He turned to speak to Donald.

'I'm not leaving Nanking. I drove down here to help these Embassy colleagues embark. Many of our staff have already gone. Now there's no petrol left in my car. It stopped just beyond the gate. If I walk back to get petrol the car won't be here when I return. The army will take it. We've very few vehicles left at the Embassy.' Kenjiro looked regretfully at the car.

'I'll give you a lift back,' Donald offered, watching Smythe and Morton sail away.

'You should have gone too,' Kenjiro said. 'That was the last launch. The *Seta* will sail soon.'

'I never make good decisions,' Donald replied. The thought of the return journey made him feel ill. 'Did you drive through that gate?' he asked.

'Is there another way?' Kenjiro answered and got into the car beside Donald. His face had a clenched, set look.

At the gate they were stopped. The stench blew in upon them again. The guard began to speak to Kenjiro through the lowered window.

'He says I can go, but you cannot. No foreigners are to enter Nanking,' Kenjiro told Donald.

'But I have just come from there,' Donald exploded.

'Keep calm. These are military men,' Kenjiro advised in a low voice.

He began to speak in Japanese. The soldier lowered his head to stare through the window at Donald, went away to confer at the gate, then with others. Several soldiers approached the car with him. Their white masks obliterated all expression. Kenjiro got out of the car and began to argue with them. He appeared ineffectual, his civilian clothes effete before powerful overcoats, iron helmets, and the spikes of guns. Soon he returned to the car.

'They refuse to listen to reason. I suggest you wait here, in my stalled car. I'll drive your car to military headquarters and get a special pass for you. I'll bring back some petrol too for my own car.' Kenjiro seemed pleased by the thought of this arrangement which ensured the safety of his vehicle.

'How do you know they'll give you a pass? You Embassy men don't seem to have much influence with your military.' Donald tried to control his desperation. To wait alone in the midst of this rotting pile of bodies filled him with new panic.

'They'll give me a pass,' Kenjiro insisted.

'I could climb the wall further down the river after dark. I've done it before, a few days ago, after I returned from the *Panay*,' Donald announced. Anything seemed better than waiting here.

'The *Panay*? You were on the *Panay*? Just wait quietly here, please. If you're seen climbing any walls, you'll be shot.' Kenjiro stared at him in shock.

Donald watched Kenjiro drive away, waved on by the guards. The shadow of the gate fell upon him. The car mounted the straw ramp and bumped its way forward.

Donald turned and opened the door of Kenjiro's car. Cold impregnated the leather. He drew his coat around him. The stench from the gate was overwhelmingly pungent although he held his handkerchief bunched tightly against his nose. From his overcoat pocket he drew out an issue of *Reader's Digest* that he had found in Martha's lounge, the last piece of mail according to her, to reach the besieged city. The words skated before him, he could catch no meaning. The sun disappeared behind some clouds, spreading shadows on the water. The *Seta* began slowly to steam away, and he looked after it with regret. A fat rat ran out from beneath a bush and crossed in front of the car. On the river the *Seta* grew smaller. He lowered his eyes to *Reader's Digest* once more. It was an hour and a half before Kenjiro returned. As promised he had a pass for Donald to re-enter Nanking.

The crushed town seemed less disturbing now, after the experience at the River Gate. Donald drove in his own car behind Kenjiro who had siphoned a few gallons of petrol into his tank. They stopped suddenly before a house and Kenjiro walked back to Donald's car.

'I live here,' he said. 'I would like you to come in. We need a drink, I think.'

Donald did not protest. He followed Nozaki up the path to the front door, wondering what was needed of him. It seemed curious after the *Panay* Incident, to be here with this Japanese. And yet, after the River Gate, something now bound them. The effort not to remember encompassed them both.

Kenjiro's small room held only the basics; a bed, a desk, two chairs. A fern stood on the window-ledge, its green feathers startling in the bareness. A bunch of what appeared to be paper chains festooned a corner. A scroll hung on a wall. It bore many large seals about a central figure.

'It is from a pilgrimage I made with my wife. The seals are those of the temples we visited,' Kenjiro explained, seeing Donald's eyes upon it. A photograph of a Western woman stood in a silver frame on the small table beside the bed. Kenjiro picked it up and held it out to Donald. He poured some brandy into Japanese teacups.

'My wife was French, you know.' Kenjiro sat down. Donald nodded politely. Did the man mean to tell him he was not like the others?

'Was your wife religious?' he asked, trying to keep the boredom from his voice. He drank back the brandy gratefully.

'Only culturally curious,' Kenjiro replied. 'I was not for going on the pilgrimage. Do you know much about Japan?' Donald shook his head.

'The *Panay* was a mistake, you know.' Kenjiro's voice was suddenly curt. He sat forward in his chair.

'It didn't feel like a mistake.' Donald replied. He knew now why he was here.

'I mean it was not officially ordered. It was the doing of a small unruly group. Some say the man responsible was a Colonel Hashimoto. He is nothing but a troublemaker, an extreme rightist. All he wants is war with the United States. On the other hand it could have been purely an accident, in which naval pilots failed to identify the American flag. The Kuomintang flag has also the same colours as the American flag. A plane flying at speed . . .'

'What good does that do now? People died,' Donald interrupted, feeling suddenly tired.

Kenjiro sat on a high-backed chair, the cup of brandy in his hands. Emotions flickered through his face. He frowned, searching for words. 'We are not a vicious people, you know. Discipline, gentleness, harmony, these are our strengths. We are also sentimental, although I do not expect you to believe me. But our people are submissive, used to obeying authority without question. Our society is structured to bring this about. People are easily open to social or political indoctrination. Our society is not like yours. With us a respect for individual personality is neglected for the personality of the larger group entity. Actions are judged according to their conformity to a set norm, not in terms of individual motivation or conscience. Our concept of virtue is different from yours.' He rose to refill their cups of brandy.

'What are you trying to say?' Donald asked, impatient.

'That I do not like this war.' Kenjiro stared into his cup. The brandy swam into his head, kicking off reticence.

There was so much he wished to lighten himself of. Every day there seemed more to digest, things that turned his stomach further. It was now known to them all at the Embassy, although little was openly said, that Japanese research into chemical and biological warfare was well established in China. Centres for this grim research stretched across the country, the largest in Harbin. What went on in these places was whispered of and seemed beyond belief. It was said experiments were carried out upon live Chinese captives. Kenjiro had refused to believe these rumours. But in the last few days further talk had alarmed him. It was said that in Nanking itself, not only captives but civilians too were being taken off the streets by the military, to be used for diabolical medical research in a centre near Shanghai. Kenjiro could not keep silent and had spoken to Fukutake.

'There is no way to prove any of this,' Fukutake also seemed uneasy about the matter. 'On the other hand, a new calibre of weapon is needed for this age of modern warfare. It is said they are at work on a mega-weapon, that would give us untold power in the world.'

'A mega-weapon?' Kenjiro questioned.

'Not a bomb as we know it, but a container of deadly gas or germs that could wipe out a whole town at one blow. Think of the power such a weapon would give us eventually, now and in the future. For all we know this war may escalate. Some people say we could one day face America. In this regard, the sacrifice of a few captives is nothing if we are to develop such a weapon.' Fukutake seemed to have convinced himself with his own reasoning. Kenjiro had made an effort to hide his agitation. If even Fukutake talked like this, then perhaps all the vile rumours were true.

Now, after the experience of the River Gate, the thought of what further layers of ghastly excess might lie submerged across the country, filled him anew with distress. He looked across at Donald Addison. He could say nothing to this foreigner, and hoped the man would never have to know the grim secrets of the military.

'Our society has no freedoms, we are ruled and indoctrinated by a military regime. It is dangerous to oppose it.' Kenjiro risked the comment. Donald looked up in interest.

'Have you opposed it?' He asked the question humorously. It was difficult to imagine this smooth, quiet man at odds with his duty.

'When I was younger and full of ideals,' Kenjiro smiled slightly.

'And what happened?' Donald asked.

'I had to leave the country or face arrest.' It was a relief to tell the man. If only for a moment, he could disassociate himself from what was happening in Nanking. He looked for some recognition in Donald's eyes.

'Then how are you here?'

'To live safely means silence in Japan.' He saw Donald did not understand.

'My daughter made these for me,' he said, pointing to the chains of coloured streamers on the wall. Donald saw then that each chain was made of small, complexly folded pieces strung together.

'It is called a *senbazuru*,' Kenjiro explained. 'Each piece of paper is folded into a bird, a crane. There are one thousand. The crane to us is the symbol of longevity. The figure of a thousand is the symbolic number for eternity. It symbolizes a wish. Usually it is made and offered at times of illness. But this is my daughter's prayer for me, at this time, in China. War is an illness I must survive.' He thought of Naomi's small fingers folding the paper, again and again, for him.

'In what way shall we survive?' Donald asked, remembering the River Gate. He heard Kenjiro sigh.

'Will you write about this, and the *Panay*?' Kenjiro asked.

'That is my work,' Donald replied.

'Neither from here nor Shanghai will anything get through. Such writing will harm the military. They will do all they can to stop you.' Kenjiro spoke slowly. It was not his place to say such things, yet he felt a bond with this man. The journey to the River Gate had changed them both.

'Your articles are blatantly anti-Japanese. They have been reported back from London to our secret police. I advise you for your own good to keep a low profile. And please, I advise you to instruct Miss Komosky to do the same. She is Russian. On her way back here from Shanghai, she got entangled with our military. She did not leave a good impression. To them all Russians are spies. They will watch her here.'

'Nadya, a spy? That's absurd.' Donald began to laugh. He had asked her so little about her journey back to Nanking. The days of illness after the *Panay* were a blank to him. Kenjiro watched him without expression and saw how the woman's name ignited emotion in his face. He knew at once there was something between them. The realization twisted sharply through him, taking him by surprise.

256

17

December 1937

A Matter of Policy

Akira Murata was cold, and always hungry. The ground was hard with frost. Battalions were packed into the town so closely that Nanking seemed a Japanese military camp, not the capital of China. He had hoped once they entered the place, the killing, the deprivations, the imminence of death from unseen dangers would immediately cease. He did not imagine it would be like this.

His unit was billeted in a school next to a temple. There was no water or electricity. Water from the Yangtze was carried in by coolies. More often there was beer or fiery Chinese spirits looted from homes and stores. Victory measures of alcohol were given them with their rations. Everyone seemed drunk. The commanding officers were also often drunk and appeared to encourage the state.

Akira crept out of the billet and crossed into the temple. No one would care where he was, all discipline had collapsed. Men dropped onto their pallets each night satiated by drink and rape. On the ground floor of their quarters there was a room of captive women for their use. The policy they had been ordered to follow in China, *kill all, burn all, destroy all*, had taken on a new life in Nanking.

He found a corner on a once decorative verandah and settled there for the night. He was glad to be on his own, away from the crowded billet. Most of the temple was already destroyed, torn apart for firewood. He pillowed his head on his arm. He did not feel well. Alcohol left him depressed. He stared at Nanking's battered walls, ringed by the colourless light of the moon, locking him into the town.

He had had no wish to go to war, but there was no ignoring the Red Paper of conscription. Moral pressure was also great, all his friends were awash with patriotism. Those who refused or claimed to be unfit without real cause, faced forced labour or a firing squad. He had been ordered first to appear for a medical examination. It had been early autumn and still hot. There were several hundred students like himself, waiting for the doctors. The crowded room was without a fan. The boys were stripped to a loincloth. Flies settled upon them, drawn by the odour of their sweat. Akira felt ill. For a week he had eaten nothing, swallowing only large quantities of soya sauce. He had been told this recipe was infallible as a means of avoiding conscription. It induced perspiration and an uneven pulse, as well as a consumptive pallor. The doctor had passed him as fit for duty. In less extreme times a 2-B pass, one grade from the bottom, should have disqualified him. The campaign in China was accelerating; more men than ever were needed.

He continued to stare at the dark rim of Nanking's walls. The moon hung bloated in the sky, low and yellow, like a huge lantern. Most moons seemed small, pale and distant, swathed in drifting clouds. This one had settled close to earth, as if to peer into Nanking. He remembered his village and how once, in the autumn at the time of the moon viewing festival, he had climbed a hill with his father to absorb the celestial beauty. The moon had looked from that village in Japan no different than it did from Nanking. It confused him now, this oneness of things, when all the time he was directed to see differences. Everywhere rivers were rivers, birds were birds, cabbage was cabbage, bamboo was bamboo, men and women were men and women with all the same emotions. If he allowed himself to think like this he no longer knew what he was fighting. None of it made sense.

The tiredness drained his memory. He could no longer recall the things he had done, the times he had pulled a trigger and seen a man slump to his knees. To thrust into a belly with his bayonet was no more now than splicing a sack of grain. He walked in a dream. He could not laugh with the others, urinating over corpses, but turned away. They nicknamed him Snowdrop for his bent head.

He awoke with a start. Within Nanking's walls he had dreamed the murdered ghosts of the last few weeks had risen like an army from the ground. They pressed about him in an impenetrable circle. He found he was trembling. Already, it was dawn. The chill of the city whipped about him in a freezing blast. The first light illuminated the sky above the walls, revealing slowly, layer by layer, Nanking's devastation.

'Snowdrop.'

A group from his unit encircled him. He looked up at them in a sleepy daze. Once in the sea he seen shoals of fish wheel and turn, as if they were one entity, not a myriad of tiny individual lives. So now, looking up at the men about him, it was as if he saw one person. Faces, minds, emotions appeared to move collectively. They had merged into a bigger form and retained no separate personality. He drew back then before them. It frightened him, this strange disintegration of individuality.

They had not risen from sleep like Akira, but had come from the theatre of some extravagant action. He observed their heaving breath and reddened faces. All night they had been at their vicious work, like a pack of dogs on heat. He sensed amongst them an emotion he could not describe. If the work of killing could be done in a state of ecstasy, then ecstasy was what he smelled. Their eyes shone with an unreal light. They were lit by a contagion.

They pulled him up and dragged him forward, intent on adding another to their crowd. He stumbled amongst them. Someone pushed a bottle to his mouth and spirit smarted on his tongue. The sun was rising. It was a fine morning. They dragged him on until they stood before a few miserable houses. Their occupants were beginning to rise. From one home came the smell of cooking.

'Wipe them out. Set them on fire,' commanded a thin man called Suzuki. He was smaller than the others, but they obeyed him.

Doors smashed easily and the screams of women and children rose about Akira. He knew the procedure well. He stood umoving as if he watched a film. They saw suddenly that he held back and turned as if at a new diversion.

'Snowdrop, that one is for you.' They pointed to the end house, pushing him towards it. On the door the characters for happiness were freshly painted. He heard a baby cry. Already, Suzuki was lighting a bundle of straw. Most of the men were still busy with the other houses. Only Suzuki stood looking at him, a leer on his face.

The door of the house opened suddenly. An old woman ran out and fell on her knees before Akira. Her white hair hung untidily about her face. She rocked back and forth, hands clasped together.

'Don't harm them, don't kill them. Only hours ago my daughter has given birth to a child. Have you no sister? Kill me, I am old.' The woman's screams filled his head. He needed no common language to understand her words.

'Shut up,' he shouted. Behind him Suzuki laughed. Others were turning to stare at Akira.

'Snowdrop? We're giving you the cream of it all. This is interesting stuff,' yelled a man behind him. 'Kill the old crone. Get rid of the Chinese baby. But not the girl, we can use another young bitch.' The woman wailed louder.

Once his mother had cried like this when one of his young brothers fell off a wall and died. He had been only a child then, but he remembered his mother's howling, as if her soul would burst from her body. She keened on her knees in just this way, disbelieving life.

'Kill me instead,' the old woman screamed again.

'Do it, Snowdrop,' the shouts rose again behind him. They were waiting.

'Have you no sister?' She tried to pull his bayonet towards her.

Why was she doing this to him? The wind took hold of her words and splayed them about him like pebbles. He heard another burst of laughter behind him. His eyes filled with tears of fury.

'Why are you saying these things to me? I am acting under orders,' he yelled at her.

Inside the hut the baby set up a fresh cry. His sister Nami had given birth when he was still in the village. The smooth skin of the child had been like a soft, ripe peach. Akira had gazed in amazement. Everything was minutely formed, the eyes with lashes, the tiny nails upon the hands. He is perfect, he had said, not knowing how else to describe his feelings of wonderment. He remembered Nami now. A sob rose in his throat. He wanted to tell the old woman. Instead, the wrong words came out.

'Shut up, you old bitch. Why must you blame me?' Anger surged inside him.

'Get it over with, Snowdrop,' they jeered from the side.

Now, at last, the words welled up the way he wished. He threw back his head and pumped them out of him again and again.

'I am just a farmer, like you. A farmer. I am a farmer too.'

He willed the words up to mix with the clouds and cover Nanking. He wanted them all to know.

'Snowdrop. Snowdrop.' The chant continued behind him.

He closed his eyes and shot the woman at point blank range. The retort of the gun shook his bones. The old crone crumpled and fell silent at last. He began to sob and could not stop and sank down on the ground beside her.

They came forward then and picked him up, looking at him oddly. The old woman they threw back into the house and after her the lighted bundles of straw. They did not bother to bring out the girl or her baby. It had been a long night. Instead they watched the hut flare up. All they wanted now was their breakfast. They dragged Akira with them along the road, the cries from the hut grew fainter. For a distance the odour of smoke hung upon the air.

At last they let Akira free and he trailed behind them. Tears streamed down his face. He could not forget the old woman. He had killed so many times before, why now must he get so worked up? Suzuki turned a cracked smile upon him, gold tooth glinting in the sun. Someone guffawed.

Suzuki was like those older conscripts who had been attached to new recruits in the military training camp in Japan. For the first three days of the training, Akira remembered, they had treated recruits like friends. Then everything changed. The day was long and the new recruits ran frantically from one task or exercise to another. At the end of the day they collapsed exhausted onto their bunks. Within ten minutes the older conscripts came, and the beatings began. There were beatings for failures during the day. Beatings for insubordination, real or imagined. Everyone was beaten for all were equally responsible for mistakes in their group. Their bodies were permanently bruised, the inside of their mouths cut and swollen from blows about the face.

'Why are they doing this?' Akira had asked the boy in the bunk below him, when at last they were allowed to sleep.

'They're turning us into machines. By day we're deprived of time for thought, at night we're beaten to a pulp. We've already lost our self-respect and any sense of achievement. Is there anyone here who wants to do more than eat and sleep?' the boy replied.

Slowly it became clear the bigger part of their training was this assault upon their personalities. Many of the new recruits had long ago learned to accept a high degree of brutalization in life. They came from rural backgrounds and endured harsh lives. In the camp they were at the mercy of their surroundings as they had always been. The men who beat them were from the same social strata. They vented upon their subordinates an anger formed long before entering the army. Everyone in the camp understood this, even the authorities, who turned a blind eye. It suited their objective of strengthening men.

It had been the excuse the older conscripts needed. 'We beat you not for personal pleasure, but to raise your fighting spirit.' In their turn they too had been beaten as new recruits.

Once, someone had tried to smuggle a letter of complaint out of the camp to his family. The next day they were called to the parade ground.

'We have a soldier in the company who is not loyal to his country.' The commanding officer read out part of the letter but ordered no punishment for the culprit.

It was left to the older conscripts. They took the recruit outside and beat him behind the ammunitions shed. Afterwards he had been sent to an outside hospital for treatment, and did not return. It was rumoured he had died.

In the camp the diet of brutality continued. They had lived in a haze of bruising and exhaustion, passing from day to day in a mechanical way. As soon as the training was finished, Akira was drafted to China. He found it difficult to react to things in the way he had before. He knew how to fight and to handle a gun. He had practised bayoneting straw barrels while thinking they were men. He knew how to break a neck or sever it cleanly with a sword. He had developed the fighting spirit and *the will that knows no defeat*. Something in him had hardened. For a time he felt hate for everything.

Now, he stared at the raucous group of men ahead of him. Suzuki's bandy legs and crooked body gave him the look of a pariah dog. And suddenly then he realized, this was what they reminded him of, nothing more than randy dogs. Their khaki uniforms were as nondescript as the mangy coats of animals. Their bony frames and bandaged legs appeared almost canine. They panted, mouths open, showing teeth, their eyes agleam. They were animals. They were all of them slowly turning into animals. Perhaps, at this very moment the metamorphosis was taking place. They would never be men again.

'We are animals. We are turning into dogs. We too will eat corpses next,' he yelled up the road to them. They turned to stare at his glazed face.

'You've gone mad,' Suzuki yelled. The men walked on, embarrassed.

Soldiers from a different unit ran out of a house some yards ahead. They had the same rapacious look about them. Akira slowed down in fear. As he came level with the house he heard a sound inside, and went in.

At first he saw only disorder. Quilts were ripped open, chinaware and furniture smashed, drawers pulled out of chests. Then, he saw the two women laying in a corner, blood thick about them. The old woman was already dead, the younger still breathed and groaned. Akira bent over them, shaking his head. It was as if someone other than himself propelled him. The words tumbled from him again, although he knew the girl could not hear him.

'I am a farmer. I am not to blame.' He repeated the words as if they would wash him clean. He found a threadbare blanket and wrapped it about the girl. Her blood soaked quickly through onto his uniform as he picked her up.

'I am a farmer.' He told her again as he staggered with her from the house. In the street the morning sun shone on the dusty road in a white glare. He could still see Suzuki in the distance. 'She is like my sister, Nami,' he called. Suzuki turned in disbelief. Akira remembered that once before he had been down this road. He knew where he must take the woman and immediately felt more cheerful.

'Soon you will be better,' he told her. The woman made no sound. He walked on awkwardly up the road with his bloody bundle, and drew level with the waiting men.

262

'She will be better soon,' he told them with a smile. He heard somebody guffaw.

'Don't go near him,' Suzuki ordered.

At last he saw the hospital, with its great arc of English words above the door. Inside, he had been told, there were foreign doctors. They would help the woman. The door was locked and he began to thump upon it. An old coolie let him in and Akira pushed past him. Once inside he was surprised to see the hospital crowded. Only the streets outside were empty. The smell of antiseptic reminded him of the prefectural hospital he had been to once in Japan, when he broke an arm as a child.

'Get me the doctor,' he shouted. The coolie did not appear to understand. Eventually, a nurse appeared and looked in horror at his uniform. He began to shout louder. He showed them the woman whose blood now covered his jacket, sodden against his skin.

'I have not done this. I am not to blame,' he yelled at them. People stared at him in silence. Frustration coursed through him.

Suddenly a foreign woman stood before him, elderly and grey-haired, wearing the white coat of a doctor. When she spoke her voice was authoritative, although he could not understand her words. He knew this was the person he had waited for and held out his bloody bundle.

The doctor's eyes blazed, although her tone of voice did not alter. Two coolies came forward with a stretcher. Akira placed the woman upon it. The doctor knelt down and drew back the quilt. There was a sudden intake of breath from the crowd of people. The woman on the stretcher no longer groaned. Perhaps, already, thought Akira, the doctor had made her better. He repeated the words he had carried about with him all morning.

'I am a farmer. I am not to blame,' he explained.

Nobody returned his smile. Instead, he saw row upon row of eyes banked silently before him. He stepped back in confusion. The foreign doctor looked up from where she knelt and shook her head at him. He realized then that the girl was dead. The doctor rose and pointed to the door. He saw suddenly how he must appear to her.

'You don't understand. We Japanese are a decent people. We are no different from you. We are not to blame for all that is happening. I am a farmer. This is a land of farmers, like Japan.' The door was against his back. He fell out into the street. While he watched, the door was shut and locked again. Tears streamed down his cheeks.

He returned to the billet in the school, and ate his breakfast at a table where children had recently squabbled, while shovelling rice into their mouths. It was as if he could hear the echo of their laughter and the

263

knock of chinaware as the empty bowls were stacked together after their lunch. It was no different from his own school in the village. Suzuki and the others sat at a table a distance away and made no sign of welcome. He got up, anxious to explain his point of view to them.

'If you've finished, the Colonel wants to see you,' Suzuki said when Akira stopped speaking, and turned his back upon him.

In what had once been a teachers' common room, the Colonel sat at a desk. He was not given to outbursts of temper, nor to unnecessary words. He was known for his fairness towards his men, and his care in difficult moments.

'I have heard strange things concerning you, Murata. What is going on in your mind?' The Colonel leaned back in his chair, and looked Akira up and down.

It was impossible to know where to begin or what was most important. Already, all the things that had happened during the day were beginning to drop from his mind. As a child, at temple festivals, he had loved to catch goldfish in a rice paper net. It was never easy. Before the net was lifted from the water the paper dissolved beneath the fish, and the creature wriggled away. One moment it was within his grasp, luminous in the sun, and the next it was gone. Things were now dropping from his mind in exactly the same manner. Perhaps he should tell the Colonel this, perhaps this was the starting point.

'Goldfish?' queried the Colonel. 'Enough. You are as mad as they say. It happens sometimes in these circumstances. It is not easy here for any of us. Follow me.'

They left the school and turned into the street. The Colonel held his face to the sun, as if enjoying its winter warmth. Wherever it was they were going the Colonel was in no hurry. He looked from left to right and seemed without a plan. He strolled up the road which curved behind the school. A pond lay at the back. The Colonel stopped some yards before it, and looked about again. A thin layer of ice edged the water, melting in the morning sun. Akira followed, puzzled at the randomness of the Colonel's behaviour.

At the far side of the pond stood a few huts. An old man poked about in a pile of rubbish, thrown out from the billet. The Colonel shouted to him, gesturing towards the pond. The old man looked up and stared in fear. The Colonel gestured again until the man began to wade out into the water. Eventually, the Colonel ordered him to stop. He stood shivering, water to his chest. Terror and bewilderment filled his lined face. The Colonel turned to Akira.

'Shoot him.'

Akira stepped back and shook his head. The Colonel repeated the order. Akira stumbled further from the pond. 'Then I will shoot *you*,' the Colonel announced, withdrawing his gun from its holster. He raised it towards Akira.

In the pond the old man, seeing the attention was no longer upon him, began to wade out of the water as fast as he could. The Colonel turned and fired a shot that skimmed across the surface. The old man stopped where he stood.

It was either the old man or himself. For a moment Akira considered the relief of his own death, but in this there was also the matter of dishonour. For the crime of dishonour, no remains would be sent to his mother. No priests would chant prayers for his journey onwards. How would his family live with the disgrace of his dishonour? He raised his rifle until it was level with the old man. The Colonel stood expressionless.

'Now,' he ordered.

The retort of the gun jumped against Akira's shoulder. The old man disappeared beneath the water. Ripples flowed out from where he had stood, in ever widening circles. Akira turned to the wall and vomited. When he straightened up he saw the contempt in the Colonel's eyes.

'I have given you this chance to show yourself a man. If you do not pull yourself together I will shoot you myself for insubordination. We have a job to do. We are under orders. We are here in the Emperor's name. His honour is at stake.' The Colonel marched back in the direction of the billet.

Akira turned to face the pond. The surface was calm again. Only about the outer edge did ripples still slap the crumbling ice.

18

December 1937

March of Triumph

General Matsui was still unwell. In the midst of war his sick-bed held him prisoner. The tubercular fever flared, coughing racked his body, distancing him as much as his newly elevated command from the vital days of the war. But Nanking was now secure. Only days before he had received a cable of congratulations from the Emperor himself. Pride flushed him as hotly as the fever; he had done as his Emperor commanded. Surely now Chiang Kai-shek would surrender. Reports came to him daily on the success of the Nanking operation. Although there had been some reports on the disorderly behaviour of troops, he hoped this had now been righted. A diplomat from Tokyo by the name of Hidaka had been to see him with complaints. Matsui had instructed Prince Asaka to enforce a greater discipline. He presumed this had been done. Because of the mistaken attack on the *Panay*, troop deportment was even more important. The eyes of the world were upon Japan.

President Roosevelt had complained to the Emperor over the Panay Incident, and set the Western world in a self-righteous uproar. Japan had apologized. The Japanese public had also reacted with shock to the news of the *Panay*'s sinking. It was said Colonel Kingoro Hashimoto was involved. He was long known for his part in intrigue and plots. It was Hashimoto's fervent hope that war with China would lead to war with Britain and America.

'Those countries are the Setting Sun. The universe will come to life only with the bright sun of Japan blazing in the sky. Watch me, I am no man to sit and talk,' he had boasted as he set foot in China.

On 11th December a Navy squadron flew into the Chinese town of Wuhu to receive Hashimoto's instructions.

'Bomb everything that moves on the Yangtze river below Nanking,' Hashimoto ordered. He might not have meant British or American craft, but nevertheless, the incident had occurred as he must have known was possible.

Matsui's outrage at Hashimoto's actions was unprecedented. The

Panay Incident was a deed of immense ramifications from which Matsui's command might never recover. He immediately attempted to discipline Hashimoto. And just as immediately found his way was blocked in Tokyo. Matsui had stormed at Prince Asaka, but he too had refused to reprimand Hashimoto. General Matsui appeared the odd man out in a dangerous, devious game.

The day of 17th December was cold but bright. General Matsui shivered beneath his heavy coat. There was to be a Victory Procession though Nanking that day. A naval launch was to take him up river to the city from his headquarters in Soochow. Now that he was to enter Nanking in triumph, his mind was full of his late friend, Sun Yat-sen. It was eight years since Matsui had stood as a mourner on Purple Mountain at the time of Sun's entombment, twenty years since they discussed their shared vision of Oriental Unity. What would Sun say now? Matsui felt the weight of responsibility for those dreams he once shared with Sun Yat-sen. He must do his best for China.

The engine of the launch kicked into life and vibrated beneath his feet. The boat nosed away from its moorings. A bleak winter landscape passed before Matsui. Burned fields or rotting bodies and crops lay beside the ruins of silent, empty villages. The migration inland had drained the Yangtze delta of its teeming life. This was not what he and Sun had dreamed about. Sadness settled upon him. He must make this sadness known to the Chinese people. He must hold a memorial service for *all* the dead, both Japanese and Chinese. That great vision of brotherhood between their two nations, and the birth of a Greater East Asia , must not die but rise instead like a Phoenix from the ashes of their dream. His sentiment grew as they neared Nanking and the devastation increased.

A car stood by the jetty. General Matsui was driven to the Mountain Gate on the eastern side of the city where the procession was assembling. From the window of the car he observed the further ruin of Nanking and his melancholy deepened. At the gate a chestnut horse with a white blaze waited for him at the head of the calvalcade. Prince Asaka, riding behind, was already astride his horse. General Matsui was helped into the saddle.

Here more than ever, at the Mountain Gate, he remembered Sun Yat-sen. The elegant gate with its triple arches that he recalled so well, was now battered, shaken by bombs and cannon fire. The great Mausoleum was up the hill to his rear. On the day of Sun's entombment a sizeable group had attended from Japan. Now, of those many men, only Matsui remained alive or without discredit, to carry on the movement for Sino-Japanese co-operation.

His horse tossed its head, disturbed. Matsui turned in his saddle. He was shocked to see Colonel Hashimoto ushered into third place in the cavalcade, directly behind Prince Asaka. The insult rang through him. He stared down the road before him, lined with tens of thousands of Japanese troops. There was nothing he could do. Nanking was Prince Asaka's command territory. To draw attention to the insult would underline his own loss of face. Especially as Colonel Hashimoto sat upon a thoroughbred horse, larger and finer than General Matsui's sturdy chestnut. His rage had no place to show itself. He could imagine the smirks behind him.

A fanfare of bugles sounded. The cavalcade set off. General Matsui, in spite of illness, sat on his horse with a bearing that became his rank. The road was lined deeply with his troops. The flash bulbs of photographers popped, blinding him for an instant. The Japanese radio had been allowed into the city for this event, as had also the cameras of the Japanese newsreels. General Matsui reared his horse smartly to face in the direction of faraway Tokyo and the Emperor's Palace. Nearby, a radio presenter announced into his microphone that General Matsui would lead a triple *banzai* for the Emperor. Three times they would cheer for the Emperor.

From his horse General Matsui looked out over the sea of khaki-clad men, and up to the sweep of sky above Nanking. The same bleak winter sun could also be seen from Tokyo. This thought gave him comfort. He took a breath. His voice had the thinness of a reed pipe, its notes released in the wind.

'*Dai Gen-sui Heika, Banzai.*' To the Emperor, Supreme Military Commander, ten thousand years of life.

He waited for the swell of voices to return his cheer. Almost immediately a sudden roar surged about him, until he felt at one with his army. He could hear the cheer curling back down the wide boulevard, into the town. As it died he waited for silence, into which to set off the next cheer. He inhaled again, preparing to release his cry anew and heard a sound like the squawking of geese. General Matsui looked sharply about but saw only the faces of his army, reddened by drink, mouths open in laughter, eyes glazed in drunken stupor. He stared in disbelief.

'*Banzai.*' Twice more he led the cheer and heard the drunken tattered echo of the sound die away. The Japan National Broadcasting Company recorded each disastrous cheer. On his horse Matsui shifted in consternation. He had no time for reflection, for already there was the order to move forward. General Matsui led his procession along the cleared route to the north of the town and the Metropolitan Hotel. The roads and the cheering men did not lift him out of himself as usual. His jaw set tightly upon his rage. He sensed already there might be little to rejoice about.

A night of feasting had been arranged at the Metropolitan. Food had been flown in and prepared in abundance. Drink flowed copiously. At the table sat General Nakajima and Colonel Muto, Asaka's main commanders in the town. Prince Asaka's headquarters were thirty miles from Nanking, and he had appointed General Nakajima in charge of the maintenance of public peace in the town. Colonel Muto had been charged by Prince Asaka with the billeting of troops in the Nanking area.

Matsui drank less than usual, and listened more. He heard new details of the Muto–Nakajima administration in Nanking. It seemed Nakajima had chosen to bring to Nanking no more than fourteen military policemen to supervise an army of eighty thousand soldiers. He heard jokes about the excellence of these policemen in supervising looting and standing guard while soldiers raped women. He listed to Colonel Muto's drunken claim that billets outside the city were inadequate, and that he had no choice but to order troops to enter town and bed down where they wished. Senior officers and colonels, Matsui was told, now had harems, culled from Nanking's most beautiful and cultured women.

Some fruits of victory must be allowed a conquering army. Matsui knew this. Ugly incidents always occurred. But the tales he now heard defied imagination. This was not as he had commanded; all his orders had been ignored. He stood up suddenly in rage and called an end to the banquet, ordering instead a staff conference.

A further room was found at the Metropolitan and General Matsui's senior staff assembled before him. Matsui could not contain his fury. He spoke again about the shame of Japan before the world and the danger of antagonizing foreign powers and inviting their intervention. He stormed at Muto and Nakajima. Muto pleaded that divisional encampments on the banks of the Yangtze were inadequate due to a shortage of water. Matsui pointed out that already in town troops subsisted on water from the Yangtze, boiled and filtered and carried into town for them by coolies. They could do the same outside the walls. Bomb damage to the Nanking municipal water plant was slight. Why was the city water not already turned on, or the electricity? General Matsui next turned upon Nakajima, chief culprit for the immediate disorder. What excuse did Nakajima have with planes at his disposal for transporting army personnel from Japan as he wished, not to install an adequate number of MPs?

'Move all unnecessary troops from the city,' he ordered General Nakajima.

'Find troop accommodation outside the city,' he ordered Colonel Muto.

Matsui slept badly and awoke in depression. He stood for so long looking out of the window at the ruined city that an aide enquired if all was well. General Matsui's voice was sad.

'I now realize that we have unknowingly wrought the most grievous effect upon this city. When I think of the feelings and sentiments of my Chinese friends who have fled from Nanking, and of the future of the two countries, I cannot but feel depressed. I am very lonely and will never be able to rejoice in this victory.'

The day ahead was busy, but General Matsui now dreaded what more he might see. Sadness pervaded his thoughts and words. He wished Nanking to know that one Japanese at least could share their pain. He built his day around it. In the morning at a press conference he was duty-bound to trumpet official Tokyo policy, but at the end he added his own address.

'I personally feel sorry for the tragedies of the people, but the army must continue unless China repents. Now, in the winter, the season gives time to reflect. I offer my sympathy, with deep emotion, to a million innocent people.'

He demanded the day keep pace with his mood, insisting on visiting Sun Yat-sen's tomb, and invoking once more that past friendship. At Nanking City Airport a memorial service for the Japanese dead had been arranged. Now General Matsui demanded that a similar service for dead Chinese warriors be conducted after the Japanese one. His mind was still full of the previous morning and his visit to Sun Yat-sen's tomb. He asked for paper and a brush and as the service meandered, composed a poem to the soul of his friend.

> In the gold-purple tomb
> was he present or absent
> the departed spirit
> my friend of former years
> in the ghastly
> field-colours of the dusk?
>
> Memories of past meetings
> on the battlefield
> came back to pierce my heart
> as I sat, head bowed,
> astride my war horse
> under the Mountain Gate.

At last the service drew to an end and Matsui prepared to honour the Chinese warriors. Before he could begin Prince Asaka came up, and explained that already the schedule was delayed. The service would be better Asaka explained, if held some other time when due respect to the Chinese dead could be offered. This was the last straw for Matsui. He turned upon Asaka.

'Everything has been lost in one moment through the brutalities of your soldiers,' he roared.

The following day Colonel Muto reported smoothly that he could find no facilities for troops outside Nanking. General Matsui, feeling now like a pawn in a game of chess, decided to show his stength. He had powers as commander of the Central Chinese Theatre that on occasions could be called upon. Now he had been pushed to the wall. He ordered operational commands that sent three of the four divisions in Nanking out on new campaigns across the Yangtze or back towards the coast. Only General Nakajima's notorious 16th regiment was untouchable. It was assigned to Nanking by Imperial Headquarters in Tokyo, by order of the Emperor.

'I wish to inspect the whole of Nanking,' he demanded. 'We must go to the observatory on Chinling Hill.' As he had only hours left in the city, it was thought best to humour him. In the observatory Matsui demanded they turn their field glasses upon one another.

'Let us look at ourselves,' he ordered and watched until the men stared into each other's faces at close range.

'Are we human beings not a curious race?' he enquired.

He swung his glasses out over Nanking. The scarred city spread out below, crushed beyond all recognition. Matsui studied the town for a long while.

'If General Chiang Kai-shek had been patient for a few years longer and avoided hostilities, Japan would have understood the disadvantage of trying to solve the issue between our two countries by the use of arms.' He put down his glasses abruptly and turned towards the door.

'I wish to talk with the refugees before I leave. I wish them to know how I feel. See it is arranged,' General Matsui ordered.

By the afternoon a suitable group had been rounded up and threatened with their lives. General Matsui walked amongst them with tears in his eyes, offering comfort and reassurance. The refugees stood silently, eyes vacant. General Matsui's words on Asian brotherhood they appeared not to comprehend. Photographs were taken. Soon, senior officers shepherded Matsui towards the open door of his car and drove him back to his hotel.

271

The next day a destroyer took him down river to Shanghai. Although the itinerary of this journey had been previously arranged, General Matsui had the feeling he had been removed, like a troubling thorn, from the area of his command. He had been powerless to avert a tragedy that he knew already was of historic proportions.

19

December 1937

A Change of Sides

The moon's gleam across the distant river stopped Akira. He stood atop Nanking's wall before the moon's oily path, spread like a skin upon the water. Now, in his village, the first snow would have fallen. Persimmons and radishes hung drying before each house to supply the winter months ahead. Persimmon. His mouth watered. In late autumn the fruit clung to bare branches, flaming against the drab land. The last colour before the winter.

It had not been difficult to slip away. From the wall he stared at the mercurial Yangtze. How many bodies did the river hold beneath its silver surface? Were the fish as fat as the dogs in the town from the supply of corpses? Below was the usual drunken caterwauling of the army. He looked back again to the river.

In his village, whatever the hardship, he had only to sit in the hills under the trees to know who he was. The valley was filled by the neat demarcation of paddies, fields of spinach or radish, and orchards. There was birdsong, and the perfume of pine. Stillness stretched between those hills. This stillness held something he could never grasp, that lifted him out of himself. And yet there was nothing but the patterns of nature before him. Only now did he begin to understand what this power might be. In some way all that was good came from that undisturbed world. The things that renewed him were of it.

He knew this now because, for the first time, he had entered a place devoid of these things. Here the sun illuminated only darkness. No green remained. No birds now sang. The air was filled with a stench nothing could contain. Within himself too, something had died. For the rest of his life he would be as if disembodied from himself. Only with death could memory cease, and even then he was not sure. What difference in the end was there between those like himself who had killed, and those who had screamed for mercy before him. They were both locked into the same blackness, wrestling with it from different sides. If they lived they could never forget. Madness was all that awaited.

There was a man in Akira's unit who had done away with himself. And there were those such as Takahashi who, like a mad animal must be done away with, for everyone's good. After shooting the man in the pond Akira knew such a fate now awaited him. It was only a question of time.

He had thought it out clearly. To avoid all shame to his family the only solution was to disappear. He had no wish to die; he saw nothing about him worth dying for. The men in command had hoodwinked the country. And how could the Emperor know what was happening so far from his cloistered palace? Akira walked on along the wall. The patrols he met ignored him. He kept his face to the river and the magical path of light upon it. At last the wall caved away before him. A mass of bombed rubble filled the breach. A short distance from the wall was the river. He began to climb down, feeling his way in the darkness, clinging to dusty, crumbling bricks. The voices of soldiers drifted up from below. His foot slipped and some stones rolled down. He heard a cry.

'It's nothing. Bits are always rolling down. Even the wind dislodges it,' somebody yelled. He waited until the men settled again.

Soon the base of the wall hung sheer beneath him. It offered few footholds and he knew he must jump. It was perhaps twenty feet to the ground and scrub grew about the bottom. He took a breath. There was the rush of air upon his face and then the coarse embrace of the bushes, closing about him like a net. Except for some scratches he was unhurt. The voices of the soldiers still argued loudly; they had not heard him jump.

He lay unmoving for a while. Slowly, his breath returned. He stared up into the sky. Thin dark clouds were pulled by the wind across the moon, diaphanous as spider's webs. Behind was nothing but a black emptiness. Stars sparked coldly. Once, he remembered riding up a village road at New Year on his bicycle. The hard banked snow either side of the lane gleamed and flashed under the light on the handlebars, like a cave of diamonds. In the same lane in summer, fireflies flitted and glowed, like creatures from another world. Summer had been the hunting season. In the hot months everything eased in the village. Food, clothes, shelter were all of less necessity. There was the smell of foliage, and long evenings on the river bank. Briefly, the village softened, flowers bloomed, trees spread. As a child, he remembered, there had been dragonflies, crickets and beetles for the taking. They hunted cicada with blobs of glue on the end of poles, thrusting the insects into cages. Such victims had been easy as compared to the bats. In the evening they twittered above the village and the children ran beneath. Dexterity was needed to claim a bat. A clog must be thrown into the air, clear of the bat

274

but breaking its beam, for the creature to plummet down.

He closed his eyes; how far now in time and distance he was from that childhood village. Perhaps he would never see it again. Exhaustion filled him. He would have dozed but instead he forced himself up. At daybreak the risk would be great. For the first time then he realized that, with escape, new dangers piled in. He was prey to both sides now. Beyond Nanking he was without the safety military power bestowed. He was not a victor but a deserter, and must live at the whim of those he had conquered. Japanese, Chinese, and even mad dogs might attack him now.

He walked quickly down the slope below the wall and headed for the river. Soon he found corpses. He began to turn them over with his foot, straining his eyes in the moonlight. They were stiff and rotted and chewed by dogs. Akira retched at the stench, but forced himself to search on in the eerie half-light. At last he found a corpse whose clothes were still in usable order. He took a breath, and began to undress the man.

Soon the rough padded trousers and jacket were in his hands. The rot of death pervaded them. He took off his own clothes and pulled on the peasant's rags. Unrolling his puttees he threw them away with his stout military boots, pushing his feet into straw sandals. Then, on second thoughts, he retrieved his boots and put them on again. He did not know what rough ground he might have to cover, straw sandals would not take him far. Not only the cold but the sickening odour of the jacket made his flesh contract. He began to run.

Now he was vulnerable to the guns at the wall, and no longer a Japanese. He had turned his back upon virtue, dead to his family and all honour. It seemed suddenly appropriate that he wore a dead man's clothes, thick with that putrid perfume. He could hear the lap of water, and stumbled frequently over bodies. They littered the dark river bank layer upon layer, for these were the execution grounds. He did not know what he looked for. Whenever the clouds cleared the silver path of the moon reappeared, always a distance ahead of him on the water. The river spread out wide as a sea.

The moon slid free of the clouds again. It seemed he could almost step onto the gleaming trail, shifting and mercurial on the surface of the water. At first he thought the dark mass a short distance away was just another floating body. Then the moon threw up its shape. He struggled towards the remains of a boat. Clinging to it, he pushed it out, hoping the raft would appear to drift by itself upon the current. Every so often he saw groups of soldiers and, once, a whole regiment camped near the

275

walls. He pushed on, willing the clouds to obscure the moon now, praying for darkness.

The splintered wood did not float well. After a while it began to sink. Each time as he rose spluttering to the surface, the cycle of sinking began again. He paddled on and at last he was free of Nanking's walls; the city lay behind him. Now there were no troops. Struggling back to the shore, he decided to walk along the river. The dripping padded clothes were heavy upon him and he began to shiver. The wind smelled again of snow. He had lost his boots in the water and now walked barefoot. Stones cut his feet. At one point he stopped to vomit up the foul river water he had swallowed. He must make his way upriver, as had the millions of Chinese before him. Only inland would he be safe. For the first time it struck him, he was already thinking like a Chinese. He was running for safety from an army he feared. He would be forever now the hunted and not the hunter.

After a while exhaustion overcame him, and he crawled under a bush to rest. The dark was impenetrable about him. The future too stretched out, immense as the great river before him. In its belly it held, like the river, dark shapes too terrible to contemplate. He knew only that he did not want to die. He did not want to return to Japan as a pile of ash in a wooden box, wrapped up in a white cloth.

The train he had taken to his village after release from the military hospital, had been full of those white boxes. Every train across the country carried the same grim cargo to village after village. At each dilapidated country station the scene was always the same. Groups of weather-beaten peasants waited to receive the urn of ashes, bowed silently and carried it away. At one station, he remembered, a great crowd had waited. People had overflowed the platform, silent and unmoving. They stared through the open windows of the train observing Akira's uniform, and bowed in respect.

Two priests and a red-capped porter had made their way through the crowd. The porter pushed a hand-cart upon which was a portable altar. In the centre was a photograph of a young man. Incense smoked before the picture, gold metal lotus in tall vases adorned the cart. The conductor had stepped from the train with a white box and placed it upon the altar. The priests began reciting sutras as the crowd on the platform shuffled forward to make obeisance. Soon the train blew its whistle and began to move forward. The scene was left behind. Akira had known then that to live was all he wanted. He crawled out now from under the bush, and began to walk again, shivering in his wet clothes.

He remembered again his village in summer. The haze of heat. A kestrel wheeling. Above all, he must remember these things. It was useless to ask himself why. *Remember.* The sun on the ripening trellis of cucumbers. The cocoons of the silkworms. The ink blue liquid of aubergines pickled in a deep brown pot. The gnarled fingers of his mother on winter evenings darning frayed kimono. *Remember.* The stillness across the valley in summer. A butterfly. A bird. A cuckoo.

He squinted anxiously at the sky, fearing daybreak. A seam of light already split the night. The dark shape of a hamlet appeared ahead. When at last he stumbled into it, he found it deserted, and sank down against a wall.

'Now what?' he yelled aloud, frustration bursting from him.

His head was jerked suddenly back, and he felt the cold blade of a knife against his throat. Three men surrounded him.

'Don't kill me.' He cried out in Japanese before he could stop himself. The men started back in shock. Why had he not pretended to be mute? Now they would know who he was. Now he would soon be dead.

The men argued incomprehensibly about him. The boy with the knife began tying his wrists. They pulled him to his feet, dragging him with them into a bare, ruined hut. One of the men bent down and appeared to rip up a portion of floor. Akira saw it was a trap-door below which there were some steps. He was pushed forward into the hole. A room was dug out beneath the house. At the bottom of the ladder a grey-haired man slept on a blanket. A kerosene lamp burned low beside him. At first Akira thought he must be another prisoner, but the man sat up at the disturbance and the boys crouched about him, conversing in an agitated way. The elderly man stared at Akira.

'You are from the Imperial Army?' he asked in Japanese. Akira nodded, gazing at the man in amazement. He was dishevelled, but he wore the long gown of an educated Chinese.

'What are you doing here in these clothes?' The man's Japanese was not fluent. He spoke slowly, searching for words, but Akira understood him.

'I have run away. What we are ordered to do no human being should consider. I am a farmer. You understand? I am a farmer, like you. Like you.' He turned to each of the men. The elderly man translated his words into Chinese.

'Why should we believe you?' the man asked, turning to Akira again.

'If you do not, I am ready to die. Do as you wish with me,' Akira shrugged. Sleep of any kind was all he wished for now. Death might be best, for he need then never wake again.

'Have you eaten?' the man asked.

Akira shook his head. The man gave an order and from a bag one of

277

the young men extracted a small bun. Akira took it gratefully. The older man bent down and poured some water into a tin mug from a pan beside his blanket.

'Drink this. We are waiting for a boat. If it does not arrive soon we must wait until tonight to move. You will come with us.' The man put the mug into his hand.

'Where are you going?' Akira asked. Panic spread through him. What would they do with him?

'We are going inland. Some distance up river is a town. From there provisions and some transport have been arranged.'

'Why are you taking me?' Akira demanded. The elderly man looked at him mildly.

'Because otherwise it is likely you will die. If not my people then your own will find and kill you. You will be safe with us. Inland there are people who will take care of you.'

'But I am Japanese,' Akira replied. It did not seem prudent to believe this man.

'Because of that no doubt some people will see a use for you. But otherwise, as far as I am concerned, you have taken a stand. You have seen the diabolical madness of all this. For me that is enough. I have friends who are Japanese. There is one who recently risked his life to save me. But for him I would not be here, alive today. For him now, in return, I take care of you.' The man spoke without emotion.

There came a hiss from above the ladder. Looking up they saw a boy signalling urgently. The boat had come.

Akira followed the men up the ladder, running after them to the river where a sampan waited. They clambered in and lay flat in the bows. The boat poled away from the bank.

'What is your name?' Akira asked.

'I am called Teng Li-sheng,' the man replied.

20

December 1937

Christmas Eve

It was Christmas Eve. Frost powdered the town in a delicate veil. The roads appeared suddenly tidier. Bodies no longer littered streets, like flotsam washed up by a tide. Because of the fear of epidemics, the Red Swastika Society were allowed again to clear them away. An epidemic, the army realized, would hit their own men as hard as Chinese civilians. Now, any open swathe of land became a mass grave.

There was the flap of wings. Donald looked up but saw only some crows settling on the roof of a building. Scavengers. He had been unable to sleep and had risen early to begin work, documenting for the Safety Committee. *Work.* There was no journalist here but himself. Nanking was his egg and he was determined to hatch it, however it repulsed him. Fortune had smiled once more, if somewhat crookedly, upon him.

At last the International Committee had realized their impotence in the face of the diabolical. There was an agreement to accept a situation in which they could do nothing, and concentrate upon documentation. Evidence must be collected and safely stored for future evaluation by the world.

Donald's reaction to this call had been immediate. Every day he was out with his notebook. His interviews with Nanking's bereaved and terrorized citizens were exhaustive. He probed always for more details. Each morning he scoured the town like a beachcomber, to gather up the remnants of the night's tide. He appeared for meals at Martha's, dishevelled and exhausted. His eyes were glazed, and his manner excitable.

He walked on up the road. Much depended upon his reportage. Yesterday he had acquired a movie camera and some films. It had been found by one of the International Committee in a cupboard at Headquarters. He had commandeered it at once and immediately began to film discreetly. Once, from the safety of a schoolroom, he had filmed the shooting of a hundred men and their burial in a mass grave. Some had still been alive. He had seen movement as the soil was piled upon them.

Christmas Eve. The date would not leave him. He kept forgetting its significance and then, remembering, the agitation began in him anew. He would have preferred to bypass the wretched event, but the International Committee were doing what they always did. Roast goose or duck or whatever could be scrounged was about to be cooked; it was difficult to believe. He was determined to be no part of any Christmas celebration. He walked on, the camera hidden in a bag. If detected it would be taken from him, and smashed.

As always, when he was out on these streets he must breathe the town's despair. Yet he feared that already he had become like Mariani, for all he could see was the same one death, over and over again. He felt nothing now when he looked at Nanking. He walked on and came to a pond. Once, at this spot, buffalo had drunk in the shade of willows, and white egrets had stood in the water. Smaller birds had picked ticks from the buffalo's ears, riding upon the animal's back. Now the willows had been hacked down, their stumps raw against the old black bark. In the distance an arched stone bridge still stood, a reminder of another world. A group of small houses was beyond it. Donald made his way towards them, his mind full of that other Christmas Eve.

They were to spend Christmas with his father, in Sussex. Cordelia had loaded the boot of the car with food and presents. John Addison's old housekeeper, Mrs Weatherington, was to cook the turkey. Cordelia looked festive. She wore, he remembered, a cherry red dress and a dark green silk padded jacket and matching green suede boots. Something glowed beneath her skin. Donald had thought it only the excitement of the moment. He had returned from India days before, after an absence of several months, and was happy to be back with her. John Addison had seemed in a jovial mood when Donald had spoken to him over the phone. He was working on a political biography that was going well, and had started no argument about India or Donald's pro-Indian views. The unusual lack of combativeness made Donald wonder if his father was well.

That Christmas Eve had been a Sunday. On their arrival at the house in Sussex there had been talk about Donald's months away in India and the political situation there. Cordelia's new job on a women's magazine had also been discussed. There was the tree to be decorated. Cordelia had been like an excited child, and John seemed newly paternal. After lunch Donald went for a walk, John said he had work to do. Cordelia announced she was tired.

He had set out alone. It was a cold and blustery day. In the persistent sun of India, he had not realized how much he missed a variety of climate. Strolling along the river, he was happy to be back, kicking at damp grass. He thought of his father's new pliancy and for once did not dislike him. Perhaps age were mellowing him and soon, at last, they might view each other as people. The wind blew up, and even when the rain began he walked on. For a time he had sheltered beneath an oak but at last turned back towards the house.

He found now he was down by the arched stone bridge, as if by thinking of that far-away river in Sussex, the Nanking water had pulled him to itself. The narrow canal was green and sluggish, lichen clung to the stone walls. The lumpen debris of bodies filled the path of water. The flat plates of lotus leaves pushed up between the corpses. A rat swam along the bank. Donald looked into the camera. The stench about him was overpowering, he remembered again the diabolical mess at the River Gate. Why was he doing this, why was he here? *I must.* He repeated the words like a mantra. *I must.* The reason had slipped through the holes in his mind.

There was the sudden sound of soldiers. Donald crouched down beneath the arch of the bridge. It was icy and his foot slipped. He caught the undergrowth for support, and saw with a shudder how easily he might roll down the bank into the water, amongst the rotting corpses. Before him the muscular stalks of lotus pushed their leathery leaves between the sodden detriment, spreading in a canopy over the putrid mess. Eastern religions might revere the flower for creating its beauty while rooted to filth but, looking at the scene before him, he felt nothing but repulsion. His thoughts were disturbed by the sound of shouting. Pulling himself up level with the lane, he took cover behind a bush.

Men were being tossed from a house by a group of soldiers. Those who protested were stuck like pigs upon bayonets and kicked to the side of the road. Donald moved to step forward, but then drew back, setting the movie camera in motion instead. He heard the comfort of the machine begin its rhythmic purr and pressed his eye to the lens. A man writhed in agony in the street. Donald's finger eased on the camera, and the machine ceased to move. He should stop the soldiers. For a moment he hesitated, then pressed the camera into motion again. This was the action he had waited for. He heard a high-pitched scream.

A woman had been run to ground. The cry filled Donald's ears, and his hands shook on the camera. As he watched the woman fled from the house. Two soldiers followed and fell upon her. Donald kept his finger on the camera button, his eye against the lens. Far away in time and place, as if through a keyhole, he watched the woman forcibly spread-eagled to receive the pumping body of a man. She did not struggle but pursed her lips to stop her screams. Her eyes were closed in stoic acceptance. His finger pressed harder upon the button, his breath choked in his throat. He could see nothing now but the scene of that other Christmas Eve.

After the walk he had returned to the house. Mrs Weatherington had gone, and thinking his father at work and Cordelia asleep, he let himself in. The place was empty. He thought perhaps they had driven to the village, and sat down with the newspapers. He read for a while then, looking up, saw through the window beyond the elderberry that the car was still in the garage. Almost at once he heard her laugh.

He walked up the stairs, disbelieving, and opened the door. At first they did not see him. Cordelia's body was partly hidden by his father's fleshy nakedness. From the open doorway he stared at the rocking mound of entwined flesh. Beneath his father's shoulder, Cordelia's head arched back. On her face he saw an expression like none he could remember. He stood for some moments before they saw him.

'Why are you back?' she screamed. John Addison hung as if suspended above her, then turned to one side, saying nothing, pulling the sheet upon himself.

Donald ran from the house and back along the river, flinging himself onto the sodden grass. The rain pelted down upon him.

Upon the camera now his hands were shaking. The nightmare welled up towards him. Before him the peasant woman's face was not stoic with terror, but alight with the ecstasy of Cordelia. Rage swilled through him. Faraway in the camera lens, bare flesh entwined. Moving. Flesh pleasuring flesh. Hate for Cordelia gripped his throat. Why should he stop it? The whirring of the camera filled his ears. Suddenly the woman opened her mouth and began to scream. With one hand the soldier continued to hold her down, with the other he raised his bayonet. Donald moved his eye from the camera. Something snapped into place. The scene sprang forward upon him, colour and emotion diffused the street. The woman was screaming now without end.

He put down the camera and ran forward then, shouting, waving his arms. The soldiers looked up and swore. One pointed a bayonet at him but Donald stepped aside. The other soldier disentangled himself from the woman, pulling up his breeches. They ran off.

The woman drew her ripped clothing together, and crawled over to her husband. Donald went into the house, but found no one. He returned to the wounded man, and knelt beside the woman.

282

'He will live, I think,' he told her, but the woman did not understand. She was middle-aged with an impassive leathery face that he guessed would survive the experience of rape, as it must have survived other trauma. He bent to pick up the man, pointing down the road. The hospital was a short distance away. The woman nodded and trotted beside him. Once she moaned and he looked at her quickly, but her face was expressionless. The man in his arms was of little weight.

He seemed to walk as if in a dream. Nothing about him appeared real. She will survive. He will survive. These people survive anything, he thought. For thousands of years they have weathered the impossible. They accept whatever they must accept, that is their strength and their wisdom, he argued with himself. And yet, within the circle of these city walls what ghosts must grieve, unending? He pushed the thought from his mind. In the distance he saw the hospital.

I could have stopped it. The thought came to him again and again. I stopped some of it, he silently argued. The woman might have died. *I could have stopped it.* The words flitted in and out of his head. No emotion seemed attached to them. He walked on, the camera in its bag upon his back. The woman trailed behind. He remembered again it was Christmas Eve.

He had returned at last to the house, on that other Christmas Eve. Cold. Dripping. Numb. The car was gone but his father was there, reading calmly in an armchair, as if nothing of moment had occurred.

'Cordelia has returned to London. You had better change or you'll catch pneumonia.' John Addison spoke in an even tone, without looking up from the newspaper.

The audacity of such coolness was shocking. Donald changed and packed. He will handle this situation as he handled all those other situations with Mother, he thought. Once, he knew, his mother had found him with a woman, a family friend, in her own bed, just as he had found him with Cordelia. Donald made his way downstairs.

'I will never see you again,' he said, his case on the floor beside him. 'Once I told Mother I'd kill you. I could not bear to see her pain. If I could I would have done it then, I hated you so much. Now I know you are not worth the effort.'

Even as he spoke he felt himself a child again, small before the power of his father. He heard his voice turn thin, and his words form ineffectually. Instead of strength he heard petulance. He hated himself for the failure.

John Addison did not reply. He nodded and returned to the paper. Donald let himself out and walked up the drive, the rain sluicing off his umbrella. It was a short walk to the station. He tried to make plans. He would stay with a friend in Hampstead, he would phone from the station. Turning out of the gate, he walked along the lane. Over the hedge he could see the lighted window of his father's study. His eyes were upon it when the shot came. No feeling of panic filled him. He did not hurry but turned and walked slowly back to the house. He knew already what he would find.

His father was slumped over the desk, the gun warm in his hand. Blood covered the wall and the desk. Part of the skull was blown away. He would never forget the mess.

21

December 1937

Christmas Day

Christmas was planned. There might not be festivity, but ritual would be observed. A goose had been cooked. The smell of the roasting bird perfumed the house. Each time Nadya inhaled its succulence depression congealed within her. Christian conviction might demand prayer, but rejoicing, even on this day, was surely here bizarre.

But perhaps, thought Nadya, it was not so insane to grasp at this pinprick of normality, like an invisible rope they might hold, if even for a moment. Christmas according to Hieronymus Bosch, was how Donald had titled the event. I want no part of it, he had told her. And shut himself up in his room with a sandwich of tinned cheese. He had brought some woman to the hospital who had been raped, and whose husband was bayoneted. He would not talk about what he had seen. The vacant expression on his face frightened Nadya more than ever. He had sealed himself off in some impenetrable world. He drifted further from her day by day, as if their relationship did not exist. Silence was all he demanded of her. She knew each of them must find their own way to live through these days. For Donald, the motive of documentation kept him functioning in an automatic way.

As for herself, like Martha, incarceration in the hospital held Nadya partially blinkered. She shut herself up within its busy, disciplined walls. Here, she faced only the end of violence, not its pitiless enactment. Had she been witness to that she could not have performed as she did in the hospital, tying up the ends of terror. She functioned because she stood as if on a shore, collecting the debris of a vicious sea. Beyond her was an ocean from which she wanted distance. Only Donald swam out each day into its bottomless expanse. Within it she feared he might drown.

The table was laid with some antique silver napkin rings into which was stuck a sprig of leaves. Flora and Lily had hung some Christmas decorations upon a branch of pine. Martha had refused to let the girls out of the hospital compound to attend the service Reverend Moeran had held. Instead, they prayed and sang hymns early in the morning.

Eventually, they sat down to the grim Christmas meal, unwilling to break tradition.

Nadya came late into the room. Mr Metzger and Mr Strang of the International Committee had been invited to eat with them. She halted in shock at the door to see Kenjiro beside them. He looked at her without expression.

'I have been sent by the Embassy. They wish me to convey to the International Committee our good wishes for your Christmas.' He gave a small, curt bow.

The words fell awkwardly from his mouth and sounded absurd. Martha had already offered him a glass of plum wine. He revolved the thin stem between his fingers, embarrassed. Nadya took a glass, and half raised it to the others. The sweet wine slipped down inside her.

'In Japan we make something like this,' Kenjiro said. 'Each year in summer my mother packs green plums and sugar into large glass jars and covers them with sake. Greetings may sound inappropriate but we wish you to know that our respect is with you are this time.' He faced them politely.

'Then you must stay and have lunch with us,' Martha insisted, her voice as level as always. It was Christmas and she was determined to be magnanimous. 'Since Mr Metzger and Mr Strang are here, we can make it a working lunch. We needed to see you anyway.' No one disliked Kenjiro. The Committee knew only too well the difficulties of the Embassy staff, who had helped them discreetly wherever possible with the military.

'That is kind,' Kenjiro replied. The pleasure was bright in his face.

He liked this room with its green oasis of plants banked up before the window, and the blue curtains patterned with a trellis of bamboo. He was returned in this room, however faintly, to his memories. It contained the same essence as those rooms Jacqueline had conjured about him. Jacqueline too had liked piling up plants before windows. Through her he knew too of the customs of Christmas. Martha guided them to the table. Almost at once discussion began.

'I must warn you that, unless corpses are cleared a little quicker, there will be epidemics. It is only because of the cold that disease has not yet broken out. Already the water supply is contaminated and has had to be drastically reduced,' Mr Metzger announced to Kenjiro.

'There will be plague before long. And you cannot imagine what that means,' Martha added, refilling glasses with plum wine.

'You know our position,' Kenjiro protested, looking at the decorative table. He remembered Christmas with Jacqueline, although he had forgotten the food that was eaten. But there had been the same flash of antique silver on the table, a pine tree laden with baubles, the same aroma of succulence in the house. He thought of his bare room in the Embassy residence, so far from that time with his wife. His life had been boxed, just as Teng said. With an effort he returned his attention to the Westerners.

'The Ambassador has cabled Tokyo, but as yet there has been no response. As you know, a report by Counsellor Hidaka has been sent to the Foreign Ministry. We hope with the New Year there will be some change.' His words were platitudes and they knew it. Everyone at the Embassy knew Counsellor Hidaka's report on the situation in Nanking was the talk of, not only the Foreign Ministry, but also the War Ministry and General Staff in Tokyo. It seemed not everyone in the Tokyo Ministries were as yet in collusion with the military. It was rumoured someone senior was already on his way to further investigate things in Nanking.

'There seems nothing left to burn or loot.' Martha looked at Kenjiro accusingly. 'And more and more cases of rape are coming to the hospital. This aggression seems to have taken on new and extreme forms, girls as young as eight or nine, pregnant women, grandmothers of eighty. And terrible mutilations. Many do not live.'

'I went myself to Ginling Women's University as you know. The cries of the women could be heard in the Embassy. But we could do nothing. We are as powerless as you.'

Kenjiro knew he should not abandon official guidelines by saying these things but, in some way, across the hatred, he wished for a bridge. Even as he spoke he checked himself. He was here under sufferance; these people were waiting to hate him. And he could not blame them before the behaviour of the army. War submerged everything. Personalities faded. To these Westerners he was part of a machine, whatever his personal convictions. He was the Man from the Embassy, nothing more. Because he was civil, they were civil. No one was deluded. If choices must be made, he knew in what manner they would be decided.

They stopped speaking as Lily and Flora entered the room, and slipped into their places at the table. Excitement brightened their faces, they had been helping in the kitchen. The cook carried in the goose, golden and steaming, filling the air with a well-basted aroma.

'Where is Donald?' asked Flora, her cheeks flushed from the heat of the oven.

'He is in his room. I think he wishes to forget what day this is,' Nadya replied. She was relieved to see a lightening in the girl's expression. She exchanged a glance with Martha and knew, if it were not for Flora and

Lily, Martha too might be inclined to forget the ritual of the day. It was primarily for them that she had made this effort. They must not know how bad things were beyond the hospital.

Kenjiro sipped his wine. He chatted to Mr Metzger beside him, but his eyes remained upon Nadya. In spite of everything the Russian woman still obsessed him. Since the day she had come to his office, Kenjiro could not erase her from his mind. He still waited for some hammer to drop, as a result of her visit to Military Headquarters. And yet even this fear seemed nothing beside the desire to see her again. A mechanism was begun that could not be stopped, and must be seen through to its end. He could comprehend nothing beyond this fact.

Across the table Nadya could not avoid his eyes. Something was laid bare, and spiralled already out of control. Why could she not reject the strange heat he filled her with? Why did she allow it, encourage it, unable to resist whatever lay coiled between them? Her body was alight.

They had not finished with the meal when the disturbance came. The old Amah hurried in to announce the Military Police. Kenjiro went at once to them. They looked at him strangely.

'I am here on behalf of the Embassy,' he explained.

'There is a Russian woman,' they replied as if he had not spoken. They were pinched-faced men, he knew the type. 'We are to take her to Headquarters.'

He returned to the room with their orders. Martha and the men rose to protest. 'It is useless to argue with them,' he explained.

Already Mr Metzger was in the hallway, his voice loud with anger. The soldier threatened him with a gun. 'I will go with her,' Kenjiro told them, stepping hurriedly before Mr Metzger. He wished he felt the confidence he pushed into his voice.

They rode in silence with the two men, to the building that only a few days before Nadya had entered so precociously. Kenjiro was silent beside her. He dare not tell her that on this Christmas Day, Prince Asaka had moved his Headquarters into the heart of Nanking, to better direct the terror. At first Kenjiro had hoped that a man of this status might, on seeing first hand the conditions in Nanking, be prepared to exert some control But he had been told in the Embassy to expect no such thing. The terror was to continue. This was a war of punishment.

The freezing building echoed as before. This time they descended to a lower level, to a corridor of small rooms. Nadya was thrust roughly through one of the doors and pushed towards a chair before a table. She drew her coat tightly about her in the icy room. Two men came in and ordered Kenjiro out. He explained his position at the Embassy.

'She is a spy,' they insisted. He shook his head.

'There is a mistake. She is a member of the International Committee. It is my job to liaise between these people and our Embassy. On behalf of the Embassy I should be present. Besides, I can interpret, it will make the interrogation easier for you,' he pleaded. Eventually he was sent to negotiate at a higher level. Nadya looked at him in terror.

'They will only question you. They will not touch you,' he promised her before closing the door and making his way upstairs. His pulse beat quickly with his own fear. His vulnerability before the Military stalked him too closely here.

He was shown into a large, well-furnished room. Colonel Kato introduced himself. 'We believe the woman is a spy,' he announced to Kenjiro.

'I have been assigned to the case,' Kenjiro argued. 'She is a member of the International Committee. Any excessive abuse could bring more pressure on Japan from international powers. After the Panay Incident we cannot risk anything more. International Committee members are already on their way here to protest her being held. It is my belief she is innocent of the charges against her.' Kenjiro faced Colonel Kato squarely.

'We have no use for Embassy interference,' Colonel Kato answered curtly. He lit a cigarette and did not offer one to Kenjiro. 'We are not convinced at all of her innocence. She is familiar with Professor Teng, a Communist. He has recently escaped from detention here.' Kato exhaled smoke lazily from his chair while assessing Kenjiro, who still stood tensely before him. 'I believe you too are acquainted with this man. Miss Komosky herself informed me when she visited this very office the other day.'

'I knew him long ago in France, when we were students. I met him here after many years. It is some time since I last saw him. I did not suspect then that he was a Communist. But these people can lie very low, of course.' At last the garrotte was being turned. He met Colonel Kato's eyes impassively. Bluff was the only chance. And Teng had already escaped.

'You met with him and the Russian woman at his house I believe?' Colonel Kato looked at him, a slight smile on his face.

'That was the time I last saw him. The Russian woman works at the university with him.'

'She might also be one of those who is lying low, charmingly so, of course,' Kato said. 'Why were you visiting this Teng at all?'

'I had some feeling he might be involved with the Communists. Even though he was a friend, I felt it my duty to determine if this was so.' Kenjiro had already rehearsed many times just such a scene as this.

289

'Ah, more detective work?' Colonel Kato replied.

'It was suspected at the Embassy that the Russian woman might be a spy. This was why I was ordered to enquire into the matter, why I had contact with her. I did not know her before this.' He resented the interrogation.

'Our own source has filed proof of her position.'

'This same source, the Indian, Dayal, first alerted us also,' Kenjiro argued. Kato showed no expression.

'I believe your own sympathies are not so far from people such as these?' Kato tested him. 'I have heard disturbing rumours about your early life.'

'In youth one often flirts dangerously with ideologies. I have seen the error of those ways. Nothing is more important than loyalty to the country. I think you can find ample proof of my sincerity in this regard.' He would not be intimidated. He must trust that neither Fukatake nor Tilik Dayal would give him away. 'I am lodged in the same house as Dayal. He would give you proof of my sincerity.'

Kato nodded. 'Your father is an eminent man.'

'His life is dedicated to the progress of the country.'

Kato was silent, nodding to himself. 'You may go. But do not forget we see everything here. Interpret for that Russian woman, certainly it will be of help. I can spare no one with proper English ability at the moment to go down there. Do not bother to investigate further yourself. We shall be keepng an eye on her.' Kato turned to the papers on his desk, dismissing Kenjiro.

He turned in relief out of the door and made his way back to the room where Nadya was being held.

'How long is this to take?' Nadya implored. Already three hours had passed. 'Their questions are ridiculous. How many times must I go over and over my life in Russia, the flight with Sergei and his meetings with Shepenov of which I know nothing.'

'It will take as long as it will take,' Kenjiro answered.

'Do not speak unless you are spoken to,' admonished the interrogator, a burly man with gold teeth. 'When did you last see this Shepenov?'

'How many times must I tell you? I did not know him. My husband disappeared with him. I was deserted. My money was used to get him out of Russia and my jewellery stolen to further his journey. He had no other use for me. I knew nothing of anything.' Her head hummed with frustration.

'If you do not tell the truth there are many ways we can find to make you tell us.' The burly man stood near her, his fist rested on the table.

'But I have told you,' she shouted, angry now. 'I left Russia to get away from Communists. I had no idea Professor Teng was a Communist. Nobody I know at the university knew this. It has been a shock to me.'

'Do not shout,' the burly man yelled. He stepped forward and slapped her across the face.

She turned in distress to Kenjiro, but he averted his eyes. If he attempted to intervene it might go worse for her, and he would be dismissed from the room. Nadya slumped forward on the table, her head buried in her arms and sobbed. The man pulled her head back by the hair.

'Sit up. Answer the questions. When did you last see Shepenov? Who are your cell members here in Nanking, other than this Teng?'

'I am not a Communist. I know nobody,' she pleaded again. It went on and on.

Already it was dark. A single light bulb now lit the small room. There was no glass in the window. Their breath froze about them.

'Take her away,' the burly man ordered Kenjiro at last. 'It is enough for today. We will watch her. Let her think we are finished with her, that we think her innocent.'

He guided her up the narrow flight of stairs, afraid she might collapse. Her body trembled. Outside the blackness was dense about them. Kenjiro shone a torch upon the road, anxious not to stumble over a corpse. In the distance were flares and the usual sounds of soldiers. They did not speak, hurrying along the road. The fabric of his life seemed suddenly transparent, disintegrating before him. One word from Dayal and he was finished. Except that Dayal too could be similarly destroyed by a word from Kenjiro. Such a double-bladed trust was now the only security. He had reckoned on it the day he spoke to the man. There was no safety but the fear they instilled in each other.

'Let us stop,' she said, out of breath, and weak with relief. Now, a short distance away, she could already see the hospital, light streaming from its many windows.

'Here.' He turned into the ground of a ruined temple. A drizzle had started. The moon shone weakly through passing clouds, giving a partial light.

'I never thought they would let me go,' she admitted leaning back against a balustrade. The numbness in her began to dissolve. Her head ached violently.

'They will watch you. They may call you again,' Kenjiro informed her.

'And you? Will they question you?' she asked. They seemed locked inevitably together now.

291

'They already tried, in a roundabout way. They will try again, more seriously. I must expect that,' Kenjiro replied.

He realized he still held her arm. He had never touched her before, and withdrew his hand abruptly. Swinging the beam of the torch about, he examined the remains of the building around them. It was dry under the deep eaves of the temple, but half the roof was smashed and rubble blocked the courtyard. All he was aware of was the woman beside him, and knew she watched him in the half-light. Without a word he turned her to him then.

'Come,' he said.

She made no reply but followed him.

He had seen by the torch that deeper within the temple there was a small pavilion. Their footsteps echoed upon the stone floor as they entered. Pieces of broken furniture lay about. The place had been looted of valuables, but not entirely destroyed. The silence fell about them, cutting them off in a separate world. They were sheltered here from the blast of the wind. It moaned weakly through cracks, or rattled at a window. There was the smell of dust and emptiness, and the fustiness of rodent droppings. Kenjiro flashed the torch around illuminating cobwebs, opulent as draperies, across a wooden screen. Great supporting columns, thick as trees, the red lacquer now splintered, rose up and vanished into blackness. Far above was the occasional rustle of wings. A rat ran across Kenjiro's feet and Nadya drew back, gripping his arm.

'It is all right,' he said. 'They will run from the light.'

He placed the torch on a ledge, its beam speared the darkness opening up a small space. He took her by the shoulders, pushing her against a wooden column. She made no move, but he felt her body tighten. Slowly then, she wound herself about him.

At first he did not kiss her but pressed the weight of himself upon her, moving against her rhythmically. He began to unbutton her blouse and she felt his lips against her breasts and upon her nipples. There seemed no urgency in his movements, as if this was a journey of pleasure he needed to extend. His hand travelled over her until he reached the centre of her body. There was no violence in his caress, but she knew the intensity of his pleasure. His tongue explored her mouth insistently. A fire began in her belly. She had wanted this she knew, with this man, as if from the beginning of time. She wanted him filling her until no space was left. She felt him rise against her and she began to loosen his clothes.

'Slowly,' he whispered, leading her now away from the support of the pillar. He laid their coats, one upon another, on the floor.

The stone was icy beneath the coats, discomfort in the extreme. Through the clumsy layers of clothing she could feel him hard against her belly, between her legs. The dim beam of the torch showed her his face, exposed to every emotion. All she wanted was to solder herself upon him. She felt she would scream if he did not now enter her. She raised her limbs to lock herself about him, and at last he thrust into her, to the deepest recess she could offer. She gasped aloud with the pleasure. And now there was nothing but the wild unstoppable race of their bodies to consume each other. She could not spread herself enough about him. The pulse of her body mounted to suffuse her, until it ripped through her. She heard herself cry out.

It seemed she had returned from some place beyond herself. Slowly, she was aware of the silence, the cold, the weak beam of the torch, the fusty smell of rodent droppings. Far above she heard again the flapping of wings. And, in the distance, the scream of a woman. The cry came again and again. It had mixed with her own, moments earlier. She blocked it from her ears. He stroked her face lightly, running his fingers over her eyes, her mouth, looking down at her in the spear of light. He bent to kiss her breasts.

'It is not right,' she whispered.

Her body was full of the languor of satisfaction, but her mind was suddenly filled by confusion. What right had they to such gratification, at this time and in this place? The obscenity of it appalled her. She hid her face in his shoulder. And she had shared this lust with a man who belonged to those who ran the killing machine.

'It is right,' he said, and drew a coat over them for warmth. He raised himself on an elbow and looked down at her. He saw there were tears of distress in her eyes.

'Why?' he asked, wiping them with his fingers.

'Because this whole town is consumed by this same evil flame; *lust*. We are no better than those animals out there. Do you not see, we have been touched by the same poison as them.' She remembered again the cry she had heard in the midst of their emotion.

He shook his head. 'You are wrong. This feeling, this lust you speak of, it has many faces. Out there it is death. But here, between us, it is life. It is only good.'

She could not agree. 'It is not love that we feel for each other; you know that. So how can it be good?' Already she knew that what she felt for him was not what she felt for Donald. There was no gentleness in this feeling. There was only a fire, burning away beneath them. It would burn until they were destroyed. If he wished she would spread herself again for him now, in an hour, tomorrow, in a week. As many times as he wished she would weld herself to him in any base manner. There was nothing left of herself. She would beg for what he could give.

'You do not understand,' Kenjiro replied. 'We are alive. Perhaps this is why we have needed each other. To confirm that, in the midst of this evil, something good can still exist. This feeling between us is proof of life, of regeneration. It is a gift. Take from it and be thankful.'

She looked at him in silence. In the darkness she was alight again. She could think of nothing but the need to be filled by him once more. Reaching out, she drew his hands to her body. If this molten shoot within her was life, then she needed to know it, again and again.

22

December 1937

End of the Day

'Is Nadya back?' Lily asked, fear rounding out her words. Flora shook her head.

'The man from the Embassy is with her. He is nice. She will be all right,' Flora comforted, and wished she herself could be so easily assured.

The hospital kitchen was deserted. Its huge cauldrons were stacked in piles or hung from hooks upon the walls, the patina of age upon them. Earlier they had bubbled upon great burners, full of rice or vegetables. It was no longer easy to feed the patients. Supplies were running out. As always there was the lingering smell of stale cooked food in the room.

'She is not a spy,' Lily burst out.

'Of course she is not,' Flora assured.

'Then why did they take her?' Lily argued.

'Nothing makes sense at this time,' Flora replied. She poured milk into a small pan and set it to boil. Martha had been called to an emergency operation.

'Mother and the others have been to wherever it is she was taken to. They were told she would be released soon, but first they have to ask her some questions. She should be home soon,' Flora assured.

Now, although she knew the worst sights were still kept from her, Flora was allowed on to the wards as auxiliary help, like Nadya. She took temperatures, helped to give bed baths, fetched and carried as directed, and did not back away from the things she saw. It was surprising to trace the rise of confidence in herself. She decided then that she wished to be a doctor. Martha was delighted.

It was only that one word, *rape*, that still reverberated icily through her. Everything else she had faced. And she knew who those women were, bed after bed of them. They lay silent, faces vacant. Something within them was destroyed. It terrified her in an inexplicable way.

'Do you want hot chocolate?' Flora asked.

Lily nodded. 'It is full moon. I want to go outside.'

'In a few minutes. I'll come with you,' Flora promised.

'I want to go out *now*,' Lily was truculent. She felt like a dog on a lead, allowed nowhere without Flora. 'I only want to go into the garden.'

'In a minute,' Flora admonished. 'First I have to take these towels upstairs. Wait here.' She put the hot chocolate down before her sister. Lily sat with a pout, and took the mug in her hands. She watched Flora disappear from the kitchen, half-hidden behind a pile of towels.

She did not want to be a doctor. She hated everything to do with the hospital, from the smells of disinfectant to the crying children, to the mangled expressions on the faces of patients. Even school would be better than this. Never again would she dismiss the advantages of school. Why was Nadya not back? She felt sick with worry. Everyone else seemed to be able to immerse their worries in yet another flurry of work. Only she seemed excluded from this relief. Instead, Martha insisted she study and had even secured a teacher from one of Nanking's schools, who spoke fluent English and French. She had come to live in the hospital. Every day with Miss Han Lily studied. There seemed no time for anything else. It was just as her mother planned. Sometimes, it was difficult to remember the city was in the midst of a sacking. The hospital was an island.

Why was Nadya not back? If it were not for Nadya she would scream from boredom. When she was older she intended looking like Nadya. Sometimes, Nadya invited her into her own room and opened the cupboards and the trunk which stood at the end of her bed. Then Lily chose. There were dresses fine as gossamer. There were the robes of Mandarins, embroidered with butterflies and peonies, like fantastical gardens. There were jade bangles that clanked upon her thin wrists and beads of sea-washed colours. There was a necklace brilliant as the setting sun. This was coral, Nadya told her and came from deep in the sea. There was the fur of a silver fox, softer than anything she had ever touched. Lily drew her breath tight when Nadya draped this about her. And scarves. Nadya had scarves of every colour, flowered, paisley, spotted, silver as the moon, gold as the sun, worked in thread or splashed with paint.

'One day we shall go to Paris together. Everyone will look at us. We will be the talk of the town. All the men will want to dance with us,' Nadya told her.

Then, when they were both dressed, the best part came. Nadya wound up the phonograph. They stuffed a towel down the trumpet so that the sound would not carry.

'One two three. One two three.' Nadya hummed. They both whirled about the room. Lily screamed with delight.

It was a secret between them. Lily told nobody, not even Flora to whom usually she told everything. She had the feeling Flora, now she had decided to be a doctor, might not approve of frivolity. Nor she was sure would her mother. Already Nadya had taught her the waltz and the fox-trot. Next, promised Nadya, they would advance to the polka.

'When?' Lily screamed.

'When there is time,' Nadya promised. For this was something they could not indulge in every day. These were serious times. And yet, now that Nadya was teaching her to dance, nothing seemed so serious.

'One. Two. Three.' Lily sipped her hot chocolate, swinging the cup before her.

'What are you doing? How can you sing when people are dying?' Flora came back into the room. 'Mother says to go home and get ready for bed. She is coming soon. You wanted to go out. Let's go.'

Flora opened the back door into the compound. Across the yard the lights were on in their home. Donald could be seen in a chair by a window, head bent, reading. It was bright in the servants' quarters, Amah would be waiting for them. Flora led the way. Lily looked up at the window of Nadya's room, dark and unoccupied. A chill passed through her.

'She is all right. Before we sleep she will be back,' Flora reassured. Lily could detect the stress now behind Flora's easy words.

They reached the square of garden in the middle of the compound. The plum tree had bloomed early. 'It is still Christmas Day,' Lily remembered.

She looked up through the flowering tree at the glint of stars. The white mass of flowers against the night took her breath away. Nadya had a black velvet jacket, padded and tightly waisted, thickly embroidered with fronds of pale leaves, that looked just like this sky. 'It is still Christmas. I want to stay out here,' Lily pouted. Any moment Nadya must come through the gate. 'See, that bright star up there, that's the Pole Star, the one the Three Kings followed.'

'You must come straight in. You know the rule. Mother will be angry.' Flora was cold. The iciness pinched her nose. Lily wore a padded Chinese suit and so did not feel the chill so acutely.

'I've only got this sweater on. Not being left on your own is for your protection,' she pointed out. Lily did her famous pout.

'Why is it only me who needs protection? Has anything happened to me yet? You go in. I shall sit here. I love it under this tree. It's like fairyland.' She stared up again at the magic blossom, massed in drifts against the dark. Just to be out of the smells and the sights of the hospital was a precious thing.

Flora pursed her lips. She had had her fill of Lily's perversity. Wherever she turned she must remember Lily. She wanted nothing now but to close her eyes and sleep for one hundred years. Martha. Lily. Lily. Martha. She felt the weight of them both upon her, like a pair of scales she must balance forever.

'Then you sit here. I am going in,' Flora announced. She would leave Lily five minutes and then come back. She strode forward and opened the front door with her key, shutting it firmly behind her.

Lily smiled. Donald's head was still bent low over his book, she wished he would look up. He had become very strange, not speaking to anyone. She wondered if he too was waiting for Nadya or if he even knew she was gone. He had been shut in his room all day. She stared up again through the blossoms at the sky. When Nadya returned she would insist that tomorrow they make a start with the polka.

The sound came from behind, and she turned at once. Nadya must be back. A shadow seemed to drop from the wall about the compound. Sometimes wild monkeys came down from Purple Mountain or the surrounding hills, especially in winter when food was scarce. They had come like this before into the hospital compound, and been chased out with brooms.

She stood up to call out to Flora and a weight fell upon her. A hand stopped the scream coming loose from her mouth. She saw then there were men, holding her tight, dragging her towards the gate in the wall. It was opened and they pulled her with them, up the road and into the night. She struggled to get her teeth into the hand over her face and bit as hard as she could. Immediately she could breathe again. She began to scream.

It was not even five minutes. It was three minutes and fifty seconds that she had waited. Flora opened the door.

'Lily.' She called but there was no answer. Again she must go out into the freezing night. Flora reached up for a jacket from the coatstand in the hallway, and struggled into it as she walked. 'Lily.'

She saw at once that the gate to the street was open. 'Lily.' How could she have gone out? Anger surged through her. How stupid could Lily get? She strode towards the gate.

'Lily.' She heard the scream and began to run.

She could already see them. The lights of the hospital spread over the road for a distance. The shadowy shapes of men appeared bunched and dark, like vultures moving over carrion. Soon they were before her.

She saw Lily pinned between them, her clothes ripped from her body, her bare limbs spread apart and held by force, revealing the centre of her body and its childish brush of hair. As she watched a man thrust himself before Lily. Even as he drew away, another came towards her.

The word that had lain so long, like a stone in the lining of her belly, swam free at last. It slice her like a knife. She screamed it out again and again.

The men turned, surprise upon their faces. They began to laugh. She was dragged with Lily into the night.

Martha put her hand on the stair rail, and stopped. The feeling was inexplicable, bursting through her. Something had happened. She ran down the stairs into the kitchen. Flora and Lily had already gone. Had something happened to Nadya? She let herself into the compound. The plum was in bloom against the black sky, lit by the lights of the hospital. She remembered it was still Christmas Day. The outline of Donald's head, bent to a book, was framed by his window. She too was breaking down under the stress and must control her feelings. She stopped under the plum for a moment, looking up through its branches at the starry sky. Then, suddenly, she noticed the door in the wall of the compound was open. Outside the street was dark and blank. The feeling she had had upon the stairs burst through her again.

'Lily! Flora!' She ran into the house, and knew already they were nowhere. The Amah and cook came running. 'Bring torches,' she ordered. She beat upon Donald's door. Life seemed to stir in his face at last, and he followed her.

She ran ahead of them into the night. Almost at once they heard the screams coming from the grounds of the temple up the road. Donald pushed past Martha, holding her back, flashing the beam of the torch before them.

She saw the men as she had seen them on that night they entered the hospital, like a pack of satyrs with their crooked legs bound tight in puttees. They bobbed like scavengers about a carcass, uttering guttural cries. She began to scream.

'Lily. Flora.' For now she saw them.

Flora was held against a wall, forced to look at what they did. In their midst Lily was as a piece of succulent meat, ripped apart by wild dogs. At the light and the noise, they let her go and ran.

'Lily. Flora.' Her limbs would not move. She met Flora's eyes and knew they had not touched her. Slowly then she forced herself forward, to pick up the torn shreds of Lily's clothing. She slipped her arms out of her jacket and bent to cover Lily's body as once before, many years ago, she had covered the baby beside the river. Behind her she could hear the loud wailing of the Amah.

299

Suddenly then she saw Nadya, and the Japanese man from the Embassy. She heard Nadya draw her breath in a sob. The Japanese man said nothing.

PART FOUR

Aftermath

China,　1938

23

Photographs

Late January, 1938

At the British Consulate in Shanghai Donald was told he must wait. The Consul General was not in town, and First Secretary Percival was at tea. He looked at his watch. There were not many working hours left to the day.

'Tell him this is a matter of national importance,' Donald threatened, impatient with petty bureaucracy. The receptionist looked apprehensively at the closed door. She entered the room, and then reappeared to beckon him in.

First Secretary Percival looked up from his desk and rose reluctantly to his feet. A cup of tea and a half-eaten slice of fruit cake lay upon a tray. Donald held out a buff envelope.

'What is this?' Annoyance deepened in Henry Percival's face. His experience of reporters was that they played the prima donna. News, in his view, could usually wait, at least until he had swallowed his tea. It was said Addison was a man who liked attention. He had read his reports in *The Times*, and did not always agree with his views.

Percival opened the envelope and took out a bundle of photographs. His lardy face did not easily register emotion. He shuffled the photographs slowly. Donald watched for shock to spear his complacency. Soon Percival sat down, hands trembling.

'What are these?' His voice had a sudden hoarseness.

'Nanking,' Donald replied, sitting down unasked in a chair. 'I have to get them out of China. And you'll have to help me. There is also a reel of movie film. I need to get the film and the photos to England or the States. I want them in a magazine that is not squeamish and has a worldwide circulation. I think *Look* would be best. And the film must go to the British or American Government.'

As soon as the gates of Nanking opened, Donald had made his way to Shanghai. The negatives of his Nanking photographs and the reel of movie film were sewn into the lining of his jacket, close to his body at all times. On arriving in Shanghai he had gone straight to a foreign-owned photographer's, monopolizing his staff and services, until all the reels were processed. Seeing the content of the film Chinese staff at the photographer's came forward with offerings of secret prints taken from reels handed in by Japanese soldiers. They asked him to send them abroad for the world to see.

Donald's nightmare was that his films would be discovered and confiscated before leaving Japanese-controlled Shanghai. It was impossible to cable news out of the censored town. Art Morton had tried to cable his newspaper from Shanghai about the conditions at the Nanking River Gate, and was asked to withdraw his article. Explicit material such as Donald now held was a danger to its owner.

Percival pushed the photos hurriedly back into the envelope, as if their touch might sully him. 'Shanghai was never like this. We've been hearing of atrocities in Nanking, but I had no idea . . . ' His voice trailed off before he continued. 'You were on the *Panay*, I believe? How did you get back into Nanking? No other reporter was there through it all. Quite the man of the moment, aren't you.'

He pulled the buff envelope towards him once more and, as if he needed verification of the horror, again drew out the photographs. 'You took these?' Revulsion filled Percival's face.

Pictures of mass beheadings or disembowelled bodies stared at him. He passed quickly over those of grinning Japanese troops, posing as if for a holiday snap beside their raped or bayoneted victims, wiping bloodied swords upon a dress. Or the killing pens where roped captives were led, as further bayonet fodder for Japanese recruits.

'My photo stills are nothing like these.' Donald spoke quietly. 'These were taken by Japanese soldiers. Many soldiers carry a camera, and they use it shamelessly, as you can see.'

'It's almost as if it were a sport for them.' Percival pushed the prints back hurriedly again into the envelope.

'Perhaps it is. War is a kind of brutish sport. Its rules are a choice of evils.' The memory of the *Panay* flooded into his mind.

Percival stood up and crossed the room to a tray of decanters and poured out two whiskies. 'I think a little of this is in order, considering what we are dealing with. How did you come by them?' He handed Donald a glass.

'Some of the Japanese troops who were in Nanking have passed through Shanghai on their way to other areas, and sent their photographs for developing without, it seems, turning a hair. They look upon them as souvenirs. Unbeknown to them the Chinese staff in the photographer's I used, at the risk of their lives, made additional prints. This war is no sport to them. I have written a covering story to the whole thing. And there is also the matter of my reel of movie film. I must put this into the highest government hands. The Japanese are likely to say the stills are faked in some way. But no one can deny a moving film.'

'How can men do these things?' Percival sat down with the glass of whisky, shaking his head.

Donald remembered the rape he himself had filmed with discomfort. He recalled again his own detachment behind the camera, for which also he had no explanation. 'They are just men like you or me. No more, no less, no different,' he replied.

'What the hell do you mean?' Percival exploded. 'Do you think you or I or any of our army would turn their hand to this inhuman behaviour?'

Donald shrugged. 'They are under orders to kill and terrorize. For some reason men seem to do what they're told under orders, especially if the cause is right to their minds. But those men, rushing about in Nanking, killing, raping, burning, looting, day after day for six weeks or more, they must suffer some after-effect. However much drink they were given to numb them, they knew what they did. Deep down in themselves, some part is alive to that fact. Perhaps that part took these photos.'

'It's devilish pride in their diabolical deeds. Nothing more,' replied Percival.

'It is that on one level, of course. But perhaps, unconsciously, the blatant gesture of printing these photos, seems to me proof of some need to confess.' The thoughts were not easy to formulate.

'Sounds like a lot of blarney to me, Addison. You're either a Jap-lover or half-mad,' Percival responded. 'You're just looking for an explanation when there is none. These men are proud of what they've done. Why otherwise are they all walking about with cameras to record their prowess? It's sickening.' Percival spoke through his teeth.

'Perhaps you're right,' Donald sighed. 'I'm tired of trying to fathom it out.' The order of everything was back to front in Nanking.

'Do you still want to send these photos? And with your name attached?' Percival enquired. Donald nodded in reply.

'You realize of course, they will make you Enemy Number One of the Japanese nation?' Percival warned.

'Probably,' Donald answered, taking a sip of the whisky.

Suddenly, after what he had said to Percival, his feelings were confused. Like Percival he was repulsed by the photos, but he queried his own motive now in needing to send them. Were they to warn the world as he thought, or were they to further his career? Was he too now taking an easy ride on the back of all this evil? He would have to deal with these

305

thoughts later. An opportunity was before him. No reporter turned his back on a scoop. If he did not send them someone else would.

Percival nodded. 'We have just been through something like this with pictures we were given from the *Panay*. We can do the same route if we're lucky. Hong Kong or Singapore is easy enough, but straight through to America is safest. No danger of the Japanese over there.' Percival picked up the phone and began to establish an avenue of escape for the films, through the collusion of diplomats.

'This will take some time. Go back to your hotel. I'll call you there,' Percival said, cupping his hand over the telephone receiver.

'The pictures still need identification and captions. I'll work on it through the night.' Donald picked up the envelope from Percival's desk, and returned to the Metropole Hotel.

Some hours went by, but at last Percival himself arrived at the hotel. 'The Americans have come up trumps again, just as they did with the *Panay* film. One of their destroyers, a fast one, is leaving for Manila at seven tomorrow morning. They have consented to carry the photographs. If there are no storms to delay the destroyer, it will reach Manila three hours before the next Clipper is due to take off for San Francisco. This is the quickest route to the Western world I can offer your photographs. The *Panay* photos went to the *New York Times* on this route. The British Consul General in San Francisco and *The Times* correspondent, as well as someone from *Look* will be there waiting for the movie and photographs. This is historic stuff,' Percival said.

At six the next morning Donald went with Percival to the docks in an Embassy car. He presented the sealed packets to the Captain, who locked them in his safe. They waited until the siren blew and the ship pulled away from the wharf.

'Those pictures will appear around the world with your name attached. I can only repeat, you'll be on a Japanese death list now, and we cannot help you there,' Percival reminded him as he dropped him back at the Metropole. Donald nodded, shutting the door of the car, turning to walk up the steps to the hotel.

In the chill early morning the wind whipped about his neck. He turned up his collar, and dug his hands into his pockets. His fingers touched the cold metal of the bullet that had punctured the lifeboat of the *Panay*, and closed about it. He kept it always upon him.

Inside the hotel he went straight to the dining room and ordered coffee and croissants. Now that the films had left Shanghai, he planned to go on to Hankow and catch up with Chiang Kai-shek. As he waited for his breakfast a Japanese Army officer entered the room, and crossed towards him. He clicked his heels smartly and bowed. Donald drew a breath. Could the photographs have brought this man here? Had they already been intercepted? Was the man from the *Kempeitai?* Donald put down his cup of coffee and prepared himself for the worst.

'General Matsui has come to know you are in Shanghai. Please make it convenient to see him this afternoon at the Shanghai Club.' The man spoke pleasantly.

'I shall be pleased to meet the General again,' Donald replied in relief.

General Matsui had the bony quality of a plucked sparrow. The stiff collar of his military uniform stood away from his frail neck. He had lost yet more weight. He coughed into a handkerchief. The room was overheated, and the fumes of the oil stove made Donald drowsy. Matsui held his hands to the flame. The tips of his fingers were dark with nicotine, his expression was morose.

'Soon I will be recalled to Japan. Every day now I await an order,' the old man sighed. He sat with inflexible military bearing, but his voice trembled at times with emotion. Except for the interpreter they were alone. Where Matsui could he spoke himself in his broken English, as if to emphasize the importance of the interview. They sat in a private room of the Shanghai Club. Hot tea and the best brandy were before them.

'I appreciate the favour you are doing me,' General Matsui announced. 'I do not wish to involve you in too much detail, but many things here are not to my liking. They have reached such a tension that either I, or somebody I wish to speak to you about, must be recalled.' There was a look of extreme weariness about the General. 'If you remember, the last time we met I said I would make you my publicity agent. Since that victory procession through Nanking, I have been a different man.' Matsui fell silent, as if re-living the event. Donald scribbled a note on his open pad.

'If, as I suspect, I am to be recalled to Japan, I wish certain things set straight to the world before I leave. Tokyo appears deaf to my voice from here. But if you publish abroad the facts as I see them, and these facts are then cabled back to Tokyo from London, I may be able to reassert my authority.'

Donald nodded. He had no intention of permitting *The Times* to be used as a vehicle in a Japanese military feud, but he was more than willing to be given this exclusive interview by Matsui.

'I will do what I can,' he answered. What would Matsui say, he wondered, if he knew of the recent dispatch of photographs?

In spite of everything, he could not dislike this tiny general. Yet, Donald knew, he must not be deceived. This man's ethics were not his own. There were distinct boundaries to his view of mercy. At a different time, in different circumstances, he would have called Matsui well meaning. But he appeared in this war as no more than a small man, locked into his own self-righteousness. It was extraordinary that Matsui was prepared to make his war views public through a foreign newspaper. The qualities that defined the Western military hero were unfamiliar to Japan. The less known by the public of their leaders' personalities, the greater the manipulation possible of the masses. Few men of position tried dramatic gestures or broke with group policy. Physical courage and obedience was all that was demanded.

'You were on the *Panay*, I understand?' Matsui stared at Donald. He raised the brandy glass to his lips. 'And, I am told, you were in Nanking during the first weeks of our occupation? How is it you survive so many dangerous situations? You have perhaps the many lives of a cat?' Matsui smiled, his small eyes lighting up. He warmed the brandy in his cupped hands. Then grimness returned to his face, and he drew hard on his cigarette. 'Did you witness these atrocities that appear to have happened? It is important for me to know.'

'I have seen things it is impossible to ever forget, and that are beyond my comprehension,' Donald replied.

'Tell me,' General Matsui ordered. Donald described whatever he could. Matsui listened impassively, occasionally clenching his jaw.

'In Nanking my men have done something very wrong and extremely regrettable,' Matsui said as Donald finished. He hung his head, staring into his glass, absently swilling the brandy.

'Do you feel the troops went berserk then, out of control?' Donald asked. Matsui looked up, his voice rising powerfully.

'I consider the discipline of the troops was as excellent as ever. But the guidance and subsequent behaviour that resulted were not. I sent a message to Prince Asaka's chief of staff at the height of things, when I realized the true extent of what was happening. I implored him to exert control over the troops, as could easily have been done. I pointed out that, especially as Prince Asaka was of the imperial blood, military discipline must be that much more strictly maintained. You can judge for yourself the good that came of my pleas.'

Everything about the Japanese attitude to war seemed poles apart from Western attitudes. Even in a war such as this, Donald had learned, the Japanese had few trained rescue teams to remove the wounded under fire or give first aid; it had no properly functioning medical system of any kind for its armies. In emergencies or retreat the wounded or hospitalized were often killed, or killed themselves, it was rumoured. Japanese society, it seemed, had no room for damaged goods in the shape of disabled soldiers. Honour in war was to fight to the death. Surrender, even if wounded or unconscious, was untenable. To Donald surrender was an honourable business, at the end of effort before hopeless odds. Prisoners of war were due a certain respect, as stated in the Geneva Convention. Such reasoning was incomprehensible to a man like Matsui. If even his own wounded were incomplete men, worthy of nothing less than disposal, what then was the value of prisoners of war? Donald grappled with these contradictions. It was as if he and Matsui approached the ethics of war from different sides of the universe.

Matsui looked at him hard. 'I also consider the mistaken decision of you foreigners to again set up a Safety Zone in Nanking, to blame in part for the tragedy,' Matsui announced.

'Their decision to stay behind was heroism of the highest order.' Donald had difficulty keeping his voice civil now to Matsui. 'My own presence there was accidental,' he explained hurriedly.

Matsui grew impatient. 'Nanking is not Shanghai. They knew this. They received no official status for their zone as we had given in Shanghai. And yet they foolishly persisted in its establishment with only a half-promise of safety. Subsequently, many refugees who might have left the city stayed on in false hope of safety and perished. Chinese soldiers who had been ordered to retreat from the town heard about this zone and, yielding to thoughts of self preservation as would no Japanese counterpart, stayed in the city, disposed of their uniforms and entered the zone. I do not exonerate my army but, I put it to you, your Safety Zone was a place of death rather than sanctuary. This is because of its organizers' ignorance and misplaced beliefs in their actions. Had there been no Safety Zone the death toll might have been reduced.'

Donald began to protest, but Matsui held up his hand for silence. 'It is the *Panay* incident that I wish to talk to you about.'

The General drew on his cigarette, his voice took on a bitter tone. 'The sinking of some of those ships was the work of Colonel Kingoro Hashimoto. I want this made clear to the world. In Japan he is a popular but dangerous man. We call him the Bad Boy of the army. He is arrogant and insubordinate. He wants Japan to fight the whole world.' Anger flushed Matsui's face. 'The Navy has been forced to take the blame for the bombing and has sacrificed an Admiral. Hashimoto is intent only on actions that will embroil Japan immediately in hostilities with Great Britain and the United States.'

'But how can he get away with it?' Donald pressed.

'In games of strategy firebrands such as Hashimoto are sometimes useful pawns,' Matsui said mysteriously.

'Things have reached such a pass that either Hashimoto goes home, or I go home. I can no longer be responsible for the actions and policies of such a firebrand. The matter of the *Panay* may already have been resolved between our countries and the attack passed off as unintentional, but I will have my say of the truth. If you wish to send any cables to your newspaper about what I have had to say to you today, I will see they get through uncensored,' Matsui promised. He indicated with a sudden, abrupt gesture that the interview was ended.

As Donald left the room he saw the General finish his brandy and, resting his head on the back of the chair, close his eyes wearily. He had a vision once more of the bird-like quality of the man, and wondered that such frailty could empower death of such magnitude. Did Matsui's indignation over Nanking spring from the wanton butchery, or from his own wounded pride? He wished to believe General Matsui, to prove decency was the common denominator of men. But, he reminded himself yet again, Matsui had made a career out of killing.

He left the Shanghai Club and made his way back to the Metropole. The town was not the place he had left so recently. Barricades were now at every intersection. Japanese soldiers stood guard, brandishing bayonets. And yet in the relatively unharmed Settlement, Donald felt returned to sanity. To look down a road and see it whole, not to stare at bloated bodies, to talk of irrelevancies without guilt; these things seemed almost novel. In the bar of the Metropole he ordered a drink and sat down at a corner table. He began to draft out a lengthy cable of Matsui's interview for *The Times*.

The bar was half empty. When full it no longer thronged with newsmen, but with Japanese personnel of the new administration. He realized then that this was the same table he had sat at with Nadya and Smollett, on that evening before the incident at the water-tower. Before leaving Nanking he had told Nadya of his departure. They had stood before each other silently.

'Are you coming back? Will we meet again?' Her voice had been emotionless. Although the gates were now open, she was not yet ready to leave the city, still pinioned to its agony. Neither of them had the energy to deal with the complexity of the emotions between them, let alone the residue of recent events. It was as if they watched the relationship slip away, like dust through their open fingers, powerless to stop it. He had turned from her without a touch, stumbling from the blighted city at last, as a somnambulist leaves a dream.

Now in Shanghai regret overwhelmed him, sharp as a pain. In the relative calm of the city it was as if he awoke. In the bar of the Metropole, his thoughts were unclear about Nadya.

24

Early March 1938

A Dark Residue

Ice no longer formed over puddles at night. Tufts of couch grass and other weeds pushed through at the sides of roads. The land beyond the moat, littered with ancient grave mounds, was now textured by the freshly turned soil of mass graves. Even here there was a hint of greenness. Nadya looked down from the ramparts of Nanking's walls at the coming spring. So too, countless times, spring must have emerged after other sackings. Then too exhaustion must have spread over the town, the living weighed down with memory. Now, people sat in doorways, unspeaking. The farmer and shopkeeper faced a new death. Seed for replanting was gone, savings for stock long plundered. The silence seemed too big to face. No bowling of rickshaws or carts or the impatient honk of cars. No hawkers' calls or children's voices. Streets were clear of bodies, the stench had left the city. Electricity and water were switched on. But upon the town was an intolerable pressure from which there was no escape. The living would walk forever with the dead. Purple Mountain darkened through the day, pale violet to inky blue, constantly renewing itself. In the town only memory remained.

The unsuccessful policy of terror had at last been abandoned in Nanking. Embassies showed some activity again, although most Ambassadors refused to return, as did those townspeople who had fled. But settled in Hankow, Chiang Kai-shek had never been more popular. The unification he sought, the Japanese had now secured for him. A hate, bigger than any hate throughout history, galvanized the country.

Patrols of soldiers were less vigilant on the walls now. It was possible to climb up once more to the view. The Yangtze River still flowed, mercurial in the distance beneath the setting sun. Thin clouds were pulled by the breeze across the sky like drifts of chiffon. Nature was impervious. Only the balances between men seemed irrevocably disturbed. Now, when she looked at the view, Nadya thought only of the vast, racked body of China, spreading away from beneath these walls.

She saw them coming from a distance, climbing the cobbled stone

311

ramp, the breath thick in their chests. Flora walked a distance behind Lily. Each day Nadya coaxed them out, until they no longer cringed before the distant trudge of army boots. She tried not to think of the months behind, taking each day as it came. They could breathe without fear once again, but the residue of nightmare left strange markings upon the personality. Each must find their own road through memory. All the old structures were smashed.

'It's turning green,' she said, nodding at the landscape.

Lily smiled. Suddenly she smiled too much. After weeks of trying to ease her from the results of trauma, Nadya wondered why Lily's brightness should fill her with such apprehension?

'Soon there will be flowers again,' Lily answered.

'Dandelions and weeds. Nobody will ever have a garden again. Even the river looks dirty.' Flora stared at the distant river.

Her silence was as heavy as Lily's brightness. These were the first whole sentences Nadya had heard her speak that day. But she noticed how, animal-like, Flora sniffed the breeze and held her face to the sun. Things as small as this counted as regrowth. Sometimes, she became impatient with Flora. Little had happened to her in comparison to Lily. And yet she sank further into depression as Lily's brightness bloomed. They needed to get away from the hospital, away from China. Even the thought of returning to the hospital appeared up here, before the glittering sun, like return to an underground burrow. At its door memory locked onto them, pulling them into a black, gelatinous mass.

'We should get back,' said Flora after a short while.

Lily nodded agreement, but tilted her face, meeting the line of the river with her eyes, as if to hold it in her mind. They were like moles who had stumbled mistakenly from the security of darkness. They clung to the terrible boundary of memory. Only the dead, thought Nadya, seemed free to forget.

'I'll stay up here a while,' she said, hoping they would wait. Instead they turned, and she watched them walk down the stone ramp, one behind the other, like strangers in separate worlds. Somnambulists.

Nadya stared at the river, bronzed now by the setting sun. Donald had gone. There was no longer any anger in her. She wished for release from all feeling for him. Instead, there seemed no erasing whatever it was that bound them together. She too should have gone like Donald, when the gates opened, but something inexplicable held her back. In this aftermath of terror, nothing cohered. There were the large incomprehensibilities, like brick walls she suddenly found herself before. How did men do the things that were done in

312

Nanking? But there were also smaller things she could not explain. Especially Kenjiro Nozaki.

The shame of it filled her once more. She knew so little about him. And yet all she could think of was the need for him still, heightening every sensation. It was as if their bodies had rocked upon the edge of a cliff, courting death, devouring each other, cell by cell, breath by breath. And in the midst of it all there had been that cry, far away from the world they constructed upon the temple floor. Lily's scream. She had heard it clearly. But the cry of her own delirium, torn from the centre of her body, had blotted out all else. At that moment of ecstasy, Lily had been destroyed. Perhaps she could have saved her. Instead, she had spread herself wider beneath the man, rapacious for escape. And, afterwards, they had left the pavilion to discover only yards away that scene she would never now forget. Lily. *It was her fault.* Nadya hid her face in her hands.

Already the sun had set and the town was melting into dusk, the river pulled towards the night. Nadya unclasped her knees and stretched her stiff legs. It was time to return to the hospital.

She found Lily sitting in a rattan chair before a glass-topped table, playing Patience. She slapped the cards down one by one. The faces of Jack and Queen and King, stared up at her, wooden and garish. Lily sat at the table all day, flicking over the cards, again and again. When asked, she moved to meals, to a bath, to bed, pliant, responsive yet absent, and returned to the table. It seemed she remembered nothing.

'I will come in a moment,' she replied to Nadya, without lifting her eyes from the table, holding onto the order before her.

'King. Jack. Ace. Queen of Spades.' Lily was safe in a one-dimensional world.

'She has blocked it all out,' Martha stated. 'She is lucky.'

Her voice was crisp with diagnosis. To label and dismiss was a relief. Martha stared at Flora to whom no such process could be applied. Why had she not sent the girls away? She had put her own need of them before their safety. It was her fault that this had happened. *Her fault.* She did not know which was worse, Lily's amnesia or Flora's distress. She could not bear to look at the girls.

Nadya pulled her chair up to the table. More than anywhere Nanking's silence seemed deepest here, in Martha's house. They ate with their heads down, hurriedly. A weight stifled everything. Nadya listened to the knock of china, and the voice of the cook in the kitchen. She traced with a finger the petals of an embroidered flower on the tablecloth.

Flora's blonde hair fell forward from beneath a band, her face was pinched. There was the machinery of desperation in her bones. She said nothing, chewing resolutely. Since that night, now almost two months ago, Flora had hardly spoken. And yet, physically, she had been unhurt. How quickly each one of them had passed into the solitariness of experience, thought Nadya. In that place no words were heard. Healing was by grace.

Even as she ate, Nadya noticed, Martha's eyes flashed over Flora. To her it was Flora, invisible victim, violated by guilt and atrocious knowledge, who suffered the greater sickness. Lily's blocked memory relieved Martha of any immediate action. It worried Nadya that Martha had taken this option. It seemed out of character with the woman she knew. There was a new tone to Martha's voice, a new firmness about her mouth. In her eyes Nadya discerned a shadow, gone almost before it was caught. It filled her with unease. Martha's usual, invincible neatness was also disturbed. Some days her hair appeared dragged into its bun with hardly a preliminary brushing. Her expression and movements lacked alertness, as if she was absent from herself.

In one or another way, thought Nadya, they were all absent from themselves. Through the weeks of terror they had hung grimly on, as if to a roller coaster. But now, it was as if she looked down a kaleidoscope where the broken shapes of once familiar patterns settled anew each day. She could never predict what she might find. All the old allegiances had disappeared, blasted apart by stress.

'I think you should go away.' Nadya looked directly at Martha.

'The Japanese are pushing everywhere, there is nowhere left to go,' Martha replied.

'To America,' Nadya announced.

'I have thought of it,' Martha said. Her voice was flat, as if she dismissed the proposal outright.

'What about the girls? What about Flora? I have heard shipping has started again. There will be a boat to America now,' Nadya argued. Martha looked at her blankly.

'Do you mean I should send them *away*?' Martha shook her head and returned to her soup. Flora started, eyes wide, watching them.

'I will stay here,' she said.

'But there is nothing here,' Nadya replied.

'They can both do correspondence courses until things are better.' The vague look grew in Martha's eyes.

'But things may not get better. And they are worse still in Europe. America has a future for the girls. Go there. Please.' She leaned over the table to Martha.

'I never go from where I am needed,' Martha replied.

'And the girls?' Nadya asked again.

'They will be fine here,' Martha answered. There was a stubborn look now in her face.

After the soup there was a stew. Flora wished she could enjoy it as before. *Before* was like another life. She wished she had a disease of the memory. There were people who, for no reason other than a bump on the head, could lose their past life for ever. She had knocked her head badly the other day on a low door frame, but nothing happened. Her memory remained intact.

She hated the stew. Its thick, rich gravy and its soft fibrous meat made her think of flesh as never before. Made her remember the bodies beside the road. Every mouthful was an effort. It was the same with ripe fruit, split open to its soft inside. Even the water, piped in from the Yangtze, purified and crystal clear, had lapped about the unspeakable. Everything must still be there, at the bottom of the river. Nothing, she had discovered, was without connections. One thing in life adhered to another as if in conspiracy. Nothing was like it had been *Before*. The stars no longer seemed eternal but flickered like bits of cheap rhinestone. And the sun shone down apathetically, upon disintegration.

Tiredness wrapped itself about her. And yet she was afraid to close her eyes for the same scene was always before her. Memory had solidified in her like a layer of bone. She knew now there were things that could never be forgotten. They sank into your blood and cells to grow like mould, destroying you from the inside out. These memories were worse than illness. Illness was treatable; pills, hot water bottles and poultices eased. There was no treatment for her, Flora knew. She was alone with the disease of memory.

She had not noticed that Lily and her mother had left the room. For some reason now she was alone at the table with Nadya, whose eyes were upon her. Flora hated her sympathy, a spongy thing that had only to be touched to spew out its unwanted warmth. She did not need it. Why did Nadya not go back to Shanghai? Soon, Flora feared, she would start up again, about the need to put terrible things behind you. Or the necessity to go out for a walk on the wall, or a voyage to America. Or to go to Lily. She knew she should go to Lily. Instead, she let the distance grow.

It was as if another identity now propelled her. Each day she became more aware of this person, pushing her away from everyone. Sometimes, it was as if she heard a voice, calling to her faintly. She had read a Greek myth about the Sirens, who called sailors irresistibly to their island. The voice she heard was of this quality, pulling her towards it.

315

'You know, Lily is sick. She needs your support,' Nadya said. Perhaps it was not right to confront Flora, but depression of the type that had seized the girl seemed to her self-generating. She could not understand the distance Flora placed between herself and Lily. It was impossible to talk to Martha about it; Martha did not want to talk about anything.

'Lily has always depended upon you. She needs even more of you now.' For a moment she saw life flicker in the girl's face.

'We've all been driven to the edge of madness by the sight of others' terror, by the knowledge of darkness. I know what you went through. But think of Lily . . . ' Nadya broke off at the emotion twisting now in Flora's face. The girl clenched her fists until the knuckles showed white, and words spewed from her suddenly.

'She has escaped. Don't you see? She remembers nothing. She's the lucky one, free of it all. It's *I* who must remember, every moment, every day.' Even as Flora shouted the words the pictures returned to her, unstoppable.

Lily had put up a wall in her mind, like a dam, so that memory should not flood down and destroy her. Martha had told Flora this. By not remembering Lily had deflected her pain, projecting it all upon Flora, forcing her to carry it. Anger at Lily spilt up anew. How dare she not remember. And yet Flora could not refuse this new burden. It was her fault. *Her fault.*

She remembered her mother the night the soldiers entered the hospital, wild-eyed, dishevelled, hysterical. The image had stayed with her. And now some further layer was displaced in Martha by what had happened to Lily. And that incident was wholly Flora's fault. *Her fault.* She had not done as her mother ordered. She had left Lily alone. It seemed suddenly unbearable. She had not the capacity to absorb yet more of Martha or Lily's pain.

'She must be made to remember, *made to*,' Flora sobbed. If Lily could remember, she would have to reclaim her pain. Then the burden upon Flora would at once be lightened.

Nadya shook her head in bewilderment. 'Be glad she does not remember. Too soon, I'm sure, she will. Until then you must help her.' Nadya looked at Flora in consternation.

'I cannot,' said Flora, pursing her lips. It was a question of her life or Lily's.

25

Mid-March 1938

Journey to Hankow

They came unexpectedly to a gorge, and walked for a while along its crest. Akira looked down at the river far below. Jagged rocks, pines and bamboo of great height packed its steep sides. The sun slipped down the ravine in long runnels. It was crowded by religious pilgrims toiling up to a temple at the top of the gorge. Kestrels wheeled in the placid sky. It was a Buddhist holiday.

Whenever he could Akira kept close to the man they called Teng. It was not just that he could speak in broken Japanese. Akira sought for a way to explain to himself the strange aura of this man. He remembered standing before a gilded statue of Kwannon, Goddess of Mercy, in his village temple. Before the calm face of that icon he knew there was nothing to fear.

They were a group now of twelve. Refugees met along the way had been encouraged to join them by Teng. There were women, and babies who cried at night. He could not bear to hear their cries, and pressed his hands to his ears. Upon their howls came memory, as if to torture him.

'Do not speak,' Teng had ordered him, after they boarded the sampan at Nanking. 'Tie this about your face. I will say you have a disease of the mouth and are mute. When the time is right I will explain who you are.' Akira knotted the scarf about the lower half of his face.

After three days they left the boat and began to trek inland. They had been weeks on the march now, sometimes stopping a few days in small towns. It was always the same. They walked in silence, concentrating on the miles to be covered. Wherever they were, the Imperial Army had not yet arrived; the countryside was whole. Sometimes, high above, planes flew on their way to raids but took no notice of them.

They did not walk alone. The whole country was on the march. At every village, people joined the moving mass. Trucks and carts towered with belongings. Besides the personal, the machinery of whole factories appeared to ride upon people's backs. Broken railway lines were patched and wagons, loaded with livestock or further machinery, were dragged forward roped to thousands of men. Engines, devoid of fuel, were pulled to safety in this way.

'Everything is going inland,' Teng told Akira. 'The infrastructure of the country must be saved. Half the factories in the Shanghai area have already been moved to safety, bit by bit in this manner. Everything is going up to Chungking. Chiang Kai-shek will move there if Hankow falls.' They had stood on the slope of a hill observing the dark caterpillars of people on the march.

'This war will be written in the hearts of a whole generation. It has come like a storm, sweeping people up like autumn leaves, scattering them in all directions,' Teng sighed.

Now the discovery of the ravine took Akira's breath away. The mass of fleeing people appeared far away. Here it was possible to believe war did not exist. Akira stared at the brightly dressed multitude. The atmosphere was light-hearted. People laughed, children ran about in play and were pulled back onto the precipitous paths by parents. Beggars lined the roads, the wealthy passed in sedan chairs. Country people, in peasant clothes of primary colours were everywhere. Some even wore clothes they would be dressed in at burial, so that the gods would recognize them. He remembered then an autumn festival at the shrine in his village. It had been like this, the holiday atmosphere, the bright clothes and milling people, the stalls of edibles and paper windmills. He remembered the chanting of sutras had mixed there too with the thick smell of incense. In the dim interior of the temple was the same dull glint of gold.

Soon, they left to make their way down the ravine to the town. Refugees like themselves could be picked out amongst the gaudy crowd by the drab, tattered quality of their apparel. Pilgrims clogged the narrow paths so thickly it was sometimes difficult to keep a balance. Suddenly, people coming up from the town began to talk of an air-raid alarm. The crowd pushed on. The holiday mood still gripped them. So often the sirens resulted in nothing.

Soon they heard a distant rumble. Far away a line of black specks appeared beneath the clouds and sped towards them, circling once before releasing bombs upon the town. Those who could made for the shelter of scrub or trees. The planes returned, low now above the gorge. Beneath the roar of the engines the crackle of machine-guns began. Bullets spat out of the sky.

Many times on the march from Shanghai to Nanking, Akira had watched squadrons of planes soar above, like glittering birds, to soften up the place of their next attack. Looking up now he saw the red globes of the rising sun on the underside of wings. His pulse quickened in pride.

Teng gestured at him to crouch down amongst the shrubs or rock. He saw then that only he stood erect, staring at the sky, as if fear was unknown.

'You are not on their side any more,' Teng hissed.

Akira pulled away from Teng's grasp, refusing to crouch down. *You are not on their side any more.* He craned his neck to hold the planes in sight as they swooped up into the sky again. He stared after them until they vanished beyond the clouds. His feelings were confused.

When they were gone he turned to look around. Below him bodies lay strewn about. Monks appeared and began to carry the victims up into the temple. Silence settled upon the ravine. The crying of a child or the moan of a woman floated up to Akira. The trail of people began to move again, up towards the temple.

Akira looked into the peasant faces climbing towards him and saw the stoic acceptance, the same capacity for endurance that he saw in the expressions of his own village. It was the look of people who lived with little. He sensed the unspoken rage in the country filling the valley now. For the first time it struck him that the silent rage of four hundred and fifty million people must be a force to reckon with. He knew then that these people would never be broken as the Japanese military wished to break them. They would endure whatever they must, as for centuries they had endured death from flood or famine, or wars against tyrants of their own. He would have stepped forward then, to help the monks.

'We must go on our way. We can do nothing here.' Teng took his arm and led him away.

Eventually they reached Hankow, now the temporary wartime capital. The city seethed with people and activity. There was no sense of a vanquished spirit here. The cry of hawkers, the frantic honking of cars and trucks surrounded them. A woman with a basket of chickens stumbled into Akira. The chickens broke free, clucking and squawking. He ran after them with her, and came back with one. She thanked him and gave him an apple. It was here, after entering the town, that he heard news of the Japanese Army. War posters were everywhere, war talk spilt from every mouth. Chinese troops and supplies were the biggest traffic in the town. Instead of Hankow it appeared the Japanese Army had decided next to attack Hsuchow, a railway junction.

'Your army will have lost six months with this blunder and we have gained valuable time,' Teng told him, dropping back to walk beside him. 'Our Communist guerrillas and the regular army in Shansi have prevented your soldiers from crossing the Yellow River. Your government should not dream of a short war or underestimate China's resistance. For the moment, for us, a crisis has passed.'

It had been difficult to come across such wide-angled news while fighting at the front. Now, slowly, Akira gained another perspective. He pushed on beside Teng and the others through the crowded streets of Hankow. He was hungry. It seemed Teng read his mind.

'Fried peppers and steamed turtle are Hankow's specialities, but where we are going we will not be served turtle,' Teng warned.

He suspected then it was to another temple that Teng would lead them. It was difficult to know exactly what Teng was, guerrilla, religious man, or something of both. They crossed the river and climbed through narrow cobbled streets to the Buddhist Red Cross War Relief Headquarters near the top of a hill. Two monks came out to greet them. It was obvious to Akira that Teng was a man of weight, with connections everywhere. Akira waited with the other refugees. He knew the conversation turned to them for the monks shook their heads and gave apathetic sighs. A long argument ensued. Eventually, it seemed something was settled.

'They are turning refugees away, but I have persuaded them to house our small band. They know me well. Everything is in short supply here; hands, money, medicine. I can arrange a little of these things for them. And I have promised them you will work alongside me. I have not told them who you are,' Teng added, seeing the alarm on Akira's face.

He was to share a room with Teng, in a small house connected to the temple by a back door. Two thin rolls of bedding were brought in for them. The room was bare, but to Akira it seemed more than a sanctuary. Outside the temple halls and courtyards were crowded with people. Many were wounded soldiers. Children played everywhere. The Buddhas in their wall niches looked down upon the rows of destitutes. Teng bent to speak to people, to crack a joke or tease a child. He looked into the saucepan of a woman cooking on an earthen stove, three children at her side. He asked if she had rice enough, and promised bean curd for the children on the following day.

'From where will you get bean curd?' asked Akira.

'I will get it,' Teng replied.

'There are wounded Chinese soldiers here,' Akira whispered, more to himself than to Teng.

'All people are one to the Buddha, and the Buddha is in all. You need think of nothing more. If you help one man you help the world,' Teng replied in the tone of a schoolmaster.

Later Akira found himself alone. He sat on a low wall surrounding a courtyard. Below him the hill descended steeply to the river. Across the water lay the bustle of Hankow, above him the sky was bruised, inky with the coming night. Behind him in the courtyard lay wounded

320

Chinese soldiers. From tomorrow he must bring them food and water, he must tend their bleeding limbs. A sudden revulsion gripped him.

He remembered his time in the military hospital in Tokyo. From the window he had watched trucks of new recruits going off to war, accompanied by supporters. He remembered the expressions on the faces of the men and the easy cheers of those who saw them off, and would never go to war. That war-intoxicated mob of supporters had frightened him. Some of those men sent off to fight may have already been killed by the soldiers he must now nurse.

Thoughts jangled about in his head. He must not forget he was dead now forever to his own world. Of no more substance than a ghost. He would never see his mother again. After being discharged from the military hospital in Tokyo, he had been allowed a brief visit home, before returning to China. It had been night when he reached his village. There was a long walk from the station across the paddies. The rasp of crickets and the croak of frogs was thick against the starry sky. Soon he saw the kilns, in long runnels up the hillside. His hands had ached to touch some clay again, to scorch his face near a firing. He made his way through the village with its heavy thatched roofs. Before most doors he saw a small Rising Sun flag, indicating someone from the house had gone to the war. Before his own home there was also a flag. He saw a light in the house and pushed back the door, calling out that he was back.

His mother came running, wiping her hands on her apron. She collapsed on her knees in shock. Her hair escaped from its knot, her spine was bent from years of planting rice with the weight of a child upon her back. She wore the same threadbare kimono as the day he left. She tried to compose herself, but her face was wet with tears as she led him in to see his father. He looked already dead, stretched out beneath a quilt. He had wasted away, his skin translucent, his breath had rasped like a cricket. Only his elder club-footed brother, Yukio was at home, useless to the military. Jiro, too young for the army, was conscripted to a factory. The three of them knelt in silence. The paper windows were torn and the thatch in need of repair. He could already hear the wind howling in winter, and feel the chill there would be in the room.

He woke at dawn the next morning and went out to the workshed in the backyard under an old sycamore tree. Shelves of unfired rice bowls still stood along one wall. Rejected pickle jars filled a corner. Most of the clay had dried up, but he scraped together a malleable lump from the bottom of a bin. He sat before the wheel, revolving it with his feet, feeling again the clay in his hand, bending it to his will. All that mattered was the clay. It was as if time stood still. A strange energy consumed him. Sometimes, as he worked, he saw his life running out, pulled slowly towards those white boxes of ashes he had seen everywhere on the train. At other moments horrific images of China returned. Even now the smell of death refused to clear from his head. In the clay then he searched for something he could not describe, a nameless thing to end the images, to return the dead to life.

It was two days before his father died. He did not regain consciousness to recognize Akira. His mother did not weep, but went quietly about preparations for the simple funeral. When the urn of remains had been buried in the village cemetery, he packed his bag to return to the front. His mother came and knelt beside him, pushing forward a piece of white cloth.

'This will protect you. Never be without it,' she had said.

He looked down at the *senninbari*, folded neatly before him on the matted floor. From the windows of the military hospital he had seen women, standing stoically, hour after hour, in the street below. And seen them again at stations as his train had stopped on the way to the village. They waited in silent vigil to solicit a stitch on a piece of cloth for a son, a husband or a brother who had gone to war. It was an old superstition that a body belt carrying a thousand stitches, sewn by a thousand different people, was an infallible talisman against death in the field. His mother had collected these one thousand stitches, walking from village to nearby village, begging a stitch from whoever she met. The stitches were decorative French knots, sewn in circles upon the cloth. He bowed to his mother and raising the *senninbari*, touched it to his brow.

He still wore the belt next to his body, and placed his hand upon it now. When he had cast off his uniform he had not thrown it away. It was all he retained of a lost self. He might never see his mother again.

On the train journey back to his village from the military hospital, the track had run precipitously along the side of a hill, like the ravine they had walked through before reaching Hankow. He remembered the paddies, terraced below him in the sun, and a bird gliding high in the sky. He had wished then that he was a bird, free of the earth. Perhaps his wish had been granted. Ghost or bird, he was free to claim himself.

26

Mid-March 1938

A Dangerous Course

Kenjiro ate the tangerine slowly, savouring its tart, sweet juice in his mouth. The fruit had been flown in from Japan, a present from Supreme Military Headquarters to the Embassy. He offered another to Fukutake. The taste of the fruit threw him back to childhood. He remembered old Chieko peeling, then cleaning the bright orange globe of its white metastasis. Then carefully, she would split the top of each segment with a nail, pulling the membrane free, popping the succulent flesh whole into his mouth.

He hoped Teng had got away, was safe by now in some distant guerrilla enclave. He had no regrets about what he had done. Certainly, he would not be judged to have acted dutifully. There was no way he could ever explain such an action to Fukutake. Perhaps only the Russian woman would understand. There too he had followed a hedonistic course, but he was not sorry about her either. He made an effort to put the woman out of his mind. Even the thought of her filled his body with inexplicable distress. He looked across the desk at Fukutake.

Fukutake, he suspected, had now been recruited by the military to probe him in a subtle way. There was a rabbity look about him. His teeth protruded slightly above a receding chin, and his eyes bulged myopically. He was easily intimidated. At Military Headquarters they would only have to grab him by the scruff of the neck for him to scuttle away and do their bidding. Now, he kept pursing his lips together over his teeth, as if he had something to hide.

Rain beat against the window with a resonant thud. Outside, the town appeared a drab watercolour in which all the paints had run. Kenjiro wondered if this town could ever rise again. On the wall before his desk the Emperor sat squarely in a thick frame. He sat upon his horse White Snow, in full military uniform. Beneath a peaked cap his eyes stared through rimless glasses, his lips full beneath a thin moustache. There was arrogance in his face. And yet, from other angles, there appeared a certain wistfulness. It was impossible to know anything of his character.

He was no God, just a mere man locked up in an ivory tower. Could he know what, in his name, had been done to this town? In what manner did things filter through to him? Had he been duped by ambitious men? Or did he willingly collude in the war?

Now, when he looked up at this portrait, to which in the Embassy they must bow each day, Kenjiro felt only sad compassion. The Emperor appeared like a distant friend in terrible trouble but beyond all help. To have piled upon one's name, even if half-unknowingly, such a wilful, primordial, wave of killing was something from which innocence could not be claimed. When he knew of the details, how would the Emperor live with himself? He could not escape guilt. He was after all a man, with responsibilities outweighing those of other men. He was to be pitied. Some day there would be a reckoning.

He saw Fukutake regarding him strangely. Had these thoughts showed upon his face? Would Fukutake report such nuances back to Colonel Kato if no substantial facts were gleaned? Would Fukutake be pleased to exonerate himself by stoking up suspicion?

'I was thinking of the Emperor, and the weight of the responsibilities he must bear at this time. In comparison our lives are easy.' He did not lie. Fukutake nodded.

There was a slight hiss to the gas fire, and a residue of fumes filled the room, making Kenjiro sleepy. After Teng's escape he expected each footstep to herald his departure to a prison cell. But nothing had happened. The *Kempeitai* had no proof, and so they had turned to Fukutake. Kenjiro's life depended upon Tilik Dayal, who had returned to Hsinking. He must trust the thread of decency that had made the man collaborate with him.

'What do they want you to find out from me? Why don't you just ask me?' Kenjiro said at last in exasperation. Fukutake started and began to blink in a nervous manner.

'I told you there is a limit to how much I can protect you. They know about your friendship with that Communist, and also that Russian woman, the one they think is a spy.' Fukutake's blinking became more rapid.

'I know how dangerous these times are. Do you think I would throw my life away? A favour here or there, or an occasional visit to a friend is one thing. When such things can tip the balance between life or death, what do you think any sane man would choose?' Kenjiro shrugged impatiently.

'I knew you were innocent of all these absurd things they're saying.' Fukutake sat back in relief.

'They have no proof of anything, otherwise they would not have come to you.' Kenjiro repeated his thoughts out loud.

'Proof is proof, but in these days suspicion alone is enough to finish a man,' Fukutake worried. 'What about the woman. Is she a spy?'

'As much as I am,' Kenjiro managed a laugh. Even a mention of the woman brought her face before him again. A bitter segment of fruit filled his mouth and he spat it into an ashtray.

'It has stopped raining. I have been told to inspect the repairs on the Embassy apartments. Personnel will be returning soon from Shanghai,' Kenjiro said, standing up. Fukutake nodded.

Kenjiro was glad of the excuse to get out, away from Fukutake's peering eyes and the fumes of the gas fire. The air was damp and filled with an unexpected sweetness. A light drizzle was clearing up. At the urging of the new government there was already some rebuilding. The smell of sawn wood smarted in his nostrils. But a defeated look was everywhere. If it were not for the soup kitchens of the Safety Committee most of the town would starve. The new government seemed in no hurry to relieve this situation.

He steered clear of the hospital, and took instead a longer route to his destination. There, he inspected the repair work in progress on the Embassy apartments. He returned the way he had come walking near a section of Nanking's wall. Suddenly he saw her, as if he had conjured her up, a startled look in her face. For a moment he considered turning away, for both her safety and his, but his feet would not move. On the top of the wall a guard appeared and stared down in some interest at them.

'I must see you,' she said. 'I have something to tell you.'

'Go to the temple pavilion,' he answered. 'I will come by a separate route. Wait there for me.' He spoke without thinking. The decision seemed made long before, as if he had expected this. He wondered at himself. It began to rain lightly again.

It was dry in the pavilion. The odour of old wood enclosed him again, as it had on that other night. Even in daylight it was a dim world. There was a smell now of urine, as if troops had made use of the building since last they were there.

'I wanted to send you a note but, I didn't dare. A boy came to the hospital with a message. Teng is safe, and in Hankow.' She shivered drawing her coat tighter. Kenjiro laughed in relief.

She turned her face apprehensively up to the rafters. There was the same rustle of wings in the darkness above. The weariness in her face gave it new delicacy. The knowledge that had been forced upon them these last months had changed expressions forever. She did not move as

325

he stepped towards her. All the old feelings were upon him again. He knew they were powerless before them. She shivered, crossing her arms before her body, hugging herself, as if to fend him off. But she made no attempt to deter him when he pulled her hands down by her sides and lowered his lips to her neck. The scent of her filled him again. In the half-light he saw a low battered Chinese altar against a wall, and led her there.

Already, the intensity of their need was so great that neither could wait as before, to journey in languor. She wanted him urgently to enter her and linked herself about him. The need was so crazed between them as to annihilate personality. There was no sound but the racing of their breath. At last he raised himself free of her body.

His heart pounded with the recklessness of all he risked. There was resentment too, now that it was over, that she had the power to guide him to her, as she guided him so quickly to the centre of her body, filling his mind each day in this way. Why could he not rid himself of her? She was a death sentence, not an ordinary woman. He was shocked at himself for coming here. Slowly, his mind began to clear.

She looked at him with an expression he could not fathom. Perhaps she sensed his feelings. There seemed this time something brutal about their coupling. Something compulsive drew them on. It seemed she too had understood the difference for she turned away, as if ashamed. He knew he must be free of her.

'I never thought I would come here again,' she said, bitterness filling her voice.

'You don't know what *I* risk by coming here,' he answered in annoyance.

'If I had not been here with you that day, then nothing would have happened to Lily or Flora. I cannot forgive myself.' Her distress was obvious.

He remembered then the scene when they had emerged from the pavilion. Dr Clayton was there and others. Kenjiro had seen Donald Addison and been filled by discomfort, knowing of his relationship with Nadya. He had slipped away quickly, embarrassed, seeing there was little he could do.

'It is too dangerous for us to meet. We risk our lives.' He stepped forward now and took her arm. She said nothing but nodded, looking down at her hands. He turned her towards him, staring into her face.

'We took life from each other, whatever else died around us. Do not forget that,' he told her. An emotion he had not seen before had risen in her face.

'Is there something you wish to tell me?' he asked.

'I think Lily is pregnant,' she whispered.

He turned out of the temple. There was still an hour of light left. The sky was full of luminosity, the clouds darkening about the edges. They formed in ripples over the horizon, like hard sand on a beach marked by waves. His pulse still beat unevenly, although his body felt heavy and cleansed. He needed to think, to examine what had happened. He walked beyond Nanking's walls, along the towpath beside a narrow inflow from the Yangtze. The sky was suffused by the setting sun. The sky was important to him. He could not understand why people, more often than not, rooted their gaze to the earth. The great walls of Nanking towered beside him, throwing a shadow over the water. He found a tuft of grass and settled himself upon it. Below him the water eddied about a rock. He tried not to think of the border of corpses, like wet bloated sandbags, that had so recently filled this stream. Now the river flowed forward anew, with a fresh charge of water. In this way too he must look at the future.

Why had he gone with the woman again? He was chasing after the past, after emotions shared with Jacqueline that still drifted through his memory. In the darkness of Nanking the Russian woman seemed to float before him, like a ghost of that past life. Just the thought of her body sent the blood rushing through him once more. He remembered the whiteness of her face beneath him in the dim pavilion, her eyes half closed. He saw suddenly that she was not Jacqueline, and never would be, and that nothing could be restored. Innocence belonged to beginnings. He was a long way now from there.

The shadow of the wall had darkened and stretched to cover the stream, enfolding him. Night was rolling in now beneath the clouds. In the distance the line of low hills was already swallowed by the dusk. He looked down into the stream. Beneath the water the weeds were a darkening mass. An object was caught amongst them, like a large moss-covered stone. The current turned the thing towards him. He stared down into the face of a man. The eyes were open and gazed at him from amongst the weeds which wound about it. Kenjiro drew back with a start. He saw again the head of that long ago rickshaw-puller in Tokyo fall with a thump at his feet, and the hiss near his ear of the executioner's sword. His heart beat in his throat. Below him in the water the current gently turned the head back into the weeds. Its hair streamed out like underwater ferns.

All his life, since the Great Kanto Earthquake, and that day of the rickshaw-man's execution, he had stood as if misaligned to life. Why had destiny now posted him here, to observe a world beyond comprehension? A feeling of loneliness filled him. He was forced always to stand outside the circle of things, as if to bear witness to the inexplicable. There must be, he felt, a reality beyond space and time and human faculty. He could give it no name, silent within him. Men were born spiritually unequal, he decided, but within them the thing that made them identical was their link with this unknowable reality. It was his task now to turn himself towards it. His own link to the strange forks in his life might then begin to show a meaning.

He looked down again at the dark form of the head in the water. He felt there were tears to shed, not only for the poor befouled creature, but also for the man with the sword. In the heart of the murderer there must also be a longing for good, misguided as it was. He thought of goodness now as like the sun. It was passive and could not move towards him. It was simply *there*, behind everything, waiting to be found. But evil was all movement, dipping and curling, swooping down like a tempest to grip its victim. It found every chink in an armour, and entered. And not until it left, if it ever left at all, would you know that it had been. He sat immobile on the bank before the rotting, severed head, and began to cry for everything he had seen.

27

Mid-March 1938

Divisions

Nadya awoke the next morning and knew that everything was changed. It was as if she stood in a flood that during the night had risen considerably deeper. At the beginning of the siege this feeling, of sinking, was with her each day as she opened her eyes. It had filled her until she realized nothing could get any worse. Now even that, like some safety net, had given way beneath her. She was in some kind of free fall.

Shaking herself awake, she remembered Lily, and then Kenjiro. The night before she had slept in a haze of exhaustion and not drawn shut the curtains. Now a strong sun filled the room. For the first time in weeks she heard a bird. What use were these indications of wholeness when the world had already cracked? There was something bizarre in the sudden tweeting of birds. Her body still held, like a shadow upon it, all the sensations of the day before. Her limbs, shedding sleep, felt heavy and luxuriant. She could not stop herself going over each movement of Kenjiro's body against her, like some slow exotic ballet. And yet, yesterday, it had been different from that first time. There had been a grim separateness. Each took pleasure as they could, before they ran. She pushed herself out of bed. She was late for her work at the hospital.

She was not as yet even sure her irrational fear about Lily was true. Why had she voiced it to Kenjiro? And if it were true, there remained the question of Martha. At the thought of Martha a chill passed through her. Because of this fear of Martha, she had waited all these weeks. And during this time Lily sat as ever in the delicate bamboo chair before the cards of Patience. She refused an offer to learn the polka. It was as if everything in her was stilled around something secret. She spoke with the ring of infancy, as if she had regressed in years. But because she smiled, ate dutifully, slept with only the occasional toss and turn, it was judged she was less in need of anxiety than the sullen, disorientated Flora. Nadya knew she must find the courage to speak to Martha, to lay bare her fears.

Martha seemed divorced from the details of everyday life. She was buried once more in her work and was glad to leave the girls to Nadya to organize in her free time. Lessons had started again for them, two tutors had been found. It gave structure to the day and space for transition before decisions were taken. Yet even here Lily sat obediently with a bland smile. She answered questions, she remembered decimals, she completed homework, and yet Nadya had the feeling knowledge hung suspended in her, never sinking beyond the surface.

It was an achievement to have persuaded the girls to walk by the river, further from the hospital than the city walls. Nadya was determined to continue her policy of getting them out. They must acquaint themselves again with the world, and breathe fresh air. They walked beside her dutifully. The sun now had a new warmth about it. It was the kind of day that in another time would have been perfect for the year's first picnic.

They came to a small gate in the old wall, which opened onto a quiet tributary of the Yangtze. Beyond the gate the scene was pastoral. The grass was a fresh new green and the water no longer stagnated upon foul garbage. There was a newness to things that infected them all, now that the city was behind them. At last there was no need to look fearfully into the sky. Bombers had lost interest in Nanking, and flew on to further destinations. At last there was a peace of sorts.

'If I return to Shanghai why don't you come with me? You could go to school and live with me,' Nadya said to Lily. She had thought over the idea for some time.

'And I?' Flora asked. There was a tremulous quality to her voice.

'There are medical schools in Shanghai. Why should you think yet of America, especially in these times,' Nadya suggested. Flora smiled for the first time in days, as if a weight had been removed from her.

'Will mother agree?' she asked. There was a note of excitement in her voice.

'We shall see that she does,' answered Nadya. 'Look, already new life is forming.' She bent down beside the river bank and, reaching into the reeds, fished out a mass of frog spawn. Lily gave a squeal of excitement. In the grass Nadya found a discarded army ration tin, and they tipped the frog spawn into it.

As the girls looked into the water for further specimens, Nadya sat back on the grass. She saw now that Lily did not move with the agility of before. A cold, sick feeling filled her. She still prayed the pictures pushing into her mind were the abominations of fantasy. And yet the more she observed the child, the surer she was of the almost imperceptible swell of her body. She must speak now to Martha. It was not yet too late.

Looking down into the river Flora could see the small darting bodies of fish, like quick moving shadows beneath the surface. There was a smell of freshness about. The terrible stench that had hung for so long over Nanking had gone. Everywhere the earth was sprouting. From the stumps of the willows she saw the first shoots of new growth. And yet, time was still divided in Flora's mind. There was *Before* and there was *Now*. Nothing seemed to join the two. It was like being turned out of a warm bed on a cold morning. All comfort was ripped away.

She looked up at the sky imagining it like a great parachute, covering the whole of China. The sun burnished it to a pale pewter, like the underside of a fish. Thin clouds of a darker shade had begun banking up, stretching for miles. God must be somewhere, even if he refused to show himself when he was needed most. The prayer she had maintained throughout the siege, muttering like a mantra all day, had stopped on that terrible night the soldiers took them. Where was God? Why did he not hear? She could ask nothing of her mother.

She walked on a distance along the river. Perhaps soon the town would bustle again. And her mother smile. Lily would argue as she had before, and boxes of Turkish Delight would arrive as always from America. They would forget all that had happened. She held her face up to the sun, even though for the moment it appeared to be hidden.

She had walked a distance ahead of Nadya and Lily, and turned to retrace her steps. Now the river ran not towards, but away from Flora. A breeze blew in her face and soughed through the coarse tufted grass. Ripples patterned the surface of the stream. As she gazed at the fast flowing current she met the eyes of a man, staring up at her from beneath the water. She stopped in shock, but felt no fear. At first she thought he might be a water sprite. Tales read long before returned to her. Now she saw it was just a head, sliced cleanly from a body. From beneath the water the man looked at her and there seemed nothing too terrible about him. His eyes bulged slightly in a staring manner, with an expression of grim surprise. His lips were thick and hung open. As she watched a minnow swam between them, and nuzzled at his teeth. She could make out his eyelashes, but it was difficult to say how old he was. There was a bloated look about him. His hair swam with the current, like luxuriant weed. It washed gently this way and that, sometimes half covering his face. At other times it streamed behind him, as if blown by the wind. She felt no repulsion. There was more a sense, as she looked at him, of things at last falling into place. A guide had been sent to find her. She knew then she had not found him by accident. Nor had he waited without reason for her here. Almost at once, with a strong tug of current, the head rolled on its side and disappeared, pulled deep into the shelving bank. Flora turned and walked back to Nadya and Lily. She knew now nothing again would be as *Before*. Everything had changed.

28

April 1938

An Unavoidable Decision

They sat alone in the darkening room. The dusk expanded shadows about a mahogany desk. The glass panes of the corner cabinet grew thick and unreflective. The scent of pot-pourri overpowered, filling the room with the perfume of dead roses. Nadya wished she could open a window. Her head had begun to ache.

At first Martha refused to believe her. Her expression compressed about the terrible idea. Silence swung between them. It had not been easy to voice her fear about Lily to Martha. Nor to suggest a termination of the pregnancy. What Nadya suggested was already, suddenly, a sizeable part of the hospital's work. Up to fifty thousand women, it was thought, had been raped during the first six weeks of the occupation. All Nadya wanted now was for Lily to step anew into life. She wished also for her own guilt to be pushed at last behind her.

'You know it is not just Lily to whom this has happened,' Nadya argued.

'And you know I don't believe in these things,' Martha replied.

Her face closed upon emotion. She herself would perform no abortions, and until recently would have none performed in her hospital. There had been a long and difficult battle with herself, before she gave in to the pressure of her medical staff. The pathetic clamour of crowds of women, and the dour-faced Chinese doctors in the hospital, had eventually persuaded her. Even then she had specified, if a woman was healthy, married and neither under-age nor over-age, she should be encouraged to bear the child. Her doctors had stared at her in pity.

'If we do not do this,' one doctor warned her, 'we may be responsible for the deaths not only of unborn children, but for a better part of fifty thousand women as well. Every quack or old crone left in Nanking will be called upon by these unfortunate women. If none are available, they'll do it themselves. We will be left to try and save their lives. And these East-Ocean devil babies when they are born, will not be allowed to live by either their mothers or their grandmothers. One way or another their fate is death. These are special times and special circumstances. God will understand. This is an act of mercy we are being asked to perform.'

Put like that Martha had been forced to look at the problem in practical terms. She knew too well the history of infanticide that in this land for centuries had been found necessary for survival. She should know, she had found Lily. *Lily.*

'What is the alternative?' Nadya asked. Darkness now encased the room. Martha's face had disappeared into the shadows of a winged armchair.

'God forgive me,' Martha whispered at last. 'She has a rare blood type. Supplies of everything in the town are down to rock bottom and have not been replenished. I will not do it unless there is extra blood of her type. She still has a child's body and the pregnancy is some months gone. It will not be easy on her.' She tried not to think of complications. 'But it will be even worse if she goes any further.' Martha sat forward, sinking her head in her hands.

'Will you tell Flora?' Nadya asked. The thought of this extra weight upon Flora worried her.

'Why did I not send them away?' Martha leaned back again in her chair. 'It was selfishness, my own need to be near them. I thought of myself before their safety.'

'I think you should tell Flora,' Nadya insisted.

'Flora is still a child. It will upset her unnecessarily. Even Lily will not know what has happened. Anaesthetic will be our magic. For the rest I'll make up some excuse. We will elaborate on the stomach ache she has complained of to you. Appendicitis or something,' Martha decided vaguely. 'In her present blocked, amnesiac state, it's not right to explain the truth to her.'

'Flora is eighteen, no longer a child. She has seen too much. You should not lie to her. What if you cannot keep it secret? She will deal better with the truth,' Nadya replied. Martha would not be moved upon her opinion. The smell of pot-pourri seemed now like a stench in the room.

At last blood, of the right type but in a small amount only, was found from the Red Cross Hospital. Dr Chen was put in charge. Martha steeled herself to stand beside him in the operating theatre. It seemed at first to have gone all right, until Lily began to haemorrhage.

Flora was conscious only of the rushing of nurses up and down the corridor. She knew it was against the rules for a nurse to run. It did exactly what it did now, instil the fear of God into those who waited in corridors. They would not let her into Lily's room, or tell her what was wrong in any certain terms. There was mystery of a chilling kind. The heavy, cold stone was there again in the lining of her stomach. They were treating her like a child. She was determined to know what was wrong.

She pushed her way into the dispensary. The sun shone on phials of pills, liquids gleamed in jewel-like colours, transparent against the light. Nurse Tan, starched and efficient, lifted a bottle of blood on to a trolley. There were long coils of rubber tubing and apparatus of a complicated nature.

'Who is that for?' Flora demanded.

'For your sister,' Nurse Tan replied.

'I want to see her,' Flora said. Nurse Tan shook her head.

'What is the matter with her then, that she needs all this blood?' Flora demanded. The old anger with Lily washed over her. The cold stone in her stomach grew heavier.

Nurse Tan frowned. Nobody had given her instructions concerning Flora, nor intimated the need for subterfuge. 'These kind of complications happen sometimes. A transfusion is a simple procedure. You'll see her in the morning,' she said.

'What is the matter with her?' Flora insisted, unable to hide her agitation.

'The same as is the matter with half the poor women in this town,' Nurse Tan replied, turning down her mouth in a grim expression. Flora still looked confused.

'Did they not tell you, she is pregnant? I didn't even know there had been a rape. I can't blame Dr Clayton for keeping it quiet. It's terrible. But she'll be all right. In the morning you can see her.'

Flora watched the shadows lengthen to consume the corridor. She would not be moved, even by Nadya. She kept seeing the clear, jewelled light of those bottles of blood, and imagined it swimming in Lily's veins. What had they done with the baby? Did it have a shape, a face? Would it have a funeral? Would it be put in the incinerator? Terrible questions filled her. She could ask no one. The words would not form themselves.

Through a half-open door she saw her mother sitting beside Lily's bed, her head bowed in her hands. She heard a call for more blood. Nadya sat with Flora on the seat in the corridor. Once, towards evening, they let Flora in to see Lily, but she ran from the room of her own accord. Lily's face was white as the pillow. There was a pearly, marbled look to her, like a waxwork of the Sleeping Beauty Flora had seen once in Shanghai. Through the night Nadya slept in the bed next to Flora, reaching out when necessary to calm her distress. Her mother, Flora knew, still sat in the room beside Lily. The cold stone in her stomach seemed to have swelled to fill every cell in Flora's body. There was nothing she could do but pray. The words eventually lulled her to sleep.

It was Nadya who told her in the morning. There had been no more blood for Lily. Without it her body had faded away, unable to sustain itself.

'There were no choices,' Nadya whispered.

Martha appeared physically to shrink, pulled by invisible strings to some deep centre of her being. She shut herself away, incapable of comforting Flora. In the grief-stricken, guilt-stricken house it was Nadya who attempted to console the distraught Flora. Nothing she said seemed to penetrate Martha's hide of sorrow.

'She needs you,' Nadya pleaded. Martha could do no more than put an arm weakly around the girl; anything else was beyond her.

In her room Martha sought shadow, drawing the curtains close during the day. The sun was an aberration. Food came, she was aware of this, but in her mouth it turned to the texture of rubber or paper, and she pushed the plate away. Each morning she reached out and took down from a shelf the great nautilus shell she had found on a beach as a child. She sat with the shell on her lap, as she had so often through her childhood. It had been found upon the sand at Tsingtao. Bradley had been with them that summer. There had been a tussle, as to who should keep the magnificent shell. Eventually, Martha won and carried it home with pride. The pearly, many-chambered interior and twisting shape filled her with its mystery. All her life she had kept it near her. Against her ear it whispered, transporting where she wished. She heard again the spill of waves at Tsingtao, the soughing of wind in the trees, and the voice of her father explaining the construction of the giant shell. It had thirty-six chambers, and in the very last lived the nautilus, withdrawn from the world.

On her lap now she stroked the smooth shell, and wondered at her connection to it after all these years. Many times she had held it to the light, seeking that inner sanctum where the nautilus once lived, and seen nothing but a labyrinth. In her mind she had tried so often to follow the twisting route to that final chamber but always, before she reached it, the map of knowledge was destroyed.

Now, she held the shell again to her ear, and let it speak to her. Scenes rolled into her mind and then retreated, like the long-ago waves upon Tsingtao beach. She was without feeling. The shell transported her where it willed.

She saw again a Jesuit church, visited once in Vienna on a voyage back from America. Its thick Rococo decoration bore down upon her, gold encrusted, layer upon layer. Great twisted pillars of pink marble rose up along the nave. Immediately, they had reminded her of the thick, muscular, bodies of snakes. The weight of the church pressed upon her. In spite of a profusion of gold, there appeared only darkness. A god of wrath and judgement lived here. She knew instinctively then, although her father was no Jesuit, this was the same God he worshipped.

'What are we to do?' she had cried when Bill did not return.

'Wait. Pray,' her father replied. Missionaries paid no ransom. It became unbearable.

'Pay, father. Give them what they want.'

'We have no resource to His Will but prayer,' Dr Keswick stubbornly replied. But later he approached with the old Bible.

'You remember this, child?' he asked. The Bible was the only possession they had with them when they were hidden in a loft by one of her father's converts during the Boxer Uprising. It had been snatched up by Dr Keswick as they fled the rebels. Her father read aloud from it through their ordeal.

Martha remembered again the terror of that loft. Kill them, kill them, the rioters cried, their yells mixed with the sound of blows and screams and falling tiles. All about was the smell of fire.

'Read what is written on the front page,' Dr Keswick had urged at the time of Bill's disappearance. She had picked up the dog-eared book.

Dr Keswick, although born in China, had no early memories of the country. He returned with his parents to America as a baby, when his father's health collapsed, and did not see China again until an adult. Before leaving China his father had written in the Bible that had carried him through unknowable tribulations – *Emmanuel, GOD is with us. Lo, I am with you always.* Under this was Dr Keswick's own writing.

To my Father   10th July 1900

We have been three days in the Riot and have been hiding in a loft. Very many miraculous escapes God has given us, but now they know we are here and it seems as if they are making arrangements to burn the building. The mission premises were destroyed and burned yesterday. Our luggage is gone. I have only saved this Bible. Several times they started smashing the roof of the very room in which we are hiding, but God stopped them doing it completely. We are in a 'tight corner'. How the Lord is going to bring us through, I don't know. But if He prefers to take us to Himself instead of our work we will rejoice. The Mandarins are not taking any steps to help us. They are afraid of the mob which is manifestly very infuriated.

I want to bear testimony to the peace God has given us all, even in the midst of the gravest danger and most trying circumstances.

337

It is wonderful to think that even by this very evening we may be with Him, and I may see my dear Mother once again. He doeth all things well. Praise Him! May blessing far surpassing aught we have seen result to China from these troublesome times.

Below this was a further paragraph, also in her father's handwriting, with a date three years later.

The blessing is coming. China is being opened up. The last provincial capital has flung wide its gates – the messenger of the Gospel has entered in. Today, any city in China may be entered without let or hindrance. The walls of conservatism are tottering to their fall; the barriers of seclusion are broken down. China yields at last – 'the Rock' has opened! Praise the Lord.

When eventually Bill's body was found in a faraway place, spliced and hacked to pieces, the coffin was nailed down. Dr Keswick would not let her see the remains. She would allow no one near her, no talk, no comfort. She shut herself in her room. Her tears were few and swelled instead inside her. For a time Dr Keswick left her alone, then slipped a note beneath her door.

For us in China there is a need of courage and joy. The day is difficult; we see not yet what China will be. We stand amid rocks and rapids. But the day is coming when all over this glorious land songs of praise shall rise from the homes and hearts that own our Saviour King. The day is coming when sorrow and sighing shall flee away. Our share in bringing it seems small; but it is a share, a part of His plan, a help toward the carrying out of His purpose. And you too, my dearest child, have a share as, step by step, you go on with Him.

She began to scream. They held her down, splashed iced-water on her face, slapped her face, and still she screamed.

She knew then there was no God. The heathens were right, not *they*. Her whole life had been a trick, played upon her by her father. He had seeded her here, in this terrible place, where they were unwanted. They were a thorn in the flesh of the massive body of China and could make not even a dent. Over all the decades of the mission in China what use were a miserable handful of converts? Did not most return to burning paper money for their dead? And what was so wrong with the heathen version of things? Its hypothesis was as cohesive as Christianity, its people no less aware of psyche and spirit. They did not preach superiority, nor pronounce God in their pocket. Her father had tricked her. He had made her a stranger to herself. He had crammed her early memories with decapitated heads on metal spikes, with the half-chewed corpses of babies, with killing and looting and strife and flight. Before her life had truly begun he had forced her to stare open-eyed at death. He

338

had stolen her childhood away. She hated him. She hated everything to do with China. Her life was a struggle to stay afloat in an alien world. At last now the floating was over.

Her scream became then a scream of relief. Dr Keswick had approached with a hypodermic. The dark limbo it brought had lasted over a year, until the day Flora found Lily.

She still had that Bible. She picked it up and once again read her father's faded writing on the first blank page. The old rage began again in her, creeping up to pulsate in her throat. No one now would approach with a hypodermic needle, pressing dark limbo upon her. The mistake after Bill had been to stop screaming, to allow her father to draw her back into a wooden life. She could scream now for ever, floating free upon the sound.

She held the nautilus high, to catch the faint light from the curtained window. She closed her eyes and let her mind travel through its numerous pearly chambers, twisting and turning against its sides, smooth as the flesh of a lychee. And at last she saw that dark, secret chamber hidden far from the world. Its beauty echoed about her. It drew her in and enclosed her at last in its silent universe.

Only Flora knew the truth. *It was her fault.* Nadya, with her usual spongy sympathy tried to dispel this as illusion. But that other person, buried deep within Flora, to whom she now turned for help, saw to the heart of it all.

'*It was you who killed her,*' said this person.

She saw again Lily's pale body, naked and thrashing, like a captured fish before the flesh of those men. Day after day without relief, she had to face these pictures now, alone. She had seen what it was they did to Lily in all its terrible detail. She had seen that secret, swollen weapon men held against their bodies. They had forced her to watch, holding her head. She could still feel their fingers gripping her skull. Making her watch. Now Lily was free of it all. Her death poured memories in a fresh deluge upon Flora. Their weight seemed many times multiplied, now that Lily was gone. How would she live with this weight?

'*If you had not left her nothing would have happened.*' The voice spoke again inside her.

When she thought of Martha a great tiredness filled Flora so immense it overflowed the world. Now, forever, there was no escape. In death Lily would press the harder upon her. And Martha in life, but carrying that death, would settle upon her like suffocation. Between them they would press her to a pulp.

'Come', said the voice. She heard the seductive sounds again, like the singing of those Greek Sirens.

She remembered again the head in the river, staring at her like a water sprite. She remembered the spiky eyelashes, and hair like waving ferns. The mouth had seemed to smile. He was her guide.

'*Come,*' said the voice again. '*Nothing need be so much pain.*'

She turned back to the room where she had first seen the bottles of blood, like liquid ruby, promising life but deceiving with death. She knew what she sought and found it.

It was still light. She turned out of the hospital towards the towpath by the river. At last she came to the water's edge. She found a tuft of weeds near where she had seen the head. The seat was comfortable, a smooth back of grass supported her. Behind rose the ancient walls of Nanking. She thought of the centuries of their existence, the wave upon wave of sorrow they had witnessed.

Dense clouds were lowering now across the sky. The horizon lay upon the earth like a dark, rent seam. The sky lifted free there, torn away from its root, ascending without end. Wide gaps opened up between the banks of cloud. Through these she could see the stratosphere beyond. A mysterious light seemed to radiate, not touching Nanking, but hanging above it, even as the clouds brought in the night.

She took the small bottle from her pocket and, opening it, began to swallow the sweet coated pills. The clouds had now parted upon the luminous sky as if to reveal a door of light. And far beneath lay the darkening earth, closing like a fist upon its own darkness, far from that magic light.

Flora looked down into the water but could not see the head. She knew he was there somewhere, waiting to guide her. Protecting her. She began to feel sleepy. It was the pleasantest sensation she had had in days. Now, at last, she could sleep undisturbed. She looked up once more to the sky. The door of light stood open still.

Martha sat without speaking in a chair. On her lap she held the nautilus. On the table beside her was an old Bible. Day after day she sat, silent and unmoving. Nadya led her to bed, helped her undress and wash, dressed her again the next day. Martha stared before her, lost to some far place, captive to its desolate landscape. Each day from the Bible she tore off two pages. These she shredded slowly, hour after hour. Scooping up the ripped bits she threw them at last in to the room like a shower of confetti. Each night she set the nautilus beside her bed, and stared at it anew. Again the next day she tore two pages from the old book, and set about the job of shredding. Slowly Nadya understood. She might never speak again.

29

April 1938

Return to Hsinking

As soon as Tilik returned to Hsinking, he went straight to Jun Hasegawa. He had thought about the matter of Teng throughout the long journey on military planes back to Manchukuo. There had been weeks of delay, first in Shanghai and then in Peking.

Hasegawa's hair was streaked with grey again. He had difficulty in Hsinking obtaining the hair dye he used in Japan. Nature's re-entrenchment gave him an air of new authority. He wore his glasses permanently now, and his lips were thin as string. The responsibility he had been given in Manchukuo sat upon him heavily. Tilik had to wait two days to see him.

Beneath the customary odour of tobacco, Hasegawa reeked of menthol. 'I have a permanent cold. This climate does not suit me. Dust and damp, and more dust.' He sniffed loudly to demonstrate the state of his sinuses. The weak warmth of the Manchurian sun did not penetrate the high stone rooms of the building Hasegawa worked in. He dragged upon a cigarette and gave a hoarse cough. Taking the report Tilik handed him, he pushed it into a drawer. Tilik suppressed his anger.

'Why were you so long? We have need of you here,' Hasegawa did not hide his irritation.

'They would not let me leave. I had no wish to stay through all that ugly business in Nanking,' Tilik replied.

'They're wasting time, energy and manpower down there. Now I hear they want to push on south, to Canton, and also continue their chase after Chiang Kai-shek. Do they not realize we are fighting on two fronts, North and South? With the taking of Nanking the main objective of the China war has been won. The principal Chinese cities and railroads are in our hands. It is time now to turn and face Russia.'

Hasegawa smashed his fist down on his desk in anger. What would happen, Tilik wondered, if this rage should ever turn upon him? After the incident with Teng in Nanking, he felt he walked a tightrope. What if it were ever discovered that the Communist had escaped because of him? Why had he done it? How had Nozaki persuaded him?

When they had first met, Tilik remembered, Hasegawa had been a Strike South man, interested only in southern expansion. His term in Hsinking, so close to Russian troops, had changed his views. He was now convinced of the need to Strike North, at the Soviet Union. Hasegawa stood up and began to pace the room.

'The Chinese have dynamited the levees along the Yellow River. It flowed back into its original course, flooding thousands of square miles of farmland. Do you know also how many thousands of our tanks, trucks and field guns have been lost in all that flood and mud, not to mention men? Tens of thousands of Chinese perished of course, but what does that matter to them? They die like ants anyway. The whole country is retreating before our troops, and as they go they flood and burn, leaving nothing behind for our army to eat.

'Soon we will face defeats. The Chinese are not stupid, and we are over-confident. And these Communist guerrillas are everywhere, worse than damn mosquitoes. If we Strike North now at Russia, Chiang would die a natural death. Instead we're making a hero of him. He gathers strength by our blundering.' Hasegawa appeared a man under considerable strain.

'They caught some Communist while I was in Nanking. I thought he seemed to match the description of that man we held here and who escaped. I asked to have a look at him, but he bore no resemblance whatever. I've put it all in the report.' Tilik was anxious to get the facts stated.

'I know all about it. They sent us a cable; wanted to know if we trusted you. Who do they think they are down there? If a man escaped it's because of their own incompetence. I replied in the appropriate manner. Shouldn't think they liked it. Those Strike South people don't want the limelight off them, that's why they're holding up a Strike North. They and the Navy! There'll be trouble soon up here. The men want to fight.' Hasegawa pulled out a small metal flask from his desk, and took a drink.

'Many of our Generals, you know, want an end to this war in China. It is a bottomless pit. It fritters away Japan's vital military resources and will prevent us waging a more essential war on the Soviet Union. We must come to an accommodation with Chiang Kai-shek. That is the only way.' Hasegawa took another mouthful from his flask.

'Why don't you let me go back to Japan?' Tilik asked, sitting forward suddenly. His relief at Hasegawa's reaction to the affair with Teng made him suddenly bold.

343

'Are you giving me orders?' Hasegawa raised his voice. 'I'll send you when I please. Get back to your desk. You'll find I've already compiled a list of instructions.' Hasegawa waved him away, coughing into his handkerchief. Tilik stood up reluctantly and left the room.

It was a relief to be back in Hsinking where everything was whole. Trees were a luminous green against a clear sun. The air was fresh, blown in for miles across the steppes. The town emanated purpose. Military cars, polished and fast, passed on the street. Barrows, piled with vegetables and fruit, gleamed with plenitude. Even the Manchurian dust seemed restrained, compared to the ash from bombs or pyres that had settled upon Nanking. He was glad to be back.

His rooms in a boarding house were small but neat. As he hoped there were letters waiting, from Michiko and Rash Bihari. He wished for a return to equilibrium. Since Nanking he was filled with painful emotions. He tore open the letter from Michiko, but the familiarity of the writing only conjured up the reality of her distance, and sank him further into depression. And the news she gave of Japan was not good. He worried about his child being born into a world of such grimness.

It is worse and worse. It is not just the lack of commodities. Now a National General Mobilization Law has been introduced, giving the Government the power of control over everything. I cannot really say this yet affects our everyday life, but there is a feeling that we are on full war footing. The newspapers are of course crammed with news of our advances in China but somehow news of a final victory never comes. We all feel rather depressed. It is as if the colour has gone out of everything. I thought once we got Nanking this war would finish, but it seems not. It seems to only get worse. And Father talks now of an even bigger war, one that might end with us facing even America. How could we ever fight America? But people are whispering these things. I am frightened. Can you not come back here? Do you think all this will happen?

Otherwise I am well. The baby moves and kicks within me. The doctor says he will be strong. Do not worry about us.

He leaned back, the letter in his hand and loneliness pressed about him. He could see the expression of worry already upon Michiko's face, the creasing about the eyes, the faint pucker of her mouth. In the beginning he had thought their life together would never settle into a truce, nor thrive. They had lived like separate people. But slowly the structure of marriage ripened about them. Once she knew a child was growing between them, acceptance came quickly to Michiko. Now, at this distance, he missed her, and could read in her letter that this feeling was reciprocated.

There was a small balcony attached to his room, and he opened the french windows. Outside the sky was thick with towering cloud. He pulled a chair out onto the narrow space and sat down with Rash Bihari's letter, drawing the thin, lined paper from the envelope. At once the old man's familiar writing filled him with nostalgia. It was as if Rash Bihari stood beside him, like a genie released from a bottle. Just the thought of his elderly, paternal presence, returned Tilik to a lost identity.

There is a feeling here of things closing in. There is no doubt that this Government has a taste for war. Here and there is talk of things in China that are not pleasant to hear. Of course the Government is very quick to suppress these accounts. For the first time now too we hear rumours of some defeats. This too is played down. What really is happening? Only from the occasional newspaper smuggled in from abroad can one get some idea of what may actually be going on. In general this seems to be triumph for Japan. And who are we to wish otherwise, even if some of their methods of war are not to our liking? War is war, unfortunately. On their triumph we must ride. Their victory is our victory. Long may it be. We must keep our minds only upon India, nothing else.

Our time in India may also soon arrive. Subash's stature grows in India. He is Congress president now. So far he is working Gandhiji's machine with some skill, but there is talk of great strains beneath the surface. I do not know how long an alliance with Gandhiji will last. I predict a split and war between them before long.

War. That is all I think about now. It seems inevitable in Europe. Japan and her conquests this side of the world, keep pace with Hitler's own. Many people speak of a greater war even, when Japan will face America. If a war of this nature should come upon us, what then will our position be? My mind turns upon this always. We must be prepared.

There are large Indian communities throughout south-east Asia. We must co-ordinate the united strength of this expatriate India, a force of perhaps two million or more. In the event of a Greater East Asia War an Indian Independence League could not only be of use to Japan, but a support to India in her struggle for Independence. We must be assured by Japan that these expatriate Indian communities will be under Japanese protection should their countries of residence fall to Japan. All this may be some way still in the future, but we must be prepared.

My gentle probing on these matters to various influential people has been very well-received. A man from the Japan Broadcasting Corporation suggested that, if events demanded, they might consider opening a short-wave radio station for us to broadcast to India.

We need to strengthen our position in Japan and consolidate all the freedom movements throughout south-east Asia. This is esssential. Let us struggle together for a free India. There is much work to be done here. I do not know what you can do there, running hither and thither across deserts and steppes. China can do without you. India needs you here. Tell them to send you back to Japan.

345

Tilik put down the letter. A sense of immediacy filled him. Rash Bihari was right. What was he doing here, jerked like a puppet on a string, at Hasegawa's whim? He must get back to Japan.

He rested the letter on his knee and looked up into the sky again. Clouds massed above, stretching and changing. An arch formed in the sky like a gate in a crumbled wall. The great walls of Nanking were at once before him. He shut his eyes quickly. So much effort now seemed to go into pushing Nanking from his mind. Everyday images crowded up, pressing against his skull. His face had taken on a rigid expression, from the effort of control. He had hoped to leave it all behind him, when he left Nanking.

Nozaki came into his mind again. Even across this distance, a taut line seemed to pull between them. Perhaps this was how twins felt, two people tied at the ankle, each aware that if the other stumbled the pain would pass through him. Did Nozaki live with the same apprehensions of revelation? What if they suspected Nozaki and tortured him and he gave way before the pressure? What then? Already Tilik saw himself before a firing squad. Why had he done such a foolhardy thing? What had Nozaki said, what were the words that had made him jeopardize not only every ideal he had worked for, but his very life? Questions piled in upon him.

He knew himself a timid man. He could not throw a bomb. In Delhi Jai Singh had died because of him. Those women loaded before his eyes upon a truck and driven off to slaughter, they too had died because he feared to mediate. And yet, for an instant Nozaki found words that had moved him to an extreme of action. *The past can fill our minds forever . . . We must know we opposed this evil . . .* Some words returned to him. Were they enough to have made him risk his life for a man he did not know? He remembered the force with which Nozaki spoke, the strange light in his eye. Why did it remain with him? He felt suddenly cold and returned to the room, shutting the windows behind him.

'This is nonsense. Have you become like a woman, asking to go home?' Hasegawa yelled and sat down at his desk to light a cigarette.

'Let me tell you a few things. We have a Russian, a general, who has crossed the border and given himself up to our Kwantung Army. He has imparted to us much invaluable information about the state of the Soviet divisions in Siberia. We are sure that now is the ideal time for a full-scale Strike North, but Tokyo orders us to wait. There is trouble on the shores of Lake Khasan where the borders of Siberia, Manchukuo and Korea meet. Soviet forces have moved into the zone and have fired already upon us. Our men are mutinous, they want to fight. If Russia has plans to intervene in China it is essential we show them they are wrong. If the army here defies Imperial orders, we are in trouble. And at this time, you want to go home.'

'Things are hotting up for India too. All these Japanese triumphs mean a spread of power. It is time now for me to concentrate on consolidating the strength of all expatriate Indians in south-east Asia. We would be an added force on the side of Japan,' Tilik argued.

'You are working for the Japanese Emperor. Never forget that,' Hasegawa hissed. 'Who is paying your keep?'

Tilik tensed in sudden fear at the expression on Hasegawa's face. He felt his courage dwindle and Rash Bihari fade into a shadowy corner. Hasegawa narrowed his eyes upon Tilik's confusion.

'We are in need of buffer zones between Manchuria and Russia. Inner Mongolia is already such a zone.'

'How will this work be done?' Tilik enquired morosely.

'We are setting up a new school to teach techniques of espionage to Koreans of our choice. They will be placed over the border of Russia to incite Koreans on that side to agitate for a state of their own, which we would then control. You will be a useful instructor in the school. It is essential you concentrate upon this. No more talk of going home.'

30

April 1938

Front Line

At midnight Donald and Art Morton began their journey towards the battle front. They were forced to travel with the China correspondent for Hitler's own paper, the *Voelkischer Beobachter*. Almost at once Heiner Zimmer opened up his typewriter. Art Morton turned to roll his eyes at Donald. The train was blacked out, Chinese guards patrolled the corridors. They smoked in silence, except the German. He wore storm troopers' boots and breeches and a semi-military jacket, and refused brandy from the flask Art Morton produced. He led, he said, a controlled life, and he spoke enthusiastically of the Hitler Youth Movement. The train sped forward through the night, swaying as if to derail itself. Donald leaned back and closed his eyes. The click of the German's typewriter was bound to the deeper knock of the train wheels. The smell of smoke and Morton's brandy hung in the air, and mixed with the German's hair oil. The door opened suddenly.

'General Pai will see you now.' A young officer put his head into the compartment and stared at the industrious Zimmer. Donald roused himself and rubbed his eyes. He felt tired all the time.

They followed the officer along the bouncing corridor. Once they were thrown heavily against the wall and a blackout blind sprang up at the window. The officer turned with a scowl, pulling it sharply into place, before striding ahead to General Pai's operations room which had once been the dining car. Maps now covered walls and tables.

General Pai Chung-hsi had the look of a thinker not a fighter. His welcome was courtly. 'The trap is about to close on the Japanese. We have them like fish in a pond. The battle should begin tomorrow. We are going to wipe out the army of a Japanese-backed Chinese warlord at Taierchuang. But I must tell you, we shall not be able to repeat this victory or to keep the Japanese from capturing Hsuchow. The town is a great railway junction, an important military gain for the Japanese. We know already we cannot defend the town for long. The terrain is unsuitable for the form of warfare the Japanese will impose upon us.

They expected to take Hsuchow as soon as they finished with Nanking, but we have not allowed them to do that yet, and can still hold them off a while. China needs at least half a year of breathing space to repair the Shanghai–Nanking losses, and prepare bases of resistance in western and south-western China. We must have a victory at Taierchuang to raise our people's spirits.'

They wrote down what the General said. Soon they returned to their carriage. Once more Zimmer opened up his typewriter, switched on the light above his seat, and began to pound the keys.

'Can't you stop that?' Morton asked. 'We need some sleep.'

'Everything I see and hear must be recorded. This is what the Fuehrer demands. My reports go to the Embassy in Hankow and then on to Berlin,' Zimmer said without disguise.

'What about *Voelkischer Beobachter*?' Donald enquired.

'They go there too, of course,' Zimmer's fingers rattled on.

'Either you stop that infernal noise or I'll throw your typewriter out of this train,' Morton announced.

'I am nearly finished, please,' Zimmer replied.

'He is no more than a spy,' Morton confided when Zimmer went to find the lavatory. 'How can they let him travel about like this? Germany probably sends his reports straight to the Japanese.'

The train roared on for hours but stopped eventually across the Grand Canal. The sudden cessation of movement filled them with excitement. In the stillness they listened to the thud and boom of heavy fighting. Sometimes the sounds were overhead, as if bombs would rain down directly upon them. They waited in silence. Soon there was the noise of opening doors. Officers entered the train, and pushed along the narrow corridor towards the operations room. Donald lifted the blackout blind a fraction. The sudden light of shells, like falling stars, illuminated the countryside. He saw also, to his amazement, General Pai with his Chief-of-Operations, pacing the furrow of a wheat field, deep in conversation. The General appeared to scorn all cover. It turned Donald's stomach to watch them as they walked up and down against a backdrop of bursting bombs only a few hundred yards away. He replaced the blind, his heart pounding.

The memory of the brilliant sky, streaked crimson as a sunset, over the burning oil ships beyond the *Panay* returned to him suddenly. He had lifted his face then as to a fireworks display, walking beside Mariani's stretcher. The burst of shellfire over the copse beyond the train unnerved him. Sometimes things became muddled in his mind, sensations and locations seemed to merge. Now, the opening and slamming of the train doors, the sudden blast of cool night air and the smell of damp wool rising off the heavy coats of the officers, threw him back to Hengtao and his interview with the double agent, Amleto Vespa. The blast of one bomb pitched him back upon another. He tried not to think of the *Panay* or Nanking. After some time the train began to move again, back in the direction it had come.

'What the hell is happening?' Donald asked, sitting forward with a frown. Morton went to enquire but was told to wait in the compartment.

Soon General Pai's Chief-of-Operations entered. 'It is bad luck for you this time. We have decided to let the Japanese stretch their lines a little deeper.' His eyes rested on Zimmer. 'You will be allowed to return next week. General Pai sends you some *kao liang*, the drink of the northern farmers. It may ease your disappointment at such a wasted journey.' He who had paced the fiery wheat field now assumed the role of genial host.

It was always the way, thought Donald. He never knew at the start of a journey whether it would end in his annihilation or an anti-climax of frustration. He was too tired to feel the kind of irritation now exploding through Morton. The German at once opened up his typewriter. Donald closed his eyes again. He did not care if he reached the front lines or not. The *kao liang* arrived and they drank the scorching liquor, letting it rip their guts apart and drug them into sleep.

When Donald opened his eyes it was morning and they were drawing into Hsuchow, the front line city and railway terminal. He had made up his mind, he was not going back to Taierchuang. One front line was like another. He had no stomach for more battle. It appeared Zimmer had also got what he wanted. He clicked shut his typewriter and reached for his cap. As they stepped down from the train General Pai's chief commander came up with a band of officers and led Zimmer, protesting, away. The commander turned to Donald and Morton.

'We are suspicious of that man. We shall interrogate him. Next week, as I said, you may return for the battle.' He snapped his heels and marched away.

Morton decided to stay on in Hsuchow and return to the front, but Donald could not be persuaded. His instinct was to go back down the track to Hankow. He did not know what his next move would be. But things turned up, they always did.

General Pai's polished, speeding train was another world from the trains returning to Hankow, weighed down with a dying cargo. Every train was a hospital train, its carriages, freight cars and open trucks crammed with wounded men. Refugees, fleeing the areas of North China taken by the Japanese, crowded upon the roofs of the trains, hanging there like a colony of bats. Thousands more walked beside the tracks.

Donald found a corner seat in a carriage of wounded men. They lay foetal-like upon the floor. They suffered in silence, and silently died before him. He offered cigarettes, settling them between their lips. There was no common language in which to ask of their ordeals. A stench of blood and gangrene hung upon the air, throwing him back to Nanking. Eventually he could stand no more and went out into the corridor. There too the same odour pressed upon him. He fought his way along the packed train, desperate to escape the overpowering reek of death. Carriage after carriage presented the same distressing scenes, the same fetid aroma, until he despaired of release. Already he neared the end of the train.

In the very last compartment a huge man sat drinking surrounded by others of lesser girth, none of whom were in uniform. The smell here was of alcohol instead of gangrene, and the ripe odour of the living. Donald pushed his way in determinedly and gestured his demand for a seat. The men made room, exchanging glances, looking at him curiously. The fat man, a bottle of liquor in one hand, appeared to be their leader. He immediately thrust a glass of *kao liang* into Donald's hand and raised his own in a toast. Donald took the drink gratefully, throwing it back. The liquor rocked through him and he began to cough. The fat man swayed with uncontrollable laughter. He gave a loud order to one of his band who disappeared and returned with a soldier who spoke some English. The fat man demanded he interpret, he wanted Donald to hear his story. He continued to laugh, showing a mouth of rotted teeth, and uttered a stream of incomprehensible words.

'His name is Fat Man Ping. Guerrilla leader,' the soldier interpreted. Donald looked at Fat Man with new interest.

'He is going to Hankow to join his friend, Grandma Chao. Many people give them money in Hankow. He will join hands with Grandma Chao. He is the leader of ten thousand guerrillas twisting the tiger's tail in the hill country. He is a northerner. They eat wheat and are big tall men. Rice-eating men are smaller. He says, Chiang Kai-shek is the first rice-eating man to be a leader in China in many years.' The soldier was given more *kao liang* as was Donald. Fat Man Ping renewed his tale.

'Fighting Japanese has saved his life. Before this war Chiang Kai-shek's men only wanted to hunt him down for being a bandit. Now he is happy. He can kill as many Japanese as he wants and not get into trouble. Now he is called a guerrilla, no longer a bandit. Only, there is no money to be made in this new game. No money either in the pockets of

351

the Japanese he kills. Just lucky charms. But their coats are good wool. Good for the snowy passes of the north. Only, if you wear them you must be careful. Other guerrillas may think you a Japanese and shoot you down. Better to leave the coat and take only the weapons of these dead Japs.' Beside the soldier, Ping rocked about with laughter, tears streamed down his face.

'From mountain ledges his men roll great rocks down upon Japanese convoys and block the narrow mountain roads. Then they pick off the East Ocean dwarfs like sparrows,' the soldier continued.

Every so often Ping slapped the interpreter on the back with a great guffaw. More *kao liang* was passed about. Donald felt his head swim and his insides bleed. Ping had tales of ambush and sleight of hand that lasted the rest of the journey. The *kao liang* seemed in inexhaustible supply. At last, to Donald's relief, Hankow was reached and they reeled from the train.

'He want to know what you do now?' the soldier asked, looking distractedly down the platform, anxious to return to his friends. Donald shrugged, his head too muzzy to think clearly about anything.

'He says you need English-speaking guide. He wants you to write about guerrillas. He wants to see his picture in a newspaper. He says you follow him.' The soldier turned and hurried away before Donald could reply. Fat Man Ping pointed to the camera and Donald obediently took his picture. Fat Man Ping posed with flourish and a wide grin, then took Donald's arm in a vice-like grip. He stumbled forward beside Ping, too demolished by *kao liang* to protest. Ping led him triumphantly out of the station, like a prize dog on a lead.

As they entered the town the sky was hazy with dusk. The hills already folded into each other in deepening layers, the remains of the sunset streaked an upper reach of sky. Fat Man Ping led them down to the river and on to a ferryboat. Had he not been pulled along by Ping, Donald would have made his way to the Terminus Hotel in the foreign concession for a whisky, food that tasted familiar and a bed of smooth white sheets. Now he had no idea where his next night would be, what food he must swallow, what dangers might assail. But this was the manner in which things turned up, by not turning your back upon them. He followed Ping's massive frame.

Behind Ping Donald struggled on to a crowded ferry and was squashed between a woman with a basket of chickens and another suckling a baby. A goat began to chew at his jacket. He pulled himself free in annoyance, the liquor now ached in his head. The dusk grew thicker about them. Across the river Donald could make out the hilly shape of Hankow's twin city, Wuchang, and the glitter of some lights. Fat Man

Ping was at the front of the boat, surrounded by a circle of admiring peasants. He craned his neck above the crowd, pointing Donald out.

Once the ferry landed they disembarked. Donald climbed a narrow cobbled street behind Ping who gasped for breath, and stopped frequently to mop his great bald head. It was almost dark. Eventually, they passed through a large gate and came into a spacious courtyard. It was crowded with refugee families. Ping and his men stopped and appeared to ask directions of people, everyone gestured them on. They entered yet another courtyard and climbed a flight of steps. The place was a temple or monastery given over now to the needy. Children ran about, people cooked in battered pans over a few coals. Wounded soldiers lay in a further courtyard, a few makeshift roofs of paper or canvas pegged above the weakest. Ping gave a sudden shout and walked towards a figure stooping over one of the soldiers. The man turned and the light of a nearby fire glowed in his face. Donald stopped in amazement at the sight of Teng. Teng stared at Donald in equal surprise. Fat Man Ping began to laugh and when told of their acquaintance, laughed even harder.

'See how things turn out,' he bellowed and called to a henchman for more *kao liang*.

Teng led them to a house beyond the courtyard and up to a second-floor room. It was bare but for some bedding on the floor and a couple of rickety chairs. Fat Man Ping did not stay long and, after elaborate goodbyes, vanished with his men.

'You take my bedding, I will sleep on a blanket,' Teng insisted to Donald. 'But first, food. I can see you are in need of it.'

He turned to a young man who followed him like a shadow, staring at Donald in a terrified way. Teng spoke to him and the man nodded and scurried away.

'If I didn't know better I would have thought you were speaking Japanese,' Donald announced as the man left the room.

'I was,' Teng replied. 'He *is* a Japanese. I speak to him only in sign language unless we are alone. It is all right with you, I know. He is a deserter. My friends picked him up near Nanking. He would have been killed by our people, if not his own. I've told everyone he is mute.' Teng sat down on the chair beside Donald and began to tell him something of his own story.

'Who helped you escape?' Donald asked.

'Oh, that is of no matter, I think,' Teng replied absently.

Akira returned with a pan of rice gruel, a few sparse bits of vegetable floating in it. He squatted down and laid out three bowls on the floor. Teng spoke to him and he gave Donald a sudden, furtive look. It was difficult to read his expression. He was in his early twenties, Donald gauged, with a thin, sensitive face. A few sentences were exchanged between him and Teng.

'He is a farmer and a potter,' Teng explained. 'I have told him he has nothing to fear from you. He wanted to know where you lived in Nanking during the siege and I explained. He said he once brought a wounded woman to Martha's hospital. Everyone thought he had killed her.'

Donald shrugged. 'He has killed others I expect.' He remembered vaguely hearing of a Japanese soldier entering the hospital carrying a dead Chinese woman. He stared at the man, who looked quickly away, as if he understood the conversation.

'Yes, he has killed others,' Teng replied slowly. 'You could say he crossed a line, along with many other men, beyond what is our everyday human evil, into the demonic. When he saw that shadow fall upon him, he had the courage to desert.'

'And what will become of him? What is he doing here?'

'I cannot answer the first question, only the second. Here, he is helping me. There are refugees who need us, and wounded Chinese soldiers.'

'The need for atonement?' Donald smiled slightly.

'Do we not all have some need for atonement?' Teng replied. 'Please, this will get cold. Let us eat. We have little enough to sustain us here as it is, without eating it cold.' He sat down on the floor and took up his bowl into which Akira had ladled the steaming gruel.

'I had thought before coming here that I would be staying at the Terminus Hotel,' Donald admitted, looking down at the unappetizing meal. The thought of a steak came to him.

'Please go if you wish. You must choose, this world or that.' Teng spooned up the gruel hungrily. Beside him Akira buried his face in the hot steam of the bowl. The room was filled with the sound of slurping.

'I long ago made my decision. After Nanking nothing can be the same for me,' Donald admitted.

'That shadow is upon us all,' Teng replied. 'And will be always. What this man here has been party to is something we must thank whatever God there is, that we were not pressed into. Goodness can so easily be uprooted. The poor man is trying to find his way out of a shadow that almost entirely consumed him. Now tell me, how is this gruel? Fit for a king, is it not?'

He watched Donald pick up the bowl and begin to eat. He noticed the clenched look about his eyes, the transparency of emotion in his face. So

354

great was the pressure of testimony locked within them all, that it could make a man appear abnormally disturbed.

'It is no easy thing, to bear witness to such a dark collective experience as was Nanking,' he said aloud. Donald looked up from his bowl, listening intently as Teng continued.

'It is as if we are asked to answer questions that have lain incomplete through eternity,' Teng sighed. 'Yet destiny planted us there for its own reason. We are the eyes of the dead, and the vision for a world that could not see. We cannot escape that role.'

It was important to affirm that destiny, Teng thought. He had no answers, he had not even a firm religion if anyone had asked him, for he had dabbled in too many. He knew only that reason set narrow boundaries that he could no longer now accept. Each man lived, unknowingly, far beyond the impoverished field of his logic. Beneath that cerebral life the world of the unconscious went on in each one, secretly accruing its own life knowledge.

'A man may spend his life with the seed of a particular knowledge within him. Only at a special moment will it flower for him to grasp its meaning. We cannot step aside from the task we have been given here.' Teng spoke mildly and returned to his food.

Donald lay awake on the roll of bedding. In the courtyard he heard the coughs and groans of the wounded, and the occasional cry of a child. In the room Teng snored lightly. Donald listened to the sound, thinking of the courage with which Teng lived his life. He stepped away from nothing. Now, he protected a man who, but recently, might have skewered him like a pig. He felt an overwhelming envy for anyone so sure of his conscience and commitment. From the Japanese there was no sound. He lay with his back to Donald, but there was a tenseness to his body, as if he too did not sleep.

Donald's mind was full of the things Teng had said. He had the feeling of receiving something, but could not determine its shape. His thoughts turned again to Nadya. Whatever it was that lay between them, his contact again with Teng seemed to ignite her in his mind. He was restless as he had not been for a long time, with thoughts of her. Something had gone wrong between them that he could not entirely clarify. His mind was full of holes. So much did not cohere. Everything had started with Smollett and spiralled down to Nanking. The thought of Nadya still in the town troubled him suddenly now. She was more vulnerable in this warring world than she knew. The idea came to him slowly then, amidst the coughs of the destitute.

Soon he left Wuchang and made his way back to Nanking. He had no difficulty now entering the smashed city. At the hospital he was informed that Nadya had left for Shanghai, and was working once more with Bradley Reed. He asked for Martha and was told she was unwell. She was being cared for by Franciscan nuns who had returned now to the city. Both Lily and Flora had died. He expressed disbelief and bewilderment. No explanations seemed forthcoming.

'Where is Martha?' he demanded. They pointed the way to the convent.

'It is better you do not see her,' said a nun at the door.

'What is wrong?' he asked.

'The grief of the world.' The nun sighed. 'We pray every day that she may find peace. Maybe later, if you are here, she could see you. God willing.' The nun smiled gently and shut the door.

There were trains now again to Shanghai. In that city the Foreign Settlement remained intact, but the Japanese were everywhere and a beleaguered atmosphere remained. He found Nadya in her old office.

'Why are you here?' Her eyes widened, then narrowed in suspicion, as if readying for attack.

'Is there a law against seeing you?' He took a chair and sat down. She leaned away from the typewriter to stare at him.

'Where have you been?'

'With Teng in Wuchang.'

She sat forward at that, questions spilling from her.

'We were worried the Japanese *Kempeitai* might have taken you again.' He looked at her anxiously.

'They seem to have other things to keep them busy. I am followed most of the time. My letters are opened. They're watching me. But it could be worse.'

She told him then about Lily and Flora. 'It has turned Martha's mind. She has not spoken since they brought Flora back from the river.' Nadya bit her lips in distress and looked down at the typewriter, trying to push away the memories. 'There was nothing I could do. I left as soon as possible.'

He looked out of the window, to the familiar view of the Bund, now full of Japanese warships. He remembered this was the building from which Nadya had viewed those first shootings, that seemed now a lifetime ago.

'Can you leave? I'll take you home,' he said.

It was the same tiny flat. Potted flowers crowded the window sill. The survival of the Foreign Settlement was something he could not get over. Beyond this island was annihilation. In the whole of China hardly a city survived, but this cultural island went on as before, with barely a geranium petal out of place. And, although in themselves so much was changed, it seemed easy here, in this room to pretend that all might be the same. He reached out to pull her into his arms, but she drew back, shaking her head. There had been nothing between them since he left Shanghai so abruptly after Smollett. Whatever it was that still tied them, she could not so readily now pick it up. She groped for words to express her feelings and then gave up.

Instead she busied herself making coffee. 'This is precious stuff. I got it from the Japanese black market.' Her hair had grown and fell wildly about her shoulders.

'I can't cope with anything more,' she said, attempting to explain her feelings about their relationship. Yet even as she said the words she knew if the man Nozaki were before her, she would not have hesitated.

'I'm going back to England,' Donald said suddenly. 'Things are hotting up there, Hitler's making advances everywhere. War is inevitable. Bad things are ahead everywhere. *The Times* wants me back. What are you going to do here?' He sipped the coffee and stared at her as she fidgeted nervously with her cup. Regret filled him again, sharp as grief. He never made the right decisions, as if to spite himself.

'Bradley is finally going back to the States for good. He and his wife want me to go. He says he'll get me a job there. But it's not so easy, being stateless. I shall find other work here no doubt.' The flat tone in her voice upset him.

'There is something I want to suggest,' he said. 'I have given it thought. I think you ought to marry me.' He had not intended to place the words so bluntly before her, he had meant in some way to prepare her. She put down her cup and looked at him with the same shock as when he had entered her office. He watched her attempt to collect herself.

'Please don't joke.' Her tone was derisive, her expression on guard.

'I am not joking. I have never been more serious.' He leaned forward. 'If you don't want to marry me in the conventional sense, then don't, although I would be happy enough to give it a try. But marry me for your own good. Don't you see how vulnerable you are? War is talked about everywhere, and not just in China, where you could say we have been bystanders. We may have a war greater than any we can conceive, involving all the nations of the world. And you are alone. You are stateless, a refugee if you like. You have no passport, no country to protect you. I can give you that protection. Don't you see you *must* marry me.' He sat back, breathless with the urgency of his speech.

It took some moments before she replied. 'Thank you for your charity.

But I don't know if I want to live my life with you, whatever the dangers I face here. You make me feel like a stray cat to which you are willing to give a home.' Her face was full of bitterness. She pushed the hair off her shoulders, and turned away from him.

He swore in exasperation. 'I don't ask that you come with me anywhere. Stay here if you wish. Do as you like. Never see me again. Just *marry* me. At least then you will have some security. You will have a passport by which to leave this country if you ever wish. If the *Kempeitai* get too near you, there will be an Embassy to call to for help. Nadya do this, please.'

'Why are you offering this? It is most suspect.' She looked at him angrily, trying to evaluate this further phase of erratic behaviour.

'In this whole war you are the only person I can help. I have done nothing to save a single human being. I am not like Teng. The gift to help the suffering has not been given to me. I have lived a useless war. You remember at the beginning of all this, when you were so upset not to hear the gun that killed those peasants? Well, I have refused to hear a single gun, while listening to them all. I can live with it no longer. This is the only honourable thing I can do. I am dying from lack of self-respect.' The feeling of his own uselessness welled up again in him.

'You are mad. A marriage like this is for the wrong reasons. How can you even suggest it? What does that make me, some form of atonement to ease your war-stricken conscience?' She stood up in new anger to pace the room.

'It *is* mad. But I would say I am doing it for the right reasons, not the wrong ones. And even if it is only to know I did one good deed, just marry me. I shall probably never feel this noble again. You will not get another offer from me,' Donald threatened.

'Oh, I'm quite sure of that,' she murmured. 'But what if in a few months, or a year or two, you meet someone you really want to marry, and you've already tied yourself up with this honourable Boy Scout deed to me? Or maybe I shall meet someone and wish to tie myself to him. What then?'

'If that should happen, something could be arranged. Annulment probably, for we could prove we had never lived together. And even if that did happen, you would still retain a British passport. But perhaps, in the future, you might even find you wish to take up your position as my wife.' He grinned with a sudden return to his old bantering style.

She shook her head. 'I have no intention of marrying anyone at present. I am happy as I am. It wouldn't work, I know it.' He sat before her, an expression of such anguish on his face, that suddenly she almost laughed.

'Maybe it will save your life. Let me at least have the pleasure of knowing I did that,' Donald argued.

'It is quite crazy.' She could see he was determined for his own strange reasons. The memory of those hours with the *Kempeitai* returned to her in a rush. She had never been without fear since that day. Even here in Shanghai, she was conscious always of a shadow. They knew what she did every hour of the day. At any moment they might take her again. She turned to look at Donald.

'It is *crazy*,' she repeated in bewilderment.

They were married by a notary within a week. She refused to sleep with him. For so strange a pact to have meaning it was important they abide by the intuitive rules. Whatever might once have passed between them, this was a magnanimous business arrangement for her safety in uncertain times. Within a week Donald sailed for England.

He kissed her before walking up the gangplank onto the ship. She doubted there would be letters from him; this was something he needed to do for himself. She looked at her new passport, its smart colour and large gold crest and the name now emblazoned on it. Nadya Addison. She turned it over in her hand. It was something held in trust between them, although she might never see him again. Soon, she was sure, he would divorce her.

31

May 1938

Disgrace

Kenjiro listened to the shuffle of footsteps on the stairs and then the march down the corridor. There was a strong decisive step and behind a quicker, irregular tread that he knew must be Fukutake, trying to keep up. As he expected they stopped before his room.

Fukutake cowered in the doorway behind the two men. He would already have said whatever it was the men wished him to say. Kenjiro did not blame him, these were difficult times. Or, perhaps, in some ways they were simple times. Decisions were stripped of complexity. Choices were stark. He closed the top of his fountain pen and placed it in its stand, as he did at the end of each day. From the window the shattered roof of the Drum Tower curled against the sky. Great cumulus clouds hung unmoving above it. Leafy fronds thrust out of the black jagged stumps of trees. Nature was reasserting herself upon the drained city. He watched a man push a laden wheelbarrow in the road before the Embassy, and wondered if this might be his last unfettered view of life? How naïve and muddled he must appear to Fukutake. How worthless to the men beside him. He stood up without emotion. The men in military uniform came forward.

A car waited outside. As it moved away from the kerb he looked up at the squat façade of the Embassy and beside it Ginling Women's University. He remembered the wave of terror, the screams that had taken him there that night weeks ago, in an effort to stop the mayhem. Soon the shadowy bulk of Military Headquarters loomed over the car. He was marched upstairs.

Colonel Kato leaned back in his chair and observed him unhurriedly. 'It has taken time for us to gather proof. What has amazed me is that you expected to get away with it.' His tone was nonchalant, almost conversational.

Then, as if a switch had been pushed, he swung forward, eyes blazing, and brought his fist down on the desktop. Kenjiro started between the two men who now reached out to grip his arms. Saliva gleamed upon Kato's irregular teeth. His lips were cracked at one corner.

'Traitor. Is there anything worse in this world? Maggots in the sewage pits, pale and fat from filth I would place higher than you. Only you knew that Communist, you and your Russian girlfriend. What were you doing the night he escaped, in a car by a broken gap in the wall? There are soldiers who saw you, whom you spoke to. How did you get that file to him? Who helped you?' Kato roared.

'I was authorized by the Embassy to liaise with the foreigners. That evening I was on my way to one of their hospitals.' He attempted to bluff again, but he knew already it would not work.

'At ten-thirty at night? That part of the wall is very far from any hospital.' Kato came round the front of the desk to stand before Kenjiro. He hit him suddenly about the face with such force Kenjiro keeled back between the two men who held him.

'Where is the woman, where has she gone?'

'I know nothing of her,' Kenjiro stammered, the blows reverberating through him.

'Liar.' Kato slapped his face again. 'You were seen with her also. She has married the British newspaper man who is filling the foreign press with evil talk about Japan. Who is giving the man this information? Who has given him the pictures of Nanking he has printed abroad? Only through a Japanese here could he have got these pictures.' Kato was incensed.

'Ask the Russian woman,' Kenjiro replied. 'I know nothing of any pictures.' His lips were beginning to swell. Kato made no sense to him. Perhaps the woman had spread some lies about to save herself.

Kato's eyes filled with fury. The slapping began again. 'As you well know, she has left the country. Gone to Hong Kong, maybe even America I am told.'

'I know nothing of her,' he managed to answer. Blood was running down his chin. Everything Kato told him was news.

'But you know the Chinese Communist,' Kato screamed. 'Where is he? Do you work as a cell? Who are your connections in Tokyo? Who are your connections in Moscow? You Communists, you liberals, you traitors make me sick.'

Soon, as he knew they would, they dragged him down into those rooms where Nadya and Teng had both been taken. The windows had been bricked up, but for a slot near the ceiling. The beatings began.

Now that the immunity of privilege was gone, now that there was no deeper place into which to fall, now that he retained nothing of himself but those thoughts that came weakly into his mind, he saw that this moment had waited for him. If he looked back down the tunnel of his life, it appeared like a dark shape, moving towards him. He looked up from the floor of the cell, to the slit of light near the ceiling. A strip of blue sky lit the dark, damp bricks. By the changing intensity of light he came to gauge the time of day. He wondered if at the Embassy they had tried to secure his release, if the Ambassador had made an effort on his behalf? Probably they would want nothing more to do with him, once the accusations against him were known. In the dimness he watched a beetle scuttle from a crevice and disappear through the slit of light out into the world. He had never expected to envy a beetle.

At times they seemed intent on killing him. Through the labyrinth of pain he clung to the thought, sinuous and unbreakable in him, that this was not his end. It was difficult to understand why this thread twisted through him, and would not disappear. And for some reason, the pain was always stopped short of that moment beyond endurance. Perhaps they had decided he had nothing of worth to say. They asked always about the Indian, Dayal, and about Teng. The questions about Teng never ended. Kenjiro said nothing.

He saw that this breaking of another's body was a job to his torturers, as was killing a job to the soldier. He had always thought such men must derive sadistic pleasure, but now he was not so sure, in spite of the energy they showed. There was something impassive in their faces. This impassiveness frightened him as much as any spark of sadistic life. They obeyed orders, as had those soldiers in Nanking, locked into their situation, powered by authority, a belief in their right and his own meaninglessness to them. It seemed as if something essential within each man had shut down, and another unknowable part opened up. In repose the men had not the faces of killers. They stopped at times to drink green tea. Once, they offered him some. And yet, they were impervious to his agony and degradation.

Half-stupefied later in his cell, unable to move for pain, thought floated strangely in and out of his head. Now that he was also a victim, like the multitudes of this city had been victims of similar soldiers, he wondered about the nature of these men. In fitful sleep questions of inordinate complexity appeared to him. The answers drifted through him as spiritual illuminations. They piled up in his mind, like scientific equations on a blackboard that attempted to answer the meaning of the universe. When he awoke they were gone. The great meanings he had grasped vanished as his sleep dissolved. Only one thing remained in his mind. He was sure now that all men were no more than the sum of their deeds. It was as the old wisdoms' said. Men *became* what they did. The deliberate decision to do evil must lead to a man becoming evil. Its root would be planted within him forever. He felt a strange compassion then, for those who waited to beat him.

He thought then too of those hundreds of thousands of his countrymen who had swarmed so viciously upon this city, and every other hamlet or town in China. He knew them as simple country boys, who lived near the earth and its laws. He knew their commanders as men of sophistication, who relished honour, beauty and discipline. Restraint was ingrained in their lives. And yet now all were touched, whether they recognized it or not, by this one inescapable darkness, like a bruise spreading through their soul. When the war was over and they returned to lives of normal humanity, how would they forget that darkness? Would they live in some state of internal crucifixion, carrying forever the tension of their opposite souls? These questions had a weird beauty and seemed, in those hours he lay inert, far bigger than his pain or the question of whether he lived or died.

The beatings stopped. He was no longer dragged in and out of the cell at unpredictable times. He wondered if they would release him, shoot him? Instead the days passed in darkness. Nobody came. At certain hours the door was opened and he cringed, but it slammed again once a bowl of food was pushed through. Strangely, the food was not bad. There was enough and it was not without taste or variety. Here prisoners were not in the normal order of things, but a rare punctuation between the shooting of criminals. The food he received was, he guessed, leftovers from the officers' mess in the Military Headquarters.

The jagged edge of terror that had sharpened each day as he waited for the beatings, was blunted. Now time entered limbo. He realized with a new and duller fear that he could be left here indefinitely, for years. Forever. People would forget him, think he was dead. In this darkness he would fade, his strength sapped slowly. Perhaps this was what they intended. Death was too easy. They wished for the destruction of his personality. Pain and fear had become his only existence and through it he had lost significance, in not only the eyes of his torturers, but also to himself. They had pushed him to the limits of their own darkness. And yet something still struggled in him to exist.

Now his past life seemed as narrow and cramped about him as this cell. He thought of the tube of a kaleidoscope through which one gazed at the illusions of light and shape. When dispassionately examined all that had held one transfixed was a slither of glass and some bits of coloured paper. Perhaps life was really like that. A great trick, an illusion, a sleight of hand. Perhaps this blackness pressing about him, and that great pit of depravity to which he had stood witness for so many weeks, perhaps *that* was the reality. Light, in every manifestation appeared unreal now. He could no longer even gauge the time he had been by himself in the cell. Perhaps the force of darkness *was* the true reality, and not the force of light. What was the sum of these two forces in the universe? Did they balance forever between them some immense, unknowable conundrum? Were they two faces of the same thing? His mind ached with confusion.

Finally Kato came, stepping into the darkness of the cell, bringing light through the open door. He stood, legs apart, haloed by brilliance, appearing huge and powerful from the mat where Kenjiro lay. He said nothing, looking down silently upon Kenjiro's inert form. The door closed upon him, there was darkness again.

Soon soldiers came, dragging him out into an open courtyard. The searing light, after so many buried days, dazzled him. He saw that there were men with guns. They blindfolded him roughly. He felt the hard wood of a post up against his back and more ropes pulled tight about him.

Now that he knew no further effort was needed, a calmness filled him. Something must lie ahead. And that journey would be stranger than this earthly one. Pain now meant little to him. This would be a blacking out, a cutting off from it all at last. He turned his face up to the sun, feeling its warmth after all the dank, nightmarish days. It appeared to him then as a sudden last gift, to guide him forward. The heat sank into his flesh. Even through the blindfold the light blazed hotly upon his eyes. He turned his thoughts then to that force of goodness he had thought about upon the Nanking river bank. It could not actively save, and yet it would save. It was there behind everything, waiting. He was filled by some immense conviction that he could frame in no thoughts or words. He found the strength then to pull himself up against the wooden post, to stand erect. At last he heard the bark of command. The shots came suddenly, slicing the air near his ear. He felt nothing and the post still pressed against his back.

Slowly then, he became aware of a sound. His knees were trembling and, but for the ropes, he would have fallen. He strained to make sense of the noise. At first he thought it the cawing of crows. Then he realized it was laughter. His blindfold was removed, and also the ropes. Colonel Kato stood to one side; he laughed, but his face held no humour. Kenjiro was pushed forward, and stumbled at Kato's feet.

The Colonel bent forward. His eyes were narrow, dark as granite. 'You are lucky, traitor. It seems you have friends in Tokyo. Very high-up friends who have spoken for you. Since we have no solid proof of your involvement in the matter of the Communist's escape, they have demanded your release. But of course, we both know, proof or no proof, that the man Teng is free because of you. We know, you and I, who is a traitor. You are to be returned to Japan. Do not think you will have it easy there. You return in disgrace. Maybe soon you will wish we had killed you.'

Kenjiro remembered little of the journey back to Japan. He was held in a cabin on his own on the ship, and not allowed up on the deck. Fukutake brought his belongings to the dock and was allowed to speak to Kenjiro before he sailed.

'There was nothing anyone could do. The Ambassador's efforts were useless. And of course there was proof against you, although circumstantial. You have brought this upon yourself, I did warn you. All I could do was to inform your father. I thought if anyone could do anything, it would be he with his connections. I was just hoping they didn't shoot you before he could arrange something. You are lucky.'

Kenjiro was taken on his return to a gaol. It was comfortable in comparison to the damp dark cell in Nanking, but nobody contacted or visited him. It was some weeks before he was released. His father came to collect him.

They sat in silence in the car. Kenjiro was shocked at the change in his father's appearance. It was several years now since Kenjiro's last visit to Japan. Yuzuru Nozaki stared straight ahead. He had suffered a mild stroke two years before and he walked now with the help of a cane. One side of his mouth sagged slightly. He had aged, shrunk into himself in a way Kenjiro had not imagined possible. Yuzuru lived now in semi-retirement, going into the Ministry occasionally, in the capacity of a consultant.

'How did you manage to free me?' Kenjiro asked.

'There are those who still owe me. People at the pinnacle of power. But in these difficult times everything seems a matter of luck.' Yuzuru nodded at the chauffeur's back to indicate discretion.

His mother wiped tears from her eyes as he entered the house. He watched emotions struggle in her face and felt guilt settle heavily upon him. Naomi had grown; already he could see the woman in her. She hung back shyly and he as yet knew no way to reach her. He pressed her arm and looked at the green eyes, so much like Jacqueline's.

Something in his father seemed irrevocably changed. He did not yet know if it was the stroke or his own disgrace that might have brought about this new submission. He had expected only rebuff from Yuzuru. No one could deny the shame he must now live with because of the manner of Kenjiro's return. And yet, instead, Kenjiro felt his father's support.

Yuzuru poured a drink. They sat together overlooking the garden where, in the past, they had so often sat and argued. Kenjiro stared at the old lantern, standing as he had left it. He felt returned to himself in this house. The last year appeared now like figments of a nightmare, dissolving before the morning light.

'Did you do what they said? Did you help this Communist escape? What is the truth? You owe me at least the truth.' His father spoke gruffly, and threw back his drink.

'It was Teng.' Kenjiro explained everything then to Yuzuru. The sake hit his weakened body hard. His head swam suddenly and he felt sick.

'They will shoot you if they ever know. Will this Indian keep his mouth shut?' Yuzuru asked, his face lined by sudden anxiety.

'I do not know,' Kenjiro admitted.

'These things you have told me, did they really happen in Nanking? Is it possible that our army can have behaved like this? Is it not an exaggeration? Here we have heard nothing. We are fed news only of victory.' Yuzuru sighed, and then continued.

'We are now all but in the hands of Colonel Tojo. He is to be elevated to the rank of General and it is rumoured is soon to be made Vice Minister for War. These military men run the country now. It is not to my liking. We no longer produce men of genius. The military takes a dim view of genius.' Yuzuru's voice was filled with resentment. 'I fear the *Kempeitai* will now marry itself to us with your return. We will be observed day and night.'

'In this country we seem not to know ourselves inwardly in anything but a rudimentary manner. If we did we could not do otherwise than assert ourselves. But self-assertion is immoral and self-sacrifice the sensible course. In this war we have all become deaf mutes. We crush anything that resists society. And we exalt anything, good or bad, that serves it. This is dangerous.' Kenjiro spoke bitterly.

'As a society we run well enough. Better than many. You have imbibed too many Western ideas. I believe in our society.' Yuzuru frowned, happy to mount his high horse for a moment.

'There is danger in these mass-produced army heroes,' Kenjiro replied. 'We lack moral courage in the Western sense, but we have physical courage in excess of any nation. Is this not a dangerous paradox in these militant times? We follow where we are led, never querying what we are told by our leaders.' He thought again of Nanking, of those killing fields that seemed to him suddenly the very image of the future. A sudden fear filled him, and he turned to his father.

366

'This lauding of physical courage in its narrowest way, has become a national industry. Ideas are feared, only instincts are cultivated. We have never been afraid of death. But this age offers something different, a debasement of those values that Japan grew strong upon. There is no nobility in this *industry* of killing. The killing of others, or of oneself or of being killed, this is now all being manipulated in our minds into a single notion of heroism. This is what the military wants. It will sacrifice our people to their ambition. Our military leaders are not men of any great stature. They set no example of greatness. And yet they demand from the people the ultimate sacrifice of greatness. They demand their very lives.' The words poured from Kenjiro.

Yuzuru Nozaki looked into his sake cup and did not answer. He appeared old and tired. Once he might have argued any number of points in Kenjiro's impassioned outburst. Now, after some moments, he changed the subject.

'I have arranged for you to work at the Ministry. For the moment, because of these circumstances, the job is not much. Ill health is the best explanation we can give for your return. And judging by your appearance many will have no trouble believing you. If times improve, we must trust so will your future. For now you must lie low. And even here, in this house, unless we are alone, do not speak freely. The *Kempeitai* are everywhere. They plant their spies amongst even the servants. Nowhere are we safe. They may come for you again at any time.' His father spoke in a whisper.

'I have brought disgrace, and persecution upon us all,' Kenjiro answered, lowering his eyes.

'It is late. I am tired. I am an old man now.' His father began to rise from the table. Kenjiro bent to help him and Yuzuru accepted his arm.

'I am indebted to you, Father.' Kenjiro bowed low before Yuzuru.

'Take care. I ask nothing more,' Yuzuru replied.

PART FIVE

The Voice of the Crane

Japan 1940–1945

32

1940–1945

Sword of Power 2

Successive German victories after the outbreak of war in Europe, impressed the military opportunists in Japan. They saw immediately that, by joining Germany and Italy in an alliance, and by taking advantage of weakened Western possessions in Asia, Japan could proceed more quickly with building the New Asian Order. An alliance would also, it was believed, deter Russian and Anglo-American interference in this New Asian Order. Such a pact demanded that, should any greater war escalate in Europe, Japan would participate on Germany's behalf.

Negotiations towards the Tripartite Pact were not to Emperor Hirohito's liking. War still raged in China, Japan did not need yet further entanglement abroad. That the China war continued to drag on, swallowing unending supplies of men, resources and armaments was a frustration to him. He wanted a positive victory, not the constant drain of an incomplete mission. Some time after the rape of Nanking he had been shown captured Chinese propaganda film, when things could no longer be hidden from him. His distaste was tempered only by the knowledge that he had no control of military operations in the field. He could not have prevented the massacre.

Although not a pacifist, he was no avid warmonger. As a monarch faced with an unavoidable war, he wished to see his country victorious. His fear was that a pact with Germany might draw Japan into battles not of her choosing, bringing disaster. The taking of risk was not part of Hirohito's methodical nature. He was a scientist who believed in the successful conclusion of carefully studied and accumulated evidence. It was therefore a shocked and further infuriated Hirohito who learned in August 1939 that Germany, whom Japan was relying upon as an ally against Russia, had signed a Non-Aggression pact with the Soviet Union. This announcement not only left the question of a military alliance with Germany in disarray, but precipitated the fall of the Japanese Government.

In Tokyo American Ambassador Grew was already concerned. *If general war breaks out,* Grew wrote in his diary, *it is almost inevitable that the United States will be unable to stay out. If Japan is tied up in the German camp in a military alliance, it will be impossible for America to remain at peace with Japan. It therefore behooves Japan to look into the future and decide where her friendship ought in her own interests to be placed.*

Prince Konoye was nominated as the new Prime Minister. Hirohito had confidence in Konoye and expected him to check the army's inordinate quest for power. But Konoye came to office for a second time full of bombast and ideas. He envisioned a World Order based on his concept of a Greater East Asia Co-Prosperity Sphere, an association of nations, grouped like a family about Japan. The age old version of *Hakko Ichiu* was about to begin anew. Konoye's premiership was not to everyone's liking. His previous disastrous vacillating leadership during the brutal rape of Nanking, had generated criticism.

Now, three days before he took office, Konoye agreed at an informal meeting with his proposed War Minister, General Tojo, and also his Foreign Minister, and Navy Chief, to make a military alliance with Germany the priority of the new Cabinet. It was felt that, in the event of a war, such a pact might avert an attack on Japan by America. The Tripartite Pact must be signed quickly however, before Nazi armies crossed the English Channel, conquered Britain and won the war. Once this were done it was feared Germany would have little use for Japan.

Ever geared for war and a clash with America and imperialistic Britain, the militarists were busy. Colonel Hashimoto of the *Panay* bombing, dashed about wildly to fuel public opinion. He urged the nation to forget the shadow of Russia in the north and turn south to face Japan's real threat for the future, Great Britain, a country ready at any crisis to send their fleet to threaten Japan. He called for immediate war upon Britain. He urged the alliance with Rome and Berlin in order to form a united Fascist front against democracy and Communism. Kill all those who oppose the alliance, he exhorted at mass rallies. Anti-Western, anti-British feeling blazed once more in certain circles across Japan. Feelings in Britain were also high. The shelling of British gunboats on the Yangtze along with the *Panay*, and the careless wounding of the British Ambassador, Sir Hugh Knatchbull-Hugessan, had raised British ire to fever-pitch. Only American hesitation prevented British action.

Hirohito's *genro* Prince Saionji, even more ancient and bed-ridden, still worried for the nation and his Emperor. To him all foreign policy must be based on co-operation with Britain and the United States. He looked bitterly at the proposed alliance. 'What can we do tied to Italy or Germany? It is ridiculous and I am suspicious. To think of Japan with the United States to the east and Britain to the west, that is meaningful. But an alliance with Italy and Germany? What possible meaning can that have?'

As well as having misgivings about Hirohito's involvement in dangerous adventures, Saionji was shattered by the Emperor's refusal to follow his advice, or share his vision of a liberal Japan. Marquis Kido, old confidant of the Emperor and back once more after a time in politics, as Keeper of the Privy Seal, agreed with Saionji's pacifist views. Kido, too, worried the Emperor would be pushed into a combative stance. Prince Konoye appeared of little help, full of his own grandiose visions, and moving as was so often his habit, with the majority opinion.

Some time before the pact was to be signed, Marquis Kido called upon the Emperor and found him relaxed after a morning swim. They talked about the Burma Road crisis.

'I suppose Britain will reject our request to end their support road to Chiang Kai-shek. In this case we shall occupy Hong Kong, and eventually declare war upon Britain,' Hirohito announced. Kido warned caution, alarmed that the need for strategy was never far from Hirohito's meticulous mind.

Hirohito however remembered Bismarck's words. *International alliances always demand that there must be one horseman and one donkey, and Germany must always be the horseman.* If the Tripartite Pact was signed, he wished Japan to be the horseman, not the donkey. *Hakko Ichiu* was now no longer a Shinto catchphrase, justifying the Emperor's right to dominate the world. It was now a slogan of practical application, a religious vindication of Japan's new power and influence.

Old Saionji from his deathbed sent one last message to his Emperor. The time was approaching, said Saionji, for Hirohito to exercise his influence fearlessly, as his Grandfather Meiji had always done. Even his younger brother Chichibu, exhorted him to take a stand against those who engineered a pact that turned Japan in direct confrontation with a war she could not win.

On the day of the Imperial Conference to ratify the Tripartite Alliance, Hirohito sat on a throne before a gold screen. A few feet below the dais were the men who now steered the course of Japan. Saionji's words and those of Chichibu were readily in his mind, but Saionji lay dying and Chichibu was ill in bed. Spread out below Hirohito were forces he knew he could not easily control. He teetered between elation and doubt. Japan's growing power overwhelmed him with excitement. But the consequences of aggressive policies that he knew no way to contain, filled him also with trepidation.

His fault was that he was not a great monarch, only a mediocre man.

Even his own father-in-law had perceived Hirohito's faults and told his daughter, the Empress, 'The Emperor is weak-willed, so it is necessary for the Empress to help him from behind the scenes. You must be strong . . .' Hirohito's childhood conditioning placed a further constraint on his ability to oppose a possible war. He believed in the orderly evolution of politics and government. When this did not happen and logical argument had no effect, his pedantic manner and retiring nature could not easily deal with the reality of violence.

Now, at this most important of Imperial Conferences, Hirohito protected himself in his usual manner, with a dour-faced silence, letting events take their course. The strategy of silence made final judgements of him difficult. And silence was all that was ever constitutionally demanded of a monarch at any Imperial Conference. In active silence Hirohito now allowed a darkness to descend upon his nation, the consequences of which he would only later realize. When the Imperial Conference was over, Hirohito looked Konoye straight in the eye.

'Well, you and I will now have to stand or fall together,' he announced. Konoye had a tendency to give up when things became difficult, and Hirohito was already unsure whether Konoye, if the worst occurred, would take with his monarch the bitter medicine of a greater war.

Hirohito put his seal to the fateful pact. On 27th September 1940, the Tripartite Pact was finally signed in Berlin between Germany, Italy and Japan. Hirohito ordered special Shinto rites inside the Palace to ask for the blessings of the Gods for this extraordinary pact. He spoke in obeisance before the Mirror of Knowledge, praying for the future of Japan. As absolute monarch he was thought by many to be in complete command. But government decisions once ratified were presented as the Imperial Will. What Hirohito thought of those decisions was immaterial. The will of the State was the will of the Emperor; unless it was requested of him, there could be no other way.

Immediately after the signing of the pact, events began to quicken. With German connivance, the Vichy Government in France was forced to agree to the Japanese occupation of French Indochina. From these bases Japan could easily later strike at both China and Malaya. President Roosevelt was aghast and made efforts to persuade Japan to alter its plans for Indochina. When persuasion failed, Roosevelt ordered all Japanese funds and assets in America frozen. An embargo was placed upon everything but cotton and food. Japan was immediately bereft of massive amounts of iron and oil, the main ingredients for war.

In June 1941 Hitler launched his attack on Russia moving the aggression in Europe towards world war. Already in Japan, at the

374

beginning of the year, the armed forces had envisaged this turn of events. At a conference of naval strategists secret plans had been laid for an attack on Pearl Harbor. Hirohito knew that war was planned. As always, he had resigned himself to the course of events. He wanted only to be certain a victory would be won. The Emperor was aware, as were also Marquis Kido and Prince Saionji, of the underlying weakness in Japan's position. But from his pinnacle, still captive to the dream of *Hakko Ichiu*, it seemed to Hirohito that Japan now rode the crest of an historical wave and might yet be victorious. Hirohito's doubts were about the manner and timing of the assault. No such doubts beset his armed forces. They waited impatiently to hurl themselves like warriors of old, into the cursed attack.

A worried American Ambassador Grew early in 1941 sent a cable from Tokyo to the State Department in Washington. *There is talk around town,* he wrote, *to the effect that the Japanese, in case of a break with the United States, are planning to go all out in a surprise attack on Pearl Harbor.* In America nobody took Grew's remarks seriously.

Although the armed forces could not wait for war, in the Emperor's circles hesitation still reigned. Hirohito once more oscillated between certainty and doubt. Admiral Nagano in audience with the Emperor could not alleviate Hirohito's anxiety.

'If war with America breaks out, our supply of oil would be sufficient for only a year and a half. Under these circumstances we would have no alternative but to take the initiative,' the Admiral admitted.

'If we do that can we then win a sweeping victory as in the Russo-Japanese war?' Hirohito wanted to know. Reports in piles were on his desk insisting a victory could be had by a German-style blitzkrieg.

'If I am told to fight regardless of consequences, I shall run wild for the first six months or a year, sweeping all before me. But I have no confidence at all for the second and third years of a war. It is doubtful we could ever win, to say nothing of the kind of great victory we saw in the Russo-Japanese war.' Admiral Nagano was an honest man.

A constant stream of Admirals and Army Generals trudged the long corridors of the Imperial Palace, summoned by Hirohito to recite their reports and hear his questions. The Emperor asked General Sugiyama, Chief of Staff of the army, how soon a campaign against Malaya could be terminated once started.

'Within three months,' the General replied.

'You made the same prediction at the beginning of 1931, before the attack on Mukden. And we could say that campaign is not yet finished after nearly ten years,' Hirohito reprimanded.

'There is a great difference between the two. China is a continent. The southern areas are islands,' Sugiyama replied.

'If you call the Chinese hinterland vast, would you not describe the Pacific as even more immense? With what confidence can you predict three months?' Hirohito was filled with anger. The embargo by America on the sale of oil and iron to Japan had placed the country in an impossible position. It could not hold out for long.

Admiral Nagano, standing beside Sugiyama, came to his rescue. 'Something must be decided quickly. Each day we delay we increase the risk of losing the game. The situation between Japan and the United States is like a patient with an illness which might require an operation. Avoiding one could mean the patient wastes away. But there is hope of recovery if a drastic act of surgery is undergone. That is war.'

'We must be victorious against America and Britain, but will it be the kind of total victory scored against Russia in 1905?' Hirohito again asked General Nagano. He could not share the optimism of his military advisors.

'We are not sure of winning,' Nagano was forced to admit.

Hirohito was depressed. Talking to Marquis Kido after this meeting he said he was not against the principle of war with America and Britain. 'But one shouldn't make war without foreseeing victory, or this will mean embarking on a war of desperation.'

If there must be war then victory was what Hirohito wanted. As this did not seem predictable with any real confidence, he urged Marquis Kido to recommend to all a continuance at the negotiating table. If America could be brought to heel through negotiations, without the need to resort to war, while allowing Japan to continue expansion in south-east Asia, that would be the best victory of all.

It was clear to not only Hirohito but to the government at large, that, even against their better judgement, a future was planning itself. War would come, even though there was no hope of winning. A future was already wilfully asserting itself against any remaining elements of reason. Of the monstrous size of the challenge ahead, or its ultimate consequences, there seemed only a dull awareness. War must be a quick Japanese blitzkrieg that would dazzle the world and lead to the negotiating table. There Japan could argue a course to retain some part of her gains in Asia.

A further Imperial Conference took place in the Autumn of 1941. Hirohito mounted the dais and sat once more before the many-panelled golden screen. Before him the Cabinet, the Chiefs of Staff, the President of the Privy Council, and the President of the Cabinet Planning Board and others waited. The discussion for war began. It was long and lively, and soon it was clear that whatever was said the decision to fight was already made. Throughout the debate Hirohito sat in the silence expected of him. A few words to end the conference was all that was needed or indeed officially expected from him.

At last the Emperor rose abruptly. His action was unexpected and the roomful of men looked up in surprise. Hirohito's glasses had misted over and he took them off and rubbed them nervously with his thumbs. He replaced them on his nose and began to speak in a high, thin voice.

'I myself have no doubt as to the answer to the great question before us.' He put his hand into a pocket and pulled from it a piece of paper. 'I would like to read to you a poem that was written by my grandfather, the great Emperor Meiji.

> *The seas surround all quarters of the globe*
> *And my heart cries out to the nations of the world.*
> *Why then do the winds and waves of strife*
> *Disrupt the peace between us?'*

He paused as he finished reading and looked at the crowded room before him. 'This is a poem which has always been one of my favourites, for it expresses what is in my heart and was in my grandfather's when he wrote it – his great love of peace.'

The room bowed to the Emperor and he sat down. For a few moments there was an embarrassed silence. Hirohito had expressed his frustration at the present state of affairs. The meaning of the poem was ambiguous. To some it argued for peace. But it could also be construed as meaning that, since the world was destined to lie under Japan's divine protection, why did so many nations refuse to accept this peaceful solution to things? Little time was wasted on defining the true meaning of the Emperor's poem. And Hirohito, in his nervousness, had gone as far as a man of timid nature, fastidious in the observation of detail and protocol, might go. There was nothing more he could do. He listened to the final decision of the Imperial Conference. It was to move towards war, if the present diplomatic negotiations with America failed.

Soon, in October 1941 under the pressure of an approaching war he was powerless to stop, Prime Minister Konoye decided to resign. Hirohito was beside himself with indecision. He had been advised by Konoye against war in favour of diplomacy. Later, after listening to military men, Hirohito sensed all hope of diplomacy was lost and returned to Konoye in an opposite frame of mind. He announced the Government must compose an imperial rescript declaring war. To many it seemed that the Emperor swung like a pendulum between two poles of thought, unable to make up his mind upon vital issues.

377

At Konoye's departure General Tojo succeeded to the Premiership. Emperor Hirohito was a frugal, conscientious man and, from his hours at a microscope, used to giving much attention to detail. He did not dislike General Tojo, who combined in his character something of these same qualities. Surrounded by legions of the obsequious, Tojo's blunt directness was refreshing to Hirohito. His strength was something concrete to lean upon after Konoye's weak leadership. Tojo's forceful sense of direction made him appear the right man for a difficult job.

General Tojo strode into office, determined to do his best by the Emperor, but clear in his mind that little would come of the strategy of diplomacy the Emperor still wished him to follow. Soon he was seen to be right. Each month of negotiation further depleted Japan's stocks of strategic resources. There was no option but to set a deadline for diplomacy. It was decided that, if nothing positive was concluded by the end of November 1941, an attack on America must be faced.

Once the path of war had been decided and return became impossible, Hirohito, as always, set his mind upon the task in hand. The dreaded thing was upon them, and Hirohito was not one to turn his back upon his responsibility. The lessons of military strategy learned at General Nogi's knee had never left him. Plans for an attack on Pearl Harbor had previously been submitted to him by the Naval Chief of Staff. On one of these regular meetings with General Sugiyama and Admiral Nagano, Hirohito made his only recorded reference to Pearl Harbor.

'What is the Navy's target date?' he asked.

'Eighth December,' Nagano replied.

'Isn't that a Monday?' Hirohito asked.

Nagano pointed out the time difference made it a Sunday. 'This Day was especially chosen because everyone will be tired after their Saturday holiday.'

'The outcome of the war depends greatly on the outcome of the first stage,' Nagano continued. 'And the outcome of the first stage depends on the outcome of the surprise attack. We must hide our war intentions at all costs.'

Within weeks, on 8th December 1941, Japan successfully attacked Pearl Harbor in Hawaii. Euphoria swept Japan. Hirohito's relief that the gamble had paid off was understandable. He had none of Marquis Kido's reservations.

'When I heard the good news of the surprise attack, I felt the will of the Gods,' Hirohito announced jubilantly to Kido.

As news of victories continued to grow during the first years of the war, Hirohito's excitement appeared almost excessive, even to Marquis Kido. In 1942, at the time of German victories in North Africa, Hirohito even wished to send a cable of congratulations to Hitler and had to be restrained. The Emperor was easily buoyed up by victory, and just as easily depressed when defeats began to accrue.

For the first time since the Meiji Restoration and the founding in 1868 of modern Japan, the country now had as its political leader an active military man. Tojo's fanaticism was not popular and once installed as Prime Minister his megalomania grew. His mind and eye were sharp enough for him to earn the nickname, The Razor. The Japanese people, naïve before international issues, were not so easily taken in by Tojo's misplaced self-importance on the domestic scene.

In imitation of Hitler, Tojo now rode around in an open black car surrounded by motorcycles. He developed a taste for appearing in public, especially on horseback, terrifying housewives at the early morning fish market or small children in kindergartens, exhorting them all to work harder. He became known for these forays as the Premier on Horseback. When dealers in the markets dared to complain of the lack of petrol to transport supplies he yelled, 'Petrol, petrol? Never mind petrol. Get up earlier. Work harder.'

The masses regarded him with a cold eye. Scandalous stories swirled about the mention of his name, and of the fortunes built by those around him. Tales circulated of a stable of beautiful mistresses and of wild carousing with his officers.

Burma, Malaya, Thailand, Singapore, Indochina, the Philippines and the Dutch East Indies fell one by one to Japan in the first months of the war. All these countries and further conquests were to be brought into the Greater East Asia Co-Prosperity Sphere. It was a prefabricated formula, riddled with slogans, served up to strip bare the countries it touched. Japan hoped to conquer the world, but lacked in itself any world sense.

Meanwhile, Prime Minister Tojo demanded respect. One by one he sacked ministers and took their portfolios upon himself. He earned a new nickname, Total Tojo. The *Kempeitai*, feared already for so long, swelled in new monstrousness. Tojo tightened his grip upon industry, forcing new economic laws through Parliament. Company presidents and plant managers were inducted into the army. They worked their businesses under military eyes and a German-style structure of responsibility. Limitations on working hours were abolished, bringing to life the danger of industrial slavery. Children were put to work in factories. Rice rations were cut. Hungry people traipsed to the countryside in search of provisions but police at railway stations confiscated their precious finds upon their return. Long-distance train tickets were curtailed and travel became almost impossible. In the stores stocks of everything vanished. A black market began to thrive.

Huge posters of Tojo's smiling face, reminiscent of those posters of Hitler in Berlin, the like of which had never before been seen in Japan, began to adorn every spare wall in the country. Such stunts of personal publicity were alien and distasteful to the Japanese nature. Hitlerism was not an ideology that appealed to most Japanese. The adulation Hitler demanded and received, General Tojo could not get.

Instead, such antics worked against him. He appeared to place himself above the Emperor, to have lost all sense of subordination to the supreme ruler of the nation. It was even said he wished to restore to the nation the office of Shogun. As military ruler he would reign over Japan, and the Emperor would fade to a ghost. Already Hirohito appeared half-hidden behind General Tojo's shadow.

Beneath their harsh burden the masses bent stoically, for the sake of the Emperor and the nation. Life became narrower, meaner, fear-ridden. The people of Japan were told nothing of the mounting defeats that had already begun in the first year of the war after the loss of the Japanese fleet at Midway. Only victories were reported. They had little idea how the war was going, trusting in their leaders. But eventually by 1944 it was no longer possible to hide defeat or, after the Battle of Leyte and then Iwo Jima, that the invaders would come. The people had to be prepared.

Colonel Hashimoto of the *Panay* bombing, leader now of the youth brigades of the Imperial Rule Association, broadcast frantic messages on the radio. 'The time has come when, like the soldiers at the front, the people in the rear must also transform themselves into human bombs. The Hundred Million of Japan must all resolve to die for the Emperor.' Hashimoto demanded suicidal resistance. If the Americans ever landed in Japan they were to find a people prepared to die rather than be conquered.

By early 1944 Tojo had dispossessed and disaffected too many of his colleagues. Plots to get rid of him abounded, but Tojo always endeavoured to keep one step ahead of this lobby of hate. Hirohito continued to trust and support the General through the dark years of war. As things deteriorated Hirohito declared to his brother Prince Takamatsu, 'It is said Tojo is no good, but who would be better? If there is no one better is there any alternative but to co-operate with the Tojo Cabinet?' Clearly he regarded Tojo's presence as in the nation's best interests. Yet, as defeats grew and desperation rose, Tojo was forced at last to resign in July 1944.

A sigh of relief flooded through Japan from Imperial circles to the common man. But Tojo had left too late. Before long Tokyo and every other major Japanese city was ablaze, razed daily by American bombing. The first raids began on Japan a few months after Tojo's fall. It was these raids and the death of Hitler that appear to have brought Hirohito back to reality.

Hitler committed suicide at the beginning of May 1945 and Germany surrendered to the Allies. This shock reverberated through Japan, as great as any earthquake. The Americans had taken Okinawa and were perilously near now to the Japanese mainland. The bombing raids upon Japan had pounded every city. In May 1945 the Imperial Palace was damaged in an air-raid. Hirohito was almost jubilant to finally be included in the great war.

'We have been bombed at last,' he said to Marquis Kido. 'Now the people will know I am sharing their ordeal with no special protection from the Gods.' The official reports he received minimized the damage of these raids, which was not in tune with the distressing information he was now receiving from more private sources. He demanded to leave the Palace and to make a tour of inspection for himself.

What Hirohito saw beyond his Palace appalled him. He left his car in horror to walk through the most devastated areas. He stopped at a shelter for the homeless to speak to people camping in holes. He was told that in the last single raid 150,000 had been killed. Oppressed, beleaguered, whipped to greater and greater sacrifices, the people of Japan now looked in bewilderment at their sovereign. God incarnate, he who was unknowable, now stepped about amongst the ruins, speaking as a human being to those who were bereft. It brought about a great confusion.

With this walk about war-torn Tokyo, Hirohito came into contact with a reality usually denied him. Nothing on his maps or tabletop operations, buried deep within the Imperial War Headquarters, prepared him for the starkness of this shock. He saw at last that defeat was truly inevitable. The great mythological dream of *Hakko Ichiu*, the eight corners of the universe under the roof of Japan, lay in smithereens before him. Hirohito resolved the war must be ended with whatever dignity could still be salvaged.

33

November 1944

A Fiery End

When the all-clear had gone, Tilik told the maid to make Rash Bihari some tea. The old man refused any longer to move from his bed and seek shelter during air-raids.

'What good are these dugouts? I'd rather die in my bed. If my time has come, it has come. It will be here anyway soon enough. Have Michiko and the children left Tokyo yet?'

A gas fire hissed in the room. The November cold filled Tilik with thoughts of approaching winter. It was one thing to crouch in a dugout in summer, another when snow was falling. From the window he looked out at the city. It was pitted and charred by daily incendiary bombing. The gaping spaces where houses had stood, multiplied each day. The town was a giant on its knees. It could not be said to have fallen, and yet it no longer stood. The dreaded raids had at last begun. Tokyo, for all its swagger, was a village of sticks and straw. From time immemorial, it knew about fire. It had few stone buildings with which to face bombs; fire was what was dreaded.

'Michiko has gone to an aunt in the countryside with her parents. These raids will accelerate. As they grow worse everyone will leave,' Tilik replied. He and Rash Bihari were awaiting the arrival of Subash Chandra Bose, who was on a visit to Tokyo.

'The family will be safe out of the city. They will also get food.' Rash Bihari began to cough. The maid hurried in and settled the old man with his tea.

Tilik looked about the small room. It was more than ten years since he had come first to this house. He remembered again that long-ago train journey from Kobe to Rash Bihari, and the fear that had gripped him. A sense of waiting filled him now. He had learned events could not be forced. Destiny runs stubbornly to its own course, like a diverted river returns to its bed. In the road outside was the sound of an approaching vehicle.

'Is that a car I hear?' asked Rash Bihari in a petulant voice. 'Why is

Subash here again in Japan?' The blue film of age covered his eyes, his flesh hung loose upon him. A faint offensive odour rose from his body. Diabetes and tuberculosis devoured him in tandem. He was alone but for the maid. Tilik visited him each day, and even slept in the house if it seemed necessary.

'Water,' he whispered and Tilik brought the glass to his lips, propping the old man up. Rash Bihari sipped and leaned back exhausted. 'There is not long left for me, thank God. There comes a time, you know, when you have seen too much, when it is no wrench to die.' He frowned suddenly at the thought of Subash Chandra Bose, before continuing.

'Tell him to go away. He listens to nothing I say. But for me he would not even be here in Asia. It was I who persuaded him to look to Japan instead of Germany for support. He has become too big for his military boots. The Japanese, you know, are not happy at this title, *Netaji*, with which he has crowned himself. The Japanese equate it, mistakenly of course, with *Führer*. To them the title smacks of arrogance. He has never understood the Japanese code of manners. I hear no one of importance has seen him on this visit.' Rash Bihari's voice trembled with emotion.

The last few years of constant journeying between Tokyo, Malaya and Singapore had exhausted Rash Bihari Bose. He was no longer the man who, once war was declared in the Pacific, had accepted leadership of the Indian Independence League in south-east Asia at the demand of expatriate Indians. Offices had been set up by the Japanese military in their newly conquered territories, to unite and make use of exiled Indians.

When his health failed Rash Bihari persuaded the Japanese to bring Subash Chandra Bose from an uninterested Germany, to take over the south-east Asian leadership from him. Since that time Subash's militancy had brought about great changes. The peaceful Indian Independence League had been demolished in favour of the militant Indian National Army.

In March 1943 a bid had been made by 120,000 Japanese troops and a contingent of the Indian National Army crossed into India over the Burma border, at Imphal. It ended in disaster. More than 65,000 men were killed. Countless others died of disease retreating through the monsoon-wracked jungles of Burma. The ludicrous inadequacy of equipment and preparations only revealed Japan's desperation in the war. Neither Rash Bihari nor Tilik wished to recall the memories that weighed now so heavily between them.

'If Tojo were still in power he would have seen Subash, I suppose,' Tilik replied. 'But the present Imperial High Command is in no mood to discuss his military schemes. For Japan the war is lost. Yet still Subash comes here. The Japanese military are losing patience with him and his constant pressing for more arms. They have nothing left with which to defend their own country.'

'He has destroyed my life work.' Rash Bihari spoke with resignation. 'In my mind, you know, although I might sometimes have dreamed extravagantly, I had no illusions. I saw no literal army in our Independence League, only a source of moral and inspirational support to our people at home and abroad. Independence in my view can only be achieved from within the country.'

'To Subash our expatriate communities exist only to fuel his ego and the Indian National Army with money and men,' Tilik replied.

'That is his way.' Rash Bihari shook his head.

There was the sudden slamming of car doors in the road outside. From the window Tilik watched Subash Chandra Bose bend to the small door in the roofed gate. For years, to Tilik, Subash had been a God-like image. The first time the man had stepped on to Japanese soil, Tilik had felt weak with excitement. There was a certain homeliness about Rash Bihari but Subash, with his trappings of uniform, salutes and fiery speeches, seemed a leader in every form. Now, he knew Subash as an obsessed and unpredictable man. Nothing had been as expected.

Soon Subash Chandra Bose entered the room. His broad face, upright back and balding head, the smart cut of his uniform, all projected energy. His high boots caught the light. He strode forward to take Rash Bihari's hands.

'I return to Rangoon tomorrow. Three weeks have passed so quickly here.' His wide smile flashed about. 'I could not go without seeing you.'

'And what is the position there, in Rangoon?' Rash Bihari asked, still petulant.

'Mountbatten's South-East Asia Command is preparing to recover Burma, of course. The Indian National Army will fight with the Japanese to block them. We must concentrate now on new recruitment to the INA.' There was no sign of defeat in Subash's voice.

'There is no longer an Indian National Army. It was destroyed at Imphal. Any recruitment of Indians now is only to fight as mercenaries for the Japanese. That is *not* what patriotic Indians want. This is *not* what I wished to live to see.' Rash Bihari shut his eyes and leaned back upon the pillow.

Subash Chandra Bose drew himself up in his polished boots and took no notice of these remarks. 'Japan will be the ultimate victor. And the INA will be expanded. Another attack will be launched into India to drive the British away. Already Japan has handed over the Andaman and

Nicobar Islands to our Provisional Government of Free India. We have a state of our own at last.'

'It was a token gesture. Japan has no intention of giving up control of such strategic islands. Do not speak to me as if I am a fool,' Rash Bihari snapped.

Subash pursed his lips and turned to look out of the window. 'Tokens count, as do symbols. *We have set foot on Indian soil.* Brief as it was, this is symbolic beyond all imagination. I think we should not forget this. I do not look upon the event as a failure, but as the greatest triumph. It was the first step on the road to victory.'

'You are an optimist of a rare order,' Rash Bihari sighed. 'I expect this will be the last time we meet.' He turned his face to the wall.

Soon Subash was gone with a slamming of car doors and a revving of engines. Tilik listened with Rash Bihari until silence filled the road again. At last Tilik stirred and glanced at his watch.

'Go now or you will be late for the radio broadcast,' Rash Bihari insisted. He gripped Tilik's hand, his voice trembled sadly. 'Each night I wonder if I will be here in the morning. Japan has no time now for our dreams.'

Eventually Tilik left the house and made his way to the studios of NHK, the Japan Broadcasting Corporation. Some time ago NHK had opened a short-wave station for the Indian Independence League, for daily broadcasts to India. From here, until his health failed, Rash Bihari had addressed his homeland and in turn each of India's leaders.

The damp odour of Autumn mixed with a sulphurous smell from the bombs. Where they could, trams still ran. Tilik groped his way along in the darkness. There were no longer street lamps, government orders for scrap metal had taken every post. Stone columns had been uprooted with their iron grilles, bridge parapets with their handrails. Nothing seemed left in place. And yet this ironware lay in a tangled, rusting mass at street corners for want of transportation to take it away. Tokyo resembled a builders' yard.

Tilik walked carefully in the dark so as not to stumble inadvertently into a dugout. It was a government order that each household should build a shelter. Or scrape from the soil a suitable hole before their home, into which to fling themselves during air raids. These unsightly craters littered roads, as if the city had been invaded by an army of moles. He could not see what good the shallow burrows were to anyone. They appeared no more than potential tombs. The Government had planned no shelter for the millions of people in its largest city. When it rained the holes filled up with black mud. They had been dug in the summer, but there had been no raids to test their use until a week ago.

385

Tilik entered the NHK building and ran up the stairs to the studio. They were waiting for him. He took his seat before the microphone. The red light came on and the man signalled to him from behind the glass. He leaned forward.

'I have come from a meeting with two great men, Subash Chandra Bose and Rash Bihari Bose. The two Boses. *Netaji* is here in Japan to replenish the ammunition of the INA. Imphal was no defeat, but the greatest of victories. We set foot upon Indian soil, upon the Motherland herself. It was the first step on the road to victory. Liberation is near. *Netaji* prepares for the next attack . . .

There was a clock high on the wall beyond the glass partition. He kept his eyes upon it. Blackout blinds covered the windows. He willed the hands of the clock to turn, to reach the half hour without the disturbance of sirens. At last it was over and he drew back from the microphone, filled by inexplicable exhaustion. Nothing made sense to him any more. He was a puppet who mouthed the empty words of others.

His house was not far from the studio. Inside he lit a few bits of charcoal over the gas in the kitchen. Carrying them into his bedroom, he placed them in the small brazier, spreading his fingers above the glowing coals. Where would anyone find charcoal this winter? In each home across the city he knew the same thoughts filled everyone's mind.

He was lucky still to have a house. Fire-trails, to stem the danger of conflagration after raids, had been incised in a grid across the city. Thousands of houses were marked for demolition. Inhabitants were given no more than a few days to evacuate with their possessions. Troops and schoolboys then tore down the homes with their bare hands and axes. From the rubble housewives scavenged bundles of firewood for the winter ahead. Strange new vistas had opened up across the city, uncomfortable in their starkness. Once he was warm Tilik lay down on the bed, pulling the thick quilt up high upon him. He never undressed nowadays. It would have been best to stay in Manchukuo. It was only anxiety about Michiko that had brought him back.

When Hasegawa refused his pleas to return to Japan he had tried to arrange for Michiko to come to Hsinking from Tokyo. Hasegawa had not been helpful, even when on one of Tilik's visits to Japan Michiko again became pregnant. It was not until after the fall of Singapore that Hasegawa announced Tilik might at last go back to Tokyo.

'It seems you will now be needed far from here. I have received word from Tokyo that you must embark on a course of direct action. The Chief of Army Staff in Tokyo supports the idea of establishing centres for your Independence League in the newly fallen British enclaves in Asia. It has been viewed as useful to co-ordinate effectively with the Indian communities in these places. We can support your struggle for independence in a concrete way now. You are to return to Rash Bihari Bose.' Hasegawa smiled and produced a bottle of brandy.

'We have many things to celebrate,' he continued. 'I too am returning to Tokyo. Now that our Empire is spreading I am also needed elsewhere.' He raised his glass to Tilik.

Since the day of his return to Tokyo Tilik's life had been one of movement, travelling constantly between Bangkok, Singapore, and Tokyo. The main centres of co-operation with the Japanese military had been set up in these places. Excitement had buoyed them all up. The Indian Independence League cartwheeled along on the tumbling Japanese victories. Now he drew the quilt further over his head. The cold would not leave his body. What would he do when Rash Bihari was dead? How would the war end? His role was already obsolete, all he had worked for was disintegrating. Even the centre of action for Indian Independence was now far removed from Tokyo. Rangoon was now that centre, nearer in access to India.

The NHK broadcasts anchored Tilik's day, but there was little more. If Japan surrendered, where would that leave him? And there was a new fear. He was being watched. He had a special status of trust and collaboration with the authorities. Yet, as the war sunk its teeth deeper into Japan, even that trust was wearing thin. Paranoia was everywhere. The antipathy Subash Chandra Bose now ignited amongst the Japanese military had filtered down to Tilik. He saw danger, moving towards him in the dark.

The siren cut a jagged edge through the night. Tilik jumped up, heart pounding, and began to run. A light rain had fallen earlier, and he hoped the wet would protect the house. The fire-fighting methods pinned up by the Neighbourhood Association in his home seemed basic in the extreme. They relied on straw mats soaked in water and a bucket brigade of women and children. It was believed such measures could save Tokyo from the power of modern incendiary bombs.

He ran from the door and climbed awkwardly into his dugout. There were several inches of water at the bottom. He was taller than most Japanese and the standard depth of the hole left his head sticking over the top. Already searchlights lit the sky. All about him people scrambled like crabs on a beach, into their muddy burrows. Children wailed. Caught in the searchlights he saw for the first time the big B-29s, chased by red flashes of anti-aircraft fire, soar across the moon. Soon, like fireworks in the distance, clusters of bombs began to explode, ripping the sky apart, shaking the ground like an earthquake. He crouched down in the hole.

A deep buzzing pulsated suddenly in his ears, vibrating through the damp earth. A geyser of flame was thrown up before him. Raising his head he saw his house was on fire. Above the city the sky was bloodied, reflecting these blossoms of the night. There was nothing he could do but watch the destruction of his home. Before the all clear went the house had already burned beyond repair. The bucket brigade lined up by the cisterns, but were driven back by the heat of the surrounding fire.

Tilik waited by the dugout for a long while, warmed by the flames and flying sparks, as if to store up a heat to keep him through the bleak months ahead. Within the furnace of his home he recognized at times the blazing shape of some familiar object, a mirror, a sofa, a child's chair. His papers were kept in a metal box, and he hoped this might survive the conflagration. About him people ran from the collapsing neighbourhood, and red hot falling beams. Only Tilik stood rooted by his dugout. It seemed to him suddenly that, in the fiery nebula before him, his own life was burning to a pile of ash.

He remembered the pyre on which his father was cremated and that he had lit as custom demanded. Not since that day had he stood before a heat as great as this. Then that long-ago fire, when he turned from it at last, had displaced him forever from comfortable acceptances. He had been fitted for nothing from that day; anger drove him on. Now, looking back, he saw in his life only one dislocation upon another. They locked together in the flames before him, amalgamating into this one, monstrous dislocation; war. When the flames died he would be bereft.

There were forces against which it was not possible to win. In taking up arms, he had joined, unwittingly, the malignant force that had killed his father. His anger had not eradicated it. Instead, by supporting violence he had propagated the very force he had wished to subdue. He had become the man who held the gun. In all the years of activism, who had he helped in the smallest way? All he could offer of decency was that one episode with the Chinese, Teng Li-sheng.

He watched the last flaming beams of his home crash down. His whole life was burning before him. Suddenly then he felt relief. If all was gone a new beginning might be possible. Perhaps, even now, a fresh journey still lay before him.

34

January 1945

The Radio

In the darkness he turned the knob of the radio and the crackle of the universe filled the room. It was as near, Kenjiro thought, as one might get to a time machine, landing unexpectedly in unknown terrain. Each day, after he returned from the ammunitions factory to which he was conscripted, he listened to the BBC news. Once, his father had crouched with him, pressing an ear to the radio. His encroaching deafness and the constant texturing of interference frustrated him. He thought it also safer to pretend to know nothing of a short-wave radio in the house. He demanded instead daily bulletins from Kenjiro.

There was the sudden creak of wood. Kenjiro sat up, listening intently, then went to the door. The corridor was empty. He returned to the radio. The old house groaned continually, one wing had already burned down in a raid. They were lucky to still have a partial roof over their heads. Usually, with a signal from him, his mother busied the servants downstairs before he came up here. The *Kempeitai* kept him under strict surveillance. The two servants who remained with them were undoubtedly informers. He could not blame them, the pressure of the *Kempeitai* was not one to stand against. Yoko would say little, she had been with them twenty years. But, Kimiko had come to them soon after he returned from China. There was no doubt she was planted. He had seen her once on the street corner, talking to a man.

He returned his attention to the radio. As he twisted the knob a voice gathered depth. Every day at this hour he heard the disembodied words of Tilik Dayal, flickering in strength over the hum of the airwaves. The first time he stumbled upon the voice shock punched through him. He realized Dayal must be back in Tokyo. The voice droned on, placing its platitudes neatly. To Kenjiro each word drew tight again the threads of complicity between them. He was tied to this man for life, as he would be to an ex-lover, some invisible exchange of spirit remaining between them. Truth was a see-saw neither could dismount.

He found at last the clear, incised tones of the BBC and listened to the news. Once it was finished he returned the radio to its place of hiding, a space hollowed out beneath the tatami mats. No one was supposed to own a short-wave radio. No one was supposed to know Japan was on the brink of disaster. Home broadcasts still spoke of victory. They harangued people to repulse invasion. Kenjiro pushed the tatami back into place and pulled the table and a cushion over the join. He heard the creak of wood and went again to the door. The corridor was still empty, but there was a tread on the lower stairs. Kenjiro heard his mother call and almost at once, from the bottom steps, Kimiko's answering words. He swore beneath his breath.

Soon he went downstairs. His mother sat darning a pair of worn *mompe* trousers, his father was reading a newspaper and looked up as he entered the room. His eyes had sunk deeply into his face and the padded kimono, once especially made for his extra large frame, was now ample about his frail body. Kenjiro pulled the door closed behind him and sat down on a cushion beside his parents. They had already, some months before when the fear of raids was imminent, sent Naomi to stay with Uncle Juichi. The way they were watched by the secret police was unnerving for her. It was also impossible to tell when Kenjiro might again be arrested. Already they had taken him once since his return from China, terrorizing Naomi.

It had been at the time of the Russian spy Sorge's detention. A Soviet spy ring had been cracked in Tokyo, bringing with it many arrests. Kenjiro had despaired of deliverance in that dark, damp place with its weevil-filled bowls of gruel. He lost count of the weeks of incarceration, of grim questioning, but eventually, without explanation, he was released again. It seemed they were satisfied that he knew nothing. But his health had been broken. Tuberculosis now filled his lungs. His father, at great expense, had sent him for a time to a sanatorium in a mountain village.

Yuzuru looked at Kenjiro questioningly, waiting for the latest news bulletin. 'Leyte has been captured at last by the Americans. Now anything is possible. From there they'll strike at Luzon and Manila. Everything now is in MacArthur's favour.' Kenjiro spoke in a whisper, listening for the approach of servants.

Back in 1941, as soon as Kenjiro had heard that Japan had attacked America, he knew the war would be lost. Their leaders had set the country on a course of madness. No one dared say a thing; no one could. Every corner of life was now tightly controlled. Myth had always been presented as history, but never more than now were the gods made to carry the unique traits of the Japanese race. Ethical studies in schools honed sharper than ever the importance of the national virtues of self-sacrifice, military discipline, ancestor worship and the Imperial cult. And as they were a nation of conformists, there could be no resistance. People like Kenjiro, when detected, were made to apostatize their principles. He too had now chosen silence. But in that vacuum, surrounded by fear, even his thoughts seemed shackled.

'Nothing yet of course on the local station. If anything is said at all it will be followed by the same old chorus, *By drawing the war within the inner Japanese defence lines, the enemy has put his head in a noose, and we are going to strangle him,*' Yuzuru sighed.

'The people are not hoodwinked so easily. All these B-29s, raining bombs upon us every day, speak louder than government words,' Kenjiro replied.

'According to the Women's Volunteer Association, if things worsen, we are all to be issued with bamboo swords to defend the country when the Americans arrive. Soon everyone will have to drill every day.' Shizuko Nozaki did not look up from her darning.

Her silk kimono, patterned with fans and clouds and birds, and obi of gold brocade were now gone. Elegance, beauty and every frivolity was frowned upon. Now, Shizuko wore the ugly baggy trousers all women were required to wear, sewn from the salvaged cloth of old kimono. Any other apparel would have brought upon them the wrath of the Neighbourhood Association. Whispers about the reason for Kenjiro's return from China and his later imprisonment meant disapproval lay heavy upon them. Already they were marked.

His mother now appeared as if carved from antique ivory, and yet there was a wiriness about her that surprised Kenjiro. She had adapted to these times. She climbed about agilely in the absurd baggy trousers of stripes or flowers, tackling tasks unknown to her in better times. Retaining her innate elegance, she reminded him sometimes in the shapeless pants, of a frail clown.

He remembered then how Jacqueline had never understood how his mother tolerated the mistresses in her husband's life. It had been difficult to explain to her that such women were a mark of a man's status, or that the position of wife was not threatened by these other liaisons. As wife a woman had a respect no husband would dishonour. The categories of relationships were kept to their appropriate compartments. Jacqueline became furious.

'She tolerates being related to her *category*, only because she has no choice. Do you really think jealousy and humiliation are unknown to her, just because she is told not to feel them?' Jacqueline always turned things around and put them to him in discomforting ways.

Shizuko Nozaki had been kind to Jacqueline. It had surprised Kenjiro that his mother, unexposed to any life beyond her own, should have established an understanding with his spirited French wife. It was as if his mother saw in Jacqueline's will and free thoughts the ghost of a girl she mourned in herself.

Never in his life had Kenjiro been closer to his parents. Never, he suspected, had they been closer to each other. Age, the eye of the *Kempeitai*, and the present grim austerity had drained his father's life of women. Geisha had been abolished, and all luxury establishments closed. Oyasu, his chief mistress, had been returned for safety to her village in the mountains. His father had sent her away, like a precious object that must be secured against better times ahead. Only for the highest government officials did a black market in geisha now exist. He sensed a new companionship between his parents.

'Kimiko was up there, I'm sure of it,' Kenjiro muttered suddenly to his father. 'I must get the radio out of the house.' They stepped through each day as if upon eggshells.

The wooden doors to the verandah were closed. In the small room their breath clouded frostily between them. A few bits of charcoal glowed in a brazier next to his mother. Shrapnel had splintered the shutters, blackout paper peeled from the hole. Through it Kenjiro stared at a brittle crescent of moon, hanging high above the garden. The sky was black and cloudless.

'There is a cold winter ahead.' Shizuko followed his gaze.

Outside, little was left of the garden. The charred remains of the camellia bushes were no more than blackened stalks. The great stones were scorched amber. Two sides of the garden, once protected by an arm of house now lay open to the road. Between where they sat and the street was a mound of charred beams and wet sodden ash, all that remained of part of the house after a recent air-raid. They trod carefully about in the crumbling structure, expecting floors to collapse beneath them.

'I have hired a truck,' Yuzuru announced suddenly.

'A truck? Who can get hold of a truck? How much did that cost you?' Shizuko looked up from her darning in alarm.

'I was lucky. Ask me no more. The day after tomorrow we move to Uncle Juichi's. The raids are accelerating. Let us get out while we can,' Yuzuru replied.

The siren began to wail. Shizuko put down her darning, folding it neatly beside her sewing box, and stood up. 'How I hate this. I would rather die here, in this room,' she grumbled. Kenjiro took her arm and guided her out of the house.

'We are lucky to have a proper shelter and not a mud dugout,' he told her.

He pushed her before him into the damp, fetid chamber. It was a crude affair, an extra large hole with concrete sides that he always expected to fall in upon them. He could not bear the wet, airless interior where his mother always crouched. The door had already been blown off. He sat on the steps, inside the open entrance. Every night now the raids came in increasing ferocity. They had all heard the new term, 'carpet bombing'.

He stared up into the black sky. There seemed such beauty in the silent emptiness, the moon drifting lazily beneath the thin clouds. Into this soon must come clamour and destruction; the chaos of men. He had lost count now of the brutal years behind him, years that defied all understanding. Soon the American bombers would appear, flying low, powerful, arrogant. He thought of the men who flew them, pasty-skinned and bland, peering through a break in the clouds for a place to deposit their deadly eggs. Did they think of those they would maim and obliterate as they pressed the button for release? Did they think at all? He felt a great wave of hate rush through him. They came, these great bombers, in the role of world liberators. What liberation could there be in the pitiful death of so many? Liberators or conquerors, what was the difference? What difference had there been in Nanking? One colonization for another. One tyranny against another. None of it made sense. Ruined cities, ruined peoples, ruined ideals, that was all there was to understand. A dark cloak had fallen upon the world.

Now, high up, the bombers threaded through the clouds. Searchlights swayed, like shafts of sun in a cellar, planes caught like flies in a beam. Bursts of light flashed through the night, falling in a fiery rain over the city from plane after plane. Jagged flames, whipped by the wind, scythed through the wooden metropolis. The thud of distant bombs shook the shelter. Behind Kenjiro his mother whimpered softly.

The sky was lit now with a pink borealis spreading in a surreal dawn. Smoke and flames rose up from the city towards this unnatural light. In its glare, dark as gliding birds, the planes could still be seen, the fiery glow far beneath reflecting on their wings. They flew on, suffused in gold light, unearthly as meteors. There was a fierce beauty in this theatre of the extreme.

There was some counter-attack in a dispatch of light Kamikaze planes. They buzzed about, ineffectual as mosquitoes, intent upon destroying themselves. One flew into a great plane and exploded in a blaze. The B-29 began to trail black smoke and careered drunkenly about. Soon it disgorged a white parachute which floated, like a feathery seed, down towards the fire. Kenjiro watched, his eyes on the black speck dangling beneath the parachute until it was enveloped in the flames. Soon the all clear went.

Now the second danger came. The wind scooped up the molten debris of the town and blew it to the inflamed sky. The air was filled with burning morsels of wood and paper, drifting like a devilish confetti back down upon their heads, starting up new fires. Before they could move to douse them, the siren went again. A second wave of bombers appeared. More dark birds upon the night.

All morning they had been loading the truck with those things Shizuko deemed essential. All valuables had long before been sent to Uncle Juichi, and buried somewhere on his land. A sharp wind whipped about Kenjiro's neck as he stood on the truck arranging boxes. A stream of neighbours had come, begging a lift out of the metropolis. The stations were bedlam, people camped for days upon the platforms for a chance to get on a train. Passengers were taken with only as much as they could carry. No extra luggage was allowed. A truck was an unheard-of luxury. They had agreed to take with them a family of three in the road behind, who also wished to go in the direction of Uncle Juichi. Already the truck was piled high, but still Shizuko kept appearing with further items.

'Mother, there is nothing more we can take,' Kenjiro protested. His own possessions were few, and consisted mainly of papers and the radio.

'Where in these times will I buy an iron pan like this? I'm lucky it wasn't taken from us already,' his mother replied. And so it went on all morning, until the truck was dangerously top heavy. Shizuko insisted on quilts, a chest, a lacquer table and any surviving cushions.

'Where will we get stuff like this again?' she repeated. 'Do we leave it here for the bombs or as pickings for the poor?'

The maid Yoko was to accompany them, Kimiko would remain in the house. At the factory Kenjiro had spoken to the supervisor, who had agreed to arrange a transfer to an ammunitions plant near Uncle Juichi's farm. The supervisor had been helpful, knowing the power once held by Yuzuru Nozaki.

Kenjiro's chest hurt. The fresh morning air in his lungs made him cough. He threw ropes of plaited cloth over the loaded truck, knotting them tight. The journey would take a few days. His mother had packed all the food they possessed, and what little rice remained. He took no notice of the noise of a car, involved as he was in knotting the ropes, until his name was called. He turned and saw two men from the *Kempeitai*. Behind them stood Kimiko.

'You are going somewhere?' they asked.

'Like everyone else we are leaving Tokyo to escape the bombing. I have informed the ward office and registered our new address. My factory has arranged a transfer to an ammunitions plant near where we shall be living. My papers are in order,' Kenjiro replied.

'Your papers may be in order, but our orders are to search everything before you leave.' They seemed to Kenjiro without personality, like clones from a master model. It was this lack of character that ignited fear. He remembered his torturers in Nanking.

The men stepped forward and unknotted the bindings of the truck, tossing out quilts, cushions and lacquer boxes unheedingly from the vehicle. Everything was opened, everything examined. Eventually, as he knew they must, they found the radio in a wooden crate beneath a padded jacket.

'Where is the aerial?' one of the men demanded.

'There is no aerial,' he replied. The man slapped him about the face.

'We know you are broadcasting messages to the enemy. You have long been suspected of being a spy. Now there is proof. Where is the aerial?'

In the house they ripped up floors and stripped cupboards. They spent a long time in the loft and emerged upon the roof. They could find nothing, and returned to him, furious. One of the men began to shout.

'Where is the aerial? Where is it?' He stamped a foot like an angry child.

'You cannot find what is not there. I am not a spy,' Kenjiro answered calmly.

They took him then by the arms, binding his hands together. He was pushed towards an armoured van. His father stepped forward to remonstrate.

'He has done nothing. Nothing,' he shouted. His agitation was useless, he was thrust roughly out of the way.

Kenjiro turned as he stumbled forward to look at his parents. His mother pressed a hand to her mouth, staring desperately after him. His father was flushed with helplessness. Behind them was Kimiko, a look of satisfaction upon her broad face. His parents stood beside the truck. Bright quilts and cushions tumbled in the road about them. Iron-bound chests spewed kimono and sweaters from their open drawers. Kitchen pans had rolled like stones into a nearby ditch. The bombed wing of the house lay like a sordid backdrop behind them. Their whole life seemed piled in tatters around them. Kenjiro felt he would never forget this scene of dispossession. Never before had he seen his father stripped of power. For the first time he saw him as an old man, waning in all those qualities he had built his life upon.

Behind his parents he could see the remains of the garden, the charred bushes and scorched stones. Only the old lantern had escaped the carnage. It stood as ever, upright, inviolable, its mossy surface singed, but intact. Suddenly, his mother ran forward crying out his name. And stopped short, realizing again the uselessness, biting down upon emotion. The brightness of her eyes was all that indicated tears.

He was pushed roughly into a van with barred windows. Through the dusty glass he peered out at the scene of devastation and knew the bleakness of that morning would live with him for ever. The van began to move. He looked a last time at the old lantern. Soon they turned a corner and everything was gone. He sat back on the floor of the lurching van and thought of that blackness he knew now so well, that must soon again encase him.

35

August 1945

Black Rain

As they finished their breakfast of stale bread and a few black beans, the air raid warning sounded. Nobody moved in the prison camp. The shed that was designated as an official shelter would collapse at a shudder. It was safer to stay where they sat with their food. The air raid warning sounded regularly at this hour as an American weather plane flew over the city.

The August heat singed the air. At night the ground reflected the stored-up fire through its baked surface. Night was the worst. The rough boards that served as bunks were layered so tightly to the ceiling no one could sit up. Prisoners were forced to climb in at an angle. Kenjiro's health had deteriorated since he entered the camp. The rations barely kept them alive. His lungs hurt, the fever and coughing had returned. As yet he spat no blood and this gave him hope. He was determined to survive.

He stared from a window. The heat and crushed conditions, the poor food and hard, monotonous work at the ammunitions factory did not bother him. He had got used to it. It seemed not worth complaining when he could see the sky each day, or smell the scent occasionally of a flower on his walk to the factory. He knew the alternatives in dark, bug-infested cells too well. It was past seven o'clock and the sun, although hot, still retained its morning freshness. At least he was alive.

They had not kept him long in the Tokyo prison. The speed with which he was brought to trial and dispatched as forced labour to this camp, was proof to him of how badly things were going. The government could not afford to keep more than an essential few in gaol. Small fry like himself must earn their keep in the factories. Once again no proof emerged of his spying.

Outside cicada crescendoed like an hysterical orchestra. The paddies glowed an acid green. In the distance stood the town and beyond it the sea. Sometimes, if the wind was right, he could sniff its briny odour. Now, all he could smell was the heat. Every day he looked up at a sky filled by heavy American planes. They sailed by amongst the clouds, like flocks of migrating birds. Wherever it was they went to bomb, they flew in from over the coast. The absence of attack upon the town filled Kenjiro with unease.

In the camp there was of course no news. Sometimes, in the factory, the workers who came in from outside as regular conscription, risked whispering the state of affairs. Since the beginning of the year there had been a change in propaganda techniques. The disinformation and false optimism had ended abruptly. No longer able to keep secret the appalling defeats of the war, the army, through radio and the newspapers, began to magnify the violence at the front. The question now was not of winning, but in what manner Japan should lose the war.

In this camp were Allied POWs, British, Australian and Dutch. They were kept apart in a hut of their own. Anyone caught talking to them was severely beaten. They were a scrawny, sickly lot, and sat now on the floor some distance away from the Japanese prisoners, waiting for the all clear. Kenjiro alone had some contact with them. He was used as an interpreter by the supervisor of the camp. Where he could he extended conversations, giving them news he had gleaned of the war situation. There were also some Koreans and Chinese, and they received the worst treatment.

'Get out on the road. Get moving.' The orders came as usual. It was past seven-thirty. They began to file out of the camp, assembling on the road to town with the factory at its edge. It was a walk of about fifty minutes from the camp. Anyone attempting to escape was shot. As they set out the all-clear sounded. The rasp of crickets and cicada pressed thickly about them. There was the smell of wet earth from the paddies. A bee buzzed about his face, and Kenjiro brushed it away. Soon they reached a spot at a higher level. From here they had a view of the town in the distance. It lay on an estuary, straddling the many tributaries of a river. Already a haze of heat lay over the city and the road ahead buckled and shimmered. A wave of dizziness overcame Kenjiro, he forced himself on. He kept his eyes on the northern suburbs, where he knew Tilik Dayal now lived.

It had been a shock to realize Dayal lived in the city. Even now he wondered at the coincidence. He had been marching as now, at exactly this time, head down, staring at the road. It had been spring, the morning was cold, and he shivered as he walked. From nowhere Dayal had fallen in to walk beside him. The shock had stopped him in his tracks, and the prisoners behind piled into him. The supervisor yelled at Dayal, who stepped back to the side of the road.

'At first I didn't recognize you,' Dayal had shouted excitedly. 'I can't

398

believe it. I'm on my way to get a ration of millet. I've moved here with my wife's family. Everything burned in Tokyo. I'll be in touch. I'll find a way to see you,' Dayal's words floated over the heads of the moving file of men. The supervisor roared his anger, thwacking Kenjiro with a bamboo cane.

There was a wait of some weeks, but eventually he was summoned to the supervisor's hut. Dayal stood before him. The supervisor's face was ugly and he did not leave the room. As they spoke in English his presence made no difference.

'How have you managed this?' Kenjiro asked.

'I have my contacts, in case you have forgotten,' Dayal smiled. 'We've only a few moments, so I'll talk quickly.' He pointed from the window to a group of houses on a nearby hill, not far from the camp, where he lived with his wife and her family. Tilik filled in the gaps of knowledge since they last met and gave a brief summary of Japan's war situation as he knew it.

'It has to be over soon. I've heard rumours already of efforts for a negotiated peace, possibly through the Russians. I'm not sure I can come again too soon. I was lucky to arrange this. Keep well. We'll meet when this is over,' Tilik said as he retreated from the room.

Now Kenjiro turned his head to look back to the hill where Dayal lived. In the sky three planes flew at a great height. Kenjiro squinted up at them. Since the all-clear had gone there could be no danger, they must be reconnaissance planes. The road narrowed, along one side was a school ground. Women were drilling, training to thrust with bamboo spears at the coming American invaders. Perhaps somewhere his mother, as she had forecast, would be doing the same. The shouts of the instructor filled his ears. Outside the school a group of soldiers dug a trench from which they would fight when the Americans came. On the opposite side of the road stood a warehouse, windowless and sombre. Upon its padlocked doors was hammered the mark of the military. Its shade fell upon him, cutting suddenly through the heat. He saw then that he had walked ahead of the others and the supervisor was shouting for him to wait. As he turned to look back a white flash of light hit the sky. There was no sound. The illumination was blinding, like a mammoth flashbulb. He saw the warehouse lift from the ground. At the same time something seemed to pick him up and propelled him through the air to meet it. It cannot be a bomb, he thought, for there was no sound. Then everything went black.

When he opened his eyes he could see nothing. A great weight was upon him. He tried to move and could not. His head was humming. His shoulder hurt. Soon Kenjiro's eyes grew accustomed to the dark, and he

399

saw high above a chink of light, like a crack at the end of a steeple. Whatever it was that pressed about him was firm but flexible to his touch. Gradually he found he could move, altering his position inch by inch. He guessed he was hemmed in by bales of raw cotton or something similar, that had cushioned the fall of the warehouse upon him. Slowly, he moved towards the light, burrowing upwards like a worm from the earth. Whatever was wrong with his shoulder, it still worked. Nothing appeared to be broken. He kept thinking, I am alive. I *think* I am alive. He feared that when he eventually reached the light he might find he was really dead. Outside might wait not the earthbound world, but some nether land beyond the living.

He did not know how long it took, but at last he reached the crack of light. He pushed his way out and found himself on top of a mountain of wood. The sun no longer shone, the day was dark. He did not recognize the scene before him. Perhaps he *was* dead. The thought kept running through his head. A thick, black dust seemed to float in the air. He climbed down with difficulty from the remains of the warehouse and looked about. The thought persisted, that he might have crossed the line of life into another world. Then he heard cries. Through the dust Kenjiro saw the other prisoners were strewn about the road.

Those still alive wandered about in a dazed manner. In the school playground the women lay in a heap, one upon another like bloodied rag dolls. The soldiers sat bolt upright but dead beside the dugout, blood streaming from their faces, their uniforms in tatters. Kenjiro looked back again at the prisoners. The supervisor lay head down in a ditch. In the distance the barracks no longer stood, flames rose from the rubble. In the area where the factory should have been, he could see nothing but a flattened mess. The houses in the road beyond the warehouse had also collapsed. He turned towards the town and stared for some time in confusion. As far as he could see a flat bowl of ash spread out before him in the darkness. He tried to think. He remembered no blast, and bombs hit specific areas. Perhaps it was not a bomb but a massive meteorite. An earthquake? He realized then that his clothes hung in shreds and he was bleeding from his chest. A wind was beginning to blow. For the first time he noticed the silence. No crickets rasped, no cicada rattled, birds had ceased to sing. In the distance he heard a strange, hollow, mewling. On the wind blew the moaning of people, welding together into a single frenzied note. Out of nowhere then a rain began. His arm was splattered with large black drops, like petrol oil. He licked his hand, but the rain tasted of nothing he knew.

He saw now that the smoke about him had taken a shape, piling up high into the sky, as if it would reach the roof of space. Twisting on a

400

black umbilical chord, a diabolical incubus hovered above the town. He stared in horror at this image. For a moment it seemed as if all the evil of the last ten or fifteen years, all the frenzied lust of killing and hate, wherever or by whoever, hovered there physically above him. He could not move, filled with terror. On the wind the moaning blew to him once more. He looked up again at that silent incubus, and knew he was not wrong. Hate had at last exploded. From this place there could be no return.

Kenjiro turned then and ran. Tears streamed down his face. He ran in the direction of Dayal's home. At last he reached the hill upon which Dayal had said he lived and began to ask for the foreigner. People pointed the way, their faces blank and bewildered. Children cried beneath the rubble of half-collapsed homes. Kenjiro stopped to help a woman pull a screaming baby from under wreckage. The child emerged almost unharmed and the woman sobbed her thanks. There seemed less damage in this district. The strange wind fanned flames from collapsed houses. One fire merged quickly into another. At last he reached a house which still partially stood. All the doors and windows had been blasted out, and most of the tiles were gone. He looked up to see Tilik standing in a ruined room, his face badly cut about.

'What was it?' he asked, scrambling up beside him.

'A new bomb, the one that's been rumoured. It'll be one bomb per city now until Japan surrenders. Michiko and the children went into town with her mother early this morning, to the doctor. I must go and find them,' Tilik gestured desperately.

'Have you seen your face? That's a bad gash above your eyes,' Kenjiro replied.

'I must go. I must find them.' Tilik pulled out a handkerchief and held it to the cut.

'I'll come with you,' Kenjiro said.

'If the *Kempeitai* see you in that prison uniform, however little there is left of it, you'll be shot. Open that cupboard, put on some of my things. Hurry,' Tilik demanded.

'Why have they bombed this town?' Kenjiro asked. He looked about in bewilderment.

'It's the base of the Second General Headquarters of the Imperial Army. The city is swarming with soldiers,' Tilik replied, already making his way out of the ruined house.

Kenjiro remembered then that Hiroshima was a military city, its wealth built upon a warring past. Troops in 1894 had set off from Hiroshima for the battlefronts of China, and Emperor Meiji had moved his military headquarters to the city. When, a decade later, Japan had gone to war with Russia, Hiroshima was once more the centre of military operations. For a moment he imagined the city like a fly caught at the centre of a web. That was why there had been no raids. They were waiting for the kill to ripen.

The closer they came to the town the worse the damage was. Not a house stood. From the flattened piles of rubble came cries for help. Kenjiro hung back, attempting to do what he could, but Tilik was desperate with impatience.

'We cannot stop. I must find Michiko.' Tilik pulled him on.

The wind seemed to have swung about and was coming now from the north. For the first time Kenjiro looked down at his arms, bare beneath the sleeves of Tilik's shirt, and saw that the splodges of black rain seemed to have sunk, indelibly, into his skin. They resembled the dark spots of age upon his father's hands.

'I don't know where I am,' Tilik said suddenly. 'There is nothing left. All the landmarks have gone.'

'Let us go to the river, perhaps from there you can find your way,' Kenjiro suggested. Walking to the factory, he passed the river each day.

Tilik nodded, 'The doctor was near the river.'

They walked on. The moaning Kenjiro had heard on the wind came now from all directions. It wrapped about him. He was overwhelmed by his helplessness before such pain and anguish. As they neared the centre of town the roads thickened with people, flowing towards them.

'Water. Water.' The cry came to them again and again.

He knew these were people. They walked, had limbs and heads that moved, but little else about them seemed recognizable. It was as if the earth had spewed up some half-formed race before their time of birth. Skinless, faceless, blind and unhearing, they flooded towards Kenjiro. He drew back in horror. Tilik pushed on before him, each sight only fuelling his desperation. He began to shout.

'Michiko. Michiko.'

They came upon a charred tram, twisted like a piece of gum. From it oozed a gluey substance in which floated blackened twigs. Kenjiro turned and vomited. The twigs he saw were burnt bones, the congealed liquid was once the passengers who that morning had boarded the tram. From everywhere people streamed at him, roasted as chickens on a spit.

'Water. Water.'

The patterns of fans or flowers from blouses were impressed like stencils upon their skin. The shadow of straps, suspenders, braces and belts were also to be seen. Soon the sheer number of people overwhelmed him. They appeared to come from all sides. Kenjiro realized

402

suddenly that he and Tilik, upright and unharmed, were like a magnet to these wounded. They lifted arms to them, chests skinless.

'Water. Water.'

Those who could not see seemed to sense their passing.

'Water. Water.'

Kenjiro helped somebody to the side of the road. He comforted a lost child, carrying it for some time upon his back but could not find its mother. He set it down beside a woman who appeared relatively unharmed and suckled a baby at her breast.

They passed a wall on top of which rested two brown gloves laid out neatly, side by side. On looking back Kenjiro realized the gloves were no more than the skin of a pair of flayed hands.

Flames whipped up about them, the heat intense upon their faces. The darkness was like an eclipse at midday. Looking up at the sky Kenjiro saw, still hovering above, that black incubus, moving, swaying, turning in upon itself. Tilik strode ahead.

They came at last to the river. In it floated a load of logs, and amongst these logs the living doused themselves with water to ease their pain. Kenjior realized that yet again, the logs were the detriment of grilled corpses.

It was late afternoon before Tilik agreed to retrace their steps, back across the bowl of ash. 'Perhaps Michiko has managed to get home,' Kenjiro comforted. Halfway across the annihilated town Tilik stopped, refusing to go on.

'Let me check the refugee centres again, and the first aid tents. Maybe I have missed her. There are also now more bodies to check.' He bent as others also bent, to examine the dead. Many people now swarmed about, relatively unharmed like themselves from the outskirts of the town, looking for relatives, anxious to help.

'You go back to the house and see if they have returned. I cannot leave. I *cannot*.' Tilik stopped again before a pile of charred bodies, turning them over, one by one.

Kenjiro walked back the way he had come, running in spite of exhaustion, to be free of the Hell. On the river now a launch pushed its way amongst the floating human debris. A naval officer stood on the deck and shouted through a megaphone. The launch was white and the officer spry in his starched summer cotton. They seemed apparitions from another world.

'Be patient. A naval hospital ship is coming to take care of you soon. Be patient.' He shouted repeatedly.

Kenjiro made his way around a smoking pile of bricks and passed a fragment of wall. His shadow stretched upon the wall, and yet there was

403

no sun. He walked forward, but the shadow did not move. Upon the wall, he suddenly realized, the shadow was all that remained of what had once been a man. It was as if that dark and sinister half of man, buried deep within himself, had shown itself at last. Upon this wall for eternity, it had imprinted its shadowy self. Kenjiro began to run.

Soon he reached the house. In the dark he stumbled across the threshold. He saw the outlines already of the two women and the children.

'I have waited here all day,' Michiko sobbed when he explained. 'I never went to the doctor. My mother felt too unwell to walk. We stopped at a neighbour's for her to recover. Then that flash came and the neighbour's house collapsed upon us. We are still alive, it's a miracle. By the time we managed to get out from under the ruins of the house, Tilik was not to be found. I thought he was dead.'

Kenjiro collapsed in exhaustion. He closed his eyes and the world reeled about him. What he had seen could not be part of any war. It was no less than the end of the world.

Eventually Tilik returned. He stared at his wife and children, sitting whole before him.

'You are here,' he said without expression. He sat down and began to cry.

PART SIX

A Choice of Evils

Tokyo, Japan 1945 – 1946

36

1945

Sword of Power 3

When the atomic bomb obliterated Hiroshima on the 6th August 1945 at fifteen minutes past eight in the morning, Emperor Hirohito was walking in the palace gardens. He had spent the previous night in his air raid shelter beneath the palace, discussing the Potsdam Declaration's demand for Japan's surrender with his brother Prince Takamatsu. He had slept little and was in an emotional state. At the news of Hiroshima he grew white and tears sprang to his eyes.

For months Marquis Kido and Prince Konoye had been urging him to think of surrender. Kido drafted a report of his own, 'Measures for Managing the Situation'. He urged Hirohito to speak out for the cessation of hostilities immediately, although the Government still talked of victory, and the Army Minister, General Anami and the chiefs of the navy and army, categorically opposed the idea of surrender. Defeat was an aberration unknown to Japan, surrender an unheard-of and alien concept. An honourable end to the war was what was sought for the nation. Hirohito seemed powerless to take an initiative. 'One more victory. One more victory', was all he seemed able to repeat to Konoye. A series of ignominious defeats, the sight of war-damaged Tokyo, and the shattering of Hirohito's dream for the era of Showa, had thrown the Emperor into a state of paralysis. Now, when informed of the nature of the new bomb, Hirohito at last began to react.

'Under these circumstances we must bow to the inevitable. No matter what happens we must put an end to this war as speedily as possible, so that this tragedy will not be repeated. My personal safety does not matter,' he announced at long last to Marquis Kido, when later they met. The safety of the Emperor and his family was everyone's concern.

But there were still fanatics prepared to fight on, who used the Potsdam Declaration's silence over the fate of the Imperial family in surrender, as a reason to continue the state of war. Hardly had the bomb been dropped than the Russians, whom Japan had hoped might negotiate a conditional surrender for them with the Americans, turned

407

instead upon Japan with a declaration of war. Hirohito was beside himself. He sent for Kido and demanded he call a session of the Supreme War Council and the Cabinet and make the Emperor's wishes known to all members of these boards. The Emperor now begged for haste. He was a scientist and could guess the potential of such a bomb.

Haste was the last thing that appeared to drive the Supreme Council. It took three days to persuade them to meet. They too, like Hirohito earlier, were paralysed by the coming defeat. The few who spoke realistically were outnumbered by those who still talked of last attacks, and a fight to the death. No consensus for surrender appeared reachable. Even news, during their discussions, of the dropping of a second atom bomb upon Nagasaki, seemed not to hurry a decision. The Americans pressed for an *unconditional* surrender. Any surrender as far as Japan was concerned must be *conditional*, but the number of conditions was still in debate. The very *idea* of defeat was unacceptable. A stalemate had been reached.

Although it was late at night, it was decided by the elderly Prime Minister Kantaro Suzuki, who had known Hirohito since his childhood, to ask the Emperor to call an Imperial Conference over which his royal presence should preside. Hirohito agreed that, if no unanimous decision was reached at the meeting, he would exercise his Royal Prerogative, and call an end to the war.

The Emperor, according to ancient metaphor, lived forever above the clouds, like a mythical crane, surveying from on high the state of his nation, but leaving its government to appointed officials. Only on occasions of rare and dire crisis might he issue direct commands to his people. At these times he spoke in the Voice of the Crane.

At this impromptu and desperate Imperial Conference, Hirohito no longer sat upon his throne before a golden screen but in his air raid bunker, fifty feet below ground. He wore a crumpled khaki uniform. It was a hot August night and there was no air-conditioning. The panelled walls of the bunker were sweating.

The conference began at 11.50 p.m. Before Hirohito sat his ministers, perspiring profusely in formal morning coats and dress uniforms as befitted an Imperial Conference. The same arguments that had devoured the previous precious hours now began again. Once more no decision was reached on suitable conditions for a surrender. At 2 a.m. Prime Minister Suzuki rose stiffly from his seat, desperation ingrained in his weary expression.

'We cannot go on like this. The situation allows for no further delay. In these circumstances I shall humbly present myself at the foot of the throne and I will seek the Imperial guidance and substitute it for the decision of the conference.' The old man left his seat and prostrated himself at the feet of the Emperor.

At last, when the Prime Minister was seated again and intensity calmed in the room, Hirohito began to speak. Agitation twisted his face, sweat had steamed up his glasses making it difficult to read the notes in his hand. He gulped visibly, and began to speak in a high, strained voice. Slowly, his voice settled and took on a sure tone.

'I have given serious thought to the situation prevailing at home and abroad, and I have come to the conclusion that continuing the war can only mean destruction for the nation and a prolongation of bloodshed and cruelty in the world . . .' He went on for some time, stopping emotionally at intervals, once taking a sip of green tea and wiping his sweating face. At last he neared the end of his speech accepting the Potsdam Declaration of unconditional surrender.

'I cannot help feeling sad when I consider the people who have served me so loyally as soldiers and sailors, who have been killed or wounded in battlefields overseas, the families who have lost their homes and so often their lives in the air raids here. I need not tell you how unbearable I find it to see the brave and loyal fighting men of Japan disarmed. It is equally unbearable that others who have given me devoted service may now be threatened with punishment as the instigators of war. Nevertheless, the time has come when we must bear the unbearable, . When I recall the feelings of my Imperial Grandfather the Emperor Meiji at the time of the Triple Intervention in 1895, I swallow my tears and give my sanction to the proposal to accept the Allied proclamation on the basis outlined by the Foreign Minister.'

Hirohito wiped his face on his handkerchief and sat down exhausted on his chair. The Voice of the Crane had spoken.

37

1946

The Journey Back

Bradley Reed returned to his office in the Dai Ichi Building in Tokyo after an interview with General MacArthur. The Supreme Command for the Allied Powers, or SCAP as it was called, was in a massive draughty building, relatively unscarred by bombs. He sat down heavily at his desk and looked across to where Nadya typed industriously. The International Military Tribunal for the Far East was about to begin.

'Now, as well as advising the Prosecution for the trial, I am to be attached to the Government Section to advise on the new Constitution. You don't refuse requests from General MacArthur. I suspect nobody knows quite what they're doing yet,' Bradley Reed announced. 'Every old China or Japan hand I know seems to have been summoned here, just like myself. It's years, you know, since I was in Japan, and it's a shock to see the state of the place.' Bradley lit his pipe. Nadya stopped typing and looked up, she could understand Bradley's shock.

Beyond the office footsteps echoed along the stone corridors of the Dai Ichi Building. A mass of uniformed Americans hurried in all directions, papers in hands, intent upon great purpose. MacArthur's American military and civilian staff appeared intimidating to Nadya. The constant rhythm of feet was like the beat to a melody that never started. Or perhaps, Nadya thought, it was that she herself waited apprehensively, as if for a curtain to rise upon some future act of life. She had obeyed Bradley's summons to join him in Tokyo with reluctance. She had been eight years in America and had no wish to leave. Most of all she had no desire to return to the Far East and the crucible of memory. Each day of the journey to Japan, as her destination drew nearer, she had felt progressively weighed down. A sense of violation filled her. She knew now that this was the real emotion left with her after Nanking. Only now could she give it a name. Perhaps there were also other emotions to discover, buried conveniently during the years in America. Her apprehension thickened.

As conditions had worsened in China in 1938, Bradley Reed returned to America to teach Chinese history and politics at Stanford University. He insisted Nadya also leave China and find a future in America. Marriage to Donald, with its resulting nationality, made this move uncomplicated. Nadya had sailed from Shanghai some weeks after Bradley. He arranged a job at Stanford for her, as librarian and assistant to his department. She settled easily and, as the years went by, felt she grafted well to the country. She enjoyed her work and the freedom at last from the trauma of war into which the whole world was progressively plunged. Bradley and his wife were forever introducing her to suitable young men. There had been several serious relationships but, to Nadya at least, none had the hope of permanence. No wave of emotion swept her away, destroying sensibility.

Every six months on average a few lines from Donald arrived, written in haste from some war zone of the world. He was alive, but she knew little more. The demand for divorce never came. She waited for his few scrawled words on a crumpled sheet of notebook. Each brought the same relief; that he was not dead, blown up by a mine or sniper fire, or shot down in a plane over Guadalcanal.

'I don't know why you need me here. Anyone can type these,' Nadya scowled at Bradley, puffing benignly on his pipe. She could not keep the anger from her voice at finding herself in Tokyo.

On arriving in the city it was a shock, after the years in America, physically untouched by war, to return to demolished worlds. The jeep Bradley sent to meet Nadya had jolted over bomb-cratered roads, towards the Dai Ichi Hotel. It was as if there had been no space of time between Nanking and now. Eight years in America appeared obliterated in a single view from the window of this vehicle.

'I didn't imagine it was as bad as this,' she said to the young GI who drove the jeep.

'Yes Ma'm, we did a thorough job of things here,' he grinned. She looked at him in distaste.

Japan. The name, during those nightmare months in Nanking, echoed of terror. It conjured a vision of irascible power. Now, Tokyo spread about her in a dust pile. A shanty town of sticks and rags and bits of paper. Barefoot, ragged children, women with babies strapped to their backs, men without legs propelling themselves upon makeshift trolleys, begged for money or cigarettes. In spite of her knowledge of the blitzing of Japan, she had been unprepared for this. The city was silent except at its centre where the GIs roamed. No street lights survived to illuminate the night. A stench of sewage corroded the place. All the old pictures of Nanking returned. She hugged her arms nervously about herself. A sudden force thrust her back into a world she had tried all these years to

411

forget. One bombed town looked much like another. One human's pain and terror, whatever their race, was the same as another's. She could have been riding through Nanking.

Since arriving in Tokyo her sleep had been blown away. Once again she awoke with nightmares. In the middle of the day she was paralysed by flashbacks. In spite of this and whatever her grumbles to Bradley, her reluctance to come to Tokyo was diluted by the knowledge that Donald must be here. Like her, he could not escape this trial. He was famous everywhere now for his war reportage, and the film he had smuggled out of Nanking all those years ago. She could not suppress the agitation filling her at the thought of seeing Donald again.

'I don't know why you need me here,' she repeated sullenly to Bradley. Her own unsettled emotional state undermined her confidence. 'The people in this building all seem to know where they're going and what they're doing. Only I feel superfluous.'

'A matter of activity hiding confusion.' Bradley puffed on his pipe, and leaned back in the chair. The smell of tobacco filled the room. 'The job before this Occupation is immense. Immediately, food must come in, millions and millions of tons. The country is starving and thousands will still die unless we act quickly. Then the educational system must be changed, religion overhauled. Democracy, justice as we know it, and the vote and equality for women must all be installed. And more, much more. A whole country and its way of thinking must be refashioned. And while all this is going on, those men who brought things to the sad pass you see beyond this building, must also be brought to book. The evil of men, many small men, who thought themselves beyond the judgement of God must be run to ground and brought to trial. The task ahead is monumental. But I have faith in General MacArthur.'

'Will General Tojo stand trial?' Nadya asked. Tojo had recovered from a suicide attempt soon after the surrender.

'Certainly he will,' Bradley replied. 'Many Japanese have lost even the last grain of respect for him because he couldn't do away with himself efficiently, as did so many others. I've forgotten how many have been arrested as war criminals to date, but hundreds, maybe thousands.' Bradley puffed again on his pipe.

'And the Emperor? Is he to be treated as a war criminal?' Nadya asked. There was much debate upon the Emperor's guilt. He still appeared to Nadya as a shadowy figure, whose true role she could not determine.

'Now, that is a much harder question,' Bradley replied. 'It is very difficult to know what to say. There is a consolidated conspiracy by all about him to protect him, not only out of reverence, but to safeguard the Emperor system. It is understandable, if you know Japan.'

'Don't they say the Emperor was a prisoner in his own palace, ineffectual against the military, without a voice of his own? It's impossible to deny he was locked up in his ivory tower, relying upon the ears and eyes of courtiers to scan the common world beyond his palace,' Nadya argued.

Bradley frowned, unwilling to agree to simplistic explanations. 'I suppose the answer to the Hirohito question must inevitably lie somewhere between innocence and guilt. We should not forget he was brought up by military men, his mind filled with the glories of past battles and talk of a united Asia under Japan. He was an expert upon military strategy, and had a rare passion for the subject. He built a War Headquarters in the grounds of his palace, where each move of the war was reported and planned. Nothing could be put into action without his knowledge and his seal upon it. I believe he is a clever man, adept at playing the role of the moment, to get his way and protect himself. I do not think of him as a warmonger, but as a man with a dream for his nation and his reign. This dream coincided with the ambition of unscrupulous men in a wilful era. He always acted constitutionally. He may have used this as a shield, but more probably, it would have been out of character and contrary to his convictions about the rule of law to do otherwise. The will of the state must always be the will of the Emperor. Sadly, he was what we see so often in history, a mediocre man caught up in the tide of great history.'

'Then why does General MacArthur not do away with the Emperor system?' Nadya asked. 'Surely, that alone would change the mentality of the whole country.'

'The goodwill of the Japanese people is needed to turn this country around. There would be also complete disorientation without the Emperor. And of course, MacArthur's main concern now is to use this country to arrest any possible spread of Communism in the future. If we leave Japan broken and weak, we leave it open to that threat. We need a stable ally now in the Far East.' Bradley emptied his pipe into an ashtray and began to fill it with fresh tobacco.

'But the Emperor met MacArthur and told him that he bore the *sole* responsibility for the war,' Nadya interjected.

'I think MacArthur was taken aback, thinking the Emperor was going to beg him not to indict him. I believe Marquis Kido, the Lord Privy Seal, had insisted the Emperor to take *no* responsibility. Anyway, MacArthur was very impressed by the Emperor. I think he has developed a great respect for him. But of course, in Japanese custom the head of any concern must take responsibility and resign for the deeds of his underlings, even if he is not guilty. Responsibility rests at the head. This is a hierarchical society.' Bradley relit his pipe and began to puff upon it again.

'Marquis Kido has been arrested, which I really don't think he deserves,' Bradley continued. 'He was more of a pacifist than many about the Emperor. He kept a diary that he has given over to the prosecution. Upon its contents rests much of our case. Although I do not think of him personally as guilty, he was spokesman in everything for the Emperor. I suppose in a way he will be tried in lieu of the Emperor. Prince Konoye took poison and died a few weeks after I arrived, rather than face this trial, as indeed did several others. I do not know sometimes how right any of this is. We hold some political civilian leaders as *criminally* responsible for this war, but thousands whose savagery was beyond belief will never even be tried. Sometimes here I feel like Alice down the rabbit hole,' Bradley sighed.

'And where do I fit in Wonderland?' Nadya asked, petulant again.

'When they told me I had to advise the prosecution on the China years, I told them I needed my own assistant, one who knew things from the inside out. And of course, you would have had to come anyway. You have been summoned as a witness by the prosecution.' Bradley looked at her cannily.

'I wanted to forget it all.' Nadya raised her voice angrily.

'My dear girl, that is impossible. Would you let such evil pass?' Bradley's clear eyes rested upon her with an expression of sorrow.

'Nothing can be undone,' she whispered, looking down at the typewriter. *You were not there in Nanking.* She wanted to say these words to him but instead remained silent.

'What happened to W.H.D.? I have heard nothing of him. Is he to come here?' she asked instead, trying to control her confusion.

'Nobody knows what happened to W.H.D. He was in Manila, returning from his first holiday in forty years when the Japanese struck. I heard Chinese friends took him into hiding in the mountains. And later I heard from an impeccable source that he had been captured by the Japanese. Perhaps he is dead. Or perhaps he will turn up and surprise us. He was always a mystery man. You could never tell what he would do or where you would find him next.' Bradley shook his head in reluctant admiration.

'Mr Keenan will see you now.' A young man put his head around the door. Bradley nodded and stood up, gesturing to Nadya to accompany him.

Joseph Keenan, Chief Counsel for the Prosecution, was a corpulent, florid man of Irish descent with a voice that carried down corridors. He pumped Nadya's hand in greeting. The redness of his nose made her

414

wonder if he had some kind of skin disease. He called for mugs of coffee, and leaned forward over his desk to speak directly to Nadya.

'Bradley has told me about your courage in Nanking. This trial will be watched by the world. American legal standards will be on show. And not only that, by it we stand or fall in the eyes of Japan. I want this trial carried out under the highest standards of professionalism and justice. We will prove to Japan what American democratic justice is. This trial must outlaw war itself. It must sentence not only military leaders but those civilians also who helped the military instigate it.' Joseph Keenan had a way with speech, discharging words in a stream of energy and spittle. Nadya drew back in her chair to avoid the shower. Keenan had warmed to his theme, his voice rose upon his words.

'The charge is, *crimes against humanity*. Those crimes we are investigating started in Manchuria. You cannot begin any investigation halfway through a crime. You must go back to the beginning and trace events from there. That is why I am so glad you are here. Manchuria then China is the fuse that led to Pearl Harbor and the world war. This we will prove beyond all doubt. The finding of witnesses for those years is in Bradley's hands.'

It was impossible to do more than sit quietly and listen as Keenan expanded on his plans. Eventually a secretary appeared to remind him of an appointment with General MacArthur. He walked with them as far as the lift, and then hurried away down the corridor. Nadya stared after him in bewilderment, unsure of her feelings about the man.

'He is a powerful personality,' she admitted to Bradley, for want of a better description.

'Let us only hope he is the right man to handle a trial such as this. I have my doubts, I'm afraid. I also have my doubts as to whether American-style justice will shine here in quite the way Keenan wishes.' Bradley re-lit his pipe as they waited for the lift. Nadya looked at him questioningly.

'MacArthur won't hear a word against Keenan, but there are rumours of a drinking problem. And he has been more used until now to defending Chicago gangsters. And, like the majority of my countrymen here to put this nation in order, he knows nothing of the history or psychology of the people we are dealing with. It worries me.' Bradley stepped to one side for Nadya to enter the lift. It was crowded and they were crushed close to each other.

'I want you to go back to Nanking to find Martha,' Bradley said suddenly, taking the pipe from his mouth.

'I have lost all contact, I know nothing. My letters were always unanswered. Before I left Nanking she was being cared for in a convent.' Nadya's body stiffened. She did not want to go back to Nanking.

But Bradley was adamant. 'She is still in that convent, looked after by the nuns. This much I know. But I do not know what her condition is. If she is in any way lucid, I want her brought here to testify.'

'You cannot do that to her,' Nadya breathed quickly. Images that she had locked away filled her mind, churning through her body.

'Many years have passed. Time does heal as they say, you know. I believe her faith in God will have pulled her through. The question is her state of health.' Bradley puffed calmly at his pipe. He averted his eyes from Nadya.

'Time does not always heal,' she protested. Do not send me back to Nanking, she prayed silently.

'Your famous *husband of convenience* is coming here too. I suppose you know that, both to report the trial for his newspaper and to appear as a witness,' he added.

'I know. He wrote me a note. Eight whole lines. Quite a tome for him.' Nadya pursed her lips. 'I suppose you had him summoned too.'

'He would have come anyway, to report on the trial,' Bradley shrugged. Nadya saw a light wash of guilt in his face. 'I have arranged for you to go to Nanking on a military flight tomorrow.'

'It seems I have little choice in the matter then.' Nadya did not hide the bitterness in her voice. Her pulse began to beat erratically.

'Who else can I send?' Bradley apologized.

It was a relief to find Nanking itself in conditions of repair. The old walls stood as on that day she left, crumbled, pitted but unbowed. There had been rebuilding in the town, and people filled the streets once more with the sense of a structure regained. Along the main streets saplings had been planted. It had taken two years to persuade anyone to return to the town. Purple Mountain still gathered blue light, untouched by time. She remembered the bombs she had watched from there with Donald. She remembered their love-making upon the grassy slope and the leaves that afterwards stuck in her hair. She passed the temple where she had lain so wantonly with the Japanese man, and outside which Lily had been destroyed. Everywhere she saw landmarks to memory. Bradley had only half understood what he was returning her to, when he sent her here.

She took a room at the Metropolitan Hotel. As soon as she could she went to the hospital. It stood as before, unchanged. Stepping in through the door she felt like a ghost forced to wander forever the echoing corridors of time. A feeling of weight came upon her. Dr Janet Allen, who

416

had run the mission hospital in Soochow for Martha, was now in charge. She was a brisk, large-busted woman with short straight hair. She greeted Nadya with a stream of information.

'On 3rd May Chiang Kai-shek will return to Nanking to reclaim his capital. Let us hope from now on all will be well. The Japanese administration has addicted the whole population to heroin. It was, I believe, their usual procedure wherever they went here in China, to weaken the populace and make money. Everyone, from children to old people, is now hooked. It is a major problem and we deal with the worst results all the time. No doubt Chiang will put it right once he arrives. There is talk now again of civil war if the Communists and the Nationalists cannot agree upon a coalition government. Without the Japanese there is no reason to keep up a United Front. However, we struggle on.'

Dr Allen now occupied Martha's house. The same furniture remained, but the curtains were new and the plants that once banked the window in the lounge had disappeared. As Dr Allen prattled on Nadya looked about the room, once so familiar and yet now so displaced. The past was all about her, like a double exposure on a negative. Here, at that terrible Christmas lunch, she had sat across the table from Kenjiro Nozaki and known, sooner or later, they would become lovers. If that had not happened, perhaps the course of many lives might have been changed. She pushed the thought away, and asked the question she dreaded.

'Dr Clayton?' For a moment Dr Allen was silent. 'She is still at the convent.'

'They want her to testify at the trial. Is she in any condition to do that?' Nadya enquired. She swallowed a sudden mouthful of hot tea and scalded her throat.

'Perhaps it is best you judge for yourself. I will phone the convent that you are coming. They say some days she is better than others. I have not seen her for a long time. I cannot really say anything.' Dr Allen fell silent for a moment before she continued.

'I remember once, many years ago, when I had just come out to China.' Dr Allen sipped her tea thoughtfully. 'I was at the Soochow hospital, and Dr Clayton came over. She was on a tour of the outlying clinics. I had the cook prepare an excellent meal, chicken, and a pie of apple and apricot I think, for she had been on the road several days in all those strange places, eating strange things. She told me quite curtly that she was well used to Chinese food, and had been brought up wearing Chinese clothes. I thought then what a difficult life she must have had, displaced from her identity and her country, living always in alienation, facing terror and death at every turn year after year of her childhood.

417

You know she was caught up in the Boxer Uprising, besides goodness knows how many other things.

'I looked into her face, I remember. I thought I could imagine only too easily even then the wild-eyed look of those poor creatures in mental asylums, driven to the last refuge of madness, by a life too painful to bear.'

Janet Allen broke off suddenly, embarrassed. 'The memory has always stayed with me. See Dr Clayton for yourself. Maybe the sight of an old friend will cheer her. Sometimes these things help. But if you find her changed, my dear, please remember, life itself can sometimes fester to a sickness in us all.'

Nadya rang the bell before the iron gate of the convent. After some moments the grating was pulled aside. She met the eyes of a watchman and gave her name. The gate was opened and she was shown in. The smell of cold stone, carbolic and incense settled about her in the waiting room.

Before leaving China for America, she had come to this same convent to say goodbye to Martha. She remembered the parting. Silence had been then an impenetrable veil about Martha. She seemed not to hear the words of goodbye, lying listless on a bed of starched sheets. The white wimples of the nuns had floated about her like great moths.

'Her mind has wandered to a far place,' Nadya recalled the nun saying, 'but she will return, with God's grace. It is a question of time and of loving care. Both these things we can give her here.'

Nothing seemed changed. The Mother Superior was still the same Irish woman. Her wimple swayed as she nodded, like the sails of a ship lifting in a breath of wind. She listened to Nadya's explanations.

'You may see her if you wish, if you are sure that is what you want,' she answered. 'I cannot guarantee how she will react.'

'Has her speech returned?' Nadya asked.

'Her speech has returned,' the nun replied.

Nadya followed her up flights of stairs and along tall corridors. Two young Chinese novices accompanied them. If Martha could speak again, perhaps it might be possible to coax from her the evidence needed in Tokyo, if she was strong enough to travel. The flights of stairs seemed endless but, at last, near the top of the building, they stopped before a door. Mother Superior motioned to the young novices, one of whom took out a large bunch of keys and selected one after some hesitation. Why must they lock Martha in, Nadya wondered? She drew back then in hesitation.

418

The room was large. The spring sun streamed in through a tall tree outside a window. Only the grille of bars before the glass gave it a sequestered look. There was a bed to one side of the room and in the middle, facing the window a woman sat in a chair, her back towards them. Mother Superior went forward.

'Martha, my dear, a friend has come to see you.' She put a hand upon her shoulder. The woman turned slowly. On the table beside her stood a huge nautilus shell. Nadya still remembered that shell. Martha had clung to it, her fingers like a vice about it on the day she had entered the convent.

'She will let no one touch that shell,' Mother Superior said, seeing Nadya's eyes upon it. 'She sits all day with it when she is peaceable, holding it up to the light, looking into its many chambers. It contains some meaning for her.'

Martha's hair had been shorn close to her head in a halo of long bristles. Her face was sunken in upon itself, the lips fallen back over toothless gums. 'If we don't cut it like that she pulls it out, strand by strand,' Mother Superior said gently, seeing Nadya's shock. 'Her teeth she knocked out, one by one. It was impossible to control her. Her mind was set upon it.'

It was the eyes that made Martha unrecognizable. They appeared pulled inwards as if by a great force, knotted deep within her skull. They were no longer the clear, judgemental eyes Nadya remembered, but as black and malicious as two small beans. Nadya wanted to say, *this is not her.*

Once, as a child, she had seen a monkey tied to a string, forced to perform the same cruel tricks, over and over again. The callousness that was visited upon the creature grew bright within its eyes. She would never forget that animal's eyes, knowing, cunning, venomous as the man who made it dance without respite. It had gone beyond the far edge of fear into another world. Nadya stepped forward.

At first there was no recognition. Martha's eyes slid from side to side, taking in the chances of escape, her lips munching on each other. Then her eyes returned to Nadya, resting upon her. They became luminous slowly with knowledge, dredged up from a locked chamber in time. Nadya waited for this recognition to peel away the madness. She took another step forward.

The sound seemed to come from far away, like a singing creature strangled in mid-song. Martha rose from the chair, and stood to face Nadya in a shapeless white shift. And now, with recognition came a new expression. Malevolence flamed in her eyes. Her mouth stretched to scream its terrible words over and over again.

419

'*You.* You killed them.' Her body began to twist and heave, like an ocean whipped by storm. She flailed about, scratching at her own eyes and face. The novices stepped forward, one on each side, and dragged her to the bed. Nadya saw then that it was hung with straps. These were bound back and forth across the struggling, demented woman, until she could not move.

'Come.' Mother Superior led Nadya from the room.

'Calm yourself, child,' she said outside. 'To expect different would be a miracle.' Nadya trembled with the shock.

'Sometimes it helps me to think of her as a visionary,' the Mother Superior said slowly. 'The visionary experience is not always blissful. There is Hell as well as Heaven. Everything that for the healthy visionary is a source of bliss, brings to her tormented soul only further nightmare. Everything for her, from the stars in the sky to the flowers in the gardens below her window, appear charged with hateful significance. We pray for her each day.'

'Pray?' Nadya looked up, her face streaked with tears. She felt a hysterical urge to laugh. 'Pray? You were not here during the sacking, you were evacuated. If you speak of Hell, we saw it here. And where was God then when he was needed? She lived her faith, every day in her deeds. She did not just waste her breath in prayer.'

'I know.' Mother Superior held her peace.

'It is guilt for being left alive that has done this to her. She cannot let go of that guilt. She is alone with a punishment she has devised for herself. Madness is the only retribution she can make.'

'In that case perhaps, for her, madness is a kind of sanity. It is her last refuge and given by God.'

'If you take it from her she will kill herself,' Nadya was sobered by the thought.

'I fear so,' Mother Superior answered. 'Strangely, that is one thing she has not yet tried to do. The infliction of self-punishment is all she is intent upon.'

Nadya sent a cable to Bradley Reed. 'Martha unusable as witness. Mental health does not permit. Have idea to trace Professor Teng, witness to mass killings of soldiers.'

At the Metropolitan Hotel sleep evaded her, even with the swallowing of pills. Every time she shut her eyes she saw once more Martha's unrecognizable face. The mad words screamed through Nadya's head. And as they died, there was always Kenjiro again in her mind, the pressure of his body against her. She remembered the icy, dusty odour of that temple pavilion and in the darkness high above, the rustle of birds or bats. She pressed her lips together; even now those feelings he had ignited still flamed through her, although she could barely remember his face. It was as Kenjiro had said. They had sought only life from each other. But immediately came that other memory, of the cry she had ignored. On the bed she tossed and turned. Sleep did not come until the first light eased into the room.

She went first to the university. The great barn of a place where once the compilers of TECSAT swarmed, was deserted. Even here the ghosts of voices echoed about her. At the university office no one knew anything about Professor Teng. There were few faces or names she now recognized in the Department of Religious Studies. The whole faculty seemed new. She sat down on a low wall outside the university. In her mind China spread out before her, vast and impenetrable as the cosmos. Where could she begin to search for Professor Teng?

A young man hurried out of the building and strode towards her. 'You wish to contact Professor Teng? I was a student of his once. Now I am teaching here. He is alive, and I have seen him recently. Some professors at the university collaborated with the Japanese during the occupation. But Professor Teng is of different political allegiance and could not have returned here without great danger. Had he done so it would have been the end for him. I can direct you to him. He is in the mountains near Hankow.'

It took some days to reach the village beyond Hankow, and a temple on a hill. Nadya was instructed to wait in a draughty hall upon a narrow chair. Light seemed to come from far away, through dusty, latticed windows. A door opened in the far wall and a shaven-headed monk appeared whom at first she did not recognize. He walked towards her and smiled. She stood up in shock. Without the mop of unruly grey hair, Teng appeared a different man. His head, now polished as a nut, reflected the diffused light.

'You did not recognize me in my metamorphosis?' His smile was the same. The robes of the monk became him.

'You are cold? Come.' He led her further into the depths of the temple to a smaller room and a brazier of coals before which he motioned her to sit.

'The war has been good to you,' he acknowledged, looking at her hard.

'Only because I was out of it all. I spent it in America working at Stanford University for Bradley Reed. I'm now in Tokyo with him.' She explained Bradley's position with MacArthur and SCAP, and then explained about the Military Tribunal.

421

'Ah,' Teng breathed. 'A trial. Here news comes to us slowly, if at all. We live in another world, both physically and metaphysically. You must forgive me. I knew nothing of this.'

'How have you come to be here?' she asked, looking out of the window of the small room upon a strip of garden. Beyond it tiers of yellow-tiled roofs descended precipitously down the hillside.

'It was a natural progression. I realize now it is the only life I ever wanted. For the first time I am at peace. Many facets have come together, like a jigsaw settling into place.' Teng poured tea from a small pot into thick, tall Chinese mugs.

'I have come from Nanking.' Nadya told him then about Martha and the two girls. The sight of Teng and his compassionate face, seemed to bring to a head everything she had tried to hold back. Teng shook his head sadly but said nothing.

'Does nothing disturb you?' she asked, drying her eyes. He smiled slightly.

'Why do you say I am never disturbed? Each one of us, saint or murderer, contains within us a divine spark. We are born with it and forget it as we grow. It is our task in this life to re-find that spark. But for this war I would not have found my way here. I would still be compiling history books,' he laughed. Nadya saw him again with his untidy grey hair and the long scholar's robe.

'Would you come as a prosecution witness to Tokyo?' she asked at last, after they had talked, drinking the clear amber tea. He seemed bemused.

'A prosecution witness? What good is a trial? What can it do?'

'Bring to justice those who deserve it. You were there in Nanking. You saw what we all saw,' she replied.

'To meet vengeance with vengeance, what good is that? I am not interested in such schemes. I cannot believe in the trial you speak of. Each man is tried by God and indeed tries himself by the deeds of his life.'

'But in worldly terms it must be done. In Germany too such a trial is going on. These criminals must be brought to justice.'

'Criminals or victims, all are caught in the same cage. Those who do violence only enslave themselves. But there is a Buddhist proverb that says, *He who lays down the butcher's knife can become a Buddha immediately*. I know such a man, a Japanese soldier,' Teng informed her.

'A Japanese soldier? Where can I find him? If he would testify it would be excellent.'

A look of annoyance passed over Teng's face. 'This man is not a man for your trial. Forget him.' He spoke brusquely.

'But we live in this world and it wants its pound of flesh. It wants also a memory defined for future generations. And would you see people who maybe helped you escape condemned because you were not there to collaborate a story?' She thought suddenly of Kenjiro, not knowing what had become of him, or what this trial might hold for him. She had found out only that he had spent time in gaol on several occasions because of his beliefs.

'The world cannot take your spiritual way. This trial is a complex thing. The world is watching and Japan is waiting. Perhaps your testimony may save the innocent rather than condemn the guilty.' She was desperate to persuade him.

He was silent for some moments. 'I will think about it,' he said at last. 'The way will be shown me. I will send you my answer.'

Outside the sun was setting now upon the roofs of the temple, the ripe crimson light reflecting across the sky, streaking the undersides of clouds and spreading to enclose them. They watched in silence as the sun sank lower towards the crest of the hills, and finally vanished beneath it.

'Like a penny down a drain, that last sinking of the sun. Here one moment and then gone the next, irretrievably. Like a man's life.' Teng smiled.

He did not let her see his confusion. Before him the world appeared peaceful, touched as it was by an omnipresent light. He had come here to find that still core in himself, to shut away experience. Now, suddenly, he wondered if such a sequestering was right. It had been a shock to see Nadya. Her face brought back the world. A trial. Trials were a game of winners and losers. Nobody was interested in the truth. The truth was incidental. What good would it do? Society seemed never to advance, it receded as fast on one side as it gained on the other. Its progress was only apparent. Civilized man might build a train, but lose the use of his feet. What good at this trial would his testimony be? Confusion pressed hard upon him.

Yet he knew already that he must go. Memory passed into history, and history was quickly forgotten. What meaning was there to his life if accountability was absent? He had been witness to the death of thousands who could give no testament. He had stood in the midst of a brutal history. If he turned his back, if he did not speak against that darkness buried in each man, the rape of Nanking might sink from sight, unknown in the ocean of time. Teng sipped his tea thoughtfully.

The world existed for the education of men. History had value only when a man could use events as a means to read himself. Then the panorama of the past, gloried or sullied as it might be, could be used for his own development. Nations, like men, had their subconscious into which Teng saw now he must place his own splinter of knowledge. Not to stand witness to experience would be to negate reality. Here in this temple, like a fisherman with a rod, he had sought the minnow of truth that swam within himself. He saw now at last that Truth stood outside him, held in the hands of the dead.

'I will speak to the Chief Abbot. Perhaps I do not need to think so much about this. Perhaps it is destined that I should come to your trial.' He bowed his head to her, as if in supplication to something greater than himself.

38

1946

Full Circle

Even on the first day of the trial, Nadya had still heard nothing from Donald. Perhaps he would not come. With Donald anything was possible. She told herself she did not want to see him, that it was no great matter if he appeared or not. But, as the days to the start of the trial drew near, she knew the tension in her body had nothing to do with the issues of impending criminality.

'Where is your boyfriend, husband or whatever he is?' Bradley stormed, as the days closed in with no news of Donald's arrival. Bradley finally cabled *The Times* in London, but they knew only that Donald Addison had already left to cover the trial. Nadya felt sick with apprehension. Adrenaline raced through her body.

'He will turn up,' she said.

'Like a bad penny,' Bradley fumed. 'Every other witness we called has already either arrived, or is in touch with us. The China evidence consists of the first phase of this trial. We can't wait forever for people. In Nuremberg the Germans are holding their war crimes trial parallel with this. I've heard Addison has been covering that too.' Nadya frowned, annoyed at not being told this news before.

The day of 3rd May was overcast, grey but breaking in places as the sun pushed through. The spring weather was at its best, not yet touched by humidity. A sense of history edged the day. From early in the morning people made their way up Ichigaya. The hill rose over Tokyo. Upon its crest sat a powerful three-storeyed building that until the surrender had housed the Ministry of War. From this hill the building had reared above the town like a temple to an insatiable God. To stage the trial here had been seen by General MacArthur as poetic justice.

It was also one of the few large buildings to have escaped Allied bombing. The great hall in which once the cream of Japan's military cadets celebrated graduation, had been transformed through months of work into a modern courtroom. Walls were panelled and floors thickly carpeted. There were special sections for the defendants and their attorneys, the prosecution, and the eleven judges. Translators had a sector of their own; the trial was to be conducted in both Japanese and English. There was a public gallery as well as boxes for special personnel. A large area for both Allied and Japanese press acknowledged world interest in the trial. Huge klieg lights hung from the ceiling to illuminate the proceedings for the cameras. The public atmosphere of the trial was undeniable. All the Class A criminals were to be tried here. Class B and C criminals would be tried simultaneously at a number of courtrooms in Yokohama and also at numerous other courtrooms across south-east Asia. Nadya sat that first day with Bradley in a box for special allied personnel. She immediately scanned the press below but could not see Donald.

All the Class A criminals were held at Sugamo Prison. From there they were brought by bus to the courthouse each day. The judges arrived first, in black limousines. There were eleven judges, nine of whom were nominated by those Allied countries who were signatories to the surrender. They filed in with expressions suitable for the sombre occasion. The courtroom hummed with excitement. At last the twenty-six Class A prisoners entered, and the great hall fell silent to observe in full these architects of death.

Their shabby ordinariness came as a shock. After months of prolonged stress and prison food, their suits now hung upon them. Several supported themselves upon canes. Amongst them General Matsui shuffled forward and seemed to have shrunk, smaller than a gnome. Marquis Kido, always sanguine, now looked ill at ease. General Tojo strode forward in his inimitable way. Behind him Colonel Hashimoto looked about defiantly as did Colonel Muto. Only the intellectual, Shumei Okawa, stood apart from his colleagues with a vague expression. He removed his jacket upon a creased shirt and clacked about upon Japanese clogs. He was asked to remove these before entering the courtroom, and given soft slippers instead. The defendants filed in and took their seats according to a prearranged plan. They would take the same seats every day for the length of the trial, however long it might last.

It was then, looking down again to scour the press box, that Nadya at last saw Donald. There was a strange constriction through her body. He sat with his back towards her, but she knew him immediately, even after so many years.

'About time,' said Bradley, when she pointed him out. 'Look at Tojo, spry as ever. You wouldn't think he tried suicide a few months ago.'

Nadya paid little attention to Bradley's comments, her eyes were still upon Donald. He made no attempt to look about, as she wished he would. It was impossible to concentrate wholly on the historic events about her, now she knew Donald was there. Eventually, the heavy doors of the courtroom closed. The defendants adjusted their earphones through which the simultaneous Japanese translation would be relayed.

'The International Military Tribunal for the Far East is in session and is ready to hear any matter brought before it,' a marshal of the court declared. There was a clearing of throats and the rustle of people settling. The President of the International Military Tribunal for the Far East, Chief Justice Sir William Webb of Australia, spoke the first words of the trial.

'We fully appreciate the great responsibility resting upon us. There has been no more important trial in history. To our great task we bring open minds both on the facts and on the law. The onus will be on the prosecution to establish guilt beyond reasonable doubt. The crimes alleged are crimes against the peace of the world, against the laws of war and against humanity, and conspiracy to commit these crimes. They are so many and so great that it was decided the appropriate forum would be a military tribunal of an international character . . .' Sir William Webb spoke fluently, his hawk-like nose seemed to fill his face.

In the dock General Tojo sat forward, his hands cupped about his earphones, listening intently, as did the other defendants. Behind Tojo sat Shumei Okawa, gaunt and tall, with thick-rimmed glasses upon his nose. He appeared not to heed the proceedings, repeatedly clasping his hands in prayer. He unbuttoned and then rebuttoned his shirt. As Webb finished reading his opening statement there was a moment of silence. In the dock the defendants surveyed the courtroom, as if they were actors in a play, expecting a round of applause. Instead there was silence in the great auditorium. Already it was midday. Soon the court recessed until 2.30 p.m.

Nadya pushed her way down the crowded flights of stairs and made her way to the press section. Donald was nowhere to be seen. She edged her way forward between the mass of people, all animatedly discussing the morning's events. The heat of the klieg lights beat down from above. She craned her neck to see across the courtroom, searching for him.

'Mrs Addison, I presume?' Donald spoke from behind her. She swung around to face him.

The same disrespectful smile, the same quizzical stare. He appeared no different to that first meeting upon Nanking's walls. The huge lights above illuminated a familiar beige linen suit.

'I can't see you for light,' she shaded her eyes in mock horror.

He came forward and gripped her arm, kissing her on the cheek. The familiar scent of him rushed through her. She saw now there were lines

427

upon his face she did not remember, grey streaked his straw-coloured hair. He looked older and had acquired an expression of austerity.

'Where were you? We expected you earlier. Bradley even cabled *The Times*,' she scolded.

'I arrived last night. Between here and Nuremberg there is no room for breath. But you look good.' He stared down into her face with a sad smile.

'If I do it's because I escaped a war,' she answered.

'No need to sound guilty. If you'd been where I've been you'd know half the world has dreamed of escape. You were one of the lucky ones. God was on your side.' He took her arm and guided her forward. 'Let's get some lunch. I'm starving.'

She sensed something new within him. Much of the old bravado seemed gone. 'I can see it's not been a good war for you? Where were you?' she asked, slipping into the old flippant tone of voice, waiting for Donald to sling the usual handful of irreverent words.

'I was everywhere. Normandy, Paris, Warsaw, Guadalcanal, Manila, Okinawa, Berlin to name a few. And the liberation of Belsen and Auschwitz.' His voice fell suddenly low. 'And what war is good? But men will fight. They'll fight again as soon as this mess is cleared up.' The censorious tone surprised her.

'I didn't mean to sound flippant, but you usually demand it from people.' She sat back in her chair and sipped a beer, observing him curiously across the table.

'Perhaps by now I've seen too much to keep up that line of defence,' he replied. He looked down at the steak that had been placed before him.

'A line of defence? Yes, perhaps that was what it was. But you were fun when you were nice, which of course got less and less. Now you don't look like you know what fun is,' Nadya replied.

'A case of temporary amnesia maybe. I'll be all right. Auschwitz and Belsen, those camps shook me up like nothing since Nanking. And I was only an observer to the leftovers.' He took a long drink of his beer. 'I'm not looking forward to re-living Nanking. I couldn't handle it then. I don't know if I can now. Who else is here?'

'I'm not sure yet,' Nadya replied and then told him about the visit to Teng, and about Martha.

'She did so much, helped so many. Nothing makes sense in this life,' Donald's voice was low and intense.

'Neither can Martha make sense of fate, I suspect,' Nadya answered. The disconcerting change in Donald gnawed at her, eroding old perceptions.

428

'We all punish ourselves for our inadequacies,' he replied but did not elaborate. 'I can always say I did one good thing in this war. I gave you the means to get to America, out of the whole damn horrible thing.' Donald grinned suddenly. 'God knows what you might have got caught up in otherwise. You always did insist upon putting yourself where the most trouble was,' he added, almost to himself.

There was an ease between them, different in quality from anything Nadya remembered. It was eight years since she had seen him. 'You know there is no binding, no obligation if you wish to be free. If you have met someone else.' She looked away, not meeting his eye. Suddenly it was important to know if there was someone else.

'You would have heard if that was so,' he smiled. 'And of course the same goes for you. We agreed on all this long before. For myself I seem to have been too busy throwing myself into the front line trenches to think of more weighty things.'

'I just thought the contract may need updating. I wanted only to be honest with you.' She was surprised at her relief on hearing his reply. As always, it was difficult to understand the strange heap of emotions that lay between them.

'You are always honest,' he smiled, remembering the night on the Lotus Lake.

They returned to the press section. He persuaded her to leave Bradley in the VIP enclosure and sit beside him, where, as he said, the action was. 'This is all so different from the Nuremberg trials. I don't like the atmosphere here. They say Keenan is a drunk. It's all arranged as pure theatre. Look at the opulence of this courtroom for a start. At Nuremberg the decor is simple, they've relied on the majesty of the concept of justice to set the tone of the trial. This trial is to be played to the world as theatre, no doubt about it.' He was already scribbling down notes. 'All these klieg lights for a start make it appear like a Hollywood première.'

'Will you write that?' Nadya asked.

'If that is what it turns out to be. I'm also honest in my way.' Donald took her hand and turned it over absently to examine her palm.

'Your life line is long,' he remarked, as if he had forgotten why he took her hand in the first place. He laid it back upon her lap.

Soon the proceedings began again with the reading of the indictment. This was undertaken in relays, for the counts were many. Once more Tojo sat forward as in the morning, to catch each word. At times he leaned back with a dispirited expression, before alerting himself again. As in the morning Shumei Okawa, seated directly behind General Tojo, rolled his eyes about like an imbecile, paying no heed to anything. He continuously buttoned and unbuttoned his shirt, scratching at his chest. Finally the shirt slipped from his shoulder as Okawa smiled inanely. Sir William Webb stopped the hearing and ordered a young military policeman to see Okawa kept his shirt on. Whenever Okawa reached for his buttons the MP placed a restraining hand upon him. Okawa continued to smile amiably. The reading of the charges advanced and Okawa created no more disturbance.

The count of indictments had reached number twenty-two. The names were read out of those in the dock, charging that 'on or about the 7th December 1941 they initiated a war of aggression and a war in violation of international law, treaties and agreements against the British Commonwealth . . '

Okawa rolled up the sheet of paper stating the charges against him, leaned forward suddenly and struck Tojo's bald head resoundingly. Tojo turned in shock, anger flushing his face. Okawa stood up and struck him a second time. MPs rushed forward and hauled Okawa from the dock. The court stirred noisily. Okawa's voice was heard, yelling in English, as he left the room.

'Tojo is a fool. I will kill him.'

Donald jumped up and rushed from the press section. Nadya attempted to follow him and then sat down, unable to push through the crowd. Outside in the corridor Okawa was still yelling.

'Tojo is a fool. I'm for democracy. America is not a democracy. She is Demo-crazy. I am a doctor of law and medicine. I haven't eaten in seventy days. This is because I have found a way to get nourishment from the air. I am the next Emperor of Japan. I must kill Tojo. I must kill him to save my country.'

Flash bulbs were popping. Okawa sat down upon a couch in the corridor. 'Give me a cigarette,' he demanded. 'Do not worry about me. I will show the world how to live on air. Shall I show you what I did to Tojo?' He stood up again and began to hit a Japanese journalist about the head. The flash bulbs popped until he was dragged away, back to Sugamo Prison.

Kenjiro Nozaki sat back in shock in his seat in the public gallery. *He's mad. Quite mad.* The whispers buzzed about him at Shumei Okawa's performance. And that, he knew, was what it was, no more than a performance. It was typical of Okawa to pull something off like this. Probably, he would get away with it. Okawa always got away with things; thuggery and murder and chicanery. There was not a political plot of the last two decades that had not been scripted by Okawa. A little acted madness was nothing to him. If, for a while, the world thought him a fool, Okawa would have the last laugh.

The Americans were naïve, Kenjiro thought angrily. Whatever the conditions of the day, a sub-culture of Okawa's adherents were buried in the woodwork of Japan. They would emerge in disguise to prove him mad, and allow him to evade a trial. Even as these thoughts flashed through his mind, he remembered that night long before when right-wing extremists had broken into his home, killing old Chieko, forcing him to flee Japan, placing him upon a path he might otherwise not have taken. No one else had the guile of Okawa. Even about Tojo, whatever his arrogance, there was a sense of directness and decency respected by those who served him. He had none of Okawa's slipperiness.

Kenjiro was depressed, the heaviness would not lift. The trial appeared to have started on a deplorably comic note. Would the drama and tragedy of the era ever come across? He had heard titters of laughter amongst the American spectators at Okawa's behaviour, and listened to comments by foreign newsmen on the theatricality of the first day. He controlled the rage of shame he felt before the arrogance of these foreigners with their superior expressions. And yet he could not deny that the nation had brought this fate upon itself. It had deceived itself by a slavish lack of criticism for those in authority. Could a people be held responsible for the society they lived in? And if they were not held accountable, how could a liberal society survive? Was that what had happened here?

Kenjiro stared at the box of elderly defendants. He dreaded re-living Nanking. It seemed strange, after a lifetime of persecution, to suddenly find his principles were fashionable. In spite of this, he could not dispel discomfort at the thought of standing in the witness-box to prosecute those of whom he knew nothing. Some of the men in the dock should not be there at all. Others, whose bestiality was beyond belief, had escaped detection or arrest.

There was also, he had discovered, to be a special immunity from prosecution for the Princes of the Blood. It was possible to see a case, rightly or wrongly, of immunity for the Emperor. But why should Prince Asaka, a Commander in the field, not stand before the court to answer with others for the rape of Nanking? Innocent or guilty, Kenjiro did not understand why so many well-known faces were deliberately to be excluded from the trial. Where, for instance, was General Nakajima? Why would he not be testifying? Was he being kept for later exhibition? How much would be manipulated to suit the American prosecution? Did they not realize they were perpetuating indefinitely by these tactics the circle of irresponsibility already present in Japanese society? After Hiroshima it was so easy for the nation to forget that Japan was also an aggressor. Kenjiro feared the responsibility for that aggression would be passed around for ever more, from the military to the police to the politicians to the bureaucrats and back again. In this cycle all need for self-examination could be avoided forever.

One part of Kenjiro had been greatly relieved that the Emperor was not to stand trial. On another less emotional level, he was unsure. By escaping trial and retaining his status, the Emperor evaded all blame for the war. It was of course difficult to determine the degree of that blame but, identification with the monarch was so strong that by allowing him to appear innocent he would become the symbol of an innocent nation. It would be forgotten in decades to come that the nation must examine the issue of its own guilt. The experience of Hiroshima would allow Japan to see itself only as a victim.

There was also the issue, that had worried Kenjiro so long ago, of medical research upon live Chinese and Allied prisoners in the pursuit of biological warfare. What Fukutake had hinted at in Nanking had been true. It was rumoured a mega-weapon of lethal proportions had indeed been developed. Apparently, no word of this criminal research, involving in its development the slaughter of hundreds of thousands of defenceless people, was to be raised in the trial. It was said a deal had been struck behind the scenes between Japan and America. In exchange for the results of Japan's long years of gruesome research, the Americans would grant immunity to those involved with it. A whole diabolical chapter of history was to be erased for the benefit of America. What other deals had been struck that nobody knew about? The whole trial had an odour. Kenjiro gave an exasperated sigh.

He had already seen Nadya down in the press section, sitting with the British journalist, Addison. Both appeared to him unchanged. Addison might look older, but Nadya seemed unscathed by war, with a freshness that took his breath away. It seemed strange now to think that once their bodies had met in a madness beyond control, risking death. The more he looked at her, the less he could believe such intimacy had passed between them. And yet, he still remembered that demented grasping at life in the midst of death.

He stood up slowly. He had now to use a cane to walk. Strange pains and symptoms afflicted him. Much of the time he felt weak, and very ill. He had lost much of his hair. Too little was known about the Hiroshima bomb to give him a prognosis. In this flamboyant trial nobody had yet mentioned that bomb, except in terms of triumphant finality. Yet was that not also as great a crime against humanity as any argued here? He felt an artificiality in the courtroom. There was the trumping up of certain facets of life and an ignoring of others of equal importance. But such things were inevitable he supposed, in a process as complex as this.

He made his way down in the next recess and at last found his way to Nadya. As he expected, she took a moment to recognize him.

'I know, it has been a long time and much has happened.' Kenjiro saw her staring at the keloid that had developed across his cheek. 'It is a minor one and I am told it will go.' He saw she did not understand. It was Addison who asked the question.

'Are those sort of things not the results of the atomic bomb?'

Kenjiro nodded. 'I was lucky. I was some distance from the bomb. A warehouse shielded me from the worst effects, and then collapsed upon me.' He explained about the prison camp in Hiroshima. Donald searched for words to adequately describe his horror, but finding nothing meaningful, remained silent.

'At the Nanking Embassy they would tell me only that you had returned to Japan.' Nadya continued to observe Kenjiro in distress. What had passed between them, however brief, still remained linking them, like a frail bridge.

'I have seen Professor Teng. I was sent to China to find him for the prosecution,' Nadya explained.

'Teng?' Kenjiro turned to her in amazement.

'He is coming here in the next few days,' she told him. She was conscious of Donald assessing the unspoken exchange between them, aware of things he did not know.

'Are you a witness for the prosecution or the defence?' Donald asked suddenly.

'Both, I think,' Kenjiro replied. 'Until now I have been a black sheep in Japan for my views. In a trial like this I feel there is little to lose in doing what I can for both sides. I saw enough in Nanking. As you know, we at the Embassy could do little to stop it. I am willing to bear witness to that.'

'And the defence?' Nadya asked. She had not seen Kenjiro's name on either prosecution or defence witness lists, but each day new witnesses were being found. It would go on like this for the length of the trial, according to Bradley.

'Tilik Dayal has been arrested on charges of war crimes and collaboration with the military regime. He too was there in Hiroshima. He was but a minor cog in a vicious wheel, and towards the end against his will. There was much human decency in him. He managed to find it before it was too late.' Kenjiro looked directly at Nadya. 'But for Dayal, Teng would not have escaped. Teng too might stand witness for the defence when he knows Dayal has been arrested.'

'Professor Teng has become a monk,' Nadya told him.

'That was always his true vocation.' Kenjiro appeared unsurprised.

The great lights in the ceiling blazed down upon them, setting Nadya's red hair on fire. Kenjiro could not take his eyes from the fiery halo, swinging about her head. It was what had first drawn him to her. Now, looking back, one part of his life appeared to fit neatly into another, like a set of Chinese boxes. Each separate entity contained its small pile of memories, yet added to the weight of the whole. He felt only gratitude that once this woman had come to him, sharing life. He felt grateful now for all experience, good or bad. Each distilled its necessary residue. He no longer mourned Jacqueline, but felt this same thankfulness fill him. Now, his thoughts were only for his daughter, Naomi. What time he had left, and he felt there was little although the doctors refused to agree, he wished to live for her. His parents were old and frail. He intended to send Naomi back regularly to France. There she would discover another side of herself and a younger set of grandparents, who would care for her if he should worsen and die.

He saw that between Nadya and Addison, as he had always suspected, lay feelings neither would admit. Time brought everything full circle, he thought. And time brought the only perspectives. Little escaped its working or judgement, however strange its ways. He thought again of Teng, and could not believe they would soon meet.

39

1946

Sugamo

News found its way about the prison quickly, especially on bath nights. Rumours twisted through the steam. Twice a week at Sugamo, gossip was as important as cleanliness. Many prisoners of the various classes were held together at Sugamo. On these nights, news of the Yokohama courthouse was exchanged for an earful of Ichigaya courthouse gossip. The news tonight was all of one thing. Shumei Okawa had gone mad. Now, instead of sitting in the dock he was in hospital being examined by American psychiatrists.

'He is a genius,' said a man called Toda, a Class B criminal who had something to do with atrocities on the Baatan death march. He spoke to Tilik from beneath a shower of hot water, before approaching the rows of steaming wooden tubs.

'I have met Okawa. He is not a man to go mad,' Tilik replied as Toda got in the bath beside him. 'If he was not an intellectual, he would have made a great actor.' He remembered the force of the man, the energy and the oratory that swayed people to his ideas. Okawa was also, he realized now, sharpened by animal cunning. He thought again of Okawa's lectures, and the pounding rhetorical stance through those books Rash Bihari had lent him at their first meeting.

'I have it from reliable sources that Okawa now regales American and Japanese doctors with accounts of visitations from Emperor Meiji, Edward VII of England, President Woodrow Wilson and the Prophet Mohammed. Japanese doctors are persuading our naïve American friends that he is suffering from tertiary syphilis. I am told this condition is irreversible and leads to insanity and a quick death. Many of us here will soon be dead, but I predict Okawa will sit out this trial in the comfort of a sanatorium. When all is over and done, he will miraculously recover from his deadly disease and live to a ripe old age. The whole thing is a hoax,' Toda chuckled.

Since he was of a different race to the other prisoners, Tilik had no cell mate. The segregation was for the sake of order. Even before the trial began in Ichigaya, the noose and the trap-door were in service in Sugamo Prison. The trial of the Class B and C criminals had started in Yokohama some time before. For them the first executions had already begun. A tremor darted wildly about the prison at the end of April, when the first hanging occurred. Sometimes, in his sleep Tilik dreamed he heard the crash of the trap-door early in the morning, and awoke with sweat pouring off him. He was not important enough to warrant a noose, being only a petty Class C criminal, but there might be years of incarceration. Or even repatriation to India. There he would stand trial with those members of the INA who had been turned over to the British after the surrender. This too was a recurrent nightmare. But somehow, nothing now seemed to matter after what he had witnessed in Hiroshima. The whole of his life, swinging away behind that one explosion, seemed now to take on new perspectives. It would live with him for ever. He did not know anyone else in the prison who had seen the bomb.

He was surprised the next day to be told he had a visitor. Visits were allowed only once a month from relatives, and Michiko had been the week before. She was not well and both children were also sick. It had been explained they were nearer the blast than he. He was now never without an underlying worry for them. A hundred yards this way or that, a wall here or there to protect, everything seemed to have made a difference with that bomb in Hiroshima. Chance drew its arbitrary lines between who should live, or die.

He followed the young American MP up to the room where Class C visits were allowed. At first he hardly recognized Nozaki. What little hair was left had turned white, and an ugly keloid covered part of his cheek. Although little more than forty-five, he already looked an old man.

'In my opinion you should not be here,' Kenjiro said sitting down before Tilik. 'This is a strange trial. The more I think of it, the more confused I become. There are of course lofty ideals involved, but also ideals that are not so lofty. This is very much a victor's justice. Who is really to judge whom? If I had not been caught in Hiroshima, I might be speaking differently. This whole trial sometimes seems no more than an excuse to prove legitimacy for the dropping of those two great bombs. I make no excuse for Japan, but lust for power is in all men and all nations.'

'I suspect we shall hear *nothing* of the dropping of those atomic bombs,' Tilik speculated.

'They have taken us into a new era of warfare and morality. What is being discussed here is already partially obsolete. The question for the future is whether it is legitimate by such indiscriminate slaughter to win

436

victory, breaking the will of a whole nation to continue to fight. Of course, the argument now is that lives were saved upon both sides, but that is not really an argument when one considers the millions upon millions of lives already wasted. Japan would have surrendered within a few days of that bomb. Negotiations were already in progress. Why did they not drop it on some uninhabited island to show us first what it could do? Nothing validates the dropping of those bombs on Hiroshima and Nagasaki.' Kenjiro clenched his teeth together.

'Governments not men create war,' Tilik answered with a sad sigh.

'I do not agree,' Kenjiro protested. 'If one man refused to kill another, governments could do nothing. Men are indoctrinated to think of the enemy as the devil incarnate. In this great tribunal the guilt of war does not appear to reach beyond the twenty-eight old men sitting in the dock. In that courtroom a war is still going on. It is the final nailing, the final retaliation. Magnanimity, understanding and charity are what we need, and they are not there. This trial is political and few of those whose deeds reached demonic levels will ever come to light. Which of us, tell me also, is free of that dark side in ourselves? Is it not better to be killed than to kill? This question comes to me always. Killing to order, killing for pleasure, for sport. Nanking still fills my dreams, you know. I shall never be free.'

They sat in silence for some moments. Then Kenjiro spoke again. 'I did not come to tell you this. Although I am to be a witness for the prosecution with regard to Nanking, I want to tell you I shall also be a witness for the defence on your behalf. We have nothing to fear now from the *Kempeitai*. I shall tell how you freed Professor Teng, a Chinese prisoner, at the risk of your own life. Teng is also expected here soon. I have no doubt he will also take the stand in your defence.'

'I am most grateful,' Tilik replied. He felt a tightening in his throat. His whole life seemed suddenly to condense before him, strange and inexplicable. The threads that should have run strongly through it were frayed beyond recognition.

The MP came towards them, signalling that their time was over. Kenjiro stood up, leaning heavily upon his cane.

On another floor in Sugamo, Donald Addison waited to meet General Matsui. Soon he was led to the General's cell with an interpreter. Matsui sat reading, and looked up as Donald entered. At first his face was blank.

'My friend Mr Addison. My publicity agent still?' The General smiled in sudden recognition.

'Yes indeed,' Donald answered.

437

Matsui gestured him to sit down upon a chair the MP had brought into the cell. The interpreter stood behind them.

'For a time I had a cell mate, Mr Okawa, but he went mad and they took him away. So now I am alone,' Matsui explained.

'Some people are saying Okawa's madness is a hoax,' Donald suggested.

Matsui looked at him hard. 'Mr Okawa was never a soldier. Those of us in the military are more used to the idea of death perhaps.'

They spoke for some moments about life in Sugamo and the General's state of health. Matsui did not look well, his frailty had a new brittleness. 'We are all preparing ourselves for the end. We read religious books, meditate, write. A priest attends us. It is a peaceful life, much as we might lead in a monastery.' The General's eyes lit up with a flash of sudden humour.

'I am sorry to see you here,' Donald said quietly.

'What else could be expected? Someone was needed to take responsibility for Nanking,' Matsui replied. 'You know my point of view. I have explained it to you already.'

'I hope it will be understood,' Donald replied. 'Where are the other commanders of Nanking? What about Prince Asaka and General Nakajima? Are you covering up for them?'

'Soon after I last saw you we were all recalled to Japan. I and Yanagawa and Prince Asaka with more than eighty officers. Counsellor Hidaka had visited Nanking and sent back a report to the Foreign Ministry. It caused an uproar, I believe. But when we returned, the Emperor personally rewarded us for the victory at Nanking. We received silver vases embossed with the crest of the Imperial Chrysanthemum. In spite of Hidaka's report, everyone except myself received promotions for their part in Nanking. But I retired to my home in Atami. I spent many hours there facing the sea and the gnarled pines that litter that rocky coast, deformed by the blast of the wind. They echoed the state of my soul.'

He explained to Donald that he had built on his estate a small shrine. Its base was of clay dug from the banks of the Yangtze about Nanking. It stood on a southwesterly point, looking out across the sea to China. Within it hung mementoes of the Chinese war dead. On an opposite wall hung mementoes of the Japanese dead. Between these knelt a priestess, chanting prayers and lamentations. Her duty was to weep. On a promontory behind the shrine, further up the hill, stood a statue of Kwannon, Goddess of Mercy. There was a crudeness about her, she was not cast in expensive bronze, or carved from costly marble. She was fired from a muddy mix of clay, half from the far away banks of the Yangtze, half from the soil of Japan.

'I have made my amends to a power greater than any man,' Matsui declared. 'I often wondered why I of all men was brought out of retirement for the battle in China. I see now that to many I appeared dispensable. The noose awaits me. And I deserve it. I should have done more to guide those in command. It is my duty now to die for the protection of the throne and the country. I am happy to end this way. Seeing now the way things have turned out, I am in fact eager to die at any time. I can face it calmly, I assure you.' He smiled slightly at the worried look on Donald's face. 'They have arrested Colonel Hashimoto too, you know. He will get what he deserves.' A look of sudden satisfaction filled Matsui's eyes.

'There are some who say the period covered by the indictment is faulty. That Japan accepted the Potsdam Declaration at the end of the 1941–45 war. If this is so, the conquest of Manchuria and of China do not come into the trial at all. The defence is to argue this point. If it is accepted then your part in the war is irrelevant,' Donald informed him.

Matsui shook his head and smiled. An expression of patience filled his thin face. 'This will not be supported. Potsdam or not, our war began with Manchuria. What occurred in 1941 was an escalation and one that from the beginning had been half-anticipated.'

'I wanted to tell you that in my reports I intend to speak of the difficulties of your position and that you tried to impose discipline but were not obeyed.'

'I appreciate your concern.' General Matsui bowed his head slightly. 'But it will do little good. They call me the Butcher of Nanking.' His thin voice broke in bitterness.

'That title should go to others. A scapegoat is needed,' Donald replied.

'I am happy to be that. I have thought for many years, day after day, upon all that has happened and pondered it deeply. My death is the only payment now that I can make.' Matsui repeated his earlier sentiments. 'All of us here regard ourselves as no more than symbols of the guilt that Japan is seen to carry by the rest of the world. We do not ourselves feel guilty in the way your western nations view it. Our guilt as we see it, is for having let our nation down, for the *face* Japan has lost. But to free the country, to purify its soul in the eyes of the Allied nations, we are happy to die as a symbolic sacrifice to the angry spirits of those Japan is seen to have wronged.' Matsui looked down once more at his book of Buddhist scriptures.

Donald stood up and bowed to the General. There was a serenity in his expression that Donald hoped was more than simple resignation to his fate. Donald turned, and the waiting MP closed the cell door behind him. At the gate, as he left Sugamo, he was surprised to see Kenjiro Nozaki and hurried to catch him up.

In his cell Tilik lay back upon his mat. He could make no sense of the future as yet. It was well over a year since Rash Bihari's death, not long after that visit from Subash Chandra Bose. Who knew also what awaited India now? At last Independence was discussed as if it might become reality. But Subash was also now dead.

His death had come as a shock to Tilik. Once more he was left adrift upon an uncharted sea. The unfinished manner of Subash's death seemed only to add to Tilik's own unresolved state. It was said Subash had died in a plane crash after Japan's surrender. In the panic of those first few days after the surrender, Subash Chandra Bose had dashed from Rangoon to Singapore and then on to Saigon. If he fell into British hands he would be tried as a traitor. The Japanese could do nothing more for him, and regarded him as a nuisance. Which country now could he turn to? It was said he decided Russia would be best and became desperate to get to Moscow. First these plans had to be finalized with his old contacts in Japan. He set off from Saigon in a Japanese plane, bound for Tokyo with several of his aides. Taking off after a stopover in Taipei, Subash's plane had crashed in flames.

Nothing but question marks surrounded his death. It was said a chest of treasure travelled with him as he fled. Japan wanted no more to do with him, it had already troubles enough. Why should he go to Russia, friend of Britain, who had just declared war on Japan? Why, if his plans had been successful, should any Japanese plane be prepared to fly him to Russia in such circumstances? Some of those on the aircraft with Subash and declared dead like him, it was whispered were still alive. Was Subash himself still alive, or really dead? Had he been captured by the British? Had he committed suicide? Was he murdered by Japan or Britain? Or even by his aides, for the treasure, and immunity from British prosecution?

These thoughts swirled about Tilik's head. Some definite knowledge of Subash's end, or a new beginning with him if he were still alive, might have given continuity. Instead, Tilik was left with question marks. He whimpered in the tiny cell.

40

1946

The Distance of Time

Chief Counsel for the Prosecution, Joseph Keenan, had earlier announced in his opening statement.

'The war which Japan waged against China and which Japanese leaders falsely described as the China Incident or the China Affair, began on the night of 18th September 1931 and ended with the surrender of Japan in Tokyo Bay on 2nd September 1945. The first phase of this war consisted of the invasion, occupation and consolidation by Japan of that part of China known as Manchuria, and of the Province of Jehol. The second phase of this war began on 7th July 1937, when Japanese troops attacked near Peking following the Marco Polo Bridge Incident, and consisted of successive advances, each followed by brief periods of consolidation in preparation for further advances into Chinese territory. Some of the accused were active in this war from the very beginning, others participated as it progressed. It is not too much to say that the fuse of the European war was first attached to the China Incident.'

Now at last that part of the trial concerning China began. Many weeks of testimony had already gone by examining not only the invasion of Manchuria, but also army intrigues that propelled events forward towards the rape of Nanking, and then the Pacific war.

The weather had progressed from spring to early summer. Now the rain beat down and in the Ichigaya courtroom the humidity was intense. People fanned themselves with reports, mopping sweat from brows with handkerchiefs. Soon there would be a summer recess, and air-conditioning installed. The great lights still burned, further heating the air unbearably.

General Matsui perspired freely in the dock. His thin face took on a ferret-like look as the evidence of witness after witness surfaced. Officers were called to the stand who had once been under Matsui's command. In the dock General Matsui stared ahead, aware of the court's gaze upon him. He wore the look of a man who wished the floor would swallow

441

him up. The courtroom was packed with spectators. Now at last the tortuous legal arguing would cease for a while, and the meat of the trial would surface. Everyone wanted to hear about the rape of Nanking.

Almost all the members of the Safety Zone Committee were present in the courtroom. They had filed more than seventy reports with the Japanese Embassy over the six week period of the siege. Now, at this distance in time, the desperation of these letters of entreaty seemed no less intense than at the moment of their dispatch. Nadya listened, sitting as she always did now beside Donald. As the trial progressed and the spectre of Nanking loomed, he seemed to regress to the state of fear that had gripped him then. The letters submitted to the Japanese Embassy, many to Kenjiro Nozaki, continued to be read. Each word seemed to push them back, inch by inch, down the dark tunnel of memory, back into the nightmare of Nanking.

'Shameful disorder continues and we see no serious efforts to stop it. The soldiers every day injure hundreds of innocent people most seriously. Does not the Japanese Army care for its reputation? In the name of humanity we appeal to you to stop the slaughter in Nanking.' Letter after letter was read.

Across the courtroom Nadya caught a glimpse of Kenjiro. He held his cane between his knees, his hands rested over its ivory knob. She knew the distress he had felt on receiving those letters. She saw him look up as Herbert Strang took the stand. Mr Metzger followed.

After Mr Strang and Mr Metzger, doctors gave their testimony, one after another, slowly building up the grim evidence. 'Our hospital filled up from the moment the Japanese entered the city and was kept full to overflowing for the next six weeks as was every other hospital in Nanking. The patients usually bore bayonet or bullet wounds. Many of the women patients were the victims of violent sexual assault and were horribly mutilated.' Dr Chen of Martha's hospital had come from Nanking to give this evidence.

A Chinese official from the Ministry of Railways spoke of his experiences. 'Japanese soldiers were rough and barbarous. They shot everyone in sight, like they would shoot rabbits.'

A Chinese merchant testified that he had been arrested with his elder brother and marched, wrists roped together to the Yangtze River. There they joined a thousand men sitting along the bank. Forty yards away a row of machine guns faced them. As the firing began he had slumped to the ground and was immediately covered by corpses and fainted.

It went on and on, until they were all sickeningly satiated by the details.

'We call to the stand Nadya Addison.'

442

She made her way to the witness-box and took the oath as instructed. In her hand she held Martha's diary.

'You were a member of the Safety Zone Committee?' the Prosecution asked.

'Yes. I worked with Dr Martha Clayton as auxiliary help in her hospital.'

'So you saw many cases of the wounded?'

The questions began and she answered as best she could.

'And will you tell us why Dr Clayton is not here,' Nadya was asked at one point.

'She is unable to leave the convent in Nanking where she has been confined by extreme ill health since 1938, several months after the reign of terror in Nanking.'

'You have a diary of Dr Clayton's with you. Would you read us some passages from it?'

Nadya nodded and opened the book and began to read.

'Many hundreds of innocent civilians are taken out before our eyes to be shot or used for bayonet practice, and we must listen to the sound of the guns that are killing them. It seems a rule that anyone who runs must be shot or bayoneted. It is a horrible story to try and relate. I know not where to begin or end. Never have I heard or read of such brutality . . .'

Nadya looked up at last from the book. Tears misted her view of the old men in the dock, who sat huddled within themselves. One or two had sunk their heads in their hands, as if ashamed to hear the details. When she returned to her seat she was shaking. Beside her Donald said nothing. She knew it was not for lack of sympathy but to control his own emotions.

Suddenly, across the court, Teng's name was called out. Nadya looked up in surprise. She knew from Bradley he was supposed to fly in the day before, but there was some delay. She had been told he would arrive a day or two later.

At first, once more, she did not recognize the monk with shaven head and robes who made his way across the court. Under the klieg lights his bald head shone like polished bone. His arms were folded across his chest, hands hidden in the wide sleeves of his gown. He mounted the steps to stand in the witness-box and prepared to answer the questions.

'You were in Nanking at the time of the terror?' The Prosecutor stepped forward.

'At that time I was Professor of Religious Studies at Nanking University. Subsequently, when the terror began I joined the Red Swastika Society, the Chinese equivalent of the Red Cross.'

'You were detailed to bury the dead?'

'The killing was prolific and indiscriminate. The policy was to let the bodies lie where they had died as a lesson to those still living in Nanking. We were not allowed at first to bury the dead. But later, because of the danger to the troops of epidemics we were ordered to begin burials.'

'How many bodies did you bury?'

'We were not permitted to keep records. During the time I worked with the Red Swastika Society it was roughly estimated we buried forty-five thousand bodies. But the actual number must be much higher. I worked with them only for a short time. Most of the corpses we were ordered to bury were those who the military had shot in large batches. Many had their hands tied behind their backs with rope or wire. It is Buddhist practice to unloose a dead body if it has been tied. We wished to bury each body separately but both the numbers we had to deal with, the state of decay and the wire that bound them, made all these things impossible. We had to bury them in mass graves.'

Sir William Webb raised his hand. 'You need not go into these details. The method of disposal of the bodies is not helpful.'

'You were arrested by the Japanese Army? Will you explain how you escaped.'

The examination of Teng's evidence was extensive, but at last it was over.

The next day General Matsui was called. He walked forward, his chin raised firmly. Although many might see him as a criminal, Donald could only view his diminutive figure with respect. Against himself, he had come to feel a bond of friendship towards the General. Matsui exuded a sad nobility as he walked towards the witness-stand. Donald was eager for the packed courtroom to see and hear the man he had met so recently at Sugamo Prison. He was sure the judges would discern that Matsui was no more than a scapegoat in a deadly game; the sincerity of the man would come through to them.

But immediately, Matsui adopted an attitude at odds with the face he had shown Donald at Sugamo. He attempted at first to feign ignorance of atrocities in Nanking, rambling on at considerable length about Chinese-Japanese brotherhood. He sounded to all half-senile.

'I was always firm in the belief that the strife between Japan and China was a quarrel between brothers in the so-called household of Asia. It was no different from an elder brother thrashing his younger recalcitrant brother after putting up with him for so long. The action was to make China come to her senses, not out of hatred, but out of love.' Matsui would not be stopped, in the gallery people yawned. About events in Nanking Matsui was at first slippery.

'You say you heard a rumour towards the end of December about atrocities. Where did this rumour come from?' the prosecution asked.

'I heard from persons who had heard these rumours,' General Matsui answered.

'In your affidavit you say that when you inspected the city on 17th December 1937, you saw only about ten dead Chinese troops lying on the streets. How many bodies of dead civilians, including women and children, did you see?'

'I did not see any,' General Matsui showed no emotion. The Prosecutor frowned.

'The reason I ask is because in your interrogation before this trial you were asked the same question. Your answer then was that *they had all been removed by that time. I saw only a few dead soldiers by the West Gate.* These were your words at that time.'

Later questions turned to his interviews with Donald. 'When did you first see Mr Donald Addison? What did you talk about?'

'I explained to Mr Addison my views with regard to respecting Foreign rights and interests in Shanghai. I explained that I wished to extend the hand of friendship to China.' A stubborn note entered Matsui's voice.

'Did you have further conversation with Mr Addison in January 1938?'

'Yes, I saw him twice. I sent for him. There were many foreign correspondents, but Mr Addison was the one I considered most trustworthy. I met him to hear what he had to say and to impart to him information I had,' General Matsui replied.

'In other words, you wanted to quell the rumours of atrocities abroad at the time.'

'I ordered an investigation into the rumour of these so-called atrocities. I ordered every unit to investigate.' General Matsui answered strongly, his voice rising on his last words.

'Did they report back to you the results of the investigation you ordered?'

'Each specific unit did not report to me directly. If I received reports it would have been for the commanders of the various army divisions.' General Matsui was again evasive.

'What reports did you receive?' Counsel for the Prosecution asked. Matsui was silent for a moment before finally replying reluctantly.

'I received none up to the time of my departure from Shanghai in February 1938, the following year.'

'Did you ask for reports?'

'Yes.'

'We were told in this court earlier by prosecution witness Hidaka, a diplomat who visited Nanking at the height of the outrages, that reports of atrocities in Nanking were sent to the Foreign Office in Tokyo, and to the army in Nanking. Where would such reports go if they went to the army in Nanking?'

'They would go to the Headquarters of the Shanghai Expeditionary Force, that is the Headquarters of General Prince Asaka,' Matsui answered curtly.

'And these headquarters were in Nanking?'

'Inside the walls of Nanking.'

'Are you aware of any communication from Tokyo addressed to anyone in China?'

'I know nothing.' General Matsui pushed his chin forward defiantly over the stiff collar of his uniform.

'Was a communication sent to Prince Asaka, Commander of the Shanghai Expeditionary Force?'

'I did not hear anything.' Matsui's voice was stubborn again.

'The claim is made that Lieutenant General Prince Asaka was a field commander who should have had some control over that part of the army that first entered Nanking. Is it correct that Prince Asaka was so placed?'

'That is correct.'

'And Prince Asaka is married to one of the daughters of the Emperor Meiji?'

'That is correct,' General Matsui was forced to admit.

'Some people claim Prince Asaka was responsible for very much of what happened in Nanking, but because of his relationship with the Imperial family little or nothing has been said about it. Is that correct?'

'I do not think so. Prince Asaka had joined our army in China only ten days before its entry into Nanking. In my view, because of the very short time he was connected with the army, I do not think he can be held responsible. I would say the Division Commanders were the responsible parties.' General Matsui appeared like an insect squashed slowly to death for all to see, between two sheets of glass.

Only towards the end of his testimony did the General, for just a few sentences, attempt to make some form of appeal for himself. To Donald his deep voice, echoing out of his shrunken frame, seemed caustic with unspoken pain.

'I am not trying to, nor do I evade all responsibility or connection with the capture of Nanking as area commander. However, I am only trying to tell you that I am not directly responsible for the discipline and morals of the troops under the respective armies under my command. I myself did not have the authority to take disciplinary measures, or to hold a court martial. Such authority resided in the Commander of the army or the Division Commander.'

'How then do you explain your previous statement to this court that you did everything in your power as Commander of the Central China Area Army to give severe punishment to those guilty of atrocities?'

'I had no authority. I could do no more than express my desires as all-over Commander of the army.' General Matsui's voice rose and wavered for a moment, before he fell silent, looking about aggressively.

Donald shook his head in distress for Matsui as at last the General was released from the stand. It was useless to talk of sacrifice to the ritual slaughter of the court, and yet that was how Matsui's performance appeared. Matsui sat once more in the dock and closed his eyes, withdrawing deep within himself.

The following day Donald was at last called to the witness-stand. There was a stir as he crossed the court. He was now a famous man. There had been much in the Japanese newspapers about his part in making public to the world all that had gone on. Across the court, standing in the witness-box, facing the dock of elderly men, he cut a tall, forbidding figure. He looked about the courtroom. The heat and humidity were intense. All the terrible details of the day seemed to hang upon the air, like a stench that would not clear. Donald felt a sudden claustrophobia such as he experienced sometimes in lifts. Nanking pressed in upon him. The questioning began.

'I returned to Nanking, after the bombing of the *Panay* in which I was involved. I climbed the walls and entered the city undetected. I returned with the intention of getting news of Nanking and what was happening there,' Donald stated.

'And how did you do this?' the prosecution asked.

'Statistics were most important. Each day I went out about the city, between other duties with the Safety Zone Committee. However grim the scenes I tried to write them up objectively for later use and evidence.' He spoke calmly, giving numbers, describing conditions. The auditorium listened in silence.

'Although we can never know the exact numbers, it is thought several hundred thousand people were killed within six weeks in Nanking. And perhaps as many as fifty thousand women were raped. Some of the worst treatment was reserved for the women. We could do nothing. *Nothing.*' Donald's voice cracked upon the word.

'You have taken film of this. Will you explain to the court how you managed to do this and what was on this film.'

Donald's mouth felt dry. The great hall was silent before him, waiting.

Wherever he looked he saw eyes, caught in the blaze of lights, moist, bright, watching him. Ahead he saw General Matsui and all the old men of the dock. Some closed their eyes in concentration, or an ostrich-like disassociation. The headphones they wore gave a strange bulbous shape to their heads. They looked to him suddenly like a box of shrivelled praying mantises, with small heads and carbuncle eyes.

'What was it that has made this movie film so special, that gave it credence to the world?' The prosecutor's voice prompted.

The dryness increased in his mouth. He looked about him, but saw no escape. The tiers of packed seats rose before him, the interpreters waited in their section. The microphone before him waited. The cupped ears of the defendants waited. The court closed about him, a well into which for eternity his words would echo, written down in print, shelved in archives. For ever.

The great lights above him threw his shadow over the sloping front of the witness-box. It moved as he moved, as if mocking him. He suddenly feared all that his shadow held locked within it. He feared it was intertwined with all that was locked in that terrible film. His terror grew as he contemplated what he must voice to the court. Things fused together in his head and would not separate. The heat in the room grew intense.

'The court is waiting.' The prosecutor's voice was now curt.

'It was a cold morning. My biggest worry was not to be seen by soldiers, otherwise the camera would be taken. As ever, there were plenty of dead bodies to record. And fires. The torch was put to so much without reason. Besides rape and murder there was also looting. I took some footage from a distance of a supply line loaded with high-grade black wood furniture. I do not know what I was looking for, except a record of Nanking as it was then. I came to a canal. Bodies were floating in it, enormously bloated. It stank.'

He felt the nausea still. He remembered the thick plates of the lotus leaves about the rotting corpses. 'There were houses beside the canal . . .'

His mouth was too dry for his tongue to move. He considered making this excuse to Sir William Webb. The shadow before him on the witness-box trembled as he trembled. He tried shifting his position, but the shadow shifted with him.

'Go on.' He heard the impatience in the prosecutor's voice.

'I heard a lot of screaming. Then a middle-aged woman and two men ran out of one of the houses. I set my camera working. There were three or maybe four soldiers, I have forgotten. But they took hold of the woman, pulling at her clothes. They began to rape her. When her

448

husband and the other man protested, they were bayoneted and fell at the side of the road.'

His mouth was so dry now his voice emerged in a cracked and uneven drawl. It was not how he wanted to sound. And something terrible had begun. It as as if a film continued now to wind on by itself without his words, pulling him into the picture. The jerking, pathetic, black and white images he had taken were now flooded by colour. The sound of screaming filled his ears. He saw again the mesh of limbs, the pumping bodies of the men, the closed eyes of the woman, stoic in her peasant endurance of pain and violation.

And even as everything had tangled in his mind on that morning, it tangled now again. He saw the image of Cordelia superimposed upon the wretched peasant woman. He saw not the scrawny limbs of those soldiers, but the pale, fleshy, heaving buttocks of his father, thrusting at Cordelia. He saw Cordelia's eyes, closed in an expression he had never aroused, her lips parted in emotion.

Desperation flooded through him. On the sloping front of the witness-box the shadow now jerked and pulled at him, its anger palpitating. It loomed up unexpectedly, throwing itself upon him, thrashing back and forth.

He looked up in terror and saw that a bird had flown into the courtroom and struck the side of one of the lamps, causing it to sway about. This did not lessen the throb of fear. The film seemed imprinted now upon his very life. He forgot why he was in the courtroom. Film and life now merged as one.

'I could have stopped it.' He raised his voice and it cracked again. 'I could have walked forward and torn those soldiers off her. But I did nothing. *Nothing.* While I was filming all I could see was Cordelia. It was as if I could no longer see that Chinese woman and what they were doing to her. I stood and watched them, like I watched Cordelia. But Cordelia wanted him, and he was my father. I always feared him I suppose. I was a coward. They thought I was out, you see. It was Christmas Eve. He shot himself. He made sure I heard the shot. That was typical of him. His brains were everywhere, all over the wall and the desk. I could have stopped him too, from killing himself. Perhaps I hoped he would do it. Perhaps I made him do it. I knew he had a gun . . .'

He slumped upon the shadow that now lay still before him. His face was wet with tears. Two MPs stepped forward and led him from the box, across the well of the court and out into the corridor. A nurse and a doctor hurried towards him.

449

41

1946

New Worlds

The remains of the house still stood. The lantern had survived, although about it the garden had died. When he had returned to the house it was the first thing Kenjiro had sought. His relief at its survival was overwhelming. That a useless weathered relic should have acquired such importance was beyond comprehension. He spread out his quilts on the rotted floor of his old room, so that upon waking he could see the lantern.

'It is a kind of icon, I suppose. And yet, it is such a useless object. I cannot understand it,' Kenjiro observed to Teng, who was staying with him until his return to China in a few days. They sat together, the large shutters pulled back upon the verandah and the smashed garden.

'I had no wish to come to this trial and testify. At first I refused Nadya's request,' Teng said. 'The evil was done, I thought it should be forgotten as quickly as possible in the seeking of a new future. But I think now this was my own fear of confronting within myself all that has happened. I saw that I must come here, for myself and for others. In a world where nothing is what* it seems, your lantern is a symbol of all that is unchanging.'

Kenjiro sighed. 'The trial appears to me to be plotted from the start. A sort of ritual before the sacrificial slaughter. I do not know what will be learned from it. Its concept of justice is, of course, a Christian one. In the Western world such concepts are based upon centuries of a particular philosophy and religion. But in Japan, you could say that we worship only nature. And in a world ruled by nature the question of individual responsibility is more difficult to assess. The cultural differences in the case have not been given enough consideration.'

Kenjiro poured into glasses some beer he had been able to buy on the black market. He half-expected Teng not to accept the drink now that he was dressed in monks' robes. Instead, he sipped at it meditatively. As always, Teng obeyed rules entirely his own.

'The whole trial is in some ways a travesty,' Kenjiro complained, taking a gulp of the warm beer. 'And too big a thing for human integrity to ever get right. They say hundreds of thousands were killed in Nanking. Each of those was killed individually. One by one. Man to man. Eye to eye killing of defenceless victims. And an almost equal number they say were killed anonymously by one bomb and a single man in Hiroshima. Tell me which is worse? On the desert where that bomb was tested they say the sand turned to glass. And yet they still dropped it . . .' His voice trailed off. A great anger rolled through him. 'Sometimes I wonder if we have not already paid a suitable price for whatever atrocities we committed in Nanking and elsewhere. In some way you could say the slate is wiped clean.' His feelings were forever in flux. He swung equally between emotions of guilt and those of rightful anger.

'Because we don't know when we will die, we think of life as an inexhaustible world. Our lives seem limitless because we can conceive of nothing else.' Teng sighed, but Kenjiro returned to more secular matters.

'Even though the Americans plan a new Constitution and a new society for us, I doubt that anything very basic will change in this country. A new dress upon the same old body perhaps? The Emperor is to be left in place, and so the country will not break with its recent past. The same bureaucracy that ran Japan in the war will now, with modifications, run it in peacetime. The same corrupt parties will remain in power. The past will be ignored, political debate stifled and this country will not grow up politically. The ghost of militarism will remain as long as the Emperor system remains.' Kenjiro spoke in a resigned manner. His anger dissipated as he pondered the future.

'Is there news yet of Dayal?' Teng asked to change the subject.

Some weeks before, at the trial of Tilik in Yokohama, on charges of conspiracy, they had both given evidence for the defence of his collaboration at the risk of his life in the escape of Teng.

'I heard only yesterday. He has been acquitted and will be released this week,' Kenjiro replied.

'I am glad,' Teng nodded. 'Very glad.'

Later they drove together to Sugamo Prison in a taxi. It looked like a run-down factory with a white wooden gate and two small guard shacks. The American flag flew on top of its three-storeyed building. Still in ill-fitting prison uniform, Tilik Dayal was waiting for them in a meeting room.

'I return to China tomorrow,' said Teng.

Tilik nodded, as if still dazed by the verdict of acquittal and his imminent freedom. 'I owe you so much,' he said.

451

'On the contrary,' Teng laughed out loud, but Tilik shook his head insistently.

'I must tell you, I am not a brave man. I might not have helped you if Nozaki had not been so persuasive. If they had tortured me, I would have told them all I knew of you both immediately.' He felt better now he had said it. He remembered again the sight of the beaten Teng, tied to a chair in the dark basement room of Military Headquarters in Nanking. He remembered his hesitation as he had hidden the metal file upon the man.

'How can you be so sure you would have told them about us?' laughed Teng. 'We never know what we will do until we are faced with a decision. Sitting here now I am sure you are perhaps surprised that you did indeed agree to help me? Is that not so?'

'Perhaps,' Tilik admitted. He recalled his fear after Teng's escape. It seemed a miracle that his part in the event had not been uncovered.

'But you did help. What else matters?' Kenjiro interrupted.

'What matters is that every day now when we read the newspapers, it is clear how ruthless the machine was that backed me. I have lived with illusions, about myself, about my ideals, about almost everything I can think of. I backed the wrong God. Vengeance devours you.' Now again he remembered Rash Bihari's words of warning on this matter, at their first meeting so long ago.

He did not tell them how much the world beyond this prison terrified him. It was a landscape devoid of the props he was used to. It was another Japan. And he was already a relic of another era. He could understand how so many had committed suicide after the surrender, rather than face the reconstruction of their world.

'You go too far, I think,' Kenjiro answered.

Tilik shook his head. He could not rid himself of his depression. Everywhere he looked in Sugamo were men who were now termed criminals. Few seemed to feel any guilt as far as he could see. Anger, acceptance, false bravado; he saw all these emotions, but the despair afflicting him seemed unique to himself.

'You have recognized that inferior part of yourself. Nothing is more important. Many live out their lives without seeing that person in themselves.' Teng spoke quietly.

'What will you do when you leave here?' Kenjiro asked.

Tilik shook his head in bewilderment. He had no idea how he would support his family. 'I was useful to a now obsolete regime. It has vanished and I too am now obsolete. Perhaps I can import tea or spices from India. I shall have to think of something.'

'I will be working soon once more, for the Foreign Ministry,' said

Kenjiro. 'As long as my health remains, I shall be in a position of responsibility. There is an era ahead of new world relations. Fresh ties will be formed between Japan and India. There is rebuilding in every sphere of life ahead. I see you as a valuable man. You have been cleared of all charges against you, and in fact proved to be on the side of right. You could work for the good of a new India in a new Japan. Independence in your country is now a reality for the future. We shall talk about this once you leave Sugamo. I see nothing for you to be despondent about.'

Tilik looked up at him, his expression clearing for the first time. 'If this could indeed be my future, there would be much to hope for, much I could do at last for the good of both our countries, and in a more rightful manner.'

Teng sat unmoving, arms crossed in his habitual manner over his chest, each hand hidden in the wide wrist of the opposite sleeve. 'Cause and effect, means and end, seed and fruit, cannot be severed from each other. The effect already blooms in the cause, the end pre-exists in the means, the fruit in the seed. Sleep hovers all our lifetime about our eyes, as night hovers all day in the boughs of the fir tree.' Teng sighed and stood up, ready to leave.

42

1946

A Break with the Past

They noticed first, like the sudden shutting of a door, a silence in the mornings. Only occasionally now was there the lone, shrill rasping of a late cicada. Already it was autumn.

'Thank God those insects are gone,' said Donald. 'They drove me mad. Screaming out all the time. Sometimes, you know, the blasted things reminded me of . . .' His words trailed into silence. There were many sentences now he suddenly lost all desire to finish. He could not round out in words how sometimes the hysterical insects reminded him of those human cries of terror, that had cut just as shrilly through his body in Nanking. They walked on up the steep hill along a narrow path between the dense slopes of cypress.

'This reminds me of Purple Mountain,' Nadya said.

She spoke about Nanking if Donald touched upon it. She knew then that tacitly permission had been granted, that his mind would not be jolted into the shock of remembrance. The doctor had advised letting Donald set his own pace for this reaching back. General MacArthur had sent his own doctor to Donald who, in turn, had recommended the American psychiatrist who now treated him. Donald had been three months in the hospital, and only now had begun to feel any wish to explore the world beyond it, or the many spectres in his past.

'It is like a road to a house he once lived in,' the doctor had said. 'Unless he goes back, unless he travels to his past, ghosts will haunt him for ever. There is only so much I can do to help him. He must find his own way to exorcize his demons.'

Twice a week Nadya made the journey to the sanatorium, a distance from Tokyo. She knew he waited for these visits. The trial at Ichigaya dragged on, and work for Bradley was never-ending. The China War segment was over and no more evidence was needed from those who had been in Nanking. Air-conditioning had been installed in the courtroom, and a greater war was now under examination. It was obvious to everyone that the six-month schedule originally given for the trial was unrealistic. It might now run into years. For as long as Bradley was here, Nadya had a job. It came as a surprise to find in this land, until now associated only with violence, so much that swung to the other extreme. The gentleness of the people she met came as a shock. She was at a loss to understand where the barbarity she had witnessed was spawned.

They climbed higher. Pine needles were slippery, like glass beneath their feet. The astringent perfume of the forest closed about them. The trees pressed in, casting shadow, light filtered down with difficulty. She saw Donald glance apprehensively about.

'It is only a short distance more,' she encouraged, hurrying ahead, so that he would not decide to turn back. She had been up here by herself before on a previous visit to Donald.

They came at last to the clearing and the shrine. It was weathered and old, its wood splintered by neglect. About it stood trees of a great size. Here too the light was of a filtered quality and a dampness settled upon them. The silence was powerful, as if they had entered a secret world.

'These trees must be of great age,' said Donald, looking up in respect. 'See the size of the trunks. They can live for hundreds of years you know. Five hundred, seven hundred, even more I believe. Think of all they must have witnessed.' Part of the old shrine was built up the slope. Stone lanterns and two ancient temple lions guarded it in front. Lichen clung to parts of its stone base.

'There must always have been a shrine here. They say it is a thousand years old. It must be the age of these trees,' Nadya whispered. 'Do you not feel the atmosphere?'

'It is the residue of centuries of human hope and pain,' Donald replied, making his way up the wooden steps to the closed door of the place. There was no lock and the doors slid open easily. He took hold of Nadya's hand, pulling her up beside him.

The smell of dampness and old wood met them as they entered the bare interior. The tatami floor was ripped in places. The many painted amulets hanging upon the walls were faded and weathered. Where the shrine backed up the hill was a narrow arched corridor, like a walled bridge. This ended in a short flight of steps and a wooden cabinet with metal-bound doors. Before it were fresh offerings of rice cakes and sake. Two small lamps glowed in the dimness beside a ritual ornament of folded brass strips.

'Somebody comes here,' Nadya said. The strange austerity of the place was unsettling. There was no icon, no decoration, just the cold, charged emptiness, the lamps and locked box.

'Why do I feel frightened here?' she whispered.

'Because in this place, as one feels sometimes in old churches, nothing can be hidden. We can no longer lie to ourselves before whatever it is that is accumulated here,' Donald replied. His grip on her hand was hard. He led her back to the bare, matted room and pointed to a beam just above their head. A polished sphere of metal rested upon a base of carved wooden clouds.

'For many weeks you know, I could not read. The effort demanded was too much. But recently, for a short while, I find I can open a book. I have learned some things. That mirror is the symbol of the soul. It directs that we look into ourselves to find every answer we seek. No false gods, no illusions, no pomp and power and calling for help upon the Almighty. Ourselves, nothing more. And in that simple wooden box on that topmost altar, the most precious thing in this shrine, is no hidden idol or secret text. There is nothing but the emptiness of the universe, from which we came and to which we return.'

He sat down on the matted floor. Nadya settled herself beside him. Donald looked about the walls, covered by the profusion of amulets, each small board inscribed with a wish.

'What do you think is written upon them?' he asked.

'I should think they must ask for sons or husbands or brothers to return from war,' Nadya replied. 'In those times what other wish could anyone have had?'

'A dying man once told me he felt covered all over on the inside by scales, like a reptile. He hated himself so much. I know how he felt. I don't want to die as he did.' Donald shuddered just thinking of Mariani and the weight he had carried to his death. 'I think I knew my father would kill himself. I willed him to. When I saw him dead upon that desk, his brains all over the wall, beneath the shock I remember there was a feeling of triumph. I had had my revenge for what he had done to my mother, for taking Cordelia from me. And for what I thought he had done to me. I was glad he was dead. Perhaps I even drove him to his death, relentlessly, deliberately. I don't know.' There were many questions he must ask himself.

It was not yet late but the afternoon sun was already shortening, cut off by the great trees about the shrine. Before the altar with its empty box, the lamps glowed with new strength in the dimness, catching brass hinges and the folded metal ornament.

She took his hand. 'You wanted to write that book about China and did not, because of that Snowman, that Edgar Snow. Why do you not now write about this whole trial, each phase of it, each part of the war and through it maybe you can reach many things?'

'Maybe,' he replied and fell silent for a moment before he spoke again.

'I cannot do it unless you are with me.' He said the words slowly, giving weight to each one.

'What are you saying?' She smiled in the dying light.

'Well, I think it is a proposal,' he answered.

'But you forget, we have been through all this before. I am already Mrs Addison.'

They stood up then to go. At the door Donald stopped and turned back as if on an impulse, returning to the few steps before the Shinto altar. He dug into his trouser pocket and drew out the bullet that he had carried upon him everywhere since the sinking of the *Panay*. He laid it before the doors of the metal-bound box, in which was trapped eternity. He closed his eyes but no prayer came to him. Silence seemed enough.

He turned back to where Nadya waited.

43

China 1946

Shadows

As he climbed higher up the mountain the heat of the plain was left behind. The mosquitoes bothered him less. A distance ahead, perched precipitously upon a crag of rock, stood the monastery. Teng walked easily. His body seemed without weight, as if it had shed many burdens.

In the distance now, on a lower promontory below the main buildings, he could make out a small figure. It jerked suddenly into life and stumbled down the slope towards him.

'Why have you come? You would be of more use at prayer,' Teng scolded Akira, but there was little astringency in his tone. They struggled in silence up the slope with little spare breath to converse.

At last they entered the cool interior of the stone buildings. The smell of incense came to them.

'What was it like?' Akira whispered at last.

'Bad. Little is left of anywhere but rubble. The great bomb left only a flat black plain of dust and a town of walking dead. I saw pictures. People looked like lizards, their skin burned off. Do not ask me more.'

'Did you find out anything?'

'Very little. Your mother is dead. Of the others I do not know. Small villages escaped the worst bombing. It is probable some of your family survived. Even now malnutrition is a big killer.' He began to untie his pack of belongings. Akira stood in silence beside him, turning the beads on a string about his wrist.

'I can arrange for you to go back. I have spoken to people about it. Many such as yourself are returning; those soldiers who were taken prisoner, and others who ran or hid like yourself. Some were prised out of Malayan jungles, or tropical island caves, and did not even know the war was ended. They are being repatriated. It will be no shame to return in the present climate. Especially with an American Occupation.'

'It will always be a shame,' Akira answered, his voice sinking low. 'I am dead to my family and to my country. No American Occupation will ever change the thoughts of our people. I am as dead. My family would be dishonoured if I returned.' He remembered again the *senninbari* his mother had given him, soliciting for his safety one thousand stitches, walking from village to village.

'I could arrange for you to go back to a monastery in Japan. You would at least be in your own country,' Teng insisted.

'My place is wherever I am,' Akira answered. There was a hard lump in his throat at the memory of his mother.

The setting sun glowed suddenly through a high window, spearing them with a shaft of light, spreading their shadows across the floor of the narrow room.

'I do not answer without thought,' Akira went on slowly. 'There are millions who have died upon this soil. A greater number of those are my Chinese brothers, and a portion are my own countrymen. In this land I have come to some realizations. I have seen the depths of human depravity. Now, from this place of peace, I tell you honestly, I am not sorry to have seen these things, although I still battle with the residue of nightmare. I feel terror in the sunshine. But I have touched the centre of evil. Many have not to take this road, and they are lucky. It was my destiny to be shown the extreme path. But, is it not through the recognition of such evil that purification can begin? I must stay here. I must pray for the souls of those I wronged. I must pray for the souls of those of my countrymen who, like myself, will never go home. I must pray for those who have returned to Japan but will find no peace. It is my duty to stay here. That is my work. It has been shown me.'

For some moments Teng was silent. 'If that is your feeling then that is what you must do. All that you say is right,' he answered at last.

The small room seemed to glow brighter in the setting sun. Teng looked up at the shaft of brilliant light and then down at the shadows it cast on the floor, of himself and of Akira. It seemed to him suddenly that, if there was an existence after death, it would have to continue at the level of consciousness attained in a lifetime. This was why earthly life was of such significance. It was not in the dimension beyond life, but only here, where opposites clashed, that the level of consciousness could be raised. And if there were rebirth, it was that level of knowledge taken over in death that would be returned to the world with each new incarnation.

Teng stepped forward and then stopped to look back once more at the shadows trailing behind them. He walked on and Akira followed.

ACKNOWLEDGEMENTS

The happenings in this book are based closely upon historical events, and many of the characters who appear in this narrative are based upon actual figures and their roles in the era covered. It is, however, important to stress that, while I hope the book may be seen as an historical document, it is also a work of fiction. All portraits of the characters portrayed are fictional, as are many of the events. My interpretation of Emperor Hirohito and other historical figures is purely my own.

Many books were vital to me in my research, and I am grateful to them all for their illuminations. I must, however, particularly mention *Japanese Terror* in China by H. J. Timperly, Correspondent for the *Manchester Guardian* at the time of the rape of Nanking. This contains the almost day by day official documentation of the International Committee of the Safety Zone in Nanking, during the time of their ordeal. It contains, as well as the official filing of reports and numerous letters to the Japanese Embassy, confidential reports, personal letters and diary entries of unimpeachable verity.

Dr Keswick's letter in the front of the old Bible belonging to Martha Clayton, is taken from *Guinness of Honan* by Mrs Howard Taylor, for which I am also indebted for an insight into missionary life in China.

I have also valued greatly the interesting recounting of his life told to me by A. M. Nair in Tokyo shortly before his death.

I would like to thank Dr Kaoru Sugihara for his advice while planning this book and also Dr Shou-ren Wang. I am most grateful to Prof. John Pritchard for his detailed reading of the finished manuscript for historical accuracy and many helpful comments. I should also like to thank Shegeki Hijino and Prof. Philip Billingsley for a further reading of the text in this regard. And my further thanks to Yoriko Kohno for her generous help with research.

PRINCIPAL FICTIONAL CHARACTERS

Cordelia Addison
Donald Addison
John Addison
Dr Janet Allen
Dr Chen
Old Chieko
Bill Clayton
Flora Clayton
Lily Clayton
Martha Clayton
Michiko Dayal
Tilik Dayal
Mr Fukutake
Jun Hasegawa

Colonel Kato
Dr Keswick
Nadya Komosky
Sergei Lekhovich
Marco Mariani
Mr Metzger
Art Morton
Akira Murata
Captain Nakamura
Kenjiro Nozaki
Jacqueline Nozaki
Naomi Nozaki
Shizuko Nozaki
Yuzuru Nozaki

Mr Ohara
Fat Man Ping
First Secretary Henry Percival
Mrs Primakov
Bradley Reed
Joe Russek
Ivan Shepenov
Hugh Smollett
Rod Smythe
Mr Strang
Professor Teng Li-sheng
Colonel Zayazeff
Heiner Zimmer

PRINCIPAL HISTORICAL CHARACTERS

General Korechika Anami
Lieutenant Anders
General Prince Yasuhiko Asaka
Rash Bihari Bose
Subash Chandra Bose
Chang Hsueh-liang
Chang Tso-lin
Grandma Chao
Chiang Kai-shek
Madame Chiang Kai-shek
Prince Chichibu
W. H. Donald
General Dyer
Dr Grazier
Ambassador Grew
Colonel Kingoro Hashimoto
Counsellor Shunrokuro Hidaka
Emperor Hirohito
Father Jacquinot
American Consul Johnson
Joseph Keenan
Marquis Koichi Kido

Prince Fumimaro Konoye
General Douglas MacArthur
Count Makino
General Iwane Matsui
Emperor Meiji
Prince Mikasa
Colonel Akira Muto
Empress Nagako
Admiral Nagano
General Kesago Nakajima
General Maresuke Nogi
General Sugiyama
Kantaro Suzuki
Emperor Taisho (Prince Yoshihito)
Prince Takamatsu
Police Commissioner Tegart
General Hideki Tojo
Mitsuru Toyama
Amleto Vespa
Sir William Webb
General Heisuke Yanagawa